PRAISE FOR *MEET CUTE*

"Perfect for fans of Helen Hoang's *The Kiss Quotient*. A fun and steamy love story with high stakes and plenty of emotion."

—*Kirkus Reviews*

"[A] smartly plotted and perfectly executed rom-com with a spot-on sense of snarky wit and a generous helping of smoldering sexual chemistry." —*Booklist*

"If a 'rom-com in book form' is what you're after this spring, you can't go wrong with *Meet Cute*." —Bustle

"*Meet Cute* is entertaining, funny, and emotional."

—*Harlequin Junkie*

"As charming as its title, but it's also so much more...Fans of Jasmine Guillory's *The Wedding Date* and Helen Hoang's *The Kiss Quotient* will love *Meet Cute*."

—*The Washington Independent Review of Books*

"*Meet Cute* is a novel where you will laugh and cry—sometimes, on the same page. It is a story of kindness and affection, sassiness and tenderness, where joy and sorrow are intermingled. You don't want to miss this book."

—Frolic

PRAISE FOR *THE GOOD LUCK CHARM*

"Fabulously fun! Lilah and Ethan's second-chance romance charmed me from the first page to the swoon-worthy end."

—Jill Shalvis, *New York Times* bestselling author

"*The Good Luck Charm* is an absolute delight.... Ms. Hunting crafted an entertaining and sexy story with a relatable cast of characters. Fans of Emma Chase, Christina Lauren, and Jaci Burton will love *The Good Luck Charm*."

—*Harlequin Junkie*

"Hockey talk, more than one steamy scene, and a hero and heroine who have a genuine respect as well as a fiery passion for each other make this romance an all-around winner."

—*BookPage*

"Writing with a deliciously sharp humor, Hunting shoots and scores in this exceptionally entertaining contemporary romance."

—*Booklist*

"Hunting sparkles in this well-plotted contemporary."

—*Publishers Weekly*

KISS MY
CUPCAKE

ALSO BY HELENA HUNTING

The Good Luck Charm

Meet Cute

KISS MY

CUPCAKE

HELENA
HUNTING

FOREVER

New York Boston

Copyright © 2020 by Helena Hunting

Cover illustration by Monika Roe
Cover copyright © 2020 by Hachette Book Group, Inc.

Forever
Hachette Book Group
1290 Avenue of the Americas, New York, NY 10104
read-forever.com
twitter.com/readforeverpub

First Edition: August 2020

Forever is an imprint of Grand Central Publishing. The Forever name and logo are trademarks of Hachette Book Group, Inc.

The publisher is not responsible for websites (or their content) that are not owned by the publisher.

The Hachette Speakers Bureau provides a wide range of authors for speaking events. To find out more, go to www.hachettespeakersbureau.com or call (866) 376-6591.

Library of Congress Control Number: 2020935792

ISBN: 978-1-5387-3467-4 (trade paperback), 978-1-5387-3465-0 (ebook)

Printed in the United States of America

LSC-C

10 9 8 7 6 5 4 3 2 1

*For the outliers who are willing to choose the
road less traveled over the easier path*

chapter one

JUST A BIG OLD PILE OF CRAP

Blaire

I have a fantastic idea for your little cupcake shop, Care Blaire!"

I cringe at the nickname, how ridiculously loud my dad is, and the reference to my first ever solo entrepreneurial endeavor as my "little cupcake shop." He doesn't mean for it to sound condescending, although it does.

My first inclination is to throw some sarcasm at him, but I'm aware he's trying to be helpful in his own misguided way, and the conversation will be over that much sooner if I play along. "What's this fantastic idea that has you so excited?"

"The café right beside Decadence is going out of business at the end of the year. I'd be happy to pick up the lease on that building and you could open up shop right next door to us! Wouldn't that be wonderful? And so much more practical than what you're doing right now."

I hold my phone away from my ear and breathe in and out

to the count of four so I don't snap at him. "My current lease is a year, Dad."

"Can't you break it?"

"Not without a penalty, no."

"Hmm. Well, I could cover that for you. I don't think it hurts for you to give this a go on your own for a few months, but then you can come back home and be part of the family business. And obviously I'd provide you with the financial capital if you decided to make the transition."

And there's the braised carrot I was waiting for him to dangle. "Can I think about it?" There is absolutely zero chance that I'm going to take him up on his offer. It's not that I don't want the financial help. It's all the strings that come along with it that I'm not interested in dealing with.

"Of course, of course. It's a great opportunity and I wouldn't want you to miss out on it. Why don't we talk later in the week?"

"Sure. Sounds good."

"Love you, Care Blaire!"

"Love you, too, Dad." I end the call on a frustrated sigh and then nearly do a face plant into the concrete trying to sidestep a pile of dog poop. I also come perilously close to dropping my Tupperware container full of buttercream-topped delights. The dog doody happens to be decorating the sidewalk right out front of my "little cupcake shop." I mentally shake a fist at the thoughtless dog owner who left it there as a special surprise.

This better not be a sign.

I glance around, looking for something to...remove the visual and olfactory offense, but the sidewalk is trash free. Normally I would be happy about the lack of old newspapers or takeout food wrappers blowing down the street, but today it's rather inconvenient. The last thing I want is a stinky mess sitting front and center outside of my not-yet-open storefront. As a helpful warning to other passersby, I pluck a yellow flower from one of the planters brightening the entrance to my brand new cocktail café/bakery, aptly named Buttercream and Booze—scheduled to open in just one week—and stick the stem in the fresh pile. I'll come back out and get rid of it so no one else suffers the same almost-fate.

Even the nearly craptastic accident and my conversation with my dad don't dim my good spirits for long. I rummage through my purse in search of my keys—they always migrate to the bottom of my purse. I finally snag them, slide the key into the lock and push the door open. It tinkles cheerily, an auditory accompaniment to the vibrant, clean interior.

I wanted simple, fresh, and chic without being overly bubblegum adorable. So I nixed any pink from the décor that doesn't include cupcake frosting. Instead I went with pale hardwood flooring, simple white tables and luxurious chairs upholstered in pale gray, easy-to-clean faux leather. Pops of vibrant yellows, pale blue, and silver accent each table's centerpiece. The windows are sparkling and streak-free, the signage across the front of the café is clean, simple, and classy in eye-catching gray with a metallic sheen.

I inhale deeply as I step inside, the faint scent of fresh paint and bleach almost entirely eclipsed by the lemon oil diffusing in the corner, and the lingering smell of the real vanilla candles from yesterday.

I forget all about cleaning up the poopy present and shriek when I notice the box sitting on the bar. I set my purse and Tupperware on the closest table and my coffee on the bar. Despite my excitement, I take a moment to wash my hands prior to nabbing a pair of scissors. I carefully drag the tip along the seam to slice through the tape.

"I thought I heard you making sex noises out here." My best friend Daphne appears at the end of the hall, scaring the heck out of me.

The scissors slip and catch my finger. "Ow! Crap!" A bead of blood wells from the cut and I suck the end of my thumb, the metallic tang making me slightly woozy. I'm a bit of a baby when it comes to the sight of blood.

"I'm so sorry." Daphne rushes across the café, heels clipping on the hardwood. She nabs the small first-aid kit behind the bar, flips it open, and retrieves a bandage.

"It's okay. I'm just clumsy this morning, and jittery."

"Everything okay?" Her expression shifts to concern as she quickly covers the wound with a Band-Aid.

"Oh yeah, you know how it is. I woke up at three because I needed to use the bathroom and my brain wouldn't shut off. Then I got another idea for opening day cupcakes so I figured I'd make a test batch while drinking an entire pot of coffee."

She glances at the adorable cupcake clock on the wall. "So you've been up since three?"

"Mm hmm. And of course my dad called this morning with another one of his amazing ideas."

She grimaces. "Oh no."

"Oh yes."

"What wonderful suggestions did he have this time?" Daphne is aware of my parents' constant push for me to join the family business. I love them, and they've worked hard to get where they are, but their dreams and mine don't line up. They love sautéing and roasting and hobnobbing with the rich and famous. I love butter and sugar and vanilla and *not* hobnobbing.

I give her the abridged version.

"And how did the conversation end?"

"All I said was that I'd think about it."

"You did not!"

I hold up a hand. "I'm not honestly going to think about it, Daph, but I also didn't feel like listening to an hour-long lecture on why being part of the family business would be better for me. I know exactly what will happen if I go back to working with my family. I won't have a say in anything. They'll take over the whole thing and change it from my cocktails and cupcakes theme into something ridiculous and highbrow. They'll strip me of all decision-making power, pooh-pooh all of my ideas, and I'll get to watch my dream go up in flames." It sounds dramatic, but it's not. My family is well-intentioned but pushy. "I didn't work this hard just to go back to kobe beef and duck fat truffle fries." Not that there's anything wrong with either. I enjoy eating both, but I don't enjoy preparing them the way my family does.

"Okay. That's good. I was worried there for a second." Daphne sheds her thin cardigan and hops lithely up onto the bar top. I finally notice her outfit; she's dressed in a pair of pale yellow jeans and a light-gray shirt with Buttercream and Booze in silver and blue letters across her chest.

"Oh my God! The shirts came in!" My volume is far too loud for the early hour, but my excitement cannot be contained. "I need to take a picture." I pat my hips, but my phone is in my purse, which is sitting on the table where I left it. I raise a single finger. "Hold on! I need my phone. Or maybe I should get the good camera. And we need a cupcake. Actually, we should stage a bunch of photos."

"Blaire." Daphne grabs my wrist. "Take a breath or six and chill the eff out."

"But we need a picture. One for our Instagram. Oh! We should host a T-shirt giveaway!"

"Done and done. I posted half an hour ago and it's already in our stories and on our Facebook page and posted to the website. Social media managed." She says the last part with a British accent, mimicking "mischief managed" from *Harry Potter*. We're both huge fans. Sometimes we have weekend movie marathons despite having seen the films quite literally a hundred times. Don't judge. There are worse addictions.

Daphne is a photographer and has her own business a

couple of blocks down. She opened her studio last year and I was right there with her, helping in whatever way I could. Unlike B&B, her place didn't need too much work, but I was there with a paintbrush and moral support. I even brought the Cupcakes to Go! truck on opening day to help entice new clients with sweet treats.

Daphne's actually the person who told me about this place. She's also been kind enough to help get all of my social media up and running. Currently, I pay her in cupcakes since I can't afford much else in the way of compensation. She's assured me this is a great addition to her portfolio and if Buttercream and Booze takes off she'll most definitely benefit. I squeeze her hand. "You are so amazing."

"I know. It's one of the many reasons I'm your bestie." She winks. "Now open the damn box so we can get excited about something else and you can freak out about more potential Insta posts."

"Right! Yes!" I take one of those deep breaths Daphne suggested because I'm speaking like I've mainlined cocaine after drinking seventeen Red Bulls and everything I say is punctuated with an exclamation mark. "Calming myself before I get more excited," I mutter as I open the flaps. That calm lasts about a quarter of a second and then I'm back to excited freak-out.

"They are so much fun!" I gently free one of the unicorn martini glasses from the box. "Aren't they the most adorable thing you've ever seen?"

"They are absolutely the most adorable things I have seen." Daphne bites her lip, obviously fighting laughter.

"Well, I think they're perfect." I can already imagine the specialty martini and the cupcakes I'll make to go with them. The glasses were a little expensive, and slightly outside of my budget, but they're so much fun and they'll look amazing in photos for social media posts.

"I wholeheartedly agree. You should display a few up there." She motions to the shelf adjacent to the bar that showcases a row of candy-inspired martini glasses.

"Ohhh! Great idea!" I carefully free two more unicorn glasses from the box and round the counter.

Daphne hops down off the bar. "I'll be right back."

I *mm-hmm*, too consumed with rearranging the shelf to be concerned with where Daphne is going.

Daphne returns as I finish positioning the glassware. She's grinning and her hands are clasped behind her back. "Close your eyes."

I slam my lids together. "They're closed."

"Arms up."

I raise them over my head and Daphne laughs. "Just to the side, like you're halfway into a jumping jack."

I lower them so they're out in a T. "Oh my God. What do you have? What came?"

"Stop jumping around and you'll find out."

I didn't even realize I was bouncing with excitement. I still and wait while Daphne drapes something over my head.

When she ties it at my waist behind my back I start bouncing again. "It's my apron, isn't it?"

"Stop moving and don't you dare peek." She smacks my butt.

"Ow!"

"It was a tap, you sucky baby."

"It was unexpected." And the most action I've had in a long time. Opening one's own business means I have very little time for anything but work, more work, and limited sleep.

"Eyes closed until I tell you." She takes me by the shoulders and pushes me forward. "Okay. You can open them."

I pry one lid open, and then the other. Daphne has moved me to the center of the café, where a massive mirror with the Buttercream and Booze decal hangs from the wall. I'm off to the right, so I can see my brand new apron without the obstruction of opaque letters cutting through it.

My hands start flapping without my permission, so I ball them into fists and hide them behind my back for a moment while I search for some calm. "It's just so perfect, isn't it?" I'm halfway to tears, I'm so elated.

But then, that's what this place reduces me to: tears and excitement. I've worked my tushy off to get here.

"It is." Daphne, being the awesome friend that she is, hands me a tissue before I even have to ask. "You've come a long way from weekend markets and a cupcake truck."

I survey the product of all my hard work. "It's been a journey, hasn't it?"

"An uphill battle to the top of cupcake mountain, really," Daphne agrees.

"I'd rather take the hard road than compromise my dream." I run my fingertips over the letters that spell out Buttercream and Booze. My phone chimes from inside my purse, signaling a call. The ringtone, which is "The Addams Family" theme song, means it's my mother.

Daphne and I look at my purse and then each other. "I'm letting that go to voicemail. I one hundred percent guarantee my mom is calling to try to argue my dad's case."

Daphne sighs. "They really don't get it, do they?"

"Nope."

"Have you told them when your grand opening is?"

"Absolutely not." I do not need them showing up on opening day throwing advice at me. And honestly, it wouldn't be that difficult for them to find the information on their own if they had the wherewithal to check out social media, but I've been extremely vague about the whole thing.

"It's too bad they can't just support you without taking everything over."

"They have the best of intentions and a complete lack of chill." Two traits I'm not unfamiliar with.

"Truer words have never been spoken." Daphne blows out a breath. "It'd be nice if they would let you access your trust without forcing their opinions on you."

"They really love the concept of conditional independence." My family owns some of the most highly regarded, exclusive fine dining establishments in the Pacific Northwest. The expectation was always that I, too, would become a chef and carry on the family legacy.

She taps on the edge of the counter. "It's just frustrating to *know* you have the money, but if you use it there are all kinds of stupid stipulations that go along with it. Sort of defeats the whole purpose of having a trust in the first place, doesn't it?"

Daphne's family is well off, too. We went to the same prep school and have been friends since we were kids. The main difference is that her family has backed every single dream she's ever had an inkling to pursue, whereas mine keeps trying to hammer the square peg that is me into a round hole of their design. "Hence the reason the money is staying where it is until this place is established and I've proven I can make it work."

Fingers crossed that's what happens. For the past several years I've been squirreling away money and living in a crap apartment because I'm determined to make a go of this, on my own merit. So I put the research in, found a storefront I could afford in an area where I thought I could be successful, worked up my business plan, secured the financing, and now here I am, opening my own place, without my family's input, much to their chagrin.

Daphne motions to the shop. "How much more proof do they need?"

"Running a successful cupcake truck business isn't quite the same as having a storefront." I run my finger around the rim of a martini glass.

Daphne taps on the counter. "I actually think the cupcake truck was probably the more difficult of the two. The crap you had to deal with on a regular basis was insane. At least you don't have to worry about slashed tires anymore."

"Thank goodness for that." The food truck business is no joke. It's wildly competitive, territorial and exceptionally cutthroat. The number of times I had to replace my tires because some jealous competitor wanted to take down Cupcakes to Go! was ridiculous.

My family was always worried for my safety. Regardless, it was my first attempt at being an independent business owner. Now here I am with my own storefront and no intention of ever working for my family again if I can help it.

Back when I was younger and still trying to appease my parents, I went to culinary school and apprenticed under renowned chef Raphael Du Beouf. He was talented, handsome, and suave. I was naïve, impressionable, and smitten. I fell for his sexy accent, his ridiculously capable hands, and his lines. So of course, like many stupid twentysomethings, I soaked up the attention and praise he lavished on me, and eventually we started sleeping together. I thought I was in love, while he thought I wouldn't find out that he was sleeping with three other aspiring chefs on the side.

Brokenhearted and totally disenchanted, I let my parents—who felt partly responsible since they were the ones who pushed us together in the first place after he started working at one of their restaurants—fund a year abroad for me in Paris. I got

over Raphael and fell in love with everything pastry and decadence. I returned with a new plan that—much to my family's
shock—did not include taking my place in their business.

So I made connections of my own and started from the
ground up. I rented a booth at the local street market and sold
cupcakes every weekend while working back of house at a
high-end bakery. Which is where I met my friend and eventual
business partner, Paul. He also worked the local street market
circuit and eventually we pooled our resources, bought a food
truck, and launched our mobile cupcake shop, Cupcakes to
Go! On the weekends we would still hit the local markets,
but during the week we made our rounds and delivered our
delicious, decadent wares.

So as much as I rue my relationship with Raphael, his
womanizing ways set me on this path. No regrets.

I shake off my trip down memory lane and motion to my
apron-clad self. "Shall we take some Insta-worthy pics?"

"Yes!" Daphne jumps to her feet and grabs her camera—it's
pretty much an additional appendage.

She poses me in various locations around the shop, holding
all manner of props, including the cupcakes I baked prior to
my arrival. "You look like the love child of Betty Crocker
and Ward Cleaver," she mumbles as she moves around me,
snapping shot after shot.

I'm a big fan of fifties-style dresses with full skirts and
up-dos reminiscent of the same era. It's not meant to be a
gimmick; it's just my thing. I pluck one of the decorative

martini glasses from the counter display and am about to take a fake sip when a massive bang shakes the entire store, making the windows rattle and the bottles on the bar tinkle. I almost drop the martini glass. It's plastic, so it wouldn't be a tragedy if I did, but still.

"What the heck was that?" I set the glass on the closest table and rush to the front window, surveying the street. I don't know what I expect to find. A tank? A wrecking ball?

"I don't know, but it felt like an earthquake."

I spin around to face Daphne. "When was the last time Seattle had an earthquake?"

She doesn't even hesitate. "2001, I think."

"Why would you even know that?"

Daphne shrugs and then covers her head with her hands when another violent bang rattles the martini glasses—the real ones—so badly, one of my new unicorn glasses falls off the shelf and shatters on the floor.

"Oh no!" Daphne slaps a palm over her mouth.

We regard the sparkly puddle with mutual horror; the gold horn sticks straight up, the eyeballs peer wonkily at us from the carnage.

"Save the unicorns!" I shout.

We scramble over to the shelf, carefully grabbing the rest of the stemware before it can meet the same sad fate. I cradle them to my chest, collecting as many as I can.

The next bang isn't as unexpected, but it's still jarring. I jump and nearly lose my hold on a unicorn. As it is, I have a horn poking me in the boob. At least the glasses are no longer at risk of falling off the shelf.

"I think it might be coming from next door." Daphne carefully sets her armload of glasses on the counter.

"What the hell is over there? A portal to another dimension?" I prop my fist on my hip and glare at the wall, as if my angry face is going to make the banging on the other side stop.

"An old bar I think?" Daphne and I both cringe with the next loud slam. "I've never really paid much attention to it, to be honest."

"It sounds like they're coming through the freaking wall! I'm going over there to see what's going on."

I grab the empty box and carefully put the shattered unicorn martini glass pieces inside. Whoever is over there needs to see what they've done.

"I'll be right back." I rush outside and manage to sidestep the doggy doo again as I stalk over to the run-down bar next door. I glance up at the faded, peeling sign above the storefront: THE KNIGHT CAP. I reluctantly admit, in my head, that it's a clever play on words.

The windows are covered with brown paper, as is the door, but another loud bang comes from inside. I knock quite vigorously and shout hello, but I'm sure no one can hear me over the ridiculous racket coming from inside. I also catch the faint pounding of bass.

I decide my best bet is to poke my head in and see what the heck is going on. I yank on the door and it opens an inch, then slams closed again, as if there's a poltergeist on the other side holding it shut. I try again, struggling with the door, which shouldn't be this heavy. There's some kind of wind vortex trying to suck it closed again, but I finally manage to pry it open and slide my body through the gap, still clutching my box with the broken unicorn martini glass. My dress nearly gets caught, but I yank it free before I get stuck in the door.

I cough a few times, breathing in sawdust. The place is absolutely filthy and a wreck. It's deceptively large and long, and the entire back of the pub is covered in plywood. Now that I'm inside, I can make out more of the song booming through the sound system, causing the floor to vibrate. It's some rock tune with heavy guitar riffs and a lot of drums.

"Hello!" I shout and take a few cautious steps across the dusty hardwood. When no one answers, I call out a second time.

A large, somewhat hulking figure appears in the doorway between the old, dusty bar and the new plywood enclosure. The garish lights behind him eclipse his face in shadow until he takes another step forward, bringing him into view.

Standing about twenty feet away is a well-built man wearing a pair of paint-splattered jeans, scuffed-up work boots, and a red-and-black plaid shirt. The sleeves are rolled up to his elbows, showing off vibrantly colored tattoos that cover both of his forearms and disappear under the sleeves. His hair is cut short and styled with some kind of product so it's perfectly smooth, not a strand out of place. An intentional, curated messiness. And he's holding an axe.

Why is this guy holding an axe?

I take an uncertain step back toward the door, because, as I was saying, *he's holding a freaking axe.*

I prop my fist on my hip and tip my chin up as axe man's gaze sweeps over me. Judging. Assessing. His left eyebrow quirks up. He has eyes the color of bourbon, high cheekbones, full lips and a rugged, square jaw with a lovely five o'clock shadow, despite it barely being eight in the morning.

"What the heck is going on here?" I motion to the mess of a bar.

That quirked eyebrow rises higher. "Excuse me?"

"What is this?" I snap.

Axe man's full lips pull up into a grin. "It's called a bar, and judging from the look of it, I think you fell down the wrong rabbit hole, Alice. Wonderland isn't here."

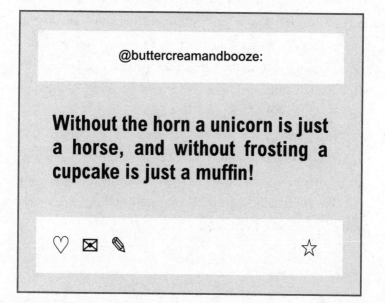

@buttercreamandbooze:

Without the horn a unicorn is just a horse, and without frosting a cupcake is just a muffin!

chapter two

HOT LUMBERJERK

Blaire

"My name is Blaire, not Alice, thank you very much." I want to smack myself for that terrible, unimpressive comeback. I blame my inability to come up with something—anything—better on thinking we were in the middle of an earthquake, the loss of one of my precious unicorn martini glasses that I honestly cannot afford to replace, and this axe-wielding hipster. Oh, did I forget to mention that beyond the fact that he's filthy and dressed like some kind of *GQ* lumberjack, he's also incredibly good-looking?

"Well, *Blaire*, you're standing in the middle of a construction zone, and I'm pretty sure those shoes don't meet the required code, so you can march them right back out the door." He uses the axe handle to point to my heels—which are adorable and surprisingly comfortable.

I take a step back. "Pointing is rude." *Where the hell has my quick wit disappeared to?*

"So is trespassing."

"I knocked, more than once, but with all the racket going on in here it's not really a surprise that no one heard me, is it?" I'm irritated and gathering steam, thanks to my embarrassment, residual fear, and frustration over the problems this guy is causing me. I can't afford setbacks—there's too much on the line for me. Plus this guy has insulted my outfit. True, I may be silently judging him for his own wardrobe choices, but I'm certainly not going to voice them. *Yet.* "I own the café next door and all your banging around in here is making my life impossible."

"You mean the cupcake shop?" Once again, he uses the handle of the axe to point in the direction of my café. It makes his tattooed forearm flex enticingly. I don't even like tattoos. Well, that's not entirely true. I don't not-like tattoos. I just don't understand how anyone can sit through hours of being stabbed with needles for the sake of wearing art that could very easily be hung on a wall instead—pain free.

"It's not a cupcake shop. It's a *cocktail* and cupcake café." *Damn it wit, I need you!*

"Right. My bad. A cupcake and cocktail café isn't the same as a cupcake shop." His sarcasm bleeds through in his dry, day-old scone tone.

I ignore the dig, because trying to explain the difference to a flannel-wearing hipster is pointless. He's clearly the opposite of my target market. "What's happening back there?" I motion to the plywood room behind him. "Is that even legal?"

"It's called an axe-throwing enclosure, and yeah, it's legal."
He pulls a piece of paper out of his back pocket and shakes it
out so it unfolds, then holds it up in front of my face. When
I try to grab it from him he snatches it away. "No touching,
looking only."

I pin him with an unimpressed glare, uncertain as to
whether that's what makes his cheek tic, and raise my hands in
mock surrender. "I wouldn't want to soil your precious paper
with my frosting fingers."

He lowers the paper so I can see that it's a permit for an
axe-throwing enclosure. "See, Alice, totally legal."

I glare at him. "It's Blaire, and you need to move this
enclosure thing because all that banging around is making my
glassware fall off the shelves."

Axe man's eyebrows pop. "Uh yeah, that's not going to
happen."

I flail a hand toward the mess of plywood. "One of my
brand new unicorn martini glasses broke because of you, and
they're expensive."

"Unicorn what?"

"Martini glasses. It's a martini glass with a unicorn face on
it, and a horn. They're adorable and they weren't cheap and all
your banging caused one to fall off the shelf and break." I hold
out the box so he can see the damage he's responsible for.

He peeks inside, but makes no move to take the box. "Can't
you just move your glasses?" His completely unaffected, blasé
attitude is driving me crazy.

I set the box on the bar rather aggressively, making the glass inside tinkle. "I'll have to move an entire shelf. Maybe more than one." I continue to flail my arms all over the place. I'm sure I resemble an octopus on some kind of hallucinogenic stimulant. All the caffeine I've consumed today was obviously a terrible idea because it's making me edgy and discomposed.

"Okay." He hooks his thumb in his pocket, obviously not understanding the difficulty this axe-throwing room of his is going to be for me and my business. He's completely self-centered as well as condescending. I hate him already. Forever. Like a kindergartner.

"It's not okay at all. Moving a shelf will offset the entire layout of the wall. You can't just take a shelf down without there being any design consequences," I tell him. "It disturbs the continuity and interrupts the flow. The whole vibe will be thrown off!"

And now he's looking at me like I'm crazy. "Well, I'm sorry that taking a shelf down is going to mess with the cupcake vibe, or whatever, *Blaire*, but unless you'd like to foot the bill to uninstall and reinstall all of this." He thumbs over his shoulder. "I'm thinking moving a shelf is probably your best bet if you don't want any more shattered unicorn dreams."

I huff my irritation, because although he has a point, the only person inconvenienced is me. And all this noise is going to make concentrating impossible today. I avoid responding, because I don't want to give in and agree with him. "How long is this going to go on for?"

"We can stop arguing about you moving a shelf anytime you want."

I've already filed this guy under Jerks I Want to Junk Punch. I hope someone puts Veet in his shampoo and all that luxurious, thick hair falls out. The thought of that alone makes me feel better. "I mean the noise, smartass."

The corners of his mouth turn up slowly until he's full on smiling. Dammit. Of course he has great teeth and a beautiful smile to go with his stupidly handsome face. All he probably has to do is flash that smile and people move shelves for him without a second thought. They probably move entire walls. And drop their damn panties, too.

He lifts a shoulder in a careless shrug. "I guess it depends on how long you want to stand here, bickering with me. I could do this all day, but that means I'm not working, and if I'm not working the enclosure isn't getting built. So it's entirely up to you how long it takes." His smile widens, likely at my appalled expression. "I'd offer to set you up with a pair of safety boots so you can keep having a go at me, but I'm not all that interested in putting a saw or a nail gun in your hands. I have a feeling it might be me you'd try to nail to the wall."

I flash him a less than friendly smile. "I meant how long do you expect these renovations to take?" I don't want them to interfere with my grand opening next week.

"Dunno. I'd say at least a couple of weeks, but it all depends on how often you decide to come over and give me shit."

"So now you're the one being inconvenienced, is that it?"

All he does is stand there with his arms crossed, wearing a telling smirk.

"Well thanks so much for making more work for me. It's not like I don't have enough to do right now. And I sincerely hope you're insulating that wall because I sure don't want an axe coming through it like some kind of B-rated horror movie!"

I spin on my heel and try to yank the door open with a dramatic flair, but of course the stupid wind-suction means I have to use both hands, which completely ruins the impact.

Once the suction seal is broken, the door flies open and I stumble back, almost landing on the filthy floor. I don't look back as I regain my composure, straighten my spine and exit his crappy pub.

"It was really nice to meet you, Blaire," he calls out after me, voice dripping sarcasm. "I'm Ronan Knight, by the way, thanks for asking, and for being so understanding about the renos!"

Well, now the name of the bar makes sense. Of course he has a super hipster, but also highly masculine name that's just as sexy as he is. Jerk.

He rattles the box with the broken glass. "Hey! You forgot your unicorn dreams!"

I consider flipping him the bird, but that would mean stooping to his level and I'm unwilling to play his game. "Kiss my cupcake!" I shout over my shoulder, wishing my wit had kicked in earlier. I stalk angrily down the sidewalk and nearly lose my footing for what seems like the hundredth time this morning when I step in something slippery. I glance down and gag, then tip my chin up to the sky. "Seriously?"

Of course I stepped in the dog-doo.

Because today hasn't been ruined enough by my new jerk of a neighbor.

I remove the offending shoe—the yellow flower is stuck to the bottom—and try not to breathe in the noxious odor. Daphne looks up from the bar where she's currently on her phone posting photos when I hobble back into my shop, my soiled shoe dangling from my finger.

Daphne's expression is somewhere between incredulous and questioning as she gives me a quick once-over. "Who are you and what have you done with my friend Blaire?"

"What?"

"Since when do you go around confronting complete strangers?"

She makes a good point. "Since I don't have enough money to replace that stupid glass. Everything I have is tied up in here." I wave my poopy shoe around. "I need this place to do well, Daph. I want to prove I can succeed on my own—with your help, obviously, and Paul's—but this needs to work out. I can't go to my family for help. They're too..."

"Crazy? Meddling? Impossible to deal with?" Daphne suggests.

"Exactly."

"Well, I gotta say, this new, bolder you is something I can definitely get used to. You're finally growing into your lady balls." She grins and nods to the shoe still dangling from my finger. "What happened?"

"I stepped in crap. Literally."

"Next door?"

"No. Out there." I motion to the sidewalk and hobble-weave my way through the tables all the way to the back door. I throw it open angrily and debate whether I should toss the shoe. I leave it outside, fairly confident no one is going to touch it.

I wash my hands before I return barefoot and still very much annoyed. Especially when the banging starts up again, and it seems like it's even more vigorous than it was before.

"So what's going on over there?"

"The lumberjerk next door is putting in an axe-throwing enclosure."

Daphne's eyes flare. "Lumberjerk?"

"He was wearing a plaid flannel shirt, wandering around with an axe. And get this: His name is Ronan, totally a hipster, right? He probably changed it from something far more pedestrian, like Robert or Bill. His hair looks like it's styled with pomade. All he was missing was the lumber-beard and the black-rimmed glasses."

Daphne holds up a hand. "Wait. Flannel in August?" Daphne asks. I'm glad she seems appropriately horrified by that fashion travesty.

"Or maybe it was plaid and I'm making up the flannel part. Regardless, he was wearing a plaid long-sleeved shirt with another shirt under it. In August. Totally ridiculous. And he's a completely condescending jerk! Can you believe he had the nerve to tell me I should move my shelf because he's putting in an axe-throwing enclosure? Who even likes throwing axes other than barbarians?"

"Uh, axe throwing is pretty popular these days."

I give her a look that tells her how much I don't appreciate her opinion on this. Or the fact that she is most certainly correct. "That's not the point. The point is he's inconveniencing me by using our adjoining wall for his freaking axe throwing! Why should I have to move my glassware for him? Moving that shelf means I'll have to adjust the entire layout. What a selfish bastard."

"Or do you mean shelf-ish bastard?" Daphne grins, and I fight one of my own.

"That was ridiculously lame."

"And yet, still funny."

I roll my eyes. "I need to tackle the shelf."

"Leave the shelf where it is."

"Why? We can't even put anything on it. Or hang stuff from that freaking wall if Lumberjerk is going to be throwing axes at it. And there's still a bar in there! How can they serve alcohol and wield axes? That seems outlandishly unsafe."

"There's protocol. And inspections."

I tap my lip, considering my options. "Inspections?"

Daphne shakes her head and raises a hand. "Don't start a war before you've even opened your doors, Blaire."

"You didn't meet him. He's a grade-A a-hole extraordinaire."

Although, she does have a point. "I'll tuck that piece of information in my pocket in case I need it."

Later, when I'm heading home for the day, I find a flyer tucked under my windshield wipers, which is odd, since I'm parked in the alley behind all the shops, where only the owners and employees are allowed. I lift the wiper and flip it over, curious and hoping that I don't have to fight a parking ticket I can't afford. It's definitely not a ticket, but it's dusk, and shadowy back here, so I climb into my SUV and toss it on the seat beside me.

It isn't until I get home and the interior light comes on that I finally realize what's on the flyer. It's an advertisement for anger-management therapy. At the top, in semi-legible man-scrawl is a note:

> *I'd invite you over for a little axe throwing to get out some of your latent aggression, but I'm not sure that's a good idea. Maybe this will help your vibe.*
>
> *~ your friendly neighborhood bar owner*

"What a jerk!" I ball it up and toss it in the trash. I don't have to wonder how he knew it was my SUV since I have a Buttercream and Booze magnetic decal stuck to the side panel.

@buttercreamandbooze:

Got a problem with me? Kiss my cupcake.

chapter three

THIS MEANS WAR

Blaire

Two days later I arrive at the shop after nine in the morning. I'm meeting Paul, my cupcake truck business partner and friend. My goal had always been to set up a storefront, while Paul really enjoyed being on the move and networking in new areas. He wanted to travel, and I wanted a home base.

We made a deal that he gets to keep the cupcake truck and the rights to the business. Instead of buying me out completely, he's agreed to continue to bake the cupcakes and I'll continue to decorate them for both of us while I get Buttercream and Booze up and running. That way he doesn't have to find someone else to partner up with, and neither of us has to hire someone to help.

I met Paul upon my return from Paris, while I was selling desserts in a booth at a local street market. Like me, Paul had his own cupcake and pastry booth, and we were right across from each other. Realizing that it would benefit us to work together—and save on booth rental costs—we ended up pooling our resources and our creativity. Having been on the street market circuit for a couple of years, Paul took me under his wing and showed me the ropes. He baked the cakes and I decorated them. We were a great team in the kitchen. Within a year we'd saved up enough to buy a food truck, and Cupcakes to Go! was born. At first Cupcakes to Go! was great and I loved having a partner. But Paul and I started butting heads since we both wanted to be in control of the business side, and by then I knew it was time to move on. It was always a temporary business venture, but it was a great learning experience.

This morning he's stopping by so he can try my newest cupcake creation and we can decide if there need to be any adjustments to the cake flavor and texture. The Cupcakes to Go! truck is parked out front on the street when I pass. The back door to my shop is already propped open with a wedge, which is considerate. It means I don't have to search my purse for my keys.

I'm busy juggling the cupcakes, my purse, and my travel mug, so I almost step in another pile of poop right in front of the door. "What the hell?" I grumble, looking around. Who would walk their dog in the back alley where there's all kinds of garbage? And who would leave their freaking dog poop behind? Maybe whoever it is has some kind of beef with the previous storeowner. Or maybe they have something against buttercream icing and booze.

The possibility that I've already made potential enemies and I haven't even opened my doors to the public unnerves me. I shake my head. I'm being paranoid. This isn't the food truck business. No one is going to slash my tires here.

I sidestep the poop and set the cupcakes inside, out of harm's way. This time I hunt down an old plastic bag immediately so I don't forget about it and no one accidentally steps in it. I make a face as I crouch down to pick it up, expecting the noxious odors to hit me, but strangely enough all I get is the faint stench of garbage. I also expect it to be squishy and gross, but it's unusually firm. Completely solid, in fact.

Once it's safely in the bag I try to lob it into the dumpster, but my aim sucks and it hits the side with a low thud and *thwang*.

I frown, because dog poop should not make that kind of sound when it hits metal. I don't know what gets into me, other than curiosity, but I open the bag and peek inside. Which is when I realize that it's not *real* poop. It's plastic.

I glance over at The Knight Cap and narrow my eyes. He must've seen me step in the poop the other day and this is his idea of being funny. "What a jerk."

Paul pokes his head out the back door. "I thought I heard someone back here. What's going on?"

I pull the fake poop out of the bag. "My neighbor is a turd, that's what's going on."

Paul makes a face. "Is that . . ."

"It's fake." I stalk over to the service entrance of The Knight

Cap. The door is propped open with a wooden wedge. The sound of a circular saw and the loud strains of rock music come from inside. I replace the wedge with the fake poop and as an afterthought, I take the wedge with me, because screw him.

"What was that all about?" Paul asks as I scoop up the box of cupcakes and he follows me down the hall.

"Apparently my new neighbor has the maturity of a twelve-year-old and thinks he's a comedian."

"Making friends already, huh?" Paul chuckles.

"Haha. As you can clearly hear, he's not the quietest, most conscientious neighbor." I set the Tupperware on the counter and wash my hands before I open it up to display my late-night endeavors.

"Oh, wow!" Paul wafts his hand over the container, inhaling deeply. "Is that maple? And bourbon? And bacon?"

"It is. Try one and tell me what you think. I'm not sure if the maple flavor is too overpowering in the icing." I tap on the counter, trying to be patient while he peels the wrapper and takes a healthy bite of the cupcake.

He closes his eyes and chews, nodding slightly. "The bourbon cream in the center balances out the maple perfectly. I wouldn't change a thing."

"Really?"

"They're decadent, Blaire. People are going to fall in love with them. Can you email me the recipe and I'll make a test batch tomorrow so I can be sure I get it right?" He glances inside the Tupperware and taps the top of two small containers labeled *icing* and *filling*, nestled among the cakes. "You're so on top of things. We're still doing the lemon drop cupcakes as well?"

"Yes, definitely. Plus the usual flavors, and the morning glory cupcakes. I have everything I need for the buttercream."

"Okay, great. Then I think we're all set. You're doing a fabulous job, Blaire." Paul gives me a kind smile.

"Thanks, I really appreciate your help."

"Well, it's mutually beneficial, isn't it? You honestly put together the most amazing flavor combinations."

I wave off the compliment, getting emotional about the whole thing. While I'm not going to miss the cramped quarters of the cupcake truck, we've been working together for a long time and he's been a good friend and partner.

He gives me a side hug, grabs the Tupperware and heads out. I'll see him at the crack of dawn on opening morning so I can decorate the cupcakes and make sure everything is picture perfect.

A few hours later, Lumberjerk passes by my front window, waving jovially.

Such a jerk.

As the week progresses I decide that my disdain for Ronan is completely justified. He's a dick. A giant, stupidly attractive dick who always wears long-sleeved plaid shirts—yes, I totally

made up the flannel part—rolled up to his elbows with another shirt underneath it. And jeans. And work boots. Every
damn day.

How do I know this?

Because every single day he passes my storefront at some
point and makes a big show of waving exuberantly while
shouting hello.

And yesterday he was wearing a pair of black, thick-rimmed
glasses. It's all too much. And annoying.

Especially since he seems to love getting under my skin.

Every day I find a flyer tucked into one of my flowerpots for
some kind of class or session to help "calm the restless soul."
One has a coupon for three free yoga sessions, which I'd be
tempted to use if I actually had time for yoga. The next day he
leaves me a brochure warning me about the effects of too much
sugar and caffeine. It's even accompanied with lavender oil.

But what really takes the cupcake are the contents of the
cardboard box I find sitting in front of my door this morning.
I'm hesitant to open it, assuming something is going to jump
out at me. I'm relieved to find nothing living, or dead, inside
the box. That relief is short-lived, though, because inside the
box is my unicorn martini glass. Except it's been reassembled
ass backward—quite literally. There are now plaid accents and
a little logo with a guy in a suit of armor wearing one of those
old-school nightcaps where its eyes used to be. Also, the horn
is sticking out of its butt.

Half of me is annoyed and the other half is impressed that

he took the time to do this to needle me. Again. It's a hideous, yet quite amazing work of art. Not that I would ever admit that to his face.

On the upside, the constant banging seems to have stopped. The paper is still on the windows, so I'm assuming it's going to be a while before the place opens. Although a new sign was put up yesterday boasting the name THE KNIGHT CAP in masculine gold letters. I'm almost surprised there isn't some kind of plaid on the signage. I'm sure there will be loads of it making the interior extra gaudy.

But today I could care less about Lumberjerk, because it's my grand opening and it's going to be amazing. My Instagram following is already over one thousand, my Facebook page has double that. More than two hundred and fifty coupons have been downloaded.

I've been here since four in the morning frosting and decorating cupcakes. We have hundreds ready to roll, and Paul has a contingency plan should I be a little too hopeful about opening day. The display case is perfectly organized and prepared; the specials board is a work of art.

I make sure today's featured cupcakes and drinks are front and center in the showcase: a lemon drop cupcake with lemon curd filling and a tangy lemon buttercream complemented by a delicious, tart, lemon drop martini. Its counterpart is a bourbon bacon cupcake with maple buttercream icing paired with a smoky bourbon old-fashioned topped with a strip of maple candy bacon. Yes, I've already Instagrammed them.

The sandwich menu is simple, yet the variety is pleasing enough for every palate and the array of savory and sweet scones, plus coffee and tea options, make this the only cupcake cocktail café of its kind.

I step outside and set up my A-frame sign boasting today's specials and my quote of the day:

"WHEN LIFE GIVES YOU LEMONS MAKE LEMON DROP MARTINIS!"

I double and triple check that the bar is stocked, the coffee is ready to be poured, the hot water is prepped for tea and Callie is comfortable with her counter duties. She's my only employee—because one person is all I can reasonably afford to pay. I'm hoping we can handle whatever gets thrown at us. She looks adorable in her Buttercream and Booze shirt, and her shoes have a lemon wedge print on them, which is beyond perfect. Thankfully, Daphne's agreed to help out this morning and not to take photos. I'm so freaking lucky to have her as a friend.

I clap my hands excitedly, smooth my palms over my apron and adjust the hem of my dress. Today I'm wearing an off-white dress with a huge lemon slice pattern. I added a temporary lemon slice tattoo on my cheek, decorated with a tiny yellow jewel.

I give Callie a brief rundown of the specials. While I expect the majority of my business to cater to the lunch, afternoon, and cocktail hour crowd, it seems spiked coffees might very well be a hit this morning, considering the line of people waiting for the doors to officially open.

We're only a few blocks from the university, and there are several student-centric apartment buildings close by, as well as plenty of local businesses.

The first hour is mayhem of the most delicious sort. It doesn't matter that it's not even noon—almost everyone seems to want cupcakes and coffee or tea. The college crowd and the Saturday shoppers fill the café in the early afternoon, the two-for-one cupcake coupons are piling up, and I'm kept busy making martinis and bourbon old-fashioneds while Callie works the cash. Daphne sticks around since we're far busier than I anticipated, which is not a bad problem to have.

Around three in the afternoon the door tinkles and Lumberjerk weaves his way through the tables, making every single woman in the place—college students, mothers, grandmothers—and a good percentage of the men do a double take.

Daphne whistles low under her breath. "Holy crap I think my panties just lit themselves on fire."

I shoot her a look. "He's not that hot."

She gives me her *seriously* face but she doesn't have a chance to respond because he's already standing in front of us. I plaster on a smile. "I think you're in the wrong place. Axe throwing is next door."

"Blaire." Daphne elbows me in the side.

He smiles back, widely. As if he knows exactly the effect he's having on me and every damn woman in here. "I thought I'd stop by and grab one of those cupcakes everyone seems to be freaking out over." He pulls a two-for-one cupcake coupon out of his back pocket. Where it's been curved around his tight ass.

Not that I've noticed how tight it is over the past week. Okay. I've totally noticed. Every single time he's walked past the front window.

He passes me the coupon and I snatch it from him with more aggression than necessary, which makes that smile of his widen even more. Damn him and his perfect teeth and his sexy eye-crinkles. I motion to the display case of cupcakes, each tray labeled based on flavor with a description of the cake and frosting combination. "What tickles your fancy?" I cringe internally at my terrible choice of wording.

Ronan tips his head to the side and his tongue peeks out of the corner of his mouth. I want to shove it back in—with a mixing spoon.

He shrugs. "What you do recommend?"

"How about some Death by Chocolate?"

He chuckles. "I'm not really a fan of chocolate cake, or death."

"Not a fan? Obviously you've been eating the wrong cake." Daphne's voice is smoky and low, like she's thinking about eating one of those Death by Chocolate cupcakes off his naked chest, while riding him.

"Maybe." He shuffles over a few steps and leans in, peering

at the options. He taps on the front of the case, leaving behind a fingerprint. "Bourbon bacon cupcake with maple buttercream? That sounds good. I'll try one of those."

"Would you like it to go?" Yes, I'm trying to get him out of my shop as quickly as possible since his mere presence is a gray cloud hanging over what's supposed to be a sunshiny day.

His gaze lifts, wry smile firmly in place. "Nah, I'll sample the goods right here, but thanks."

I slip my hand into a pale pink non-latex glove and pluck one of the cupcakes from the display case, then wait for him to decide on his second one.

"The lemon drop cupcake is a featured special today if you'd like to give it a try."

"Hmm. Is it sour?" The *like you* is clearly intimated, though unspoken.

"It has some pucker power, if that's what you mean. It's a good balance of sweet and tart."

"So exactly like its creator, then?"

Daphne chokes on a cough and turns away so she can help the next customer while I finish up with Ronan. He hems and haws for another minute before he finally decides to go with the lemon drop cupcake.

"Would you like anything to drink with that?" I set the plate on top of the glass display counter.

"Nah, just the cupcakes, thanks." He passes over a five-dollar bill.

He braces a forearm on the glass case, despite the fact that there's a sweet little sign that reads DO NOT TOUCH THE GLASS. Peeling the pale yellow wrapper from the lemon cupcake, he jams half of it into his mouth in one bite, making a small noise of surprise—likely a result of the sweet-tart combination of flavors. Cake crumbs litter the glass top and there's now a small line of customers waiting.

Instead of moving aside, he continues to devour the cupcake in a less than polite manner, while leaning on the display case, making it impossible for anyone else to check out what's available. Not that any of the waiting customers are particularly upset about it, considering the way many of them are eyeing him, probably wishing they're that freaking cupcake he's mowing down on.

He eats the first one in three bites and licks the icing from his fingers before he starts in on the bourbon bacon and maple one. His brows pull down on the first bite, and a deep groan follows. He chews quickly, his Adam's apple bobbing as he swallows. "Holy fuck, that's awesome. It's like sweet, but not? Savory, but...decadent?" He jams the rest of it into his mouth, leaving more crumbs on the glass top counter and making a general mess.

He also groans his way through the mouthful. It's ridiculous. "Wow. That was amazing. They both were, but the bacon is the winner for me. Can I buy half a dozen of those?"

"Of course you can!" Callie appears out of nowhere. "I can help, Blaire, and you can take care of the new customers." She gives me a slightly manic, bright smile.

"That'd be great. Thanks."

Ronan glances at what has now become a significant line. "Oh shit. I'm kinda holding things up, aren't I?" He winks at the waiting customers, who all happen to be women. "Sorry, ladies."

There's a collective murmur of "it's okay" and "no problem" and I'm pretty sure someone says "marry me."

I let Callie take over his order since she's already loading up a box for him.

His little performance seems to have an impact on the rest of the customers standing in line, because every single one of them orders a bourbon bacon maple cupcake.

On his way out, he stops at a couple of tables to chat with some of the customers. I eye him suspiciously, but I don't have time to contemplate it much since he's created quite the backlog.

"You failed to mention Lumberjerk is also a super hottie," Daphne mutters as she bumps my hip so she can get to the cupcakes.

"That's because his personality ruins all the pretty," I reply. But that's not entirely true, because despite the jerkiness, I can still definitely appreciate how nice he is to look at, unfortunately.

"I don't know. Is he really that bad? He came in to support you, and now everyone is ordering cupcakes by the half-dozen, so it's not like he's bad for business."

I grunt instead of answering, because she might be right, but admitting it is against my current moral standards.

We run out of bourbon cupcakes so I have to run to the back to restock the display case while Callie and Daphne manage the front counter.

It's nearly four thirty before things calm down and I can finally take a breath. I move through the tables, checking on customers. I pause to clear some plates at a two-top with a pair of women in their mid-twenties and notice a couple of pieces of paper sitting beside an empty coffee cup. Upon closer inspection, I realize it's a coupon. For half-price wings and beer at The Knight Cap. And it's for today.

As if on cue, the low rumble of bass coming from next door makes the floor vibrate under my feet.

I plaster on what I hope is a pleasant smile and tap the coupon. "Do you mind if I ask where you got this?"

"That super hot guy who orgasm-moaned his way through his cupcake at the display case dropped it off at our table on the way out," she offers.

"I'm stuffed, but I would totally pretend to sip a beer so I could stare at him for a while." Her friend pats her belly.

They both laugh and I join in, although I sound like I'm choking on a squeaky toy, or like I've swallowed the Wicked Witch of the West. "Do you mind if I take one of these?"

"Go right ahead! I say you should treat yourself after you close up for the night and enjoy some eye candy." She pushes one of the coupons toward me.

"I might do that." I wink and slide the coupon into my apron pocket, then clear their empty plates and cups.

After I drop them in the bus bin, I sidle up to Daphne at the till and slap the coupon on the counter. "Looks like our neighbor wasn't being quite so supportive."

Daphne scans the coupon. "Where'd you get this?"

"He gave it to our customers on his way out. Invited them to his Grand Opening. So kind and thoughtful, huh?"

"But you said that place was a construction site last week. How could it be ready to open so soon?"

"Who the hell knows?" I glance at the tables and notice that there are several women holding the same damn coupon. *That slimy bastard.* "But I'm going over there to confront him. Hold down the fort." I grab the coupon, stalk around the counter and head for the door, my anger gaining steam as I step outside and notice the giant GRAND OPENING banner plastered to his storefront and the sign that looks almost exactly like mine, but reads DONE WITH TEA AND CAKES? NEED A BREAK FROM WONDERLAND? HALF-PRICE BEER IS HERE!

"Sonofdouchecanoe!" I mutter and stomp my way up the front steps. I yank on the door, expecting the same suction vacuum as last time. However, the problem must have been fixed last week because it opens surprisingly easily, almost sending me flying backward. Again, but for the opposite reason.

I recover before I end up sprawled out over the sidewalk and step inside the low-lit pub. It's the exact opposite of my bright, airy café. However, I can easily pick out at least six tables with familiar faces—because they were all recently patrons of mine before they defected here.

I loathe to admit that in the week since I stepped foot in this place, it's come together quite nicely. Despite the dim lighting, I can see the tables are pale pine, and the décor, although lacking in sophistication, is cozy and comfortable. And, as I predicted, there's a red-and-black plaid theme throughout.

Perfectly publike. It's a great place to sit back, drink beers, eat wings and hang out with other hipsters while getting your axe throw on. Which is exactly what's happening in the back half of the pub.

It's even manned by a huge, ominous-looking bouncer who doesn't let anyone through the door without first signing a waiver and passing a sobriety test.

I drag my attention away from the axe-throwing enclosure and search the bar for the backstabbing turd who owns the place. I find him behind the bar, a black towel thrown over his shoulder, matching his black-rimmed glasses.

I cross the hardwood floor, noting that it's been freshly varnished, and step up to the bar as Ronan places a pint in front of one of his customers with a wink. She also happens to have recently been a customer of mine.

He grins when he sees me and props his thick, gloriously tattooed forearms on the bar. *Gloriously tattooed*? What is wrong with me? "You taking a break from Wonderland to join the madness, Alice?"

"I'd like to talk to you."

"I'm a little busy." He motions to the already crowded pub.

"But you can pull up a stool and tell me all your woes over a pint." He winks.

I want to poke him in the eye.

I ignore his semi-flirtatious behavior, aware that these are probably the lines he uses on every single woman who bats her lashes at him, which I don't do. Instead, I slap the coupon on the bar. "Would you care to explain this?"

"It's a coupon for half price beer and wings. Not sure you're much of a wing eater since that would mean getting your fingers dirty." And there's that smile again. So condescending.

"I know it's a coupon and I know what it's for, thanks. I'm fully capable of reading. What I'd like to know is what the hell you think you're doing coming into *my* café under the guise of being supportive, when really, you were planning to steal my customers."

His smile drops. "I wasn't trying to steal them."

"Oh, really?" I wave the coupon in front of his face. My voice continues to rise over the thumping bass. "So you just happened to stop by and drop a handful of coupons at my patrons' tables inviting them to leave my place and go to *your* Grand Opening, which you also happened to schedule the same day as *mine*?"

He bites his bottom lip, glancing at the women sitting at the bar to his right, who all recently came from my café. "Can we talk over here?" He tips his head to the end of the bar.

I follow his lead and meet him at the other end. He uses his hip to open the swinging half door that separates the bar from the rest of the pub and motions me down a short hall. Old, framed photographs line the wall, a few of them slightly askew, as if someone has brushed them with their shoulder on the way past and tried to right them, but only ended up setting them even more out of line. For some reason it's endearing, annoyingly so. He ushers me into a small office, which was clearly left out of the renovations based on the ancient desk and the rolling chair that looks like it's from the seventies.

He leaves the door slightly ajar. In this confined space I'm noticing how big he is compared to me. At five-five I'm not exactly fun-sized, and my heels put me at a solid five-eight, but Ronan is well over six feet.

Not that I'll allow his size to intimidate me.

I toss the coupon on his desk—it's messy and there is a pile of them scattered all over it—and cross my arms. "Real dick move, hijacking my Grand Opening, Ronan. You said your place wouldn't be ready for at least a couple of weeks. It somehow miraculously came together in one?"

His brows pop. "It's not like we're appealing to the same client base. You serve fruity drinks and cupcakes, and I serve beer and bar food."

"That might've been a decent argument if you hadn't come by pretending to be all nice-nice, putting on a great show for my customers, having yourself a foodgasm in front of them, buttering them all up and stealing them right from under my nose with this." I stab at the coupon.

He half-rolls his eyes. "I didn't steal them."

"Like hell you didn't!" I throw my hands up in the air, agitated, and nearly hit him in the face since there isn't much room for flailing in here. "More than half the women lining your bar were in my café before you pillaged them."

"Okay, *pillaged* intimates something a lot more sinister than handing over a coupon and inviting them to stop by when they were *done* at your place."

"They might have stayed longer, had another drink, ordered some cupcakes to go if you hadn't stopped by and flashed your pretty smile and special offers at them." I flick his glasses, which is admittedly crossing the invisible *don't-touch* line, veering into assault territory, but I'm really fired up and we're less than a foot apart so it's almost impossible to not touch him. "Are these even real or are they a prop? What about your tattoos? I'd hardly be surprised if you ordered those fake sleeves online so you can look more hipster than you are." I don't know what it is about this guy, but he brings out a side of me that I didn't even know existed. Sure I can get worked up about things, but not usually to this degree.

"So I can...What?" He shakes his head and holds up his hands, maybe to prevent me from flicking him again. "I've been pulling twenty-hour days for the past week, and if I wear my contacts it feels like I have sand under them. The glasses are real, and so are the tattoos."

"So you're a legit thieving hipster. Good to know."

He purses his lips. "I'm not trying to steal your business."

"And I'm supposed to believe you after you drop by and flirt with all my customers and leave these coupons for them?"

"I wasn't flirting with them."

"Oh my God! Yes you most certainly were with the smiles and the banter and the damn winking."

"I don't wink."

"Oh yes you do."

"I do not."

I hold a hand up, unwilling to argue about this. "The winking isn't the point. The point is that you're a lying, conniving bastard and I'm on to you."

I reach for the doorknob at the same time he does, so his fingers skim the back of my hand. I jolt from the contact, because it honestly feels a little like I've been electrocuted. Not in an *I'm going to die* kind of way, but more of an unexpected stimulating way. I'm not sure which is worse, actually.

He raises both hands in the air and adopts a contrite expression. "My intention wasn't to steal your customers, Alice."

"It's Blaire, not Alice!" Of course he's still making fun of me. "As if I'm going to believe that after you leave fake poop in front of my back door and all the anger management, get Zen with yourself flyers! Not to mention what you did to my poor unicorn martini glass!"

He rolls his eyes. "Oh, come on, I was playing around and you have to admit the unicorn glass looks way cooler now."

"It's an abomination! And of course it's funny to you since you're the one doing the pranking!"

His expression sobers. "Look, it's too bad you took it the wrong way, but you came in here that first day guns blazing and I figured it might lighten you up. Obviously I was way wrong about that. As for the grand opening, I just thought it would be better for both of us if they happened on the same day, more like a two-for-one kind of deal, you know?"

"You mean you thought it would be better for *you* since I'd already done the work to bring people to the area. If you really thought it would be better for both of us you should've approached me, but you didn't."

He crosses his arms. "Well maybe I would have if you'd been more approachable."

I prop a fist on my hip. "And you think playing pranks on me would accomplish that."

"Okay. So I should've told you my plan—"

I cut him off, triumphant that he's finally admitted he's wrong. "Of course you'll admit it was a mistake now, when the damage is already done."

His eyes go wide, as if he's trying to look innocent. "I can see how this might look to you, but I really wasn't trying to steal your customers. Besides, it's not like people can survive on cupcakes and alcohol indefinitely—"

He did not just say that. "Do not try and justify your actions to me." I point a finger at his face. "I see right through you. Just remember, Ronan, you threw the first axe."

"What? I didn't throw anything."

"It's an expression." I roll my eyes. "I'm being cheeky. You threw the first stone, took the first shot. It's on." And with that I yank open the door. "You may have started the war, but I'll be the one taking you down, one sweet treat at a time." I wink and sashay through the bar, slipping my hand into my apron. I pull out a handful of my own coupons and toss them on tables, inviting customers to stop by before they head home so they can bring their loved ones something delightful to sink their teeth into.

@buttercreamandbooze:

I BAKE the world a better place.

chapter four

I'M NUMBER ONE

Blaire

Things heat up with my neighbor post–grand opening. A little not-quite-friendly competition, so to speak. Things like, when Ronan has a special, I try to make mine better. On Friday night I hand out two-for-one cocktail coupons to combat his half-price draft beer and house wine. Everyone knows that house wine is the cheap crappy stuff.

So what if the two-for-one martinis aren't made with the premium vodka? They're also full of things like crème de cacao and other sweet, minty, chocolaty, or fruity booze and juice, so it hides the taste and does the trick.

Twentysomething-year-old guys might not mind cheap draft beer, but most women in their late twenties would much rather sip a pretty martini over a cheap glass of wine any day of the week. How do I know this? I polled my followers, of course.

And don't think Ronan is an innocent. His prankster ways

continue—this week I stepped in what I believed was poop—again—but it just happened to be poop-shaped Play-Doh. It also contained sparkles, which I got on my hands and which subsequently were all over everything I own for the next three days.

In addition to the fake sparkle poop, Ronan has taken to dropping off a daily coupon for me, except they're modified to whatever it is he's been serving to customers that day. He always includes some kind of tongue-in-cheek comment about what he regards as my less-than-friendly personality. I am friendly. Just not with him. Today's coupon was for half-priced salt-and-vinegar fish and chips and some honey lager—which I hate to admit sounds kind of yummy. He scrawled a note on the back about drawing more flies with honey than vinegar.

Two weeks in, and things are going well on the business end. Better than well, actually. We're busy throughout the day, we have orders for pickup and takeout all the time, the cupcakes are flying off the shelves and people love our daily cupcake cocktail themes. My social media feeds are full of tags and picture perfect photos of B&B, of groups of friends gathered together in the café, and of delighted smiles and rave reviews.

Even so, I'm barely eking by right now. On the upside, I'm close to being able to cover my expenses without digging too deeply into my line of credit. Am I eating a lot of leftover cup-cakes and close-to-the-expiration-date sandwiches that would otherwise be destined for the garbage? Most definitely. But I knew finances were going to be tough at the beginning.

It can take up to three years for a business to grow its legs and with the way things are looking, there is a chance I'll be able to turn a profit within the next few years. Notwithstanding an annoying neighbor who is taking some of my business.

"This is amazing. You must be on top of the world right now!" Daphne sips her salted caramel martini while scrolling through the Instagram feed.

The last customer left about twenty minutes ago, probably heading next door for whatever Lumberjerk has planned for tonight. I closed up shop and made us a drink and now we're relaxing at the back of the café, stretched out on the comfy couches and chairs.

Daphne snaps a photo of me lounging on the couch and Paul returns from the bathroom in time to peek over her shoulder. "Definitely post that."

"Right? It'll get tons of likes," Daphne agrees.

Paul comes by first thing in the mornings to drop off the cupcakes for the day, giving me plenty of time to decorate them before opening. But tomorrow he has an out of town event, so he dropped everything off this evening and I con-vinced him to stay for a drink. There's no way I could've made this work without his help and I'm eternally grateful for his friendship over the past several years.

I wait for Daphne to pass her camera over. "Can I at least see it before you post it? What if I look like a shrew?"

"As if I would post a bad picture of you." Daphne is appropriately offended; she and I have spent a ridiculous amount of time perfecting posed photos over the past several weeks.

I hold my hands up in supplication. "I know. It's a conditioned response. I got a message earlier in the week from my sister telling me she thinks my right side is more flattering."

Daphne's lip curls in disdain. "I hope you told her to suck it."

"It's her way of trying to be helpful."

"It's her way of being a bitch," Daphne argues.

I shrug. Maddy is pretty much always a bitch. I've spent my entire life dealing with her, so her random comments are nothing in comparison to some of her other antics.

"Anyway, the only time I've seen you possess shrewlike qualities was when you and Raphael broke up," Daphne continues.

I glare at her. "We do not talk about Raphael."

"Raphael? How come I've never heard of this guy?" Paul asks.

"You have. He's more commonly known as The Douche."

"Oh. You mean the guy who was boning you and three other chefs at the same time?" Paul drops into the chair beside mine.

"The one and only. And can we not discuss him, please? It was years ago, before you came along and made me realize there's more to life than kobe beef and truffle fries. Unlike you, he was more interested in showing me his bratwurst than he was in teaching me anything of value." I pat Paul on the arm. One of the things I appreciate most about Paul is the fact that our relationship has always been strictly professional and platonic. Which was what I needed after the nightmare that was Raphael.

"Back when you were still trying to please Mummy and Daddy." He takes a swig of his Manhattan.

"Those days are long gone." I take another, deeper sip of my martini. It's more like a gulp. I love my family, but they are ridiculously highbrow in their approach to the food industry. They're also crazy.

I have no desire to serve people who think it's reasonable to spend two thousand dollars on a burger. I don't care if God himself blessed the freaking cow and then dusted it in edible gold.

"Have they seen this place yet?" Paul asks.

"Uh no, they haven't." And if I can prevent it, I'm hoping they won't ever manage to make the trip out here to my "little cupcake shop." They chose their side the day it became clear they were more concerned with the success of their business and keeping star chef Raphael happy than with my own broken heart. At least I'd gotten my trip to France out of the deal.

While I've been lost in my head, thinking about my family, Daphne and Paul have been chatting. Paul reaches over and pinches my arm, almost causing me to spill my martini on my dress. "Ow! What the hell?"

"Did you hear anything Daphne just said?" He gives me a look.

"Sorry, I was thinking. What'd I miss?"

"You know Tori Taylor the famous YouTuber?" Daphne asks.

"Sure. What about her?" I know the very vaguest basics about Tori. She has an insane number of subscribers and has made a career out of "Best of" videos. Last year alone she put at least ten small businesses on the map. The second she promotes something, thousands of people are right there, buying whatever it is, or going to whatever location she deems popular. She has incredible influence.

"Check this out." Daphne hands me her phone so I can watch the video she has cued up. Tori appears on the screen, makeup on point, looking stunning as usual, name dropping the brands she's currently wearing, citing the discount code you can use to get the same look/purse/shirt/shoes before she pans out to show her viewers the cool interior of her favorite local bar in LA.

"I've been coming here since I was legal to drink." She winks. "Every time I come home this is the place I go to meet up with friends. It has the perfect ambiance. It's quirky, cool and has the most amazing drinks." She goes on to talk about the special cocktail she's currently drinking, and her love of jalapeño-infused margaritas. "So it got me thinking, I have this road trip coming up and I need to know where the best bars are in the Pacific Northwest. What are the funkiest places, the ones with the best drink menus, the coolest vibe, the best food between San Francisco and Seattle? I want the bars that have it all. Drop your nominations in the comments and make sure you link their social media so I can check them out! And don't forget to use the hashtag 'toritaylorbestbars!' Maybe your favorite bar will be a stop on my road trip! And best of all, the winner will not only be featured on my channel, but I've made a deal with the Food and Drink network to showcase the best bar! Check my site for more details!" She makes a heart with her hands, kissy lips the screen, winks and signs off.

"You have to enter this!" Daphne declares. "We need to get everyone we know to nominate Buttercream and Booze for best bar! Can you even imagine how amazing it would be for business if you were featured on Tori's channel, let alone on Food and Drink?"

"It could make your career." Paul starts scrolling through the comments. "This video has been up for an hour and there are thousands of nominations. What's the name of the pub next door?"

"The Knight Cap," Daphne and I say at the same time.

"It's already in here a bunch of times." Paul shows me his phone.

"Of course it is." I roll my eyes. "I'm sure Lumberjerk held everyone at axe point until they gave him a raving review."

Daphne slides her chair closer, pulls up The Knight Cap's social media and starts comparing our social media posts, because that's her specialty. I'm getting better at staging photos, but since Daphne is still building her portfolio, she's happy to give me advice when I need it.

"You have twice as many followers as The Knight Cap. And your posts are way prettier. Although, I have to admit, the Lumberjerk isn't hard to look at."

Paul makes a face. "Man, this guy wears a lot of plaid."

I throw my hands up in the air. "Yes! Exactly! Every freaking day it's plaid, plaid, and more plaid!"

"Well that's the uniform over there, isn't it?" Daphne says. "Don't defend the plaid."

Daphne shrugs. "It kinda works for him, though."

"You're supposed to be on my side!"

"I am on your side, but I'm also allowed to appreciate a hottie, and this guy is smokin', with or without the plaid. I will say, though, it's clear that he doesn't have a professional helping him with this. All of these pictures are candid and based on the number of selfies from the bartender I'm going to hazard a guess that he's the one posting most of this stuff." Daphne shows me an image of a younger guy, smirking at the camera while Ronan pours a pint in the background.

"Let's hope they don't hire anyone then, because I'd like to keep the social media leg up on him. And hot or not, we need to do better than the whole axe-throwing thing he's got going on over there."

"Mmm, it's a double draw, isn't it? Hot guys and axe throwing in a college town is high on the yes-please scale."

As if they can hear us talking through the wall—which they can't, the plywood is thick and the music is loud enough that the low thump of bass makes the floor vibrate—a thud, followed by shouts of approval and some muffled chanting, makes all of us jump. "Someone hit the target." And based on the chanting, it was the resident Lumberjerk.

Daphne taps her lip with a manicured nail. "You know what we need to do?"

"Steal all of the axes and break off the handles?" Paul suggests.

"Axes can be replaced and theft isn't a good way to get ahead. We need to fight axes with cupcakes." Daphne makes a face and waves that comment away. "What I mean is that we should roll the cupcake-drink theme into events."

"You want to have a salted caramel event?" I ask.

"No. Well, yes. Kind of. Like we come up with different theme nights to draw in new customers the same way we have theme cupcakes and drinks every day. We need something buzz-worthy that's going to help us get more nominations."

"Okay. So what can we do that's better than axe throwing? And I don't want to do something that's super dangerous." The last thing I want is someone chopping off a vital body part. I can barely handle a paper cut without getting woozy.

"We could hold a cupcake-decorating contest. Winner gets a fifty-dollar gift card? That way the money goes back into Buttercream and Booze."

"Ooooh! I like this. That could be super fun."

"Exactly!" Daphne agrees. "I don't know that we need to try to compete with The Knight Cap. Your clientele is during the day and into the evening, where Lumberjerk caters to the evening and late night crowd. So I think we need to focus on what attracts people here and what we can do to keep them entertained for as long as possible."

"Okay, so we need to poll our customers and find out what other kinds of events they'd be interested in. Karaoke is always a winner, and trivia nights are super fun. I always loved a good poetry slam night back when I was in college."

Paul scoffs.

I cross my arms. "What? Poetry slams are fun."

Paul cocks a brow. "I'm sure for you they are."

"What is that supposed to mean?"

"You look like a cross between a librarian and a fifties pinup girl. The fact that poetry slams excite you isn't even a remote surprise."

"Whatever. You just wait, my poetry slam nights are going to make axe throwing seem like a trip on a snooze cruise."

"Gettin' your rhyme on already?" Daphne smirks.

"It must be the booze."

They chuckle and groan.

"But seriously, when it comes to poetry slams, I never lose."

@buttercreamandbooze:

YOU'RE A GREAT SINGER. ~love, Wine

♡ ✉ ✎   ☆

chapter five

POKE THE AGITATED ALICE

Ronan

The books look good so far." My grandfather pushes his glasses up his nose, bushy white eyebrows furrowed, shoulders hunched as he leans in close and leafs through the printed reports. Being in his eighties means everything gets lost in translation when he's looking at a computer screen with the exact same numbers, so I print things out for him, even though it makes forests cry.

He rolls his shoulders back, sitting up straighter as he looks around the bar. His eyes crinkle in the corners, the lines in his face deepening with his wistful smile. "The renovations look good, too."

I lean on the bar, pride choking me up, so my reply comes out a little gruff. "Thanks Gramps." It was hard for him when I started changing things, so he hadn't come in much for a while, but he's back to popping in almost every other day.

He pats my arm with his big, knobby fingers. Gramps and

I are about the same height, although he's lost a couple of inches with age. His white shock of hair is slicked back and styled neatly, and as usual he's wearing a white button-down and a pair of black dress pants. "Back in my day the only guys who decorated their skin were the ones who were in the Navy or spent some time behind bars." He tells me this pretty much every single time he sees me, which is often, especially now that I'm helping run his bar. Mostly it's a joke. Although the first time he saw my sleeves he asked me why I couldn't hang my art on my walls like regular people.

"I can make you an appointment, get you set up with your own art if you're jealous of mine. We could get matching ones."

Gramps snorts a laugh. "I don't even like it when a pretty nurse takes my blood. Not gonna have some guy coming at me with a bunch o' buzzing needles."

I rap on the bar and point a finger at him. "Just remember that when you tell a nurse she's pretty nowadays it's called sexual harassment."

"It's really a woman's world, isn't it? Can't say we didn't have it comin' or that Dottie didn't tell me it would happen. God rest her soul." He makes the sign of the cross, and I do the same.

Grams passed away a little over a year ago, and for a while there I was worried Gramps was going to follow in her footsteps. They'd been together for more than sixty years and had been working side by side every single day since they met. In all the time they'd been married, they'd never spent a night apart. Sure, Gramps would go out with his friends and play poker, and Grams would have "knitting" nights with her friends—which were really gin martini socials with a few balls of wool and sets of knitting needles lying around for decoration—but there wasn't a single night in over sixty years that they didn't sleep beside each other.

I'm not sure if I'd consider that romantic, clingy, or an extreme case of codependency. Regardless, they loved and bickered fiercely. So when Gramps woke one morning to find that she'd passed in her sleep, I wasn't so sure he was going to be able to manage the world without her. And more selfishly, I worried about how I would handle it if Gramps couldn't deal with the loss.

My dad—his oldest son—and my mom were killed in a car accident when I was twenty. I was old enough to survive on my own, but it still shook the foundation of my life. I'd always been close to my grandparents, so they stepped into the role of surrogate parents. Which is how I ended up back here, running the show instead of just bussing tables and tending bar—although I still do those things, too.

I'd been working my way up the ladder in finance, because that's where the money is, but it isn't my passion. Not even close. It was a nine-to-five grind that lined my pockets but gave me zero in the way of job satisfaction.

For the past several years I've wanted to open my own brewery, but to do that I need cash. So I went to Gramps for a loan, hoping to circumvent the bank's high interest rates.

Having immigrated from Scotland to America as a kid and growing up in a middle-class family that sometimes struggled to make ends meet when they first came to America, he's a big fan of working for what you get. Which means he didn't just hand over the money. Not a big surprise.

However, he offered me an opportunity. The Knight Cap has been in our family for three generations, and he can no longer handle the responsibility of managing the place on his own. Plus, it was in serious need of an overhaul. He would fund the renovations and if I could breathe some life back into the pub, he would loan me the start-up money for the brewery—no interest. It would give me the experience I needed running a business and hopefully keep his pride and joy from going belly up.

So far, I'm keeping up my end of the bargain.

"I have to admit, I wasn't real keen on the axe-throwing business, but it looks like once the renovations are paid off, you'll be turning a real profit there, as long as no one hacks off an arm, anyway." He winks. "It's a real good start, son."

"Thanks. And there are some pretty strict rules around the axe throwing, so everyone's limbs should stay safely attached to their bodies."

"That's generally where ya want them, eh?" He drums his fingers on the bar top, his grin wry. "And I appreciate that ya kept the wall o' photographs. Means a lot to this old man."

"Well, I might not have been there for all of them, but they mean a lot to me, too." I know it's been hard for Gramps to have to step down from running the bar. It's been his second home for most of his life, and all the memories in it contain Grams.

My phone lights up with new social media alerts. We both glance at the screen.

"What's that all about? You get yourself a new girlfriend? You started dating one of the ladies you hired?" His expression brightens and I laugh.

"Once again, asking my employees out is on the list of no-no's these days. Too many potential complications."

Gramps throws his hands in the air. "Dottie and I would n'er 'ave gotten married if we'd worried about complications, now would we?"

"This is true. However, my employees are college students."

"Ah well, you're bound to meet a lass eventually, especially working 'ere."

I decide to veer the topic away from my dating life, since it's not very exciting these days. Besides, if I let him keep going he'll eventually get on me about settling down before I'm too old.

It's not that I don't want a partner, but from what I've seen, you can't be married to your job and married to another person unless you're like my Gramps and Grams who worked together. Otherwise, the career or the partner ends up neglected.

And right now, my career is paramount. I have an obligation to Gramps, and the brewery is actually within my grasp.

Besides, I haven't been able to meet anyone since I'm always at The Knight Cap.

At least this is the justification I give anyone who asks about my relationship status. Honestly, losing my parents at twenty was rough, and that was a kind of pain I wanted to avoid. It didn't help that I'd had a girlfriend when they passed away, and that relationship hit some major turbulence, eventually crashing and burning because I couldn't handle the loss and she didn't know how to help me grieve. It wasn't her fault, we were college kids, but it sure did have an impact.

Relationships make a person vulnerable to pain, and losing my parents and the end of that relationship was more anguish than I could deal with. Watching Gramps degrade quickly after Grams passed was another reason to avoid getting serious with anyone.

"For now I'll focus on the pub, which reminds me, I haven't told you about the golden opportunity that might put us on the map and make it rain."

His mouth turns down. "Is this some young person slang I don't understand?"

"Uh yeah. 'Make it rain' means make lots of money. There's this huge YouTuber—"

"YouTuber?" More frowning ensues.

"Yeah, it's a woman who makes videos—"

"Videos?" Gramps's eyes go wide, and he gives me a disapproving look. "Not the dirty kind. Ya won't be using my Dottie's bar to be makin' those naughty films."

I choke back a mouthful of coffee and cough into my elbow. "No, Gramps. Just videos, not of sex. Why in the world would you think I'd do something like that?"

His eyes shift away and he shrugs, then takes a big gulp of his beer. "I was looking something up on the computer this morning and you know how it likes to fill in words for you sometimes. Well, it took me to a site with all kinds of things no one should be looking at at nine in the morning. Felt like I needed to go to confession after that."

"Not the best way to start the day, huh?"

He shakes his head. "Those images get stuck in the brain, they do. Anyway, you were saying something about this YouTuber?"

"Right, yes." I smack the bar, happy to move the subject away from my grandfather accidentally stumbling on a porn site. "She has a channel."

"Like a TV channel?"

"Yeah, kinda. I mean, they even have commercials that you have to watch—"

"Can't you DVR and fast-forward through the junk?"

I introduced Gramps to DVR back when I lived with him and Grams after my parents passed and it's probably his favorite thing in the world. Apart from this bar and the memory of Grams. "Not on YouTube. Anyway, this woman, Tori Taylor—"

"Sounds like one of those dirty film stars."

"I promise she's not a dirty film star. Anyway, she has a channel with over ten million subscribers."

"Geez, that's a lot of people. She do neat tricks or something? Is she a dancer?"

"No, Gramps. She's not a dancer. Just let me finish." I wait to see if he's going to interrupt again, but he stays silent, for now. "Anyway, she runs a 'Best of' feature on her channel. Best products, best places to visit, that kind of thing. She's running a Best Bar in the Pacific Northwest competition and The Knight Cap is entered." I pull up the video on my phone and play it for Gramps, then show him The Knight Cap nominations before I shift to Instagram where he can check out all the other bars that have been nominated, too.

He pauses my scroll a few pictures down. "Isn't that the place next door? Buttercream and Booze?"

"Yup. Sure is." Of course she's been nominated, likely by every single human being she knows. And despite her super prickly attitude, apparently she has a lot of friends because she's clogging up the feed with all the damn nominations.

Gramps takes my phone and starts scrolling. Then he hits her profile link and keeps on flipping through pictures. He lets out a low whistle and holds the phone out two inches from my face. "Have you met her?"

"Sure have."

"She's quite the looker," Gramps mutters.

"I guess, if you like the whole June Cleaver get-up."

Gramps cocks a brow. "Does nae matter what she's wearing. Could be a burlap sack and she'd still have the face of an angel."

Gramps isn't wrong. She's stunning in a very classic,

wholesome way. I have to admit, as unconventional as her clothing choices may be, they also make her alluring. She's a mass of contradictions. Her entire look screams sweet and retro, but she's a real take-no-prisoners spitfire. And I have to admit I kind of like how easy it is to get under her skin. It's addicting, really.

The flyers were meant to be a joke and so was the fake poop. I'd watched her step in it the day before and thought the best way to clear the air would be to make light of it. Apparently Alice and I have very different ideas as to what is funny and what isn't. She didn't seem to appreciate the fake turd. Or the anger management flyer, or the lavender oil— who doesn't love the smell of that? And I didn't so much as get a thank you or a chuckle over the reconfigured unicorn martini glass. Which I put a lot of time and effort into for my own personal satisfaction.

I thought she'd laugh and soften up, but that isn't at all what's happened. Then again, what would I expect of someone who'd rather mix drinks with fourteen freaking ingredients instead of pouring a nice hoppy beer instead.

"Does she own the place next door, or just work there?" Gramps asks.

"I think it's hers? She runs it, that much I know."

"Well, it's been empty a long time. Every single business that crops up there ends up going under within the year. Here's hoping she's got better luck than the rest. I'm guessing she got a deal on the rent with all the bad juju coming outta that place."

I'm not a big believer in things like "bad juju" or luck. Places fail or succeed for a lot of reasons, not because the businesses that occupied the same location prior tanked. Regardless, the fact that she probably got a deal on rent tells me something about grumpy Alice in Wonderland. She's clearly a fighter and savvy. I've got my work cut out for me if I'm going to beat her as The Best Bar in the Pacific Northwest.

Was it the smartest way to handle things by piggybacking on her Grand Opening? Probably not, and I hadn't intentionally copied her, but it definitely ended up working in my favor. Good thing I like friendly competition.

"Live bands, they're always popular." Lars, my fulltime bartender, polishes a glass while checking out his reflection in the mirror. "I'd be happy to be the first live performance if you can get Lana to bartend."

He's good at his job, and the women love him, which is why I deal with his inflated ego. He's also my twenty-three-year-old cousin who's still waiting for his big break to rock stardom, hence the bartending gig. "So you can serenade her with songs you've written professing your undying love?"

"Women eat that shit up."

"Too bad you can't date her since you work with her." It's more of a reminder than anything.

"Why are you always such a buzzkill? This is a bar, not some office."

"Why are you always such a fuckboy?"

He smirks. "I'm surprised you even know what that means, old man."

"I'm thirty, not collecting my pension."

"Whatever. I'm in my sexual prime and I plan to capitalize on that for as long as my dick will allow."

"Just not with any of the women who work here and preferably not the patrons, either."

He rolls his eyes. "What's the point of being a bartender if I can't use it to get laid?"

It's my turn to give him a look. "Okay, first of all, think about what you're saying, Lars. Do you really want to entice drunk, not fully coherent women into your bed? Consider the potential ramifications of that. Carefully."

His entire face scrunches up. "When you put it that way..."

"Consent is best sought when sober." I'm aware that I am, in fact, being a huge buzzkill—but for good reason. Serving alcohol is a big responsibility, especially in an establishment that has been in my family for years. I'm all for having fun... within reason. And twenty-one-year-olds aren't known for high-level thinking skills when they're under the influence.

If Lars and Lana end up dating, there's really not much I can do about it, but by telling them a no-dating-coworkers-and-customers policy exists, I figure I'm at least putting the fear of unemployment into them. Although, I will say that as much of a player as Lars presents himself to be, he doesn't like to disappoint people. So I'm banking on that to keep him in line.

I rap on the bar top. "Anyway, back to live bands. Won't we need sound equipment for that?"

"Yeah, but I have two sets at home, so I can bring one to keep here if you want. Most bands have their own equipment, but they're not all created equal." He smirks. "Plus, we can host a karaoke night. Everyone thinks they're a singer when they're drunk."

"Hell yes, they do," I agree. And I can just imagine Alice in Wonderland throwing an epic fit over it.

"Look at how excited you are." Lars mirrors what I'm assuming is my wide smile. "You win this thing and you definitely better credit me with some of the ideas, man."

"It's a long shot. Literally hundreds of bars have been nominated."

"Yeah, but this one has history and a great story. I vote we start posting about our grandparents. Tori Taylor ships pretty much every famous couple out there."

I frown, feeling like I'm missing something. "Ships what?"

"She's always posting about couple goals. Anyways, it's something else we can post about if we need to, you know, to pull in the lady crowd."

"Right, yeah." I don't want to have to worry about things like couple goals and romance. I just want laid-back and easygoing. A nice chilled-out environment where people come and drink pints and enjoy conversation or sports or whatever, as opposed to my uptight neighbor and her perfect prissy cupcakes and fruity drinks. "I'll get some graphics made so we can start promoting the live band. You think this Saturday will work for you?"

"Yeah man, I can get the guys together for Saturday."

"And you'll be ready to perform?"

The bell over the door chimes, and a group of women who look to be in their early twenties walk in.

"I was born ready." Lars winks and turns to the group of women. "Evening, ladies. Looking thirsty."

I shake my head and leave him to his flirting. It's after seven and I have yet to make a stop next door for my daily dose of sweet and sour. My neighbor might be an annoying pain in the ass, but those cupcakes are addictive. I'm starting to wonder if they're laced with something.

I stop by every night before closing—she shuts down around nine, but stays open later on Friday and Saturday. It has to make for insanely long days for her. But her hours aren't my problem. Besides, I pull long days, too.

I nab a coupon from behind the bar. "I'll be back in a few," I call out as I pass Lars chatting up the group of women who now span the four barstools directly in front of the draft taps.

He tips his chin up at me and goes back to checking IDs as I push through the door and step outside in the waning evening sunshine. It's still warm and balmy for early September. I miss the nights where I used to have time to sit outside on my balcony and enjoy watching the sun set. Now I'm always here, at the bar, watching the light fade through the windows.

I'll get that back someday, though. For now, I remind myself that there's a bigger plan and a few missed sunsets aren't the end of the world if I'm able to pursue my dream.

When I was young—in my teens, and long before I was of legal drinking age—my dad used to dabble in home brewing. I learned from a very early age to appreciate the science behind creating superior craft beers. It had always been a hobby for my dad and somewhere along the way it became a passion for me. Now, aside from my grandfather, it's the final connection I have with my dad, the one thing I don't want to give up, especially as the memories of him continue to fade.

For a while money mattered more than dreams, but when Grams passed, it shifted my perspective. I needed the memories to stay fresh and I needed time with Gramps, so here I am.

I glance up at the sign I had custom made, expensive but worth it. Your storefront is your main source of advertising for passersby, and the more alluring it is the more likely people are to come in. I snicker as I pass Alice in Wonderland's sidewalk sign. Today it reads: DON'T BE BITTER. TREAT YOURSELF TO SOMETHING SWEET!

I open the door and survey the shop. Despite it being a Tuesday, the café is busy, almost every table occupied by latte- and martini-drinking women. In the corners, young couples huddle, their textbooks lying open but ignored as their owners pick at cupcakes, their feet intertwined under the tables while they flirt.

Alice-Blaire is behind the counter, hands propped on her hips, bottom lip caught between her teeth. Her dress is pale pink with a huge rainbow swirl lollipop print. The skirt flares wide; obviously there's some kind of material underneath to make it so . . . poofy. It accentuates her lush, curvy figure. Her hair is pulled into some kind of intricate up-do, making her look like she's stepped straight off the set of a fifties-era sitcom. She sure is an interesting woman.

Her head turns and her welcoming smile turns saccharine. "Well, if it isn't my favorite neighbor." She bats her lashes. "I've been expecting you."

My own grin widens with genuine happiness. For reasons I don't quite understand, part of me really enjoys the daily dose of snark I get from Blaire.

"Miss me, then?" I lean on the glass display case. Yes, I'm very aware it says I shouldn't. I'm also aware that the second I leave she'll be out with some environmentally friendly, lemony-smelling glass cleaner, wiping away the mark my forearm leaves behind.

She makes a guttural sound, rolls her eyes, and mutters something under her breath. I don't quite catch all of it, but I swear it sounds sexual.

I probably need to get laid.

"What was that?"

"Nothing." She keeps that smile plastered on her face, but

her cheeks have flushed pink. "What can I get for you today, Ronan?"

"Dunno, what'd you recommend?"

"I'd recommend Death by Chocolate again, but we're fresh out and you always seem opposed." She taps her pink-glossed lips and *hmm*s. They're full. A little pouty. Probably perfect for kissing.

Yup, definitely need to get laid.

"Oh! Actually, I have something special for you today."

"Special?"

"Mmm." She arches a brow and spins around, her skirt flaring impressively. There's a bow knotted at the center of her back. Even her apron is tied perfectly, which seems impossible since she can't see the back of it. Unless she has someone do it for her.

She's in the middle of retrieving something—not from the cupcake case—when a lanky guy wearing a polo that reads CUPCAKES TO GO! over his left pec appears from the back of the café.

"All set for tomorrow morning. You need anything else before I take off?" He runs a hand through his thinning hair.

She abandons the box, which I'm assuming is for me, and takes a few steps in his direction. "Thanks so much for taking care of all of this tonight instead of tomorrow morning, Paul. I know it's going to be a busy day for you."

"Well, I wasn't going to leave you hanging." His shoulders roll back and his smile oozes pride and satisfaction.

"You're a godsend." She puts a manicured hand on his forearm. "I would've been here all night if I'd tried to pull that off on my own."

That smile of his widens further and he tips his chin down as she tips hers up. "Can't have you turning into a zombie on me."

"I appreciate your concern for my well-being and my non-zombie status." She gives his arm a squeeze and steps back. "Now you should go because it's getting late, and I don't want *you* to be the zombie on account of being here so late."

She turns away from Paul and his gaze follows her. She crosses over to the sink, turns on the tap, and lathers up her hands. She hums a tune under her breath as she rubs her palms together. She also does a hip shake.

He glances at me as he takes a step back and his expression shifts to hostility. Huh. That's interesting.

He knocks into the bussing cart, which gets Blaire's attention.

"Oh! Thank you so much for taking that to the back, Paul. Callie has been running off her feet all day and we'll both definitely appreciate the help."

"Oh, right, yeah, of course. Have a good night, Blaire."

"You, too."

He backs down the hall, throwing me one final glare before he disappears. I wonder if she's mentioned me to him, and if so, I'm guessing whatever she said wasn't all that pleasant. Blaire sashays across the small space, holding a plate with a single cupcake. She sets it down on the counter and pushes it

toward me. "Here you go. I made this one special for you."
She winks.

I glance down at the cake. There's a tiny cookie-shaped
decoration on top with the phrase EAT ME in block capital
letters.

I lift my gaze to hers. "You made this for me?"

She blinks once—that same, almost unnervingly placid
smile plastered on her gorgeous face. Wait. *Gorgeous?* Since
when do I find her and her odd fashion sense attractive?

"I did," she replies.

I glance back down at the cake, assessing the details more
carefully. The tiny cookie looks like it's made out of candy
and the letters have been painted on with an incredibly steady
hand. I touch the edge, gently and with care. "What about
this? Did you make this?"

"Yup. It's not laced with arsenic or anything. You can eat it
without worrying about your health."

"I wasn't until you said that."

"I wouldn't risk the welfare of my entire business over you."
She's still smiling, but there's a sharp edge to her tone, like a
razorblade slice.

I laugh a little. "You're killing me with your kindness, Blaire."

"Are you gonna eat it or what?" She leans against the edge
of the counter.

Obviously I've reached the limit to her patience, which is
exactly what I've been waiting for. I love it when she gets sour
with me. Like one of her lemon curd-filled cupcakes.

"You gonna jam it in my mouth for me if I don't?"

"Maybe." Her lips twitch.

"Don't you want me to savor the experience?" I pluck the tiny candy cookie from the top. "It doesn't say devour me, it says EAT ME. Slow or fast is always the question. Slow is usually better, though, don't you think?" What in the actual fuck am I doing? Am I using sexual innuendos?

The design on the cupcake is clearly an *Alice in Wonderland* reference, not an actual invitation to eat her. And why am I suddenly thinking about what that would be like? Is she quiet or loud? I bet she's demanding. Probably bossy. And there's nothing sexier than a woman who tells you exactly what she wants.

I pop the tiny candy into my mouth, to make sure none of the thoughts floating around in my head ends up coming out of my mouth, and also to get this over with. Because I need to get out of here instead of continuing this conversation. She's my competition in the Best Bar challenge, not a prospective date.

Fast is how it's going to be, apparently.

Except that tiny little candy dissolves on my tongue, fizzing unexpectedly. And the flavor is familiar.

Blaire smirks and clasps her hands behind her, rocking back on her heels.

I peel the wrapper from the cake and drop it on the plate. I bring it to my nose and sniff it. "Is that . . . coffee?"

"Just take a bite," she snaps.

Her tone, however, doesn't match her expression, which I realize she's trying to keep neutral, but is failing at quite painfully. Her gaze is trained on my face—eager, expectant. She bounces a couple of times and I glance at the reflection in the mirrored bar behind her, lined with bottles of top-shelf spirits and liqueurs. She's wringing her clasped hands behind her back, but trying to keep them hidden.

I take a bite, not as big as I originally intended, because that's probably what she expects and I want to prolong the agony of her anticipation as much as I humanly can. I intend to tell her it's just okay, but the moment the flavors hit my tongue I groan. Loudly. "Oh my God," I mumble, crumbs tumble out of my mouth and sprinkle all over the counter. Which I realize is disgusting.

But Blaire doesn't seem to care. She grins widely, satisfaction and triumph making her face even more stunning. I consider asking what this is, but decide I don't care enough to stop eating it. There's coffee in the icing, but it's not overly sweet, it's light and buttery and decadently creamy. The cake practically melts in my mouth, hints of . . . whiskey, cocoa, and vanilla and with the next bite I get a hit of creamy custard with a gentle hint of . . . almond.

Blaire doesn't seem to notice the mess I'm making. At all. She's sucking on her bottom lip and bouncing on the balls of her feet. Her lip pops free, teeth marks still evident. "Enjoying yourself." It's not a question, more of an accusation.

I want to shove the rest of it in my face instead of answering, but I lift my hand to cover my mouth so I can ask a question instead of affirm what she clearly already knows. "What is it?"

A slow smirk spreads across her lips.

She doesn't say anything right away, so I jam the rest of it in my mouth. Half of me wants to beg her for more, but I know if I do, then somehow I've managed to give her the upper hand. Which is ridiculous. It's just a cupcake, and regardless of what she thinks, we're not really competing with each other. For the YouTube thing sure, but I don't see how she can win against me and my kickass cool bar and the axe throwing. And now the whole live bands idea and karaoke.

The cupcakes-and-cocktails theme is cute. But that's about all it is.

I try to keep my groan in this time, but a sound of contentment slips out.

"So you like my screaming orgasms?" she asks.

Which is when I start coughing. I also try to inhale with food in my mouth and choke. And cough some more. Blaire takes a step back since I'm spraying the counter with half-chewed cupcake. It's a travesty because I want that all in my belly and not on the counter.

"Are you okay?" she asks when I continue to cough for another solid fifteen seconds.

"Yeah." *Cough.* "I just"—*cough*—"didn't expect that."

"It's the name of the cupcake," she informs me.

"I figured, since you didn't scream even once."

"I'm not a screamer." Her eyes flare, as if she didn't mean for that to slip out.

Now it's my turn to smirk. "Is that right?"

She spins around, but I can see her face in the mirrored wall in front of her. Her ears have gone red and she mutters something to herself, nabbing the box from the bar behind her. She rolls her shoulders back and turns to face me again. Her cheeks are the same color as her ears. She drops the box unceremoniously on the counter. "I figured you'd want more than one."

"Yes. Definitely." I nod.

"Multiples really are the best." Her cheek tics, and the tips of her ears look as if they're going to light on fire and take all her hair with it. I wonder how much product she uses to keep it looking so perfect and if it's soft to the touch or not.

"I love multiples." Both the giving and the receiving. I leave that part out, because I would prefer to eat the cupcakes, not wear them, and I feel like we're suddenly treading a very fine line. Either that or we've already jumped right over it. I shake my head to clear it. "Uh, what do I owe you?"

"Those are on the house. Enjoy your night."

Blaire usually happily charges me full price for my cupcake addiction. Although she does tend to toss in an extra one for good measure. I'm tempted to ask if I'm going to end up hogtied in the trunk of a car if I eat the rest of these, but I figure that might be pushing it. "I can't imagine anyone has ever said no to free multiple screaming orgasms."

She gives me a patronizing look. "Okay, Ronan, the joke is over. Off you go." She shoos me away. "I have customers to serve and they want what you had."

I leave the cupcake shop feeling a lot like I lost that round. I even forgot to pass her a coupon for free beer and fried pickles.

Lars has moved on from flirting with the group of women so he can serve other customers. I round the bar and flip the box open, intent on eating another one of the cupcakes. I shake my head when I see the rest of them. Each one has a message written on tiny sugary cookies: EAT ME, BITE ME, SUCK IT and there's one rogue Death by Chocolate cupcake, complete with skull and crossbones.

Huh, looks like Alice has a sense of humor after all.

@the_knightcap:

Stop trying to make everyone happy. You're not beer.

chapter six

SO HILARIOUS

Blaire

My customer poll shows me that poetry slams are not quite as popular as I thought. So my plan to open our events with one is vetoed by Daphne and Paul in favor of Comedy Night.

It took all of two days, a few social media posts and two hours of auditions to secure our night of entertainment—I will say that there are a lot of people out there who think they're funny but are not. We're paying our entertainment in free cupcakes and booze, and even with the entry fee, which I was originally on the fence about, the café is packed. We have a fabulous selection of drinks, cakes, and savory treats. And Daphne has offered to make a few video clips of the entertainment to post on YouTube, which is amazing since I'll be too busy mixing cocktails to handle something like that.

I fully believe nothing can ruin this night. That belief is naïve and likely shortsighted.

However, since the EAT ME cupcake incident, there's been a shift with Ronan. One I'm not sure how to take. Yes, I still think he's an asshole. Yes, I'm still wary. Yes, we still stand outside on Friday afternoons and toss coupons at customers, trying to get them to spend their money on our wares. But he's addicted to my cupcakes. He comes in here every single night to get a hit of my special treats, and he can't even hide his excitement or his enjoyment.

Normally I charge him, but that night I was feeling extra generous because he's inadvertently sparked my cupcake creativity. I knew I had a winner on my hands, and that his reaction would inspire customers to buy what he was getting off on.

Every time he puts on a performance, I usually sell out of whatever's left in specialty cupcakes, so the initial out of pocket was totally worth it. Is it annoying that he constantly leaves me coupons for wings and asks me if I'm ready for a "big girl drink"? Sure, but toying with him is as much fun as watching him scarf down my cupcakes while grudgingly moaning his delight.

He hasn't made his daily stop yet, although generally he comes in later, within a couple hours of closing and after his dinner rush. I give my head a shake, because fixating on when Ronan stops in for cupcakes is unhelpful when I should be focused on my event.

Twenty minutes later, the opening act hits our small makeshift stage. Chairs and tables have been rearranged so everyone has a great view. At first I'm worried, because the guy is clearly nervous, but as the jokes start flowing and the crowd begins to chuckle and then laugh boisterously, he gains confidence. He finishes to a huge round of applause, and the bar is flooded with orders between the acts. Three comedians are scheduled tonight, which is perfect. It means rounds of drinks, appetizers, snacks, and desserts come in waves, which we're prepared for.

Everything is going as smooth as buttercream frosting until the final comedian sets up. It's almost nine and the sound of bass and feedback filters through the wall I share with Ronan's bar, making the floors vibrate.

As the final act begins, she's rudely interrupted by the sudden, very loud banging of…drums? It's followed by equally loud guitar riffs, and a growly voice belting out lyrics, which eclipse the comedian entirely for a few seconds.

It stops as abruptly as it begins and the performer makes a joke, setting off a round of nervous chuckling. Unfortunately, not thirty seconds later it happens again. "Dammit." I drop a stack of plates into the bus bin. The clatter would be loud if the noise coming from next door didn't drown it out, along with Karen the Comedian. She tries speaking louder, but it doesn't help. "I'm going over there."

Daphne, who's been filming and taking photos, makes a face. "Maybe I should go."

I give her the hairy eyeball. "So you can drool all over Ronan and forget to ask him to tone it the hell down?"

She arches a brow. Whatever. It's the truth, even if me calling her out on it in a less than pleasant manner is probably unwarranted. But this is my first event, and he's ruining it with whatever he has going on over there. People always remember what happened at the beginning or the end of an event the best. So my customers are going to remember the fun start to their evening and how it was ruined because a loud band drowned out the last damn act.

I rush over to Ronan's bar in time for the really loud music to start. Pounding bass, drums, and excessively aggressive guitar riffs blare through the sound system. The place is packed, bodies crowding the small stage positioned to the right. No wonder it's so loud in my café—the band is pretty much playing right against our adjoining wall. I notice that it's the young bartender up onstage. I think his name is Larry or something. He starts scream-singing. It's pretty unpleasant, not that I think scream-singing is ever really all that appealing.

I scan the dimly lit bar, searching for Ronan in a sea of black rim glasses-wearing twentysomethings. I finally spot him, in all his plaid glory, behind the bar, pouring pints. It takes me forever to squeeze my way through the crowd, but when I get to the bar the lineup is three deep. I try to edge my way between waiting customers, but it proves impossible.

Annoyed and frustrated, and frankly, grossed out by the number of sweaty bodies pressing up on me, I do another cursory scan of the bar and notice an opening a ways down.

I settle my hands on some guy's hips, trying to skirt around him. Unfortunately he takes it as a sign that I want to dance—or make out.

He spins around, eyes flaring as he takes me in. I'm glad I'm wearing heels because I'm not particularly tall and he certainly is. A slow smile spreads across his face. His cheeks are baby smooth, indicating he's probably just old enough to be here legally.

"Sorry, excuse me. I'm just trying to get to the bar. I need to talk to the bartender."

"You can talk to me while you wait if you want," he shouts over the noise.

I'm not sure how that would even be possible because it's too loud to hear myself think, let alone have any kind of meaningful conversation. I tap my ear to indicate that I can't hear him.

"We don't have to talk." He winds an arm around my waist, catching me off guard as he pulls me closer. "I'm totally into cougars."

"Cougar?" I slap my palms on his chest—which is ridiculously bony—and turn my head as he leans in.

"Yeah, you're like, close to thirty, right? That's hot."

I am seriously going to throttle Ronan. It might not be his fault that this clueless git is suddenly mauling me, but I'm blaming him since he's the reason I had to come here in the first place. I purposely step on his foot with my pointy heel.

He lets me go with a yelp. *Such a baby.* I elbow my way

through the crowd, done with the *excuse me*s and *sorry*s. I decide the only way to get to Ronan is by going behind the bar, which means shoving my way all the way down the line of thrashing and waiting customers. I finally free myself from the wave of bodies—I might go out the back door and brave the stench of garbage to get back to the café in lieu of having to fight the throng a second time—and try to wave Ronan down at the end of the bar.

He glances in my direction, tips his chin up and goes back to pouring pints. *Bastard.* There's no way I'm going to let Ronan ignore me. I unlatch the waist-high door and slip in behind the bar. I tread carefully across the honeycomb mat, waiting while Ronan slides two pints over the bar and rings the money through the till before I tug on his sleeve.

I feel very much like a kid seeking the attention of someone who definitely doesn't want to give it to me.

Ronan startles at the contact and frowns when he realizes it's me and not one of his employees. "What the hell, Blaire? You can't be back here."

"I need to talk to you!" I say, just as another particularly loud aggressive drum solo starts up.

He motions to his ear, signaling he can't hear me.

I pin him with an unimpressed glare and he rolls his eyes. I grab his arm, digging my nails in and try to pull him down so I can shout directly in his ear.

He gives me a look like I'm insane. "I'm kinda busy here." He points to the sea of bodies.

"You're ruining my Comedy Night with this!" I gesture in the direction of the band.

He huffs and shakes his head while he tries to pry my hand free from his arm. I stumble back a step, heel caught in the honeycomb mat meant to keep the bartenders from slipping on spilled beer. "You're gonna get hurt back here. You gotta go." He points to the end of the bar.

"Not until we talk."

"For fuck's sake, Blaire. I don't have time for this shit tonight." He circles my waist with one arm and hauls me up against him.

I gasp and flail, forced to hug his neck as he stalks the length of the bar. I don't want to notice how firm all of him is, or how good he smells when he's this close. "What the hell are you doing? Put me down! You can't manhandle me like this!"

"I can when you're behind my bar, wearing fucking heels, and at risk of spraining your damn ankle," he shouts, his minty breath washing over my cheek, lips brushing the shell of my ear.

"You're ruining my night."

"Maybe your comedians suck. Ever think of that?"

Instead of opening the waist-high door, he swings me up, catching me fireman style under the knees, his cold palm wrapping around my thigh briefly as he lifts me over it and then unceremoniously dumps me back on my feet on the other side.

"My comedians don't suck! Your scream-o band is the problem." I keep flailing, which is frustrating because it makes me look like more of a lunatic.

"I need to work." He turns and starts to walk away.

"I'm not done with you!" I call after him.

He motions to his ear again.

Ugh. I hate him. I flip him the double bird. "How's that? Can you hear that?" I shout.

He has the audacity to salute me, gives me his back and leans on the bar, turning his head so some scantily dressed college girl can yell her beer order in his ear. He really is a jerk.

By the time I get back to B&B the last comedian has given up on account of the noise and the crowd is starting to clear out. Probably heading next door to enjoy the stupid band. I apologize to Karen, and while she's understanding I don't think there's much of a chance that she'll come back anytime soon, if ever.

I start to clean up with the help of Daphne, who hasn't asked what happened yet, likely because I'm so angry it's a wonder there isn't steam coming out of my ears. Only a few diehard customers are left in the place and I'm pretty sure the only reason they're hanging around is the possibility of half-price cupcakes.

I offer them the deal and they polish off what's left of their martinis, pick a half-dozen each and take off, muttering about stopping at their car before they head over to The Knight Cap to check out the band, leaving my place totally empty. I'd planned to stay open until ten tonight, but it looks like I don't have to anymore.

I flip the bird at the wall between our two bars as yet another bass-pounding song starts, and then box up the few remaining cupcakes.

Daphne dumps what's left in the coffee carafe down the drain. "Guess the talk with Ronan didn't go all that well, huh?"

"He's a dick."

"What'd he say?"

"He pretended he couldn't hear me and then man-handled me."

She sets the carafe down. "He did *what?*"

"He was behind the bar, ignoring me, so I went back there to confront him and he picked me up and carried me back out!" My cheeks heat as I recall exactly how forceful he was, and how strong, and also how easy it was for him to carry me. I'm not particularly petite.

Daphne's eyebrows rise. "Can't say I'd be all that upset if it was me he was manhandling."

"He ruined the night!"

"Well, to be fair, he only ruined the last act and I'll be honest: She was the weakest of the three, so maybe it was a blessing in disguise. Plus you do usually close at nine, so maybe he didn't realize you were still open?"

"She was distracted, and do not defend him. It's thoughtless of him to schedule a live band on the same night as our first event. He couldn't have not known about it. We had signs and flyers out all week. He should've consulted me!"

Daphne crosses her arms. "Because you two are clearly besties."

"It's common courtesy!"

"Which would hold some water if you two were actually on some kind of friendly terms, but all you do is push each other's buttons. I'll honestly be surprised if you don't either kill each other or end up boning each other's brains out."

I scoff. "Not in a million years."

Daphne grins. "Want to put some money on that?"

"You know I don't gamble."

"Uh huh. However you want to play it, Blaire. But I see the cupcakes you set aside for him every single day, and there's an awful lot of effort going into something for someone you supposedly hate."

I glance at the box still sitting on the counter with the cupcakes I decorated and specifically set aside for Ronan. "I do it because it's satisfying to watch him helplessly devour them."

"Okay."

"It's true."

"Uh huh."

I dump the box in the trash to prove my point, but it feels a lot like I've proven hers instead.

The next morning, once the brunch rush is over I steel my resolve and head to The Knight Cap to talk to Ronan about last night before he opens. I can see him through the window, leaning on the bar, wearing one of his plaid shirts, thick fore-arms exposed.

I bet it's purposeful so he can show off his tattoos. I take a deep breath, determined to keep my cool and try to open the door, but it's still locked. I knock on the window and he glances my way, pushing his black-rimmed glasses up his nose.

Stupid sexy hipster glasses.

I rattle the doorknob to demonstrate that I can't get in.

He lifts his left arm and taps his watch. It's very old school, something I would like to *not* find endearing and generally don't, especially since he doesn't make a move to come out from behind the bar and let me in.

So I keep knocking. And knocking. And knocking some more. In fact I start knocking out the rhythm of a song. He shakes his head, tosses his pen down on the bar top, and shambles slowly to the end of the bar. He stops three times on the way to the door to adjust stools and once more to fix a picture that's hanging askew on the wall. His back is to me, and he strokes his chin, tipping his head to the right before he readjusts the picture in the opposite direction. I take the opportunity to stare at his butt, which I would like to smack and also kick with my pointy heel. I'm not sure what would be more satisfying, although I do know what would be most embarrassing. For me.

He finally saunters over to the door and taps the sign with the opening times posted on it. "We don't open for another fifteen minutes."

I bite back a bitchy retort because as he's pointed out before, you don't attract flies with vinegar. "Can we please talk?"

He jams a thumb in his pocket and rolls back on his heels. "You seemed to communicate just fine with hand signals last night."

I clasp my hands behind my back and fire the middle finger at him from there, while I plaster a smile on my face. Immature? Yes. Does it make me feel better? Marginally. "You manhandled me."

"You shouldn't have been behind my bar with heels on. You were a distraction and a liability." His gaze moves over me in a slow sweep. It's not unappreciative.

"Can we please do this without a door between us?" It's demeaning to be kept out here on the street, speaking loudly to be heard through the pane of glass.

"Are you gonna try to maim me with your talons again?"

"Maim you?" What in the world is he talking about?

He flicks the lock and steps back, not bothering with chivalry. I open the door and slip in out of the cold as he unbuttons his plaid shirt and pulls the collar aside.

"What are you doing?"

"Showing you the evidence."

"Of what?"

He bends, bringing his shoulder down to my level. There are crescent-shaped nail marks in his skin defined by bruises.

"I did not do that."

"You sure did."

"I'm sure that was from whatever college girl you had a quickie with in your office when you took a five-minute break last night, not from me."

He blinks a few times, inked forearms flexing when he crosses them. The right one is covered in beautiful flowers, and the left is some kind of landscape. I can't see enough of it to figure out what exactly it is. One of those arms was against my bare thigh last night when he picked me up. "First of all, I have no interest in college girls."

I scoff and mirror his pose. "Could've fooled me with the way you were eyeing them last night."

"I was tending bar. My job is to be friendly when I'm serving booze. Secondly, I don't fuck where I work, and third, the word *quickie* isn't in my vocabulary. I'm an all-or-nothing kind of guy."

I fight to hold my smile. "So you're saying you like to savor instead of devour."

"That's exactly what I'm saying."

I have to tip my head up to meet his gaze. His caramel-colored eyes are hot, burning like a shot of whiskey. "You treat sex the opposite of how you treat my cupcakes."

He licks his lips and swallows thickly, like he's tasting the memory of one right now. "I devour the first one and savor the rest when I'm alone."

"Hey, Ronan, sorry I'm a bit la—" Ronan's usual bartender—and the screamer from last night—is at the end of the bar, hands in the air as he takes deliberate steps backward and thumbs over his shoulder. "Oh, sorry, man, I didn't, uh...I'll go grab a couple cases of beer or something." He disappears around the corner.

I don't understand what that was all about until Ronan's attention returns to me. We're literally inches apart, and his arms are no longer crossed. He takes a step back and so do I, bumping into the door.

I clear my throat. "We need to set a schedule for our events. You ruined the last act of my comedy night with your live band."

"I'm sure it wasn't that bad."

"It was." On many levels. "Look, you're open until two and I'm only open until nine most nights, ten when I have entertainment on the weekends. You can hold your band until nine thirty, can't you? How much could that possibly hurt your business?"

"Why should I have to be the one to make concessions?"

"I already moved all my glasses and had to adjust my entire interior wall that adjoins your bar. The least you can do is give me an extra half hour."

"What're you gonna do for me?"

"I can start my comedy nights at seven instead of seven thirty. It's only half an hour and then we can both benefit. My customers can move over to your place and I can close when you have live bands." I don't want to bend, but I realize compromise is the only way to win this. I need him to be willing to work with me so I don't keep losing out. "Unless one of us switches days?"

"Live bands are best on Saturday nights." And he's back to crossing his arms.

"And comedians usually have nine-to-five jobs." Or they're booked somewhere better than a café in downtown Seattle.

"Unless they're actually good." It's like he's living in my damn head.

"They were good." I'm extra defensive, which is frustrating, especially since it makes him smile. "And the last one would have been a whole lot better if not for the noise over here."

We stare each other down for several long seconds that slowly turn heavy and uncomfortable. He finally sighs and runs a palm down his face. "You're not going to leave unless I agree to this, are you?"

"That's correct."

"Okay. I can push back live bands until nine thirty, but make sure you wrap up the yukkity-yuks by nine so you're not back here next Sunday griping at me for something else."

"Do you have anything else planned for this week?"

"Do you?" he shoots back.

I roll my eyes. "I'm trying to be proactive."

"If that's what you want to call it. Maybe you're trying to steal my ideas."

"So far you've been the one piggybacking me, not the other way around."

He leans in and lowers his voice. "Except last night when you were clinging to me like I was carrying you on a tightrope, not across a bar, one you weren't supposed to be behind in the first place."

I open my mouth and snap it shut. He's goading me. On purpose. I brush a wayward curl from my forehead with my middle finger and spin around, yanking the door open.

His laughter follows me all the way back to my café.

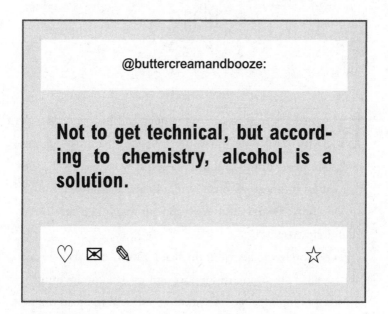

@buttercreamandbooze:

Not to get technical, but according to chemistry, alcohol is a solution.

chapter seven

WHAT HOUSE ARE YOU?

Blaire

Ronan stays true to our agreement and his band doesn't go on until nine thirty the following Saturday, giving my last comedian time to finish his act. It works out well, and it's great for business—Ronan's more than mine, since it means a good chunk of my customers end up migrating over there when I close up.

I even pop in to check out the band, mostly out of curiosity. Not because I'm trying to support him or ogle, or anything.

After polling my regular customers and setting up an online survey, Harry Potter Trivia Night is born. The winner gets a dozen HP-inspired cupcakes and a round of drinks for them and three friends.

I'm a huge Harry Potter fan. I've read all the books, listened to the entire series on audio more than once, and I own all the movies. I also saw every single one in the theater on opening night. "Big fan" is an understatement. I'm pretty proud of the fact that I didn't need to go online to research tough questions since I'm so well versed already.

I've gone all out. Every drink and cupcake is HP themed. My posts are getting a record amount of likes, and we have twenty individuals entered in the contest. It's going to be fabulous.

I'm decked out in my Gryffindor dress, wielding my Hermione wand and wearing my Hogwarts cape. It's almost like a pre-Halloween party. If this event gets the same amount of attention as the comedy nights do, trivia night will become another monthly staple at B&B. I'm thinking *Stranger Things* deserves its own event, too.

At seven, the café begins to fill with entrants and their friends. Callie is kept busy behind the counter, Daphne is helping with drinks, and the hardcore HP fans are dressed in their house garb, devouring cupcakes and house-themed drinks.

I call out the names of the competitors and am completely shocked when Ronan walks into the café dressed in a Slytherin hoodie. The Slytherin part isn't much of a surprise—he definitely fits the profile with his dark hair, less-than-aboveboard business tactics, and prankster ways, but the fact that he's an HP fan is unexpected. Unless he borrowed the hoodie from one of his employees. I wouldn't put it past him to use it as an opportunity to piggyback on another one of my ideas.

"You're a Harry Potter fan?" I ask when he approaches the counter to register.

"Hell yeah."

"The movies or the books?" I demand.

He scoffs and makes a face like he can't believe I'd ask such a thing. "The books, of course. I own all the first-edition hardcovers and the soft ones, too. Plus Jim Dale nails the audio."

"Oh my God, I love his voice!" The audio books are amazing, and I listen to them all the time when I'm at home, testing cupcake recipes.

We grin at each other, and for half a second I dislike him a little less. I register him to play, and he grabs a drink before he takes a seat at the table up front where all his fellow HP competitors are already waiting.

There's a sizable crowd of non-entrants lining the fringe of the café as we get ready for the contest to begin.

Word to the wise: HP fans are ultracompetitive. The first three rounds of trivia weed out the *I saw the movie but never bothered to read the books* crowd. By eight we've narrowed it down to the best six contestants. Ronan manages to stay in the top three.

He nails the rapid-question round, putting him in the finals. His adversary is Shanna, a twenty-two-year-old lit major at the local college who's writing her thesis paper on Harry Potter lore, so he has his work cut out for him.

I pull the final question, which has been selected randomly, and whistle into the microphone. "Wow, this one's a doozy. For the title of Harry Potter Trivia Champion, a dozen of my magically delicious cupcakes and drinks for you and three friends, name every ingredient contained in Polyjuice Potion."

Ronan and Shanna both slap their hands on the buzzer at the same time, but Shanna gets there a fraction of a second sooner, the red light bathing her face in a sinister glow.

"Shanna, what's your answer for the win?"

She leans in to the microphone, closing her eyes—it's how she's answered every single question. "Lacewing flies, leeches, knotgrass, fluxweed . . . " Her brow furrows and she hesitates for a second before continuing. "Shredded Boomslang skin and a bit of the person you want to turn into." Her eyes pop open and she smiles triumphantly.

"Is that your final answer?" I prompt.

"Yes. That's my final answer."

I admit, I'm disappointed when I have to say, "I'm sorry, but that is incorrect." Shannon's face falls like a pile of crumbling bricks.

"Ronan, would you like to respond and try to steal or would you like a new question?"

"I'll try to steal, thanks." He clears his throat, eyes fixed on mine as he leans in, lips almost touching the mic. His voice is a low, confident rumble. "The ingredients in Polyjuice Potion are lacewing flies, leeches, knotgrass, fluxweed, shredded Boomslang skin, a bit of the person you want to turn into *and* . . ." He pauses for dramatic effect. "Powdered Bicorn horn."

I have to bite the inside of my cheek to keep from smiling. "Is that your final answer?"

A cocky grin spreads lazily across his face. "Yes, Blaire, it's my final answer."

"You're sure?" I arch a brow.

His smile doesn't waver. "Absolutely."

"You are correct. We have a winner!"

"Hell yeah!" Ronan jumps to his feet and raises both fists into the air as if he's won a round in the boxing ring. He turns to me and in what I can only assume is an impulsive show of victory, he wraps his arms around my waist, picks me up off the floor, and swings me around in a circle.

When he sets me down, I take a dizzy step back. He keeps his hands on my waist to prevent me from falling off the makeshift stage. "I gotta head back to the bar, but I'll take a raincheck on the drinks." He winks, jumps off the stage, and fist bumps his way to the front door.

The brief warm and fuzzies disappear the following night when Ronan hosts a Beer Pong Tournament. The loudest beer pong tournament in the history of the universe, apparently, because every thirty seconds there's a collective "ooooooh" or "yeeeahhhhh" coming from his place.

It takes everything in me not to go over and check it out after I close up. And even then I peek through the window, just to see. It looks ridiculously fun. But I know if I go in there Ronan will find a way to make me participate, and I have terrible aim. I'm guaranteed to lose, which would also mean drinking beer. I have an early morning tomorrow, so I back away slowly and head home, where it's mostly quiet and there are no twenty-one-year-olds playing beer pong in the apartment next door to mine.

Over the next several weeks my competition with Ronan heats up, both of us trying to outdo each other with new events, particularly since we've both made it through to the top one hundred bars from the over five hundred who were initially nominated for Tori Taylor's Best Bar contest. The next round will bring us down to the top fifty, and both of our bars are currently hovering in the thirties thanks to social media votes. After that, the competition is going to get steeper with the quarterfinals, taking us down to the top twenty-five bars. I don't want to get cocky or complacent though, since we still have a long way to go to number one.

I hold a poetry slam night and despite the initial lack of excitement, it turns out to be a totally popular event, especially with the drama students at the college.

Unfortunately, Ronan plans another one of his loud events—all his events are loud—on the same night, so we're forced to wrap it up early. I should really know better by now.

On the upside, every new, fun event I host does better than the last. We hold a Halloween cookie-decorating contest and sell a ridiculous number of gory cupcakes and fun, horrifying drinks. Orders for cupcakes for the local businesses continue to pour in, which means I'm endlessly busy and still managing not to dig too far into my line of credit. It also means I'm light on sleep, but I can deal with being tired as long as B&B is staying afloat.

Tonight I have a bachelorette cupcake and cookie-decorating party. It's actually one of Daphne's engagement photo shoot clients who came back looking to secure her for additional dates—including the wedding. When Daphne suggested the bachelorette party I absolutely ran with it, with her input, of course. It gives her another opportunity to take some fun candid photos to add to their engagement and wedding albums and I have the opportunity to do something new and different.

Daphne came in earlier to snap some shots of the setup, and then popped back in before the bride and her wedding party were scheduled to arrive.

The bride's sister arranged the event and rented out the entire café. Customers can still come in and purchase cupcakes to go, but there's a warning on the door and the entire place is full of women decorating treats.

We decided the cupcakes are fun, but you can't make interesting shapes the way you can with a cookie. We start with a cupcake-decorating tutorial—Daphne records that part—but that's quickly devolved into turning cupcakes into vaginas. And the cookies…well, those are just as entertaining. Once the debauched decorating begins, Daphne takes off back to her studio, half apologizing for not being able to stay. I wave her off; honestly, this is the most fun I've had with a decorating class.

At eight Ronan pops by—he still makes a daily stop for a cupcake—and gets a gander at the penis cookies the ladies are working on.

The entire wedding party stops to watch him cross the café.

"Ooooh! Hey there, cutie, you can come sit with me!" The bride's sister—Stephanie—is on her third martini and lost her filter an hour ago. The drinks aren't even that strong. Every time she decorates a cookie, she ends up taking a picture of her biting into it and then she forces her friends to send her the picture. She then promptly posts it to all her social media accounts. She's also tagged the café in every single post. I should probably mention that the cookies she's most fond of posting are the penis ones.

I consider untagging the café, but decide that based on the number of likes the posts are getting it doesn't hurt to let it ride. Who knows, it could become another new revenue stream.

"What're you ladies up to?" He shoots a smile and wink in my direction—the wink is probably unconscious—and veers toward the women.

"We're decorating cookies. See!" Stephanie holds up her most recent work of art. A very orange penis, complete with pubic hair. It looks like it was decorated by a six-year-old. Or a drunk woman, the latter of which is accurate.

Ronan's eyes go wide and he coughs into his fist. "That's very convincing."

"I even gave it pubes! They're made out of licorice."

"I manscaped mine," one of the other bridesmaids declares and holds up her less orange, much more aesthetically appealing bald-balled cookie.

Stephanie's eyes rake over Ronan, pausing at his crotch. "Do you manscape?"

"Uhhh—"

"Ladies, this is Ronan, owner of the bar next door. When you're done here, you should drop by. You must have some kind of special drink promotion you can offer these lovely ladies, right, Ronan? And don't you have some kind of event going on? Is it a live band?" I know it's not because I stalk his IG profile. I don't follow him, because I don't want him to know I'm watching him, but after the loud, live entertainment started I needed to know ahead of time what I was facing every week.

His gaze moves from the penis cookie two inches from his face to me. He looks like he's plotting my murder. I can completely understand why. These ladies are already halfway to rowdy drunk. They're all on some ridiculous pre-wedding keto diet—which died a sad, necessary death once I told them the cookie calories don't count tonight—and they've been sipping martinis for the past two hours. They'll fit in perfectly next door.

"Ooooh! You own The Knight Cap?" Stephanie puts her hand on his forearm, leaving icing smears on his tattooed skin. She's definitely on the prowl based on the way she's eyeing Ronan's crotch the same way he eyes my cupcakes.

Ronan either chooses to ignore her or maybe he's too busy giving me the death glare and missed her simpering question. She strokes his forearm, rubbing in the icing. I'm sure it's sticking to his arm hair.

"He does, don't you, Ronan?"

"I don't actually own it, I just run it. It's my grandfather's—"

"Oh, wow, isn't that sweet? You work with your grandpa? I love guys who are close to their families. I'm close to my family, too." Stephanie is still petting his arm. Still holding her penis cookie up in the air, as if she's waiting for Ronan to praise her efforts.

The rest of the women are watching the one-sided exchange with something between fascination and mortification. Mostly it's fascination, though.

The woman on Stephanie's right snorts. "You haven't talked to your mom in three years."

"I'm close with the rest of my family, though," she snaps, sending a rage glare at the other woman. I think her name might be Laura or Laurie. Stephanie returns her attention to Ronan. "I'm close with everyone else. Even my stepmother."

"Well that's...nice." He takes a deliberate step back, away from her petting and the phallic cookie. "You ladies enjoy the cookie decorating." He makes a move toward the door.

"Aren't you forgetting something?" I call out.

"Huh?" His gaze shifts to me.

I hold up the small box I set aside for him. It contains two cupcakes. They're themed for tonight's bachelorette party. Although I decorated these especially for Ronan, as I always do.

"Oh, right."

He rushes over and tries to grab the box from my hands, but I maintain my protective hold on it, smiling serenely. "Don't you want to know what kind they are?"

"I'm sure I'll love them."

"Me, too, but you should sample one, don't you think?" I bat my lashes and smile wider. "These ladies have yet to try the cupcakes. I'm sure they want your seal of approval, don't you?"

A chorus of "Yes!" comes from the table, followed by some additional hoots, hollers, and taunts. You'd think we were at a strip club, not a freaking cupcake cocktail café.

Ronan narrows his eyes.

"You heard them. You don't want to disappoint the bride-to-be." I flip the lid open and his eyes flare and meet mine.

For the first time, Ronan is less than 100 percent composed. In fact, his cheeks have turned a lovely shade of pink. "You gotta be shitting me." He rubs the back of his neck.

"They look real, don't they?"

"Ooooh! What are they? Can we see?" Stephanie claps her hands together excitedly. I should probably hydrate this group before I send them next door.

"Why don't you show them, Ronan?" I hold my smile.

"No way."

I go for the cupcake on the left.

"Hell no." Ronan smacks the back of my hand and his eyes dart to the women. "I'm not eating that in front of them."

That little smack seems to reverberate through my entire body, pinging around like a marble in places that haven't had attention in a long time. Ironic considering the design on the cupcake I'm about to make him eat in front of these women.

"So this one, then?" I lift it from the box and turn it so it's facing the right way for him.

"I'm going to get you back for this." His tone is low and dark: equal parts threat and promise.

"Totally worth it." I nod to the cake perched in my open palm.

He grudgingly takes it.

The women have abandoned the table and their cookies to gather around the spectacle that Ronan has become. Because he's holding a vagina cupcake. The other option is, of course, the male anatomy. Both are convincing in their authenticity.

"Eat it, Ronan!" Stephanie shouts. The rest of the bachelorette party join in and chant his name.

His ears are red, his glare tells me he's so freaking pissed off, but he's also aware that these ladies are going to come over to his bar and drop stupid amounts of money on shots and girlie drinks as soon as they're done here. Customers are worth more than his pride in this moment. Also, Ronan has proven that he isn't the kind of man who backs down from a challenge, and for some reason I hate him a tiny bit less because of it. For now.

I covertly slip my hand in my pocket, searching for my phone as he peels the Bride-to-Be wrapper from the cake. Thankfully, Ronan is sufficiently distracted by Stephanie, who's snaked her arm around his waist and is screaming his name like she's the one about to get eaten.

I manage to pull up the camera app, switch it to video

mode, and hit Record before he fully unwraps the cake. He holds my gaze as he brings it to his mouth, opening wide. I lift the phone, making sure I catch him when he takes a robust, rather sensual bite.

And all the while his eyes tell me he wants to mash the cupcake in my face. But he doesn't. Instead he puts on a show. I'm hashtagging this cupcake porn. Because that's 100 percent what it is, literally and figuratively. Even the bite placement is purposeful, and so is his groan when the flavors hit his tongue. The sweetness of vanilla cake, the hint of cocoa in the thin layer of icing before the light buttercream registers and then there's the vanilla custard center, because come on, I'm nothing if not detail oriented.

He obviously doesn't expect the filling, which of course is the point. Custard dribbles down his chin, but he's so busy glaring at me while I record this epic moment that he doesn't notice.

I can't resist the opportunity. I bite my lip, fighting my own smile. "Oh! You're making a mess, Ronan. Here, let me help." I make sure the video is still rolling and I catch the dribble before it drips off his chin.

Before I can pull my hand away, he wraps his fingers around my wrist. There have been very few instances in which Ronan has made intentional, prolonged physical contact with me. The most body-to-body contact we've had to date was when he picked me up and removed me from behind his bar. After the fact, I can admit that he was right in that situation and

I was not. Did he really need to fireman-carry me out from behind the bar? Probably not. Have I thought about all that physical contact countless times since then? Not at all. Okay, maybe a few. Hundred times.

So when he yanks me forward by my wrist I stumble and my hips meet the counter. I have to remember to keep the phone trained on his face when he bites my finger at the first knuckle. And I have to swallow down the gasp when his tongue swirls around my finger, cleaning off the custard.

He releases my finger with a wet suctioned pop, drops my wrist and jams the rest of the cupcake in his mouth. The whole thing. I cut the video because he's killed the sexy, but I know I can edit it into something useable.

He chews quickly and swallows, swiping at his mouth with the back of his hand. "Post that and you'll regret it."

"I'll regret it or you will? That was cupcake porn gold, wasn't it, ladies?"

The women cheer and he jerks back, like he's suddenly aware there are other people here besides us.

He nabs the box, halfway to crushing it. "Just remember you pulled the pin, Alice." And with that he spins around, excuses himself, and leaves the café.

"Okay." The bride-to-be raises both of her hands like she's trying to stop traffic. "Please tell me you're sleeping with him. You have to be sleeping with him. I'm pretty sure I just came vicariously through you."

"I'm sorry." I splutter and smooth out my apron—totally a

nervous move. "I don't know what you're talking about. He's my rival, not my . . . boyfriend."

Stephanie grabs my arm, eyes wide and alarmed. "Fuck buddy? Please tell me you're boning him."

"Uhhh—"

"You will be soon if you're not already," the bride-to-be says.

"I don't even *like* him," I scoff.

She smiles. "You don't need to like him to ride him; you just need to want to use him for stress relief. That's how me and Tristan started out and now we're getting married. I see wedding bells in your future!"

I see a whole lot of retribution and Ronan doing whatever he can to get back at me, probably by making a crap-ton of noise, but I don't bother to tell these ladies that. They're the end of my night, and whatever trouble they have brewing isn't going to be mine to endure. It'll be Ronan's and I'm more than happy to let them wreak havoc on him.

Forty-five minutes later, my bachelorette party has defected next door and I've finished cleaning up. I consider stopping at The Knight Cap to see how things are going over there.

Off-key singing filters through the barrier of the wall separating our places. I decide I can drop in for five minutes to check how the girls are doing.

I reapply my lipstick, check my hair, and grab my purse. I'm almost out the door when I realize I'm still wearing my apron. I take it off—careful not to mess up my hair—and throw it in the washing machine, knowing I can toss it in the dryer in the morning when I come in to decorate the cupcakes for tomorrow. Then I lock up and head next door.

The place is packed with people, and I spot the bachelorette ladies on the stage, one of them belting out a tuneless "Wrecking Ball" by Miley Cyrus. Everyone is cheering, likely because of her backup dancers twerking their way around the stage. The ladies are significantly more intoxicated than they were when they left my place. The song finally comes to an end, which is a relief because the horrible singing gets worse the longer it goes on.

Ronan steps up and takes the microphone from the bride-to-be before she can start another song. "That was fantastic! A round of applause for Amanda. You definitely outdid yourself with that one!" The crowd bursts into applause and laughter. Thankfully the bride is way too intoxicated to know that she sounded like a dying goose on methamphetamines.

I turn to leave, satisfied that I've accomplished what I set out to—make Ronan's life a little more difficult—but people have moved in behind me, so I can't get to the door.

"Blaire!" Ronan's deep voice echoes through the speakers and I freeze. "I see you out there. Come on up! The cupcake queen from next door has graced us with her gorgeous presence. Who wants to hear her sing?"

The crowd erupts in a cheer.

"You heard them, Blaire. They want you to sing for them. Don't be shy!" A spotlight is suddenly on me, the glare blindingly bright. "Come on, ladies, go get Blaire and bring her up here for me."

Of course he commissions the drunk bachelorettes to help.

I don't blend in very well in my fifties-inspired dress—tonight it's pink and has a diamond ring theme—so it means that every single person is now staring at me.

The bachelorette crew grabs my arms and pulls me toward the stage. Ronan is grinning like the cat who ate the canary. He did promise to get me back for the vagina cupcake. And I totally posted the video in my stories as soon as he left. I figure it's great advertising for future bachelorette parties.

I don't bother to fight. If Ronan thinks dragging me onstage in front of a bunch of drunk college kids is going to embarrass me, he's got another thing coming.

When I reach the stage, he holds out his hand in faux-chivalry. I slip my palm into his, and warmth zings through my body at the contact. I climb the stairs and he tugs me against his side, smiling down at me, eyes twinkling with malicious mirth. "I'm so glad you stopped in to see what was happening here tonight, Blaire."

I wrap my fingers around his wrist and angle the microphone down. "I couldn't miss hearing my girls sing!"

His grin widens. "They were certainly a delight, weren't they?" He addresses the crowd, and they all clap and whistle.

Ronan is ridiculously charismatic. It doesn't matter that the bride and her wedding party sucked more than a Hoover on the highest setting; they love him and in turn they love the ladies' terrible performance.

"Well, now that I have you up here, what should I do with you?" Ronan's tongue peeks out and the right side of his mouth quirks up in a half-smirk. He tips the microphone toward me.

"What do you want to do with me?" I'd like to say my voice is purposely low and smoky, but honestly, the question and the way he's looking at me seems almost lascivious.

"Hmmm." He sucks his teeth. "Not so sure I should answer that honestly."

That gets a loud cheer from the crowd.

He gives them all a look and I roll my eyes. "Aren't I up here to sing?"

"Right. Yeah. What's your jam? How about 'Let's Get It On'?"

I scoff and take the microphone from him. "Mmm, I think we can come up with something better than that." I tap my lip. "Have you been up here yet, Ronan?"

"I'm running the show, not in it." He laughs, but his eyes glint with a warning look.

"Why can't you do both? Who wants to hear Ronan sing? What do you guys say, should we do a duet?"

The cheer is so loud it makes my ears ring.

"You heard them, they want us to do it together."

"There's only one microphone."

I lift a shoulder in a light shrug. "We can share, can't we?" I drop the mic and whisper. "You're not getting out of this."

He gives his head a slight shake, but his smile tells me he knows he's screwed himself with this. "What're we gonna sing?"

"Hmm." I pretend to think about it for a few seconds. "How about 'You're the One that I Want'?"

Ronan laughs. "I should've known you'd be a *Grease* fan." He motions to the deejay. "All right, you heard the lady. Let's do it."

What Ronan doesn't know is that I've probably watched the movie a thousand times. And I've seen the play at least twenty times. I also have the soundtrack and I listen to it in my car all the time. I don't even need the lyric feed. My love for *Grease* is a good part of the reason I wear the dresses I do.

When I adopt an obsession, I don't half ass it; I commit fully. Much like my obsession with Harry Potter and cupcakes. When I was a teenager, I used to love drama class. Even in college I would join the theater groups for fun. I didn't ever want it to be a job. Once I was the understudy for the role of Sandy, so I know the entire song by heart, actions included.

I smooth my hands over my skirt and hand the microphone back to him. I love that he has to start.

I have to hand it to Ronan. He really does try to hit the notes and he doesn't do a half bad job, but he has to keep looking at the screen. His gaze keeps darting back and forth. It makes it that much more satisfying when I cover his hand with mine, tip the microphone down and sing to him, telling him he's the one that I want.

It's obvious he's shocked, possibly because I don't need the lyric prompt, possibly because I'm not a half bad singer. He almost misses the cue to join me, but I nudge him and nod to the screen, forcing him to drag his eyes away from mine.

He tries to keep up. It's rather commendable, and I will say, what he lacks in vocal range he makes up for in hip shaking.

When the song ends, the crowd bursts into uncontrollable applause and shouts for an encore. I slip my hand into Ronan's, noting his damp palm, and we take a bow.

I hand him back the microphone and tug on the collar of his shirt, pulling him down. My lips brush the shell of his ear and his skin pebbles as I whisper, "Not quite how you thought it was going to go down, huh?"

@buttercreamandbooze:

You're the Cupcake I Want

chapter eight

SHOULD'VE BEEN MY WIN

Blaire

The next morning I'm still sort of floating on the high of last night's win. I have to say, I'm feeling pretty damn awesome right now. I continue riding that same fabulous wave all the way in to work. Everything is awesome. Nothing can ruin my fantastic mood, not even the fact that I haven't slept much.

I find a box sitting on the front step and carry it inside with me. I don't recognize the name of the company, but maybe Daphne ordered something for our next event as a surprise.

I pluck a pair of scissors from the jar next to the cash register, sliding it carefully along the seam.

Before I have a chance to open it, the back doors swing open and Paul wheels a cart of boxes down the hall. "Hey! You're here early!" He's smiling, but he looks tired.

The scissors clatter to the floor, narrowly missing my foot. "Geez! You scared the crap out of me. I expected you to be long gone by now."

"I had to shift around some deliveries because of the holiday." Paul has had to do that a lot more recently. Either dropping off cupcakes in the evening, or coming in extra early so he can get specialty ones done for me. A few times it's been down to the wire.

Paul agreed to help me through Thanksgiving, but after that he'll be done paying me back for the truck, and I'll have to either hire another baker or take on the job myself. Based on finances, it looks like it's probably going to be me taking on the extra workload, so my already limited sleep is going to suffer even more.

He maneuvers the cart of cupcakes behind the register so I can check them out. I flip the box on top open. They smell delicious—like pumpkin pie spice—and will be even more amazing once I add the cream cheese center filling and vanilla buttercream icing, topped with an adorable pumpkin candy. "These smell like heaven."

"Well, it's your recipe, so you can take the credit for that." He's still grinning. "You feeling like a rock star this morning?"

"Uh, not particularly, no." I lean against the counter, legs still shaky from the scare.

His smile fades and his face scrunches up. "I take it you haven't heard?"

"Heard what?" I drag my attention away from the cupcakes, imagining how perfect they're going to look when I'm done with them.

"There's a video of you."

"What kind of video?" A shot of panic hits me. I'm not sure why. It's not like I've ever made one of *those* kinds of video. And honestly, there are loads of videos of me posted on YouTube since I have a channel and I upload there all the time.

He arches a brow. "Wow, your face right now makes me want to ask a lot of questions, many of which I don't necessarily think I want the answer to."

I wave the comment away. "Stop being dramatic and cryptic and tell me what's going on."

"Someone posted your performance from last night." He tips his chin toward the wall connecting us to The Knight Cap.

"Oh, that. It wasn't a big deal." I pull a tray of cupcakes from the cart and begin arranging them carefully in the display case.

"Well, maybe not to you, but it's sure getting lots of attention."

"What kind of attention?"

Paul fishes his phone out of his pocket and opens YouTube. It appears the video was uploaded by Ronan's bartender Lars— apparently his name isn't Larry. Paul hands me the device.

"This can't be right. It's been viewed more than a million times?"

"He tagged that YouTuber Tori in the video and she shared it." He taps the screen right under the video, where Lars has captioned it "Best Bar in the Pacific Northwest Challenge"

#toritaylorbestof #TheKnightCap #BestBarPNW and about seven hundred more hashtags. The video has tons of likes.

"Damn it!" I grouse, scrolling through the comments. "I can't believe this."

"You sound great. I mean I always knew you could sing, but you really nailed that performance."

"I know I can sing."

Paul's eyebrows lift. "Humble much?"

I give him a look. "It's not ego talking. I was always in theater. I can sing. It's a fact, and now Ronan is getting the accolades for it." I hit Play on the video for additional self-torture.

Ronan and I appear on the screen, although only half of me because the focus is on Ronan, at least at the beginning since he's singing and the center of attention. He doesn't have a terrible voice, and he's annoyingly nice to look at. The camera really loves him and all his pretty man angles.

When it's my turn I nab the microphone from him and start singing. "Damn!" Lars turns the camera around and there's a closeup of his face and wide eyes. Like Ronan, he's also nice to look at. "Listen to that voice." He flips the camera around again, turns it sideways and pans back to me.

"How the hell am I going to beat him now?" I pass Paul his phone back before I do something like throw it against a wall. I don't have the funds to replace it. "He didn't even tag me or B&B in the comments! What a jerk."

"If Tori ends up coming to Seattle, you'll have a chance to

prove you're the better bar." Paul gives my shoulder a squeeze. I hate that his expression holds guilt as well. "I can try to help out for a little longer if you need me."

I wave the offer away. "We both know that won't work. Especially not with you moving an hour away. I can totally handle this." I motion to the naked cupcakes. I can definitely do all the baking, but I'm worried about how it's going to impact everything else. Running a business is a lot of work. Especially with all the paperwork and keeping track of inventory and ingredients. It's been nice to have the help while it lasted. "Anyway, let's check this out." The box is unusually light, so maybe it's sample napkins or something. The company we bought ours from routinely does that.

I fold back the flaps and a balloon with the word BOOM! floats out, heading for the ceiling. Paul and I give each other a quizzical look as a second balloon rises out of the box. Both of them pop at the same time and suddenly I find myself covered in a shower of hot pink glitter.

"Oh my God! The cupcakes!" I shriek and try to push Paul out of the way so I can save the open box from the glitter bomb, but it's too late. The cakes are already sparkling. I shout a bunch of nonsense profanity, because Paul's hard work and two dozen of my income source are now trash.

"What the hell is this stuff?" Paul raises his hand, about to run his fingers through his hair.

"That was a glitter bomb! You can't do that in here! You'll

make it worse!" I guide him to the back door, hoping to minimize the damage.

"A glitter bomb?" Paul asks as I help him shake the glitter out of his hair and brush it off his shoulders.

I give my own head a shake. My palms are sparkling. "Glitter is the herpes of crafting. It'll be everywhere for weeks! I'll never get rid of it."

"Who would send you one of those?"

"How the hell—" I stop mid-sentence and glance next door. "That sonofabitch. First he steals all the goddamn glory last night and now this?" There's only one person I can think of who would do something like this. Freaking Ronan.

I spend the rest of the day trying to clean up glitter between customers, but it's literally everywhere and anyone who comes into the shop is an immediate victim of a glitter attack. Thankfully I have a couple of short breaks between the lunch and afternoon rush, so I have time to de-glitter my café. Apart from a mangled pumpkin spice one and the glitter-covered ones that weren't for sale I manage to sell out of cupcakes.

I'll be closed on Thursday for Thanksgiving and will have a skeleton staff the day before and through the weekend so Callie can spend the holiday with her family. I would try to get out of my own family obligations, but I haven't been home to visit since I opened Buttercream and Booze, and my dad would be disappointed if I didn't come for dinner. As much as I don't love their interfering ways, or their general bossiness and insanity, I do love them.

Ronan stops in as I'm shutting down for the day, grinning like a fool. "Hey, super star! You get my awesome present this morning?"

I don't return the smile. "I sure did." I spin around and grab the box of ruined cupcakes from the shelf behind me and set it on the counter in front of him.

He tips his head to the side, and lifts his hand as if he's about to touch my face. I jerk back. "What're you doing?"

"You have some glitter on your cheek."

I throw my hands in the air. "I have glitter literally everywhere. It's even in my damn underwear!"

Ronan's smile turns into a grimace at my unnecessary overshare, and his face falls even further as I flip the box of cupcakes open. "Oh shit."

"Oh shit is right. Thank you so much for your kind, thoughtful gift."

"I figured you would've opened it in your office."

"Well I guess you figured wrong."

He chews on the corner of his plush bottom lip. "I'm so sorry, Blaire. I thought it would be funny."

I cross my arms. "Do you have any idea how impossible it is to clean up glitter? I'm going to be finding sparkly crap where the sun doesn't shine for weeks."

He fishes his wallet out of his back pocket and glances at the menu board where the price list is posted. He peels off four twenties.

"What are you doing?"

"Well you couldn't sell those today, could you?"

"Not covered in glitter, no."

"So I'm paying for them because even though they're bathed in glitter they smell fantastic and I bet you would've sold them if they hadn't been ruined."

"You really don't have to do that." But I could use the eighty bucks right now, which is sort of depressing. He obviously feels bad if he's willing to fork over the money I lost as a result of his prank.

"Yes I do. I honestly didn't mean to make such a mess of your day, or cost you potential revenue." He pushes the money toward me and picks up one of the glitter-covered cakes. He proceeds to shake it off, and then he tries to brush off the rest of the glitter, which means he ends up getting it all over his hands.

"You're not going to eat that, are you?"

He gives me a look. "And let it go to waste?"

"It's not even decorated." Wow, he must really feel bad.

"Sure it is, with glitter."

"Glitter isn't really digestible, or particularly safe to eat. Might be advisable to leave the top if you're going to give that a whirl."

He reluctantly pries the top off, then takes a huge bite and chews exaggeratedly. His expression is priceless and he makes a lot of noises, some of delight and some of surprise. "It's a little—"

"Gritty?"

He nods and raises his hand in front of his mouth. "But still delicious."

It's hard not to laugh. "I do have one left over that's mangled but isn't covered in glitter."

"Really?"

"You can have it on one condition."

"Sure. Anything."

"You help me de-glitter my counter space." It's clear that he really didn't mean to cause me problems today, but it doesn't mean I'm not going to make him suffer at least a little for it.

I hand him a damp cloth and he goes to work wiping down all the surfaces that still hold traces of glitter. The best part is that no matter how careful he tries to be, sparkles get stuck to his face. I guarantee he'll be glittering all night long, like a disco ball.

On Wednesday morning I've just arrived at B&B when Ronan comes busting out the back door. He looks frazzled and exhausted. His hair is also an unusual mess. It's actually quite sexy, to be honest. Like he rolled out of bed and came straight here. His clothes are even rumpled. "Hey. Hi. I'm so glad you're here."

This is a new greeting. "Um, it's nice to see you, too?"

"Can I ask you a huge favor? Please?"

"Ahhh. Now the friendliness makes more sense. What do you need?"

"I'm supposed to get a whole load of Thanksgiving supplies delivered this morning, but the guy is running late and I have to take my grandfather up to my brother's. I'm supposed to leave"—he checks his watch—"ten minutes ago. And Gramps hates being late for stuff and I have to drive four hours there and back. I tried to call Lars, but I doubt he'll get the message until it's way too late."

I hold up a hand. "I can sign for the order."

"It all needs to go in the fridge."

"I can make sure that happens."

"Really?"

"Really."

He drops a key to The Knight Cap in my hand and pulls me in for a shockingly tight hug. "Thank you so much, Blaire. I really owe you big time. I always enjoy seeing you, even when you're tearing me a new one. I gotta run. Thank you. A million times over." And he's off.

"You're welcome," I mutter and head back to B&B to start on the icing for today's cupcakes.

Forty-five minutes later the delivery truck shows up. I'm in the middle of a particularly tricky caramel filling and Paul is on his way out so he accepts the delivery—which I ask him to sign for—and makes sure it's safely in the fridge before he takes off.

chapter nine

NOT THE PAYBACK I WAS LOOKING FOR

Blaire

Even though B&B isn't open on Thanksgiving, I still head into the shop first thing in the morning. I need to frost the cupcakes for my family's dinner and all my supplies are there. Plus I want to drop off yesterday's unsold goods at the local soup kitchen, along with any other treats that won't be fresh by tomorrow. Usually one of their staff comes to pick them up, but they couldn't make it yesterday and I figured it was easier for me to do the dropping off on the way out of town.

I'm surprised to see Ronan in the back alley outside The Knight Cap. He usually isn't in until sometime after ten, and it's barely eight thirty. He's pacing as he talks on the phone, his tone clipped and annoyed. He's not wearing his usual plaid-and-jeans uniform, either. Today he's in a pair of gray sweats and a hoodie, his hair is a mess, again, and he has a serious five-o'clock shadow going on. He's wearing his glasses, like he rolled out of bed and came straight here. Amazingly, he still manages to look delicious.

"Well what the hell am I supposed to do now?" He spins around and stalks back into The Knight Cap.

Looks like it's his turn to be in a mood.

I'm about to go back inside, but a tired-looking Lars steps out and sags against the wall, cringing when Ronan's loud, angry voice filters through the gap in the door.

"What's going on?"

He startles and holds his finger to his lips. "I'm hiding."

"Why are you here this early?"

"Because I was supposed to help with food prep and get double pay today, but it looks like that's not happening."

Ronan comes busting out into the back alley again and the door nearly hits Lars in the face, but his reaction time is at least decent, because he manages to get out of the way before the steel connects with his nose.

"What the fuck am I going to do?" Ronan grabs his hair and kicks the giant metal trash bin.

I've never seen Ronan anything but calm. "Are you okay?" I ask, even though it's very obvious that he's definitely not okay.

"No!" He throws his hands in the air. "I'm not fucking okay!"

"Is there anything I can do to help?"

"Unless you can magically thaw twenty-five damn Cornish game hens in the next three hours, then no."

A sinking feeling hits me. I let Paul sign for the order

yesterday and then I got busy with customers. It was nonstop all day. "Oh my God. Is this my fault? Did they go in the freezer instead of the fridge?"

Ronan's brow furrows. "What? No. The freaking company I ordered from messed it up. I ordered fresh Cornish game hens and they brought me frozen ones and a bunch of cans of damn pie filling instead of pie."

"Oh no! I hope they're giving you your money back." I can't even imagine what it would do to my bank account if something like that happened to me.

"Yeah, but that's not going to help me tonight. Now all I have to serve for Thanksgiving is potatoes, stuffing, and freaking vegetables."

He paces the alley, hands still in his hair. I try not to ogle his tattoos, or the way his jogging pants do a great job of hugging his butt, but it's a challenge.

"What if we put them in a cold water bath?" I suggest.

"They're rock solid. It'll take at least six hours and then we'd still have to prep and cook them. I spent eleven damn hours in a car yesterday so I could be open on Thanksgiving and this is what I get. I should've checked last night." He scrubs his face with both hands. "Lars, you might as well go home. Enjoy the day off."

"We could do wings or something," he offers.

"It's Thanksgiving. People don't want wings. They want a proper dinner, and we don't have one. We don't even have a dessert to serve. There just really isn't a point."

"Sorry, Ronan. I know you had big plans for today."

He waves him off. "It's fine. It's not your fault."

"I guess I'll see you tomorrow?" Lars takes a step toward the door.

"Yeah. Thanks for coming in early. I know you'd rather be sleeping."

Lars leaves and Ronan slips his hands in his pockets and drops his head with a sigh.

I feel awful for him. Thanksgiving can be a good opportunity to make money, if you have the food to serve. "Do you need any help with anything?"

He rubs the back of his neck. "Nah. Guess I'm gonna sit on the couch and watch football today."

"Why don't you come over and I'll make you a boozy coffee." I incline my head toward B&B. It's really the least I can do.

He blows out a breath. "Yeah, sure. Why not? It's not like I have anything better to do."

I'd be offended, but I don't think it's a personal attack, more that he's upset about the sudden and unexpected crappy turn his day took.

I make us both special lattes, his spiked with booze, mine not since I have some baking to do. "I need to frost some cupcakes. If you're interested in hanging around, you can be my taste tester."

"Uh sure, yeah. I could do that."

I lead him to the kitchen and set him up with a stool.

I pull the naked cupcakes from the fridge so they have time to warm up, don a hairnet—hygiene before vanity—wash my hands and slip out of my heels and into a pair of flats before I get the rest of the ingredients out.

"Do you need any help?"

"Nope. You're good to just hang out and drink coffee. I'm sorry about the delivery. We had a busy day yesterday and I let Paul accept it. I didn't even check what it was."

"It wouldn't have mattered. I didn't tell you what was supposed to be delivered and I should've checked everything last night, but that drive was hell. There was an accident on the way back and it took seven hours instead of four, which is already long enough, you know? I just didn't plan this as well as I should have. Rookie mistake, I guess."

"You can always do a post-Thanksgiving dinner this weekend, can't you? Maybe on Saturday you can do a Cornish game hen special?" I tie my apron and set up the industrial mixer so I can work on the buttercream.

"That's what I'll have to do. They've already been in the fridge overnight. I'm hoping by tomorrow afternoon they'll be thawed and then the kitchen staff can prep and cook them."

"At the very least you'll be able to thaw them the rest of the way in a water bath, won't you?"

"Mmm. Yeah." He watches me measure ingredients, turn on the mixer and set the timer before I move to a smaller one to prepare the chocolate buttercream for the triple chocolate cupcakes. My dad put in a special request for those. He put in several special requests. Sometimes it's hard to understand why he just won't let me live my dream when it's so clear I know what I'm doing.

"I can't believe you're wearing a dress and working with chocolate."

"I do everything in a dress."

One of his eyebrows lifts.

"Almost everything," I amend. I don't know why my mind immediately goes to sex on account of his eyebrow raise. Possibly because Ronan's hair is sticking out all over the place like he's just been screwed? Or because he looks half–book nerd and half badass with the glasses, sweats, and full sleeves. Or because I haven't had it in forever.

I'll go with the last one.

I stick my head in the fridge and take far longer than necessary to retrieve the milk so he can't see my embarrassment.

"Do you ever wear pants?"

"Not often."

"What about when you're at home?"

"I still prefer dresses most of the time. I mean, of course I have things like leggings for when it gets cold, but this is how I'm most comfortable." I push up on my toes to try to reach the container of icing sugar. I don't know why Paul insists on putting it up this high all the time. Probably because he gets a chuckle out of it.

"Why?"

I look over my shoulder. "Why did you cover your arms in tattoos?"

"Because I want to wear my memories, see them every day and remember." It seems a lot like an unfinished sentence. He hops off his stool, plucks the canister from the shelf and hands it to me. "You still haven't answered my question. Why are you more comfortable in dresses than pants? You have killer calves, and the waist up is easy on the eyes. I gotta imagine whatever you're hiding under those skirts matches the rest of you."

I give him a sideways look. "Is that a compliment?"

"It's an observation, and if you'd like to take it as a compliment, feel free."

I laugh. "This is my style." There's actually a lot more to it than just being my style, but it's not really something I tend to share with people, let alone a rival bar owner who barely tolerates me and is probably humoring me. "Just like plaid shirts and black rimmed glasses and sleeve tattoos are yours."

"I'm going to say something, and I don't want you to take offense to it."

"Does that mean it's going to be offensive?"

Ronan chuckles. "I think it could be misconstrued as an insult when that's not how I intend it."

"Go ahead then." I check on the icing and start measuring out the ingredients for the chocolate buttercream.

"You give off this classy pinup girl vibe crossed with a fifties housewife, but you're an entrepreneur. It's sort of a contradiction, isn't it? And here you are, all dressed up at nine in the morning, making me coffee and whipping up buttercream icing."

"I made you coffee because you looked like you needed a break and a shot. And do you mean to say I don't look like I should be taken seriously because I'm not wearing a pantsuit?"

"That's not what I said."

"Sometimes it's good to be underestimated, don't you think?" I set another timer for seven minutes while I let the butter cream.

"I don't think it's about underestimating you. I mean, clearly you have vision and business savvy, but you don't come across as . . . threatening, I guess."

"Sort of goes hand in hand with being underestimated." I dip a spoon into the chocolate ganache and hand it to him, before I do the same for myself. My sample is much smaller than his. I wait until he's done groaning his way through the spoonful before I ask another question. "So tell me about The Knight Cap. Your grandfather owns it and you decided to come work with him? Or take it over?"

"He lost my grams a little over a year ago; they worked here together since they were teenagers, so doing it without her was . . . hard. That's what all the framed couple pictures are about on the wall opposite the booths. It's the story of their life together, which was spent at the bar for the most part."

I press my hand to my chest. "Did they meet there?"

"They did." He nods, his eyes suddenly far away. "The bar has been in our family for three generations. Gramps bartended and Grams was a waitress. Fell head over heels in love with each other. Caused a big ruckus since she was a few years younger than him and her parents were hoping she'd marry up, but no one and nothing could keep them apart." He smiles softly; it's full of fondness and sadness. "They even dated in secret for a while. Lots of backroom and closet stories, I'm sure. Not that Gramps would ever disrespect Grams by telling any of them."

I laugh and then sigh. "Did she get sick?"

"Uh no, she was healthy all the way to the end, thankfully. She had a heart attack and passed in her sleep." He flips his spoon absently between his fingers.

The timer on the vanilla buttercream goes off, and I slow down the speed so I can add the sugar and vanilla. "Your poor grandpa. Was he with her?"

"Yeah. It was rough there for a bit and running this place on his own was just too much, so things kind of slipped. I was working in finance and hating it, so Gramps gave me an opportunity I couldn't refuse."

"Which was to bring this place back to life?" I supply.

"Yeah. He said if I could run it successfully for a year he'd loan me the money to start up my own brewery, which is something I've always wanted to do, but banks aren't all that excited about giving you money for that kind of thing when you don't have the entrepreneurial experience behind you."

"Don't I know it. It took me three years before the bank would give me a freaking loan for this place."

"What'd you do before you set up shop here?"

"I had a cupcake truck."

"Seriously?" He looks like he wants to laugh.

"Don't knock it. I started out with tents at food festivals and then weekend market booths until eventually I had a pretty decent following. When I saved up enough I invested in a truck."

"And you did that on your own?"

"Paul helped, actually."

"What's the deal with you two?" He gives me a curious look.

"He's a friend, and he helped me get started. We worked together for almost five years."

"And that's all you've ever been? Friends?"

"Yup. We were good at being in business together, and even that had its limitations. But I learned a lot from him and he was a great mentor."

"He never tried for more?" Ronan presses.

"Nope. Selling cupcakes out of a truck puts you in seriously close quarters with another person. He's seen all my sides, the good, the bad, and terrifying. Besides, getting in bed with a coworker or colleague is a recipe for disaster. Pun completely intended."

He laughs and shakes his head. "Yeah, can't imagine it's a great idea for a lot of reasons, although my gramps would likely disagree."

"Those were different times, weren't they?"

"Less complicated in a lot of ways, and yet more at the same time." Ronan nods.

Twenty minutes later, I have batches of icing ready for decorating.

Ronan is practically drooling as he watches me put it in piping bags, so I get out a bunch of spoons and bowls and let him sample a bit of each as I decorate the cupcakes for dinner.

"I thought you weren't opening up today."

"I'm not." I pipe chocolate mocha buttercream on the triple chocolate cupcake. "These are for my family dinner." Although, half my family will probably make the sign of the cross at them. My mom and sisters are huge keto fans. The easy conversation shifts into that slightly awkward *what-now* limbo. "Do you usually spend Thanksgiving with your gramps?"

"Typically he was always here for Thanksgiving. Grams really loved the holiday and always wanted to make sure people who didn't have family to celebrate with could go somewhere and have a nice dinner, which is why I ordered all the Cornish game hens. It's been hard for Gramps to be here without her, though, so I told him I'd run things today. He went to my brother's place. He's staying there for a few days and won't be back until Sunday sometime. You're going to spend the day with your parents?"

"Yup. I haven't seen them since I opened this place, so I'm due for a visit." Before I can really consider what I'm saying I blurt, "You should come with me."

Ronan's eyebrows lift. "To your family Thanksgiving?"

"Yeah. Yes." I nod slightly more vigorously than necessary.

"You can't spend the holiday alone. My parents always make a huge production of it. You need to stuff yourself with turkey and beer. It'll be fun!" I'm not sure that *fun* is really the best description for my family events, but it's too late to take it back now.

"I don't know. I should probably plan for the rest of the weekend," Ronan says slowly.

"You already have a plan, a post-Thanksgiving dinner. Come with me. No one should be alone during the holidays."

He grins. "You're sure?"

"Absolutely positive."

"Can I sample the cupcakes before we go?"

"Of course." The eye roll and the *duh* are implied in my tone.

"Okay. I'm in."

"Fabulous!"

What the hell have I just gotten myself into?

@buttercreamandbooze:

I'm just a cupcake, looking for my stud muffin.

chapter ten

TURKEY TIME

Ronan

I'm not sure how to read Blaire's reaction to my saying yes. If I'm completely honest, the cupcakes are the clincher. They're dangerously addictive. Like nicotine, or heroin, or cocaine—none of which has ever been an addiction of mine. Hence the reason I hastily agreed to spend an entire day with Blaire and her family when I know very little about her.

If nothing else, this should prove to be an entertaining day. Blaire is...a lot of personality. And I don't mean that in a bad way. I'm still trying to figure her out and I guess now I'll have the opportunity to do that.

I put a note on the front door of The Knight Cap apologizing for the closure today, and indicating we'll be open again tomorrow, which is when I notice a sign on the empty building across the street. "Is that new?" I ask Blaire. She's busy inspecting all the framed photos of my grandparents that line the wall opposite the booths. I'm sure they have new meaning for her now that she knows the story behind them.

"Hmm?" She drags her gaze away from a black-and-white photo of Gramps and Grams when they were young—younger than I am now.

I point across the street. "Looks like someone finally leased that place. I wonder what's opening there."

She crosses over to where I'm standing. "It's a big building. Wasn't it a law office before or something?"

"I think so, yeah?" It's changed hands a number of times over the years.

"So it's probably something similar, which will be good for both of us." She tips her chin up and looks at me. "More business professionals to cater to."

"Let's hope that's what it is, then." More patrons means The Knight Cap has even greater potential to do well.

"Should I follow you back to your place so you can change, and then we can head to my parents' place?"

I look down at my old white T-shirt and my sweats. "Probably a good idea. Not sure sweats are appropriate for much other than the gym and lazy days at home."

Blaire takes down my address so she can follow me to my place. It's not far from the pub. Making her wait in the car is rude, so I invite her up to my apartment.

It feels weird to have her in my personal space. Although, honestly, the only thing I do here lately is sleep.

"Wow. I don't think it gets more man cave than this," Blaire says as she takes in my loft apartment. It's not huge, but it's comfortable.

"It's just me." I'm not sure if I should be defensive about her assessment or not.

"I can see that." She runs her fingertips along the edge of the distressed wood table I rarely use. I'm not here enough to entertain, and eating dinner alone at a table meant for six is kind of depressing. Mostly I eat at the bar, or on rare occasions when I'm not in a rush, in front of the TV.

"Let me guess: Your place looks like a unicorn vomited a rainbow of happiness all over it?" Mostly I'm poking fun at her.

She laughs. "You would be guessing wrong."

"So you don't have eleven million throw cushions with inspirational phrases on them?" I toe off my shoes and toss them by the door.

"Ahh, just ten million or so, and only a few have cute unicorns farting inspirational phrases." The way she rolls her shoulder back and her narrow-eyed glare tells me everything I need to know.

I've totally hit a nerve. I don't know why I enjoy needling her as much as I do. Maybe because she's so prone to reacting. "I bet your place is decorated for the holiday. All sorts of cute pumpkin stuff everywhere, a papier-mâché turkey centerpiece that you made at some workshop on your dining room table."

Her cheeks flush pink. "I don't have a dining room table."

"But you have a papier-mâché turkey?"

"I had several construction paper ones when I was a child. I probably would have kept them for all eternity if my parents hadn't thrown out my box of homemade crafts when I was a teenager in the name of decluttering."

I file that little piece of information away, feeling like she's told me a secret she didn't intend to. "Pumpkin, then?" I press.

I can tell it irritates her that I can read her so easily, but all anyone has to do is step foot inside Buttercream and Booze to see how much she loves the holidays. "Ceramic, not papier-mâché."

"And you painted it yourself?"

"Maybe." She pokes me in the shoulder. "Enough with all the questions. It's an hour and a half drive; you'll have loads of time trapped in a car to make fun of me."

"Right. Yeah." I'm not sure what a long ride in a car together is going to be like. "I'll just change real quick. Can I get you something to drink while you wait?"

"I'm fine, thanks."

I leave her to wander around my apartment while I change. She doesn't seem the type to snoop, but you never know. Considering Blaire is wearing one of her dresses complete with festive holiday print, I decide a pair of black casual pants, dress shirt, and plaid tie are appropriate. I don't bother with contacts since my eyes already feel gritty from lack of sleep.

I find her in my living room, staring up at a collage of family photos. "Ready to roll?"

She turns her head slowly, her expression soft. "I'm so

sorry." She reaches up and adjusts the wooden picture frame, and suddenly her apology makes sense. That was the last family photo we took, and the phrase "In loving memory" is etched into the matte in silver letters.

It's never level, always listing to the right because the frame itself is unbalanced. I refuse to change it, though, because it was one of my first woodshop projects, and my dad and I worked on it together. It's old and cracked and a whole lot ugly, but it's a memory I can't let go of. I nod and swallow around the lump in my throat. "Oh, uh, thanks. It was a long time ago." But on days like this it feels like it was yesterday, not a decade ago, that they passed.

"How old were you when you lost them?" She presses her hand to her chest. "You don't have to answer that if it's not something you want to talk about."

"It's okay." I jam my hands in my pockets and clear my throat again as I step up beside her. "I was twenty."

She blows out a slow, tremulous breath, her smile sad. "That must have been so hard. It looks like you were close."

"We were a tight family. My brothers are both older, so they were more settled, with careers and partners. It shook us all up pretty good. I ended up living with my gramps and grams for a couple of years after they passed."

She nods, putting together the pieces of the puzzle, like why I took over The Knight Cap and why I kept all the pictures of him and Grams up.

"I'm sorry you're not with your family today."

"I'm used to celebrating after the fact." If my brother's place wasn't so far away I might have made the effort to drive out there again today. But after spending all day yesterday taking Gramps up there and coming back, I just don't have the energy. And sometimes the family stuff is harder on days like today, especially since my brothers are in committed relationships, and everyone gets on me for being alone. I force a smile and change the subject. "We should probably hit the road, huh?"

She gives her head a slight shake, as if she's been lost in her own thoughts. "Oh yes. Definitely." She squeezes my forearm gently. "Endless food awaits."

Blaire wasn't lying about her love of the movie *Grease*. The soundtrack is saved as a playlist. Apparently she's a huge fan of movie and musical soundtracks.

"Feel free to change it to whatever you like. I know this isn't everyone's cup of tea." She motions to the stereo system.

Blaire drives a midsized SUV that has a pretty prominent rattle in the engine. It also boasts a Buttercream and Booze magnetic sign on both the driver and passenger side doors. The engine rattle makes me wonder what kind of restaurant background she comes from and how much her family has struggled to make a living at it.

"You said your family is in the restaurant industry, right?" I ask, making small talk.

"Yup, they are." Blaire taps the steering wheel, like she's drumming to the beat of the song.

"So why don't you work with them? Why go out on your

own?" Clearly they're at least somewhat close if she's willing to drive an hour and a half for dinner.

"They're more steak and lobster, and that isn't where my passion lies," she replies. "They like to hobnob, and I like . . . not to."

There's clearly more to that story, but I don't know if I should push it too much since despite all our interactions—which have been mostly Blaire being pissed off at me for something—I'm not sure we're at a place where she feels comfortable sharing too much personal information. Although I'm attending Thanksgiving dinner with her family, in part because it was better than being alone, and also because I'm curious about Blaire. It's a bit of a strange situation all the way around. "Do you want to expand on that?"

She grips and releases the steering wheel, blowing out a breath. "My family is a little . . . odd."

Considering Blaire dresses like she's June Cleaver's pinup-worthy sister I can't say I'm all that surprised. "Aren't all families odd?"

"Mine more than most, I think. They're all very Type A and concerned about money and being the best. And of course I want to be the best, too, but on my own merit and not theirs. I could've worked my way up the ladder in one of their restaurants, but I love baking, and that was never going to fly with them, so I went out on my own instead." She signals right and takes the next exit off the freeway. "They're also kind of insane, and I spent the first twenty-five years of my life dealing with it on a daily basis. I figured I deserved some separation from that."

"That's fair. I love my brothers, but they drive me nuts on a good day. We worked for the same company for a while, but they ended up going out on their own and I don't know that I could ever really work for them." Which was part of the reason I went in a different direction. They wanted the three of us to go into business together and I already didn't love the job.

"Mmm. Family businesses can be tough. It would be a lot easier financially if I went in the direction they wanted me to. They'd love to have me as their pastry chef, designing intricate, elaborate creations that would get them written up by all the highbrow foodie bloggers. But that's not my style. I'd rather struggle to make ends meet for a while than give up my own dream."

"I can't imagine how intense it must be doing it all on your own." It makes me even more grateful for Gramps's support.

"The first couple of years are always hard, but I'm hoping in the end it'll pay off. Someday I'll be able to get more than five hours of sleep a night and my diet won't consist mostly of leftover cupcakes and almost-expired sandwiches."

"Because you don't have time to cook?"

She lifts a shoulder. "Everything I have is tied up in Buttercream and Booze so if the money's already spent on the food, then I might as well eat it rather than buy groceries that are going to rot in my fridge because I'm never home."

"Do you remember the last time you had a lazy Saturday?" I ask.

"Nope." Blaire raises her finger in the air. "Wait. I had the flu two years ago and had to take a Saturday off because of it."

"I don't think that counts as a lazy day." This conversation makes me highly aware of just how hard Blaire has to work to get where she is. It explains why she was so hostile the first time I met her.

Blaire turns down a country road and the distance between houses increases. The farther we get from the freeway, the antsier Blaire becomes. She stops asking questions and her answers grow shorter, more clipped. She starts to nibble on her bottom lip, eyes darting to me and away every so often.

"Having second thoughts?" I'm kind of joking, kind of not. We don't know each other all that well and while I find myself strangely attracted to her, I'm not sure if it's completely one-sided or not. I believe the invite was more her feeling bad for me, but there's also been more than one interaction that's included thinly veiled innuendo and what seems like flirting.

"No. Not really. I mean—" She cringes. "I should probably warn you; my family is a bit...unconventional."

"Unconventional how?" Maybe they're circus-performing restaurateurs.

Blaire slows the SUV and makes a careful right. She stops at the gated entrance. For the first time I notice the eight-foot wrought-iron fence that stretches out on both sides into the distance. It's surrounded by forest. Maybe they're part of a commune. Or a cult. I sincerely hope I make it out of this alive.

Blaire punches in a code and the gate opens slowly. She clutches the steering wheel until her knuckles turn white as we make our way down the narrow tree-lined driveway.

"Holy crap," I mutter when the house comes into view. Because it's not a house. It's a goddamn palace. A seriously eccentric, gaudy as hell, gothic and creepy palace. Okay, that's a bit of an exaggeration, but based on the vehicle Blaire drives, the knowledge that she had a freaking cupcake *truck*, and the cheap rent she must pay for Buttercream and Booze, I'm a little shocked. This doesn't really add up. "Your family lives here?" Maybe they're the help and we'll be eating in the servant quarters. Or we'll have to actually serve dinner before we get to eat it.

"Yup." Blaire nods stiffly.

No fewer than three Bentleys are parked in the driveway. There's also a black Ferrari and some obscure European sports car I can't identify. That's almost three million dollars in cars parked out front.

"Am I underdressed?" I feel like a tux would've been more appropriate.

She waves a nervous hand around in the air and smiles almost manically. "Oh no. You're perfect. It's really anything goes."

She parks her crappy SUV, leaving lots of space between it and one of the six-figure cars, and practically throws herself out of the vehicle. She pops the hatch and I help her carry the boxes of cupcakes up the massive staircase—I'm almost out of breath by the time we get to the top.

She shifts her hold on the boxes, which makes me nervous since she seems shaky and more high-strung than usual all of a sudden. I don't want any cupcake casualties. Although if they're ruined they can't be served and then I could bring them home and eat them all.

She punches in a code and the doors open on their own. Andddd...it only gets weirder. Two statues take up the space on either side of the massive entrance. They're naked butlers, and their butler trays are not held up by their hands. More naked statues function as the banisters on the winding staircase with a tacky gold inlay. It's like a Greek mythology museum, a medieval knight, and bad porn slammed into each other, and the result is this strange mash-up. Blaire places the boxes of cupcakes on one of the naked butlers' trays. She tips her head toward the ceiling and murmurs something I don't catch, then takes a deep breath. She smiles stiffly and gives my arm a squeeze. I'm not sure if it's meant to be reassuring for her or me. Or both.

"Hello! I'm here! And I brought a friend with me!" Blaire shouts, her voice echoing off the ceiling of the cavernous open foyer. A butler—*an actual fucking butler*, dressed in one of those suits with the long tails—appears out of thin air. "Miss Blaire, it's wonderful to have you home today."

"Buster, it's so lovely to see you."

Buster the butler. Classic. I wonder if it's his real name or if they changed it for the alliteration.

He lifts the lid and peeks inside one of the boxes resting on the naked butler statue tray. "Oh! All of my favorites, Miss Blaire. You've outdone yourself."

"One of those boxes is for you and the staff. You might want to hide it so the cupcakes don't all disappear before dinner." She takes the smaller box I'm still holding. "And these are for you to take home."

"You're too good to me." His smile is fond and warm.

She winks. "Not nearly good enough, considering what you put up with on a regular basis."

He laughs. "It's like living on the set of one of Margaret's soap operas." He nods to me. "Welcome to the Calloway house, Mr. . . ."

"Oh, this is my friend, Ronan. All his birds were frozen so I brought him along for dinner." She pats my arm.

The weird phrasing doesn't seem to faze Buster. "Well, keep an eye on him in this house." He winks and strides off.

I'm about to ask her what that means, and why the hell she drives an old SUV when it appears her family has enough money to buy a medium-sized country, but she takes a deep breath and squares her shoulders. "I should mention that my parents are divorced but still friendly with each other."

"So they'll both be here?" I'm starting to wonder what I've gotten myself into.

"Yes, and they're both remarried—"

"Care Blaire! You finally made it! Cocktail hour started at

noon!" A woman crosses the expansive, marble foyer. Based on her features, she's most definitely Blaire's mother. Although Blaire is softer around the edges with Marilyn Monroe curves, and her mother looks more like an aging Twiggy. She's also wearing a short, tight and sparkly dress more appropriate for a nightclub. "Oh! I didn't know you were bringing a date! Lawrence, Blaire brought a date!" she calls over her shoulder.

"I'm sorry that you're trapped here with me now. I promise the booze and food will make it worth it," Blaire mutters before her mother pulls her into one of those loose, fake hugs and air kisses both of her cheeks.

Her mother grabs her by the shoulders. "You look tired. I think you're probably working too much. Have you gained weight? I have a great juice detox that will shed some of that baby fat like—" She snaps her fingers beside Blaire's ear, making her jump.

"Mom, I'm almost thirty. The baby fat is here to stay."

"It's all the carbs, honey."

"I like carbs more than I like food deprivation. Anyway, Mom, this is Ronan." She motions to me. "Ronan, this is my mother—"

"—Glinda. Like the good witch from *The Wizard of Oz*." Her hand shoots out. "Enchanted, I'm sure. And I'm sorry for my terrible manners, but we haven't seen our Care Blaire since the summer. So much catching up to do! How long have you two been dating?"

"He's a friend, Mom. We're not dating."

"Yet?" she asks, hopefully. "When was the last time you had a boyfriend, darling?"

"Not since Maddy stole the last one," Blaire replies.

"They were better suited for each other." Glinda gives her a patronizing look before she turns her attention back to me and looks me over as if I'm an accessory she's unsure of. "Where did you meet my Care Blaire?"

"I own the bar next door to Buttercream and Booze."

"Next door to what?" Glinda looks confused.

"My café," Blaire mumbles.

"Oh!" Glinda claps her bony hands. "So you're the rival! How fun that you're here."

I glance at Blaire, whose lips are pursed. "Thank you for that, Mom."

"I don't know if I'd call us rivals. I serve beer and wings, and Blaire serves the most delicious cupcakes in the universe." I'm not trying to suck up to her mother, but I am sort of sucking up to Blaire. Mostly because I have a feeling that her relationship with her family is complicated. Her mother has basically called her fat and chastised her on her dating habits. In front of me.

I wonder if Blaire invited me so I'd be a distraction of some kind. Or a shield.

"Hmm, she is quite adept with the buttercream and a spatula." She pinches Blaire's side. "As is evidenced by all the taste testing we must be doing."

A man who looks like Hugh Hefner from two decades ago appears in the foyer. He's wearing a velvet smoking jacket, burgundy silk pants, and black slippers. He's also holding an unlit cigar. "Blaire! We were wondering when you were going to arrive."

"Hi, Uncle Lawrence."

He glides across the room and does the same air-kiss thing as her mother did before he shakes my hand.

"We didn't realize Blaire was bringing a date."

"He's a friend, not a date," Blaire corrects.

"Well, you're introducing him to the family so that must mean you're interested in turning him into your date." He turns to Glinda. "Doesn't it, darling?"

"I would agree, but maybe Care Blaire would prefer to keep that little detail to herself in case Skylar gets an idea to steal him away."

"I guess that means my cousin made it back from San Francisco for dinner tonight." Blaire smiles tightly.

"You know how she hates missing family events," Lawrence says.

I can't tell if they're joking. Or what's going on, because Blaire's mom is now caressing Lawrence's arm in a way that seems overly friendly for someone who's either supposed to be her brother or her brother-in-law. This whole thing is hella confusing and eye-opening.

"I thought I heard your voice! How's my baby girl?" A balding, potbellied man wearing a white linen suit ambles into the room. He looks more like he's ready for bed than for a Thanksgiving dinner party.

"Hey, Dad!" A huge smile breaks across her face and she opens her arms, wrapping them around his expansive belly.

He kisses her on top of the head and his gaze shifts to me. "You brought a date?"

"She's telling everyone he's just a friend," Glinda supplies.

"Because she doesn't want Skylar to try to steal him," Lawrence adds.

"It doesn't have anything to do with Skylar." Blaire tries to defend herself, but is interrupted by yet another woman.

"Care Blaire! Please tell me you brought your cupcakes! Gran-Gran has been asking about them all afternoon!"

"Hi, Aunt Nora. I certainly did." And we go through another round of introductions.

I'm once again confused when Blaire's aunt moves in beside her dad and pats his belly. I can see the physical resemblance between Nora and Glinda, which I'm assuming means they're sisters. Either that or they are uncannily similar.

We're ushered through a massive sitting room, and into the kitchen where everyone dons an apron and returns to whatever station they were at before we arrived. It smells amazing, and the kitchen is insane. It looks like a very high-end restaurant kitchen merged with more gaudy glitz and glamour. Now I need to know what restaurants they actually own, because I'm thinking they must be pretty damn successful if this is their pad.

The sound of mixing, stirring, and chopping is accompanied

by orders being given, and in the middle of all of this they're also trying to carry on an actual conversation. It's impossible to follow.

Blaire opens a door and searches through the aprons hanging from a hook until she finds the one she wants. She hugs it to her chest before she pulls it over her head and reaches behind her to tie it.

"I can help with that." I step up and brush her hands out of the way.

She jumps at the contact. "Oh, thanks." She picks out a black apron and hands it to me, returning the favor. She slips her arm through mine, and tugs so I bend until her lips are at my ear. "I meant to tell you before you met them, but my mom is married to my uncle and my aunt is married to my dad."

I turn my head to see whether she's kidding, because that is some next-level fucked-up shit, but don't take into account how close our faces are, so the end of my nose brushes hers.

"Ah ha!" Someone shouts, startling the hell out of us. "I knew it! You were kissing! Ronan *is* your date."

Blaire drops my arm and takes one excessively large step away from me. "We weren't kissing. I was bringing him up to speed on the family dynamic."

Aunt Nora claps gleefully. "I saw it with my own eyes."

"Then you need new glasses," Blaire grumbles.

The accidental nose brush incites a ridiculous slew of questions, beginning with how long we've been secretly dating, how we met, and whether I've ever been incarcerated. In the very short time I've been here, I come to the conclusion that Blaire's family is entertaining, but definitely a whole bag of WTF with a side of *this reminds me of a bad reality show.*

Another woman who looks to be a couple of years younger than Blaire glides into the room, a well-dressed man lagging behind her. Everyone looks like they're ready to attend some kind of formal event, apart from her uncle in his Hugh Hefner getup and her dad in his pajama suit.

"Care Blaire! Yay!" She waves her arms in the air like the inflatable balloon guy while she shuffle-runs across the room in her extra high heels and throws her arms around Blaire. She's at least four inches taller and looks like her last good meal was probably five years ago. I don't understand how people who cook food that smells this delicious can be that thin. She does the same thing Blaire's mother did and holds her at arm's length. "This dress is so cute! Have you gained some weight?"

"At least thirty pounds," Blaire deadpans. "Madeline, this is my friend Ronan. Ronan, this is my younger, more attractive and thinner sister, Madeline."

"You can call me Maddy." She giggles, gives me a simpering look, bats her lashes, and holds out her hand.

I shake it, because it's rude not to, and bite my tongue, because all I want to do is defend Blaire and give her hell for not doing it herself when I know for a fact that she's got bigger balls than most men I know.

A tall, somewhat wiry guy slings his arm over Maddy's shoulder and extends his free hand. "I'm Matthew, Maddy's husband."

"Ronan."

He's still shaking my hand, but he's not looking at me. His eyes are on Blaire, and the way he's looking at her seems really inappropriate. "Ballsy move, bringing a date with Skylar on the rebound."

She rolls her eyes. "Skylar is always on the rebound."

Maddy chuckles and claps her hands together. "This is going to be so much fun!"

As if on cue, another very thin woman enters the kitchen, wearing a club-appropriate minidress and holding a half-empty martini glass. Her gaze hones in on Blaire and a slightly evil smile tips up the corner of her mouth.

"Care Blaire!" Her voice is high-pitched, like nails on a chalkboard. She saunters over, the sway of her hips highly exaggerated as she crosses the room. Instead of taking the most direct route to Blaire, which would be to go around Maddy, she slides her chest along Matthew's bicep, gives me a very blatant once-over, and then air kisses Blaire's cheeks. "Your dress is so cute! It makes your waist look so narrow!"

Sweet baby Jesus riding a skateboard down a freeway without a helmet, Blaire's family is a bunch of assholes.

"And your dress makes you look like you belong in the red light district," Blaire says through gritted teeth and a brittle smile.

"That's exactly where I got it!" She turns to me. "And who might your delicious friend be?"

Blaire introduces me tonelessly to Skylar, the cousin on the rebound everyone seems to think is going to try to steal me. Based on the way she presses her entire body against mine and kisses me on both cheeks, I'm inclined to believe it wasn't a joke.

The last person I'm introduced to is Blaire's Gran-Gran. I'm relieved when all she does is shake my hand and tell Blaire she's so happy she could make it for dinner and that they need to schedule a proper lunch date so she can whup Blaire's ass at gin rummy—those are her exact words.

I'm offered a drink and Blaire mutters that I should definitely take it, even though she declines the alcohol, citing that she'll have to drive home later.

"You two can always stay the night." Skylar dons an apron, grabs me by the arm, leads me over to the kitchen island, and pushes me onto one of the high-back stools. "Let's all get to know each other!" She picks up a knife and starts chopping carrots into thin discs without even looking at what she's doing.

"How's your little bakeshop doing, Blaire?" her uncle asks as he stirs some kind of sauce. Blaire is drinking ginger ale and whisking something in a bowl—at least two people suggested sparkling water or a diet variety of soda. I want to punch everyone in the room out, apart from Gran-Gran, who hasn't said anything mean. Yet.

"My little bakeshop is doing fine, thanks for asking."

I glance over at her—she's standing on my right, keeping an eye on Skylar, whose arm keeps bumping mine she's so freaking close.

"It's actually doing amazing," I interject.

I stretch my arm across the back of the stool and angle my body toward Blaire and away from Skylar. Whatever the reason I'm here—whether as a distraction for her crazy-ass family or because she honestly felt bad that my day was shot and I would be spending Thanksgiving alone—I decide I'm going to play the role of the boyfriend everyone thinks I am tonight, if for no other reason than to keep Skylar from humping my leg while her family watches.

"Awww, isn't that so lovely to hear." Her mother's tone is patronizing at best. "Well, you know that there's always a place for you back here if you get tired of the grueling hours. It must be hard to make a living on five-dollar cupcakes."

"People buy them by the dozen. You've all been by to see it, haven't you?" I ask, which gets me a swift elbow to the ribs.

"Oh no, Blaire made it seem like it wasn't a trip we needed to make with our busy schedules." Her mother smiles, but I can't quite read the emotion behind it. Indulgent? Hurt? Accusatory?

"Really, Blaire?" I can't bring myself to add Care in front of it. It's the worst fucking nickname in the history of the universe. It's condescending and it doesn't fit her at all. Alice, which is terrible in its own right considering the implications, is still a million times better. "I can't believe you haven't invited your family down for the full Buttercream and Booze experience."

"They're busy," she says through clenched teeth.

I should probably back off, but I'm pretty pissed off at how little regard her family seems to have for her and what she's accomplished, apparently all on her own. I also don't like that the strong, in your face, demanding, combative woman who I thoroughly enjoy riling up is just...taking their shit.

I reach out and pull Blaire into my side and make a show of pressing my lips to her temple. Neither of us expects the static-like shock that accompanies what should be a very innocent display of affection—were we actually dating. She grabs my thigh and I breathe "Sorry" in her ear.

Even though I'm not. And that becomes even more obvious when I say, "But not too busy to celebrate their daughter's accomplishments."

"Of course not," her father jumps in, sending a hard look my way. "We didn't want to push ourselves on Blaire. She has her own way of doing things and we don't want to step on her toes."

Gran-Gran Calloway, who reminds me of a younger Betty White during the *Golden Girls* era and is clearly senile, jumps into the conversation to ask when Blaire's due. I decide I need a break from the crazy before I tell someone off on Blaire's behalf.

"Sweetheart, can you show me where the bathroom is?"

"I can show you!" Skylar's knife clatters on the counter and she grabs my free arm.

I don't even look in Skylar's direction when I respond. "Thanks, but Blaire can take care of me." Yes, I mean for it to sound 100 percent suggestive.

I stand up and extend my hand. Blaire has no choice but to take it, unless she wants to make more of a scene. She leads me out of the kitchen, down a hallway, passing three doors before she finally stops. I push it open and take the opportunity for what it is by pulling her inside and closing her in with me.

The light isn't on, though, so we're submerged in darkness.

"What're you doing?" Her voice is all pitchy.

"What are *you* doing?" I slap around on the wall, trying to find a switch.

Half a second later we're both blinded by light. "Showing you where the bathroom is." Her gaze bounces all over the room.

As does mine, but for very different reasons. "What the hell is going on in here?" Everything is gold. The wallpaper, the vanity, the sink, even the toilet. The floor, however, is black marble and reflective.

"My family is eclectic," she replies, not defensively, but matter-of-factly.

"Is this real gold? Actually, don't answer that, I don't want to know." I motion toward the door. "Why am I here?"

"Because I invited you, which in hindsight may not have been the best idea, at least not without some preparation. I'm used to my family, so I forget how crazy they really are." I've never seen Blaire quite so fidgety.

I give her a look that tells her I think that's utter bullshit.

She throws her hands in the air. "Okay, I didn't forget that they were crazy, but I felt bad that you didn't have plans for Thanksgiving and no one should be alone on the holidays, so it was kind of a kneejerk reaction to invite you along. It wasn't until we were on the way here that I really considered what it would be like for you, and me, frankly."

"Right, okay. So what's the deal with Skylar?"

"She's harmless."

"She's a sexual harassment lawsuit waiting to happen."

"She's actually a total professional at work. She just enjoys getting under my skin and putting on a show."

I point a finger at her. "Your job tonight is to keep her away from me."

"I can try, but she's persistent."

"And what the hell is with you letting your family treat you like garbage?"

"They don't treat me like garbage."

And there's the defensiveness I've been waiting for. "Your *little bakeshop*? When you get tired of the grueling hours you can work for the family? And they haven't even come out to see your place." I don't know why I'm so pissed off about this. Maybe because I know how hard she works? I'm always fighting to keep up. I'm lucky that college kids are willing to pay money for things like throwing axes.

"It's better they don't interfere. Otherwise I'll have to start serving hundred-dollar kobe beef cupcakes."

I make a face because that sounds disgusting. Although she did make a Guinness and bacon cupcake that nearly killed me, it was that good, and I really expected to hate it. "Since when do you let other people dictate your actions?"

"I don't; that's the point."

"But they should see how hard you work."

Blaire sighs. "Look, Ronan, your irritation on my behalf is endearing, but you don't know what you're saying. You've spent less than half an hour with them and we're already locked in a bathroom together and you have a million questions. Which I will answer. Later. On the drive home. But for now I need you to trust me when I say I do not want my family visiting B&B because it will inevitably mean they will try to take over. They are well-meaning but insane."

I stare at her for several long seconds, digesting, accepting. "You are spilling the beans on the drive home."

"There probably won't be much to spill by the time we leave, but sure." She shrugs and turns to open the door.

I stop her from leaving by pressing my palm against it. "Hold up."

She sighs and her shoulders curl forward. "Can't it wait?"

"What's the deal with Matthew?"

She doesn't turn around, but her head drops and she seems to deflate even further. "We used to date."

"Excuse me?"

"We dated. It didn't work out. He married my sister. Oh, and I think Skylar slept with him, too, before they started dating, but then she's done that a few times with various boyfriends, so sometimes it's hard to keep track."

"Wait. What? Skylar slept with your ex-boyfriend before your sister stole him from you?" I feel like my head is going to explode from this information.

"Yeah. Can I go now, please, before we get accused of grabbing a pre-dinner quickie in the bathroom?"

I lift my hand from the door, and she slips out without another word.

Blaire's offhand mention of a quickie is apparently an appealing idea to my man parts, so it takes me a minute to calm down before I'm able to relieve myself.

As I wait I decide two things: I'm not drinking any more alcohol tonight and I'm going to play up being Blaire's boyfriend for the rest of our time here. It's not like her family is going to see me again. I might as well leave them with one hell of a lasting impression.

@the_knightcap:

I prefer my KALE with a silent K.

chapter eleven

THIS ISN'T THE GAME
I WAS PLAYING

Blaire

Hindsight. It's a bitch. I should have warned Ronan about my family and how insane they are. But at the same time, he's been messing with me since day one, and a little payback never hurt anyone.

However, I'm not excited about the prospect of Skylar mauling Ronan all night, as she likes to do with other people's significant others. Between her and Maddy, I've lost at least four dateable prospects.

I realize it doesn't say much about the guys I went out with, but Skylar will fuck a long john if she's desperate enough. As for Maddy and Matthew, they belong together. They're both vain, shallow, and entirely too wrapped up in taking staged photos with celebrities and enjoying the perks of the family wealth.

Despite all this, my family generally has good intentions. It's just their execution is quite lacking. Also, the fact that my mother and her sister swapped husbands is just plain weird.

So, yeah. Thanksgiving dinner is turning out to be a bit of a clusterfuck. Dinner should be served shortly and we can leave right after dessert. I'm still standing in the hallway outside the bathroom. I don't know that Ronan and I should return to the kitchen together, but I'm not certain he'll be able to find his way back on his own. There's also a significant chance that Skylar will be hiding around the corner, ready to pounce on him, so I wait.

Thankfully, dinner is ready to be served when we return and there's too much commotion and passing of dishes for anyone to comment on our brief disappearance.

Ronan stays glued to my side, palm resting against the small of my back as we make our way to the dining room. Skylar has obviously been in here, tinkering with the seating arrangements because originally Ronan isn't even sitting next to me, but he switches the name cards around and pulls my chair out.

Maddy makes a joke about being careful, since we like to play musical chairs in this family. I want to sink into the floor and disappear. And they wonder why I never bring dates over to meet the family. Dinner is a decadent affair, as usual. It's family style instead of plated, but every dish looks like a work of art. The turkey is a deep-fried masterpiece.

My mother, aunt, cousin, and sister are all on some keto bullshit or other so they refuse all carbs or anything that might contain sugar but load up on fried brussels sprouts and whatever other keto-friendly stuff they've prepared.

There are even cauliflower "mashed potatoes" loaded with cream and butter and lord knows what else. Skylar goes on about how all she had today was her detox tea so she could enjoy her dinner.

My dad, however, samples everything, dissecting the delicacy of the flavors. And beside me, Ronan quietly groans his food lust. "This is unbelievable," he mumbles through a mouthful of turkey.

"Don't forget to save room for dessert." It's sort of tongue in cheek since half the people at the table balk at dessert. Or there will be some kind of carb- and flavor-free option that tastes like sadness and cardboard.

Every single member of my family has their phone beside their plate and keeps checking messages between bites. "The manager at the LA location of Decadence wants to meet about the New Year menu. Maddy and I are flying out in the morning to hit up the one in San Diego. Do you want me to stop there, too?" Matthew asks my dad.

"That would be great. If you have time, you might want to make the trip to Vegas while you're out that way. Nora and I are heading to New York, and Glinda and Lawrence, you're taking the Midwest locations, is that correct?"

"What about me?" Skylar asks.

"We need you here to keep an eye on things."

"Or I could go to Vegas with Matthew and Maddy. Why do they get to go to all the fun places and I have to hang out here?"

"We can discuss it after dinner, sweetheart," Lawrence says with a practiced smile.

My parents shift the discussion to which big stars are hiring them for catering over the holidays—it's always a particularly busy time for them—and it's like name-dropping central.

"You've met Daxton Hughes? That teen actor who became an entertainment lawyer?" Ronan dabs at his mouth before he continues. "My ex in high school used to be in love with him."

"I have a crush on him now," my mother replies with a grin.

"He hit on me," Skylar adds.

"No, honey, you hit on him. It was me he was hitting on." Gran-Gran Calloway winks in my direction.

The rest of dinner is spent listening to Gran-Gran tell stories about all the famous people she's met over her lifetime.

Buster brings in the cupcakes I made on a special platter, and of course my mom, aunt, cousin, and sister all have their special keto-friendly dessert brought out. It looks like some kind of chocolate thing served with three berries and a mint leaf, which are on the approved carb list, I guess.

"You're not going to have one of Blaire's cupcakes?" Ronan looks dumbfounded. I'd like to say it's an innocent question, but based on his expression and his tone, it's not.

I don't know why he's so annoyed on my behalf, but I can't say I don't appreciate it.

"Too many carbs and far too much sugar. Sugar is more addictive than cocaine, you know," Skylar says haughtily.

"You would know," I mutter.

"Well, at least I can't end up with a deviated septum or psychosis on account of my sugar consumption," Ronan replies and then asks Buster for one of each cupcake flavor.

Ronan proceeds to inhale all of them while making noises that sound a lot like the ones I'd hear were he naked and I was riding him. And now that image is in my head.

I start to wonder if maybe the ink on his arms spans his back, and possibly his chest as well. In my mind, I decorate the rest of his right arm in more, pretty flowers and the left side in an expansive landscape.

His exuberance seems to compel my mother to fold. She peels the wrapper off, wipes her hands on her napkin and daintily uses her fork to take the tiniest bite. Her eyes go wide, and she blinks several times. "Oh, this is heavenly. Lawrence, did you try this one? You really must."

My aunt also folds and offers to share a cupcake with my dad, who has polished off three already, based on the stack of discarded wrappers.

Skylar is watching Ronan devour cupcakes like it's porn. And honestly, so am I.

When he's finished the last cupcake, he sucks the icing off his fingers—loudly—and turns his gaze on me. His eyes are half-mast, making it look like he's recently had an orgasm. The effects of a sugar rush, the crash soon to follow.

His brows rise. "Everything okay?"

I can't even imagine what my expression must be. "Did you enjoy those?"

He grins. "Immensely. The only cupcake I enjoyed more was the one you made me eat in front of those women at the bachelorette party."

I can feel the heat rising in my cheeks and his grin widens. I will never forget how he looked biting into the vagina cake. Or the way the custard center dribbled down his chin. We're still staring at each other, possibly both lost in that memory.

The stare-off ends when my mother asks what kind of cupcakes they are, and of course she and my father decide to guess the ingredients, arguing about the merits of cooked versus uncooked buttercream.

While this takes place, Skylar keeps edging closer to Ronan, which means he keeps edging closer to me. At this point, his arm is draped over the back of my chair, and he's halfway into my lap. It's kind of funny and also highly distracting because every once in a while his fingers graze the back of my neck and I have to fight off a shiver.

I'm still nibbling my way through my own cupcake, savoring instead of devouring. Despite the fact that Maddy and Skylar refused to try one, there are none left. I'm pretty sure my dad ate half a dozen.

"If you don't hurry up and finish that, I'm stealing it," Ronan whispers, warm breath fanning across my cheek.

"Try it and I'll stab you with my fork." I slide another small bite between my lips and *mmm* my delight.

I can feel his eyes on me. He's so close, if I turn my head

there's a good chance we'll be brushing noses again. "You've got icing on your lip."

I lick them self-consciously and lean away so I can turn my head and make eye contact—the kind that should signal him to back off. "All gone?"

"Nope. Still there."

I raise my napkin with the intent of wiping my face, because there's nothing more embarrassing than having icing on my face, but he covers my hand with his. "I'll get it for you."

"Really, I can do it myself." Now I'm embarrassed because my entire family is watching and Ronan seems oblivious to all the attention. Or maybe this is on purpose.

"Really, I got it." He's right in my personal space, his grin full of villainous mirth. Which I finally understand when he licks the corner of my mouth.

A hot feeling shoots down my spine to settle between my legs. He freezes, his eyes wide, likely with the same shock I'm currently experiencing because *Ronan just licked my face.* I don't understand why he looks so horrified since he's the one who licked me and not the other way around.

"What the hell, Ronan?" I swat his chest and wipe his saliva from the corner of my mouth.

He recovers, expression returning to that same mirthful deviousness. "Hold on. I didn't get it all." He leans in again and I put my hands on his chest, trying to keep him at bay. I honestly have no idea what his plan is, or why he's being so damn flirty.

He backs off as quickly as he tried to attack me, his grin ridiculously wide as he pops what's left of my cupcake into his mouth.

"You jerk!"

"Oh my gosh, you two are so freaking cute. Aren't they the cutest?" Maddy claps excitedly, reminding me that we are not alone. In fact, my entire family is watching this display with rapt interest.

Except Skylar. Her arms are crossed over her chest and she's pouting. "You should probably get a room," she says.

"Maybe you two need another bathroom quickie." Maddy's smirking. Of course she was just waiting for the opportunity to draw attention to our disappearance right before dinner.

Skylar looks scandalized. "Ew! You did not."

Ronan wipes his mouth with his napkin and swallows the rest of my cupcake. "I prefer to take my time and savor the experience when it comes to anything that has to do with Blaire, apart from her cupcakes." He takes my hand in his.

I try to yank mine free, but he tightens his grip and brings it to his lips, biting my knuckle with another one of his mischievous grins.

"Well, I think it's great that these two lovebirds can't keep their hands or tongue to themselves, even at the dinner table. That's the kind of passion every couple should have." Gran-Gran slaps the table. "I need a glass of brandy. Let's retire to the sitting room."

I take the out while I can. "We should probably think about

heading home, actually." This time Ronan lets me yank my hand free from his grasp. I push my chair back, looking to put some space between us.

"You're not staying the night?" My father's disappointment is obvious.

"We both have to be up early for work tomorrow." It's not a lie. Also, the charade with Ronan has gone on long enough. I'm not sleeping in the same room as him to keep up false pretenses. Besides, I don't trust Skylar not to pick the lock and try to hump him in the middle of the night.

"That's too bad. Next time you'll have to plan to stay," my mom says.

I doubt I'll be able to do that anytime soon, but I don't bother to argue. We spend another ten minutes debating whether we really need to leave. Ronan yawns. I can't tell if it's real or forced, but I use it to our advantage.

"Looks like someone is crashing from all the buttercream."

The entire family walks Ronan and me to the door. Then it's a round of awkward hugs and lots of people whispering in my ear about how they hope I bring him back at Christmas. Ronan uses me as a shield to avoid a hug from Skylar. Quite literally. He moves to stand behind me, his forearm coming to rest against my collarbones, fingers curling around my shoulder. The entire front of his body is pressed up against the back of mine. I find myself sort of melting into him as Skylar does some kind of weird dance move like she's trying to find a way between us.

He rests his chin on my opposite shoulder and extends his hand. "It was a pleasure to meet you, Skylawn."

"Skylar." She gives it a dead-fish shake, pouting the entire time.

"Right, my bad." He brushes the shell of my ear with the tip of his nose. "Time to go home, *Care Blaire*. Dessert round two is calling my name."

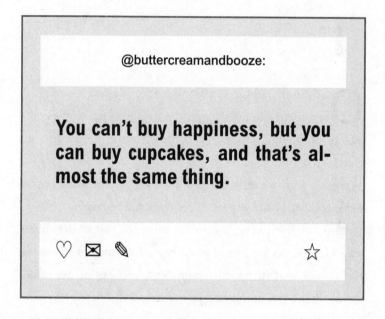

@buttercreamandbooze:

You can't buy happiness, but you can buy cupcakes, and that's almost the same thing.

chapter twelve

THE REVEALING RIDE HOME

Ronan

Okay, so the whole sexual innuendo, "dessert round two" comment was a little over the top, but I felt it was completely justified considering Blaire's cousin needs an ego check.

It isn't until we're in Blaire's SUV and we've made it past the gates that I finally speak. "That was interesting."

Blaire glances at me before she turns left out of the driveway. Her cheeks are tinged pink, likely from the embarrassing end to our visit in which I insinuated, in front of her entire family, that I was going to take her home and devour her like one of her cupcakes. "Sorry I didn't adequately prepare you for the experience."

"I don't think anything could have adequately prepared me for that."

"They're well-meaning but crazy." She tucks a few wayward strands of hair behind her ear.

"You can say that again. How the hell did your parents end up swapping partners?" I wonder how many people Blaire's had to explain this to and whether it ever gets easier.

Blaire blows out a breath. "Uh, I don't really know what precipitated it, but my whole family has always been really close, traveling together to get new restaurants up and running. Skylar, Maddy, and I were pretty much raised as sisters, and whoever wasn't on the road looked after us. The parental roles were basically interchangeable."

She grips the steering wheel tightly. "When I was a sophomore in high school, Mom, Dad, Aunt Nora, and Uncle Lawrence sat us kids down and explained that things were going to change." She shakes her head, maybe remembering how it all went down. "It was the weirdest conversation I've ever been involved in. At least until Maddy and Matthew told me they'd started dating."

The whole Maddy and Matthew situation is its own crazy nightmare, I'm sure. I'd have to come back to that, though. "You were in high school when it happened?"

She nods once. "Yup."

"That must've been rough."

"Uh, well, not much changed to be honest. I mean, there were obvious things, like my mom and dad stopped sleeping in the same bedroom, but the actual family dynamic stayed pretty much the same. Outside the house it was a whole different story, though."

"Can I ask how, or do you not want to talk about it?

Because honestly, I can totally understand if you don't want to, but I can't lie and tell you I'm not curious."

"It's like a bad daytime talk show episode."

I can't tell if she's embarrassed or what, so I give her an out. "We can change the subject."

"It's fine. It was a long time ago. I'm mostly over it. I'm pretty removed from the situation at this point. I love my family, but the whole situation is weird and kind of squicky, you know?" She grimaces. "Actually, you probably don't know, which is a really good thing. Anyway, my parents thought the best plan would be to have everyone move into the house together, less disruption for us kids, and my aunt and uncle were always over anyway. So they pooled their resources and built that tacky monstrosity and we all moved in there. My mom and my uncle took a wing, and my dad and my aunt took a wing, and us girls were just supposed to deal with it."

"Is that how it worked out?" Having two families mesh together like an incestuous Brady Bunch doesn't seem like something teenage girls would just be able to roll with.

She lifts a shoulder in what I assume is meant to be a careless shrug. "Yes and no. Was it awkward? Definitely. We went to this really exclusive, expensive private school where everyone was super gossipy, and my parents own some insanely successful restaurants all over the world, so..."

"It did not go unnoticed." I can't even imagine how awful it would be to have your family's messed-up drama become public knowledge.

"Nope. Teens aren't very forgiving when your parents and your aunt and uncle switch partners. I think their lack of convention made me crave normalcy. I became obsessed with family shows, especially *Leave It to Beaver*. I loved everything about shows with stereotypical family units who were solidly average."

"I can see how that would be appealing." I take in her appearance, from the perfectly styled hair and makeup to the full-skirted dress and cute heels. "I'm assuming it also inspired your fashion sense."

"Kind of, yeah. The whole thing sort of came out around Halloween and I was already in my *Leave It to Beaver* phase, and I was in the play *Grease*, so I started wearing the dresses and never really stopped. It was easier to have people whispering about my weird fashion choices than it was to have them talk about how my parents were probably swingers."

"People said that to you?"

"There was speculation, and honestly, I wouldn't be surprised to learn that it was true, however I'm happy to be blissfully ignorant on that front for the rest of my damn life."

Everything I've learned about Blaire tonight shifts my perception of her. She's even stronger than I realized, not taking the easy road where everything could've been handed to her on a silver platter.

She sighs. "Anyway, I love them, really I do, but there's just too much crazy. I know my dad would've tried to find a way to let me pursue my passion for baking if I'd really pushed for it, but I needed the separation and I didn't want to have to compromise. Besides, Maddy and Matthew are up to their elbows in the family biz, and I would really like to steer clear of that whole situation. Not to mention the Skylar situation."

She's opened the door to the topic, so I'm happy to walk right through it. Also, she's right: This is totally like a horrible Jerry Springer episode. "You mentioned you and Matthew dated before?"

Blaire grips the steering wheel tightly and nods once. "He was sort of a rebound. I knew he wasn't the right one, but he seemed like a decent in-between. I guess that sounds bad. I'd gotten out of a particularly toxic relationship and Matthew came along. He was safe and... very even."

"Sounds boring."

She laughs, which is good because this conversation has been a whole lot of heavy. "He was *painfully* boring. *Is*, not past tense. I've never met a more monochromatic human being in my life, apart from Maddy anyway. They are perfect for each other. All they want to do is work for the family because of all the perks and their ability to take selfies with famous people and travel all over America, while depriving themselves of carbs so they can be Insta-pretty."

"Doesn't sound like your type at all." I don't know what her type is, but boring and vapid sounds like the opposite of what she'd go for.

"He wasn't. Like I said, he was a rebound. He was uncomplicated and he seemed to like me. I went out of town for a convention and by the time I came back, well, he and Maddy had hit it off."

"How freaking long was the convention?"

She gives me a sidelong glance. "Five days."

"She stole your boyfriend in five days?" Her family really is a bunch of jerks.

"*Stole* sounds harsh. Matthew and I were not destined for white picket fences, two-point-two children, and a purebred poodle. Besides, we'd only been seeing each other for a couple of months."

"That's still shitty."

"What was shitty was when they ambushed me the second I got home and sat me down together to ask for my blessing to date."

"And you obviously gave it." I want to be angry that she folded, but clearly Matthew is a douche and so is Maddy, so it's better they ended up together. Or at least that's my assumption.

"Seemed pointless not to when it was obvious they planned to date regardless. I also got to be a bridesmaid at their wedding. On the upside, I'm well aware that Matthew is painfully average in every way." She motions toward her crotch, as if it needed further explanation.

I don't want to think about Blaire with that asshole. I don't want to think about Blaire with anyone, which I realize should raise some serious red flags. However, I'm inclined to ignore those at the moment.

I decide to leave that information alone. For now it's enough to know he's barely adequate and vapid. "And what's the deal with Skylar?"

"She's always been a hot mess. She was young when the swap happened, so I honestly think it messed her up more than the rest of us. She doesn't have any kind of moral compass at all, or direction, or independent thoughts. I actually sometimes wonder if she's my half sister and not just my cousin."

"That's a mind fuck, right there."

"My whole family is a mind fuck. And like I said, I love them and I know they love me even if they suck at showing it. I just want a normal life where I can do what I love without my family trying to railroad me and make all the decisions for me."

"You're incredible. You know that, right?"

"My family doesn't think so."

"No offense, but your family is fucked."

She laughs. "This is very true. I knew I would fall short if I tried to work with them."

"Fall short how? You're amazingly talented."

She chews her bottom lip for a moment. "I don't share the same values as they do. They're all about appearances and who they know, and that's never really mattered to me. Our goals just don't align. I want to do what I love, not necessarily what's going to make me the most money. And maybe that's naïve, or shortsighted or whatever, but it's how I feel. So I avoided the potential disappointment by going in a completely different direction and now here I am, eking out a living, but doing it on my own."

"They won't help you?"

"My dad has tried to loan me money half a dozen times. He's constantly offering to transfer funds into my account, but if I take their money, I also have to take their advice, and that is not something I want. Like when I wanted to buy the cupcake truck, my dad was there with a big old check, but it came with all kinds of stipulations, so I thanked him and told him I wanted to do it on my own and that's what I did—well, with Paul's help, anyway."

This explains why Blaire is all about doing things her own way. "Do they get how hard you're working?"

She shrugs. "Maybe? I'm not looking for their approval, or a pat on the back, though. I stopped doing that a long time ago when I realized their view of success and mine were so different."

"My brothers are a lot like that. It's always been about how much money they can make and how fast they can make it. For a while I was the same way, but it was making me miserable. No matter how hard I worked, my heart wasn't really in it, so when they wanted to go out on their own, I had to reevaluate my own goals."

"That makes sense." She smiles and glances at me before focusing on the road again. "It seems like you really love the bar."

"I do. It's not going to make me rich, but it makes me a

hell of a lot happier than working in finance ever did. And eventually I want to open a small brewery, so this is a great stepping stone." It's definitely something we have in common, loving what we do.

"A brewery? Really?"

"Yeah. It's a passion project, but it'll take time to make it happen."

"Hmm, what about your brothers? Do they love what they do or do they love the money?"

"Both, I think, and they're good at it. Finance is a natural fit for them, but it really never was for me."

"So are you kind of a black sheep like me?"

"You're not a black sheep. You're an outlier, Blaire. My parents were always about doing what made us happy, as long as it wasn't rotting our brains with garbage TV and hours of video gaming. But I guess in some ways I'm the black sheep. Both of my brothers have significant others and lucrative careers. They kind of fit the conventional stereotype of success: big house, nice cars, gorgeous wife or girlfriend—and my oldest brother, Daniel, is going to be a dad this year, so they're on their way to the two kids and a dog scenario."

"So you're going to be an uncle. That's exciting! I'm not sure if Maddy and Matthew will have kids or not, since Maddy is terrified of stretch marks."

I laugh, but realize she's serious. "That's kind of . . ."

"Sad and self-centered?" Blaire supplies. "Honestly, I don't think Maddy would be all that involved in raising her kids.

She's more the kind of person who would Insta-pose them and make it look like her family is picture perfect and then hand them over to the nanny to deal with the feedings and dirty diapers while she gets a facial." She grimaces. "God, I'm making her sound horrible. She's really not. We just had an atypical upbringing, and our parents made some less than perfect choices when it came to smoothing over the fallout of the partner swap, like overindulging us."

"You're not overindulged."

"I'm a different person than she is, though."

I have to agree with that.

She waves a hand around in the air. "Anyway, enough about that. Tell me more about you and your grandpa. You seem like you're really close."

"Mmm, yeah, we always have been, even before my parents passed. My first job was bussing tables at The Knight Cap as a teenager, and then later I became a bartender there. Plus, I ended up living with him and Grams during my last two years of college after my parents passed, and that brought us closer. We're a lot alike. Same core values, same work ethic."

"He sounds like a good guy." Her voice has that soft edge, somewhere between empathy and envy.

"He is. Thinks you're quite the looker." I cringe, wishing I'd kept that detail to myself.

But it gets another chuckle out of her, which I like. We talk about our childhoods, all our time spent in family restaurants—it sounds like her experiences were a lot different than mine and I love the way her face lights up and her eyes go all dreamy when she talks about the patisseries in France and how they solidified her love of all things sweet.

The rest of the drive passes quickly, and soon she's stopping in front of my building. I consider inviting her up for a drink. It sends a message I'm not entirely opposed to, but it could add a layer of complication. Especially since we work side by side and today is the first time we've spent more than five minutes in each other's presence without arguing. So I decide against it and just go with: "Thanks for the entertaining evening. I had fun."

She graces me with one of her gorgeous smiles. "Me, too. Thanks for coming along, and for not being all weird about my crazy family."

"They made this the most exciting Thanksgiving ever. Nothing will top it."

She widens her eyes and whispers. "You should see what Christmas is like with them." Her gaze darts to my mouth, but she looks away just as quickly. "Anyway, see you tomorrow."

"See you tomorrow." I get out of the car. "Drive safe, Blaire."

"I will." She waits for me to let myself into my building before she pulls away, her SUV clunking down the street.

Under those layers of pretty fabric, full skirts, and perfectly coiffed hair is one hell of a dynamic woman. Yeah, it was probably a good idea *not* to invite her up. Otherwise I might have wanted to make good on that comment I made about a second helping of dessert in the form of a Blaire cupcake.

@the_knightcap:

Alcohol: Because no great story ever started with a salad.

chapter thirteen

DICK AND BOBBY INVASION

Blaire

Despite my rather short sleep, I'm in a surprisingly good mood this morning. Maybe because I had fun at a family event for once in my life, and even though Skylar was her flirty, obvious self, Ronan didn't so much as give her a second glance. It was a refreshing change from past events when I brought a date and Skylar basically tried to hump him in front of me. Despite the boyfriend thieving and how inappropriate she is, I do love her. We went through a lot together as teens, so as much as I can't stand the crap she pulls, I'm aware that she's more messed up than the rest of us.

I would be lying if I said I didn't like all the attention he threw my way, either. I'm sure he did it to play up the whole fake-date situation, but still. He's a good-looking guy who smells nice. Who wouldn't want a hot man to lick icing off their mouth in front of their boyfriend-stealing sister and cousin?

I check my reflection in the rearview mirror before I get out of my SUV and cross the parking lot. The Knight Cap is still locked up, but it's barely after eight in the morning, and usually no one is there before nine thirty. Although with Ronan needing to deal with the frozen bird situation, I'm sure he'll be in early.

Daphne is visiting her parents, and Paul is with his family and after next week I'm on my own with the cupcakes. Callie offered to come in later, so it's just me this morning.

I pare down the menu to specials in celebration of the holiday. My diehards who have to work like me pop in for coffees, scones, the festive turkey, brie, and cranberry wraps I ordered in, and cupcakes. Most of the cupcake orders have already gone out for the weekend, apart from a few stragglers, so it's a quiet day.

Ronan pops his head in to say hello just before eleven, but I'm with a customer, so he doesn't stick around. By six it's a ghost town, which is to be expected, and I close early.

I pack the daily leftovers and make up a box of cupcakes for Ronan. My stomach does a twist and leap as I check my reflection in the mirror. I look tired, but otherwise I'm presentable, so I head over to The Knight Cap to deliver the cupcakes. Maybe I'll stay for a drink tonight.

I glance at the building across the street, the one that's been empty since we both opened shop. Brown paper still covers the windows, but there's a new sign plastered across the front that wasn't there yesterday. In huge gaudy red letters is the very familiar logo for Dick and Bobby's, a chain of restaurants that boasts massive TVs and broadcasts every major sporting event in existence, even that not-real sport where people ride those hobby-horse things. Plus they televise all the MMA fights. And they have pool tables and all sorts of games. It's the grown-up version of Chuck E. Cheese with booze, horrible greasy food, and sports. I'd like to believe it's not going to be an issue since B&B caters to a slightly more sophisticated crowd, but we really don't need new competition around here.

I open the door to The Knight Cap. It's pretty quiet, only a handful of tables occupied. There are a few older men sitting at the bar, nursing pints and watching the football game.

Ronan glances at the door when it chimes, signaling my arrival. A fluttery feeling in my stomach makes me pause as images and sensations from last night flash through my head: the way he pulled me into his side, how I seemed to fit quite nicely under his arm, how it felt to have his fingers brushing along the back of my neck when we were seated at the dinner table. A warm shiver runs down my spine as I remember the shock of him licking me close to the corner of my mouth.

It's so silly. He was just playing the part of my date, mostly because he couldn't believe that my cousin was actually hitting on him in front of the entire family. Still, he's smiling, and that's a whole lot different from his usual "oh, you again" scowl.

He wipes his hands on a bar towel. "Hey, Alice, how's Wonderland?" He winks, though, so I know he's playing around.

"Wonderland was empty and I was bored, so I thought I'd stop by." I set the box on the bar top. "Have you seen what's going on across the street?"

He wipes down a pint glass before he shelves it, tattooed forearms flexing enticingly. I drag my eyes up to his face, which is also nice to look at. He's wearing his glasses today, and I've decided they're sexy. He looks like an intellectual lumberjack. A badass one. The plaid is definitely growing on me and so is the man wearing the plaid.

"Earth to Blaire? You sure you're not still in Wonderland?"

"Huh?"

"You said something was going on across the street." He arches a brow. "Have you been sampling the martinis this afternoon?"

"Oh! Right! No. I haven't." I crook a finger at him. "Come with me, I want to show you something."

He looks pointedly at his customers and I roll my eyes.

"It'll only take a minute and it's better if I show you, rather than tell. Besides, Lars can watch the bar, can't you?"

Lars winks at me. "Anything for you."

"Thank you." I wink back and give Ronan my attention again. "Why can't you be so accommodating?"

"I can be accommodating. When the situation warrants it, and don't encourage this one. His ego is already big enough. He doesn't need you flirting with him to inflate it even more."

Ronan whips him on the back of the arm with the towel

as he rounds the bar and saunters toward me, apparently in no hurry.

As soon as he's close enough I slip my arm through his, noting how nice and firm his bicep is. I have the urge to trace the outline of the delicate, colorful blooms decorating his forearm. I notice, for the first time, that there's a woman's face set in the middle of them. I realize it's the same woman in the picture on Ronan's living room wall: his mother. And now I understand what he meant about wanting to see his memories and remember.

I pull him toward the door, yank it open and step out onto the sidewalk. It's cold and dreary, so I press myself closer, using him as a barrier against the wind and rain. "Look." I point across the street at the ugly sign.

"Oh shit," he mutters and looks down at me, eyes wide. "Is this a joke? This has to be a joke. That place was a damn law office three months ago." I still have my arm threaded through his, so when he moves toward the edge of the sidewalk he takes me with him.

He checks for traffic before he drags me across the street. To be fair, I could let go of his arm, but I don't really want to. He smells good—like beer, cologne, and laundry detergent. It's a nice combination.

I snuggle in closer, trying to claim some of his body heat as I read the notice taped to the inside of the window beside the Dick and Bobby's sign.

"Damn it, they're supposed to open in a month. How is that even possible? They have to gut this entire place."

"It's a chain, though, right? They have loads of money. It wouldn't take much for them to be able to afford to renovate."

"Why aren't you upset about this?" Ronan snaps.

I shrug, trying to understand why he's so panicked. "It's a huge, impersonal big box place. Loud, awful, and the food is terrible."

"Newsflash, Blaire, college kids don't have discerning palates. This is like an indoor play place for grown-ups, with food and beer and gross coolers that only college students can stomach."

"And I should be upset that they're going to serve disgusting coolers, gross beer, and bad food?" My teeth start to chatter because it's cold and even though I'm wearing my jacket, my legs are bare and there's a breeze up my skirt.

"It's all cheap. Cheap and shitty, but still cheap and do you know what college kids love?" He doesn't give me a chance to answer. "Cheap shit, Blaire. They love cheap shit. When are we busiest? When we have some kind of event and a promotion. Five-dollar pints draw college kids, three-dollar garbage draft is going to kill my business."

"I think you're getting your knickers in a knot over nothing, but I'm willing to listen as long as we can talk about how their awful beer is going to ruin your business *inside* your place of business before my legs turn into popsicles."

His gaze moves over my bare legs, all the way back up to my face and more specifically my mouth. My teeth bang against each other, which explains why that's where his focus is. "Yeah. Of course. You must be freezing."

I hold my fingers apart a fraction of an inch. "Just a bit."

We rush back across the street. "Take a seat and I'll get you something to warm you up."

"Sure. Okay." I climb up on one of the barstools close to the draft taps. I rub my arms and blow warm air into my clasped hands. It's really starting to feel like winter is on its way now. I should've put on tights today, but I was in a rush having slept in later than usual this morning.

Ronan brings me a steaming mug with THE KNIGHT CAP logo on it. It's topped with whipped cream and chocolate drizzle. I grin and flip up the lid on the box of treats I brought over. The cupcakes are still Thanksgiving themed, but these I made special. They're turkey butts that read EAT ME!

He smirks and plucks one from the box. "These don't have some kind of chocolate filling in them, do they?"

"I guess you'll have to eat it to find out."

He shrugs and peels off the wrapper, taking a big bite. "So fucking delicious," he groans. Once he's polished off a cupcake he leans on the bar. "So D&B are going to be a problem for both of us."

I sip my spiked hot chocolate. "Explain why you think that. Buttercream and Booze has a fun vibe, we serve specialty drinks, gourmet cupcakes. You serve local craft beers and great pub fare. Sure, you have the staples, like fries and wings, but you also have a great variety of other options to appeal to a more upscale customer. We also both have cool entertainment, which the people around here love."

"I agree with all of those things, but do you know what D&B has that we don't?"

"Bad ambiance and a tacky name?"

"Yes and yes, but also money for marketing. Lots of it."

He waits for that to sink in. It doesn't take long. I pull my phone out of my purse and bring up their social media. They have a massive following and they've just announced their new location coming soon on its own social media profile. I click on it and of course they already have double the followers I do. Neither of us has the kind of money they do to throw at TV and billboard ads. "And no matter how crappy a bar they are, that money equals visibility we don't have, plus a recognizable name."

"Exactly." Ronan raps on the bar with his knuckles.

"You really think they're going to be a threat?" For the first time since I saw that horrible sign, I'm struck with a niggle of worry.

"I honestly don't see how they can't be. Chain restaurants are notorious for killing off small businesses. They're huge competition. I don't know about you, but I have reno costs I still need to recoup and losing business to that nightmare is going to make it that much more of a struggle."

I chew on my bottom lip. "I'm barely scraping by," I admit.

He seems surprised by that revelation. "It's that bad? Your place is always hopping."

"I got a really good deal on rent, which is basically the only reason I can afford the storefront, and Paul paid off the cupcake truck in actual cupcakes. At the end of next week I'm going to be on my own with cupcake production. Honestly, any loss of business is going to be bad for my bottom line." And my bank account.

Ronan taps his bottom lip with his index finger. "You know what we need to do?"

"Find a new storefront that isn't across the street from Dick and Bobby's?" Not that I could even hope to afford it. Also, this location is prime, which is obviously what the owners of D&B realized.

"It really is an awful name for a restaurant." He gives his head a shake. "Anyway, we need to get as many loyal customers as we can before that place opens."

"Agreed."

"We should host combined events to get even more people to come out. Have big simultaneous promotions."

I stare at him from over the rim of my delicious alcohol-laced coffee.

"You have to admit it's a good idea." He plucks another cupcake from the box.

"What about the Best Bar competition?"

"We can still compete against each other for best bar thing, but this is a way bigger threat, and more important because it has the potential to flush both of our businesses down the toilet." He bites into the chocolate cupcake.

"So you want us to work together?"

He nods. "Yeah, what do you say?"

"Okay. We can do it, but it's an even split on events and promotions. And we have to promote each other equally on our social media."

"That's a good idea." He wipes his hand on his pants and holds it out. "Deal?"

I slip mine into his. "Deal."

There are far worse people I could get into bed with—proverbially speaking, of course.

@buttercreamandbooze:

Making the world a better place, one cupcake at a time.

chapter fourteen

COORDINATION NATION

Blaire

O ver the next few days, Ronan and I work out a calendar of events leading up to the Christmas holidays. I'm a visual person so I color coordinate everything, and send it to him via email, but I also print a copy and have it blown up in color so we can post it in our respective shops. On top of that, I have daily social media posts prepared.

It's Thursday and tonight I have trivia night followed by Ronan's karaoke. The timing is great, since the quarterfinals for Best Bar are going to be announced next week, narrowing it down to the top twenty-five bars. I'm pretty excited about it, because now that we're working together, I don't have to worry about him starting early and stealing my business, although he stopped doing that a while ago. Plus we both have specials, and if they move from one bar to the other they get an additional coupon to use for a future event, which means more incentive to keep coming back.

I have a plan, but to orchestrate it I need to acquire some pertinent information about Ronan and free up a couple of hours this afternoon. I could get the information by asking him, but I kind of want it to be a fun surprise. It's nine in the morning, and Ronan usually isn't in until closer to ten, so I step out into the back alley. As I expected, the back door of The Knight Cap is propped open with a wedge.

I peek inside but don't make my presence known. Instead I sneak down the hall. It's a bit of a feat, considering I'm wearing heels and have to go extra-high on my tippy toes so they don't click on the floor.

I pass the bar to get to Ronan's office. I scan the area, spotting Lars and one of the female servers close talking. They're too wrapped up in each other to notice me, so I make it past them undetected and slip into Ronan's office. It still hasn't been updated like the rest of the place, but it smells like his cologne. The same old dilapidated chair with a full-blown butt groove and picked-apart armrests sits in front of the ancient, pitted desk.

Originally, I found this office rather disgusting, but now, knowing what I do about this place it's sweet that Ronan hasn't changed a thing about it.

In the corner is a coat rack. I smile when I spot what I'm looking for—two plaid shirts hanging from the hooks. I nab one and check the size. It's an extra large, as I suspected, considering his broad shoulders, not to mention how thick his biceps are. I bring the shirt to my nose and inhale. It holds the faint scent of laundry detergent, his cologne, and the pervasive odor of fried food that comes from working in a bar. I always smell like vanilla, butter, icing sugar, and sometimes coffee. I decide it's a good idea to take the shirt with me, because sizing can vary depending on the store, so it will be good to bring it along for comparison's sake.

I turn around, still holding the shirt up to my nose, humming contentedly. And slam right into a chest, which happens to be wrapped in exactly the same plaid shirt I'm huffing.

"Oh!" My gasp is muffled by the fabric.

I tip my head up and meet Ronan's inquisitive, amused gaze. "Are you sniffing my shirt?"

"I was checking to see if it was clean." It's only sort of a lie. Okay, it's a complete lie and I can feel my face turning red.

"Right. Okay." He nods once, eyes narrowed. "And where exactly are you going with my shirt?"

"I uh, I need to borrow it."

He crosses his arms over his chest. "For what?"

"It's supposed to be for a surprise, which you're currently ruining." And now I'm snappy to go along with my embarrassment.

He smiles, eyes moving over my face slowly, lingering on my lip, which I'm currently biting. "Am I going to get my shirt back?"

"Yes."

"In one piece?"

"Of course."

"Okay." He steps aside. "You can borrow it, then."

I smile brightly, trying to mask my mortification as I brush past him. "Great."

"Blaire."

"Hmm?" I pause and glance over my shoulder. He's right behind me.

He dips down, nose brushing the shell of my ear. He makes a low sound in the back of his throat, a purr, and murmurs, "I like the way you smell, too."

"Good to know." I leave feeling slightly less embarrassed and a whole lot turned on.

Two hours later I return from my shopping trip. I've been getting my dresses from the same store for years. I always hit their sample and sale rack—even before I had to scrimp and save every penny—so I get my dresses for around forty dollars each, often 25 percent of the full price. It means I have a closet full of dresses that I've amassed over the past decade and a half, and because they're very much fashioned after the fifties, they never really go out of style.

The lunch rush is in full swing, so I leave my purchases in my office and dive back into work. It isn't until after two that we finally have a lull in the constant stream of customers. Not that I'm going to complain.

I pop back over to The Knight Cap to somewhat reluctantly

return Ronan's borrowed shirt. I resist the urge to get in a couple more sniffs because I'll be able to sniff the real thing shortly.

I find Ronan sitting in the last seat at the end of the bar with his laptop propped open, reviewing spreadsheets. Like my place, his is quieter this time of day—between lunch and dinner. Several tables are occupied with groups of college students studying over afternoon pints and local business people grabbing a bite while they work.

"Hey! Do you have a minute?" I have to fight with my body not to get all bouncy because I'm excited.

Ronan glances up from the laptop, a wry grin pulling up the corner of his mouth. "Sure. What's up?"

"Can we go to your office? I have something to show you." I'm holding a huge bag behind my back, most of which is hidden by my skirt.

"Why can't you show me here?" He tries to peek around me, where my hands are clasped behind my back.

"No peeking!" I shrug, trying to remain nonchalant. "And because I don't want anyone else to see yet."

He closes his laptop, tucks it under his arm and slides off the stool. He motions toward the hall leading to his office. "Ladies first."

I practically bounce down the hall, giddy with excitement. I hang his shirt on the rack, set the bag on his executive chair and spin to face him. He's standing in the doorway, leaning against the jamb, arms crossed over his chest, expression halfway between curious and amused.

I pull him inside and close the door, trapping us together in the small, crowded room that smells like him, paper, and more faintly of food.

I pull the garment bag out of the shopping bag and lay it over the back of the chair. "So I had this idea." I turn away from him, unzip the garment bag and pull out the dress I picked out for tonight's event.

"And you need my opinion on a dress?" He seems confused.

I give him a look. "No, silly. I don't need your opinion. Although you're welcome to give it if you'd like." I pull out the plaid shirt that matches the color scheme of the dress— blue with yellow neon accents, also on sale—spin around to face him and hold them both up. "Ta-da!"

Ronan's eyes shift back and forth between the shirt—in his size—and the dress. "I don't get it."

I roll my eyes. "You're such a dude. Look at the colors."

"What about them?"

"They match."

He blinks.

Obviously he requires more of an explanation aside from the visual, which I thought made it pretty clear. "It's for when we do combined events, so we match." I motion between us.

"So we match?" he repeats.

I expected him to be more excited about this, which is maybe naïve of me. He's a guy who lives in jeans and the same kind of plaid shirt every day of the week. It's possible it's his forever uniform and he even wears it when he's at home. Or sweats, which I've only ever seen him in a couple of times. I lose a little of my zeal at his lack of reaction. "Or maybe not. Are the colors too much? It was just a thought. I can return the shirts."

"You got me more than one?" He moves into my personal space and peeks inside the garment bag. It's stuffed pretty full with my dresses and the shirts I'm now probably going to have to return.

"It's not a big deal. I thought it might be fun, but it's okay if that's not something you're interested in. I should've talked to you about it first." I try to brush his hand aside so I can tuck the shirt and dress back in the bag. I'm so embarrassed right now, and deflated to be quite honest.

He covers my hand with his. "I think it's a great idea, Blaire."

"You're just saying that," I mutter.

"No, I'm not. I honestly think it's a good idea. An amazing one. I just didn't get it at first, but it totally makes sense for us to match when we're doing these shared events and it was really thoughtful of you to go out and get all this stuff as a surprise."

"You're sure you think it's a good idea?" I can't tell if he's just trying to save my bruised ego or what.

"I swear, I think it's fantastic." He gives me the Boy Scout salute. "It sure isn't anything I would've thought of."

"Really?"

"Really." He nods.

"Great!" I beam up at him and get lost in his smile. Our eyes lock and hold for several long seconds, warmth blossoming in my stomach and radiating through my limbs. I give my head a shake. "Let me show you the rest of them, and you can try them on and make sure they fit properly. I used the shirt I borrowed to cross reference the size because sometimes they don't all fit the same. There's this great store a few blocks away and they have a crazy selection of plaid shirts. I stumbled across it online and thought it would work out really well." I'm excited-rambling now, but with Ronan on board I can see in my mind exactly how well this will work, and Daphne is going to love it. "If you're game for it we can take some fun pictures to post on social media being all matchy-matchy. I think it'll look great and really help unify the collaborated event."

"I like the sound of all of this."

"Really?"

"Yeah. I think it's super smart."

"Can I ask you something?"

"Sure." Ronan starts unbuttoning his shirt.

"Why do you always wear plaid?"

"The same reason you always wear dresses, I guess."

"You're obsessed with *Leave It to Beaver*–style shows?"

He laughs, but his expression sobers quickly and he focuses on the task of flicking open buttons. "After my parents passed, I had to go through the house and clean it out. My dad had all of these plaid shirts. It was his thing, I guess. I couldn't really conceive of getting rid of them, so I started wearing them and never really stopped."

"So it became your thing, too." Another way to stay connected to a person he loved and lost.

"Exactly." He gives me a wry smile as he shrugs out of his button-down. He's wearing a white undershirt beneath his usual red and black plaid. The fabric is thin and stretched tight, conforming to the contours and planes of muscle. "It wasn't long after that I started on the body art."

I allow my gaze to soak in the designs decorating his exposed arms. Based on the slightly sheer quality of the shirt, I discover that Ronan's artwork extends to his chest. Muted colors seep through and I wonder if I'll ever have the chance to see all of it. "How many tattoos do you have?" I finally manage to drag my eyes back up to his face—it's not a hardship.

"Quite a few."

Maybe how many is the wrong question. "Are they just from the waist up?"

A slight grin appears. "Most of them, yeah."

He reaches around me and grabs the first shirt with the navy and neon yellow plaid print and shrugs into it. It fits perfectly.

"I can throw that one in the wash right now so it's ready for the event tonight."

"You don't need to do that. I can wear it as is."

"I don't mind, and it'll feel nicer if it's been washed and not so stiff. I'll add which shirt to wear and when on the calendar to make it easy for you."

"I don't want to put that all on you. We could do it together."

"Sure. Okay. We can check out calendars later and figure out what works best?"

"That'd be great."

"Hey, Ronan, a couple of the girls need you to sign off so they can cash out." Lars peeks his head in the office. "Oh, hey, Blaire, I didn't realize you were here." He gives me a once-over. "You look pretty, but then you always do."

"Save the flirting for someone you actually have a chance with, Lars," Ronan says tonelessly.

I chuckle. "I should go. I'll see you both later tonight."

"Looking forward to it, Blaire," Lars calls after me as I walk down the hall toward the back exit carrying the garment bag of dresses and shirts.

I wave at them both over my shoulder and head back to B&B in a buoyant mood.

My matchy-matchy plan turns out to be a great one. We look adorable in our coordinated outfits, and they make for fantastic social media posts. The first few collaborative events go over really well. Both of our businesses see an increase in revenue, and the more we work together the busier we get. Meanwhile, we're holding our own in the Best Bar competition, although Ronan's a few spots above me.

We each end up having to hire another bartender so we can keep up with the new demands on our promotional nights. As the holidays approach, I suggest that we collaborate on a New Year's event and Ronan agrees.

It's much more involved and means planning sessions take place outside of business hours, not in our respective bars where interruptions abound. Which is how I end up at Ronan's apartment on a Sunday night after hours. Well, my hours, not his. He left work early so I wouldn't end up completely bleary-eyed in the morning.

"Do you mind if I change real quick so I don't smell like stale beer and wing sauce?" Ronan asks once we're in his apartment.

"Not at all."

"Great. Just make yourself comfortable. I'll be back in a minute." He motions to the living room with the oversized dark leather furniture. The whole place is rustic with warm tones, like an open-concept cottage transplanted into an apartment building in the city. The floors are dark, rough-hewn hardwood and although I'm wearing tights, I shiver as the cold hits the soles of my feet and travels up my spine.

I cross over to the pictures hung on the walls, taking them in with new eyes now that I know more about the history of the bar and Ronan's relationship with his grandfather. It makes me sad that he lost his parents at such a young age.

As whacked out as my family may be, I'm lucky to have them. They love me in their own weird way. There are a few more photos of an older Ronan with his grandfather and grandmother. I don't know if it's just me, but his smile doesn't seem quite as bright. Maybe they were taken not long after he lost his parents.

Ronan returns a minute later wearing a pair of loose jogging pants and a T-shirt. He's changed from contacts to glasses. His hair is less than perfect, as if he rushed to change. The shirt pulls tight across his chest and hugs his biceps. I can't complain about the view.

He holds up a pair of wool socks—the kind with a cream and red band at the top. "The floors are kind of cold in here. I thought you might want these."

He meets me halfway across the living room to pass them over. Without my heels on he's quite a bit taller than me, so I have to tip my head back to look up at him. "Thanks, my feet are perpetually cold. I'm pretty much in slippers between October and April."

"Or heels." He inclines his head toward the kitchen. "Come have a seat and I'll make us a drink before we get down to business."

I hoist myself up on a stool and pull on the warm wool socks. They're so big they almost reach my knees. Ronan roots around in the fridge and returns with four bottles, which he lines up in front of me. "Do you like craft beer?"

"Depends on the beer, but I'm always game to try something new." I pick up the one closest to me and read the handwritten label. "Rhubarb ale?"

"I have a few new flavors I've been trying out and I need a guinea pig. I can pour us each a flight and you can sample a few?"

"Sounds good. Can I help with anything?"

"Nope. I've got it covered."

While Ronan pours us beers, I take the opportunity to inspect his body art more closely. From my vantage point, I have a great view of the woman's portrait surrounded by blooming roses. I reach out and trace the contour of her face.

Ronan's in the middle of pouring a beer, and I startle him with the unexpected contact, so some of it sloshes onto the counter.

"Oh! Sorry. That's my fault; let me clean that up." I hop off the stool and grab the closest rag.

"That's okay, I got it." His fingers wrap around my wrist and that warm, buttery feeling coasts through my veins. I'm sure my face is red. You'd think with the amount of time we spend together that I'd have gotten over my fascination with his art and the way his touch seems to affect me, but if anything it's gotten worse, not better. Or maybe more intense is a more accurate way to explain it? I don't know, but I'm definitely attracted to him.

Acting on that would not be a good idea. Too complicated. What if he's bad in bed and we still have to cohost all of these events? Or worse, what if he thinks I'm bad in bed? And why am I suddenly thinking about sleeping with him just because he's making innocuous physical contact?

"Blaire, I got it. No big deal," he repeats, and I realize I've been staring at his hand wrapped around my wrist, lost in my own head. I hope it wasn't for long.

"Really, I startled you. I can clean it up."

"Blaire." This time his tone makes me look up.

"Just let me help," I press.

"You're not holding a dishrag." He's sort of smirking, but his cheeks are pink.

"What?" I glance back down to the cloth in my hand.

"Just give it to me, please." He tries to pry it from my fingers, but his sudden desperation to take it away makes me want to hold on tighter.

"Just let go," I tell him.

"No. *You* let go."

Are we really having a kindergarten-style fight over this? He spins me around so my back is against his chest and bars his free arm around me, but I'm wiggly and for once it's him who seems to be embarrassed. And suddenly I realize why.

Instead of a dishcloth, I'm holding a pair of boxer briefs with a cartoon Santa holding a beer on them. "Oh my God! Why the hell do you have boxers on your counter! Are they dirty?"

Ronan lets me go and raises both hands in the air. "They're fresh from the laundry, I swear. They fell out of my laundry basket and I found them on the floor and tossed them on the counter this morning on the way out the door. I know I live alone and I'm a dude, but I don't normally keep my underwear on the counter."

This time it's Ronan who's red-faced instead of the other way around. I decide I should savor the experience since I have no idea when it's going to happen again. I hold them up and frown at the way the peen pouch holds its shape. "What's going on here?" I poke at the pouch.

He makes a noise that sounds half like he's choking and also a groan. "Don't do that."

"Why not? You said they're clean. Are you lying?"

"I'm not lying," he croaks.

I know he's telling the truth because the fresh smell of his laundry detergent prevails as I wave around his festive underwear. This is more fun than it should be. I peek inside. These aren't like regular underwear at all. "Are these for sports or something? Like they have a built-in jockstrap?"

He tries to grab them from me but I spin out of reach, putting the island between us as a barrier. He pokes at his cheek with his tongue. "They offer support." He uses his hand to demonstrate, but in the air, not by cupping his actual junk.

"Like a bra for your balls?" I make the same cupping motion in front of my chest. His underwear dangle from my pinkie.

"Yeah, sort of like a bra for my balls."

"So it lifts and separates?"

"Same basic principle." He closes his eyes for a few seconds, exhaling a long slow breath before he opens them again. "Can we stop talking about this now?"

"You're the one who leaves underwear on your counter. I don't think it's unreasonable for me to be curious about them."

He swallows thickly. "Is your curiosity sated?"

"Partially. I might have more questions later. Why? Is this conversation making you uncomfortable?"

He blinks a couple of times before his eyebrows rise. "We're talking about my balls and your tits, Blaire."

"And?" I play dumb, because this whole conversation is making me think about cupping his junk, so I have to assume it's making him think about the same thing and possibly him acting as a human bra for my boobs.

"Well, Blaire, you're fondling my underwear, we're discussing cupping balls, you're drawing attention to your chest, and men are visual creatures. So as you're talking I'm imagining every single one of those things. And I'm wearing gray sweatpants and I'm commando now."

"Seriously?" I push up on my tiptoes and try to get a look at his crotch, which is a silly thing to do because it's not like I can see if he's commando through his sweats.

He points a finger at me. "You stay right where you are."

"Why?"

"Do you really need to ask?"

I shrug and give him a look that tells him I do, in fact, need to ask.

He plants his fists on the counter and huffs a laugh. He keeps his head bowed but lifts his gaze. "This conversation is *stimulating*."

"Oh." I glance down and back up a few times. "*Oh!* Are you *aroused*?"

All he does is glare at me.

"I see." I nod primly and place his boxer briefs on the counter. I carefully smooth them out, bite my lip, and push them in his direction. "You know." I wrinkle my nose. "I think I'm just going to excuse myself to the bathroom for a minute. It's down the hall, isn't it?" I motion in the direction he went when he changed into gray sweats.

"First door on the left," he grinds out.

"I'll give you a minute to...calm down, then," I whisper. Yes, it's sultry and on purpose.

"Much appreciated, Blaire."

I wait until I'm halfway down the hall before I allow myself to smile. It's nice to know I'm not the only one affected.

When I return from the bathroom—I take an extra long time and wish I'd thought to bring my purse along so I can fix my makeup—the underwear is no longer sitting on the counter, and Ronan has relocated to the couch.

In addition to the flights of beer, he's set out bowls of chips, nuts, and popcorn. I grab my laptop and clipboard and join him.

I leave a cushion of space between us and adjust my dress so I can tuck my legs under all the fabric. If I'd been thinking, I would have lost the crinoline. It makes the skirt extra poofy—and hides my thighs and butt, which Maddy and Skylar had a habit of smacking anytime I wore jeans because, unlike them, I actually have a butt. Crinolines, while great for keeping the booty under wraps, are not necessarily the most comfortable thing to sit around in.

I battle the fabric down and use a throw pillow—there's only one and it looks like it might have been cross-stitched by a grandmother—to keep it from poofing up again.

"I'd offer you a pair of jogging pants, but I think you'd swim in mine."

"It's fine. I'm used to it."

"You don't look all that comfortable."

He gives me the raised eyebrow and I stare at him for a few more seconds before I finally give in, stand up, pull the crinoline down and step out of it. It holds its shape for a few long seconds, resembling a pretty fabric volcano before it sinks into a puddle on the floor.

"Happy now?" I sit back down and tuck my legs back under the skirt again.

"As long as you're happy and comfortable, I'm happy and comfortable. You wear that thing every day?"

"It's comfy, for the most part."

"I'll take your word for it." He motions to the spread. "Help yourself, but let me give you a rundown of the beers and what goes best with which snack." He describes each craft brew: pumpkin, orange, rhubarb, and a hopped mango ale and tells me which snack to pair it with. I take a sip after each description, then follow it with a nibble of the accompanying snack so I can experience the way the flavors complement one another. "Where did these beers come from? They're all delicious." I go back to the rhubarb ale, because I favor the hint of sweetness and the tart, gentle tang that follows the initial bitterness of the hops.

"I made them."

"What? When would you have time for that?"

"Gramps let me set up a brew in his garage. It's just small

batches, but I think it'll be enough to have some decent options for New Year's. What do you think?"

I set my beer down and clap my hands excitedly, and then grab his. "Oh my God! What about a craft beer and champagne theme! We can have specialty cupcakes based on the beer flavors and champagne. You can host the dinner and I'll handle dessert. Do you think we can apply to have a gated outdoor space so people can go back and forth between our places as long as there's security? Or is that too much? It might be too much."

"I think it's a great idea, and it's sort of exactly what I was already thinking."

"I'll shut down B&B at ten and move the party over to The Knight Cap. We can have a cupcake table and appetizers and all the delicious craft beer. This is going to be fantastic."

We spend the next hour sipping beers, eating snacks, and planning our New Year's co-celebration. I start to get tired—beer hits me a lot faster than vodka for some reason—and when Ronan excuses himself to the bathroom, I stretch out and close my eyes for a few seconds.

I blink and try to roll over, but my face hits...a wall? No wait. Walls aren't soft, and they aren't made of...leather? I blink a couple of times, but close my eyes right away because the morning sun is streaming through the windows, blinding me. It's enough time for me to come to the conclusion that I'm not in my own apartment.

Panic takes over for a few disorienting seconds until the

familiar smell of Ronan's cologne registers. I blink again, still trying to adjust to the light beyond my eyelids.

I can't believe I fell asleep. Well, that's not true; I've been burning the candle at both ends, working long hours, basically seven days a week, since the beginning of the summer. That I passed out on Ronan's couch isn't much of a surprise. That he didn't wake me up and send me home sort of is.

Or maybe he tried and failed. That would be both embarrassing and not entirely impossible given the above facts.

I note the soft pillow tucked under my head—not the cross-stitched one I was hugging last night. I'm also covered in a blanket that smells like Ronan. On the table beside me is a glass of water.

The food and drinks from last night have been cleared away and sit on the counter across the room. I must have passed out so hard. I check the time. It's barely after seven, but I have to stop at home to change at the very least and manage my makeup situation, so there's no way I'm going to make it in before eight thirty. I'm glad I had the foresight to prepare most of the cupcakes for today last night, otherwise we'd be in real short supply this morning.

I throw off the covers, consider leaving them in a heap, but decide that's super rude, so I fold everything—half-assed folding, but still—and look around the floor for my crinoline.

I spot all my stuff—purse, laptop, clipboard, and crinoline—on the club chair across from the couch. I can sincerely appreciate Ronan's tidiness.

Once my mess is straightened up, I find a piece of paper,

scribble an apology and a thank you, and gather up my things, shoving the crinoline in my purse because carrying it is awkward.

Of course my attempt to make a stealthy exit is thwarted when my purse knocks into a wooden sculpture of a beaver and it clatters to the floor. I carefully put it back, glad it wasn't glass, and tiptoe to the door, careful not to bang into anything else. I realize I'm still wearing Ronan's socks, so I have to take those off before I can slip my feet into my shoes. This also requires me to set down all the things I'm carrying because the socks are clinging to my tights.

"Morning." The gravelly voice gives me pause.

"I'm so sorry I fell asleep on you." I turn to give him an apologetic smile to go with the verbal one, but I'm pretty sure all I'm capable of is drooling. "Oh." I'm excessively breathy as I murmur, "Good morning to me."

Ronan is standing about ten feet away, wearing the same gray sweats as last night. Except he's gloriously shirtless, all his artwork and his lovely, defined muscles on display. There's a lot of both to appreciate.

I'd like to say I make an attempt to conceal my gawking, but I don't. I scan his torso, drinking in the ink that covers the left side of his chest and merges with the ink running down his arm. I also admire the delicious V of muscle that disappears under the waistband of his sweats.

Eventually I make it up to his face. Even the smirk he's wearing is adorably delicious. A five o'clock shadow covers his jaw and sleep lines cut across his face. His hair sticks up all over the place. *This is a sight I wouldn't mind waking up to more often.*

"Blaire?" His right brow arches.

Damn it, he's asked me a question and I've been too busy thinking about how it's too bad he doesn't sleep completely naked to be bothered to pay attention. "I'm sorry if I woke you. I knocked a beaver over." I thumb over my shoulder. "But I didn't break it or anything. And I'm sorry I fell asleep on you. I know I'm impossible to wake up."

He runs a hand through his hair, making more of it stand on end. "I would've moved you to the spare bedroom, but you were out like a light and I figured you probably needed the rest. I hope you slept okay."

"Like the dead, actually. I should go, though." God, this is awkward.

Ronan gives me a lopsided grin. "You don't want to stay and make me breakfast?"

It's my turn for my eyebrows to climb my forehead. "I need to shower and change before work." Plus Daphne said she was going to stop by this morning with a few things she thought might be helpful for the New Year's celebration and she seemed particularly excited. No matter how many times I tell her I can manage, she always makes herself available on the nights with special events.

"It's only just seven, and I'm kidding about you making me breakfast, Blaire. But *I* could make *you* breakfast."

"Oh, you don't need to do that. I've already overstayed my welcome."

"If that was true, I would've stayed in bed and let you leave. You can let Callie open up, can't you? I won't make you late. I can whip up a mean breakfast sandwich." His tone is light and playful, but his expression is earnest.

Warmth courses through my veins and pools in my stomach. "I guess I could stay for breakfast. I need to call Callie, though."

"Great. I'll put on a pot of coffee while you do that." His warm fingertips graze the back of my hand as he passes. I don't think it's an accident.

After I call Callie, who's happy to open up for me, I message Daphne about coming in a little late this morning.

Her response is immediate:

Daphne: Are you sick?

Blaire: No. Late night planning with Ronan. I'll explain when I see you.

Daphne: Please tell me he has a big 🍆 and you rode it all night long.

I ignore her text.

Blaire: See you in a couple hours.

"Everything okay? You still good to stay for breakfast?" Ronan asks.

"Yup. All set. What can I do to help?"

He hands me a mug. "You can get this ready to be filled with coffee. I'm going to throw on a shirt, and then I'll start breakfast."

"Okay." I can't remember the last time a guy made me breakfast. Especially not after an accidental sleepover, which did not include sex. I think I kind of like it.

He pads across the living room and I get a look at his back, also covered in art. He's a living, breathing canvas. One I'd love to explore every inch of. And not just with my eyes.

@buttercreamandbooze:

You're the icing to my cupcake.

chapter fifteen

MISS MISTLETOE

Blaire

Look at the traction this post is getting!" Daphne shoves her phone in my face and waves it around, making it impossible to focus on the image.

I grab it from her, so I can see what she's so excited about. I frown, not because it's a bad image, but because I have no idea who took it or why it has so many comments or likes. It's a picture of Ronan and me, his arm slung over my shoulder and mine wrapped around his waist. We're smiling at each other, and while it's on his feed, it was taken in my shop. Based on what's happening in the background and my outfit, it was taken a couple of days ago when we had a post-Christmas, pre–New Year's collaborative event—which is what most of our events are at this point.

And it's turned out to be incredibly positive in terms of the Best Bar competition. We both made it through to the quarterfinals, although The Knight Cap managed to secure spot number twelve, while B&B ranked as number fifteen. I think it has a lot to do with our duets during karaoke nights, not that I'll say it out loud.

I read the caption. I'm aware that Ronan leaves that stuff to Lars and one of his servers, who sometimes pass things by me or Daphne, so they can manage what to post and when. This is clearly not a pre-approved post, but people seem to love it. Because they've dubbed us The Knight Cakes and have given us a hashtag.

"Who approved this hashtag? It's terrible."

"Really? I think it's cute." Daphne gives me her innocent look, which isn't innocent at all.

"Blonan is not a cute hashtag. It's too close to blowjob. Was this your idea? Who took this picture?"

"I had nothing to do with the hashtag. Your followers came up with it, and they're loving it. Everyone ships you two."

I roll my eyes. "We're not dating, we're collaborating."

"*Yet.* You're not dating *yet.*"

We've had this conversation several times over the past three weeks—ever since the night I fell asleep on Ronan's couch. "Am I attracted to him? Yes. Is it a good idea to get involved with him? No."

"Says who?"

"Says anyone who knows what it's like to date someone you're working with. It's a recipe for disaster. See Raphael for details." She can't argue with that logic, considering the way that entire situation blew up in my face.

Although, if that hadn't happened I might not be here, working for myself. I may barely be making ends meet, and I may also be very much in need of a month-long nap, but at least I'm doing what I love.

"Raphael was a douche canoe, and it's not the same situation at all. You were not his equal, you were his student and he took advantage of a position of power. And then he seriously screwed you over because he likes to stick his dick in everything that moves. Including Baked Alaska."

I shudder at that image. "It's still not advisable. We're competing against each other for Best Bar *and* we're working together to keep our businesses afloat so those fuckers don't push us out." I motion across the street to the yet-to-open massive adult indoor arcade and bar.

Their grand opening is New Year's Eve, of course. Which is why Ronan and I have been spending an inordinate amount of time together planning our own New Year's bash.

We've gone over all the fine details relentlessly. I have not, however, been back to his place since the night I fell asleep on his couch. Has there been a suggestion that we might want to work at his place? Maybe, but since B&B closes earlier than The Knight Cap, it makes sense for us to plan at my shop. At least that's been my rationale, and he hasn't really pushed it.

Not to mention, that morning when I went into work late one of Tori Taylor's people, who happens to be local, stopped in before I arrived. I missed my chance to make a good impression—or any impression at all, really.

And of course that same person ended up at Ronan's, because he's in the competition, too—only Ronan made it to the bar in time. I might find him attractive, but I don't want to lose out on any other opportunities, should they arise.

It doesn't mean we're not flirting, or that I don't find myself staring at his mouth, wondering how his lips would feel on mine.

It just means I've been circumventing the potential for further complications and excessive distractions. Until this Best Bar competition is over and done with and we see what the impact of this whole Dick and Bobby's grand opening has on our respective bottom lines, I don't think it's a great idea to jump into his bed. Or jump him in general.

I do think about it frequently when I'm in the shower, and in my own bed. And everywhere, really.

"Earth to Blaire." Daphne snaps her fingers in my face. At the same time her camera goes off.

I jerk back. "What?"

"You were totally thinking about boning Ronan just now, weren't you?"

"I was not!"

"You definitely were. Look at the expression on your face!" She holds up her phone so I can see the picture she took.

I'm biting my lip and touching my throat, lost in a daydream. About riding Ronan. I push her phone away. "Whatever. Thinking about it and doing it aren't the same thing."

Daphne wiggles her eyebrows. "I give you max two weeks before you fold."

Fortunately, Callie arrives for her shift, ending that conversation.

During the lead-up to New Year's Eve I average about four hours of sleep a night, and it sure as hell isn't the restful kind. On the upside, the cohosted events with Ronan have been keeping me from digging further into my line of credit. It's a little less terrifying to pay the bills when I know I'm not turning my overdraft into a black hole every time or adding to my debt.

New Year's planning means lots of expenses, but ticket sales for the event have been incredible and we sold out completely last week, which helps offset all the costs.

On New Year's Eve, I'm up before six in the morning even though I went to bed at two. Ronan and I sat at his bar and went over the plan for tonight, double and triple checking that we have everything we need. Our cohosted New Year's party has been getting a lot of attention and rumor has it Tori Taylor is planning to come our way soon as the semifinal round closes in.

When I arrive at B&B, I notice that Ronan's truck is already there, which seems a lot early for him. Imagine my surprise when I walk into my shop and find Ronan behind the bar, making cappuccinos. "What're you doing here?"

He glances at me, eyes moving over me in that familiar way that makes a shiver run down my spine and heat pool south of the navel. "Good morning to you, too."

"Sorry. It's just a surprise to see you here at this hour." Ronan usually doesn't roll in until nine thirty or ten. "Oh God, nothing happened next door? We don't have another wrong delivery, do we?"

Ronan wipes his hands on his apron—he's wearing one with the B&B logo; actually, it's mine because it has the cupcake with the crown decoration—and wraps his hands around my arms. "Take a deep breath, Blaire. You look like you're on the verge of panic, and there is absolutely nothing to be worried about."

Over the past few weeks I've grown accustomed to Ronan's touch. The way he casually slings his arm over my shoulder. The frequent occasions where he picks me up and moves me out of the way when I'm ranting about something and he wants to multitask. And although I'm accustomed to it, I'm definitely not immune. I clear my throat before I speak; otherwise I'm liable to sound all breathy. "It's barely eight in the morning. How are you here and did you even sleep last night?" His hands slide down my arms and I fight a shiver.

He shrugs, looking sheepish. "I got a few hours. I plan to sleep all day tomorrow. I borrowed Daphne's key. I figured you might need some help this morning since you likely went to bed around the same time as me."

"Oh, well that's incredibly sweet of you. I'm going to

sleep all the sleeps tomorrow, too. It's going to be magic." I fight a yawn.

His eyes widen comically. "Oh no! Don't do that! They're contagious." We both cup our hands over our mouths and yawn at the same time. My eyes water. Lord, I'm going to be exhausted tomorrow.

A loud clank and hiss comes from behind him and we both startle.

"What the heck?" I grab on to his arm and hide behind him as he spins around.

I peek over his shoulder and get a glimpse of the cappuccino maker, which is currently steaming in places it shouldn't be.

"Oh shit, that doesn't look right." His expression reflects his horror.

"That's because it's not." I move around him, pulling the plug before it blows.

Ronan helps me clean up the mess. It turns out one of the seals has broken, so we're down a freaking cappuccino maker. I call around frantically, looking to see if someone can come in and fix it today. While we can usually get by with one machine, it's going to be busy tonight.

I manage to find someone who can come in this afternoon, but of course it's going to cost me a freaking arm and a leg. Ronan apologizes profusely, obviously feeling bad about it. I assure him it wasn't his fault, and that it's just crap timing.

The morning flies by; people working half-days stop in to grab a quick bite, orders are picked up for events, and by the time two rolls around we're almost completely sold out, which is great because it means little in the way of cleanup before we set up for tonight.

The cappuccino maker is fixed, thankfully, before three in the afternoon, and a test run indicates that it's back in working order.

By three thirty B&B is ready for the evening, tables set up to display tiers of dessert cupcakes, glittery decorations everywhere, a perfect complement to the beer and champagne theme. Everything is gold and black and sparkly and beautiful.

I stand in the middle of the shop with my hands on my hips. "I think it looks perfect. What do you think?"

"Definitely perfect." Ronan is still wearing a Buttercream and Booze apron, but his focus isn't on the decorations.

"You're not even looking." I motion to the shop.

"I don't need to. I helped put them up, so I already know how they look."

"But it's everything put together. That's what makes it perfect."

"And you're the cherry on top. Or maybe you should be one of those little Eat Me candies instead. Those are delicious. You got any lying around?"

"You realize that made no sense at all, right?"

"Sure it did. This place looks perfect and not just because the decorations are on point, but because you're in the middle of it, looking radiant and proud as hell, as you should be. Now where are those Eat Me candies?"

"There aren't any Eat Me candies."

"Well, that's a disappointment. I guess I'll have to settle for a leftover cupcake." He plucks one from a box—that's all there is left—peels off the wrapper and devours it in two bites, groaning his enjoyment.

When he's done, we head over to The Knight Cap and enlist the help of his staff to decorate. Much to Ronan's dismay, I hang mistletoe above the bar and over the tables.

"Aren't we a little late for this?"

"It's never too late for mistletoe."

"Like people don't already have an excuse to make out on New Year's; now you're adding this?" He motions to the pretty sprig tied with a red, gold, and black plaid ribbon hanging from one of the lights above the bar—which I'm standing on top of, while wearing a pair of the steel-toed boots reserved for the axe throwers.

On account of tonight's festivities and the very high likelihood that many if not most of the patrons will be "super wasted," as Lars put it, the axes have all been locked away. Standing tables have been set up and stools line the walls so there's more room for mingling and dancing.

"Oh, come on, don't be a Scrooge. These should have been up all month!"

"I'm just saying, Lars doesn't need an excuse to make out with the customers."

"Maybe some poor shy girl who would never in a million years have the guts to kiss the guy she's interested in will find herself under this mistletoe and end up kissed by her very own Prince Charming."

"More likely a bleary-eyed, horny, drunk guy, but I get that you're throwing off your wonderland vibes tonight and prefer to live in a land of fairy tales and make-believe where college guys aren't a bunch of dirtbags."

"Were you a dirtbag?" I ask. Ronan is flirty, but not in a slimy way.

"Not as a general rule, no."

I move down the bar to the next hanging light so I can wrap the glittery garland around it, affixing yet another sprig of mistletoe. "So that means you occasionally *were* a dirtbag." It's more statement than question.

"I'm not perfect, and I was once a drunk, horny twenty-something. Try not to judge me too harshly."

I move on to the next light. "How old were you when you started with the body art?"

Ronan hands me another set of ribbons. "When I was eighteen, but it wasn't until after I lost my parents that I started on the sleeves. Why?"

"I bet the college girls loved you, all tatted up and badass." I tap my lip. "And I'm sure that hasn't changed at all."

He barks out a laugh. "Lars is more the college girl catnip."

I glance at Lars and shrug. "I mean, he's a cute kid, and I'm sure there are plenty of college girls who would fall all over themselves to get his attention, but he's got the grace of an elephant trying to be a ballerina when he's hitting on women. I mean, he told *me* he'd love to take a ride on the cougar express."

Ronan's jaw drops. "He said *what?*"

"It was a joke." At least I'm going to pretend it was.

"Like hell it was. When did he say that? Was it recently? It better not have been recently." If looks could kill, Lars would be the ashy remains of a cremated corpse.

I prop a fist on my hip. "I think it was actually meant as a backward compliment."

"He was trying to get into your pants, like he tries to do with every single female he encounters that he isn't related to. Or under your skirt, since I've never seen you in a pair of pants. Ever." His gaze moves over my legs. I'm wearing a pair of sparkly tights.

"So really you're saying he'll screw anything with a pulse, no matter what she looks like?"

"He's not very discerning."

"Well, thanks." That's a blow my ego certainly doesn't need from the guy I'm crushing on. "I know I'm not a model-esque, highly fashionable beauty queen, but I'm not an ogre, either!"

"I didn't mean that you're unattractive—"

"No, just that Lars will bone anyone with a vagina, so don't be flattered that he hit on me. I get it." I've reached the end of the bar and crouch so the jump down isn't as far. The last thing I need tonight is to roll an ankle. I'm super tired and stressed about the event tonight, and for whatever reason the whole Lars thing gets my back up.

"Let me help you down." Ronan holds out a hand.

I swat it away. "I don't need help."

"Are you serious right now? Why are you suddenly all pissy?"

"I'm not pissy," I say rather pissily.

"Really?"

"Move out of the way so I can get down." Now I'm snippy to go with the pissy. And because I'm extra overtired, and maybe a little too hopped up on caffeine, I'm also very close to irrational tears. I better not be getting my period on top of everything else.

"Or you could just let me help you."

"I told you, I'm fine." I put a hand on the edge of the bar so I can hop the three and a half feet to the floor.

But before I can make a move Ronan steps closer and wraps his hands around my waist. I don't expect him to lift me off the bar, so I tip forward. Grabbing his shoulder, I slide down the front of his body. His very firm, hard, muscular body.

Ronan has a lot of ridges and planes and angles. But as my hips glide down his abs I'm suddenly aware of a very significant, prominent lump as I make the trip past his fly.

He's still holding on to my waist, and I'm still clutching his shoulders. I attempt to step back, but his grip tightens. I tip my chin up and blink up at him.

His expression is mostly flat as he dips his head down until his mouth is at my ear. "I would appreciate it if you didn't call me out right now, Blaire, but as I'm sure you can feel, the head below the belt, which happens to respond to messages from my brain, does *not* find you unattractive. In fact, based on my inability to control said head, I would say that's evidence that we find you rather appealing and both of us would prefer it if Lars would keep his commentary to himself and his damn eyeballs off you."

He backs up enough that his face comes into focus. His expression is far from remote now; it's full of heat. The same kind of heat pooling in my belly. I'd like to say something cheeky about the fact that he's referring to his penis as if it's an independent thinker, but my mouth has gone dry.

I manage to whisper, "Noted."

"Great. I'm going to take a minute to get a handle on things." He cringes. "Not an actual handle. I'm just going to think about unappealing things. I'll be back."

He lets go of me and I drop my arms. I watch him walk away, stiffly.

Lars appears beside me. "Where's Ronan going?"

"He's taking a minute to collect himself." I don't mean to go with such blatant honesty.

Lars smirks and jerks his chin up. "I bet he is. Dude's been staring at your legs for the past half hour like he's watching a damn striptease. You two just need to hook up and get it over with. The sexual tension is making *me* all edgy and shit." He slings his towel over his shoulder and saunters back to the bar where he's skewering fruit for cocktails.

I glance up at the mistletoe hanging from the lights and consider how it might come in handy later.

By four thirty in the afternoon we're completely set up, the food is prepped, tables are decorated, and menus are laid out. Now it's just a matter of changing, freshening my makeup, and mainlining about four gallons of coffee.

The evening doesn't go off without a hitch; there are glitches. B&B runs out of the top-shelf vodka, but Ronan is there to save the day with his own stock. Thankfully we've agreed to split costs and revenue, so it's not a big deal. One of the servers slips on a French fry and loses an entire tray of cupcakes, but overall it's an incredible success. And while there's a line outside of Dick and Bobby's celebrating their grand opening, we're at max capacity and end up having to turn people away, which is unfortunate but also a good thing.

The adrenaline pumping through my veins means I'm probably going to crash hard when the bar finally closes, but for the time being I'm enjoying the success of the event.

As midnight approaches, I find myself behind the bar with Ronan, mixing drinks. His fireworks-patterned tie is thrown over his shoulder so it doesn't soak up anything spilled on the bartop. Despite the extra staff, they can't seem to keep up with the demands and the lineup to get to the bar is three deep as people order champagne cocktails to toast the New Year.

I lost my heels hours ago in exchange for the steel-toe boots required behind the bar, which means I've also lost three inches of height, and I have to stretch to reach the bottles on the high shelves.

Ronan reaches over me and grabs the bottle I need, then bends so his mouth is at my ear, shouting over the music so I can hear him. "Tell me what you need, and I'll get it for you." His lips brush the shell as he speaks, sending a warm shiver down my spine.

I nod because I've been shouting most of the night and my voice is pretty much gone. The front of my fireworks-and-champagne-glasses dress is damp from leaning over the bar, and I smell like champagne and beer, but I couldn't be happier.

We work together, passing bottles and garnishes without having to speak because we each seem to know what the other needs. He reaches around behind me, our bodies touching constantly as we pour and serve, pour and serve.

Then the countdown begins, and there's a tiny pause in the mayhem behind the bar as the crowd raise their drinks in the air, shouting and laughing their way into the New Year.

"Here, take this." Ronan wraps my hand around a shot glass and clinks his own against it.

"What is it?"

"Just drink it," he shouts.

We raise our glasses to our lips and I knock back the shot. Shouts of "Happy New Year!" rise to almost unbearable levels as it burns its way down my throat.

"Happy New Year!" Lars screams and gives us a double hug and then points to the light above us. "Look up." And then he's off down the bar, yelling *"Happy New Year!"* at the top of his lungs.

Ronan and I look up at the same time and realize that we happen to be standing directly under one of the sprigs of mistletoe. Our gazes meet, and I can see the resolve in his eyes. I'm sure the few shots we've done behind the bar tonight are fully responsible for what happens next.

Ronan slips one hand around my waist and pulls me against him. He tips his head to the side fractionally: a silent question. I respond by sliding my hands over his chest to lock them behind his neck, tugging gently as I tip my chin up.

His other hand curves around my nape as he dips down and his warm, minty breath mingles with mine. "Happy New Year, Blaire."

"Happy New Year, Ronan."

A shock of energy lights me up like a neon sign, zinging through my veins as our lips meet for the first time. It's a full-body tingle, starting at my scalp, working its way down my body. Heat funnels straight between my thighs and my toes curl.

We tip our heads in opposite directions, lips parting, tongues sliding against each other. He groans and I moan as we open wider, tongues stroking deeper. I grip the back of his neck and the hand on my waist drifts lower. Cupping my left butt cheek, Ronan pulls me tighter against him. I feel him hard against my stomach, and I press my hips closer.

I'm pretty sure the kiss would have lasted forever—or until

we got naked—except the sudden hoots, hollers, and shrill whistles remind us that we're not even remotely alone.

We break apart and I worry for a second that maybe this wasn't the best idea. Realistically it's not a good plan to get involved with my competition/neighbor, but that was one hell of a kiss.

Ronan blinks a couple of times and blows out a breath. "I don't think we're in Wonderland anymore, Alice."

I laugh, glad he's broken the tension.

"You're coming back to my place after we close tonight, right?"

I cock a brow.

"Or we can go to yours if that's better. Or closer," he adds.

"Are you saying you want more of this?" I motion to my lips.

The music has started again and there are patrons clamoring for drinks, but Ronan holds a finger up in their direction and leans in close so his lips are at my ear again. "I want all of this. Repeatedly. And while my office has a door that locks, I'm not sure I'll give my best performance in there."

"Mmm. Good point. Your place it is."

chapter sixteen

RINGING IN THE NEW YEAR

Ronan

It's after three in the morning by the time we get an Uber back to my place. I usher Blaire inside, lock the door, and turn around.

She's standing in the middle of my front hallway, still wearing the steel-toed boots I forced on her because there was no way I was risking her twisting an ankle behind the bar, which was where I wanted her. Right beside me all night long. Not on the floor where she'd get hit on relentlessly by drunk assholes.

It might sound chivalrous. It's not—my motives were purely self-serving.

She clasps her hands in front of her, looking demure and sexy in her fireworks dress with black and plaid accents. We matched, of course. Her teeth sink into her bottom lip. I kissed her lipstick off hours ago and she didn't bother to reapply, mostly because there was no time.

"Do you want something to drink?" My voice is rough like sandpaper.

Her brow furrows for a moment, as if she finds the question confusing. "Do you?"

I take a few steps in her direction. "Not particularly, no, but I figured I should be hospitable and offer rather than just attack you with my mouth and hands." *And parts below the waist.*

"Hmm." She taps her lip, a playful smile on those luscious lips of hers. "Water for hydration purposes might be a good idea, but that can probably wait until after you attack me with your mouth and hands." Her eyes move down my chest in a slow, hot sweep. "And other parts, hopefully."

We are so on the same page. And then we're on each other.

Blaire loops her arms over my shoulders and links her hands behind my neck, pulling my mouth to hers. I grip her waist and walk her backward through the short entryway, careful not to bump into the side table on the right. The bedroom seems too far away, so I swipe a hand blindly across the kitchen counter, knocking a few things out of the way before I lift her up and deposit her on top.

The kiss slows for all of two beats, and then we're right back at it, full force, teeth clashing, tongues battling, moaning into each other's mouths. Blaire tugs my shirt free from my pants, then starts on the buttons while I search the back of her dress for a zipper. All I find is smooth fabric.

She breaks the kiss long enough to say, "Hidden zipper."

I pull back, because that makes no sense. "What?"

"It's hidden." She abandons my shirt and pushes on my chest, forcing me back. I'm about to protest, but she reaches under her skirt and MacGyvers her poofy under-skirt thing off, tossing it on the floor. Then she grabs the front of my shirt and yanks me between her legs again.

I start feeling up and down her spine, in search of this hidden zipper. I finally find one, but it's tiny and I keep losing my grip on it.

"How do you get the zipper down?" I mumble around her tongue.

"Don't worry about it, all the important parts are easily accessible." She hikes the skirt of her dress higher, trying to shift the fabric out of the way.

I pull back so I can see her in the dimly lit kitchen. The lamp on the other side of the living room is weak, and the hall light leading to my bedroom is on a dimmer switch, set to low.

"I would like the full experience here, not just access to what's between your thighs." I motion to her crotch. "I mean, I definitely want that, but I plan to explore every last inch of you in the process."

I have every intention of devouring her, but I'd like to do that while also savoring the experience. I take my time unzipping the dress—actually, the tiny zipper tab is a pain in my ass, so half the slowing down is forced because it's a struggle and I'm determined to be the one to undress her, on my own, without her help.

I finally manage the zipper situation, but there's a freaking hook thing, too, which means more struggles on my end.

She chuckles against my lips, sucking on the bottom one. I finally unclasp it, but instead of removing the dress I delay my own gratification and hers. It's like unwrapping the best, belated birthday present.

I pull the bodice down, freeing her arms to reveal her bra. I let out a low, appreciative whistle. Under the dress with the gold and black plaid accents she's wearing a black bra with red and gold plaid accents. I'm willing to bet the panties match, because this is Blaire we're talking about and her wardrobe is always meticulously planned. I lift her skirt so I can take a peek. Yup, they totally match, which begs the question, "Were you planning to seduce me tonight?"

Her brow furrows. "What? No, of course not. Why would you think that?"

"Because . . ." I run my hands up her thighs, warm and soft, bunching up the skirt, exposing more skin as I do. I savor the feel of her under my hands, the way her breath stutters when I skim the edge of her panties with my fingertips. "This bra and panty set looks like it was picked out with me in mind."

"I wanted to coordinate it with my dress."

"Which you bought so we'd match." I slip my hands out from under her skirt, much to her dismay, so I can cup her full breasts in my palms and run my thumbs over her nipples through the fabric.

She arches and sucks in a breath. "I like things that match."

"So that means you did inadvertently buy these for me."

"If you need to stroke your own ego over my choice of bra and panties, go for it."

"Do you have matching sets for all of your dresses?" I slip my pinkie under the satin.

"Some, not all."

"Hmm." And now it's become my mission to unwrap her like a present as often as she'll allow so I can see what kind of lingerie she's wearing underneath. For that to happen, I need to guarantee that she's going to want a repeat of tonight. Which means bringing my A-game.

We get back to making out, her half-dressed, me still fully clothed. I loosen my tie with one hand while she tackles the remaining buttons on my shirt. They join the other clothes on the floor and I break the kiss long enough to get my undershirt off.

I'm ready to dive back in, but Blaire's palms connect with my chest, preventing our lips from meeting. She drags her nails from my pecs down to my abs. "So sexy," she murmurs on a soft sigh. She lifts her gaze. "You know, I never thought tattoos were hot before you, but now . . ." She traces the outline of the tree that decorates my side and disappears into the waistband of my pants. "So much yum."

I laugh and then groan when she goes lower and cups me through my pants.

"I was so disappointed when you put on a shirt the morning after I accidentally fell asleep on your couch."

"I was kind of disappointed that you fell asleep and didn't end up in my bed with me."

"Really?" She slips my belt through the loops and starts to unbuckle it.

"I went to the bathroom so I could brush my teeth and freshen up. I was thinking maybe I'd make a move, but when I came back you were out like a light."

"I had no idea." She pops the button.

"I've been flirting with you since day one."

"I was too busy being aggravated that you were my competition and you were so hot, and composed, and I was always too flustered to notice that you were flirting. Plus, it's your job to flirt." She drags the zipper down slowly.

"I'm friendly with customers, but I flirt with *you*. There's a difference."

"Hmm. You'll have to explain that difference later, so I'm in the know." She slips her index finger under the waistband of my boxer briefs and pulls them away from my skin, peeking inside. I doubt she can see much since the lights are low and it's dark in my underwear.

"What're you doing?"

"I want to see what I'm dealing with."

"You can touch him, he doesn't bite."

"Him?" She peeks up, her expression amused. "Does he have a name?"

I scoff. "Of course not." I call him The Sword of Destiny in my head, though.

"I don't believe you." She reaches inside and skims the length.

I groan and prop one fist on the counter, the other still cupping her breast. I have plans to take that bra off eventually, but I'm kind of in love with it and also distracted by the fact that her hand is in my pants.

She wraps her fingers around me, giving me a tentative squeeze before she frees me from my boxers. Her bottom lip is between her teeth and she peers down, exhaling what sounds like a relieved breath along with the words. "Thank God."

"Thank God, what?"

Her gaze flips back up to mine, and I have a feeling she didn't mean to say that out loud. Her cheeks might be turning pink, but the lighting makes it hard to tell.

"I just wasn't sure where the tattoos started and ended."

I bark out a laugh. "That's a hard pass area for me. There isn't much going on below the waist."

Blaire raises a brow and gives my erection a squeeze. "I'd beg to differ."

"I mean tattoo wise."

"Ah yes, well, I guess I'll be able to confirm that soon enough."

She pulls my mouth back to hers and I continue to tease her nipple while she strokes me. It's probably an awkward angle for her hand, considering I'm standing between her thighs, but I'm not all that interested in stopping her and she doesn't seem to mind.

When the sensation gets to be too much for me to handle—meaning when I'm worried I'm going to blow in her hand—I start kissing my way down her neck.

Reaching around behind her, I flick the clasp of her bra open. It slides down her arms and lands on the counter, then drops to the floor with the rest of our clothes. I kiss my way across her collarbone and down over the swell until I can cover a nipple with my mouth.

Blaire moans, and she loses her grip on my erection. It's not a bad thing, considering I'm already close to an edge I don't want to be near when we've hardly even started with the foreplay.

Her fingers slide into my hair, the other hand moving to grip my shoulder. I use her distraction to my advantage and tuck myself back into my pants so I can focus on making her feel good. If I can make her come before the sex—if we get to that, I'm not making assumptions but I'm hoping—then it'll take some of the pressure off.

I ease my palm up her thigh, moving inward. Her legs are parted to accommodate me, so when I reach the apex I brush my knuckles over the satin.

"Oh yes, please." She spreads her legs wider.

This is what I want, for all that uptight Instagram perfection to fall away. I want her uninhibited and unworried about anything but how she feels. I keep sweeping my knuckles back and forth, barely skimming the damp fabric. "Do you like that, Blaire?"

"Mmm, it's nice." She wriggles her butt.

I slip a single finger under the elastic and I'm met with hot, wet skin.

"Oh, that's so much nicer." Her eyes flutter closed as I stroke her center, easing a finger inside.

She props herself on her arms and she bites her lip, moaning softly when I add a second finger. Her head rolls on her shoulders and her lids flutter open, gaze dropping to where my forearm disappears under her skirt. "God, that is so hot," she groans, and her fingertips graze my inked arm.

"It is, isn't it?" I agree. "You look like a good girl who got caught up with a bad boy." She looks like she fell right out of the fifties with her perfect hair and retro dresses, which makes her current position, with the top hanging at her waist and my hand under the bunched-up skirt, seem that much more illicit. And those steel-toed boots paired with her thigh-high stockings are the icing on the sexy cupcake.

She drags her skirt up higher, exposing my hidden forearm and wrist, all the way up to where her panties are pushed to the side and I'm buried inside her.

I curl the fingers of my free hand around the back of her neck, thumb stroking along the edge of her jaw. "You like watching what I'm doing to you, Blaire?"

She fists the fabric and moans again. "Yes."

"You gonna be a good girl and come all over my hand?" I pump faster, taking cues from the way her breath catches.

"Oh God," she groans and tries to close her legs, but her knees hit my hips. And then her orgasm hits—she contracts around my fingers, hips swiveling as she rides my hand.

"You are so damn sexy," I assure her.

Before the orgasm wanes, I withdraw my fingers. She makes a plaintive sound, probably unimpressed that I stopped mid-orgasm, but I'm planning to make up for that. I yank her panties down. They get caught up on her boots, but I manage to get them off without shredding them. I grip her by the hip and drag her to the edge of the counter as I drop to my knees.

"What—"

The rest of her question dissolves into a gasp when I lick up her center.

She falls back on one elbow, the other hand sliding into my hair and gripping tight.

"Mmm, just like one of those cream-filled cupcakes you made me eat in front of that bachelorette party." I cover her sex with my mouth. "But tastes even better."

That gets a moan out of her, slightly embarrassed, but also totally turned on based on the way she rolls her hips and rides my tongue back to another orgasm.

As soon as I rise up, she grabs the nape of my neck with one hand and fuses her mouth to mine. She mumbles something completely unintelligible, mostly because she's sucking on my tongue. She frantically searches for the waistband of my underwear with the other one and jams her hand down the front, freeing me from my boxers.

She breaks the kiss. "You have condoms, right?"

I pull my wallet from my back pocket, flip it open, and slap it on the counter so I can retrieve the condom that's been in there since before August.

As soon as it's in my hand, Blaire nabs it and squints at the date before she tears it open. Her tongue peeks out as she rolls it down my length and uses her foot—the boots are still on, and I'm still wearing my pants—to pull me closer.

"Hold on. Raise your arms."

She frowns but complies, maybe because the orgasms have made her less argumentative, or possibly she's just as ready as I am for sex, even after two orgasms. I grab the bottom of her dress and lift it over her head. It messes up her perfect hair a little, but all that does is make her sexier.

And totally naked.

"You're a vision, Blaire." Anticipation makes my erection kick in my fist, but I force myself to slow it down for a beat. I drag the head of my condom-covered length along her sex. "You ready for me?"

"So damn ready." She bites her lip.

"You want slow and soft or fast and hard?" I line myself up and meet her hot, needy gaze.

She gives me a saucy grin. "Surprise me."

I chuckle. "Such a good bad girl." I grab her hips to steady her as I push inside.

She scrambles to lock her hands around the back of my neck. When I'm sure she's latched on good and tight I pull back out, almost all the way before I thrust again. Her jaw goes slack and her eyes roll up on a deep groan.

"Okay?" I ask, before I do it again.

"Yes. Please don't stop."

I shift her so she's right at the edge of the counter and pump into her, taking my cues from her moans and her pleas not to stop. As it turns out, Blaire seems to be a fan of hard and fast.

It doesn't take long before I'm warning her I'm about to come. I can always improve endurance on round two. She pries one hand from my neck and dips her fingers between her thighs. "Hold on, I'm so close."

I'm teetering on the edge, barely hanging on. "Listen to you, wanting more when you've come twice already."

"I know, I know, but it's so good. Please, Ronan."

"Better work fast," I warn.

I try to think of something, anything to stop the inevitable, but Blaire's lip is caught between her teeth, pressing in hard, and her fingers are moving at a furious pace between her legs, as if she's trying to light a damn fire.

I thrust one last time before the orgasm rockets down my spine, and I explode. That sensation is magnified a thousand-fold when Blaire contracts around me.

My legs threaten to give out, so I lean against the counter, letting it take some of my weight while I regain the ability to function. Blaire runs her fingers through my hair.

Eventually I lift my head and kiss a path up her shoulder to her mouth.

"Hey."

"Hey." She nibbles my bottom lip. "So that was fun."

I laugh, which makes her gasp and clench and my chuckle

turns into a groan as I slowly ease out. I remove the condom, tie it off and toss it in the garbage by the sink. "You're gonna stay the night, right?"

She blows out a breath. "Well, I mean, it's probably a good idea since I've been pretty greedy and I think we probably need to even out the orgasm totals so I'm not winning by such a wide margin."

@the_knightcap:

The hangover only lasts a day, but the memories last a lifetime.

♡ ✉ ✎   ☆

chapter seventeen

AFTER THE ORGASMS

Blaire

I wake up to Ronan wrapped around me, although it's the sound of a phone ringing that drags me out of the delicious sleep haze. Based on the tone, it's not mine.

"Ronan?"

He grunts and shifts his hips.

I'm not entirely convinced he's awake.

His tattooed arm is wrapped around me, his forearm across my chest, his hand tucked under my shoulder, fingers curling around the back. I think we've been spooning the entire night.

While I can certainly believe last night happened because the attraction is strong with this one, what I didn't expect, and maybe should have, was exactly what kind of lover Ronan would be. Demanding, intense, giving, and insanely attentive.

We stumbled into his bed at four in the morning, and I

would have gone to sleep wearing those steel-toed boots if he hadn't been lucid enough to take them off for me. I did not have a chance to make good on my promise to even out our orgasms because we promptly passed out.

I crane my neck to check the clock on the nightstand. It's already one in the afternoon. That's not a huge surprise, given the ridiculous time we went to bed or the fact that we've both been running on a massive sleep deficit.

Regardless, sleeping the entire day away seems like a waste, since I have so few free ones. I wiggle around in Ronan's arm and he mutters something about being impatient and greedy and nuzzles into my neck.

His phone goes off again, and then again a minute later. Someone is clearly trying to get hold of him.

"Ronan, your phone keeps going off."

"I'm not awake." His raspy sleep voice does tingly things to my body, specifically in the area between my thighs.

"Then how come you're talking to me?"

"I'm not. You're dreaming."

I laugh and he rubs up against me.

"I can go get your phone for you so you don't have to leave this bed," I offer.

"No."

I try another tactic. "I need to use the bathroom, and when I come back I can help even out the lopsided orgasm tally from last night."

He releases me from his hold, rolls onto his back, and throws the covers off, giving me a great view of how excited he is about that prospect. "We'll be right here waiting for you."

Muscles ache that I didn't even know existed. And my tailbone is sore, probably from the counter sex. I use the bathroom first, then go in search of his phone. I find it on the edge of the kitchen counter; it looks as if we very nearly knocked it onto the floor last night. It starts ringing again on my way back to the bedroom.

"Six missed calls in the past twenty minutes. I think you should probably answer before we get sidetracked with extracurriculars." I toss the phone on the bed beside him.

He eyes it like it's a poisonous spider. He's ridiculously appealing, lying in bed, hair sleep-messed, pillow lines on his cheek, body art on display. I want to spend some time exploring all the designs and learning what each one means. After morning sex. Or afternoon sex, as it were. I climb back into bed and snuggle into his warm body. He slips his arm under me and pulls me closer. His lips find my temple as he glances at his phone.

"Oh shit, it's after one?" Ronan brings the device to his ear. "Hey, brother, I know I'm late. I'm sorry. It was a busy night and I slept in." He's silent for a few seconds. "I just woke up. Give me an hour and start without me if you need to, but save me a few of the cinnamon raisin ones, please. No, fuck off. And I'm bringing a friend." He ends the call and tosses his phone on the nightstand.

"What's going on?"

"We have to go to Gramps's place in a bit."

"We?"

"Yeah, you're coming with. It's a family tradition that we get together on New Year's Day. I was supposed to be there at noon, but forgot to set my alarm. I'm not letting you out of my sight for the rest of the day. But first, orgasms."

Half an hour later we have a very quick shower since our antics have put us even further behind. I'm forced to put my dress from last night back on. Not ideal, but then I didn't expect to ring in the New Year in Ronan's bed.

We have to Uber to the bar to get Ronan's truck before we can do anything else. "We'll stop at your place on the way so you don't have to wear last night's dress again."

"That'd be great." I slide into the passenger seat.

Since we're already running late, later than before, I rush up and decide to forgo the dress today, and throw on a pair of jeans and a sweater. I don't often wear jeans, but I do own a few cute pairs. I also pull my hair up into a ponytail. I'm mostly makeup free, but I give my lashes a quick swipe with the mascara brush and throw on a coat of lip gloss. I shrug into my winter coat and rush back down to Ronan, who's busy scrolling through his phone.

I slide back into the passenger seat and buckle up. His eyes move over my legs and up my thighs. From mid-thigh up, they're covered by my coat. "Is this okay? I don't need to be more formal, do I?"

"No. You look great. Jeans are perfect." He puts the truck into gear. "I've just never seen you in a pair before."

His gaze lingers on my legs before he shifts his focus to the road.

"So who's all going to be there?"

"My brothers, their significant others, and Lars may or may not come. Depends on what he got up to after the bar closed." Lars had a lot of attention last night. And I'm pretty sure three girls took advantage of the mistletoe hanging over the bar, and that was only what I saw when I wasn't too busy serving drinks. "Daniel is the oldest. He's thirty-seven, and a big-time financial advisor. His wife, Celia, is a teacher."

"Is she the pregnant one?"

Ronan nods. "Yup. And she's kind of at that weird in-between stage where she just looks like she's put on weight but there isn't enough of a bump that you can be sure she's pregnant, so she's taken to wearing shirts that advertise the fact that she hasn't eaten too many Christmas cookies, and my brother is ridiculous about it. So fucking proud that his sperm managed to hit the mark."

I chuckle at that. "Aw, that's kind of cute, though, isn't it?"

"Kind of, I guess. Mostly it makes me want to gag. You'll see what I mean."

"I literally cannot imagine Maddy or Skylar having children. God forbid they don't get a full night's sleep or have to change a messy diaper." I'd ask Ronan how he feels about kids, but I don't feel like that's a great conversation post first-sexy-times sleepover. "Okay, so Daniel is the oldest and he's married to Celia, who's a teacher and is pregnant. And your other brother, is he married, too?"

"Engaged, actually. Aiden and Leslie have been together for eight years, and living together for six, so the wedding is pretty much a formality. They were going to elope in Vegas, but she's an only child and her mom would have been devastated if she didn't have a real ceremony, so they decided a destination wedding was the best option."

"Oh, that's fun."

"We'll see. She's also in finance, and so is half of her family, so most dinner conversations revolve around the state of the stock market when they're all together."

"That sounds..."

"Boring?"

"Normal?" I offer.

"Boringly normal. Anyway, with Celia there we'll at least have some balance and I'm sure they'll ask you all sorts of questions and try to get you to let them manage your financial portfolio."

"I don't have much of a financial portfolio to speak of, so I'm not sure I'd be worth managing."

"Buttercream and Booze is doing amazingly well, though."

"Oh yes, definitely. But I'm putting pretty much everything I have into it right now, so there's not much extra to play around with. For now, anyway." I'm hopeful things keep going the way they are, but with Dick and Bobby's across the street we're bound to see a dip, at least while it's shiny and new. Hopefully it will all balance out after the initial excitement is over.

Ronan taps the steering wheel. "I really think it's commendable that you're doing it all on your own."

"It makes the reward of success that much greater, you know?"

"Yeah. I can see that, especially for someone like you." We pass over the freeway, heading away from Pioneer Square and the downtown area into the more residential neighborhoods.

"Someone like me?"

"You come from this family who could easily push you around, but you managed to stand your ground and prove to them that you can make your own mark. And they don't even really know." Ronan makes a right down a quiet residential street with older homes that have been well maintained.

"Their version of success and mine aren't the same. I don't want creepy statues with hard-ons all over my house. Or so much space that I could literally get lost on the way to my bedroom and never find my way back. I just want to do what I love and be surrounded by the people I care about."

"I feel exactly the same way." He gives my hand a squeeze, then pulls into the driveway of a quaint, brick, two-story house.

When we reach the front door, I have a moment of panic. "Oh no! I'm showing up empty-handed. Maybe we should stop somewhere and grab a bottle of wine? There has to be a convenience store open somewhere that sells wine, right?"

"Don't worry about it, Blaire. There's going to be more food and booze than an army can consume. And even if we found an open store, all they're going to have is cheap wine that tastes like tomorrow's headache. Trust me when I say it's okay that we're coming empty-handed. Plus I dropped stuff off a few days ago for this occasion, and my brew shed is out back, so we're all set."

He doesn't knock on the door, just lets himself in, ushering me ahead of him. I'm greeted by the most delicious combination of scents. I breathe in cinnamon and cloves along with hints of citrus and cranberry. But more pungent is the aroma of something fried and sweet. "Oh, wow, what is that smell?"

"New Year's cookies, but they're more like donuts and they're the perfect cure for a post–New Year's Eve hangover."

"I'm not hungover, though."

"Well, we're about to start drinking again, so these should help prevent one." He helps me out of my coat and groans. "Ah hell, Blaire."

"What? Is everything okay?" I'm about to spin around to see what's going on, but he grabs me by the hips.

He pulls me back into him, dropping his head so his lips are at my ear. "These jeans are going to kill me. Now I have a perfect visual of all those curves you keep hidden under those skirts. It's going to be a long, uncomfortable afternoon for me."

I grin. Unlike Maddy and Skylar, I have curves. I learned very early on to embrace those curves and love the hell out of them.

One Halloween—around the time the parent swap

happened—I dressed as June Cleaver. And surprisingly, I felt the most comfortable in my skin. Maybe because my conventional family unit had been obliterated. Maybe because I liked the idea of an uncomplicated life. Of pot roasts, family dinners, and parents who worked normal jobs.

While I might not fit the entire June Cleaver mold, considering I have my own business, it's the style I adopted so I could hold on to that comforting idea of family values and morals. Plus I love dresses, but I don't mind sliding into a pair of jeans once in a while, possibly more often if this is the kind of reaction I get.

"I thought I heard the door. Oh, Miss Cupcake! When Ronan said he was bringing a friend I didn't realize it would be you." Ronan's grandfather ambles slowly toward us. "What a pleasant surprise." He grins, and his eyes almost disappear under his bushy brows. I would guess he's somewhere around eighty. He's a few inches shorter than Ronan, although I'm sure he was closer to the same height in his younger years, before his shoulders rounded.

"Hi, Mr. Knight. I hope it's not an imposition." I've met Ronan's grandfather a couple of times in passing, and we've exchanged hellos and an introduction, but I've always been busy during the day and he's never been around by the end of the evening.

"Not at all, dearie. And you can call me Henry; no mister anything is necessary, or Gramps works if yer comfortable with that." He winks and clasps my hand between his gnarled fingers. "I wondered when my grandson would finally find his balls and ask ya out on a date."

"Really, Gramps?" I can practically feel Ronan's embarrassment.

"What? She's been all you can talk about for months, riles you right up and puts a smile on yer face. It was bound to happen when ya got yer head outta yer ass."

"Okay, Gramps, you're killin' my game."

"Is that Ronan?" Another man appears in an adjacent doorway. Based on his facial features, he's definitely one of Ronan's brothers. He's shorter than Ronan, but just as broad and athletic, with the same hair and eye coloring, except he has a little gray flirting at the temples. "'Bout time you got here!" He pulls his brother into a hug, and they exchange firm back pats. He lowers his voice, keeping Ronan close. "Celia's still got freaking morning sickness, so she can't help with shit. And Leslie thinks every single cookie needs to be uniform in shape, so we've only managed one damn batch. All I want to do is drink scotch and eat cookies. Help a brother out."

"I'm on it, don't worry." Ronan pulls me into his side. "And I brought reinforcements. Daniel, this is Blaire, and she can bake every single person here under the table."

"Hi, Blaire." He extends his hand. His palms are soft, like the most strenuous thing he does is swing a golf club. "Ronan didn't mention having a girlfriend at Christmas."

"Oh, I'm not his girlfriend." I glance at Ronan.

His gaze meets mine and he shrugs with a questioning expression. "Well, I mean..."

"Am I your girlfriend?" It's an actual question, because riding his metaphorical bologna pony doesn't necessarily mean we're a thing.

"I brought you to a family function, so that generally means I wouldn't have a problem introducing you as my girlfriend."

Daniel snorts, and Gramps's smile widens.

"I invited you to a family function when you and I were barely civil to each other." I'm not sure why I feel the need to bring this up, because all it's doing is making this awkward situation even more awkward, since Daniel and Gramps are ping-ponging between us, watching this go down with something like gleeful amusement.

"Yeah, but we had a connection right from the start. And you invited me because you felt guilty, so it wasn't an actual date. And come to think of it, I was a shield more than anything." Ronan's grinning, like he finds this entire thing entertaining as well.

My cheeks heat at his instant-connection reference since he's correct, even though I was determined not to find him sexy, at least when he was being inflexible and breaking my unicorn glasses. "You weren't a shield. It was a spur-of-the-moment invitation, and yes I felt some guilt, but that wasn't the sole impetus for asking you to come along. I mean, look at you." I motion to his casual attire, which consists of a long-sleeved shirt, pushed up to expose half of his forearms, and his dark wash jeans. "You're not exactly hard on the eyes. And while you were certainly a convenient distraction from my family's lunacy, it wasn't the dominant motivating factor."

Ronan cocks a brow. "I see how it is. You just wanted to objectify me."

I shrug. "Didn't hurt to have someone nice to look at while the insanity ensued."

Daniel claps Ronan on the shoulder. "You've finally met your match. This is so great. Just don't get hitched before Aiden and Leslie, or she's never going to let him live it down, and it'll be the rest of us who suffer."

Ronan gives him a *what the hell* look. "Thanks for making this introduction not awkward at all, Dan."

"I'm here for you, bro. Now please get your ass in the kitchen so I can eat some damn donuts."

"Watch yer language in front of Blaire," Gramps warns. He's been quietly standing off to the side, hands clasped in front of him, rocking back on his heels. Until the profanity anyway. Now his expression is adorably stern.

"It's fine, Henry." I put a comforting hand on his arm and wink. "I'm a big girl; I've heard all the bad words."

He pats my hand. "Oh, I'm sure you have. And they're not donuts, they're New Year's cookies. Dottie could nae stand it when the boys called them donuts. Drove her batty. Rest her soul." He makes the sign of the cross and blinks a few times, eyes shadowed in sadness for a moment before they clear. "Come, dear, let's get you a drink."

A full bar is set up, and I opt for one of Ronan's beers, because they're delicious and if I sip it slowly I won't have to worry about getting tipsy too fast.

We find Leslie and Aiden in the kitchen. This time Ronan introduces me as his girlfriend, and I don't dispute him. Aiden pulls Ronan in for a hug. "Thank God you're here, man. Save me, please."

Leslie looks frazzled and like she would rather be doing anything other than standing in front of a pot of boiling oil.

The kitchen probably hasn't been renovated since sometime in the nineties if I had to guess based on the cabinets. There's a new stainless steel stove, fridge, and dishwasher, though. I'm assuming either Ronan or his brothers were responsible for the updates to bring his grandfather into the twenty-first century, at least from an appliance standpoint.

I survey the counter, the giant bowl of dough, the variety of adds-ins in the form of cinnamon and sugarcoated apple chunks, chopped dried fruit, and raisins. "Oh! It's *oliebollen*!"

"Huh?" Everyone in the kitchen turns to look at me.

"*Oliebollen*. Mennonite New Year's cookies. They're the same thing. I loved these as a kid!" I motion to the spread.

"You know what these are?" Leslie asks. She sounds somewhere between hopeful and desperate.

"I haven't had them since I was a teenager, but definitely. My grandmother was Mennonite."

"Seriously?" Ronan's shock is actually reasonable.

"Non-practicing. She passed when I was fourteen, but up until then we had *oliebollen* every New Year's. They just bring back so many great memories." Before my family let all their crazy hang out. I realize I'm getting misty, which is embarrassing in front of a bunch of people I've just met who are related to my new boyfriend.

Thankfully, Leslie seems oblivious. "Do you know how to make them?"

"Blaire runs Buttercream and Booze, the place next to The Knight Cap."

"This is Alice in Wonderland?" Aiden's eyes dart between the two of us. "I mean. Damn."

"You've mentioned me before?" I arch a brow, waiting to see how he's going to try to get out of this.

"Mentioned you before? Dude was obsessed at the end of the summer, pretty much every single time I got on the phone with him he was moaning about how good your cupcakes were."

"Aiden," Ronan snaps.

"What?"

"You're a dick."

"Yeah. I know. I have zero social skills; just ask Leslie." He thumbs over his shoulder at his fiancée.

"He's right," Leslie chimes in. "But his brain is big and full of numbers, and I find that hopelessly sexy, so I decided to keep him." She passes her apron to me. "Please help us. All I want to do is eat donuts. I've been saving myself for these so all I've had today is a yogurt cup with blueberries and the ones I've made so far aren't all that great." She pokes at the overdone balls.

"They look super for your first time!" I lie. "Give me twenty minutes, and I'll have a fresh batch for you."

"You don't have to do that. I'm fully prepared to make cookies," Ronan interjects.

"Or we could do it together." I pull the apron over my head.

He grins. "Okay. Sure."

"Sheesh, I feel like I'm watching foreplay. Come on, babe. Let's leave them alone." Aiden claps Ronan on the shoulder. "Make sure you wash your hands if you put your fingers in places you're not supposed to."

"Aiden! Enough, or she'll never come back!" Leslie swats him on the butt with a dishtowel.

"Get your head out of the gutter. I meant places like his *nose*. All the pheromones must be getting to you. Should we go upstairs for a few minutes and check on that light bulb that needs to be changed?"

"What—" Her confusion turns into an eye roll. "Celia is napping upstairs, but nice try."

He ushers her out of the kitchen, leaving the two of us alone. I split the dough into several bowls so I can add the cinnamon apples, dried fruit mix, and the raisins to some. While I work on the add-ins, Ronan puts on a seventies-era apron and starts dropping balls of dough into the pot of boiling oil.

"Sorry about the razzing from my brothers. And the

girlfriend designation. That probably should've been a conversation prior to me opening my big mouth."

I shrug, not wanting to give him a hard time about it. "It's cute."

He cringes. "Cute?"

"Okay, maybe *cute* is the wrong word, considering you've turned a really horrible green color. How about sweet? I think it's sweet that you introduced me as your girlfriend. I like you, Ronan, a lot. And as your girlfriend, I can say I'm definitely interested in repeating the events of last night on a very regular basis."

He pulls me into him. "I can certainly accommodate that request. Once we're finished stuffing our faces with donuts." He gives me a quick peck, and then we get back to work.

Half an hour later, we have three bowls piled high with *oliebollen*. We have honey, sugar, powdered sugar, cinnamon sugar, and a delicious maple butter for dipping.

Celia comes down from her nap as we're getting settled at the dining room table. Ronan introduces me, and she promptly bursts into tears, blubbering about how she's so glad Ronan is finally settling down and how they've always wanted him to find someone.

Once she's no longer sobbing all over Daniel's shirt, he tucks her into the table and flits around, making sure she's comfortable. Then he loads up a plate for her, careful to make sure the maple dipped ones don't touch the cinnamon sugar.

"Sorry about that," Ronan mutters as we fill our plates.

"I think it's sweet that your family cares so much about you. It's nice to see." So much nicer than my boyfriend-stealing sister and my attempted-boyfriend-thieving cousin.

No one talks about which famous person they ran into last week, or the newest keto diet, or which plastic surgeon botched up what surgery. As predicted, the stock market comes up a couple of times, but Ronan is quick to shut down the hard sales pitch Daniel lobs my way.

They regale me with stories about Ronan and his science experiments as a teen. Apparently the desire to brew started early. Pre-legal drinking age early. By sixteen he'd made his first batch of moonshine.

He shrugs. "Booze was expensive and hard to get ahold of. I found a way around it."

After we stuff ourselves silly, we retire to the living room. Just like the rest of this house, it's a time warp back to the nineties. The carpet is an awful rose color, the furniture is boxy and worn, and the curtains boast a garish, retro floral pattern. It's horrible and homey and wonderful.

"I just need to help Daniel with something. You'll be okay for a few?" Ronan asks.

"Of course, you go right ahead."

He kisses me on the cheek and I cross over to the fireplace so I can check out the pictures on the mantel. A sixtieth wedding anniversary photo sits in the middle, Henry and the late Dottie dressed up as though they were ready to party. As I take in the background I realize they're in The Knight Cap.

"That was my Dottie." Henry picks up the framed photo, his smile fond but also sad.

"You look like you belonged together."

"Aye. We did. Met when we were just kids. I was eighteen and a fool. She smiled at me and I was a goner."

"Just like that, huh?"

"Sometimes you just know." His thumb smooths along the edge of the frame.

"I believe that. I love the wall of photos in The Knight Cap. It's like watching the progress of your love through still shots."

"Every year I made sure to put a picture on that wall so we could walk by and see our good times together. I know in this day people don't really make photo albums, but we always had one going."

"Will you show me?"

Henry's face lights up. "I'd be happy to." He ambles over to a bookshelf lined with photo albums. It's five shelves high, and there have to be at least ten albums on each shelf. He taps his lip. "Where to start. Ah!" He lifts an album from the shelf and motions for me to take a seat on the couch.

Setting the album between us, he flips to the first page. Old, yellowed, black and white images with captions and dates line each page.

The very first image is of a young woman, a teenager based on the softness of her features and the innocence of her smile.

"That's the first picture I ever took of Dottie." He taps the image. "Our parents were against us dating. I was a few years older and she was serving tables at the time, but love doesn't care about approval. We kept it a secret."

"Eventually they must have realized you were made for each other, though."

"Aye. Got married in that bar the day she turned eighteen, and then there was nothing anyone could do to keep us apart." He winks. "And grandbabies have a way of making people come around no matter what. We did every little thing together. She was my entire world for more than sixty years."

"I can see that." I flip to the next page and find more pictures of a teenage Dottie in various stages of laughter.

He clears his throat. "She had a heart condition. Born with it, and there wasn't a thing we could do to fix it. Despite that she loved damn hard, and you couldn't stop her from doing things she wanted to because she always said life was too short to be afraid of the end."

"Sounds like a smart woman."

"She was damn smart. Would've been some Wall Street working woman if she'd been born a few decades later. She's the one who kept The Knight Cap going all those years. She made me promise if something happened to her that I'd stick around to make sure our boy Ronan got himself settled."

"There's that big heart you're talking about."

"Aye. She loved that boy like he was her own, 'specially after Jim and Cindy's accident. Broke all of our hearts, but

Ronan's the most, I think. He's a lot like me, needs a partner even if he's done his damnedest to avoid it since we lost his parents." He shakes his head, like he's breaking himself out of a sad spell. "Anyway, the moment I heard about you giving him hell I thought: There she is, the reason he's back here with me. She's the woman who's going to settle his restless soul."

"Restless soul? He seems pretty settled here."

"Now he is," Gramps agrees. "But when he was younger he had a hard time staying in one place. He was always on the move. Even when he was in college, he took on a million things. Except for when he had a girlfriend."

"Did he have a lot of girlfriends?"

Gramps gives me a sly look. "That I met? No. But you better believe Ronan was serious when he brought a lady to a family event like this one."

"So you've met a few girlfriends then?" Ronan hasn't even mentioned an ex, although I'm sure there must have been some along the way.

"Only one, other than you."

"What happened?" I wave the question away. "You don't need to answer that. It's personal and I'm just curious."

"It's okay." He pats my hand. "Ronan isn't likely to talk about it, but it might help you understand him better. After his parents passed, he transferred colleges between his sophomore and junior year. I think his heart was already too broken, and he didn't want to risk it getting any more mangled than it was, so he found a way to end things without causing either of them too much heartache."

"That couldn't have been easy for either of them."

"It wasn't, but he put all of his energy into school and working at the bar. He went on dates, but it never got serious, which was hard to watch, because Ronan has a big heart, and he needs someone who's going to take care of it." He winks and squeezes my hand. "Someone like you."

We don't leave Ronan's grandfather's until late in the afternoon.

"That was so much fun." I buckle myself in. "Your family is so . . . normal."

"I don't know if I'd exactly call us normal, but I'm glad you enjoyed yourself."

"I had a fantastic time. Your brothers are great, and I can see why you and Henry are so close. He really loves you, you know."

Ronan nods. "Yeah. I'm pretty lucky to have him."

"That bar is so special to him. He has so many fantastic memories all caught up in that place, it's a wonder he let you renovate."

"Well, it helps that I made the suggestions a few years back and Grams had been on board. Gramps had a harder time with the possible changes because of how much of his heart is tied up in the place."

"I can see how that would be difficult. What do think is going to happen to The Knight Cap once you start your brewery?" It's heartbreaking to think of that legacy coming to an end.

"I don't know. I'm hopeful Lars will take more of an interest in the management side of things, but he's young yet, so we'll see." He taps the steering wheel, his expression hard to read, but it softens quickly. "We should stop and grab your SUV, shouldn't we?"

"Oh yes! That's a good idea, then I don't have to worry about how I'm getting to work in the morning."

He pulls into the lot behind the building and parks beside my SUV, tapping the wheel restlessly. "It's still early, did you want to come back to my place?"

"Or you could come back to mine?" My apartment isn't as nice as Ronan's, but it's cute and homey and a few minutes closer so getting up and out in the morning won't be as much of a challenge.

"I could definitely do that." His gaze moves over me in a slow sweep. "I haven't quite had my fill of you yet, today."

"I feel exactly the same way." I lean over and kiss him on the cheek. "See you back at my place, then."

@buttercreamandbooze:

Have your cupcake and eat it, too.

chapter eighteen

PURSE STRINGS

Blaire

W"ow, you're in a good mood," Daphne observes the next morning. "It's almost like you've got the post-laid afterglow going on."

I stop writing the daily special on the chalkboard to look at her.

Her eyes go wide. "Holy hell! You *did* get laid!"

I slap her arm. "I don't think the people outside heard you!"

She rushes toward the front door. I'm not sure if she's kidding or actually planning to scream it down the street, but I chase after her and slide my body in front of the door before she can open it and shout my private information to the world.

She rolls her eyes. "I wasn't really going to tell the entire neighborhood, you loon. What the hell happened?" She grabs me by the shoulders. "Oh my God, you slept with Ronan, didn't you?"

Judging by her expression, I don't need to respond with words.

"You did! How did that happen?"

"Well, Daphne, when a man and a woman get naked—"

She waves her hand in the air to stop me. "Don't be sarcastic. I mean, I guess it was bound to happen because you two have turned bickering into foreplay, but what happened to make it finally happen?"

"Mistletoe."

"Mistletoe?"

"He kissed me under the mistletoe at midnight on New Year's."

Her face falls. "That's actually romantic."

"Why do you look so disappointed?"

"Because I assumed you two would get into an argument and end up hate fucking each other or something. But that just sounds sweet."

"If it makes you feel better, he's a bit of a dirty talker."

Her expression is a mix of surprise and glee. "He is not!"

"Oh, he very much is."

"So the sex was stellar? He's got it going on?" She motions to her crotch.

"Oh yeah, he totally has it going on, and the sex was mind-blowing. He actually stayed over last night." I can feel my face heating up, partially at the memories of what happened between the sheets, and on top of them, and in the shower.

"Whoa, wait, so this isn't a one-time thing?"

I'm not sure what to make of her shock. "Uh, no, not a one-time thing."

She props her hip against the counter, concern furrowing her brow. "Is that really a good idea? I mean, sure, scratch the itch, but now you're what? Sleeping with the enemy on the regular?"

"He's not the enemy."

"Aren't you the one who said he's your competition? You're both in the semifinals for Best Bar, and he's got a lead on you." She makes a hand motion below the waist. "You don't want to let the D distract you when you're in the home stretch."

She makes a good point, one I'm not all that interested in admitting, if I'm going to be perfectly honest with myself. It's been a very, very long time since I've had great sex, and while she's right about not losing sight of my goals, I feel like I can balance having my cupcake and eating it, too.

I motion across the street to the gaudy, ugly glowing D&B sign. "We have bigger competition to worry about now."

Daphne raises a hand. "I know. I just don't want you to get taken for a ride." She rolls her eyes when I arch a brow. "You know what I mean. I don't want you to get taken advantage of. He's a smooth mother-fudger and damn pretty and you're gorgeous and definitely beddable. I want to make sure he's not using you to get what he wants aside from orgasms. There were orgasms, right?"

"Several." I smirk. "I don't think he's using me. I mean, he introduced me to his family yesterday."

"Seriously?"

"Yup. We went over for New Year's cookies at his grandpa's place and I met his brothers and their wives. Guys don't usually do the family-intro thing when their plan is a hump and dump."

"This is true." Daphne leans against the counter. "So this is a real thing?"

I shrug. "I think so. He introduced me as his girlfriend."

"Oh, wow. You must've been amazing in the sack." She rounds the cupcake display case. "You need to tell me all about it over coffee. I need details."

I fully expect there to be a bit of a lull in business after New Year's, especially with Dick and Bobby's opening across the street. January can be a slow month for businesses, everyone tightening their purse strings thanks to big credit card bills post-holiday spend.

What I don't expect is for B&B to be a virtual ghost town apart from when Ronan and I have our joint events. I was barely scraping by before, and now I'm veering into dangerous territory, dipping into my overdraft more and more often to make ends meet.

Even the attention we managed to garner from our New Year's party on social media doesn't buffer the impact of D&B opening up across the street. The great press from Tori Taylor and the fact that both The Knight Cap and B&B have made it into the top ten Best Bars doesn't seem to be helping me keep my head above water.

I'm terrified, because Tori Taylor is planning her trip to Seattle this month and now more than ever, I need business to pick up.

To combat the slowdown, Ronan and I coordinate more joint events with deals and promotions to help entice the college kids to come to us rather than Dick and Bobby's. I try not to let my desperation show, or to let Ronan know how bad things are getting. I know he's feeling the pinch, too, but I don't think it's nearly as dire for him as it is for me since The Knight Cap is long established and he only has to recover the renovation costs.

It's a Thursday morning and tonight I have a trivia night, followed by karaoke over at Ronan's bar. Our duets have become a thing over the past few months, and we've started allowing patrons to request songs. I figure it's a smart co-event with Tori coming to town because it always generates tons of posts and lots of interaction on social media before and after.

It's only nine in the morning when Ronan drops by, far earlier than usual for him, even on an event night. "Hey, you got a minute? I need to show you something next door."

"Sure, everything okay?"

"Oh yeah, I just want you to check something out."

I leave Callie in charge and follow Ronan next door to The Knight Cap.

He ushers me down the hall to his office. "In here."

I step inside, expecting there to be some kind of surprise, but it looks like the same old in-need-of-updating office. "Okay. What do I need to check out?"

I turn around and he takes my face between his hands, tips my head back, and slants his mouth over mine. I gasp in surprise but sink into the kiss.

His hand eases down my side and curves around my butt, over my dress, and he pulls me closer, grinding his erection against my stomach.

I fight a moan, not wanting anyone to know there are non-business-related things going on behind Ronan's office door. His other hand leaves my cheek and his ancient and very squeaky rolling chair bangs into the wall. A few seconds later he picks me up and deposits me on the desk.

"What're you doing?"

"Reenacting the fantasy I've had since New Year's." His left hand slides under my dress, up my thigh.

I have to press my knees together so they don't automatically part for him. "Someone will hear."

"They won't."

"I can't be that quiet and you can't *not* say dirty things." I'd like to say I can bite my tongue, or his shirt, or something, but whatever his plan is, there is no way in hell he's going to be able to keep his mouth shut and neither will I.

He gives me a knowing, satisfied grin. "We're alone. There's no one else here."

"No one?"

"No one. I came in early on purpose." He slides his other hand under my skirt and up my thigh.

"So you planned this?"

"Only after waking up for the seventh day in a row from the same damn dream."

"Which was what?" I lift my butt, allowing him to drag my panties down. I help by removing my crinoline.

"A repeat of New Year's, except on my desk." He tosses my panties and crinoline on his chair and drops to his knees, making good on that repeat performance from start to finish.

When I open his office door, I'm a little sweaty and definitely flushed, but oh-so-sated. I accidentally kick something on the floor.

"What's that?" Ronan grabs me by the hips to keep from knocking me over since he bumps into me from behind when I bend to retrieve it.

I hold it up for Ronan to see. "Air freshener?"

"Weird. I don't remember leaving that in the hall, but clearly I'm on the ball. Oooh, and it's festive scented." He releases a spray into his office. It smells like a cinnamon roll. It's probably a good idea since it helps cover the latex and sex.

He walks me down the hall and I come to an abrupt stop when I spot Lars behind the bar, cutting lemon wedges. Ronan bumps into me from behind. "Oh, hey!" My voice has that high pitch associated with surprise and embarrassment.

He pauses his chopping to tip his chin in our direction. "Hey."

"Lars? How long have you been here?" Ronan sounds more annoyed than embarrassed.

"Long enough." A wide grin spreads across his face.

"Oh my gosh," I mutter as Ronan ushers me down the hall toward the back entrance.

Once we're out of hearing range I turn to face Ronan. "He heard me."

"Us. He heard *us*." He rubs his jaw.

I throw my hands up in the air. "I thought you said we were alone!"

"We were." He glances at his wristwatch. "Looks like we got carried away with the foreplay."

I twist his wrist so I can check the time. "It's ten! We were in there for an hour!"

He shrugs. "I was hungry, and you didn't seem to be in a hurry."

I poke him in the chest. "This isn't funny! What if that had been Gramps and not Lars?"

"Gramps doesn't leave the house before eleven these days."

"Not the freaking point and you know it."

"Babe, relax. Lars isn't going to care, and it wasn't Gramps so we're safe."

"But he probably heard me coming and saying...things!"

"I'm sure he didn't press his ear to the door. He probably passed by, heard some noise, got cheeky with the spray, and steered clear."

"You can't know that."

"Well, he better hope that's what he did. Look, I'm sorry. Next time we'll wait until after closing before we get freaky in my office."

"What makes you think there's going to be a next time?"

Ronan cocks a brow and smirks. "Because you loved that just as much as I did."

I don't respond to that, because he's right; I did love it. "I have to get back. Callie is probably wondering where I am." I turn to stalk off, but Ronan grabs my arm.

"Hey. Don't walk away angry." He pulls me in for a hug and presses his lips to my temple.

"I'm embarrassed, not angry," I mumble against his chest.

"I love the sound of your orgasms," he murmurs in my ear. "I love the way you moan my name. I love that you're not quiet about what feels good for you. It's sexy as hell."

"And now I'm really leaving. We can talk more about that later. When we're not at work and have to function for the rest of the day."

He gives my hip a squeeze and releases me. I stand outside in the cold January morning for a couple of minutes to allow the sweat to dry and the heat in my face to calm before I go back in and apologize for taking as long as I did. Not that I regret it all that much.

As January rolls through, I do everything I can to pull in more customers—fun new cupcakes, bachelorette parties, cupcake-decorating classes in the evenings—but I'm still struggling to compete against D&B's super cheap prices and their endless marketing money. I manage to find a great part-time baker to help alleviate some of the strain on my time and demands. Financially it's going to be a bit of a struggle for a while, but I can't reasonably run a business on no sleep.

On the downside, hiring a new baker means I have to find a way to reduce other costs. I end up cutting back on Callie's hours. It's the beginning of a new semester and the workload is heavy so she's not heartbroken over it, but it still doesn't feel good.

The new part-time baker is great about helping to get the shop open, but cutting back on Callie's hours means I'm working just as many as I was before. There have been a few occasions when I've been able to enjoy sleeping past five in the morning, usually with Ronan, but if business doesn't pick up soon I'm going to have to put an end to those altogether.

The only saving grace seems to be our cohosted events. I'm grateful that Tori is planning her stop around one of those events, because those tend to be the busiest nights. She always makes her appearance a surprise, but based on her previous stops over the past week, Ronan and I predicted she'd be coming our way this week, and we were right.

She stops by during one of my comedy nights and Ronan's live bands. Of course, that morning I got a call from the best of the three comedians saying she had the flu and there was no way she could get up onstage without a bucket and a toilet. I was prepared to host it with just the two comedians, but Lars said he had a friend who was hilarious and would love the opportunity.

His friend was hot, which was a bonus, and had a pretty big following on social media so I took a chance, shuffling the acts around so he could go last. As it turned out, his pretty face was the only palatable thing about his act. It was more frat boy humor than anything my clientele would find funny, so he was met with some embarrassingly pathetic chuckles and not much else.

To make matters worse, Tori has the pleasure of witnessing it firsthand. If she'd shown up at the beginning, when everyone was crying with laughter, it would've made the final act seem a little less awful, but since she's missed the best part, it's taken the shine out of the evening. She stays for a drink and samples the cupcakes, expressing how much she loves the décor and the concept.

She's certainly done her homework, asking about my family and why I chose to go out on my own with a low-key local vibe instead of catering to celebrities. I explain that my heart is in baking and that I wanted the opportunity to prove myself, which she seems to appreciate.

She heads over to The Knight Cap while I close up. I'm feeling disheartened. I know B&B is a great place with an awesome atmosphere, and usually my entertainment is top

notch. Tonight we were packed, not an empty seat in the
house, but if I'm honest with myself, The Knight Cap has
something special—beyond the axe throwing, which I hate to
admit is really fun.

One night when I stayed to help him behind the bar during
a cohosted event, Ronan convinced me to leave on the steel-
toed boots and give it a shot.

Watching Ronan demonstrate how to throw and then getting
all up in my personal space so he could correct my form became
its own brand of foreplay. Every time I hit the target, he'd praise
me, and if I missed he'd step in and give me pointers that con-
sisted mostly of him adjusting my stance. After a while I started
missing on purpose, and eventually he caught on. That night
ended with me pressed up against the wall, legs wrapped around
his waist while he groaned about how sexy I looked wielding an
axe. Obviously, I'm kind of in love with the whole thing now.

It's hard to compete with Ronan's incredible charisma,
not to mention the history and romance connected to The
Knight Cap.

And Tori is certainly not immune, considering the dreamy
look that came over her face when she mentioned Ronan. I
can totally relate, because it's the same look I wear all the time
around him. I finish cleaning up, send my servers home, and
make sure everything is prepped for the morning. In the quiet
that follows, I take a quick look at the books. I'm not entirely
sure what the point is, since I already know I'm balancing on
a fine line these days.

Even more discouraged, I close up and head over to The Knight Cap to check out how Ronan's night is going. Of course the band is on point and the crowd is going wild. I spot Tori over by the bar, chatting it up with Ronan. Every once in a while, she throws her head back and laughs at something he says.

Tori is a stunning, perfect woman. She's camera ready and a successful entrepreneur who travels the world. She's smart, savvy, and gorgeous. Yes, she has a high-profile athlete boy-friend, but there have been some rumors lately about trouble in paradise, and Ronan is a professional flirt. It might be harmless, but I'm a little sensitive after the way my night has gone.

Lars appears beside me from out of nowhere and hands me a shot. "You gotta stop trying to kill her with your laser beam stare."

"Huh?"

"Tori. You look like you want to destroy her. He's not flirting. He's just chatting and really fucking oblivious." Lars is smirking.

"I know he's not flirting." I toss back the shot.

"Your chill is at zero, though. I mean, I know you two got it bad for each other, but I didn't realize it was this bad."

"I don't know what you're talking about." I'm mentally preparing myself to go over and say hello without also saying or doing something stupid. I want to tell Lars his comedian friend sucked, but I figure I'm in too much of a mood not to be a total jerk about it, so I decide to save that for later.

Lars snorts and hands me a cocktail. I don't know where he's keeping the cocktails, or the shots, but I'm not about to say no to them. "Whatever you say, Blaire. Give him a few more minutes before you go over there and stake your claim. I know you're together and stuff, but he wouldn't sabotage you, so you should extend the same courtesy."

"I wouldn't sabotage Ronan!" I say, indignant.

"Not intentionally, but you've got that look in your eye, like you want to catfight her. And I think it's human nature to protect what's yours."

"That's rather insightful. Although, I've never actually been in a fight, and I don't want to get into one with the person who has the potential to help put mine or Ronan's business on the map."

"I don't mean that you'd actually fight her. I think you're more likely to do or say something that could mess up your chances when you're feeling this territorial, so it's best you just hang with me until she moves on." He drapes his arm over my shoulder and gives it a squeeze. "He's going home with you, and that's really the only thing that should matter."

Tori doesn't seem to be in any hurry to move on, and I'm tired and prickly, so I decide home is a better option than spreading my bad mood to Ronan when he's clearly riding the high tonight.

"I'm going to head out."

"You want me to give Ronan a message?"

"That's okay. I'll text him that I'll see him tomorrow."

"You all right to drive?"

"I just had that one shot, and like three sips of this." I pass him my mostly full cocktail.

"You're sure you want to leave?"

"He needs his focus to be where it is, and I don't want to be the clingy girlfriend."

I leave out the front door instead of going through the bar and using the service entrance, mostly so Ronan doesn't see me. I get what Daphne was saying when I first started sleeping with my competition and how it would complicate things. She wasn't wrong. I don't want him to lose, but I also want to win. It's a weird spot to be in, and right now I could really use the positive press to help bolster business.

I shoot Ronan a message when I get home, letting him know I stopped by, but that he and Tori were talking and I didn't want to interrupt, so I'll see him tomorrow. I throw in a couple of kissy-face emojis to make it seem upbeat and not like I'm a jealous girlfriend, or mopey, when in reality I'm both.

I change into a comfy sleep shirt, get my dress ready for tomorrow, and decide I've had enough of today. I brush my teeth, grab a glass of water, and climb into bed. I've just turned off the light when my phone buzzes, not with a message, but a call, from Ronan.

I debate letting it go to voicemail, but I decide that would be a jerk move. It's not Ronan's fault that my last act wasn't great and his band was. Or that he's ridiculously attractive and charming and women go gaga over him. Myself included.

I accept the call. "Hey."

"Hey, yourself. You took off without saying good-bye. I thought I was coming back to your place." There's no accusation in his voice, just a hint of disappointment.

"You were busy with Tori, and I didn't want to interrupt."

He's silent for a moment. "Everything okay?"

"Yeah, just tired after a long day." It's more of an omission than a lie.

"Is this you uninviting me over tonight?" And now there's hurt to go with the disappointment.

I should give myself the night, especially with my mood, but I'm feeling selfish and needy. "Of course not, I always love having you in my bed. I'll leave the door unlocked so you can let yourself in."

"I'll be there in fifteen."

I'm still staring at the ceiling, no longer quite as exhausted as I was when I slid between the sheets. I know I'm going to be tired tomorrow as a result, but my brain is too busy to settle.

When the door to my bedroom creaks open I flick on the lamp beside my bed and whisper "Hi."

"Hey, yourself." I watch as Ronan strips down to his boxer briefs, warmth spreading through my limbs as any residual tiredness fades away, replaced with want. As soon as he joins me in bed, I pull his mouth to mine and lose myself in him.

Half an hour later I'm tucked into his side, my head resting on his shoulder, fingertips tracing the tree limbs that climb his shoulder and morph into birds taking flight. It's a gorgeous, intricate tattoo.

"The band was great tonight," I say softly.

"They were. I was impressed. How was the rest of comedy night?" He'd stopped in during the first act, when everyone was laughing their heads off.

"Started great, fizzled out at the end."

"Oh no, I'm sorry, babe." He presses his lips to my forehead and tips my chin up. "What happened?"

"The last act was a dud. I should have cut it at two when Betty canceled, but I figured it wouldn't hurt to give someone new a chance. I think Tori being there unnerved the guy and he just kind of shit the bed."

"Maybe it's not as bad as you think."

"It is. Or was. It's okay. I'm glad your night went well, though."

"Me, too, but I don't like that yours didn't." His sincerity makes me feel conflicted. I want him to succeed, but I want my own success, as well.

"It would've been nice to make a better impression on Tori. I could really use some positive press and more customers."

"Your place was packed tonight."

"It was, but you know how quiet it's been when we don't

have cohosted events. I don't want to cut Callie's hours more, but if things keep going this way, I might have to."

His brow furrows. "It's that bad?"

I backtrack, not wanting to rain on his parade with my dark cloud. "I'm just being preemptive. I can't afford to go too far into the red, so I have to cut costs where I can." Not to mention I've been pulling out all the stops in anticipation of Tori, and that means spending more than I probably should have.

He's quiet for a few moments. "I have an idea."

"I'm all for one of your ideas because I'm fresh out."

"Why don't we have a street event?"

I adjust my position so I can see his face better. "How do you mean?"

"So when we cohost events both of our businesses see higher returns, right?"

"Definitely."

"What if we apply the same principle to all the restaurants and shops on the street? We could involve everyone and have a big weekend event with a focus on small businesses. We could plan it for Valentine's."

I perk up at the idea. "Like a Love Is in the Air event?"

"Exactly. It could be good for all of us, and a nice middle finger to Dick and Bobby's for screwing it up for the rest of us."

"I love this! And Valentine's is pretty much my favorite!"

"Why am I not surprised?" Ronan tucks my hair behind my ear, smiling wryly. "We can start canvassing tomorrow and see what kind of interest we have. I'm sure we're not the only ones who've been impacted by D&B, and there's no way in hell I'm going to let them steal your dream from you."

My heart stutters, and my worries take a back seat, at least for tonight, because I know we're in this together. Or at least I hope so.

@buttercreamandbooze:

We go together like cupcakes and buttercream.

chapter nineteen

BEST BAR AWARD GOES TO...

Blaire

It turns out that every single small business on the street is interested in being part of the event. The bars and restaurants are feeling the effects of D&B and everyone agrees that the cross-promotion certainly can't hurt.

Ronan sets up a meeting at The Knight Cap, where we come up with a weekend-long themed event that will take place in the middle of February, piggybacking on Valentine's Day celebrations. I'm grateful that Renata, my new baker, has managed to slide into the role fairly seamlessly. Sure, there have been a few hiccups, but she's got great vision and is a master baker, so I can be assured she'll be able to handle the demands that are coming our way.

Daphne came up with an idea to set up a photo booth outside of Buttercream and Booze to showcase the event. Ever since the bachelorette party she's been getting loads of bookings for weddings, engagement parties, and birthdays. Since Valentine's

Day thrives on romance and couples, it's a great way for her to get more visibility and meet some potential new clients.

It definitely doesn't hurt that the local newspapers and TV stations have picked up on the event, which helps us spread the word. Business has picked up again—not like it was before D&B came in, but at least I'm not quite as worried about having to cut more of Callie's hours. For now.

A few days before the Love Is in the Air event, my phone chimes with an alert about a new video from Tori's YouTube channel. Over the past few weeks she's made her way through the top ten bars, narrowing it down to five. I watched the one she put up the day after she visited B&B and The Knight Cap. She was kind enough to edit her video to highlight the few funny moments from the final comedian—there weren't many—and focused more on the fun, fresh vibe, the themed drinks and cupcakes, and my eclectic sense of style that was reflected in the ambiance of the café.

I consider calling Ronan before I watch the video, but Daphne's here, setting up her photo booth and taking pretty pictures for the upcoming Valentine's Day extravaganza, so we crowd around my phone as I cue up the video.

"Ready?" Daphne asks.

I nod and we both cross our fingers as I hit Play. Of course Tori takes her sweet time talking about all the amazing bars she visited while she was touring the Pacific Northwest. "I'll admit, it was a tough competition and there are some amazing bars out there. I'm going to post a top ten on my site because narrowing it down was such a challenge, but there is one bar that really stood out among the rest!" She pauses for effect. "It's not just the food or the ambiance that makes one bar stand apart, it's the whole package, and my winner has it all. A charming, homey environment, the most amazing selection of craft beers, delicious food, fabulous entertainment and a seriously charismatic, smokin' hot owner." She fans herself dramatically.

"He won," I murmur and Daphne squeezes my hand.

"The Knight Cap is the whole package and more, which is why it's getting the Tori Taylor seal of approval and the title of The Best Bar in the Pacific Northwest! I can't wait to celebrate this win with Ronan Knight!"

The video goes on to show some highlights from her visit to The Knight Cap. Ronan was wholly captivating, and Tori was happy to wax poetic about the bar, the vibe, and the gorgeous owner.

"I'm so sorry, Blaire. I know how much you wanted this." Daphne slings her arm over my shoulder and gives me a side hug.

"Thanks. I guess at least if I had to lose, he's the one person I don't mind losing to?" It's more of a question than anything, because as happy as I am for Ronan, I'm disappointed for me.

"You're still allowed to be sad about it, though. You're a big part of the reason his events were so successful, especially the karaoke, and your customers were always in his bar after, not really the other way around."

She's right. While we both benefited, Ronan was the one who got the most out of our deal, and now he gets the benefit of all the extra promotion. "The Knight Cap has a history and a story I can't really compete with, though."

"And you did amazing, despite that." She taps the comments where Tori has posted a link to her top 10 favorite bars in the Pacific Northwest. Buttercream and Booze has taken the number two spot, right under The Knight Cap.

It's positive promotion no matter what, but I still give myself a minute to be disappointed, especially since we were just so close at the end, and if my final comedian hadn't sucked, I might have stood a chance. I remind myself that it's not Ronan's fault that my original act got sick, or that his cousin offered a poor replacement. It still really sucks, though.

"I should probably go over and congratulate him."

"Probably, but if you need to eat a pint of ice cream later and be sad about it, I'm your girl, okay?"

"Thanks." She hugs me and fixes my hair before she lets me head over to The Knight Cap.

It's barely ten thirty in the morning, but I find Ronan behind the bar, tossing back shots with Lars.

His huge grin widens when he sees me, and he motions to the TV above the bar with Tori's vlog playing out on the screen. "Babe! Did you see?"

"I did. Congratulations on the win." I slip behind the bar and he scoops me up, spinning me around.

When he sets me down, I grip his arms to keep from toppling over. His wide smile falters. "I'm sorry it wasn't you."

I curve my palm around the back of his neck, determined not to put a damper on his win. "Don't apologize. If I was going to lose to anyone, I'm glad it's you."

He drops his head, his lips finding mine. He tastes like tequila. "I wouldn't have won if it wasn't for you. Without the cohosted events, I wouldn't have stood a chance. I wish there could be two winners."

"Well, that would cheapen the award." I smooth my palms over his chest. "Does Gramps know yet?" I've taken to calling Henry that all the time now. He pops by the bakery quite regularly to say hello, and also for cupcakes. He makes me promise not to tell Ronan about his little addiction.

"I haven't. Should I call him? Or maybe I should tell him in person? Probably in person, right?"

"Definitely in person." I smile at his excitement.

"Yes. Good call. You'll come with me? I want you to come with me. Can you leave Callie in charge for an hour?" He kisses me again, making it impossible for me to answer.

When he finally pulls back, I assure him that I can most definitely come with him if that's what he wants. I pop back over to B&B to let Callie know she's in charge for a bit.

Ronan meets me out back and holds out his keys. "I'm too amped to drive."

I chuckle and get behind the wheel, marveling at how smooth the ride is compared to my SUV. It takes twenty minutes to get to Gramps's place, and Ronan talks a mile a minute, his excitement infectious and adorable. "We should have a big party to celebrate, shouldn't we? Do you think tonight is too soon? Can we get something out on social media that quick, or should it be tomorrow? Is that too close to the street party?" He taps the armrest, pausing only long enough to suck in a breath. "Maybe it should just be a staff thing, you know, to show my appreciation for all their hard work in helping make this happen? Oh! I should call the band and tell them. If they're not busy, they could play a set tonight!"

"I think we can totally get a party together tonight as long as you're not looking to have it catered, and we can keep it going through the weekend as a celebration of the win."

"Do you think Daphne would be interested in taking pictures?" Ronan asks. "I'd be happy to pay her."

"As soon as we get to Gramps's I'll message her and see if she's available. And I think you can have a separate staff party to acknowledge how much you appreciate them after the event this weekend. You could even close the bar to the public one evening and have the entire thing catered. And yes, definitely call the band and see if they're available."

"I really don't know how I would've done all of this without you." He squeezes my hand and brings his phone to his ear.

By the time we get to Gramps's house, Ronan has secured the band for tonight. It's not a stretch since they were already booked for the entire weekend event. I fire off a message to Daphne and before we even get to the front door she's already agreed to take pictures, but she's adamant that she doesn't need to be paid. I'm not sure Ronan will let her get away with that, but Daphne has always been exceedingly generous, so he might have to find another way to compensate her, like free beer and food. He knocks before he lets himself in with the key. The low drone of the TV filters through to the foyer.

"Gramps?"

"Ronan? What're ya doin' here at this time in the morning?"

"I have some exciting news," he calls out.

"I'm in the living room watching *The Price Is Right*!"

Ronan holds up a finger and drops his voice. "Give me a sec. Sometimes he likes to lounge around in his underpants and it's not a pretty sight."

"Standing by."

He peeks around the corner and then gives me a thumbs-up so I follow him into the living room.

Gramps's gaze bounces from Ronan to me and back again. "Oh, praise the lord!" He makes the sign of the cross. "Ya heard me prayers, Dottie. It's finally happening." A massive grin breaks across his face. "Yer gettin' married!"

"Uh." Ronan and I exchange questioning glances. "No, Gramps, we're not getting married."

Gramps's face falls. "Yer not?"

"We've only been dating for a couple of months."

"When ya know, ya know, though." Gramps's eyes round again and then narrow. "Ya better not have knocked Blaire up or I'll whup yer ass, boy."

"Okay, first of all, you will not whup anyone's ass, let alone mine, and secondly, no, I did not knock Blaire up."

"Oh." He slumps back in his chair. "Well, whatever the news is, it can't be that great, now can it?"

"You were ready to give me an ass whupping for knocking Blaire up two seconds ago and now you're disappointed I didn't?" Ronan sounds amused.

"I figure if you knocked her up, then you'd have to do the noble thing and marry her."

"Well, I might if it wasn't the twenty-first century. People have kids without getting married all the time." He turns to me. "Not that I don't want to get married or have kids. I just wouldn't expect you to suddenly want to tie the knot should I happen to knock you up accidentally."

"That's reasonable."

"Do you want to get married and have kids?"

"Now? No. But down the line I wouldn't be opposed, when the timing feels right. We can talk about this later, though. Like months from now, even." I put a hand on his arm and incline my head toward Henry, who is smiling gleefully.

"Oh, right, yeah." Ronan clears his throat. "Remember that YouTuber I was telling you about?"

"The lady with the really long eyelashes who makes all the videos that aren't the dirty kind?"

I fight a laugh.

"That's the one," Ronan confirms. "So she came through Seattle a couple of weeks back."

"That's right, I remember."

"And she stopped by The Knight Cap."

"She's not using my bar to make dirty videos."

"Gramps, we already established she doesn't make dirty videos. She named The Knight Cap the Best Bar in the Pacific Northwest. It's going to be featured on her YouTube channel, and she's partnered with Food and Drink and *The Seattle Morning Show*, so they'll be featuring us, too. We did it, Gramps! We got the bar back on its feet, and this is going to keep it standing."

Henry folds down the footrest on his La-Z-Boy and slowly pushes to a standing position. He hobbles over and pulls Ronan into a hug. "I'm so proud of ya." He smacks him on the back a couple of times before he grabs him by the arms, eyes watery, smile wavering. "Dottie would be too if she was here. I know she's looking down on you from heaven with a big smile on her face. She always believed in you."

"I know she did."

He pats Ronan's chest and turns to me, pulling me in for a hug. "You're the one who lit a fire under his ass, so I hope he's told you how much he appreciates you."

I hug him back, choked up about the whole thing, especially since I know Ronan's story and Henry's, and how much this bar means to him and this family.

Ronan tells Henry that he's planning to throw a party tonight, and he would love it if he would be able to come to the bar for dinner at the very least to celebrate.

"Are you kidding me? I'm coming right now. You kids hold on a few minutes while I get ready." His slippers make a *whoosh-whoosh* sound as he shuffles down the hall.

"I can't believe he thought I knocked you up."

I can't believe he thought Ronan asked me to marry him. "I like that he got all righteous about it."

"Yeah, well, I think fifty percent of the reason he couldn't wait to marry my grandma was so he could finally get into her pants, because back in the sixties that was how things went."

I roll my eyes. "That's how you think things went. It wasn't any different than it is now. Teenagers had sex back then just like they do now, only now it's easier to get contraception and kids actually know that standing up after sex doesn't prevent pregnancy."

"Okay, we need to stop talking about sex and teenagers and pregnancy, because it's sending mixed messages below the waist and I'm having some conflict over that."

I glance down at his crotch. "Are you aroused?"

"Not fully." He's amusingly defensive.

I poke the front of his pants. "You have a semi?"

"You said 'sex' twice and 'contraception,' and some parts of me don't realize it doesn't mean right now."

"You're ridiculous."

"I'm excited, about a lot of things, not the least of which is my girlfriend spending the night with me. Tell me you can get Callie to open for you tomorrow. I really want you to celebrate this win with me because it never would have happened without you."

"I'll talk to her as soon as we're back at The Knight Cap."

"This is as much your win as it is mine."

"This is yours, Ronan. Don't feel bad about being excited."

"I know how much this meant to you, though."

"And it means a lot to you, too, and to Gramps." As much as I wanted the win to be mine, I can't begrudge Ronan this. There's so much love here. History and connection and family. It's impossible to compete with that kind of beautiful backstory. "I can't think of a better way to honor your grandmother's memory."

Henry appears in the hallway. "What do ya think? Not too dressy for the occasion, is it?" He tugs on the hem of his suit jacket and I want to burst into tears. Like everything else in this house, it's a throwback to the nineties, and it's obvious he's lost some weight since he put it on last.

"You look perfect, Gramps. You're gonna knock 'em all out," Ronan says, his voice breaking.

Henry looks to me and winks. "Blaire, I need a woman's opinion, not this hipster jackass."

A half giggle–half sob bubbles up, but I manage to swallow it back down. "You look absolutely dapper."

"I haven't worn this suit in a while, but I figured if ever there was a reason to wear the family tartan, this is it." His smile is huge, and my heart melts for the man who stepped in and brought his grandfather's bar back to life.

@buttercreamandbooze:

We all deserve an ALCOHoliday.

chapter twenty

DON'T LEAVE ME HANGING

Blaire

The Knight Cap celebration is fantastic.

Ronan stays over at my place afterward and keeps me up until an ungodly hour in the morning. I tamp down my resentment over his peaceful, sleeping form sprawled over my mattress, dead to the world as I tiptoe around my room and try not to trip over our discarded clothes while I get ready for work.

We only have three days left to prepare for the street party, which means I have a lot of things to take care of. I leave Ronan in my bed, ruing my lack of sleep, but aware it's my own damn fault for staying out until two in the morning and then letting him persuade me to have slightly drunk marathon sex until four. My short sleep seems woefully inadequate right now.

I'm running behind this morning, so I have to rush through decorating today's cupcakes before B&B opens. I'm grateful that Callie is around to help, because I'm still in decorating mode when the doors open. The shop is bustling with morning customers and people picking up orders. I help Callie get things under control, tragically under-caffeinated for this level of on-the-ball. I can't say I'm disappointed by the number of customers we have, though. It's busier than it has been as of late, possibly because of the best bar winner announcement and the Top 10 list Tori posted on its heels.

Once we're past the initial rush, it slows down until lunch, which means I can start tackling the event prep and the eleven million questions that come with it. I expect Ronan to stop by and say hello, get his cupcake fix, and go over the last-minute stuff we need to get in order for Saturday. Except that doesn't happen.

I pop over to The Knight Cap after the lunch rush dies down, hoping to touch base with Ronan, but he's not there. Lars isn't on until the evening shift and Lana, one of the other bartenders, doesn't seem to know where Ronan is or when he'll be in.

I send him a message, asking about an ETA and when we'll have time to go over any last-minute emergencies. Two hours and another influx of customers later, he still hasn't responded so I start fielding questions on my own.

It's almost four in the afternoon by the time he rolls in, looking a hell of a lot more chipper and rested than I feel. "Hey, babe." He leans over the counter and kisses me on the cheek. He sweeps a thumb across the hollow under my eye. "Sorry I kept you up so late. You hanging in there?"

I fight that melty feeling I always get when he touches me and remind myself I'm kind of annoyed that the day is more than half over and he's been MIA. "I'm okay. Where have you been?"

"Oh, you know, running around, picking up stuff for the weekend."

"Did you get my message?"

"Huh?"

"I sent you a message hours ago." I can feel my irritation building at his less than remorseful expression.

"Really? I must've missed it. What's going on? What do you need?"

I blink at him, trying to figure out why he's suddenly so . . . off. Preoccupied? I don't know what it is, but I find it frustrating. "We have an event in two days. I could've used some help fielding questions from all the other local businesses and coordinating with them, but you were nowhere to be found."

He seems to realize I'm pissed off. "I'm sorry. I didn't mean to leave you hanging. I was taking care of last-minute stuff. Who needs questions answered?"

"No one anymore, for now."

"Fantastic. You're always so organized. This is going to be smooth sailing until Saturday." He pats his pocket when his phone starts buzzing. He checks the screen. "I gotta take this. I'll stop by later." He kisses me on the cheek again, grabs the cupcake I plated for him—like the sucker I am—and disappears out the front door, his phone at his ear.

He doesn't stop by later, though. And when I drop by The Knight Cap again to see if he's around to go over the fine details, I discover that he left a couple of hours ago to take care of some *things*, according to Lars.

"Do you know when he's going to be back?" It's already after nine and I've been going all day. I'm barely functioning on the limited sleep I managed last night.

Lars shrugs. "Dunno. He left in kind of a hurry and said he'd try to be back before closing."

"He'd *try*?" I parrot. "What the hell could he be doing at this time of night?"

Lars gives me an apologetic look. "I honestly don't know. He's been holed up in his office most of the day, and when he's come out he's stuck around for a few minutes before he had to field another call. Do you want me to tell him you stopped by?"

I wave him off, feeling pathetic and highly annoyed. "No. Don't bother. I'll just talk to him tomorrow. I'm beat, and I need actual sleep tonight."

"Celebrations went well into the wee hours of the morning, huh?" He tips his chin up and nods knowingly.

I don't bother to respond. I'm sure my expression says everything.

"Aren't you a wild one? All sweet and pretty and proper and buttoned up on the surface, but you leave some marks behind when you really let loose?" He cocks a brow in question.

I glare at him while my face turns the same color as the

red in his plaid shirt. There were some scratch marks on Ronan's back last night and my handprint on his butt from me smacking it, telling him to go harder. The handprint was likely gone by the morning, but I'm sure the scratches are still there. "What the hell has he been saying to you?"

Lars's grin widens. "Absolutely nothing. Ronan couldn't be more tight-lipped if he tried. It was just a guess on my part, and obviously I was right. Ronan's a lucky asshole."

I laugh, unsure how he managed to turn that into a compliment. "I'll see you tomorrow."

I consider texting Ronan when I get home, but I figure it's his turn to reach out. I change into comfy clothes but don't even manage to wash my face or take my makeup off before I pass out. On top of my covers.

The next morning I'm slightly better rested and feeling less like garbage and more half-human. I have a text from Ronan about being sorry that he missed me last night, but he'll make it up to me. It's followed with a slew of emojis, including eggplants, the panting-tongue thing and a bunch of hand symbols that indicate what he may be planning to do with them.

Normally I'd think it was cute. But this morning I do not. I decide not to respond right away because I'm inclined to say something snarky and less than friendly in my current, grumpy state. Clearly the sleep wasn't enough.

As it turns out, I don't run into Ronan.

Because he's not at The Knight Cap. His car isn't in the parking lot and hasn't been there all day. I may or may not have looked outside every single hour to check.

"Okay, what's the deal?" Daphne asks when I come back down the hall after checking for the seven millionth time if Ronan is here. "I don't know what's going on, but maybe you need a cupcake and some valium so you can chill the eff out."

"I'm totally chill," I snap.

She grabs me by the elbow and steers me toward the office.

"What're you doing?"

"Avoiding a scene. In you go." She shoves me inside and closes the door behind her, barricading me in.

I fling my arms in the air. "I don't have time for this! There's too much stuff to do!"

"Take a breath, Blaire. We are ninety-five percent ready for tomorrow. It's just little things that need to be taken care of. Social media is blowing up and people are excited. But you're freaking out poor Callie the way you're snapping every time she asks you a question."

"I'm not snappy!" I close my eyes and rub my temple. "Sorry. I'm just...overwhelmed and I thought I'd get some actual help from Ronan, but he's nowhere to be found and left me to do everything."

"Isn't he next door?"

"No. He's not. He hasn't been there all day and he wasn't there yesterday."

Daphne's tone softens. "But you know where he is?"

"Running errands, apparently. The last time I actually saw him for more than five distracted seconds was two nights ago when he stayed at my place after he found out he won Best Bar." I pace my small office. It's not big enough for effective, angry pacing, though, so I'm forced to turn around after two steps and then I run right into Daphne. "What if he's using me as a means to an end? What if it was convenient to bone the chick who's super organized and loves to take control of events? What if he was having his cupcake and eating it, too!"

"Pretty sure he *has* been having his cupcake and eating it, too," Daphne mutters.

"This isn't a joke. He's been MIA the past two days and I've had to manage everything! With your help, obviously, and Callie's and his staff, but he's supposed to be here and involved and he's not."

"Have you tried asking him where he's been and what he's doing?"

"Well, he'd have to answer his damn messages for me to be able to confirm that. And now that he's won the competition and his grandfather's bar is doing well he's probably going to go ahead and open that brewery, and that'll be the end of us."

Daphne arches a brow. "You're in a pretty fatalistic mood."

"I'm being realistic. Think about it. First all the pranks, hijacking my grand opening, the freaking glitter bomb. And then we call a truce when D&B opens and start throwing all these events together. They benefit him more than they do me. And there was that time one of Tori's people came to scope things out. It was the same morning Ronan convinced me to stay at his place for breakfast."

"That seems like a pretty unfortunate coincidence," Daphne hedges.

"Except he made it to work in time to meet up with Tori's people and win them over with his charm and his charisma." I throw my hands in the air. "What about the time I found him making cappuccinos, only the damn machine crapped its pants while he was right there! If I hadn't had someone to fix it, I would've been in a huge bind on a seriously busy night."

"I didn't know about that." Daphne chews her bottom lip.

"It got fixed, but it was expensive, and then everything was fine and I forgot about it. But then Lars gives me the name of a shitty comedian on the *same night* Tori shows up. What if Ronan's distracted me with his exceptional bedroom skills and all along he's been sabotaging me! Remember how crazy it used to be in the food truck business? People constantly slashing tires, fighting over what area they were allowed to target. It was nasty. Maybe he's only been sleeping with me so he can win this damn thing and get what he wants, which is his brewery!"

"That would be a pretty calculated, somewhat sociopathic thing to do, don't you think?" Daphne sounds less like the voice of reason and more like she's just as worried as I am now.

"Well, he won the entire competition, and Gramps will fork over the start-up money for his brewery, which is always what he was working toward. And now here I am, with no win and an absentee boyfriend who's probably going to dump me." I flap my hands in front of my face as if that's going to stop the tears. "Damn it! I can't afford a meltdown right now!"

"Take a deep breath, Blaire. I get that you're upset, and all of these individual things together might seem bad, but until you've had a conversation with him you really can't know for sure, can you? And honestly, this is nothing like the food truck business, which is literally insane."

"Doesn't it seem like a pretty big coincidence that he's suddenly impossible to get ahold of right after he wins the award and we have this huge event we're trying to pull off so our businesses don't end up in the shitter?"

"Yes, I agree that it does, but I also don't want you to go off half-cocked and blow up this relationship without having the whole story."

She has a point. "I just don't want my shop to fail. I can't afford for it to fail because if it does it means my dream is dead."

"Let's not borrow trouble. You have a weekend of awesomeness planned, and we've done everything we can to promote it. Have some faith in yourself and your ability to make this a success, regardless of whether Ronan pulls through for you."

"I'm supposed to have a partner in this." And maybe that's the biggest kick in the pants for me. Because that's what this felt like, a partnership. A real one on all levels. So it hurts more than I'd like that the man who I thought was with me on this whole thing was only here for as long as I was useful and necessary, sort of like how Raphael used me to get closer to my family. In the end, my parents cared more about his skill set than my broken heart. I thought I'd been smarter this time. I thought I knew better.

"*I'm* your partner right now. You don't need Ronan to make this a success. He's great arm candy and I'm sure he's a rock star in bed, but he isn't essential to pulling this off. You've been the one to set up all the cohosted events. You made those a success."

"Well, they weren't successful enough."

"So what if you had one bad comedy act? So what if you didn't win the Best Bar title? Put that aside and focus on the here and now. You have the respect of your peers. They've come to you with every question, so remember that when you're getting down on yourself or thinking you're not enough. And honestly, if Ronan did just use you for a ride I'll happily kick him in the balls for you."

"While wearing steel-toed boots."

"Yes. Or cleats. Then he could be textured for your pleasure."

"That is not a pleasant visual."

Someone knocks on the door timidly and Daphne opens it up. "What's up, Callie?"

"Um, I'm really sorry to interrupt." She wrings her hands nervously. "But the McClellands are here and they have an order for pickup, but I can't find it in the stack."

"I'll take care of it. I didn't put it out front because it has a custard filling and needs to be refrigerated. Tell them I'll be right out," I say, much more gently than I have all day.

I push Ronan's absence to the back of my mind. I can't afford to fixate, and Daphne is right: I'm scaring Callie when I should be building excitement for the weekend.

I retrieve the McClelland order and reset my attitude. It helps put everyone else at ease, and we're all in a far more positive mood by the end of the day.

I send Callie home an hour early and post a sign that our hours will be modified for the weekend so we can stick around for all of the festivities.

The specials have already been added to the board, tomorrow's cupcakes are decorated and in the fridge, and we're well stocked with drinks and everything we could possibly need to make Love Is in the Air a success.

I pull up my Instagram account to check interaction, and the first thing that pops up on my feed is a post from Tori Taylor, which isn't all that surprising. But the fact that it's a picture of her and Ronan sitting in a cozy-looking bar that *isn't* The Knight Cap sure is not what I expect to see. And it was posted half an hour ago. So much for running errands and helping prep for the event. I'm tempted to comment on the post, but I decide it's not in my best interest to be petty where Tori is concerned.

I pop over to The Knight Cap before I head home, not because I'm looking for Ronan at this point since clearly he's too busy making plans with Tori to be bothered with the event, but because I want to touch base with the bar staff and make sure they don't have any questions.

Lars is tending bar along with Corbin, who was hired last week and seems to be a great addition to their team. He's got the whole surfer dude look going on, long blond hair, tanned, and always calling everyone "bro" and "sweetheart." The women eat it up.

Lars cringes when he sees me approach. I hold up a hand, feeling even worse based on his response to my presence. "I'm not looking for Ronan. I just want to make sure you're all set for tomorrow."

He blinks at me a couple of times but says nothing.

"Do you need any clarification on anything?" I ask.

"Uhhhh...I don't think so. I'm supposed to be here at nine thirty to help prep the bar and the doors open at eleven. I'll be serving drinks all day and managing whatever else needs to happen to make things go smoothly."

"What about the rest of your crew?"

"I think we're all good. We got your to-do list, and Lana is huge on the decorating shit." He motions to the heart garland strung all over the bar interspersed with lei-wearing cupids. The hearts are red and black plaid, to match the rest of the décor. "So I think we're okay unless something major happens tomorrow."

"Okay, great. Text me if you need anything or if there's something you're unsure of."

"Will do." A couple of college girls approach the bar.

"I'll let you get back to it."

As I turn to leave, Lars calls out, "Blaire."

I pause and give him a questioning smile.

"Try not to think the worst."

I nod, and he turns back to the girls.

It's easier said than done, though. I give in and send Ronan a message before I go to bed. I don't anticipate sleeping well, or much at all, but I figure it's worth a shot. It's well past midnight before I fall into a restless, fitful sleep. And still nothing from Ronan.

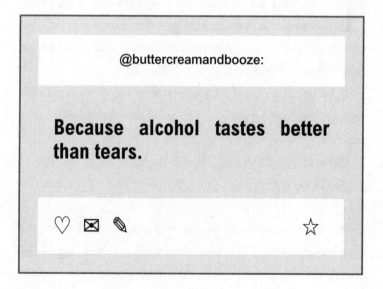

@buttercreamandbooze:

Because alcohol tastes better than tears.

chapter twenty-one

WELL THAT EXPLAINS IT

Blaire

The first thing I do when my alarm goes off is groan my displeasure at how quickly morning comes. Then I remember that the Love Is in the Air event is today, and I have four billion things to take care of before B&B opens.

I also check to see if Ronan ever responded last night. He did. At four in the morning. The message is lackluster.

Ronan: Sry it's so late, tmrw is going to be awsm, see you in the A.M.

No kissy faces, no hearts or eggplant emojis. I leave the message unanswered. My reaction is slightly passive-aggressive, but I'd rather say nothing than something nasty. I don't need to start my day with an argument.

I set the coffeemaker to brew, then shower and get ready for what I hope will be a fantastic day. The Seattle paper is supposed to come by and spotlight the local businesses participating in the Love Is in the Air pub crawl. I'm hopeful the positive press will help us all and bring to light the harmful impact big chains have when they come and undercut small businesses.

My dress boasts an adorable hearts and cupids-slinging-arrows theme. It's an old one that I embellished with a wide plaid ribbon with a cupcake, cocktails, and beer pattern tied at my waist. I also have a special apron for today.

I swallow thickly as I take in my reflection. I'd hoped that Ronan and I would've spent last night together, that he would be here to see me get ready for this event that we worked so hard to make happen.

I push aside the negative thoughts, aware they don't do me any good. I'm out the door by seven thirty. We're not opening until later this morning, but I want to be at B&B nice and early so I can make sure everything is set up and help calm anyone with event-day jitters.

I park my SUV behind the shop, surprised to see Ronan's truck there already. The moment I walk into B&B, I'm assaulted by Daphne. She grabs me by the shoulders. "You need to go next door. Right now."

I set my purse on the counter. I'm not in a hurry to see Ronan this morning. "Why are you here so early?"

"Because I couldn't sleep and because of...reasons." She tries to turn me around, but I refuse to budge. "Come on, you have to see this."

"See what?"

"I can't tell you. I have to show you."

"Well, show me later. I have lots of stuff to take care of." I glance out the window and notice there's already a crowd gathered, even though we're not supposed to open for several hours. I squint. "Is that a camera crew? What's going on out there?"

I head for the door but turn abruptly. Daphne is following so closely she slams into me and nearly knocks over a table. "Do I need to reapply my lipstick?"

"No. You're perfect. But you should lose the coat."

"It's freezing outside."

"You'll survive. I promise." She tugs my parka down my arms like I'm a toddler who needs help. Once I'm coatless, I open the door and step outside. The street has been blocked off so people are able to walk down the road and traffic won't interfere with the event. We had to petition the city councillors to make that happen.

In the middle of the street is Ronan looking damn gorgeous in his plaid shirt and black sports jacket. He's also wearing a pair of dark-wash jeans and his usual steel-toed work boots. And he's surrounded by media. There are several news crews, people from *The Seattle Morning Show*, and Tori.

"What the heck is going on?" I mutter.

"Your boyfriend is awesome; that's what's going on." Daphne squeezes my arm.

It's as if Ronan can sense my presence the moment I step out the front door and onto the sidewalk. His gaze shifts from Tori—who's standing beside him looking ridiculously perfect for this horribly early hour—and lands on me. His smile widens, and he extends a hand. "And here she is, the reason behind all of this."

"He's talking about you! Go on." Daphne elbows me in the side.

He takes a step forward, breaking from the group, and winks. "Come on, beautiful, don't be shy on me."

I give him a look, feeling my cheeks heat. He said those same words less than a week ago when he wanted to have sex on the bar of The Knight Cap. After hours, of course. Even with no lights on and the mostly opaque sign covering the front windows I was apprehensive. I gave in eventually, though. And then made him sanitize the hell out of the bar afterward while I watched, and told him he was a bad influence, and that we should maybe consider doing that on the bar in his apartment next time instead. He wondered why he hadn't thought of that himself.

"What is all this?" I ask when I reach him.

He doesn't answer at first. Simply takes my face between his cold hands—because it's frigid out here—bends down, and presses his lips gently to mine. "You look good enough to eat."

"Can you stop saying things that make me turn red?"

"Your cheeks will match the hearts on your dress." He smiles against my lips and then backs up so I can see his face. "I'm sorry I haven't been around the last couple of days, but now you know why."

"I'm confused as to what all is happening here. Is that Thom Thomas from channel five?"

"It is."

"And Claudia Carmichael from Food and Drink?"

"You're correct. Come on, let me introduce you." Ronan threads his fingers through mine.

"Do I look okay?" I smooth my hand down the front of my dress.

"You look good enough to eat, remember?" He tugs on my hand and brings me over to the group of media professionals. People I've watched on TV for years, and they're here because of Ronan. "This is Blaire Calloway. She's the reason all of this is happening."

I want to argue since he was the one who suggested the street party, but I'm suddenly shaking hands with all these influential people. Tori extends her hand. "It's so great to see you again, Blaire. I think what you're doing here is amazing. I'm a big advocate for small business owners."

"Your parents started Organically Yours," I mention.

"That's right, back when I was just a kid. I know how hard they worked to promote their business and stay current and relevant, which is how I ended up here."

"You've done amazing things for so many independent businesses," I say. Because it's true. She's always focused on new products or start-ups, giving preference to smaller companies trying to find their footing. A recommendation from someone like Tori creates buzz and awareness. It's a powerful marketing tool.

"So have you." Tori smiles like she's in on a secret.

"I'm sorry, I don't think I understand." I glance between her and Ronan.

"All of this..." Tori motions to the businesses setting up for the day, at the decorations that line the street.

"You're the one who made this happen, Blaire," Ronan says.

"It was your idea, though."

"I just made a suggestion. You're the one who ran with it and made it reality. I was just a bystander taking orders from the cupcake queen." He smiles down at me, his expression reflecting so many emotions. The most dominant is pride and it makes my heart swell.

"I just wanted us to have a fighting chance, and the best way to do that was to band together," I explain.

"And you were absolutely right to do that. I wanted to make sure that all the right people could be here to see it happen, so I talked to Tori."

I'm sure my confusion is clear on my face.

"Ronan thought it would be a good idea to showcase not just The Knight Cap but the entire community here, since you're all so involved with each other," Tori says. "It's amazing to see so many businesses come together instead of making rivals of each other. I thought it was a fantastic idea, so I made some calls and explained what was going on, and of course I needed Ronan's help to make it happen."

"Which is why you've been MIA the past couple of days," I whisper. I feel awful for assuming the worst, although to be fair I've had my share of being burned.

"I know I kind of left you in the lurch, but I wanted to make sure I could pull this off. That we could pull this off." He motions between himself and Tori.

Ronan forfeited his spotlight so we could all benefit, and here I was, thinking he was out to screw me over. I wave my hand in front of my face, trying to control the emotions, which apparently want to leak out of my eyes in the form of tears.

He pulls me against him and dips his head down so his lips are at my ear. "Are these happy tears?"

"So happy," I mumble against his chest. My boyfriend is the best.

There are lines out the door all day, which is fantastic. I almost pass out from shock when my family shows up late in the afternoon. My parents, aunt, uncle, Maddy, and Skylar sort of suck the air out of the place with their presence. They're dressed up like they're going to a diamond-level restaurant, but then, my family loves to make a statement. And I suppose I'm no different with the way I dress.

"What are you guys doing here?" I peel off my latex gloves and toss them in the trash. Wiping my hands on my apron, I round the display case so I can air-kiss them.

"Your boyfriend called and said you were hosting an event and that it would be great if we could come out and see what you've accomplished," my mom says.

"This place is so cute!" Maddy says.

"It really is," Skylar agrees, albeit reluctantly.

My dad pulls me in for a hug. "This really is incredible, Blaire. You've done amazing things, and all on your own."

"I didn't do it all on my own. Ronan was a lot of help with the event." Minus the past couple of days, but clearly he's forgiven for that.

"I mean with this place." My dad motions to the line of people waiting for cupcakes and cocktails—or mocktails, since there are loads of families at the event. It's standing room only, with customers ordering cupcakes to go so they can sample more vendors. "You followed your dream, and you did it on your own. I'm proud of you, honey."

I get misty-eyed at the praise and the acknowledgment that this accomplishment is well and truly mine.

My jaw nearly hits the floor when they all try a cupcake and a cocktail. Even Maddy and Skylar—although they both talk about the two-hour run plus detox they're going to have to endure because of the single cupcake they consumed.

My dad mingles with everyone, happy to tell them that he's my father and that I inherited my excellent business sense and my baking skills from him.

By the time we close the doors, the only thing that's left are a pair of lonely Death by Chocolate cupcakes.

I bring them next door to The Knight Cap, where the band has already started playing. Ronan and I are going to be dead on our feet by the time the bar closes, but we're taking a day off after all of this is over, so we should be able to catch up on some much-needed sleep and some alone time.

I spot Gramps sitting at the end of the bar, nursing a pint of Guinness. When he sees me, a huge grin lights up his face. I give him a hug from the side and shout over the noise. "Having fun?"

"I sure am. This is the busiest I've seen this place in a long time. Dottie would be proud 'a both of you." He thumbs over to the band. "But I gotta be honest, this just sounds like noise. Gonna finish my pint and head home."

"Want dessert with that?" I flip open the lid on the box.

"You don't have to ask me twice." He winks and takes one.

I leave him to his pint and I sidle up next to Ronan behind the bar. "Gramps is having a great time."

He glances down at my feet, but doesn't comment on my lack of proper footwear. "I'm impressed that he's still here. I would have thought he'd bail so he doesn't miss the late night rerun of *Jeopardy*."

"Thank goodness for DVR, I guess. Did he used to watch it with Dottie?"

"Every night at seven thirty. They'd compete to see who could answer the most questions correctly."

"Did they keep score?"

"Sure did."

"He must miss her so much."

Ronan nods. "He does. We both do. But I think I'd rather have someone to miss than never have the opportunity to witness that kind of devotion. They were each other's everything."

"Makes it tough to settle for anything less, I would think." I tip my chin up, overwhelmed by the sudden surge of emotion. I don't really know what it's like to watch a love like that. My parents are the most unconventional people I know, and the idea of finding a soul mate seemed elusive.

Lars interrupts—his timing sucks—to ask Ronan for some help behind the bar, because they're swamped and I'm monopolizing him. I change into a pair of boots and mix some drinks.

When the band finishes, the crowd slowly starts to dissipate.

"I can't believe how well this has gone." I load barware into the washer and dry off the clean ones before I stack them. "Or that you managed to get Thom Thomas from channel five here, or that you forfeited your spotlight with Tori so we could all be in it."

Ronan puts the beer steins in the freezer. "To be fair, it was Tori who pulled all the strings since she has all the connections. I just proposed the idea and she ran with it. I'm sorry I left you hanging the last couple of days, but I really wanted to be able to pull this off and give you and Buttercream and Booze the attention you deserved."

"I feel bad for being annoyed with you." And for doubting his sincerity and his loyalty. Although I was under a lot of stress, and he did sort of screw right off immediately after winning the Best Bar in Town award, so there was some room for doubt and worry.

He laughs. "Lars said you didn't look all that impressed the couple of times you stopped in here. I told him I was trying to make some things happen, but I wouldn't tell him what exactly because I couldn't be sure he'd keep his mouth shut. And I knew if I saw you I'd want to tell you what I was planning, but on the off chance I failed, I also didn't want to disappoint you. It was a real conundrum."

"I'm so sorry I was less than sweet to you the past couple of days." If I'd known he was planning something then maybe I would've calmed my tits and not been so passive-aggressive. It's a good reminder that I can't base my opinions or assumptions on past experiences and that Ronan isn't like Raphael.

"It's not your sweetness that keeps me coming back, Blaire." He winks.

I'm about to give him some sass, but Tori appears at the bar. "Do you have a few minutes for an interview? I'd love to get your thoughts on how today has been for you and the rest of the family-owned businesses on the street."

I make a move to step to the side. "I'll just give you a few minutes."

Ronan snags me by the waist before I get too far. "I think Tori actually wants to interview you, Blaire, since you're the one who orchestrated all of this."

I glance between him and Tori. "But it's your spotlight."

"I'd actually love it if you could do this together. Ronan's already answered most of these questions for me over the past couple of days while we've been getting everything together to make this happen, but I'd love to get them on camera and hear your side of things, too, Blaire. Are you okay if we go live with this? It's more organic this way, you know? Feels a lot less scripted."

Ronan defers to me. "Are you okay with that?"

"Sure, of course. We can go live." As if I'm going to pass up this opportunity.

"Great." Tori motions for her crew to get set up and three women swoop in with makeup brushes and attack her face. "Can we touch you up, Blaire?"

"Um, sure?" One of the women flits down the length of the bar and makes her way to me, brushes and makeup case in hand.

Tori taps her lip. "I think you two should stay behind the bar. I like the lighting and the backdrop is fantastic. Are those your grandparents?" She points to the picture behind Ronan.

"That's them."

She looks from the framed photo to us and back again. "It's like history repeating itself." She does a little shimmy. "This is beyond perfect."

Two minutes later I'm all touched up and when the girl moves in to get to Ronan he raises both hands in the air. "Is it okay if you don't use that stuff on me?"

Tori waves her off and she takes a seat at the bar. I make her a pretty cocktail and we plate the lone Death by Chocolate cupcake for her. She's all about product placement, making sure the coaster with The Knight Cap logo on it is situated so viewers can read it easily and that the cupcake box with the B&B sticker is equally visible and prominent.

"You two, nice and close, please." Tori makes hand gestures until our shoulders are touching. "You can put your arm around Blaire, Ronan."

He slings it over my shoulder and I wrap mine around his waist. I tip my chin up as he looks down and we both smile and laugh. He bends to press a kiss to my temple.

"Oh my God, cuteness overload," Tori sighs.

"You ready?" the cameraman asks.

Tori gives him a thumbs-up. "Okay, we're going live in, three, two, one." The camera guy focuses on Tori and she squares her shoulders. "Tori Taylor here and tonight we're celebrating Love Is in the Air with the Best Bar winner, The Knight Cap, but Ronan Knight, our designated winner, wanted to share the limelight with the rest of the family-owned businesses in the area, so they created this amazing Love Is in the Air event, and it has been outstanding! I've never had so much fun in my entire life! Ronan, tell me what inspired you to put together such an incredible day."

"Alice in Wonderland," Ronan blurts.

To her credit, Tori hardly misses a beat. "The Tim Burton remake?"

"That's what he called me the first time he met me," I supply.

"Oh? This is definitely a story. Do tell!"

Ronan and I look at each other. "Go ahead. I'm interested to hear your version of events." I nudge him playfully.

His smile widens. "Are you sure you want me to share this story?"

"Just remember whose bed you're sleeping in tonight." I bat my lashes.

Ronan bites his lip, likely to prevent his grin from growing any wider. He tips my chin up and kisses me softly. I don't think he's even in tune with the fact that he's being recorded anymore because he doesn't look at the camera.

"I'll never forget the moment I met you. God, you were just so angry and beautiful and righteous. And I never would have admitted it then, but now I can say that it was a total jerk move to start renovations and not come by and introduce myself first."

"Tell us more about that." Tori pulls his attention away from me.

Ronan blinks a couple of times and realizes he's not talking just to me but a million plus subscribers. "Uh. I'd just agreed to help my grandfather with The Knight Cap. We lost my grandmother a while back and they were the epitome of soul mates. They did everything together, including run this place. After she passed, it was hard for him to run it on his own."

Tori nods, her expression sympathetic. "You're very close with your grandfather."

"I am." He goes on to explain the deal he made with his grandfather to get his brewery capital.

"You worked here before, though, right? It was your first job," Tori adds, shifting away from the heavier topic of losing his grandmother.

"I washed dishes, bussed tables, served them—and sucked

at that part—before I finally got to tend the bar. It's all a lot different than running the place."

"And you added some new features."

"I did, and they weren't particularly convenient for my neighbor." He smiles down at me. "She came in here, all fired up about problems I was causing her."

"He wasn't very receptive at first," I add.

"Oh, I was more than receptive, and that was the problem."

I cock my head. This is the first I've heard of this.

"I didn't need a distraction. I needed to take this bar from red to black and then I could move on. That was my plan, and then Blaire happened. I've never met someone so determined to succeed. She comes from a family of restaurateurs and she's a baker. You might think it's the same, but it's not. We shouldn't have been each other's competition, but we were. Blaire is a force; she's smart and beautiful and driven and uniquely herself. And I think it took me about two weeks to fall for her, but man I tried so hard not to."

"You fell in love with your rival?" Tori presses her hand to her heart and I stare up at Ronan, trying to figure out what in the world is happening here.

His expression turns panicked, like he suddenly realizes what he's said and where. He doesn't address Tori, but he does address me. "I'm so in love with you," he says softly, with conviction.

"And I'm so in love with you," I whisper back. If I hadn't made the decision to go out on my own I never would have met him, or had the chance to fall for him.

His smile is beautiful. He dips down and presses his lips to mine. "I can't wait to take you home and show you how much I love you," he murmurs.

I'm all for that, but I'm not sure all of Tori's subscribers need to know about it. "There are cameras rolling," I say against his lips, trying my best to keep his tongue from sliding between mine.

His gaze darts to Tori and the cameraman. "Damn it. Right. I keep forgetting this is a live thing."

We all burst into laughter and Tori turns to face the camera. "I think we all know this one has a happy ending. So make sure to come visit The Knight Cap and Buttercream and Booze, and maybe you, too, will find your very own happily ever after."

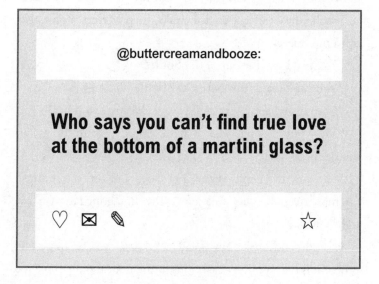

@buttercreamandbooze:

Who says you can't find true love at the bottom of a martini glass?

I LOVE YOU MORE THAN CUPCAKES

Ronan

Three months later

Gramps hoists himself up onto one of the barstools and pulls a bottle of my homebrew out of the inside pocket of his coat and sets it on the bar. "Uncap that for me, Ronan."

I shake my head but do as he asks, then retrieve a pint glass from the freezer.

"No, no. I want it out of the bottle."

"You can't drink this out of the bottle, Gramps."

"I can do whatever the hell I want. It's my damn bar."

"This guy giving you a hard time?" Blaire sidles up beside me.

"He won't let me drink my beer out of the bottle." Gramps gives me the stink eye. "I'm not gonna start a bar fight with it."

I laugh and shake my head. "I know you're not. The problem is that we don't carry this in the pub, and if people see they might want to know what it is and you'll be drinking the only one 'cause you brought your own beer into the bar."

"Well, start serving it and I won't have to bring my own."

I shrug. "I don't have enough space to brew it in large batches yet."

"I already said I'd cut you the check," he grumbles.

I lean an arm on the bar. "When'd you say that?"

He waves a hand around in the air. "I'm old, how am I supposed to remember when. After you won that Best Bar award, I said I'd cut you a check for the start-up cost."

"Are you sure you said it out loud?"

Gramps gives me a look and turns to Blaire. "Are you listening to this? Giving this old guy a hard time, making me question my memory. It's ageism is what it is!"

"Maybe you already cut him the check and he's messing with you to make you think you didn't," Blaire teases.

I lean on the bar and fight a smile. "Whose side are you on?"

She grins up at me. "I'm not taking sides on this."

"Sounds like she's taking my side." Gramps gives her a wink and an affectionate smile. "When you putting a ring on Blaire's finger? Everyone's waiting for it, ya know."

"Yeah, Gramps, I know. Everyone needs to find some chill about it, too." I kiss Blaire on the temple. We've only been together for a few months, but I can't see my life without her. "And I've been thinking about the brewery situation lately."

"I'll miss driving in to work with you." Blaire gives my arm a squeeze.

"Well, that's the thing...Lars is a good kid, but he isn't anywhere near ready to take over this place, and I kinda like what we've got going on here." I put my arm around Blaire's shoulder and pull her in closer. "People really love what we're doing, and I figure I can put the brewery on hold until we can settle on a location."

"But that's what you've been working toward," Blaire says.

Gramps nods and sips his beer, a hint of a smile there, like maybe he knew this was coming. "The McCurdys next door have been thinking about selling. At least that's what Bertie says pretty much every time I go over to buy some cold cuts."

"If they decide to sell we could look at what it would take to convert it. Wouldn't take much to make a doorway to connect the two," I say.

"Things to think about." Gramps shifts his attention to Blaire. "Might be a good time to mention that thing *you* were thinking about. Pretty sure you might be on the same page."

Blaire gives him a meaningful look. "I'm not sure now is the time."

I look between them, unnerved that Gramps and Blaire are having conversations about whatever, apparently behind my back. "Now isn't the time for what?"

Gramps wears an expression that looks a lot like a smirk and then turns away as a couple of his friends walk through the front door—they've taken to coming out at least once a week for beers and wings—and he slips off the stool. "I'll leave you two lovebirds to talk."

"Are you going to explain what that's about?" I motion between Gramps and Blaire as he ambles over to one of the four-tops.

He's been in such better spirits lately. So happy with how the bar is doing, glad to see it full of life and people again. And honestly, so am I.

Blaire slips her arm through mine. "Come on, let's go talk in your office."

"Are you going to try to distract me with sex?"

Blaire laughs. "I could, but I won't. Especially not while Gramps is here."

I slip into the office first so I can quickly shuffle some of the papers around on the desk, hiding the ones I'm not sure I'm ready for Blaire to see yet. I close the door and sit on the edge of the desk, giving her the new executive chair. As much as Gramps loved the old one, it was falling apart. Literally. One of the arms fell off two weeks ago and it was really all the encouragement I needed to buy something comfortable.

"So what have you and Gramps been talking about behind my back?" I go for light, but I'm not sure it comes out that way.

Blaire reaches up and takes one of my hands in hers, skimming along the design on my wrist. "It was just something I mentioned a few weeks back, more as a joke than anything."

"Okay." I wait for her to elaborate, but after a few seconds of quiet, I press. "Blaire? Are you gonna tell me?"

"I just made a comment that it would be a lot easier to run

all of our cohosted events if we put a doorway between B&B and The Knight Cap." She laughs, but it's high and nervous.

I have to give it to Gramps; he really knows how to force a conversation I wasn't sure I was ready to have. I lace my fingers with hers. "Oh yeah? And what did Gramps say about that?"

She waves her free hand in the air. "Oh, you know Gramps."

"So you were just joking about that? About a doorway between our places?"

Her expression is somewhere between embarrassed and nervous. "I'm already moving in with you. It's not like you want me in your face all day every day, too. Besides, Gramps has had to manage enough change with all the renovations this year."

Last month I suggested she move in with me. It's maybe five minutes farther from the bars, but my place is also twice the size of hers and nicer, and my bed is bigger. And she actually kind of lives in a shithole, not that I would say that out loud. But it isn't great. So she's been driving stuff over by the carload.

"I'd be more than happy to have you in my face all day every day and every night." I raise our twined fingers and kiss the back of her hand. "But I totally understand if that would be too much of me for you."

"I can't ever get enough of you, Ronan. You know that. Anyway, it was just a silly idea I threw out, because it was cold and rainy and I didn't have an umbrella with me."

"What if I said I didn't think it was that silly of an idea."

She blinks up at me. "What do you mean?"

"I mean what if we joined forces permanently? I love you and I love this place, and I think we work really well together."

"So do I, and I love you, too." She gives me a gentle, inquisitive smile.

"I know how important it is for you to do this on your own, and I don't want to take that away from you, but my favorite nights are when we cohost events. And the thing I look forward to the most every day are the times I get to see you."

Blaire's fingers go to her lips. "You're serious?"

"I think we make a great team."

"Me, too." She smiles, and then her expression turns serious. "We'd have to open up a wall."

"The adjoining wall doesn't have anything but electrical to worry about, and that's easy to shift around."

She cocks her head to the side, considering. "What about the booths and the wall of photos?"

"We'd only have to lose one booth to put the doorway in, and we could have a host stand between the two."

"You sound like you already have a layout for this." She laughs.

"I might have drawn up a rough sketch and looked into a few things."

"Wait. You've already thought about this, too?" A small

wry smile tips up the corner of her mouth. "So that's what Gramps meant by we're on the same page."

"I don't want to push you into this either way, Blaire. I know how important your independence is, and how hard you've worked so you don't have to compromise your dream. I just want you to know that if you're ever interested, I'd love to do this together with you, but it's really okay if you don't like—"

She launches herself out of the chair and wraps her arms around me. "I'm interested. I know I've always talked about not compromising my dream, but I realized I really love having a partner. Having the *right* partner. I only wanted to do it on my own because no one ever thought I could, and now I know I can. My favorite place to be is right next to you. I want us to do this together." She smooths her hands down my chest. "But what about the brewery?"

"I don't want to let this go—us, the bar, the connection I have to you and this place is far too important. I came into this thinking I would make it work and then move on, but I got so much more out of it. I got you."

"And cupcakes. Don't forget about those."

I chuckle and bend to kiss her. "And cupcakes. So we're in this together?"

"There isn't anyone else I'd rather do this with than you."

"Let's go tell Gramps the good news. He's been hounding me to ask you."

"How long have you been thinking about this?"

"A while." I've thought about it since I won Best Bar. But I started falling for her long before that.

I tug her by the hand and give Lars a covert thumbs-up on the way over to the table where Gramps is sitting. Lars gives me a quick nod and pulls his phone out of his back pocket, speed typing a message.

I survey the booths close to Gramps's table, glad everything seems to have fallen into place today. Like fate has stepped in once again and thrown something undeniable in my path, forcing me to stop and see what's in front of me. Or in this case, hugging my arm and practically skipping toward Gramps.

His gaze meets mine, and anticipation churns in my gut. He and I have sat down countless times over the past several months, hashing this out, me questioning whether I'm moving too fast, him telling me I'm moving too damn slow. I've been worried about making more changes to The Knight Cap, but he's assured me that Grams would be all for it. Grams always said it wasn't about fixing broken things; it was about giving them a lift to make them feel new again.

And that's exactly what we're going to do.

Gramps pushes out of his chair, a little unsteady, just like me. "So? Do you like the idea?"

Blaire laughs and releases my arm so she can hug him. "I love it. I think it's perfect."

He hugs her back and winks at me over her shoulder. "I knew you would."

When he releases her I step in and give him a hug. "Thank you for believing in me."

"Always, son, always." His voice cracks, and I feel the emotion rising, the sadness over our mutual loss—first his son, and my father and mother, then Grams. But he gives me a pat on the back, then he takes my hand in his, giving me the last piece of the puzzle. "Now stop stalling."

I nod once and turn to face Blaire, who looks like she's on the verge of tears—happy ones, though—and I drop to one knee.

Her eyes flare with surprise, but stay locked on mine as understanding dawns. I've taken a lot of big risks today and I'm about to take the biggest one of all.

I smooth my thumb over the worn velvet box, finding strength in it. It isn't a new ring, but it's special and it has meaning, because it was my grandmother's. I flip the lid open, the diamond catching the light, and rainbows dance across the back of my hand and Blaire's dress.

"Oh, Ronan," Blaire whispers. Shaking fingers touch her lips and she smiles behind them, even as a single tear tracks slowly down her cheek.

"Blaire, for a long time I didn't want to fall in love, because the reality of losing someone you love is so hard, especially when you don't expect it. But this, being here"—I motion to the bar, and all the people in it, watching me take a huge chance on the woman I love—"and meeting you changed everything. You came slamming through that door and you made it impossible not to fall in love with you and your determination and your beautiful, creative mind." I squeeze her hand, and she squeezes back. "I want you at my side every day. I want your good days and bad. I want your fight and your warmth and your effervescence lighting up my world. I want your forever. Marry me, please."

"Of course I'll marry you."

I slip the ring on her finger and push to a stand. "She said yes!"

Everyone bursts into raucous cheers as I wrap my arms around her waist. I kiss her, probably longer than is appropriate with the number of people watching. But I don't care, and neither does she, apparently. We've found forever in each other, and now I never have to let her go.

Blaire

6 months later

"One year ago today I stepped in a pile of dog crap."

My stylist, Frangelica—yes, like the liqueur—meets my gaze in the mirror briefly and smiles. "Oh?"

Daphne snorts and takes another photo.

The cameraman steps to the right, presumably so he can pan in on my face.

"Is this the story of the first time you met?" Tori asks.

She popped in as soon as my makeup was done so she could get a few minutes with me while Fran finishes up with my hair. It's my wedding day and I'm clearly nervous since it's going to be livestreamed on Tori's YouTube channel.

"It is." I'm about to nod, but remember Fran is working on my hair.

"Oh! I've only heard Ronan's version! I want to hear yours!" Tori claps her hands excitedly.

So I tell her my version, including all the little details, the bang we thought was an earthquake, the broken unicorn glass, the way I lost my ability to speak and string together logical sentences because he was so disarmingly handsome and ridiculously composed. I recall how annoyed and flustered I was, so much so that I stepped in the dog poop I'd marked with a flower and forgot about. Recounting the story helps settle my nerves.

So much has happened in the past year, but the last six months have been an amazing whirlwind. Lars recorded Ronan's proposal and shared it on social media after I said yes. From there things went a little crazy, especially with the incessant requests from people who wanted to see us tie the knot live.

So we agreed to let Tori do the honors, in part because of her role in bringing us together. Yes, there were other variables and factors at play, but if we hadn't been competing against each other, and then eventually banding together to outdo D&B, we may not have fallen in love. Shoddy plumbing shut D&B down after the Love Is in the Air event, and they ended up relocating to another end of town. The building across the street has been turned into a software company with fifty new employees, which means more business for us.

Which means The Knight Cap & Cupcakery is thriving.

When we opened the wall between B&B and The Knight Cap we needed to find a way to blend the two very distinct, very different themes. Instead of a complete overhaul, we found a way to work the plaid into my side and the whimsy of cupcakes into his without emasculating it entirely.

My family shows up as I finish the story. There's a whole lot of hugs and hands flapping in front of faces to ward off the tears. My parents have really come around in the past year, offering support and praise without trying to take over. Although Ronan is pretty good at standing his ground and politely telling them to back off. I've even gotten better at it, too.

Eventually we shoo everyone out of the back room—it's not really made for more than two or three people—so Daphne can help me into my dress.

My dress isn't quite the typical bridal gown. It's far more representative of me and Ronan and where we met, which is here. It's champagne colored and the entire bustier top is red and black plaid. It matches Ronan's tux with his red vest and plaid tie.

"Ronan is going to lose his freaking mind when he sees you in this dress," Daphne mutters. "Let's hope he can make it through the reception instead of dragging you into the office."

I snort indelicately, as though the idea is completely ludicrous. "As if." I can feel my face going red, especially since my mom is also in the room with us.

"Not according to Lars," she mumbles.

"What did you just say?"

She gives me a serene smile. "Hmm?"

I poke her in the shoulder. "Since when do you and Lars gossip about what Ronan and I do behind closed doors?"

Her smile turns into a smirk. "You mean closed *office* doors, which happen to be right across the hall from the stockroom."

I don't get to grill her about it because there's a knock on the door, but I make a mental note to give Lars hell for telling Daphne about the office incident. He was supposed to take that to the grave.

Daphne opens the door for my dad. "Care Blaire, you look gorgeous." He pulls me in for a huge hug and for once I don't hate that nickname. He holds me at arm's length, eyes watery, a sad smile on his face. "You ready for this?"

"I've never been more ready for anything in my life." And it's true. I can't wait to marry Ronan, because then we can officially start our forever. I slip my arm through his. "You ready to walk me down the aisle and give me away?"

"Never, but I can see how much you two love each other, so I'm willing to put my own feelings aside on this one." He winks and gives my arm a squeeze. "I don't really feel like I have any words of wisdom to impart to you where marriage is concerned, all considering."

I lean my head on his shoulder. "You taught me that love doesn't always fit into a neat little box, and I'm a better person for it. Plus, normal families are boring."

He chuckles and bends to kiss me on the cheek. "I'm glad he loves you enough to deal with the rest of us."

"We're kind of a package deal, aren't we? Now let's get out there so I can marry the one that I want."

The wedding march starts—bagpipes, of course—and we walk down the short hall, turn left at the end of the bar and there's Ronan.

His hand goes to his chest and he tips his chin up to the ceiling; his eyes fall closed for the briefest moment and he murmurs something that makes Gramps squeeze his arm. Of course he's Ronan's best man.

As I make my way down the aisle, past our family and friends and Tori and the camera crew, I feel like I'm falling backward through time, Alice traveling to Wonderland, to the moment when Henry and Dottie found their forever in exactly the same place, on exactly the same day, sixty-three years ago. History sometimes repeats itself in the most magical ways.

When I finally reach Ronan, my dad kisses me on the cheek and I take Ronan's hand. He looks magnificent and happy and a tad nervous, and like he's on the verge of tears. So am I.

"God, you're beautiful." He squeezes both of my hands. "You look like you were made for me."

I squeeze back. "That's because I am."

And I know without a doubt that Ronan is mine. That we'll stand beside each other through all the good times and the bad, that we'll argue and cry and laugh and love.

He's the icing to my cupcake. My happily forever after.

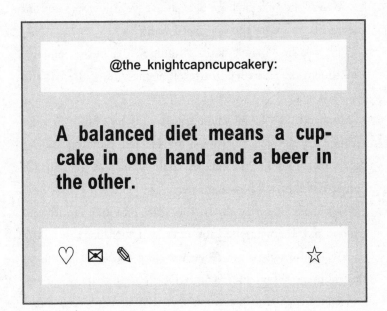

@the_knightcapncupcakery:

A balanced diet means a cupcake in one hand and a beer in the other.

ACKNOWLEDGMENTS

Hubs and kidlet; you are my rocks and I'm incredibly lucky to have your love and your support. Mom, Dad, and Mel, you're amazing cheerleaders and I adore you.

Deb, you are always there to lift me up when I need it, to make fun of me when I'm being dramatic and ridiculous, and you never fail to celebrate my victories, no matter how small they are. You're a once in a lifetime friend and I'm so lucky to have you.

Kimberly, I'm so grateful for your friendship and your incredible business brain. Thank you for being such a force to reckon with.

Sarah, I am beyond blessed to have you in my corner; you are the keeper of my sanity, and I adore you. Hustlers, thank you for being such an endless source of support and friendship.

Tijan, you're such a warm hug and a gentle soul, thank you for being you.

Leigh, thank you for always being a voice of reason when the doubt kicks in.

Huge gratitude to Leah, Estelle, and my team at Forever for

all the amazing ideas, support, and enthusiasm for each new project. I'm lucky to have such wonderful, innovative women to work with.

Sarah, Jenn, Hilary, Shan, and my team at Social Butterfly, you're an amazing group of women and I adore you. Thank you for everything you do.

Sarah Musings, you create such gorgeous graphics, thank you for sharing your talent with me.

Gel, you are a graphic wizard, and I adore your creative mind and your out of the box thinking. Thank you for bringing my words to life.

Beavers, I'm so grateful for all of you. You are my safe space and the place I go to when I want to laugh and share my excitement.

I have so much love for the incredible women in this community who are my friends, colleagues, teachers, and cheerleaders: Deb and Katherine, Tijan, Marty, Karen, Teeny, Erika, Shalu, Kellie, Ruth, Kelly, Melanie, Leigh, Marnie, Julie, Lou, Laurie, Kathrine, Angela, Holiday's. Thank you for being such influential people in my life. I'm so fortunate to have all of you.

To my readers, bloggers, and bookstagrammers: Thank you for loving books and believing in happily ever afters.

ABOUT THE AUTHOR

New York Times and *USA Today* bestselling author Helena Hunting lives outside of Toronto with her amazing family and her two awesome cats, who think the best place to sleep is her keyboard. She writes all things romance—contemporary, romantic comedy, sports and angsty new adult. Helena loves to bake cupcakes, has been known to listen to a song on repeat 1,512 times while writing a book, and if she has to be away from her family, prefers to be in warm weather with her friends.

PRAISE FOR ALEXA MARTIN'S PLAYBOOK SERIES

"Martin is an incredible storyteller and has a unique ability to blend fiction with real-life situations in the sports world."
—*New York Times* bestselling author La La Anthony

"Get ready for sparks to fly . . ."   —PopSugar

"An emotional journey with an intoxicating romance."   —NPR

"A fun and sexy romance novel set in the sports world."
—Bustle

"If you like steamy romance with a side of sports, this fun, fast-paced novel is for you."   —HelloGiggles

"The writing is snappy, the pacing is quick, the romance is sublime, and the humor is off-the-charts. Alexa Martin delivers a stellar love story, and I can't wait to see what she writes next."
—*USA Today*

"Martin scores a touchdown of a debut with *Intercepted*, a witty rom-com set in the world of professional football players and their wives."   —*Entertainment Weekly*

"Fast, fun, and absolutely engaging. A smashing debut!"
—*New York Times* bestselling author Kristan Higgins

"Alexa Martin's books are the ultimate reading escape filled with fabulous characters; witty, dazzling prose; and swoonworthy romances."   —*New York Times* bestselling author Chanel Cleeton

"Alexa Martin is so good at this; I'm so impressed by how nuanced and thoughtful this book is, while still being hilarious and sexy!"
—*New York Times* bestselling author Jasmine Guillory

SNAPPED

Alexa Martin

JOVE
NEW YORK

A JOVE BOOK
Published by Berkley
An imprint of Penguin Random House LLC
penguinrandomhouse.com

Library of Congress Cataloging-in-Publication Data

Names: Martin, Alexa, author.
Title: Snapped / Alexa Martin.
Description: First Edition. | New York : Jove, 2020. | Series: The playbook ; vol 4
Identifiers: LCCN 2020007423 (print) | LCCN 2020007424 (ebook) |
ISBN 9780593102503 (trade paperback) | ISBN 9780593102510 (ebook)
Subjects: GSAFD: Love stories.
Classification: LCC PS3613.A77776 S63 2020 (print) |
LCC PS3613.A77776 (ebook) |
DDC 813/.6—dc23
LC record available at https://lccn.loc.gov/2020007423
LC ebook record available at https://lccn.loc.gov/2020007424

First Edition: October 2020

Printed in the United States of America
1   3   5   7   9   10   8   6   4   2

Cover art and design by Colleen Reinhart

To Anna and Paul, my grandparents.
I miss you every single day.
I'm forever grateful for every moment I spent with you.
Thank you for loving all of me.

AUTHOR'S NOTE

WHEN I FIRST STARTED MY WRITING JOURNEY, I SWORE I WOULD never write about football. Having lived the sport for a while, I was having a hard time believing anybody would think this life was glamorous or romantic. However, as I wrote *Intercepted* and began the Playbook series, my opinion changed. I realized I didn't have to tell the story that was expected of me; I was able to use my experiences to create stories that felt authentic to me.

And that's what happened with *Snapped*.

I very clearly remember doing my first-ever podcast and Jenny Nordbak asking me if I was planning on writing a book that touched on players taking a knee on the field. I'm not sure I could've said no any faster. It was not in my plans to write this book. My husband retired before Colin Kaepernick began to take a knee on the field and in the height of the "controversy," I wasn't sure I could properly tell that story.

But when I found out I was able to write a fourth book for the series, it was the only idea I wanted to pursue. I figured enough time had passed that I would be able to tell the story I wanted to tell. I finished writing *Snapped* in October 2019. Little did I know that this book would be more relevant as it released than it was while I was writing it.

This is not Colin Kaepernick's story. I respect him and the bravery he showed by kneeling on the field in 2016. He made a stand that has gotten more powerful over time. He was definitely an inspiration for this book, but I can't tell his story. Only he can. This is a story about Elliot and Quinton. I know I do not speak for all Black experiences, or even all biracial ones. This is my story, coming from my perspective, based on my lived experiences.

Like Elliot, I am biracial. Also like Elliot, my Black parent died when I was very young, and I was raised with my all-white family. Understanding and accepting my racial identity has been a long journey for me. I grew up in the most amazing home with my mom and grandparents who loved me. Because of that, it was hard for me to see or acknowledge many forms of racism. Partly because I didn't want my family, who loved me, to feel betrayed.

I also constantly felt like I was being pulled in different directions outside of the house. Being told that I wasn't Black enough by some and that I was too Black for others. There was even a time when we went to visit extended family and one of my cousins could not understand how it was possible that I was Black and related to her. We were both in our teens. It was incredibly hurtful, but because it was what I always did, I laughed it off.

It wasn't until I became an adult, got married to a Black man, and had Black children that I finally began to come to grips with my identity and process the way a lifetime of microaggressions had affected me. And it was painful. Painful to come to grips with the way the people I loved and who loved me had left a long-lasting impression. Painful to realize I had quieted and doubted my own feelings for others' comfort.

As for Quinton, I really wanted to narrow his focus on the football league, their treatment of retired players, and racism within the organization. As more people are seeing the realities BIPOC face in this country, these are problems that are impossible to escape. I knew I couldn't do the story justice unless I narrowed it down. As the wife of a former professional player, I've been hearing more and more about the mistreatment of former players, specifically players who retired before 1993. After hearing personal accounts from their spouses, listening to interviews, and then finding FAIR—Fairness for Athletes in Retirement, a nonprofit that lifts the voices of players who retired before 1993—I knew this was the story I was capable of telling in a meaningful and effective way.

This book, which I hoped would be full of laughs and fun, took on a much more personal and serious tone. Though I hope everyone still finishes this book with a smile on their face, my main hope is that you, the reader, will feel the love and heart I tried to insert in these pages. And I hope that if you started this book set in one perspective, you finish it more open to understanding the journeys of self-discovery and acceptance that so many of us are on.

Prologue

Quinton
Game One

THE CROWD'S CHEERS ECHO IN THE TUNNEL. SCREAMS OF EXCITE-
ment bounce off the concrete floor and vibrate through my cleats
and into my veins.

I live for this feeling. The anticipation of running onto the
field. Never knowing what is coming or what might happen.

I've always kept my head down. I've listened to the coaches.
Made the plays. I've done my job like the good little athlete they've
trained me to be.

But today is different.

The piece of black tape feels as if it weighs a thousand pounds
hidden in my glove. My knee itches to touch the ground.

I can't keep quiet any longer. I won't keep quiet any longer.

No.

This is the day I will take a stand by taking a knee.

Today is the day I look up.

One

Elliot

I'VE NEVER HAD ACTUAL WORK BENEFITS.

I mean, sure, I've got medical and a 401(k), but I'm talking about benefits that mean something. Like my friend Liv's Nordstrom discount or Marie's endless supply of cupcakes.

But now, I'm finally on their level. I have perks. The *best* perks possible: discounted and readily available Denver Mustangs tickets.

Sure, the parking costs a mint, the food is outrageous, and don't even get me started on the drinks . . . but I'm here! My first ever professional football game and I'm part of the Mustangs family.

My dad would've freaking loved this.

"Why'd you make us get here so early?" Marie's freckled arm stretches in front of me to nab one of the cheese-covered nachos in my lap. "I'm going to burn to hell and back."

I made her apply sunscreen in the car, but even so, she's right.

She's still going to burn. She burns just thinking about the sun. When we took a trip to Vegas for her twenty-first birthday, she burned so bad at the pool that I thought she needed to go to the emergency room.

"Because, if we didn't get here when we did, the parking would've been impossible, the lines to the concessions would've been a mile long, and you would've been complaining that you were hungry and needed beer when I wanted to watch the game."

"Okay, but now the team's about to come out and I'm almost out of beer and you're not being a good nacho sharer, so I'm going to complain anyways." She grabs the last cheesy nacho in the tray and shoves it into her mouth before I can steal it back. And, because I work for the organization, I can't punch her in the arm like I really want to. Maybe if I was a trainer or something that sounded a little more aggressive, I could get away with a light swat. But, since I work in public relations—aka the department that extinguishes fires, not ignites them—it's probably not the best idea.

In my next life, I'm so going to be a wrestler.

"Asshole," I mumble beneath my breath, which turns out to be unnecessary because that's the moment the announcer decides to let his presence be known.

"Denver, Colorado! Get on your feet! Let's hear it for your Denver Mustangs!" Jack, the announcer the Mustangs have used for the last five seasons, shouts through the speakers. I met him this week; he was kind of obnoxious, but I guess that's perfect for his job.

The metal floor rattles beneath my shoes with synchronized anticipation as everyone jumps to their feet.

Everyone, that is, except for me.

This is the first professional football game I've ever been to. I've wanted to come to one of these games forever and I promised my dad that he'd be by my side when I did. We were going to celebrate his remission with the best seats and all the beer he could drink.

Grief is such a bitch.

Because even though I woke up with a smile and have been looking forward to this for weeks, grief has decided to take this moment to drop a brick on my chest and wrap itself around my throat. The tears fall before I even have the chance to stop them and the only coherent thought I have is that I hope none of my new coworkers are around to witness this absurd meltdown.

"Hey." Marie squeezes my shoulder and sympathy emanates from her sapphire eyes. "I know he would love this. But I also know he'd have a fit if he thought he was the reason you missed the Mustangs' grand entrance you both obsessed over. So wipe those tears away before he comes back and haunts me for not straightening you out."

That gets a laugh out of me. More like a chorkle—laughter mixed with crying does not make for pretty noises. My fingers linger over his watch, which he had resized for me right after the doctors told him the chemo wasn't working anymore, before I swipe the tears off my face. "You're right." I stand up with the rest of the crowd, who are thankfully too busy watching the offensive starters get called out of the tunnel to notice the crazy girl hysterically crying in the plastic chair next to them. "I'm done. We're going to have a fucking blast for the rest of the game."

"Yeah we are." She lifts her hand into the air for a high five that is purposefully too high for me to reach. "Plus, you pulled it together before they called that new hot quarterback out."

I decide to keep my dignity intact and not jump for the high five. Instead I let her hand linger above me and focus on the field in front of me.

Because—even if I'm not sure I can say this anymore, since I work here—Quinton Howard Junior is very hot.

Like smokin'.

He's a legacy player—his dad was a lineman in the eighties and early nineties—but it was his ability to lead his team to a championship win last year that brought him to Denver . . . and a contract worth a lot (and I mean *a lot*) of money. He was originally a sixth-round draft pick and didn't have the opportunity to start until the quarterback he played under suffered a season-ending injury during Quinton's fifth season. This is his seventh year and so far he's had a killer preseason. Every time I turn on ESPN, there's another commentator placing their bets on him leading the Mustangs to his second championship ring.

As if conjured by pure willpower—or really good timing—his picture appears on the JumboTron. The screams that held an undertone of bass from grown men transform to the screams you hear at a boy band concert. And Marie, who has made her disinterest of the sport clear to me throughout our entire friendship, is suddenly staring at the JumboTron like she's preparing to write a paper on the juxtaposition of having a perfect face and getting tackled for a living.

Even though I want to give her shit and pretend like I'm above ogling the hot quarterback—I mean, can you say cliché?—I give in and stare right along with her and just about every other person in the stadium.

Quinton Howard Junior is the physical representation of tall, dark, and handsome. His dark brown skin has not a single imperfection; even amplified and broadcast on a giant HD screen, there isn't one thing marring his prefect face. While other players are smiling huge, goofy, yet adorable grins in their pictures, Quinton is the epitome of determination. His almond-shaped eyes are so dark, they're practically black, and are framed by the thickest, darkest lashes I've seen outside of Instagram ads. His thick eyebrows have perfect arches that I doubt have ever been touched by tweezers or wax and I will never get over the unfairness of it all. Granted, maybe if I hadn't gone tweezer crazy in seventh grade, I wouldn't be living the eyebrow struggle now. But what really kills me, more than the eyes and the skin, is his mouth.

Oh sweet heavens. His mouth. Last season, he was clean-shaven. His square jaw on full display. He was adorable. He had a little bit of a baby face and always sported this shy smile that made him look modest and surprised by his own abilities. But not this season. Now he's sporting a full beard around his plump lips. Nothing about him looks modest or young. No, this version of Quinton Howard Junior is a man who knows exactly what he wants and how he's going to get it. Which might be hotter than every single physical attribute he was blessed with.

God help any woman who ever comes in his sights.

"In his first official game in blue and orange, Mustangs fans, give it up for Quinton Howard Juuunnnior!" Jack's voice reverberates through the stadium as fireworks shoot from the sides of the tunnels.

Whereas all the other players ran out of the tunnel with contagious energy and excitement, Quinton takes his time. His steps are slow and his expression is of pure intensity. Everyone around me is eating it up. Their shouts grow louder as if he's putting on some kind of act for them to enjoy.

But it's my job to see a media event before it happens.

And my spidey sense is telling me that whatever this is? It's not going to be local news. No, this is going to be national coverage.

As he walks, he begins to lose the cocky tilt of his head. I don't see the spark of hunger in his eyes that says this is for show.

No.

There's hesitation in his movement. Fear and nerves written all across his face as he gets closer and closer to the cameraman blasting his image for everyone to see.

Then his feet stop moving and he stares straight into the camera. If my nerves weren't eating me alive, I'd probably be enjoying the close-up of his full lips and dark brown eyes like everyone else. But instead, my eyes are locked on the screen and I watch as he pulls a piece of black tape out of his glove and very carefully places it over the League's emblem embroidered on his jersey.

"Oh my god," I whisper in the midst of similar sentiments floating around me.

"I don't get it." Marie's voice sounds like a shout in the suddenly quiet stadium. She's completely oblivious as she lifts her beer to her lips and takes a final sip. "Is that some kind of quarterback thing?"

The only time Marie has ever watched football was when her ex-boyfriend played on our college team. He wanted her to support him. She broke up with him after the second game because no man was worth that kind of torture—her words, not mine. She came today after letting me know that in no way, shape, or form was I to yell at her when she started playing Candy Crush in the first quarter. I was honestly just so proud that she knew football was comprised of quarters and not periods or innings that I couldn't argue with her. So when she says she's confused, she means it.

Usually I can clear things up, but not this time.

"Not that I know of."

I think she keeps talking, but I can't hear her anymore. All I can do is track Quinton's movement on the field like everyone else. I think of any positive way to spin him blatantly disrespecting the League paying him millions of dollars. I have to be misunderstanding his intentions.

Time ticks by and both teams go to their benches. Most of the fans seem to have let whatever the hell he was doing roll off their backs and I relax a little. I grab my phone out of my purse, wanting to make sure nobody from the Mustangs has sent a panicked email as the first beats of the national anthem start to play.

Then it happens.

I'm waiting for my email to refresh when I hear the cascade of whispers and boos beginning to build.

I hope it's just the poor performer forgetting the words, but when I look up, my eyes are laser focused on Quinton Howard Junior.

On his knee. During the national anthem.

He's making a stand. He's not the first player in the League to take a knee, but he is the first Mustangs player to do it.

I get goosebumps on my arm. As a biracial Black woman, I'm aware of the injustices Black people face daily and respect Quinton's protest. But pride wars with panic over how this will affect my new job.

"Oh shit." Marie doesn't even try to hide her smile. "Looks like your job just got more interesting in the best possible way."

I'm about to spout off some sarcastic response when my phone starts vibrating in my hand, my boss's number on the screen.

I'm not sure the fallout at the Mustangs will be the "best," but Marie wasn't wrong. It did just get a lot more interesting.

Two

THE WORLD IS ON FIRE.

Okay. Fine. That's mad dramatic.

The world is not on fire, but my job has for sure taken the first crazy train straight to chaos.

I'm the strategic communications manager for the Denver Mustangs. Most people have no idea what that means and look at me like I have two heads. Then I tell them I'm basically Olivia Pope . . . but for football players. This helps most people. Or, at least it helps Shondaland fans. And why would I even talk to someone who doesn't appreciate the greatness that is Shonda Rhimes?

Anyways, it's my job to fix problems when they arise and to place the Mustangs organization in the best light possible. When I found out about the opening for this position—the position I put on my dream board my freshman year of college—I already had a binder full of strategies. Drunk driving? Covered. Injuries? Check. Failed drug test? I have ten different emails ready to send out. I had any and everything that could possibly happen mapped out with at least five ways to spin each one.

I even had a tentative plan for one of the players taking a knee.

One I hoped would keep the player, the community, and the organization happy. What I didn't expect? The quarterback blacking out his logo and protesting his employer too. I mean . . . what in the world?

Like I said: Crazy. Train.

"Did you see what Glenn Chandler said?" Paul, my coworker, asks.

Glenn Chandler is the latest person to throw their hat into the upcoming presidential race. It's just that the hat he threw in is covered in outrageous statements trying to get him the most coverage possible. And boy is he eating up this Quinton thing. "That Quinton is an ungrateful and entitled American, spitting in the faces of our troops?" I repeat the talking points Glenn really harped on. "I did. And people seem to be eating it up."

Thanks to YouTube and social media, everyone has a platform. That can be wonderful. I mean, it brought us Issa Rae and who can ever be mad at that? But for every creative genius using it for good, there's a Glenn Chandler using it to fuel their fire of anger. So when Glenn stood in front of the American flag, with a flag pin attached to his lapel, and started making accusations? It didn't matter that he didn't have anything to back them up with. His conviction was enough to convince his followers that Quinton had one motivation: to attack America and all it stands for.

And now I'm left scrambling to catch up. Normally I'm great at getting ahead of a situation. If Quinton had just told us about his plan, I could've helped. I would've had the press briefed, prepared, and on topic. But now we're two steps behind in a gap that seems to be growing every second.

"Yeah, that's what he said. But we sent your statement to ESPN and for what it's worth, you did a great job defusing the situation for most people." Paul rolls his chair next to mine and tosses his phone on my desk. "Just don't look at the comment section."

"Obviously. That's the first rule of the Internet." Also, I spent all last night reading the thousands of comments on the Yahoo homepage. There's no need for me to dive back into all of that vileness at work. People are terrible.

Even though I won't admit it out loud, I'm not sure how I feel about everything.

After his pregame routine, Quinton was on fire. And as he threw touchdown pass after touchdown pass, the fans seemed to forget about him taking a knee and covering the League's logo. I got hopeful that maybe this would blow over and not be a big deal. It wasn't until I tuned in to watch the postgame press conference that I learned how much work I was in for. Because even though the fans seemed to forget, the reporters did not.

The very first question had nothing to do with plays made or points scored. Nope. The only things they seemed to care about were his actions on the field. Why the tape? Why now?

I held my breath. Waiting to hear what he had to say, to hear him explain. I didn't understand the tape. Plus, he didn't kneel at all last season when players on other teams started to.

"I blacked out the logo because I work for a company that doesn't value our lives. Retired players are struggling and they are being met with silence. The same men we 'honor' with banners, the men who paved the way for us to get here, are wasting away and nothing is being done to help them. This company owns us, they exploit us, and once we're injured and battered, they throw us to the side like garbage. The League is a microcosm of our country and just like in our country, racism and discrimination run rampant. So the tape is for my teammates, but the knee is for the Black lives all across the country." But despite his serious words, his tone was conversational—happy even. He rubbed his hand down his beard, the picture of calm and collected. "I can't ignore the fact that racism and police brutality in this country are killing Black men, women, and children. This crisis must be addressed. I have a platform and I intend to use it." Then, without hesitation or his smile fading at all, he nodded to the press and stood up. "Thanks, guys. I think I can count on talking with you all soon."

I watched the clip approximately a trillion times, until his words were etched inside my skull like an ancient Egyptian text. They even echoed in my dreams during that pitiful hour of sleep I managed to get.

I've never been in a position like this before.

I've never been made to feel off-kilter by a situation I'm supposed to defuse. Obviously, the downside of this job is I don't get to have an opinion. I'm one part of the greater whole. And my job is to make the greater whole look good no matter what my personal feelings are.

What Quinton Howard Junior did—and said after the fact—has forced my insecurities to the forefront of my mind.

I've never known where I fit in the movement for social justice or if I even belonged. And now, that struggle—the ever-constant push and pull—with who I am is happening at work.

"Elliot?" Paul takes his foot and sends my desk chair gliding across the carpet. "You still in there?"

"Yeah, sorry." I shake my head and force a smile to spread across my face. "Just trying to come up with other ways to spin this since the media is clearly trying to confuse intentions."

"Welp." The wrinkles around Paul's blue eyes deepen and I get the distinct feeling that he's laughing at me. "I hope you pull something together fast, because Mr. Mahler wants to see you in his office."

"Just me?" I squeak out, my voice deciding to take a hike.

"Just you, new girl."

"Now?" I grab the edge of my desk as my eyes go wide and my knuckles turn white.

"Right now."

Fuck.

Mr. Mahler is the owner of the Denver Mustangs. He sat in on my final interview and literally did not say one word to me. When he had something to say, he would write it down on the clipboard in front of him and pass it to Paul. Then, he would stare at me with an unwavering gaze as I answered. He didn't even crack a smile. I actually went home and polished off a bottle of wine as I made cookies because I was convinced he hated me and I wouldn't get the job.

Obviously I got the job, but I'm still not so sure Mr. Mahler doesn't hate my guts.

I stand on shaky legs and take a deep breath. "It's been nice working with you, Paul. Remember me when I'm gone."

Even though I've only known Paul for less than a month, I feel like he was meant to be my work husband. The thought of having it annulled so soon breaks my heart a little bit.

"Don't be ridiculous." He rolls his eyes and grabs his abandoned phone from my desk. "I never remember anyone after they're given the axe."

At my gasp, he dissolves into a very unprofessional fit of laughter. Rude.

THE NEW HEELS I splurged on after landing my dream job drag across the carpeted floors as I make my way to hear of my untimely demise. Thank goodness I didn't go ahead and buy the cream coat too. Even with Liv's discount, it would've been an obscene amount . . . although it did totally look like one Kerry Washington wore once.

Our offices are located inside the Mustangs training facility. A perk I found to be almost as cool as the discounted game tickets.

Almost.

Now, looking at the empty practice fields through the window-lined hallways, I feel like I'm being mocked. But as Mr. Mahler's office comes into view, a sense of peace settles over me and confidence infiltrates my veins.

I'm a woman in a man's world. A biracial woman in a man's world. I've had to work twice as hard as most people to get a foot in the door. I got this job because I was the best choice. Because I'm damn good at my job. I raise my chin and steel my spine. The statement I sent out to the media was great. It was apologetic as well as stern. It made it clear we were taking things seriously while at the same time not jumping to conclusions. It was the best anyone could've made of this hectic situation, and I'm sure Mr. Mahler knows it too.

"Hello," I greet Mr. Mahler's secretary. The older woman has her white hair pulled back into a graceful chignon that highlights her classic features that have not been dimmed by age. "I'm Elliot Reed. Mr. Mahler asked to see me."

"Of course, dear." Her expertly painted red lips split into a genuine smile as she motions toward a seating area filled with navy chairs and orange pillows. "Take a seat and I'll let him know you're here."

"Thank you." I turn to take a seat, but before I make any progress, a door swings open.

"Miss Reed!" Mr. Mahler's gravelly voice takes me by surprise. Considering he didn't speak to me at all during my previous—and only—encounter with him, the smile on his face and apparent eagerness to see me is a pleasant surprise. "Please come in."

When I imagined what Mr. Mahler's office would look like—which happens much more often than I'd care to share—I pictured tons of dark wood with lots of gold accessories. And I'm pleased to say, I hit the nail on the head.

Whereas the rest of the Mustangs facility is filled with modern touches and shades of orange and blue everywhere you look, his office is like stepping back in time. Dark wood panels line the wall. His oversized desk is very obviously missing a computer of any type. Newspapers and magazines are strewn all across the workspace. Even though Denver is a smoke-free city, a gold ashtray with a lit cigar sending swirls of smoke into the air and a glass filled with some type of amber liquid are sitting on the desk. The only clue his doorway was not a portal back to the 1950s is the wall filled with television screens showing every sports channel available. All of which happen to have Quinton Howard Junior's name and face plastered on them.

I settle into the plush leather chair across from Mr. Mahler. Keeping my shoulders squared, I run through all of the talking points I'd been writing down this morning.

Mr. Mahler takes a seat in his wingback leather chair that is most likely older than I am and lifts his cigar to his mouth. He takes a deep pull and exhales the smoke slowly. It takes all of my self-control to ignore the billowing smoke cloud heading straight into my face.

"I'm sure you're well aware that we are facing a little bit of a media problem." Mr. Mahler keeps the cigar in between his fingers as he grabs one of the newspapers off the table and hands it to me. Finding newspapers nowadays is surprisingly difficult, but I managed to track down a few this morning, so the headline proclaiming that Quinton Howard Junior is an overpaid toddler doesn't catch me off guard.

"Yes sir, I am." I set the newspaper back on his desk, careful not to disturb the rest of the mess cluttering the surface. "We sent out a statement this morning that has gone over pretty well. It was vague, but we were waiting to hear the response from the public before releasing anything else." I pause to see if Mr. Mahler would like to interject, but when he just takes a sip out of the crystal glass, I carry on. "We want to make sure our message doesn't get twisted. The only thing worse than saying nothing is saying everything. We want to make sure we have a direction when we speak so that the public doesn't feel like we are just saying what they want to hear."

"Hmmm." He pulls from his cigar again, his eyes, which match the amber liquid he's sipping, narrowing as he assesses me. I hold his eye contact and refuse to cower under his gaze. "You are so young, I wasn't sure you could handle the job. But you're very articulate. I'm impressed."

Well, that's a backhanded compliment if I've ever heard one. But, it is still a compliment. And considering my last interaction with Mr. Mahler, it does for me what the liquor he's sipping does for him. Warmth flows through my system and the tension I woke up with finally begins to dissipate.

"Now here is the problem as I see it." He sets down the glass and his cigar and steeples his fingers in front of his face. "We can put out as many statements as we want. We can listen to the public and try to take a stance that keeps their anger in check, but nothing is going to change if every time we get them settled down, Quinton steps back on the field covering logos and kneeling during the anthem."

This is the problem that's been haunting me since I saw Quinton walk out of the tunnel yesterday. How do I support his message, but also the organization I'm paid to represent? "We can only say so much if the entire organization isn't on the same page, and that includes Mr. Howard."

"Exactly." He smiles wide. His bright white teeth are on full display and instead of feeling reassured, a spiral of unease blooms in my gut. "That is why I'm assigning you to Quinton."

"I'm sorry, what?" Until that moment I had all of my emotions in check, but there's no masking the panic lacing my words.

"Quinton will be expecting you at HERS this afternoon. The owner, Brynn Sterling, works closely with our organization and will make sure you will both be comfortable for what may be a very uncomfortable conversation." Suddenly, Mr. Mahler's posture changes as he sits up and levels me with the same intense stare that haunted my dreams after my interview. "It's imperative that you get Quinton on our side. The damage his accusations could cause not only our organization, but the League as a whole, is enormous. From this point forward, you are to work only with him and the mess he created. Understood?"

"Yes." The word comes out weak. I close my eyes and take a deep breath and try again. "Yes, I understand."

He nods his head. Satisfaction is written across his time-weathered face, but I speak before he can, because for some reason, I know that he's not finished with me yet. "Just so you know, Mr. Mahler, this job means more to me than just a paycheck. My father passed away earlier this year. We spent his final months together watching the Mustangs play. My favorite memories of him are wrapped up with your organization. I want what's best for everyone."

His gaze softened as I spoke, but I have a sick feeling in my stomach. It was less because of what I said, and more of what he hadn't. "I'll hold you to that. We can't have an entire season of bad press, and if you don't have a handle on this by playoffs, we will have to find someone who can get it done."

Dammit.

Sometimes I really hate being right.

Three

"WAIT," LIV'S VOICE BOOMS THROUGH MY CAR SPEAKERS. "YOU'RE meeting who?"

"You heard me." If the bumper-to-bumper Denver traffic wasn't enough to make a sane person go crazy, listening to Liv's voice rise approximately twenty decibels would be mad entertaining. "Quinton Howard Junior. The stubborn quarterback who just had to do this on his own and possibly put an end to my career before it even started."

I figured a lunch meeting would mean avoiding rush hour. However, I forgot that with the influx of Denver residents over the last few years, every hour is rush hour. It has taken almost an hour to finally reach my exit and I'm most definitely not amused.

"By stubborn, do you mean extremely hot?"

"No, I definitely do not mean hot." I used to think he was hot, but the whole "could cost me my job" thing has changed my mind. "Do you understand how good I am at my job? I'm really fucking good. All he had to do is reach out to me and I would've helped him organize this! Do you know how many people would love to have me at their back? Now the Mustangs—"

"Whoa, whoa, whoa," Liv cuts me off. "I know you love a good rant, but I think you forgot that I don't actually care about the Mustangs. I just wanted to talk about his pretty face and white spandex pants."

"This is why I didn't invite you to the game."

At least Marie will pretend to care about football.

"And this entire 'the Mustangs turn me into a ranting lunatic' is the reason I would've said no even if you did ask."

"Fair point."

I've known Olivia Pearson since freshman year of high school. I don't know if it was because my dad thought nuns could replace the missing female presence in my life, but he sent me to an all-girls Catholic school when I was in kindergarten and kept me there until high school. It was fine. I definitely didn't hate it. Still to this day, I have a soft spot for plaid pleated skirts and cable-knit tights—it's probably the only reason I joined the field hockey team too. But I wanted to have the full "what you see on TV" high school experience. Mainly, I wanted *Friday Night Lights*. And lucky for me, so did my dad. He played hardball, but I promised straight A's and he gave in. But the luckiest part for me was that Liv was assigned the seat next to me in my first period class and had an affinity for the spoken word. And since I really like to listen, we decided we'd be best friends.

She still likes to talk.

"So, since this is a work lunch, does that mean they are going to pay? HERS has really good cocktails, you should order a few of those bad boys."

I almost don't see the light turning red with how hard I roll my eyes. "I'm not sure if you caught the part where I told you my job is literally hanging by a thread, but I think getting trashed when

I'm supposed to be wrangling a grown-ass man is probably a bad idea."

"Well, I get off in a couple hours, want me to meet you there?"

"Doesn't that mean you should be working now? Don't you work on commission?"

Liv has had her job at Nordstrom since we graduated from high school. She's the most stylish person I've ever met. Which is why her fashion blog has taken off the way it has. She doesn't need her day job anymore, but she loves her clients . . . and I love her discount. She's a true freaking friend.

"Eh." I can picture her tossing her perfectly highlighted mane over her shoulder. "I had a huge sale this morning. I'm in the back going through inventory now. But yes to drinks, right?"

"Yes." My phone buzzes in my cupholder, telling me I've arrived at HERS. "I have a feeling drinks will be mandatory after this."

"Yay! Best Monday ever!"

At least for one of us.

IF I HADN'T sat in traffic for half of my life (only a slight exaggeration) to meet the man who holds my dream job in his hands, I'd be stoked to get an afternoon, work-sponsored trip to HERS. I don't like the term "guilty pleasure," because if I've learned anything the past couple of years, it's to not feel guilt over things that bring me joy. But if I had to label one thing as a guilty pleasure, it would be my love of reality television. And *Love the Player* is at the top of my reality TV obsession. Not only does it take place in my city, but it's based on my favorite football team! It's the only reality show my dad actually liked watching with me. I've wanted to go to HERS for the longest time, since so much of the show is filmed there. It's too bad that my first time going might also coincide with the fiery crash of my career.

I luck out and find a parking spot on the street in front of HERS. But as soon as my feet hit the pavement, I don't want to move. So many conflicting thoughts run through my mind. I want to prove to Mr. Mahler that I'm the best person for this job. I worked my ass off for this job and I didn't get it by running from a challenge. But on the other hand, I'm having a hard time sorting out my thoughts about Quinton Howard Junior. I completely respect the stance he's taking. It's brave and admirable. But on a personal—and selfish—level, I hate that I feel like I'm being forced to choose between two parts of myself . . . again. This is my dream job. It's been my rainbow after the darkest, worst year of my life. I refuse to just walk away. There has to be a way I can keep everyone happy and I guess it's my job to figure it out.

With that thought, I pull back my shoulders, plaster a smile onto my face, and open the door to HERS like I own the place.

Even on a Monday, the place is far from empty. Music drifts from the speakers just over the rumbling of conversations taking place and glasses clinking. The wall by the front door is covered in flowers and a pink neon HERS sign that I know for a fact is used as the background for many an Instagram post.

"Welcome to HERS," a woman with the thickest, blackest, most beautiful hair I've ever seen greets me. "Would you like a table or are you going to the bar?"

Bar. God. I wish I was going to the bar.

"I'm actually meeting someone, but thank you." I feel myself cringe, but if she noticed, she doesn't let on, which makes me like her even more. Maybe if I get fired, I could try to get a job here and she can be my friend. Plus, I'm really good at drinking . . . maybe that could translate to my skills behind the bar too.

"Great." She smiles and her teeth gleam against her brown skin that, even inside, sparkles. "Please let me know if I can help you find them."

Unfortunately for me, Quinton Howard Junior is the only thing more noticeable than the meticulously decorated bar I'm standing in. I was hoping he would be in some spot that made him hard to find, or even better, would be late. But luck just hasn't been on my side these days.

For the second time today, I thank Liv for convincing me to splurge on my shoes. It's impossible to have a timid stride when you're wearing four-inch, five-hundred-dollar shoes . . . and that's science. Even if on the inside I'm a nervous wreck, at least I look confident in my approach.

Not that it matters much, because even though Quinton looks directly at me as I'm walking toward him, he dismisses me just as quickly.

Rude.

"Hello, Mr. Howard," I use the voice that Marie mocks me endlessly for. "Nice to meet—"

I don't finish, not because I don't want to, but because he doesn't give me the chance to.

"I'm sorry, I'm waiting for someone." I assume that he's talking to me since I'm the only person standing at his table, but I'm not positive because he hasn't looked up from his phone.

Super fucking rude.

"Actually, I—"

"What do you want me to sign?" He holds out his hand expectantly.

"Nothing, I—"

"Listen," he cuts me off again and actually takes his eyes off his phone this time to look at me. "I appreciate a forward woman as much as any man, but you're not my type."

I know I'm no beauty queen—Liv is definitely the one in my group that would take that title—but this was harsh no matter how I look. I'm sure his type is a six foot tall, size zero model with flowing blonde locks and eyes as blue as the ocean. Basically the complete opposite of my five-foot, three-inch frame that hasn't fit into a size zero since middle school . . . and even that is pushing it. My hair did have gold highlights for a while, but because I blast it with a flatiron at least once a week to tame my wild curls, I stopped dyeing it so it didn't all fall out. And my eyes are more the color of trees—not the leaves, the trunks. They're brown. I'm about as average as they come and I'm usually fine with that because most people have at least a sliver of manners.

In any other situation, I would be completely and utterly horrified. I mean, that's not just rude, it's hurtful! But thankfully for my tear ducts—and my pride—I'm just pissed. Who the hell does he think he is? Just because he was blessed with perfect, smooth dark brown skin and sharp cheekbones that are noticeable even with the thick beard that is infuriatingly even more gorgeous up close, does not mean that every woman who approaches him wants in his pants.

At my sides, my hands form into fists so tight that my neatly trimmed nails start digging into my palms, and I can actually feel the heat rising in my face like my head might explode at any second.

Even through my brown skin and peach blush, Quinton must see the red in my cheeks. He just reads it the wrong way.

I know he gets it wrong because instead of running away screaming, he has the audacity to touch me. His oversized hand wraps around my fist that is now shaking with the almost unbearable urge to punch him.

Much to my dismay, my body isn't on the same page with my mind. Because as soon as his calloused palm rubs against the sensitive skin on the back of my hand, it's like the fireworks that went off as the Mustangs ran onto the field moved into my pants. This only makes me more furious. I mean, I didn't even know touching hands could do this! The freaking audacity! And, by the way, why couldn't my body have reacted like this for any of the guys who actually weren't jerks to me?

"I didn't mean to embarrass you." He squeezes my hand and his voice is so patronizing that if I didn't know the value of the hand touching me, I'd consider breaking it. "I'm just not interested."

I yank my hand away from him, ignoring the way my skin still tingles from his touch and using every last bit of restraint I have, I pull out the chair across from him and take a seat. He opens up his mouth to speak, but this time, *I* talk over *him*. "As I was trying to say, I'm Elliot Reed. Mr. Mahler sent me."

His mouth falls open and finally—FINALLY!—no words come out.

If I wasn't so out-of-my-mind furious, I might even get some pleasure out of this moment.

But I can say, with one hundred percent certainty, that nothing Quinton Howard Junior does will ever bring me pleasure.

Four

"YOU . . . YOU'RE . . . I MEAN . . ." QUINTON STUMBLES OVER HIS words so hard, it's nearly impossible to think this is the same graceful man out on the field every Sunday. "I thought you were a man."

"Did Mr. Mahler tell you I was a man?" I ask. "Do you think I look like a man?"

The truth is, because of my name, this has happened before. But unlike now, nobody has ever made me feel so small during their confusion. So the joy I'm feeling watching him stumble around is profound.

"No, no!" He holds his hands out in front of him as his eyes damn near bulge out of his head. I swear I can see a blush creep up his dark brown cheeks. "That's not what I meant. I just assumed I was meeting with a man."

"Well, you know what they say about people who *assume* things." And yes, while I know my job depends on me working with this guy, I can't help but to stress "ass" because . . . well, because he's a giant one.

"Yeah, about that," he starts, but I've heard enough and I already want this meeting to be over.

"No need. You made yourself clear and that's fine. I'm here to do my job." The rejection was bad enough, the last thing I need to do is sit here while he lists all the reasons I'm not his type. I like to torment myself enough on my own, I do not need the physically flawless jerk to do it for me. "I'm hoping we can both be professional from this point forward."

Considering I just called him an ass, I definitely need the reminder just as much as he does.

"Yes, of course." He nods his head vigorously. "I really am so—"

"Sorry. You're so sorry, got it. Moving on." I'm here for a reason, and every second we sit here with the bullshit apologies is a second I could be doing my job. I just want to hurry this along, and, ultimately, go drown my sorrows at the fully stocked bar less than twenty feet away from me. I grab the fully decked-out iPad that the Mustangs supplied me with from my purse and swipe out of the Twitter app covered with endless tweets about the man in front of me before opening my notes. "So, we both obviously know why we're here."

"Because I'm making Mahler and a large portion of the country uncomfortable." The words come out conversationally, but there's an undercurrent of anger powering them.

I was not expecting it.

And from the way he shakes his head and then aims a perfectly white, perfectly straight, perfectly fake smile at me, he wasn't expecting it either.

I'm not sure which part surprises me the most, the fact that he showed me his anger or that he's so good at hiding it. I never saw it during his interview.

I put the iPad down on the table and level my stare with his. "Is that why you're doing this? To make people uncomfortable?" My words don't have any of the malice the reporters had. I'm honestly curious. Unlike Mahler, I don't disagree with the stance he's making. I just can't help unless I understand his motives and goals.

"No." He slumps down in his chair as he deflates before me. Like the confidence helium he sucked down before meeting me has finally dissolved. "It's not that at all and I hate that the point I'm trying to make is now being lost in the politics of it. That people are saying that I'm trying to get attention. They have no idea how personal all of this is to me."

Aha!

I move to write it down, but I'm not a therapist and I don't want to spook him out of telling me more. So I make sure to tuck that little nugget of information into the depths of my memory.

"Of course it's personal. If it wasn't, you wouldn't do this at all." I try to relax in my chair, which, though insanely cute, is not the epitome of comfort. "I think I have an idea that could make everyone happy."

He doesn't say anything, but the expression that crosses his face says everything. He thinks I'm full of shit. Which could be accurate. I want everyone happy, but I really don't want to take a journey down to the unemployment office.

But, last night, as I was reading the comment section filled with the scum of the world, an idea popped into my head. And sitting in front of him, seeing that this is something he actually cares about and not a publicity stunt, I know it's the only angle I have with him.

"You don't have a foundation." I open my email and click on one of the six messages I sent myself for this meeting. "Why not?"

He shrugs his shoulders, but that's all he gives me as far as answers go.

"I think you should start one." I open one of the links in the email, a player's foundation website, and hand him the iPad. He tentatively takes it from me, another win in my column. "With a foundation of your own, you can put actual action in place. You can raise money and help the causes you're so passionate about. I put together a list of about fifteen different player foundations, just go back to the email and you can click through the list."

I don't say anything else as he scrolls and reads. Instead, I watch him. I watch the way his eyebrows furrow together, the slight tilt of his lips, the way his spine seems to lengthen. He's into it. This might actually work!

"I started to set up a foundation last year." His words catch me all the way off guard. Not that he would notice, because he still hasn't looked away from the screen. "I did all of the paperwork and was approved for 501(c)(3) status at the beginning of the summer, but let it fall off after that."

"Wow. Okay, good." The paperwork would've taken us half the season, so this is great for my plan. But even though it makes things easier on me, I can't help but be irritated that normal people can't get approved before they have all of the details. Of course, for the rich and mighty Quinton Howard Junior, he can just make things happen with no real intent to follow through. "Do you have anything else for it?"

"Nope, just the approval." He glances down at the iPad again, like more than a few seconds of eye contact with me is impossible for him. "I filed the papers and then life happened and I didn't do anything else."

Life happened?

By that, does he mean he signed a ginormous contract guaranteeing he'll make more money in a month than I'll likely see in a lifetime? When life got in the way for me this past year, it was because I was burying my father next to the plot where we buried my mother thirty years ago.

How sad for him.

The embers of leftover anger and irritation begin to spark and I struggle to smother them.

"Yeah, I get that. Life can get pretty tricky." Luckily for me, none of the frustration I feel comes out when I speak. Unluckily, however, the quivering that tends to happen every time my dad crosses my mind is completely evident, and apparently is the only thing that can pull Quinton's attention from the iPad.

Dammit.

"Are you alright?" He pushes the tablet across the table as if nothing else matters besides me. And man, what a total freaking mind fuck that is. Because as much as I've been telling myself that I hate his guts, the second he turns his attention to me and those black eyes soften, it's like all of my resolve slips away.

"Yeah, I'm fine." I force a smile on my face and focus on the task at hand, reminding myself of his harsh words from only moments ago. "The fact that you already have the tax part done is huge. Now, it's all about the details, and I'm a total details girl, so this is the part I love."

"What's next?" I can tell he wanted to know what caused my near meltdown, but thankfully he moves on. Or, more accurately, he doesn't actually care. Either way, it's a win for me.

"Well, I know you're busy now that the season has started, but I'll need your input and help for a lot of this. It's your foundation after all." I close my email and open up the calendar app. "If you could tell me days and times that work for you, I'm more than happy to work my schedule around yours. If you are really serious about getting this done, I think we can have a launch event in a month. And I know you aren't going to love this part, but we're going to have to set up a few interviews and press conferences for you. If we want this to work, it's up to you to take control of the narrative. After we flesh out what your foundation is really addressing, I'll compile some statements and key talking points for you to focus on. This means that when you aren't doing football, you'll be doing this. It will be a commitment. Are you ready for this?"

And as much as I want this to work, the little voice in the back of my mind shouts that he's worth more to the team than I am, if things go south.

"I know you don't know me. I get that. And I know that people think because I play football and came from a family where my dad also played, that I'm some entitled fuckboy who has been handed everything in life."

Well fuck me! Not literally. Maybe literally? No. Definitely not.

Is he a mind reader?

"But the people who know me know that's not true. I work for everything I have . . . and now I'm ready to work for the Black community, whose voices are being ignored." He leans toward me, his voice somehow getting quieter, yet more powerful at the same time. "We got off to a bad start and that's on me, but I need you to know that I'm in this. I'm not doing this for attention or because I didn't get the contract I wanted or whatever other bullshit reason people are coming up with. This matters to me and I work for what's important to me."

Even though he's rude and I hate him, I still respect him. This stance isn't gaining him many fans. And as a person who has a deep desire to be liked, I think it's commendable to do something you believe in, consequences be damned.

Also, as much as I hate myself for thinking about it, I can't help the way every time he looks at me with that dark intensity that my imagination drifts away and I picture him saying those words about me . . . me being what matters to him. To feel like the most important thing to anyone. Something I haven't felt since I last held my dad's hand.

I shake away the memories. "Great. Because I think this can be the perfect solution for you and the Mustangs organization. My job is to make everyone happy here."

"Good luck with that. I'll try this, but I don't care about making everyone happy. I want change and progress, and I won't stop kneeling or blacking out my logo until I see it."

Well, crap.

One step forward, two steps back.

Story of my life.

"Well, I would never ask you to stop." I lean across the table, meeting him in the middle before lowering my voice. "And I do love a good challenge."

He sucks in a hiss of breath and his eyes widen a fraction. Then, without warning, he leans back and starts to laugh. A laugh so raspy and deep, it's as if he hasn't done it in years and I can hear the rust falling away. And fuck me now if it's not the hottest thing I've heard in a long, long time. Maybe ever.

"Looks like I've finally met my match." He takes the tablet back and I watch as his fingers dance across the screen before he pushes it back to me. "Tomorrow at noon. I put the address in for you. I'll see you then."

"Tomorrow." The amount of work I have to do in less than twenty-four hours causes a weird sense of calm and determination to come over me. "Hope you'll be ready."

"Haven't you heard?" The cocky smile I'm so familiar with from watching him play flashes across his face, his midnight eyes gleaming with mischief. "I'm always ready."

"We'll see about that."

Then, in a move I've only seen executed in movies and just about every reality show on Bravo, I get up and leave without a goodbye.

Like a boss.

Quinton Howard Junior was right. He has met his match.

Five

IT TOOK UNTIL I GOT TO MY CAR BEFORE I REMEMBERED THAT I WAS supposed to stay at HERS to meet Liv for drinks.

And nothing ruins a boss-ass exit more than having to walk back in with your tail between your legs.

Which is exactly why I sit in my car until I see Quinton leave.

I mean, the guy shot me down with barely a glance. I wouldn't consider myself a prideful person, but even I don't want to be embarrassed twice in the span of a single afternoon.

Liv texts me while I'm hiding—I mean, waiting—that she's stuck in traffic and running late, but to order her any drink that looks fancy and has gin. I'm more of a whiskey girl, myself. Call it an Irish thing . . . or being raised by an Irish-American single dad thing. But the only time I've had a drink anyone could refer to as fancy, it's been ordered for me, not by me.

I walk back in just as two women are leaving the bar. It's that awkward time after lunch, but before happy hour. I don't think HERS is ever empty, but it's far from crowded now. Which works for me because now I can rant to Liv as soon as she gets here and not worry about tons of strangers hearing.

From watching *Love the Player*, I recognize everyone behind the bar immediately. Especially Brynn Sterling (not Lewis—I swear, her not taking Maxwell Lewis's name was an entire story-line last season). I don't know why, but I assumed in real life, she wouldn't be as pretty as she is on the show. Some of that had to be TV magic. You know, soft light, glam squad, something. But nope. Somehow, behind the bar with what looks like not even a scrap of makeup on her face and a messy bun on top of her head, she's even prettier. And how unfair is that?

All of this to say that even though I want to play it cool, I'm pretty sure I have hearts in my eyes as she walks my way.

"You're back!" Her smile is so white that I swear it brightens the entire room. I look over my shoulder to see who came into the bar, but nobody seems to talk to her. When I turn back around, she's standing in front of me with a menu in hand. "I'm so glad you decided to stay and grab a drink. That conversation looked like one was needed."

"Um . . ." My eyes shift from side to side. I'm still unsure that she's actually talking to me. "Me?"

Her eyes twinkle as her laugh fills the room, and suddenly I realize why HERS is so wildly successful. One second around its owner and I already feel like she's my best friend.

"Yes, you!" She places the menu in front of me and a glass that she starts to fill up with water. "Elliot, right? Gemma, Mr. Mahler's secretary, told me I should be expecting you."

"Yeah, well, people usually call me Elle." I take the menu, grateful to have something to do with my hands.

"Is it okay if I call you Elliot? I've always liked that name, but it's just so kick-ass for a woman."

"An opinion I'm sure you'd reconsider if you had an encounter like the one I just had."

Lovely. I haven't even ordered a drink yet and I already have loose lips.

Oh yeah, Brynn is a freaking master at what she does.

"Really?" She props her elbows on the bar and leans in closer, as if she wants to both protect my privacy and expose all my secrets at once. "It did look really intense, but I figured that was just because of the subject matter at hand."

"Actually, when we were talking about that, things were fine." I hold the menu tighter, the memory of total humiliation making me tense. "It was his initial reaction to seeing me and letting me know that, in no uncertain terms, I'm not his type and he's definitely not interested that wasn't so pleasant."

The smile she'd been rocking falls off her face almost as fast as the color rises in her cheeks.

"Are you fucking kidding me?" she damn near shrieks. "What an idiot! First of all, not like you're probably not already aware, but you're drop-dead gorgeous. And second, even if you weren't, who says that?!"

I know I'm thirty-one and being self-conscious is supposed to end in high school, but loving the way I look has never been something that comes naturally to me. So having a stranger—a beautiful and successful one on top of that—tell me I'm gorgeous actually means a lot to me. Probably too much, if I'm being honest with myself.

"Thank you!" I finally let go of my death grip on the drink specials and throw my hands in the air. "That's what I was thinking! I mean, in what world do you assume that a person is approaching you just to sleep with you?"

Brynn purses her lips and gives a wicked side-eye. "I'm married to a football player." The fact that she acts like I have no idea who she is or that she's married to Maxwell Lewis makes her that much more endearing. "So I'm not the kind of person who likes to paint all athletes with the same brush. So many of them are the shit. They can be the nicest, most generous, smartest guys in the world." The way her eyes gloss over as she talks makes it clear she's describing her husband. It's disgusting . . . but also freaking adorable. "But there are also guys who have heads so big, it's a miracle they can find a helmet to fit them. And their heads stay that big because people feed their egos all day, every day. And have been their entire life."

I can read between the lines.

Quinton thought I was coming to try to sleep with him because people actually approach him to try to sleep with him.

"I guess I can see that happening. I mean, I am a woman on the Internet so I've gotten my share of unsolicited dick pics."

"Are they ever not unsolicited?" Brynn asks.

That is the question of a person well versed in the subject of dick pics.

I also assume it's rhetorical, because really. They're *never* solicited.

"So women approaching him in public is like getting a dick pic in his life?"

"What an odd conversation to come in the middle of." Liv slides into the chair next to me.

"Oh! Hi!" I lean over and give her a hug. "You've never come into a room unnoticed before."

"Well, I was prepared to shout, but then I heard the subject at hand and decided to keep my mouth closed." She grabs the menu from me, but the gleam in her eyes lets me know she's not finished. "As one does when dicks are being thrown around."

"Alright! Topic change!" I can't hear that word again. Ever. In life. "Brynn, this is Liv. Liv, this is Brynn. We were just discussing my lunch meeting with Quinton and how it started as a disaster."

Liv's eyes triple in size and for the first time, concern crosses her face. "He didn't try to—"

"No, no. Not even close." I cut her off before she lets herself go there.

Olivia's shoulders sag in relief, and guilt causes mine to fall along with hers.

My experience at my last job wasn't a great one. Ever since I can remember, I've always wanted to work in sports. And being raised by a man who never questioned or doubted my intelligence or capabilities at working in the sports world, I'd say I was woefully underprepared for what awaited me. The harassment I dealt with, in part because of my gender, part because of my ethnicity, was terrible on a good day. And considering my dad was diagnosed with cancer while I was there, it was soul crushing.

Liv stood by me every step of the way. Even coming over to force me into the shower when things got really bad. Even though I know she's happy for me for landing my dream job, I know she's holding her breath, terrified that I'll fall apart again.

And Brynn, like the bartending goddess that she is, clearly reads the change of tone. "You know what?" She pulls out two martini glasses from beneath the bar. "I think we need cocktails before we continue. What are you ladies drinking? This one's on me."

Liv perks up immediately.

Hey. We're millennials. Home ownership might not ever be in the plans for most of us, so we find pleasure where we can. And a complimentary cocktail is definitely one of them.

"I love everything I've ever had from here." Liv pushes away the menu. "Gin is my booze of choice. Could you surprise me?"

"Oh my goodness!" Brynn practically vibrates with glee. "Yes!

None of my friends will drink gin, so I've needed a person like you to experiment with!"

I can see the dreams of unlimited free cocktails floating across Liv's face and just like that, all fears of me again falling apart have disappeared.

"What about you?" Brynn looks at me over her shoulder as she reaches for a bottle of Bombay Sapphire. "Wanna be a test dummy?"

"As much fun as that sounds"—I do have a secret dream of having a drink named after me—"I think I need to stick with comfort today . . . and with something that I know won't result in a hangover. Scotch on the rocks, please."

Her hand freezes above the gin. "Seriously?"

I glance at Liv, who is giving me the "I told you only old white dudes order that and you need a new drink" look, before cringing a bit and looking back to Brynn. "Yeah, I'm a whiskey girl."

"This is even better than the gin! I've been wanting to have a whiskey tasting for so long and nobody will do one with me!" She grabs the gin and spins around to face us. "I've been buying all of the stuff to do one. Maxwell is going to be so excited that I found someone else to push this on. He hates the stuff, but humors me."

"I'm in." At the mention of Maxwell, I'm reminded that I have my own Mustangs player I need to humor me. "But maybe make mine a single for now. I'm meeting with Quinton again tomorrow and my career literally depends on it."

"Well." Brynn puts away one martini glass and pulls out a lowball glass before ignoring my request for a single. She pours a healthy serving of a scotch I haven't heard of before and drops in a couple of whiskey stones. "Lucky for you, I consider myself something of a Mustangs expert and I do my best work with a drink in hand."

"I may not know anything about the Mustangs," Liv chimes

in, "but I am an Elliot Reed expert, so I think we have you covered."

I freaking hope so. Because I have a feeling Quinton is not going to make this easy on me and I'm going to need help from somewhere . . .

And good scotch and friends is always a solid starting point.

Six

WHEN QUINTON GAVE ME THE ADDRESS TO WHERE HE WANTED ME
to meet him, I assumed it was for another restaurant. Guess I'm
the ass now.

Because parking on this super residential street in front of a
house, not a business of any kind, I realize that Quinton Howard
Junior might've given me his address . . . to his house . . . where
he lives . . . and sleeps . . . maybe naked.

His house is exactly where I thought it would be. I remember
all those years ago when Gavin Pope came to play for the Mustangs. He bought a condo not far from where I grew up. Granted,
his condo cost probably triple what my childhood home was
worth, but it was still exciting that he lived close.

Quinton, on the other hand, lives in the suburbs of all suburbs.
Like, I think they built this subdivision because other suburbs
weren't suburby enough. I passed seven Starbucks, two mega-
churches, and one private school once I got off the highway. On
the plus side, I now know of two new spin gyms because the one
by my place is always packed and I'm never able to get into any

classes. And because it's in the suburbs, it could only be reached by the tollway, so I didn't have to deal with traffic and I get to send the bill to the Mustangs.

I will give it to him, though; even though the location wouldn't be my top choice, his house is pretty amazing. It looks like a super modern cabin that you'd find in Vail or Breckenridge or any of those other places I never go to, but maybe would if I could sit inside a house like this and look at the snow instead of being in it. The exterior is all wood, black steel, and glass. The only stone is the intricate paving of his driveway and the chimney jutting out of the roof.

I don't know if this was a power play on his part, inviting me to his home, surrounding me by his wealth, but I'm trying to keep an open mind. Plus, I dressed down today, hoping looking casual would make him feel more comfortable around me. Like jeans and Birkenstocks would somehow make him forget that his boss's boss's boss sent me. Plus, I can think much better when I'm comfortable and my feet aren't screaming in stilettos.

I'm climbing up the steps leading to his front door, admiring the simple landscaping that really enhances the entire house, when I hear the door open. I look up, a smile and a compliment on my lips, when instead of seeing Quinton, I see a woman who is so gorgeous and put together that I want to turn and run and not return until I'm fully armored in heels and a pencil skirt.

"I'll give you a call later." She leans in to give him a hug. "Thanks for this morning, it was really helpful." Her blonde hair is cascading down her back in perfect waves and her tan skin glows against the emerald green of her shift dress. She's basically a goddess.

And the polar opposite of everything I am.

Exactly what I pictured when he said I wasn't his type.

She turns to leave and finally notices me standing there . . . in fucking Birkenstocks.

"Oh!" She jumps back. "I'm so sorry. I didn't see you."

Clearly.

"Oh no, you're fine. I'm sorry I startled you."

"Elliot." Quinton steps out from behind her and I get my first glance at him, barefoot and in gray sweatpants. "You're early."

And I mean, honestly! Gray sweatpants? How fucking dare he? Gray sweatpants are like my kryptonite!

But once I move past the sweatpants, I see his face.

And he looks pissed.

"Oh." I look down at my watch. I am early, but only by ten minutes. "I'm sorry. Do you need me to wait in my car?"

"It's fine. You're here already, just come in." He steps back and waves me inside without even saying goodbye to the blonde beauty.

She gives me a small, encouraging smile before slipping past me and making her getaway, unlocking the doors to the white sedan I parked behind.

I walk inside and all of the hope I had leading up to this meeting drifts away. Instead, I'm left feeling unwelcome, uncomfortable, and confused.

"Sorry I got here early." Even though I'm not exactly sure what I'm apologizing for. Professionalism? Punctuality? Both? "I was expecting more traffic and when I got here, I didn't know how long I could sit in my beat-up Camry with Mustangs stickers before one of your neighbors called the cops thinking I was a stalker fan."

This is not a lie. Once I saw blinds starting to crack open, I got out of my car immediately.

I stand inside the entryway, unsure of what I should do. Between the stark white walls, the cement floors, and the industrial beams scattered across the room, it's like the tension is vibrating throughout the space, bouncing from one cold surface to the next, intent on latching onto me.

"I said it's fine." Quinton throws over his shoulder as his bare feet pad across the cement floor.

It's all so awkward that I have to wonder if working with him for the next four months is actually worth it. If I've learned anything over the last couple of years, it's that life is too short to be miserable.

"Are you just going to stand there or come in? I'm guessing since you got here early, it's because there's a lot to do." It's a good thing he's a better quarterback than he is host.

He's standing behind an island in the kitchen that—like the rest of the house—has no personality. He leans forward, cracking his knuckles against the white stone covering the island, the black pendant light dangling above his head only highlights the shadows crossing his face that make him seem even less approachable than he did in HERS yesterday.

But since I can't quit today—bills can't be paid with happiness—I pull up my grown-up panties and get to work . . . still wishing I wasn't wearing Birkenstocks.

"Yes, as I told you yesterday, while this won't be hard, it will be time-consuming." I cross the room and place my bag on the counter across from him, pulling out my sleek and shiny laptop. After years of buying secondhand computers that were usually covered with half-peeled-off stickers, seeing it still sends a thrill through my system. "So, first things first. Why do you want a foundation?"

"You're the one who wants the foundation."

I not so successfully fight the urge to roll my eyes. But, because he's acting like a petulant teenager, he's not looking at me to see it anyways.

"Well, we both know that's not true since you applied for your 501(c)(3) before I was even a blip on your radar." Which, by the way, I still can't believe he got approved for without having anything else in place. Ahhh, to be rich and famous. Must be so freaking nice. "Did you at least have an idea in place before life got in the way?"

"Let's move this to my office." He lets out a deep breath before pushing off the countertop. "I didn't have much for it, but what I do have is in there."

He doesn't wait for me to respond before he starts to walk away. I slam my computer shut and hurry to follow him. The last thing my nosy ass needs is to be left alone anywhere in this man's house. Even though, from what I can see, he lacks anything that could possibly have any personal or emotional meaning.

And, when he pushes open the door, his office is more of the same.

Not one picture to be seen; his desk—which I'm sure cost as much as my mortgage—has nothing on it besides his computer. It's actually sad. I may be broke compared to him, but at least the things I do have mean something to me.

"Take a seat." He motions to the very attractive, very uncomfortable chair across from his desk as he rounds it and plops into the rolling leather chair opposite me. "You were asking if I had anything ready when I submitted papers to the IRS, right?"

"Yeah, sorry." I cringe at the noise the chair makes as I try to scoot closer to his desk. "There are certain things we have to have in place before we start asking for money, which is part of the goal for the launch event we want to throw."

"That makes sense." He leans back in his chair, some of the irritation finally fleeing from his expression. "Nobody wants to give money if they don't know what it's for."

"Exactly." I flip open my computer again and quickly type in my password before pulling up the checklist I created last night. "Which is why we want the mission statement to be as clear as possible. You've made quite a stir. ESPN has been hounding me and I already scheduled a couple interviews with local channels. Getting publicity isn't going to be the problem. The hard part is going to be getting your message across in a way that can't be misinterpreted. It will just be guiding the conversation to the place you want it to go. And you can only do that by precise, strategic planning."

"Is that even possible with the Internet? Twitter alone is wild." He quirks a single eyebrow, skepticism thick in his voice. "With everyone spouting off their opinions all the time, how do we overshadow that?"

We. YES!

I knew going into this that the biggest challenge was going to be Quinton not feeling like I'm on his team. I mean, I am being paid by someone who wants him to stop doing something that's very important. So him including me in this, no matter how minor it may seem, is a giant step to this plan succeeding.

"First, don't go on Twitter or any other social media platform from now on. That's my job. I will schedule posts for you if you want to keep a presence online. The last thing you need is to get caught up with online trolls." I've spent enough time on social media trying to gauge people's reactions to him to last a freaking lifetime. I doubt he wants to see all of the "spoiled millionaire complaining over nothing, why don't we send him overseas and see if he can respect the flag then" and the #ShutUpAndPlay tweets. People also seemed to forget that he led a team to the championship. Way too many people were saying he sucks and isn't worth the trouble. "But yes, it is possible. I know it sounds difficult and it can be. But there are things we can do to keep the focus where we want it to be. Big companies do it all the time."

"Big companies? Like the one we both work for."

Oops.

And just like that, we're back to square one.

"Yes, just like the company *we* work for." I don't even try to mask the truth; that will only cause his distrust for me to grow. "But lucky for you, you're the one in charge of this. You control the narrative and can pretty much demand that they support you."

Fuck. Loose lips again. That was probably not the best thing to tell him. But it's true. And maybe if he can realize the power he has here, he can focus on finding another way to express his feelings.

And let me help.

He nods his head—that hopefully isn't getting even bigger from his newly held power—so I continue. "From there, we'll want to appoint your board, create bylaws, and then the fun part: setting up funding guidelines and picking the first organizations you'll fund."

"That all sounds really good. I did some research last night into foundations and what was needed to get started." He pushes his chair back and opens the drawer to his desk. Pulling out a spiral notebook, he eyes me as if he's still deciding whether or not he should trust me. Then I guess he decides he does because he opens the notebook and hands it to me. "I listed out some potential members for the board, some ideas on what I want the mission statement to say, and a few organizations I think would benefit from funding."

My mouth falls open as I read through his scrappy yet pleasantly neat handwriting.

THE MISSION OF THE QUINTON HOWARD JUNIOR FOUNDATION IS TO FIGHT FOR JUSTICE AND EQUALITY ACROSS THE BOARD. BY SUPPORTING AND FUNDING

ORGANIZATIONS THAT ARE DEDICATED TO ENDING RACISM
AND HELPING PEOPLE LIVE A LIFE WITH DIGNITY, WE WILL
HELP MAKE THIS COUNTRY A BETTER PLACE
FOR ALL PEOPLE.

His mission statement isn't some messy, thrown-together thing. It's short, to the point, and perfectly describes his objective. He melds together two problems and makes them seem so cohesive that I couldn't find a place to separate them even if I tried. There are pages and pages of organizations. Some local, some national, all listed with what they do and why he thinks they'd benefit not just from funding, but funding specifically from him. And finally, he has a group of about twenty potential board members.

"This is amazing." I look at him once I'm finished reading everything. "Why did you act like you didn't have anything ready when I asked?"

"People tend to act like I'm incapable of doing anything by myself." He shrugs, but there's tension in his shoulders that wasn't there a minute ago and his smile no longer reaches his eyes. "I like to gauge how big of an idiot people think I am. What's the point of letting someone in who isn't going to ever take me seriously?"

Ouch.

I know that he showed me in the end, so that means that on some level he senses how much I want this to work. But it also shows that I'm not doing a very good job of hiding some of my personal feelings and he was able to pick up on that.

Just like it wasn't my fault that I got dealt a hand that held a dead mom and a dad who died a slow and painful death, Quinton didn't choose to be the son of a professional athlete. And even though I think he was the lucky one between the two of us, it doesn't discount his feelings and his hurt.

In the end, all people care about is themselves.

I'd do well to remember that.

My sob story doesn't matter here. It won't change anything. If I want this to work, I have to focus on Quinton. That means taking him and all of his childhood problems—no matter what I think of them—seriously.

He has a point to make. I have a job to keep.

And there's only one way to make that happen.

I hand him back his notebook.

"It looks like the Quinton Howard Junior Foundation is well on its way." I crack my knuckles, a habit my dad detested, and reposition my computer in front of me. "You ready to get busy?"

"I thought you'd never ask." No smile crosses his face, but he pushes his shoulders back and any shadows of irritation still lingering on his face are replaced by pure determination.

And I can work with that.

Seven

IN THE TWO WEEKS SINCE OUR FIRST MEETING AT QUINTON'S house, the probability that I will become the newest hostess at HERS has decreased exponentially.

Whereas when I was first assigned this "project," I was one hundred percent certain I'd be heading to the unemployment office at the end of our four months together, now I'm only ninety percent sure.

But hey, progress is progress! Am I right?

I mean, yeah, Quinton is still covering the League's logo on his jersey as soon as his cleats touch the field and is definitely still kneeling. And fans are starting to become restless, so their reactions are growing before every game. Plus Glenn Chandler, who is now in full-on campaign mode, has made Quinton a crucial part of his speeches. Every single night, my phone starts to go crazy with alerts showing me the newest YouTube video of Glenn Chandler standing behind a podium in whatever new city he's traveled to, attacking Quinton. I especially like when he looked directly into the camera and said, "This spoiled child has the audacity to go out on a football field, in stadiums that taxes funded, and disrespect our flag, our troops, and our men and women in blue!"

Those are fun.

And his supporters are eating it up. As soon as he's finished speaking, there's an endless influx of tweets about Quinton's disrespect to our country and how he needs to learn his place. Apparently, if you have a job in sports, it doesn't matter if you're an American citizen or not, you are not allowed to have an opinion. #ShutUpAndPlay has been trending all week long. And while I still don't know where exactly I belong in this movement, I get pissed every time I see the way they twist his motives into something else completely.

On the bright side, we have made a ton of progress on his foundation and the launch party is shaping up to be pretty phenomenal if I may say so myself.

"I'm thinking balloons. Lots and lots of balloons." I look at Quinton over the top of my computer, the screen filled with balloon displays by a local company.

"Balloons?" Quinton quirks his left eyebrow up, something I've noticed he always does when he thinks I'm being absurd. "Like a kid's birthday party?"

"I mean, kind of, yeah. Balloons are at celebrations because they make people happy. They're joyous. Which is a good feeling for people to have when you want their money." I turn my computer toward him when his face still doesn't change. "See? We can have a big backdrop by the entrance where people can take pictures. Some of the balloons will have your logo on them, so it will be just like a step and repeat, except better. Then, inside"—I walk around the table to stand next to him and point to the arrangement I want—"they can snake up the wall and cover the ceiling. It will be so much more fun than flowers. This isn't a wedding and we don't want it to read that way."

"These are pretty dope. I didn't know they did shit like that with balloons."

"Balloons are super dope and shit." I repeat his words back to him, but the words that sounded so natural coming out of his mouth sound so ridiculous coming from me that we both start laughing.

Besides the very first time we met, this is the only other time that I've heard him laugh. I mean, the man barely smiles. I guess he has transformed from quarterback extraordinaire to one of the most controversial figures in sports in the matter of three games, so I can see where the stress would come from. But I have a feeling there may be more to it than that. And even though we're cordial with one another, I don't feel comfortable asking. Even so, an annoying sense of happiness floats through me for being the person who finally wiped that serious expression from his face.

Once his laughter has faded away, he looks me straight in the eyes and if I hadn't witnessed it, I'd think I'd imagined him laughing. Not one trace of humor lingers in the hard edges of his face. "Don't ever say that again."

My spine straightens. "What?"

Then it happens.

He winks at me.

WINKS!

"Wait? Are you teasing me?" I've been shocked by quite a few things during our time together, like how much he seems to genuinely care about the causes he's choosing to support, how smart he is when the mask he always seems to be wearing accidentally slips, the Diet Coke I found in his fridge that he let me drink. I mean, I would *never* give up the last Diet Coke. But this, a hidden sense of humor, might be the biggest shock of all.

"You aren't the only funny one here."

Well, that's a stretch. I'm definitely funnier than he is.

I don't say that, though.

"You're not funnier than me," he says.

But apparently my face said it loud and clear. I really need to learn to check my facial expressions.

"Whatever. I guess humor is subjective." I grab my computer and move back to my seat. I open up the spreadsheet I've created for the party and add a column for balloons before confirming. "So yes on the balloons?"

"Yup." He lifts his chin. "Pop yourself out."

I groan and rest my head on my computer. "Puns. Dear God. He really thinks he's punny."

His throaty chuckle reverberates off the still-empty walls and rugless cement floor.

I sit back up in my chair, closing the party tabs and tucking the piece of hair that has fallen in front of my face behind my ear. I look up to ask Quinton a question. My head jerks back when instead of seeing the top of his head like I expected, we are making direct eye contact. And he's got some weird expression on his face that I haven't seen before.

"What? Do I have something on my face?" I narrow my eyes at him before wiping at my cheek. "Why are you looking at me like that?"

"I wasn't looking at you." He drops his eyes and stares at the paper that has no words on it, fidgeting with the pen between his fingers. "I was looking at the door, trying to think of something when you tried to see into my soul."

You know that feeling when you wave to the stranger in the grocery store because you think they're waving at you, but they are really waving to someone standing behind you? That's how I feel.

"Oh, sorry for interrupting your thinking." I hope the heat I feel in my cheeks is hidden beneath my brown skin and Fenty blush I slathered on this morning. "But do you have the finalized list for your board members?"

I had him reach out to everyone he had in mind for the board after our first meeting at his house. Some people were immediate—and enthusiastic—yeses. Others had too many commitments already to get involved and the few maybes were supposed to get back to him over the weekend. They didn't say anything outright, but I think a couple of them were nervous to attach their name to his until they saw which way all of this media attention started to swing. But because I'm good at my job, I drafted an email for him to send over. In it, we showed them the world Quinton was intent on creating. A world where, even if there were some people who were angry—you can't please everyone—history would show that he was on the right side. This was going to have a lasting impact and they had the opportunity to create a legacy of change.

"Yeah." He flips through the spiral notebook. The only time I've seen him use a computer is when I push mine in front of him. "They said yes."

"Told you my persuasive emails were a surefire thing." I resist the urge to shimmy in my seat, the embarrassments of today's meeting still too fresh in my mind to add another one.

"You did." He slides the notebook across the table so I can enter in all of the details to my foundation spreadsheet. What? I like a spreadsheet! "Between you and the balloons, we're sure to raise a ton of money."

"You've never said a more accurate statement in your entire—" I stop talking. Rereading the list of board members, there's one name that is glaringly missing. "Is this everyone?"

He pulls the notebook back. "Yeah." His eyebrows furrow as

he tries to figure out what has me so confused. "Why? Am I missing someone?"

"Why isn't your dad going to be on the board?" When I didn't see him on the list of potential members, I assumed it was just because he was a shoo-in, not that he wasn't being considered at all. "The optics of having you both work together, generations of players fighting for equality and the fair treatment of players who have been forgotten, is really important. Not having your dad involved is going to cause problems. Somebody will twist that into him not supporting you."

I don't know what part of what I said has pissed him off, but the guy I thought was just starting to warm up to having me around has reverted back to the asshole I first met at HERS.

"Then I guess they're going to talk because he's not going to be on the board." He glares at me and makes no effort to hide his distaste.

But you know what? Fucking same! I'm not here because I need a new friend. I'm here to do my job. And I'm not going to let him sabotage all of the work we've done together. And keeping up with his mood swings is giving me whiplash.

As much as I want to say I can't stand him, spending time with him has softened my resolve. He's intense in a way that I respect and admire, like he's the kind of friend who will push you out of your comfort zone because he sees your true potential. I hate to admit it, but that's something I'm missing in my life. I love my friends, but after all they've seen me go through, they ache to see me comfortable. Quinton is forcing me to be better. And I thought I was doing the same for him.

"I'm not even going to pretend to know the ins and outs of the Howard family. But if this is because you want to separate your name from his"—even though they literally share a name, so that seems like a dumb hill to die on—"this is not the time. One mistake can take this from a success to a failure. You're going to need to put on your big boy panties and go ask your dad to help you out. If you don't, I will."

Okay. So after it leaves my mouth, I want to shovel it back in. Telling him to put on his big boy panties is definitely not the way to get what I want. Unless I wanted him to look at me like I was the actual scum of the earth, because that's what I'm getting right now.

"My dad will *not* be involved in this. Do you understand me?" His voice has dropped to a whisper, but the anger is still coming through loud and clear. "I don't want him anywhere near this project. If I find out you tried to go behind my back to change that, I will take a knee on the sideline and not throw a single pass for the rest of the season. We'll see how Mahler feels about that, but I don't think he'd be very happy with you. Do you?"

Now, to be fair, I never told him about my meeting with Mr. Mahler and my possible termination if things don't go well. But it doesn't take a rocket scientist to see that I'm not spending all my free time with the rude, moody man in front of me for fun. So his threat hits his intended mark. But that's not the part that has my sinuses burning and my eyes threatening to flood.

I would give anything . . . ANYTHING! . . . to spend time with my dad. Even when I'm not actively thinking about him, I know he's only a scent, an image, a word away. And Quinton has the chance to not only spend time with his dad, but to create an actual legacy with him, and he's spitting on it.

What an asshole!

The inside of my cheeks begin to hurt from how hard I'm biting them. I unclench my jaw and throw my hands in the air at the same time. "Fine." I shrug my shoulders, shifting my focus back to the computer screen. "This is your foundation. Do whatever you want."

I expect some kind of response, but thankfully, I'm met with silence.

Unfortunately, though, that silence only lasts a couple of minutes.

"You know," he says, interrupting my daydreams of him sustaining a minor—but season-ending—injury so I don't have to deal with him anymore, "I was wondering something."

When he doesn't continue, I look up to see him staring at me, waiting for me to say something.

"What, Quinton?" I can't scrounge up the effort to hide my eye roll or mask the irritation in my tone when I answer. "Please, tell me. What were you wondering?"

"I mean, you seem smart." He starts in the worst possible way ever. "I've just been trying to figure out how you let Mahler trick you into being the token Black girl. Why would you let him use you like this?"

Out of everything that I thought would come out of his mouth, that was worse than anything I could've possibly imagined. I'm stunned speechless.

"Did he convince you that you're a meaningful part of his organization? Did he say something that convinced you he didn't put you on me clearly for the optics of hiring a Black woman and supporting diversity?" He tilts his head to the side as if I'm some puzzle for him to solve and not a person he just insulted. "What even is your role in this?"

I try to take some deep cleansing breaths, to remember the coping skills that I had to use almost every day at my old job. The techniques I vowed I would never have to use again because of somebody making me feel small at work.

Yet here I am again.

"Here's what's going to happen." I keep my words calm and measured as I slowly close my computer, afraid that all of the anger sizzling through my veins will cause a Hulk-like blowup. "I'm going to leave and try to forget that you ever said that. Tomorrow, you will meet me in my office when you get out of practice and we will only meet there unless we have to go to the venue for the launch. We will only speak when we need to speak or when you decide that you're ready to apologize for insinuating that not only am I not qualified for my job, but that I only got it because of my skin color."

"You really don't think that he's using you? So that when the press comes sniffing around, he can parade you in front of them and say that I'm misguided in calling out the racism in his organization because look at you. You're Black *and* a woman." He leans back in his chair, a sadistic smirk tugging on the corner of his mouth. "You can't be that naive."

My dad raised me with the mentality to be color-blind. I try to live my life like that. I don't know what Quinton has experienced. I see the struggles Black men in this country face and I'm not so "naive" to think racism isn't a huge problem. But I'm not okay with him projecting his problems onto me. I've had enough people question my validity as a biracial woman—and where they think I belong in this world—that I can't bite my tongue any longer.

"What's your problem? Seriously, there's something wrong with you. I've been working with you for two weeks. In that time, name one moment where you've felt I'm not qualified to be here. You can't. Because I'm damn good at my job." I shove my computer in my bag and start walking to the door before I spin back around. "No! I'm not done here. You've made your stance clear. You have a problem with racism and mistreatment in the League. Everyone should! But did you ever consider that by implying I got my job solely because of my skin color, and not because I've worked my entire life for it, you're creating problems too? Yes, I'm Black. And I'm white. I was raised by my white dad. I have white friends. And they've never insinuated anything like what just came out of your mouth. So maybe before you go throwing around insults like that, you should check your own bias first."

And finally feeling satisfied by the look of something other than smugness on Quinton's stupid face, I make my exit with the sinking feeling that my career is ending with the door slamming behind me.

Eight

ICY.

If there is one word that could be used to describe the state of my relationships with everyone involved with the Mustangs organization, it's icy.

As much as I wanted to dismiss everything Quinton said as pure bullshit, I'd be lying if some of it didn't worm its way right into my brain and feed all of my insecurities. Like the fact that Mr. Mahler didn't even seem to like me before placing this huge task on my shoulders. Or the fact that since he assigned it, I haven't heard a peep from him. I send him an update every Friday, but he has yet to respond to one email. I'm starting to wonder if he's giving me enough rope to hang myself. I feel like he took the first opportunity he could find to sabotage my time here.

He set the stage so that if Quinton decides to stop taking a knee, he looks great for working things out. Or, on the flip side, say Quinton keeps kneeling and covering his logo, he can place all of the blame for the lack of progress on me.

I asked Paul if this level of disinterest is normal from him and he assured me that it is. That Mahler is known to give big assignments and then leave us to do our work without micromanagement. But now I'm even wondering if I can trust Paul to tell me the truth. I spent all weekend drafting statements for coaches and the general managers to use when they're confronted with questions about Quinton. The messaging is in line with what Quinton has been saying, but takes pressure off the organization. Paul thanked me and told me I did a great job, but when I watched the press conference after the practice, the coaches were singing a completely different tune. It's like Paul took my message and gave them the polar opposite statement. I can feel the distance growing between me and my coworkers. That feeling of never quite fitting in or belonging grows more pronounced every time I walk in the room.

If Quinton's intentions were to plant a poppy seed of doubt that would bloom into full-blown paranoia, he was wildly successful.

And now, unlucky for me, I get to start my weekend by spending this beautiful Saturday morning waking up way too early and listening to Quinton's annoying voice echoing around the empty room where we'll be hosting his launch event in exactly ten days. And would you like to know how I'm feeling about that? In the infamous words of Dorinda—New York is the best *Housewives* franchise, don't @ me—Medley, "Not well, bitch!"

"What do you think of setting up the bar here?" Brynn points to the corner of the empty event space. "We can bring in our chalkboard, and Paisley, one of the bartenders working that night, is great at hand-lettering so it will look pretty too."

"Ask Quinton, it's his event. I'm just here to take notes for setup. All the decisions are his to make." I can't even be bothered to care anymore. I already have plans to spend tonight with a pint of Ben & Jerry's while I update my résumé.

Apparently, Quinton is capable of making friends with some people, and Maxwell Lewis is one of them. Between their relationship and Brynn's longstanding one with the Mustangs organization, she volunteered to donate her services to this event. And because of Quinton's and the venue's schedules, she was nice enough to come out during the only time they could squeeze us in.

If I wasn't too busy hating my life right now, I'd be really excited to be spending time with her.

But instead, all my enthusiasm for anything including Quinton Howard Junior is long gone and I have adopted the mood of an angsty teen instead.

"Um, yeah. Okay, I'll ask him." Brynn turns to find Quinton, but only takes a few steps before she's walking back to me and grabbing my arm, dragging me out of the room.

"Brynn!" I hiss out. "What are you doing?"

She doesn't answer until we are in the bathroom with the door locked behind us and the faucets all turned on.

"What happened?" She stands in front of me, her hands firmly on her hips and fire behind her eyes.

"Nothing happened. I don't know what you're talking about."

"Oh, don't even try that shit with me." She jabs a finger into my shoulder and I'm convinced I'll have a fingertip-sized bruise later. "If you knew my friends, you'd know that I've been witness to Mustang drama for what feels like my entire life. I've even gotten Vonnie Lamar to break. You don't stand a chance against me."

"Lavonne Lamar? From *Colorado Everyday*?" My attention is that of a squirrel. "I loved when she was on that show! Did you see the episode where she did the fish pedicure? I laughed so hard I almost peed myself. Why'd she quit?"

"Oh my god." She closes her eyes and lets out a deep breath. "You're just like them. As soon as you and Quinton admit you're into each other, you're going to fit in perfectly."

"Me and Quinton?" I put my hand on her forehead. "Are you sick? Do you have a fever? Do you need me to call nine-one-one?"

She slaps my hand away, which, like the finger jab, also hurts way more than it probably should.

"I think you're underestimating my deep knowledge when it comes to Mustangs romances," she says. "I was a bridesmaid in Gavin and Marlee Pope's wedding for a reason. TK and Poppy's rekindling basically took place in HERS. I've conducted a deep dive over the courtship between me and Maxwell. And I won't even get into how many wives and girlfriends I've counseled in my office after Wednesday meetings, but hint? It's a fucking lot."

"Well, 'fucking' is the largest form of measurement, so I can only imagine."

"Sarcasm is the lowest form of wit."

"But the highest form of intelligence," I finish for her. "Why does everybody always forget the end of that quote?"

"I think the real question is why do you know the entire quote?"

I have no good comeback for that. "Fine. Whatever. You win this round." I revert back to my angsty teen routine.

"Ha! Victorious again!" She does a double fist pump before the realization that a double fist pump is way worse than knowing an iconic quote and lowers her arms in defeat. "Call it a tie?"

"I can live with that."

We shake hands and suddenly, this feels like a very formal bathroom meeting.

"So now are you ready to tell me what's going on with you?" she asks. "I know you weren't thrilled about this stint with Quinton, but Liv and Marie both said you were making it work and actually feeling really good about the work you two were doing."

"Wait." I replay her words in my head. "What?"

I know Liv and Marie have been going to HERS. They've

invited me a few times, but because I'm busy trying not to get fired, I haven't gone. Friday nights spent writing statements that are continually ignored—but still requested—isn't as much fun as I initially thought. Plus, I have the added benefit of sorting through the hate mail aimed at Quinton, which has been rerouted to me. Speaking of, if people who love the Second Amendment so much had the same enthusiasm for the First Amendment, my job would be so much easier . . . and less scary. What I didn't know, however, was that I've been the subject of their conversations when they went to HERS without me.

"They've been coming in and doing gin tastings. They've been super helpful. I have three new cocktails ready for winter." She doesn't even pretend to be a little bit sorry that she's boozing up my friends to gain intel.

And I'll be having a conversation with Liv and Marie soon. I mean really? Betrayed in the name of gin?

How rude.

But also, relatable. I'd totally turn on them for whiskey.

"Okay, so yes, things were getting better." I start to sit on the ground before remembering we're still in the bathroom and activate my glutes and hamstrings harder than I ever have in my entire thirty-one years on this earth. Maybe if I get fired, I can start a new workout trend that takes place in public restrooms? I mean, spinning is so last year.

"That was, quite possibly, the greatest squat save I've ever witnessed," Brynn says.

"Thank you!" I shout, even though I know it's probably heard throughout the entire venue. But nothing gets me more excited than a simple compliment. "My knees didn't even pop!"

"Even more impressive," she says. I get the distinct feeling that now she's mocking me. "Now that I know how you have the world's nicest ass, would you like to explain to me what the hell is going on with you out there?"

"He's just a jackass." My eyes start to twitch just thinking about that day at his house.

"And . . ." Brynn motions me to continue. "More than four words would be helpful."

"I went over to his house on Tuesday to plan like we've been doing and it was going really well. Liv and Marie weren't lying when they said I was enjoying it. His foundation is setting up to do some real good in the world. He is really looking into fixing problems within the League—I guess there are a lot of problems with the way some of the older retired players are treated. But he doesn't want to stop there. We've been finding projects and charities that address inequality in their communities."

I've been reaching out to a lot of the organizations he's researched. One of my favorites is an organization that provides professional clothing to men and women. It seems like a small thing, but they provide haircuts and classes to prepare people for interviews. It's life changing for the people it helps. One thing I've noticed about the causes Quinton seems to champion is that, at their core, they provide dignity. Helping underprivileged people out in a way where they can help themselves and not feel like they're begging for charity. It's really beautiful.

"I understand why he chose the football field and the national anthem to make a stance. There's so much passion behind his actions and we were taking it to the next level. It was going surprisingly well, then it wasn't. He said some really hurtful things and made it clear that he didn't respect or value the work I was doing."

I leave out the details. I don't want to hear the words that have been bouncing around in my head for the last two weeks aloud.

Some part of me thinks that even though they've already consumed my mind, speaking them will cause them to become a truth.

"It sounds like that means you two need to talk more, not less." Brynn gives the advice of an adult, which is not what I'd like to hear.

"There's nothing he can say that can excuse his behavior." Or that can slow the avalanche of self-doubt he set in motion. "For a person so set on using his voice to create change, I'm not sure he truly understands the power his words have. And how damaging they can be."

Brynn leans against the door and I know she's prepared to stay in the bathroom for as long as it takes to get me to agree to take her side. What she doesn't know is stubborn is my middle name, so we could be in this bathroom all damn day.

"Have you told him that?" she asks.

"No." Is she crazy? Maybe she had some gin before she came over. "I'm not his mom and he's a grown-ass man. He should've learned basic manners a long time ago."

"I can understand that. It's not your job. Except wait!" She perks up. "It literally *is* your job!"

"Oh no. Not even close." I shake my head. Setting up press conferences, curating emails and Instagram posts, drafting speeches and statements, and planning this event was enough. I know I'm not emotionally stable enough myself to take on a twentysomething rich boy, with what seems like some serious daddy issues. I'm still a disaster, but therapy at least taught me how to set basic boundaries. "I know you mean well, but I've been through a lot this year. I really can't add someone else's baggage to the mounds of my own issues."

"That's fair." She bites her bottom lip and taps an embroidered tennis shoe–covered foot against the beige tile. And I think my little conundrum might've finally broken Brynn. I don't know if I should be proud or apologetic.

"We can be cordial. I can stand near him and not say something rude." *Maybe.* "But from now on, I'm just going to show up and try to hoard my paychecks before I get fired in January."

"That's it!" Brynn brightens and pushes off the door. Not the reaction I thought she'd have after I informed her of my impending unemployment status. "Have you told him that you have a stake in this too? That you could lose your job?"

I feel all of the wrinkles in my forehead when my eyebrows try to high-five each other. "Of course I haven't."

Is she insane? I know I haven't been the most professional dealing with Quinton, but that's a little too low even for me.

"Why not?"

I don't know if she is messing with me or not, but I answer anyways.

"Because my job isn't to trick him into submission." I mean, it honestly might be. Something tells me there aren't many lows Mr. Mahler won't fall to. "It's to give him another option to feel heard. I support the protest he's making. If he wants to stop kneeling, it will have nothing to do with me. I won't hang my burden on him. I won't try to manipulate him with my problems."

Not that he'd even care if I got fired. He basically taunted me with his ability to make that happen at his house.

She walks toward me and takes my hands in hers.

"It's not manipulating him, Elliot." Her voice is softer and so are her eyes. It's a look I know well. One people gave me for weeks after my dad died. Until their lives moved on and I was still stuck in the cyclone of mourning. "I don't know what you're going through and neither does he. But maybe, if you opened up to him, he'd be understanding and you could both get along better."

"I shouldn't have to tell him my sob story for him to not be a jerk. You never know what a person is going through. But he doesn't seem to understand that."

Brynn squeezes my hands and her lips pull into a straight line. "You're right," she says. "And have you thought that maybe you don't know what he's going through?"

With that, she turns the faucets off and leaves me alone in the bathroom with a hell of a lot to think about.

What could Quinton possibly be going through that can compare to the loss I've experienced this year? The problems he's dealing with are only there because he created them.

We don't have anything in common. Of that, I'm positive.

So I don't know why I look so ashamed when I catch a glimpse of my reflection in the bathroom mirror.

Nine

WANDERING BACK INTO THE NOW EMPTY EVENT SPACE, I GO OUT
of my way to avoid the corner where Brynn has pinned down
Quinton. The loafers I threw on this morning are blissfully quiet
as I cross the room as quickly as possible to talk with Jen.

Jen Ingram, manager of the Rue, the event space we're using,
has been a lifesaver throughout this project. While I fully knew
I could create a beautiful and memorable event in a month for
Quinton, finding a space large enough to host it that wasn't
booked was another story. So when she called to let me know the
Rue had opened up, I jumped on it.

The distressed hardwood floors and the exposed brick walls
give this historic building instant character. Between the hundreds,
maybe even thousands of balloons—I may have gone a little
overboard—the acrylic chairs, and the string lighting that will
soon be going up, this event will be the perfect mix of old and
new. Something that goes hand in hand with the issues at the
heart of what the evening is going to be about.

"Hey! Don't forget to give me the caterer's and the balloon

lady's numbers. I need to store them in my computer," Jen says when she sees me approaching. "And I'll email you the new contract with the updated price. Sound good?"

As Jen sat with me and Hannah, the owner of Modern Balloon, her eyes got wider and wider as the designs set in place for the event space were listed out. Hannah had barely left the table before Jen offered to take fifteen percent off the price she'd given us if we let her use the professional pictures from the event in her marketing campaign. I probably should've asked Quinton if he was okay with it before I agreed, but what can I say? Your girl's a sucker for a deal!

"Sounds perfect." I pull my phone out of my pocket and forward her the phone numbers before I forget. "Done!"

"You're the best." She tucks the clipboard with the checklist I emailed to her yesterday under her arm. "I'm just putting it out there: We've been thinking about hiring an in-house event planner. I know you have a job, but if you ever consider a career change, the job is yours."

I file that offer in the back of my mind. "Just wait a couple months and I might take you up on the offer."

"I'm serious," she says. "You're really talented at this, both visually and with the numbers. We'd be lucky to have you."

I decide to let her think I wasn't being serious when I told her to wait a couple of months. Nobody needs my heavy baggage laid on them on a Saturday. And despite really not wanting to care about this event anymore, I'm secretly really excited for it.

It has nothing at all to do with Quinton, but I wasn't lying when I told him I'm a details girl. And big events like this are comprised of nothing but details. From the napkins to the color scheme to the guest list to the budget, no detail is too small.

After my dad passed, I was able to distract from the pain by throwing myself into planning his funeral. And it worked so well that I haven't really stopped. I guess you could say busywork has become my coping mechanism. Because ignoring the problem completely instead of facing it head on has never backfired on anyone in the history of humanity.

"I appreciate you saying that, really." Especially since I'm not sure Quinton is actually aware of how much work I've put into this event. We spend the majority of our time together focused on the foundation itself. I only ask him questions for the launch when I really need to.

"Appreciate what?" Quinton, the stealthy fucker, says from right behind me.

"Nothing." I plaster on my professional "the person who just became a potential job lead is watching" smile and turn to face him. "Are you ready for the launch?"

"I am." He looks around the empty venue and an almost wistful look crosses his face.

"I think this is going to be one of the best events we've ever hosted. Elle really did a great job picking all of the vendors," Jen cuts in. "And I know this is to launch your new foundation, so what exactly is your foundation about?"

Quinton looks to me for permission to answer. I told him in no uncertain terms he was not allowed to discuss his foundation with anyone. I mean, what's the point of a reveal if everyone already knows what it is? But I'm still kind of shocked he's listened to anything I've told him.

"She signed a nondisclosure agreement," I tell him. "You can give her all of the details."

"Aw shit, looks like I found my new therapist," he says and a surprised snort slips from my mouth.

It's not that he's funny, per se; it's that he's always so serious and even when he jokes, he does it with a straight face. My dad had the driest sense of humor ever, so even though I will never tell him, I do find him pretty funny when he's not being a total jerk.

"No, but seriously." He shakes his head and reveals a smile that is almost fragile. "The Quinton Howard Junior Foundation will support at-risk communities while also bringing attention to the problems within the League. I think it's really important to point out the problems in these massive corporations because they tend to mirror or set the tone for issues in our communities. Whether it's racism, greed, corruption, or violence, the League is a microcosm of bigger issues, and too often players are afraid to speak against them—you can't bite the hand that feeds you. So I'm going to take the lead, stir things up so that the players, past and present, can have their voices heard."

"I had no idea players felt this way. Is it really that big of a problem?" Jen asks.

"It's bigger." Quinton doesn't hesitate. "You know, with the news about CTE starting to make ripples, some people are acknowledging the real danger in playing football. But we're only talking about it because so many former players are suffering and dying. CTE is just one aspect. Nobody is talking about the rest and that's one of the things I want to do. And as a society, we need a hard time talking about racism, but we need to have that dialogue. In a company where seventy percent of its players are Black, but only nine percent of managers and zero percent of owners are? That's a problem. Racism isn't just saying mean things. It's a system that makes it impossible for minorities to reach certain levels."

"Wow, this is really amazing." Jen breathes out, enthralled with Quinton—lost in the passion behind his words. And I don't blame her.

Even though I know what the foundation is and the passion he possesses for his causes, I've never heard him speak this way. With me, he's guarded. He's precise, but never emotional. Listening to him talk to Jen, however, there are feelings I can't even begin to unpack fueling his words. This isn't just a cause he wants to champion, this is his life's mission. Like every year spent perfecting his craft wasn't for a huge contract or championship ring, but for this moment . . . for the opportunity to speak and have people listen.

I wait for Quinton to say something, to thank her, but instead it's like he has gone somewhere else. Like the mask he's always wearing slipped and he's struggling to put it back in place.

"I told you it was going to be big," I cut into the silence and give Jen a quick hug. "Thank you again for letting us come in today. We'll get out of your hair now, but I'll shoot you an email with the updated spreadsheets later."

"Yes." Quinton's deep voice comes out strong and confident—and very close. Whatever was going on with him a few seconds ago is in the past. "We appreciate your help."

Then he mimics my goodbye and leans in, wrapping his long, strong arms around Jen. And poor Jen, who has been the epitome of professionalism, turns into a blushing, giggling disaster. "It's been my pleasure," she says once she's gotten herself under control, aka when Quinton stops touching her.

Poor Jen.

I mean, I get it! Technically speaking, he is very handsome with his stupidly flawless skin, full lips that look both lusciously plump and firm, his hair that is long and unruly on top—like he's begging you to dig your fingers into it—and the bone structure of a god that is highlighted with a perfectly maintained beard. And on top of all that, he just gave her this impassioned speech about all of the good he wants to do in the world. Who wouldn't giggle? Maybe if she spent more time around him, she'd become immune to the charms that are few and far between when he's around just me.

"Later!" I wave to Jen, who still looks a little light-headed as we turn to leave.

We push open the door and are met with the chaos of Down-town Denver on a weekend. Fall has just arrived, but it's chilled the air just enough to make for a perfect Colorado day. The glare of the sun off the glass windows surrounding us reminds me that I have somehow managed to forget the sunglasses that I keep in my car *and* the ones I try to keep in my purse.

But even in the midst of crowds of people on their way to lunch and the women chatting on their phones with oversized bags slung over their shoulders, nothing can seem to distract from the awkwardness lingering between us. The noise around us is still not enough to break the uncomfortable silence and tension as we walk to the parking lot Jen told us to park in.

"That was a good speech." Even though his head—and ego—is already inflated, I can't help but say it.

"Oh yeah. That? Thanks." His steps falter a bit.

Huh? Look at that. I guess me being nice to him is the one thing that can knock him off balance. I'll have to remember that.

"Have you been practicing what you're going to say at the launch?"

I wanted to prepare a speech for him, but he won't let me. He's okay with it for press conferences, but he wants what he says at the event to be all him. Which I get.

A thing I've learned about Quinton by observing him these last few weeks is that he's quietly very smart and dedicated, so I wouldn't be surprised if he's been practicing in front of mirrors. He's always writing something down in his notebook or on his phone. He's able to come to meetings in my office hours after the cars have left the player's parking lot because he's studying film. But when reporters talk to him and ask about something other than the stance he's taking, he never really takes credit for what he does. When he throws a great pass? It was all the receiver for running a perfect route. No interceptions? The offensive line blocked for him all night.

It's actually really admirable. But I've already complimented him once and I will NOT do it again.

I refuse.

"No . . . I mean, yeah, I have been practicing, but it wasn't that. That was just from yes—" He waves a dismissive hand through the air and clears his throat. "Uh, never mind. No, it wasn't planned."

"Well, it was good." I'm curious about what he was going to say, but decide not to push it. "Hopefully she'll remember it after you scrambled her brain cells before we left."

I laugh remembering the dazed expression on Jen's face, but when I glance at Quinton, he's staring at me with a blank look.

"Scrambled her brain cells? What are you talking about?"

"You know." I shrug. "When you hugged her all tight and it looked like her head was going to explode all over the place."

"You hugged her first." His voice takes on a hard edge. "Why was it wrong when I did it?"

"Whoa there, killer." I raise my hands up in surrender. Not sure how me trying to be nice to him got us here. "I didn't say it was wrong. Just that, well, you're you. A hug coming from you is a lot different than one from me."

"What does that even mean? I was just being nice."

Looks like being nice is backfiring for both of us.

"Come on, dude." I stop walking and turn to face him, ignoring the not-so-nice words the man behind me mutters as he passes by. "You have to know what you look like. On top of that, you're the starting quarterback for a professional team. So you're young, famous, rich, handsome, and occasionally not a jerk." I tick off my fingers one by one. "There's a lot of people who would love the chance to try and shoot their shot."

He mumbles something beneath his breath that I don't quite catch and starts to walk again. His strides are long and measured, but his shoulders are slumped and his spine is bowed. It's like he's trying to curl into himself. By itself, that's concerning body language, but from the ever confident Quinton Howard Junior? It's downright alarming.

"Hey!" I call after him and try to pick up my pace. But he's moving really fast and his legs are a lot longer than mine, so this really isn't fair. "Wait for me!"

He doesn't answer, but he does slow his steps until I reach him again. And I'll take what I can get.

"Are you okay? I missed what you said before you walked away," I ask when I've caught up, only slightly out of breath.

"I didn't say anything."

He ignores my question about whether or not he's okay, but after spending the time I have with him, I know he can be short with words. Most of the time, I'd brush this off as him being a dismissive asshole again. But something is wrong. I can see it in the way his throat is working, as if he wants to say something, but the words are stuck . . . threatening to choke him.

And it's something I recognize. I know all too well what it looks like to pretend everything is fine when in reality, you're in so much pain you don't know which way is up or down anymore.

Brynn's parting words from the bathroom run through my head again. Maybe I don't know what this man is going through. And it is my job to find out. So instead of ignoring him and hopping in my car that's finally come into view, I make a new plan.

"Hey." I rest a hand on his forearm to stop him, ignoring the jolt of electricity that flows through my fingertips at the feeling of his skin. It somehow feels even smoother than it looks. "I'm actually starving right now and there are still a few little things I'd like to discuss with you about the event. I know you have to be at the team's hotel later, but would you want to grab some lunch and go over everything with me?"

"Um, yeah." He glances down at his Apple Watch. "I have time for lunch."

"Oh good!" I try to find some excitement that I don't really feel. Fake it till you make it, am I right? "Are you in the mood for anything?"

"I'm fine with whatever. I'm still new to the city." He looks along the building-lined streets of Downtown Denver, probably ready to shout out the name of the first restaurant he sees to get this over with. "I don't know what's good here."

"Well, lucky for you, you're with a Denver native and I grew up not far from here. I know a place and it's never crowded." I reach into my purse and grab my keys and phone. "I'll text you the address. It's not far."

"Sounds good." He taps on his watch when the text goes through. Technology is so wild. "I'll see you there soon."

"See ya." I open my car door and slide into the seat, then, before I can close the door, he does it for me, like the old-school gentleman he's most definitely not, then turns and walks away without a backward glance.

What an odd, odd man.

Jen

I DIDN'T THINK THIS PLAN THROUGH.

When my dad died, I made the decision to stay far away from the neighborhood that housed too many memories to face on a daily basis. And I've managed to do just that.

Until today.

Driving down the tree-lined roads, memories I've been avoiding like the plague hit me hard and fast. The corner where my dad helped me set up a lemonade stand every summer until I decided I was too cool to do it anymore. The street where he dropped me off for the bus each morning. The park where we would play basketball together. All of those amazing memories that should bring a smile to my face, but are chased away as I drive past the street where our house is.

Was.

Where our house was.

The hospice nurses setting up his bed. Watching the rise and fall of his chest until it stopped. The funeral home coming to take him away. Handing the keys to the house I was raised in to the real estate agent and walking out of the door for the last time. It all slams into me at once.

It's been months. And it somehow hurts even more now.

The air in my car gets thicker, heavier. Inhaling and exhaling becomes a struggle as tears begin to cloud my vision. And I want to give in. I want to pull over and punch my steering wheel until my knuckles bleed, scream until my throat is raw about the unfairness of it all.

But I don't. *I won't.* Because it will do nothing. It won't bring him back or help me grieve. Instead, I'll still be just as alone as I am now, except the physical pain might distract from the emotional pain of it all.

I relax my grip on the steering wheel, push my foot down a little bit harder on the pedal, and stuff all of those feelings down so deep that I forget they even exist. Or at least pretend they don't exist until the next reminder threatens to finally crack the exterior I've spent so long building.

Stanley's comes into view and I parallel park right in front. Tucked on a quiet side street and owned by a man who thinks Facebook is "hogwash," it's a hidden gem. It's been here for as long as I can remember and if you didn't know before you walked in, the decor inside would tip you off. I'm pretty sure they haven't changed a single thing since they first opened. They even have their "smoking section" sign still up, even though Denver went smoke free when I was in high school.

I open the door and the bell dings over my head. My eyes go immediately to the empty stool sitting outside of the kitchen and I almost fall to the floor in relief. When Mr. Stanley is here, his butt never leaves that stool. And if he was here, he'd ask about my dad and that's the last thing I need to happen in front of Quinton.

A waitress yells from across the room for me to sit wherever I want. Without thinking, my feet automatically cross the checkered linoleum floors until I'm sliding into the booth that my dad and I always used to sit in.

I run my fingers over the tattered vinyl covering the seat and look at the long scratch in the table. The one I put there when my dad let me color with a pen and I got a little out of control.

I order a Diet Coke and look at the menu I memorized years ago while I wait for Quinton.

"Elliot?" A voice says from somewhere behind me. "Elliot Reed? I knew that was you!"

The voice is nearly as familiar—and now, foreign—as my dad's. And while my heart flutters with aching and yearning for the comfort and love it's been missing, my brain sends signals of panic and fear. My palms begin to sweat and I've never wanted to be Barry Allen so badly.

But since I don't have super speed—or the superconvenient power to become invisible—I turn to face my old neighbor. "Mrs. Rafter, how are you?"

I slide out of the booth and stand to give her a hug. My hands shake as I touch the person I was resigned to never see again after I last saw her . . . at my dad's funeral. The scent of her signature perfume wraps me as tight as her frail arms. I lean back, but neither one of us lets go of the other. Her blue eyes shine bright against her pale skin, and her yellowing teeth still look perfect against the pink lipstick she always wears. The comfort of the familiarity she brings me causes the first crack in my defense system.

"You would know if you ever came to see an old lady, wouldn't you?" She scolds me, but even though there's not any anger in those words, there is hurt.

"I know." Shame washes over me and the guilt I've been pretending I didn't feel makes a sudden appearance.

Mrs. Rafter has lived in her little bungalow since 1969. Twenty years before I was even born. Her husband passed away and she wasn't able to have kids. So, when my parents bought the house next door and—from the stories Mrs. Rafter told me—my mom took special care to not just be a friendly neighbor but to bring her in as part of our family, Mrs. Rafter didn't hesitate. And I became the grandchild she never thought she'd have. We baked cookies together and watched old black-and-white movies together. She gave me money every time I brought home a good report card, and a serious lecture the one time I didn't. And when we found out my dad was sick, she was there every Monday with a new casserole and a story about the crazy ladies from her knitting group at church.

"I'm sorry. I just couldn't go back." I focus on the french fry on the floor that needs to be swept up, unable to look her in the eyes.

While the priest was speaking at my dad's funeral, I made the decision to do everything I could to never feel pain like that again. And that included cutting off just about everybody from my past. The only reason Liv and Marie made the cut is because they are fucking stalkers and wouldn't let me avoid them. Mrs. Rafter, on the other hand, doesn't have the social media or Internet detective prowess to find me.

I've picked up my phone to call her so many times, but I could never go through with it. After the weeks went by, I regretted my decision, but it felt too late to go back. Part of me was afraid of the pain hearing her voice would cause. But mainly, it was the fear that she would be mad at me for running away and wouldn't want to talk to me anymore. I couldn't deal with losing another person. At least not knowing kept the possibilities alive.

"Oh, you stop that right now." Her delicate touch lifting up my chin is in total contrast to the fire in her voice. A fire, I should add, that I've never heard from her before. "You don't apologize for protecting yourself. I know how much you loved your dad, how much he loved you. You know I talked to him not long before he passed. And the only thing he was worried about was leaving you. He knew you needed to sell the house, but he was worried you wouldn't. That'd you'd stay and all of the laughter buried in those walls would be washed away by sadness."

The tears I work so hard to keep locked away start to beat against the barriers I have in place and I know I'm not going to be able to fight them much longer.

"I miss him." I give life to the thought that runs through my head on an endless loop, but never dare say out loud. "I miss you. I miss the life from before. I don't know how to be around everything that I want back and still move on."

"Sweet girl." Her hand, covered in wrinkles that only point to the wisdom in the life she's lived, reaches up to wipe the tears I didn't even realize had fallen. "You will miss him for the rest of your life. We never move on, we just learn to not only live with the pain but to welcome it. Because it's all we have left of a love so great."

I hate that for her. I hate knowing how long she's been living with pain. But man am I grateful that it led her to me.

"Would you like to come see my place soon?" I sniffle and try to pull myself together. "I can make dinner and we can watch reruns of *Scandal*."

"Oh yes, you know how much I enjoy that Olivia Pope. Just don't try to make me eat any of that kale crap." She pats my hand and I know we're okay again. "I'm old. I don't need to worry about my figure anymore."

You make someone a kale salad one time! I swear.

"No kale, I promise."

She lifts her hand like she's about to wave when something catches her attention out of the corner of her eye. "Oh my, Elliot." Color rises in her cheeks and she pats the stark white hair curled on her head. "I didn't realize I was interrupting a date! Why didn't you tell me?" Reality punches me in the stomach and I feel like I might literally throw up when I realize that not only has Quinton arrived, but he's witnessed this deeply personal moment.

Anger, hurt, and embarrassment swirl through me as I watch Quinton slip his large form out of the booth like nothing happened. Like he didn't encroach on my privacy by listening to this conversation. "Pleased to meet you, ma'am." He extends a calloused hand to Mrs. Rafter, the epitome of a gentleman . . . and all I want to do is slap it away. "I'm Quinton."

"Oh, I know you!" She ignores his hand and claps hers together, drawing the attention of a couple at the table behind us. "You're that football fella! The one who's been causing all sorts of hubbub! Oh yes, I do love it. Tell those greedy old bastards where to stick it, won't you."

I gasp. "Mrs. Rafter!" I've never heard her call anyone out like that!

Quinton's deep laughter fills the room and causes Mrs. Rafter to blush . . . again.

"Thank you, ma'am," he says. "Actually, Elliot has been helping me set up my foundation. We're having a party next Tuesday and I would love for you to come if you're free. You can see all of the work she's put in. I couldn't have done it without her."

I want to object. I hate that Quinton knows my personal business at all, the last thing I want is him getting even more information . . . having a greater hold over me. But by the way Mrs. Rafter's eyes light up at the invitation, I can't say anything.

"Oh, well spoil an old lady, why don't you? I'd love that!" Mrs. Rafter pats him on the chest and her hand lingers just long enough that I know she's trying to see if he feels as hard beneath that T-shirt as he looks. "Who would've thought a trip to Stanley's would get me my girl back and an invitation to a party? Well, I'm going to head home, I don't want to use all this luck in one spot. Maybe I'll buy a lotto ticket on the way."

She leans in, giving me one more hug, and then shouts out her goodbyes to the rest of the patrons. I watch through the window as she makes her way to her car, and I try to get ahold of the anger that feels like it's spinning out of control.

"Your Diet." The waitress places my soda on the table before turning her friendly gaze to Quinton. "Can I get you something to drink?"

"A water'd be great, thanks."

"Easy enough!" She smiles, putting her untouched notepad back in her pocket. "I'll be right back with that."

I'm still trying to rein in not only my thoughts, but my emotions as well, when she walks away. I grab my Coke and take a deep sip, wishing Stanley's had vodka.

We sit in the silence. Neither one of us seems to know what to say. I'm hoping this means he'll just pretend he didn't hear or see anything at all.

But I've never been particularly lucky.

"I'm really sorry about your dad. I had no idea." He's so quiet that I almost didn't hear it.

I wish I hadn't heard it.

"Of course you had no idea, why would you?" I keep my voice even, indifferent.

"I know, it's just . . ." He scrubs a hand over his head before leaning back in the booth—leaning back in my dad's spot in the booth. "It sucks, you know? I'm sorry you had to go through that. Life's not fair."

"You got that right." Humorless laughter I can't contain bubbles up from the ugliest part of my soul.

"I'm really sorry." A look I can't decipher crosses his face. It looks like he's having a battle in his head until he squares his jaw and leans forward, coming to a decision on whatever it was. He reaches his arm across the table and gently squeezes my hand.

Oh. Apparently he was deciding whether or not to initiate physical contact with me. Like I'd throw myself all over him at the slightest touch. And that's annoying, but not infuriating. No.

"I know," he says. "Losing a parent—"

That's infuriating. And it's all I let him say. Because is he fucking kidding me?

"You know?" I pull my hand back and let his fall flat against the table. "You know what it's like to watch your father, your only living parent, slowly waste away until he's so sick, so tired of it all, that he quits treatment?"

"Well, I mean . . ." he stutters and pulls his hand back.

I don't wait for him to finish because I don't really want to hear what he has to say anyways.

"So you know what it's like to spend those months pretending everything is going to be fine, when in reality everything is on fucking fire? But instead, you let him think you're fine, and watch football games with him while you try to memorize each moment with him because you know pretty soon there won't be any more?"

I pause and raise my eyebrows to see if he has an answer yet. When I'm met with silence, I keep going.

"Then, it happens and he dies. So even though you feel like you're literally walking through hell and you want to do nothing except stay in bed and cry forever, you get up and work your ass off. And then you get it—the job of your dreams, working for your dad's favorite team. Only to be stuck with someone who insinuates that you don't deserve that job? You know what that's like?"

"No." He shakes his head, hardness set in his jaw. "I don't know what that's like."

"Of course you don't." I lean across the table, disdain dripping from each word. "Because you just think about yourself. You make these grandstanding gestures. You create this foundation. You make these impassioned statements all to say what you want to say and make everyone believe you have all the answers. Forget everything except what mighty, righteous Quinton has to say. You want to fight against racism and problems plaguing the League, but only if it's on your terms, right? God forbid anyone say anything you don't like. You've gotten everything you've wanted your entire life and that's not gonna stop now. Am I right?"

His expression is blank and those black eyes of his look soulless, not one ounce of remorse or regret shining through. "So I'm guessing we're going to skip lunch?" He pulls his keys out of his pocket and doesn't acknowledge anything I've said.

Which for some inexplicable reason pisses me off even more.

"Yeah," I snap. "I think we're finished here."

He doesn't say another word as he unfolds his large body from the small booth and walks out of the restaurant.

"That went fucking great." I say out loud before waving the waitress back over. "Cake. I need cake."

Eleven

THE SOUND OF MY PHONE RINGING WAKES ME UP THE FOLLOWING Sunday and a few things stand out.

I do have friends, and said friends do call me on occasion. However, they never call on a Sunday—they know how I am about Sundays during football season—and never before eight a.m. because that's just rude. The other thing that stands out is the ringtone. The obnoxious ringtone that I set for the obnoxious person on the other end of this call.

"Quinton?" I try my hardest to sound wide-awake, but fail nonetheless. I was up until almost four going over the final details for his event on Tuesday and writing up statements for the coaches and GM to use when they're undoubtedly questioned about Quinton after today's game. "Is everything okay?"

"Yeah, why wouldn't it be?"

"Because it's not even eight and we've never spoken on the phone, that's why."

"We've talked on the phone." He says the lie with so much

confidence that even I doubt myself for a second. "We just talked last night."

I've been avoiding Quinton since our lunch from hell last weekend. It's actually been really easy. I've been so busy finalizing details and meeting with vendors for the launch party that we've only had time to communicate via text and email. At first, I was super thankful for this. I was pissed and wanted nothing to do with his stupid, but still handsome, face. But as the days have passed and my temper has cooled, I know I need to apologize for how I reacted. But because I can be an adult sometimes, I want to do it face-to-face.

"No we didn't." I fall back onto my pillow, wishing I was still asleep. I wonder if he can hear my eyes rolling from wherever he is. "We were texting, and texting is not talking on the phone."

"We've communicated on the phone before. Is that better?"

If I weren't so tired, I might be impressed that we're managing to fight about this.

"Sure, fine. Tell me what you want or I'm hanging up."

His deep sigh in my ear is a not-so-gentle reminder of my ability to grate on his nerves. "Dammit, Elliot. I was hoping this early you would at least be too tired to have an attitude."

"There isn't an hour of the day I wouldn't be fully prepared to have one with you. I'm hanging up now." I pull the phone away from my ear, fully intending on hanging up when his voice comes over the line.

"Fine! I just got off the phone with my agent," he says like that should mean something to me.

"And you're telling me this because?"

"You make everything so difficult." He compliments me without realizing it. "He's been trying to make it out here for the last couple of weeks and now that he's here, he wants to talk with you before the launch. I was wondering if you could go to the game with him? He'll pick you up so you can talk on the way. I share a box with Justin Lamar's wife, but she's cool and you guys will be able to have some privacy if you need it."

Here's the thing, even though I would like to make Quinton squirm and worry that I won't get on board, he's offering me box tickets! I would've said yes to driving myself and sitting in the nosebleed section. But no hassle *and* a box? With Lavonne freaking Lamar?! Hell. Fucking. Yes!

I don't say that to him, though. He can never know that he's unintentionally fulfilling one of my bucket list items.

"I mean, it's kind of last minute, but I think that should be fine." The cobwebs of sleep still in my voice hide the excitement.

Totally the epitome of cool. *Crushed it.*

"Alright, yeah. Okay. This will be fine. Yeah. It will be good."

Now, I'm fully aware that I'm not an expert when it comes to Quinton Howard Junior, but the nerves and uncertainty as he speaks are so unlike the smug jerk I'm used to being around, that even I know something is up.

"What's wrong with you?" I scoot up in my bed. There's not a chance in hell I'll be able to go back to sleep. "Why do you sound so weird?"

"Nothing. I don't sound weird." He says it so fast and loud I know I'm right. "It's just that, well, Donny can be a lot. And since I did the whole knee-and-tape thing, he's been even more . . . outspoken. I'd say he'll be on his best behavior, but I'm not sure he has a best behavior."

"I'm sure you're exaggerating." God. If he's giving me this warning about the guy he trusts with his career, I wonder what he's said about me? "He can't be that bad."

"If anything, I'm downplaying it." He mutters something else I don't quite catch. "Just . . . can you try to keep an eye on him? And promise you won't quit."

Wait. Is he anxious and *kind of admitting that he needs my help? This might actually be serious.*

"Or at least just wait until Wednesday to quit," he adds on.

Annnnndddd there it is. He's fine.

"Stop acting like I'm not equipped to spend an afternoon with your agent. I'm not a child and like I've told you a million times, it's my job to handle people." Ugh. See? This is why I shouldn't be on the phone before coffee. I can't have people messing with my energy this early. "I'm hanging up for real this time. Bye."

I don't wait for him to say anything before I end the call, but I do hear something that sounds suspiciously like laughter before it disconnects.

I can't stand him.

THERE'S A KNOCK on my door three minutes after the time Quinton told me I should expect Donny to arrive.

Normally, I'm not one to be standing by the door and ready to go, but I'm going to sit in a box at the Mustangs game. I was standing at the door twenty minutes ago.

I open the door and am met face-to-face with who I can only assume is Donny. I'm five feet three inches and he's only got a few inches on me. He's wearing a suit that does nothing less than tell anyone who goes near him that he's a very important person. And even though it's a rare cloudy day in Colorado, he's still wearing black sunglasses.

"Hi." I extend my hand. "You must be Donny."

"Yeah." He returns my handshake and goes a tad bit overboard with the firm grip thing. "And you must be the broad that old bastard Mahler stuck on Q." He lets go of my hand and starts to walk away before calling over his shoulder, "Fuckin' move it, lady. I'm parked in a handicap spot and you live in fuckin' Kansas. I have to get in that box early. I don't play well with the general public and if the Lamar boys beat us, they'll eat all the good shit."

Okay . . .

So it looks like I might owe Quinton another apology. He definitely was not exaggerating when it came to Donny.

My condo is on the second floor of my building in Aurora—not Kansas. Thankfully I'm wearing flats, so I'm able to catch up to him faster than if I'd gone with the heels I was contemplating since this technically is a work event. When we reach his rental, he barely waits for me to close the door, let alone put on a seat belt before he's speeding out of the parking lot.

"So let's just get this shit out of the way. I'm not trying to chit-chat and drag this bullshit out when I could be watching my boy play." He turns off the sports radio he was listening to, but doesn't so much as glance my way as he talks. "I don't trust that racist fucker Mahler as far as I can throw the bastard. So that means I don't trust you."

"Considering you don't know me, I wouldn't think you'd trust me." I dig my fingernails into my palms, hoping it will distract me from my rising temper. "But open hostility seems a little out of hand too."

"Oh, hostile is one of the nicest fuckin' words used to describe me," he says like I just offered him a heartfelt compliment. "Q told me you've been helping him with his foundation, but I want you to know what I told him. I told him not to stand unless the entire fucking stadium is on fire. And even then, he better stay on a knee until the damn turf is melted to those tight-ass pants and the only thing he can smell is the charred old boy's club this league has been clinging on to for the last three decades."

Whoa.

That was . . . descriptive . . . and unexpected. Yeah, def owe Quinton an apology. After I yell at him for telling me to get into a confined space with this lunatic, that is.

"My only job is to help Quinton make his point. If, by making these off-the-field accomplishments, he feels like he can stand on the field again? Well, that's up to him. I've never insinuated otherwise and quite frankly, *Donny*, fuck you for implying I would and that I'm just here to do Mr. Mahler's bidding." Alright, so maybe I am just here to do Mr. Mahler's bidding, but I can't tell Donny that. I really do want to help Quinton; I can't have them thinking I'm the bad guy here.

Silence fills the midsized sedan before Donny's—unsurprisingly loud—laugh takes over.

"Well, hell!" He finally takes off his sunglasses and looks at me. "I might like you after all."

"Lucky me." I deadpan before moving my attention to the moving cars outside my window.

"Yeah, lucky you." He focuses back on the road. "I don't know what Q told you about me. It's my job to make sure my clients are covered. And unlike some of the fuckin' hacks out here doing this job, I actually really do care about all of my clients. All the guys I represent are stand-up guys, but Q? I've known him since he was a kid. He's on another fuckin' level and he's got enough shit goin' on in his life. I'm not going to let the fuckin' Mustangs ruin his career."

"So what you're saying is that you think I'm out to ruin his career?" What has Quinton told this man about what we are working on to give him these outlandish ideas about me?

"Never said that, babe."

Babe? Is this guy serious?

"Call me babe one more time and I will jump straight out of this car, Donny. Swear to god, don't test me."

He raises a hand in surrender. "Right, sorry."

"Thank you." I'm honestly shocked he knows how to apologize, so I focus back on the topic at hand before he revokes it. "Why do you seem to think I'm intent on bringing Quinton down? Has he told you he's unhappy with the direction his foundation is going or the community outreach I've been working on? Or that any of the press I've set up for him has been counterproductive?" There was a local host who was a bit of a jerk, but Quinton handled it perfectly.

I want to be annoyed that I'm asking these questions, but then I think back to my outburst in the restaurant and fight it back. We haven't exactly earned each other's trust yet.

"No," Donny says. "He said you're good at your job and that he's really happy with the direction everything is going behind the scenes. What I think you're missing here is that nobody is accusing you of being a shit fuckin' human. What I *am* saying, though, is you work for one."

"I mean, sure, Mr. Mahler probably doesn't deserve the Nobel Prize"—and he is threatening to fire me over someone else's actions—"but that seems a little extreme."

"You know football?" he asks out of nowhere.

"No, I just chose to work for a professional team for shits and giggles. Do you know football?"

"She's a smart-ass too. What's with Colorado?" he says to himself . . . or the people in his head. Who knows with this guy? "Anyways. What do you know Quinton for?"

"For stepping up when the quarterback got hurt, clinching the starting position for himself, and then leading Atlanta to their first ever championship." You don't even have to know football to know that.

"Exactly. 'Cause Q is a quarterback. Everything about that man is leadership, quick thinking, and the best fuckin' throwing arm I've ever seen, and Gavin Pope is one of my clients, so that's saying something."

Considering Gavin Pope was my fantasy pick every year until last year when I swapped him for Quinton, I cannot disagree.

"Okay." He's piqued my interest. "What's your point?"

He glances over his shoulder before changing lanes. "My point, dear naive one, is that after the general manager reached out about possibly getting Quinton in orange and blue, we had to table the negotiations because Mahler said he'd only want him if he'd make the switch to wide receiver or running back."

"What?" My head jerks back and bounces off the headrest. "Why would he want to put him at wide receiver? That doesn't make any sense."

"Mahler said that players like him are better at speed than quick-thinking, high-pressure situations."

My eyebrows knit together and I couldn't hide my confusion even if I tried. "Players like him? What does that even mean?"

Donny's mouth falls open and he takes his eyes off the road for about two seconds too long before he snaps out of it and focuses on driving. "You're fuckin' with me, right?"

"No." I shake my head, genuinely confused. "I really don't understand why Mr. Mahler would've wanted him at wide receiver. Especially after all of his success at quarterback."

His knuckles go white around the steering wheel. "Because he's a fucking racist, that's why."

"Oookay." I shake my head and roll my eyes. "I could see how it makes Mahler look incompetent at his job, but racist? I feel like that's pushing it."

"Fucking hell. Q told me you were a little wet behind the ears but this is fucking unbelievable." He takes a hand off the steering wheel and undoes the top button of his shirt. "It's some old-school, racist bullshit that Black athletes can't be quarterbacks because they aren't smart enough. That all they're good for is hitting people and running fast."

I purse my lips, trying to come up with another explanation, but I can't think of anything. "Not everything is racist."

"Yeah, not everything is racist, but this is." A vein on Donny's head I didn't notice before is all of a sudden very pronounced. "I don't get it, aren't you Black?"

"I'm biracial." I don't mean to snap, but I hate this conversation.

I'm fully aware that I didn't inherit my dad's blue eyes or freckled skin and that I look like my mom instead. Something my dad thanked god for all the time, never missing an opportunity to tell me how beautiful he thought I was. With my full lips, espresso eyes, and wide nostrils, I know I don't look like what most people see as "mixed." So when people make the assumption that I'm Black, they aren't wrong, but they aren't right either.

I know they don't mean any harm, but what those people don't see is a lifetime of feeling like I was just on the outside of everything. Always wanting to feel accepted, but never feeling like the world ever truly would. Always being made to feel like I had to pick one side over the other, but at the same time, being forced to pick the side that I resembled . . . not the side who actually raised me, the side that for some reason nobody can understand me connecting to.

"You know what?" Donny reaches over and turns back on the sports radio he was listening to. "As a person with some real fucked-up issues, I can recognize them pretty easily in other people. And if I know one thing, your problems aren't with me . . . or even Q."

"I don't know what you're talking about."

"Sure you do," he says. "I just hope that you can put aside whatever issues are fuckin' with your head and start seeing Q for the man he is, not the man you think you're supposed to see."

I don't respond to that. I can't.

And thankfully for the throbbing starting to creep into my brain, Donny drops it.

All I know is this box better be the fanciest fucking box on the planet to make today worth it.

Twelve

THE BOX IS EVERYTHING I EXPECTED AND SO MUCH MORE.

The walls are covered with TVs showing the pregame shows from not only the Mustangs but all the other games from around the League preparing to start. The front of the box has a glass wall with a glass door seamlessly built in that blocks out the noise from the stadium. But as soon as you open that door and take a seat in one of the many chairs, you are right in the mix with a perfect view of the field. Then on top of all that, there's a buffet table stocked with my favorite foods and a bar with three different kinds of whiskey.

It's literally a dream come true.

"Why the fuck isn't Brynn here?" Donny grumbles as he struggles to pick which alcohol he wants.

I have to admit, out of all the ridiculous First World problems I've ever encountered, having to pour your own free booze in a private (also free) box might be at the top of the list.

"Oh my god." I pull the glass out of his hand and nudge him out of the way after he picks up then puts down the fifth bottle. I scoop some ice into the glass, pour in some Jameson, and top it off with ginger ale. "Take it."

"Jame-O and ginger?" He gives the drink an approving nod before opening the glass door and picking his seat.

I almost scold him for not saying thank you. However, in my short time knowing Donny, I get the distinct feeling he's physically incapable of not arguing back. So instead, I bite back the sarcastic remark on the tip of my tongue and appreciate the quiet now that he's gone.

I breathe in the stillness and pour myself a Jameson and ginger as well. Just like my dad used to make us on game day before he got sick. He was definitely more of a nosebleeds type guy, but he would've gotten such a kick out of this. I close my eyes and raise my glass into the air, hoping he's somewhere doing the same.

I take a deep sip and open my eyes just in time to see three boys barreling through the door and aiming straight for the food.

I'm guessing these are the Lamar boys and I'm also guessing that Donny wasn't too far off about them eating all the food.

"Jagger, Jett, Jax, you better not act a fool today." A booming voice I instantly recognize as Lavonne Lamar's enters the room before she does. "And before you even think it, I don't care what Donny says, you know I don't listen to one word out of his fool mouth."

And I'm in love.

I love Lavonne Lamar.

"I think you meant foul mouth," Donny yells from his seat outside of the box.

"I said what I said, Donny! I don't have time for any of your nonsense today."

Okay.

So I was wrong.

Now I love her.

If only she rode in the car with us, my day would be going so much smoother.

Lavonne finally strides into the room, making her grand entrance one thigh-high boot in front of the other and—It. Is. Glorious!

Whereas two of her boys are wearing matching Lamar jerseys like probably thousands of other people in the stadium and the tallest—and I'm guessing oldest—boy is in a hoodie and basketball shorts, she is decked out to the nines. The red soles peek out from the inside of her heels as she walks, signaling that she's wearing my mortgage payment on her feet. Like her oldest, she's also wearing a hoodie. But instead of a Nike logo spread across her chest, there is a massive crystal-encrusted crest with a football in one corner, her husband's number in another, the Mustangs logo in one, and a cursive L in the last.

The sparkle from it almost competes with the sparkle coming from the giant diamond on her ring finger. And even the clear plastic purse she's carrying somehow looks designer.

There's a new rule that says you aren't allowed to bring a purse or backpack into the stadium unless it's a clear bag. Not even diaper bags are permitted. I think it's the stupidest f'ing rule ever.

All I know is it's supposed to be for "security" but seems to mainly affect women, even though we aren't the ones typically committing the crimes they're trying to prevent. If they're so worried about safety, maybe they should donate a couple of those millions they throw around to places that help domestic violence victims. I mean, I'm pretty sure one thing most people who commit mass murder have in common is a history of violence against women . . .

But I digress.

That is a good idea, though. I reach into my back pocket to grab my phone so I can make a note to remind myself to bring it up to Quinton later when I hear my name yelled.

"Elliot!" Brynn crosses the box, her model-long legs making quick work of the short distance separating us. "If I had known you were coming, I would've picked you up."

Lavonne clears her throat and gives Brynn the most wicked side-eye that I've ever personally witnessed outside of housewife GIFs.

"Fine. Vonnie would've picked you up." Brynn waves a dismissive hand through the air. "The point still stands, though, we could've come together."

Being that I don't know Lavonne or her children—and still don't—that could've been awkward. Not more awkward than my time with Donny, but awkward nonetheless.

"It's fine." I shrug my shoulders and take a quick sip of my drink. "It was a really last-minute thing and Donny gave me a ride."

Thank goodness they hadn't gotten drinks yet. They both look so shocked that I'm pretty sure if they had, I'd be doused in alcohol right now.

"Donny who?" Lavonne asks.

Because I don't know her, I'm not sure if that's a rhetorical question or not, but I decide to answer just in case it's not. I point toward the seat where Donny is now tapping away on his phone.

"What the hell girl!" She swivels to Brynn. "I thought you said they were into each other?"

"I thought they were!" Brynn takes a step back before narrowing her gaze my way. "I thought you were!"

"Whoa whoa whoa!" I hold my hands up in surrender because I really have no idea what they're talking about. "You thought I was what?"

"Into Quinton, duh. Keep up." Brynn rolls her eyes and if they weren't so pretty, I'd hope they got stuck back there. "You said you two were getting along."

My head snaps back. "I did not. I said he wasn't being as big of a jerk."

I also didn't tell her that we haven't really been talking because I was the rude one this time.

"Same thing." They both say in unison.

I wonder if this box is actually a portal to another dimension or something, because this can't be real life.

"But if he likes her, there's no way he would just stick her in a car with Donny's crazy ass." Lavonne's voice is beautiful and bold and loud.

So Donny hears exactly what she says.

"I'm a motherfucking delight, Lamar!" he shouts from the other side of the glass. "The sooner you accept that, the sooner your life changes for the fuckin' better."

"Children!" she scolds him and points a manicured finger at her boys. "Remember what I said when we walked in here, I don't want to hear anything Donny says coming out of your mouths or you'll be grounded for a month."

"I'll give you each two hundred bucks if you tell your mom to shove it." Still not moving from his seat, Donny waves two hundred-dollar bills over his head.

Now, to the immense credit of Lavonne and her parenting skills, two of her boys shake their heads no and walk away immediately. The other one—the smallest one—however, looks like he is seriously considering it.

"Jax, I wish you would. It's been too long since I put the fear of god in someone and I've been waiting for a reason to do it," Lavonne warns and even I get scared.

Please don't do it, Jax. Please don't do it!

And like he heard my silent prayer, or most likely, the truth in the words his mom spoke, Jax says, "No thanks, Mr. Donny," before joining his brothers as they attack the gummy bears on the table.

"I know you're their mom and can't pick favorites, but Jax is totally mine." Brynn ignores the death stare Lavonne is trying to shoot through her skull. "That kid's gonna rule the world."

"He'll rule something, alright. Maybe if football wasn't still taking over their dad's life, he'd be around to help more. But nope! Gotta love men and their priorities, am I right?" Lavonne exhales as if her life has fully and completely exhausted her. She's smiling and I think I'm supposed to believe that she's joking. When I glance at Brynn, there's a look of concern on her face too.

"Anyway, I'm so rude." Lavonne reaches out her hand to me, successfully diverting Brynn from calling her out in front of me and diving into her possible marital problems. "Brynn told me about you and all the work you've been doing for Q, and I feel like I already know you, but I don't! I'm Vonnie, so nice to finally meet you, Elliot . . . even if it's after you saw me nearly have to end one of my children."

Ohmygod! Lavonne Lamar just told me to call her Vonnie. A nickname! Nicknames mean we're friends. Vonnie is my new best friend. That's just how it works, I don't make the rules.

"It was honestly the highlight of my day so far," I tell her truthfully. "And you can call me Elle."

LIKE FOR REAL now, I think Vonnie and Brynn might actually be my friends. I don't know how I will break the news to Marie and Liv that they've been replaced, but if they really love me, they'll understand.

We're sitting in the seats in front of Donny and I'm picking at the chicken finger I'm too full to eat, but want anyways, when Jack's voice comes over the speaker and the audience comes alive.

Unlike the peons in the rest of the stadium, I have no need to stand. Instead I lean back into my seat—with cushion, not the plastic junk like everyone else has—like the overlord I am.

Holy shit.

It's in this moment that I know this should be my last game in a box, if I ever even have the opportunity again. Clearly, it has all gone to my head very quickly.

"Denver Colorado! Get on your feet!" The instruction seems redundant, given that everybody—except for me, obvi—is already standing, but go off I guess, Jack. "Make some noise, Denver!"

It's week five of the season and the Mustangs are currently 4–0. And while yes, football is a team sport, a large portion of the credit is due to Quinton. Much to the dismay of his critics, who believe that his actions will distract from his—and his teammates'—performance, he's on track to set a new record for the most touchdown passes thrown by a quarterback in a season.

The commotion is finally enough to pull Vonnie's boys from the food, and they skip the steps until they're at the front of the box.

The cheers explode as fire shoots from the sides of the tunnel and a real mustang runs onto the field being ridden by a woman in a full-on cowgirl outfit waving a huge Mustangs flag. The cheerleaders sprint onto the field, rubbing their pom-poms together as they split into two separate lines, a human extension of the tunnel.

"Here they come!" Jack's voice, mixed with the screams and clapping, causes the floor beneath my feet to rattle. "YOUR DENVER MUSTANGS!"

A stampede of blue and orange bursts from the tunnel as players jump, sprint, or jog onto the field. They all raise their hands in the air, feeding the crowd, fueling up off of our energy.

"Look!" Jett points to the field before he starts waving. "There's Dad!"

"And there's Mr. Maxwell!" Jax shouts out.

The Lamar boys go crazy whooping and clapping up a storm and it's not long until Brynn is standing next to them, blowing outrageous kisses to Maxwell. I look over to Vonnie, expecting her to be doing some version of the same, but instead, she's doing the opposite. She's not even looking at the field. Her focus is on her phone, like she's looking at the most interesting thing ever. But since I tried with no avail to check my emails earlier, I know there's no service here. In the back of my head, I know I should look away. Leave her be. I mean, I don't even know her.

Her shoulders that were held back, in line with her perfect posture, are slumped down and the grip she has on her phone is so tight that her hand is shaking. Her legs are crossed and her Louboutin-booted feet won't stop bouncing. Everything about her says this is the last place she wants to be right now. But it's when I notice the glassy sheen of her perfectly lined eyes, that my heart breaks a little for her.

I look away as fast as I can and pretend I don't notice anything when I see her wipe away a tear out of the corner of her eye.

It's not long until the Lamar boys are calming down and Jack's voice comes over the speaker again. The JumboTrons light up as the starting offense's pictures flash on screen as they are announced one by one.

Unexpected knots fill my stomach as I wait with bated breath for Quinton to come out.

I haven't been to a game since he first made his stand and this part of the game is never televised. Sure, I've found clips on YouTube, but this is the first time I'll witness it in person since the confusion has cleared and fans have started picking their sides.

When his name finally shows up on the screen, it's like my body can't help but react. I stand automatically, taking in the crowd around me. Listening as the boos blend together with the cheers. Knowing what I know now about Quinton's intentions and the mission at the heart of this, I feel an elevated sense of pride watching him now. And while I know that it's controversial for some, I hope that once people learn what he's actually fighting for, the boos will disappear. And maybe then people will worry less about where he's protesting and more about the reason he's doing it in the first place.

That wishful thinking is lost when I'm snapped back to reality by Donny's unmistakable voice shouting from the front of the box as Quinton slowly and precisely covers the League's logo with black tape. "Hell yeah, Q! Don't ever fuckin' stop what you're doing!" Then, I guess somebody from somewhere says something to him, because his attention moves from the field and he yells, "Yeah? How about fuck you too, motherfucker? How about you say something when you've done something with your pitiful fuckin' life, fuckin' scumbag!"

And just like that, I slide back into PR mode.

"Whoa there." I grab Donny by the sleeve and pull him up the steps. "I think Quinton has the bad press thing down without any help from you."

While babysitting Donny isn't exactly my dream job, at least the booze is free and he's sure to keep me entertained. Today definitely could've been worse.

Thirteen

THE DAY OF THE LAUNCH IS PURE PANDEMONIUM.

Between the vendors coming in and out all day, helping with setup, and Brynn forcing me to give my opinion on the signature cocktails she came up with, I've hardly even had time to go to the bathroom. My feet already hurt, I'm jittery from a caffeine overload, and my back is tighter than it's ever been. And I'm loving every freaking second of it all.

Hannah and her crew are still putting up the balloons and someone else is stringing white lights across the ceiling. They aren't even close to being finished.

The caterer is setting up stations all around the room so the crowds will have access to food no matter where they are. Brynn's finishing up arranging her bar while Paisley is creating a chalkboard menu that is basically art.

Everything is coming together beautifully, but there's still one giant dark cloud looming over everything.

Quinton.

I was hoping I'd have a chance to apologize to him face-to-face after Sunday's game. But when the Mustangs were up by over 20 in the fourth quarter and Vonnie offered me a ride home early, I couldn't refuse.

It wasn't at all because I chickened out and was looking for a hasty exit.

Nope, not at all.

Now I just have to hope I can avoid him until after the event and when I do finally see him, he'll be so thankful for how amazing it was that he won't have any other option but to forgive me.

"Can I help you with anything?" I ask Hannah, not because I don't have a hundred other things to do, but because I'm obsessed with the balloon sculptures she creates and I want to learn from the master.

"Sure! We need to move these toward the entry." She always sounds as if she's just finished drinking espresso shots, giddy and energetic. But I guess that's just what happy people sound like? Weird.

She stands up from behind the balloon structure. It's so massive that her legs physically cannot just climb over the balloons to get to me, she has to walk around it instead.

She's walking toward me, pointing a bright pink fingernail near where I'm standing. "See that gold balloon? You should be able to feel some string beneath it—just grab that and lift."

I lean in, wincing as I go, so afraid that I'm going to pop a balloon and ruin this magnificent creation.

"Don't worry, I've never popped a balloon doing the transfer," Hannah says. She must have seen the look of terror on my face. "It will be fine."

I want to believe her, but she must not be aware of my aptitude to fuck shit up.

"I think she's just worried it will be too heavy for her," a deep voice says from over my shoulder.

Because why would my hope for Quinton staying away until after the event happen? Oh, that's right, because that's how my life always works!

But at least he's joking? I mean, it is at my expense, but it's a joke and I feel like that means he doesn't hate me still?

"Hardy har har." I look at Hannah, who is suddenly sporting very rosy cheeks, and roll my eyes. "He thinks he's a comedian, don't mind him."

He looks like he's about to grab some balloons too when Brynn calls him over. "Howard!" she shouts across the room. "Get your ass over here and come have one of these lame-ass vodka drinks you made me make."

I guess Brynn likes to get extra creative when she does a gig outside of HERS and wanted to explore her creativity during this event. So, when she invited Quinton over to her and Maxwell's house for dinner and a cocktail tasting (something I was HIGHLY upset not to be included in) and he told her he thought they'd just have wine and maybe a vodka tonic (his drink of choice apparently), she did not handle it well. I feel like she's already super creative at HERS. But when she was telling me the story, she seemed super annoyed and I didn't want to get yelled at, so I kept my opinion to myself.

This resulted in her forcing me to sample cocktails too, because much to Maxwell's dismay, she decided to ignore Quinton and do what she wanted. Which is why she told me she'd be handing him a cocktail when he came in and breaking the news to him that way. Wasted effort because I'm ninety-nine percent sure he doesn't care one way or another.

"Do you boss Maxwell around like this? Or am I just special?" he yells back before dropping his backpack by my feet and heading her way.

"Oh, trust me, Maxwell loves it when I boss him around," she says loud and proud and for everyone around us to hear.

"Oh my god," Hannah—poor, sweet, innocent Hannah—gasps from beside me, her cheeks no longer rosy and instead fire-engine red as Quinton's deep laughter fades away as he crosses the room.

I'm holding the string like she instructed, but I'm still afraid it's going to pop in my hand. "Sorry about that, not the most professional setting," I apologize in hopes of getting her moving.

"Right!" She claps, no doubt still trying to erase the last five minutes from her memory. "Let's get working."

Carefully, Hannah and I weave through the different vendors walking around and setting up. By the time we make it to the front, my nerves are tattered and driblets of sweat I've been too afraid to swipe are trickling down the back of my neck, but no balloons have popped. Also, it has diverted me fully from any future career switch to anything revolving around balloons. So, wins all around!

"Thanks for your help." Hannah—who I'm pretty sure is *not* thankful for my help, and is just relieved that my anxiety will no longer be rubbing off on her—waves me off as her assistant takes my place beneath the balloons.

I turn to take everything in and see that the tablecloths are now being laid on the tables. Wanting it to feel more like a cocktail party than a formal event, but still wanting to give guests a place to sit, we decided on having smaller tables scattered throughout the room with no seating arrangement. It was the best compromise we could come up with and we're hoping that it invites an atmosphere of community and getting to know one another.

I head in the direction of the acrylic chairs that are stacked in the corner to start placing them around the tables when I see Quinton headed my way with his eyes directly on me.

Well crap.

I guess there's no way to avoid this conversation any longer.

"Hey." My awkward wave reveals the killer butterflies attacking my nervous system. "Wanna come talk with me real fast?"

He nods without answering and follows me as I make my way to Jen's office. She told me to take it over if I needed any privacy and while I thought I wouldn't, it's coming in handy now.

I hold the door open for him, turning the lock as soon as he's in the room. The last thing I need is another person hearing all of my business.

"The way I behaved at Stanley's was unacceptable." I opt out of small talk and dive right in. I keep my eyes on him, even though the urge to inspect Jen's ceiling instead is really calling me. "I'm not sure if you've noticed this about me yet, but sometimes I overreact to things. You caught me in a very raw, very private moment. I don't like people seeing me like that, especially someone I work with. I took my hurt out on you and I'm sorry."

His eyes widen just a fraction. I'm sure he never thought I would dole out an apology. But I'm an adult, so I own my mistakes . . . occasionally.

"Um, thank you." He drags his fingers through his thick beard and lets out a deep sigh. Which—inappropriately—makes me want to reach out and touch it as well. As bumpy as our time has been together, I still can't pretend like he doesn't affect me. He's infuriating, but he's passionate and so flipping pretty it hurts my eyes. "I wanted to apologize to you too."

My hair slaps me in the face with how hard my head jerks back. "Apologize to me for what?"

"Donny." He says the name like it should explain everything. And it does.

"Oh." I wave off his apology. "No need."

By the end of the day I couldn't help but like Donny. He's nuts and probably needs intense therapy, but honestly? Same.

Plus, he really does seem to care about Quinton and it was almost endearing.

But, instead of looking relieved that we're good, he looks more nervous. He shoves his hands in his pockets and starts to inspect the floors, which are very nice, but not at all interesting. "And I'm sorry for inviting Mrs. Rafter tonight."

Oh yeah. That.

That was pretty fucked up, but like, in the kindest of ways. And knowing how much he's coughing up per person for this event, it was really nice of him. But it did upset me and I've had a really hard time putting words to my feelings about it.

"It's okay, she's really excited to come tonight." And she is, which is another reason I felt so shitty about my reaction.

"It's really not okay, though," he says. "I told you how upset I would be if you went behind my back to talk to my family and then I did the same thing. That wasn't my place. More than anything, I understand wanting to keep your personal life personal. I should've talked to you before I overstepped."

My mouth falls open, but no words come out.

Because Quinton, of all people, is the only person who seems to understand how I was feeling and put words to it.

And that's something I can't even begin to process right now, but I can accept it.

"Thank you. I really appreciate it." I hold my hand out toward him, feeling like an understanding has finally been reached between us. Hope and excitement bloom at the difference we can make now that we're on the same page. "Now, are you ready to have the best launch party ever?"

His strong grip shakes my hand and the sparks that were there the first time we touched come racing back. The warmth from his touch winds around me and my insides go soft. His eyes crease at the corners as a genuine smile lights up his face and for a split second I hope he's feeling what I am. "I've never been more ready for anything."

"Good." I drop his hand, not letting my mind go there, making myself remember his words about me not being his type. I open the door and shove him out of it. "Now go home and get ready, I want the finished product to be a surprise."

Fourteen

FORGET ANYTHING I'VE EVER SAID ABOUT BALLOONS. THEY ARE A terrible idea and now I see why parents always seem about two seconds from losing their shit when they're around.

As the who's who of Denver start filtering in, filling the Rue with their expertly coiffed hair and thousand-dollar shoes, visions of balloons popping and causing mass hysteria resulting in a stampede flood my mind.

However, for the less paranoid attendees, they seem rather impressed by the decorations and the way the event has turned out.

"You planned this?" Mrs. Rafter looks around in awe, taking in everything with a cocktail in one hand and a plate of appetizers in the other. "I knew you were creative, but I had no idea you could do all of this."

"Well, it's less creative and more able to hire a lot of really creative people." Even though I have a hard time accepting her compliment, that doesn't mean I don't enjoy hearing it. And coming from the woman I've known my entire life, it means even more. I wish my dad could be here.

I give Quinton a thumbs-up, seeing if he needs anything when I spot him across the room. Not that he's easy to miss—and not just because of the constant buzz that has been following him around. Always in the middle of a group, it's like I hired a spotlight to follow him around all night. I swear, he's glowing—pride even evident in his long strides.

When he first walked in for the grand reveal, I thought he was going to cry. Tears are always my goal. I love nothing more than making someone so happy that they can't help but cry. Unfortunately for me, Quinton held it together. Also unlucky for me? The fact that he has never looked more handsome in his entire life, of this I am sure. And this is coming from a person who doesn't even really like him.

He's wearing a velvet fucking suit, for god's sake! He should look ridiculous. Who gave him permission to be this hot at an event for charity?

All of this is terrible for me in a lot of ways, but especially for two big reasons. One, I don't want to have to acknowledge his hotness. I work really hard not to think about it every time I'm around him. It's super rude for him to thrust it in my face after he's apologized and I don't hate him as much. Two, if he's looking this good, it takes away from all of the work I did around him. He was born good-looking, I worked really hard to make this come together.

Mrs. Rafter follows my gaze, watching as Quinton excuses himself from a guest I recognize as the sports reporter and news anchor from 9 News. "That is one handsome fella you got there." She takes a sip of the manhattan that Paisley made just for her. "Your dad would definitely approve."

I laugh because the thought of Quinton being "my fella" almost makes me need to get a drink of my own. "He's not my boyfriend, he's not even a friend," I correct her. "I'm just working for him. He's basically my boss."

"Is that why he invited me to this fancy thing?" She keeps her eyes focused on him as he shakes hands with guests but never stops heading our way. "Plus"—she finally moves her attention to me—"I saw some bosses look at their employees back in the day, but I think that'd get him sued these days."

I open my mouth to tell her all of the mortifying details of our first meeting, when he put it in no uncertain terms that he was not interested, but he beats me to her.

"Mrs. Rafter!" He pulls her into his arms, wrapping her in a giant hug. "I'm so glad you made it."

"Thank you for inviting me. The ladies in my knitting group were spitting nails, they were so jealous." She looks up at him, not letting him go. "But I told them my granddaughter planned it, so her boyfriend was obligated to invite me!"

My face goes cold. Which is I guess what happens when all the blood drains from it.

The last thing I need is Quinton thinking I'm going around telling people he's my boyfriend. This is like that nightmare when you're naked in front of everyone.

Except worse.

And real.

I'm staring at Mrs. Rafter with eyes so wide that it hurts and shaking my head no, hoping she'll catch what I'm throwing. But instead, she just looks at me and waves me off.

"Oh, stop it, dear," she says to me before patting Quinton's arm. "You're beautiful and talented, he's a smart man. He knows what a catch you are. He's lucky to have you."

"Oh my god," I groan, wishing I could hide behind my hands, but knowing I have on way too much makeup for that. "I'm so sorry," I mouth to Quinton, who looks way too entertained by all of this.

Or you know what? Maybe I'm not sorry. Quinton could at

least have enough grace to look like he's not enjoying this so much. But instead his smile grows with every word out of Mrs. Rafter's mouth and his body is shaking with pent-up laughter. The jerk.

"You're lucky to have Elliot? I thought she fuckin' hated you!" Donny moves in between us and stands by Quinton. Supporting my hypothesis that whenever I think things can't get any worse, they actually can.

I close my eyes and throw my head back. "Somebody kill me now."

"Of course he's lucky to have her, just look at her!" Mrs. Rafter gestures at me like I'm a prize on *The Price is Right*, before motioning to the rest of the room. "Look at what she did here. She's a catch, this one—I've known it her whole life."

I decide if there's ever a time to break my no-drinking-during-an-event rule, it's right now. "I'm going to go check on the bar, you know . . . make sure they're fully stocked and whatever."

"Oh good." Mrs. Rafter hands me her empty glass. "Do get me another one, won't you, dear?"

"Of course." I probably have a million things to do right now, but I can't say no to Mrs. Rafter . . . even after she's embarrassed me.

"And I'll take you to your seat," Quinton says.

She frowns, her eyebrows furrowing together. "I thought it was just open seating?"

"It is," he confirms before leaning closer to her ear, "but I have a special VIP table for a select few, and of course you're one of them."

The empty glass nearly slips from my hands as my jaw falls to the floor. He does have a VIP table, just one, and not even Mr. Mahler is sitting there. But now, Mrs. Rafter is.

Shit. I might cry.

He offers her his arm and she slips hers through it without hesitating before he starts guiding her through the crowd. I'm frozen to the spot, watching them as they go, and he waves off some huge potential donors in order to give Mrs. Rafter his full, undivided attention. And the look on her face? Her smile being the sole focus of his? She is gleaming.

Yup.

I'm totally going to cry.

"Still think he's a fuckboy?" Donny elbows me in the ribs. While he does ruin the moment, at least he saves my makeup.

I aim my sweetest smile his way and pat his shoulder. "Not as big as you." Then I walk away, pretending I don't hear his obnoxious laughter as I go.

When I get to the bar, I'm hoping to get in Paisley's line because, well, she doesn't ask me questions. But of course, as luck would have it, a group just ordered a round of shots and she's busy tending to their needs. I cross my fingers they get so drunk that they forget how much money they donate tonight.

"This is amazing! I can't believe you put all of this together. I'm totally calling you for the next event we have at HERS," Brynn says as soon as she sees me.

"Thank you." I look around for the millionth time, taking everything in. "I did do a pretty good job, didn't I?"

"Fucking killed it!" She hands me a shot that I should not, but do, take.

I cringe as the familiar burn warms my chest. "Tequila?"

"The only shot I'll make. If you want something fancy, join everyone else." She points at the long line building in front of Paisley before leaning across the bar and crooking her finger. "Hey! Before I forget to ask, how was Vonnie when she was driving you home? Something has been off with her lately. She thinks she's good at covering it up, but she's not and I'm getting worried."

"She seemed okay? Even though . . ." I think about the tears I saw her shed before the game. I don't know if I should tell Brynn or not. It seemed like a deeply personal moment for her and I'm not sure if it's my place to say anything. Even to a well-meaning friend. "She did seem a little upset before the game."

"Yeah." She nods. "I noticed that too. Just do me a favor and keep an eye on her if you're around her again."

I doubt that will happen as yesterday was a one-time thing, but I agree anyways. "Yeah, of course."

"Now that that's out of the way"—she points a finger across the room—"who's that with Q? She must be coming out of pocket a lot for that level of attention."

I follow her line of sight and see that Quinton is now sitting beside Mrs. Rafter, throwing his head back in laughter at something she said. Probably the story about the time I stole her bra and tried to wear it to the playground or some other mortifying childhood tale.

"Oh no," I tell her. "That's just Mrs. Rafter."

Instead of her curiosity diminishing like I assumed it would knowing that Mrs. Rafter isn't some eccentric millionaire with a hoard of cats, she somehow looks more curious.

She plops both elbows on the bar top. "Who's Mrs. Rafter?"

I start to think Brynn might possess some secret, superhero-level ability to sniff out gossip.

"She's my neighbor," I say before realizing that she isn't my neighbor anymore. "Was—she was my neighbor before I moved," I correct myself and still, with every word out of my mouth, Brynn's interest seems to grow and grow some more.

"How random," she says in a way that says she doesn't think it's actually random at all. "How does he know your ex-neighbor?"

"Umm . . ." How the eff am I supposed to navigate this land-mine? "We ran into her while we were having a business lunch."

I scoot to the side when someone comes behind me and try not to snort-laugh at the face Brynn makes when they order a vodka tonic.

She squeezes lime wedges into the cocktail and slides it over to them with a grimace on her face that I *think* is supposed to be a smile before turning her attention back on me.

"Okay, so where were we? Oh! That's right! We were talking about Q inviting your ex-neighbor to an event that's costing more per head than some of the nicest weddings I've been to." She rests her chin in her palms, smugness dripping off her like the condensation of the cocktails she's been serving. "But I thought you hate each other."

"Listen, you don't even want to know all of the details behind him asking her, but let's just say I wasn't happy and he has since apologized."

"Oh, you are *so* wrong about that. I always want details." She stands up straight and looks over my shoulder. "And if you didn't have an incoming visitor, I'd want them now. But I can be patient . . . well, patient-ish."

I brace and turn around, thinking Donny has come back to torture me again, but instead I'm met with the skeptical smile of Mr. Mahler and the swirling smoke of his wife's cigarette in a long cigarette holder.

And as that sick feeling I had walking to Mr. Mahler's office five weeks ago returns, I realize that I would much rather talk to Donny.

I guess there really is a first for everything.

Fifteen

"THERE YOU ARE!" MR. MAHLER'S CIGAR-RASPED VOICE CALLS OUT over the music.

"Mr. Mahler." I paste on my prettiest smile and extend my hand as he gets closer. "I'm so glad you could make it tonight."

Even under the dim lighting, Mr. Mahler's unnaturally tan skin stands out . . . as does the bright white of his teeth. "I wouldn't have missed this for the world."

That's nice to know now, after he ignored the email I sent him about the event and the formal invite I hand delivered to Gemma for him.

His wife, unimpressed by our conversation, comes to stand right beside me. "Brynn, darling!" She takes a deep drag from her cigarette holder and blows the smoke out of the corner of her mouth . . . and directly into my face. What a peach. "You remember my drink, don't you?"

"Like I could ever forget." Brynn grabs a martini glass. "The dirtiest martini for the dirtiest woman!"

My eyes widen a fraction and my heart stops until I hear Mrs. Mahler's gravelly laughter.

"That's why you'll always be my favorite," she says.

And now it's no wonder Brynn wasn't disappointed Mrs. Rafter wasn't an eccentric millionaire; she has an eccentric billionaire of her very own.

Now that I know Brynn isn't going to cost me my job by insulting my boss's boss's wife, I focus my attention back on Mr. Mahler, who is busy shaking hands.

"Elliot!" he calls me over. "I'd like you to meet one of my business partners, Charles Carlin. Charles, this is Elliot Reed. She's the one who's planned this event we're putting on."

If the shock of him acting like he's had any part of Quinton's launch shows on my face, neither of the men in front of me acknowledge it.

"A pleasure to meet you, Mr. Carlin."

"Yes." His clammy hand takes hold of mine in a very firm handshake. "Nice to meet you as well."

"I've been thinking about that project we've been discussing." Mr. Mahler directs all of his attention to Charles, as if he didn't just call me over. "What do you think about having her plan the event?"

Now, I have a lot—and I mean *a lot*—of pet peeves, but people talking about me like I'm not standing right there is at the top of the list.

"Oh yes." Charles looks around the room, stopping on the balloons cascading across the ceiling before looking back at Mr. Mahler and nodding his head. "Yes, I think she would do very well."

He nods once before the pair turns to face me. "I have been tasked with hosting a very important event. It's a fundraiser, much like tonight, but a little more . . . traditional. Does that sound like something you could handle?"

"Yes, of course." A traditional, formal sit-down would actually be easier for me to put together. "Does this mean that you want me to stop working with Quinton?"

For some reason, the thought of not working with him anymore—not seeing the aftermath of this event—makes me hesitant to accept this offer.

"Oh no." Mr. Mahler and Charles laugh like they're both in on a joke but don't want to fill me in. "This will be separate from the Mustangs and as such, compensation will be separate as well. Or will this be too much to do while you handle Mr. Howard?"

I ignore the way he seems to growl Quinton's name. Been there, done that.

"No!" I almost jump at the opportunity. "I would love that!"

Because my mom died when I was young, my dad made sure he had life insurance to help me out if anything ever happened to him. That, along with the money I got from selling a house in Denver, was enough to pay off hospital bills, give him the funeral he deserved, and put a down payment on my place, but I'm not rolling in money . . . not even close.

"Wonderful, just wonderful!" He clasps his hand on my shoulder. "Stop by my office on Friday and we'll go over some things."

"I'll be there." My cheeks hurt from smiling. Tonight is going better than I ever could've imagined. "Thank you so much for this opportunity."

"You're welcome, now just don't let me down," he says before someone calls his name and he wanders in their direction.

My conversation with Donny from our drive to the game pops unbidden into my head. And sure, maybe Mr. Mahler has ignored me until he saw that I could do this, but Paul told me this is his leadership style. He's got that "throw them in the pool and let them swim" old-school kind of thinking. But now he's offering me a job that he could've given to anyone. Me! Would a racist do that? Give me not one but *two* jobs? I don't think so.

"What was that?" Brynn asks once Mrs. Mahler leaves with what might be her third martini in her hand.

"Mr. Mahler just offered me a job planning a fundraiser for him."

"Wow!" She holds a hand above the bar, which I high-five with a reckless abandon. "Look at you! Kicking ass and taking names."

"Thank you." I hold out my blazer jacket and curtsy. "Thank you very much."

But before I get the chance to tell her more, my phone vibrates in my pocket with the reminder that it's time for Quinton to welcome everyone and finally unveil what we've been working on.

"I'll be back," I tell her. "I'm going to need a celebratory cocktail once everyone leaves tonight."

"Oh man." She rubs her hands together, looking more evil genius than bartender. "I'm so getting you drunk tonight."

"Sounds good to me." I eye the bar for her whiskey stash. "I know how to Uber."

EVEN THOUGH QUINTON is no longer wooing Mrs. Rafter with his charm, he still isn't hard to find.

As he is the person everyone in the room is vying to have a moment with, all I have to do is find a large group of people and work my way into the middle.

"Excuse me, sorry, excuse me," I say as I weave my way to the front of the crowd. The look of relief when Quinton sees me is a stark contrast to the looks I usually get from him. "Mr. Howard?" I've learned that sounding overtly professional is the best way to intimidate drunk people into being quiet. "It's time for you to give your speech."

"Thank you, Miss Reed." He nods, amusement lighting his dark eyes at this weird, very formal thing we have going on before he looks back to the group surrounding him. And I know it shouldn't, but him calling me Miss Reed kinda turns me on? I'll explore that later. "Thank you everyone for coming tonight. Now, if you would like to gravitate toward the front of the room, I'll finally get to tell you all of the details behind the reason you're here tonight."

I swear, as he talks, the men and women all begin to swoon.

It must be the velvet suit.

That shit is straight magic.

I lead the way to extract him from the madness, feeling very Secret Service and wishing I had an earpiece on. As we're moving, my back goes straight when Quinton rests a hand on my shoulder to make sure we don't get separated. And maybe it's because I haven't been touched by a man in many months—fine, years! Leave me alone!—but those sparks I feel every time he touches me seem to explode from his fingertips, causing my entire body to tingle.

And let me tell you, nothing makes you feel more pathetic than getting hot and bothered from the completely platonic touch of a man whose first reaction to you was only slightly below disgust.

When we're finally out of danger from the crowd sucking him back in, he drops his hand and falls into step beside me.

"Are you ready for this?" I try to use small talk to distract myself from the electrical current still lingering.

"I've been waiting years for this." He's stretching his neck and cracking his knuckles. This is just another game for him, one he seems to be taking very seriously.

I look at his empty hands. "Did you write your speech down? Do you need me to go find your speech?"

"No speech." He doesn't look at me. His eyes are focused on

the area we've designated as the stage. He points to his head. "It's all in here." He drops his hand to point at his velvet-covered chest. "And in here. I wanted it to feel real, not rehearsed."

Even though he told me from the beginning he didn't want me writing a speech, I hoped he'd eventually see the light and write one himself. Or you know, just do it to get rid of hearing me nag. I've been to enough events to know not having something on paper isn't a good idea. But I'm keeping my fingers crossed the stubborn man standing in front of me will prove me wrong. And if he doesn't, at least I get to say "I told you so."

I give the signal to the DJ to introduce him once the song that's playing has ended. And it's like that simple motion causes Quinton's nerves to skyrocket. His confident stance is now bouncing due to his tapping foot and all of his nervous energy is contagious.

"Relax, you've won a championship, this will be cake." Really though, a couple hundred guests versus millions watching? How hard could this be?

But instead of my words lightening the mood, I think they do the opposite.

Actually, I know they do the opposite because instead of laughing, he shoots his hand out like a rocket and latches on to mine. He stares into my eyes for a second, fear written across every hard edge of his face. "But this actually matters."

"Hey." I turn my entire body to face him and grab his other hand, ignoring the way my stomach is doing flips from not only feeling his touch, but getting to be the person he's confiding in. "You're going to be amazing. I know we haven't exactly seen eye to eye during this process, but even so, I've never seen someone more dedicated and passionate about something. Everyone here will see that too." I maintain eye contact with him, watching as he shakes out his shoulders and takes deep, measured breaths.

"You're right. I got this." He drops my hand and I mourn the heat almost instantly. "Thank you. And if I haven't told you before, you're more than qualified for this job. I couldn't have done this without you."

Before I get the chance to respond, the DJ is calling Quinton to the stage and I'm left staring at him as he goes, trying to wrap my head around what just happened between us.

"Good evening, everyone. Thank you so much for joining me here tonight." Quinton's voice booming through the speakers shakes me out of whatever spell he put on me, and I slip to the back of the stage so I can take in everyone's reactions as he speaks.

"As I'm sure everyone in here is aware, I've caused a little . . . disturbance . . . this season." Quiet laughter rumbles through the audience. It's the perfect start to his speech. "During the first regular season game I decided to use the platform I've worked so hard for to speak out against issues that are plaguing not only our society, but the company I work for. I placed black tape over the League's logo and I've taken a knee during the national anthem."

He pauses for a second, letting the audience get their applause . . . and a few boos . . . out of the way before he continues.

"You see, just like with the small group that's gathered here tonight, everyone has different opinions on what I'm doing. And although I've had more interviews this last month than I've had my entire career, I still need to share my truth. You've heard that I'm upset with the way the company I work for treats its players and the way society treats marginalized groups of all kinds, but you don't know everything. And that's why we're here tonight.

"I've heard from people that even though they might support the causes I'm fighting for, they don't necessarily agree with my methods. I understand that." He finds me on the side of the stage, flashing a quick smile at me before turning to walk across the stage. I don't want that little speck of attention to mean anything to me, but it does. In this room full of people, he sought me out.

We shared something that nobody else knows about and it makes those butterflies that only seem to make an appearance around him flutter back to the surface. "Football is one of America's favorite pastimes, fans are coming to games to escape the reality of their life to watch a game for a few hours, and why should I take that away? Do my job. Hashtag shut up and play, right? Leave the politics to the politicians. I've heard all of you. I have. So now, I'm asking that you hear me.

"As you all know, I've grown up with football. My dad, who wishes he could be here tonight, retired from this great game in 1992, ten years after he suited up for his first professional game. When he retired, there were three African American head coaches. The League was almost seventy percent Black, but only three head coaches were. That was a problem, but that was also progress.

"Now, I want to fast-forward to this year. The demographics are still pretty much the same. The League is still made up of nearly seventy percent Black players, which means there has to have been some progress on the coaching front, right? Wrong. Today, there are only two Black head coaches. There are only five Black general managers. And owners? Oh, there are none." He pauses and lets the statistics he's just rattled off sink into everyone in the room. "In an industry that could not continue without Black players, we're still struggling to hold a position of real power inside it. I've been told I shouldn't be a quarterback, I'd be more successful at running back . . . and that was after I got a ring. Black coaches with comparable records to their white counterparts are being fired while white coaches are given another chance. Discipline within the League isn't evenly distributed, with Black players getting harsher punishments than their white teammates. If this is happening in the League, if systemic and overt racism affect men who are often well known and respected, what do you think is happening to Black people across this country?"

Oh. Shit.

I find Mr. Mahler in the crowd and even from beneath the harsh pink tint of his skin, I can still see the heat rising in his face. He looks pissed.

"And I'm using this platform for the men who, like my dad, retired before 1993 and have been completely left by the wayside. These men who made the League what it is by playing their hearts out without any knowledge of the dangers we know about now. Without access to the insurance we players have now, without the pensions we have, they are suffering in silence. They have been dealing with the neurological issues we're now taking steps to avoid, but without means to provide for themselves or their families. These men are dying and it is our job as players to fight for them. It's imperative that I use my platform for a cause that means something to me. And that is to fight for the people who cannot fight for themselves."

Whispers begin to roll through the crowd as they start to feed off the energy Quinton is bringing into the room.

"'Put your money where your mouth is.' That's something else I've heard. And I've been thinking about that a lot, which is part of why the Quinton Howard Junior Foundation was created. I'm making a stance on the field, but tonight I want to tell you about my actions off the field. I brought all of you here hoping that you would open up your hearts and checkbooks to help me fight this fight. But I realized I have to lead by example, which is why I'm here to tell you that I will be donating my salary for this season to different charities whose causes support the mission of the Quinton Howard Junior Foundation."

The whispers completely dissipate and I could hear a pin drop with how quiet the room is. Quinton was slated to make twenty-one million dollars this year and I'm not sure anyone thinks they heard him right . . . myself included. Out of all the things we discussed, this was *not* one of them.

"That's my fuckin' boy!" Donny—of course it's Donny—
jumps to his feet and breaks the silence.

It's not even a second before everyone in the crowd has joined
him on their feet, the applause and cheers causing the distressed
wood beneath my feet to rattle with hope and energy and faith
that this man, that Quinton, can not only lead the Mustangs, but
everyone around him, to being better humans.

"Thank you." His voice is barely audible over the cheers still
going strong. "But I want to tell you who the first check will be
going to. Earlier today, I sent a check to Pro Players for Equal
Treatment, an organization run by a former player's wife that is
committed to working with the League to find a solution that al-
lows these retired players and their loved ones to live with dignity.
I'm honored to bring attention not only to them, but to the important cause they're fighting for. Thank you everyone for coming
out tonight. This is the beginning of something wonderful and I
truly appreciate all of your support."

And just like that, the room explodes with excitement and applause once again. The reporters who were here for a fun evening
all have their cell phones plastered to their faces, no doubt calling
their stations to send a camera crew over, as the rest of the crowd
rushes across the room trying to get to Quinton. Thankfully, I
already had an interview with ESPN set up after this event. Good
thing I'm good at my job. But hopefully some of these reporters
are now changing their questions from "Why?" to "How can we
help?" I do know that, without a doubt, they're all seeing him
through a completely new lens. One that no longer sees him as a
spoiled, entitled brat, but as a selfless, caring individual who is
going to change the world.

And how the hell am I supposed to keep my guard up around
that?

Sixteen

TO SAY THE EVENT WAS A SUCCESS IS A MASSIVE UNDERSTATE-
ment.

Quinton was trending before the crowds cleared. The news of his outrageous pledge damn near broke the Internet . . . or at least his website, which crashed approximately fifteen minutes after his announcement.

The other thing trending? Pro Players for Equal Treatment, the first organization receiving a donation from Quinton.

When I told him about all of the traffic to his site, he was annoyingly blasé about it. But when I pulled him to the side thirty minutes later to tell him that? He excused himself and locked himself in Jen's office. When he came out a few minutes later, his smile was the biggest I've ever seen. Before that moment, I actually thought maybe the muscles around his mouth weren't quite working (which did *not* lead my mind down a rabbit hole about Quinton's mouth that I'd rather not recount. *No. Absolutely not.*) and all pictures of him smiling with this many teeth showing were actually photoshopped. But when he stepped back into the hallway with red-tinted eyes, his full lips were pulled wide and framing his perfect smile.

And it was the best moment I've had doing my job . . . ever.

"Never doubted you for a fuckin' second." Donny slaps my shoulder and holds a shot in front of me. "Brynn said it's her specialty."

"You had no faith in me and told me so." I remind him of our car ride that he couldn't have forgotten, given it was only two days ago. "I thought Brynn only does tequila shots?"

The guests left an hour ago. Mrs. Rafter left an hour before that, refusing to let me take her home because she's "old, but not incapable." And a few of us stuck around to help clean up.

And by that, I mean tidying up the bar.

And by *that*, I mean drinking vodka tonics.

After Quinton's declaration, Brynn seemed to lose her distaste for the drink. I guess being the drink choice of a full-fledged activist made it more appealing. And maybe it does? I don't own a bar, so what do I know?

"I do!" Brynn shouts from behind a balloon tower she's dissecting. "Just slam it!"

Tequila shots are not my favorite, but because tonight ended up getting me on Mr. Mahler's good side with another job for him, I do just that.

"Eeeeek!" My entire face puckers as the bitter burn of tequila hits my throat. "It's so bad! I need a lime."

This is why I stopped taking shots in college. Now I get drunk the classy way. Slowly and generally hating myself during the process.

"Training wheels are for wimps and you're no fuckin' wimp, Reed!" Donny puts another shot in my hand. "You're the fuckin' boss who just put together one of the most memorable nights in sports!"

Wow.

I totally get why these guys hired Donny. If Donny was my alarm, telling me what a boss-ass bitch I was every morning, I feel like my life would improve drastically.

"You're right! I am a fucking boss!" I snatch the small glass from his hand and throw it back.

Bottoms up, bitches!

"Fuck yes!" Donny punches the air before yelling—or just talking? I can never tell with him—to anyone who will listen, "Reed's taking shots! Turn-up time has arrived!"

I regret agreeing to shenanigans with him for a split second before I decide, what the hell? Live a little.

I can't even remember the last time I got drunk for a reason that wasn't sad. Not only do I deserve to celebrate after a job well done, if I know anything, it's that life's too short to wait to celebrate.

Donny is walking back holding glasses. Not shot glasses, water glasses—filled with what I can only assume is tequila. Is he insane?

I take the glass from Donny and pour some of it into the shot glass I just used.

Because while turning up is a party, alcohol poisoning is not.

"It's starting to not taste as bad," I tell Donny. I learned my lesson on this my senior year. It tasting better does not mean it's actually tasting better, it means I'm fully inebriated. "That means I have to tap out soon."

"But you just fuckin' turned up!"

"Yeah," I agree. "But I'm not very good at this. I don't have a Donny-level tolerance."

"Funny." Quinton slides into the empty seat next to me. "And I just don't have Donny tolerance."

"Ha-fucking-ha." Donny rolls his eyes. "I don't know why you

Denver people always want to act like you don't love me. Everyone loves me!"

Quinton and I both look at each other, but neither of us say anything at all until Donny walks away mumbling how the altitude has ruined us.

"Tequila, huh?" He points at my empty shot glass. "I didn't peg you as a shot girl."

I don't know if it's the adrenaline rush I get after an event, the vodka tonics, the tequila, or all of the above, but the response I would've lassoed in yesterday just falls right out of my mouth.

"Well, considering you didn't peg me for a girl at all when we first met, this doesn't surprise me."

And then—definitely from the tequila—I laugh really hard . . . at my own joke. Lucky for me, it's not long before Quinton's thick, raspy laughter is mixing with mine.

"Oh shit!" He leans back in his chair, covering his mouth with a fist. "You got jokes?"

"I got a few." I bounce my shoulders a few times, and the urge not to brush them off is just obtainable in my drunken haze.

I've obviously seen him all throughout this event . . . and after too. But it's in this moment, with all of the overhead lights on and the top buttons of his shirt undone, that I realize I've never seen Quinton look like this before. The shadows and edges usually covering his face are gone and there's a softness to him. It's the first time I've seen him look happy and relaxed. And it makes him even better looking.

He opens his mouth to say something, but doesn't get it out.

"Elliot!" Brynn yells from across the room, her arms stuffed with balloons. "Are you sure you don't need a ride?"

"Yeah, I'm just going to get an Uber. Thanks, though."

"Okay, if you're sure! We're going to fill up our cars with these bad boys and then stuff them in Poppy's living room." She uses her head to nod in Paisley's direction and I see that she's also holding balloons. "TK hates balloons for some reason, but Posie's obsessed with them. She's going to be so excited and TK can't say no to her. It's going to be epic. You sure you don't want to join?"

Not to sound like a total fucking creep, but hell yes I want to go to TK Moore's house! He was my favorite Mustangs player ever. He did these ridiculous dances and just always seemed like he was having the best time. I get why he retired, but I'm still kinda bummed I don't get to watch him on the field anymore.

I don't say any of this because I don't want to get booted from the cool kids table. But also because I'm ninety percent sure that I'm not just drunk, but I'm druuunnnnk. And as such, I need to take my drunk ass home.

"As much fun as that sounds, and it really is the best invite I've had in months, I think I'm going to have to skip this balloon bombardment."

"Oooh!" Brynn opens her arms and lets the balloons fall to the ground. "Balloon bombardment! That's a good one, I'm writing that down."

"For what?" The fear of whatever diabolical plan Brynn is cooking up is clear in Paisley's voice.

"Not sure, but I do love a themed party." Brynn starts to gather the loose balloons before she sees Donny sipping another cocktail. "Donny! Either make yourself useful and help us mess with TK or you're paying for that bottle."

He puts down his glass without hesitating. "Where do you want the balloons?"

"Hey." Quinton pulls my attention from the train wreck in front of me. "I'm about to head out and Donny told me where you live, it's on my way. Let me give you a ride."

"Oh. No, that's not necessary." "No" is my automatic response to anyone offering to do anything for me ever. "I'll be fine."

"Of course you'll be fine," he says. "Just let me? Please. You did such a great job with this and I know I wasn't the easiest person to work with. A ride is the least I could do."

I actually am not a fan of Uber. I mean, I feel like climbing in a car with a total stranger and giving them directions to my house is the first thing I was taught not to do. A ride with Quinton wouldn't be the worst thing in the world.

Well . . . maybe.

He's watching me closely and I get the feeling that my thoughts are playing out across my face. "You know what?" I slap the table. "I think I will take you up on that offer."

Quinton pulls his bottom lip in between his teeth. Maybe trying not to laugh. Definitely drawing unwanted attention to his mouth.

At least there's a good chance that being trapped in the car with him will rid me of all these pleasant feelings I'm having toward him right now. Because right now I feel like it's messing with the balance of the universe or something.

"Cool. Then are you ready to go or do you need to check on anything else?"

The fact that he thinks I'm capable of doing anything productive right now is very generous of him.

"Nope, I think I'm good."

I look around to find Jen and spot her in the corner talking with Donny. He's got an armful of balloons Brynn forced him to collect, and it looks like he's hanging onto every word coming out of Jen's mouth. And Jen isn't just talking. No, she's twirling her hair with one hand and touching his arm with the other. The two cornerstones of flirting. "Hey!" I whisper-yell as I elbow Quinton in the arm to see if he sees what I do. Tequila has tricked me into reading signs that weren't there before. "Are Donny and Jen flirting or am I seeing things?"

"Oh shit." He leans in, squinting his eyes. "I've never seen Donny not wildly gesturing at somebody. So maybe?"

Out of everything that happened tonight, this might be the most surprising. Well, you know, after Quinton donating his entire salary to charity.

"I was going to say bye to her, but I don't want to ruin their moment." I think. It is Donny she's talking to. Maybe I owe it to her to ruin this. But Donny is loyal to a degree that's almost impossible to find, and even though he makes me nuts, he also keeps me laughing. "No, I'll just shoot her a text later. Let's hit the road."

His hand with his keys in them freezes in midair.

"Hit the road?" he repeats. "Oh god. You're the kind of person who sings in the car, aren't you?"

I am.

I so totally am. And I'm the kind of person who will actively try to outsing the radio. Turning up the volume only makes me sing louder.

"I guess you'll have to wait and see because it's too late to back out now." I waggle my eyebrows before bending down to pick up my shoes that I took off as soon as the last guest left.

"Fuck." He groans, but the smile is still on his face and it feels more like a friend giving me a hard time instead of him hating me. "Is this what I get for doing a good deed?"

"It is, you lucky son of a gun."

I don't know if it's the tequila or the lingering buzz of adrenaline from tonight, but for the first time in a very, very long time, I don't feel sad. My limbs don't feel weighed down by grief, my smile doesn't ache with guilt. I just feel like me, like the Elliot I used to be. Happy.

And to my immense shock and total displeasure, I think that Quinton might be part of the reason why.

Seventeen

"THANK YOU AGAIN FOR DOING THIS." I LOOK UP AT STREETLIGHTS as they blur together. The dark Colorado sky above them is even darker through the heavy tint on his windows. His BMW whatever series is a lot nicer than my beat-up Camry.

"I told you, you're on my way home. It's not a big deal." The glow from the lights on his dashboard makes everything about him look soft. His eyes, his skin, his lips . . .

"No, not for the ride." I sit up in the seat. Between the long day, the booze, and the plush, heated seat, I'm in serious danger of dozing off. "I mean, yes, thank you for the ride, but I meant thank you for tonight."

"Why are you thanking me? You did all of the work and the idea was yours." He sneaks a quick glance my way before focusing back on the road in front of him.

Now, I love a compliment as much as anyone—more, if I'm honest—but only when they are warranted. And the reason tonight was so successful wasn't because of the balloons, lighting, and excellent food. Don't get me wrong, that stuff helped, but the reason it was trending, the reason it worked, was all because of Quinton.

Pledging to give away millions didn't hurt either.

"I didn't do all of the work, not the important stuff. You did that." I shift in my seat, turning to the window, knowing I can't look at him while I say the next part. The gloating I'm sure he'll do will ruin the moment. "I mean letting me be part of this. I love my job, but a lot of times it's cleaning up messes I don't agree with. Spinning a domestic violence case, defending a DUI. But this? This I can be proud of . . . even if you're a total pain in my ass."

His laughter fills the car and even though I don't want to look at him, I can't resist. Seeing his eyes crinkled in genuine amusement is so rare, I can't deny myself the opportunity to take it in.

"Glad you added in that last bit. I almost rerouted us to the hospital," he says. "A compliment from you must mean something is seriously wrong."

"Ha ha. You're hilarious." I roll my eyes but it's half-assed. It's nice being like this with him. Trying to hate him all the time is exhausting.

"I know you're being sarcastic right now, but I think it's imperative to tell you that Mrs. Rafter thinks I really am funny." He risks our lives and looks away from the road to stick his tongue out at me. "So there."

I feel my eyes go wide in my face as I just stare at him, unable to say or do anything. Quinton Howard Junior, arguably the best quarterback in the League, just stuck his tongue out at me. Like a kindergartner . . . a very large kindergartner.

"You did not just do that!" I shove his arm and try to ignore how firm it feels beneath my palm but fail miserably. There was literally no jiggle. I didn't know that was possible!

"I did." He doesn't seem to notice my fascination with his limbs, thank goodness. "It felt like the right thing to do."

"Well, I wouldn't want you ignoring your instincts."

"Exactly." He taps his brakes, slowing as he takes the exit for my place.

"Question. You don't really listen to anything I say to you, right?" I ask. "Like, I could word vomit all over your car and you wouldn't remember any of it by the time you drove away?"

"Right." He rolls to a stop at the red light before directing all of his attention to me. "You can say whatever you want and it will never leave this car."

Even though he's smiling, there's a seriousness behind his words. Like he understands just how much I need to talk to someone. How vital it is that I don't go home to an empty house and still have these words bouncing around inside of my head.

I don't know if it's because in this moment I feel like he might be the only person who understands me or because I have drunk mouth—yes, that's the technical term—but everything I'm feeling just falls out of my mouth.

"I kept picturing my dad sitting with Mrs. Rafter tonight and what he would've thought about everything. It's the first time I've been able to do that and not get swallowed by grief. It actually made me happy. And I know my dad wouldn't want me to be sad forever, but not feeling sad is making me feel guilty. Is that crazy? Because I think I'm going insane."

"I'm not an expert on this, but I think that being happy when you get a memory of him is something you should embrace." He keeps his eyes on the road. I'm sure after the way I flipped during our conversation at Stanley's, he's choosing his words carefully.

"Oh, trust me, therapy has told me that you are correct." I drop my hand between the seat and the door until I feel the button to recline the seat. I close my eyes as I let the seat all the way down. "But even though I know you're right, I feel bad that I participated in this huge thing that he would've loved without him. And that when I did think of him, it wasn't because I was sad he wasn't there, it was because he just would have been so proud."

"I don't like calling people crazy," he says. "And if I know anything, I know that grief and pain never make sense. So you just feel what you feel and do the best that you can with it. And after seeing everything that you've done, I think you're doing pretty fucking good."

Considering I'm drunk and lying down in his car while talking about my dead dad, this is probably the nicest lie he could've ever told me.

"That's nice of you." I should stop talking. I know I should stop talking. But I don't. "What's so crazy is that I thought because my mom died, I'd be okay. Right? Like, if you have one dead parent, the other one shouldn't be as bad. That was bad logic. Like, really fucking bad. My mom died when I was a baby. I didn't know her. And as fucked up as this sounds, I don't miss her. I mean, how can you miss a person you never knew? I miss the idea of her. I miss the idea of having a mom. But this? My dad? Fucking hell. And I want to talk about him all the time. Have you seen *Coco*?" I don't give him a chance to answer and even though I remember that this, the loose lips part of being drunk, is the reason I stopped drinking tequila, I still keep talking. "Don't see it. Or do. It's beautiful. Just be prepared. I was not prepared watching that on Netflix one night when I thought a nice Disney movie could distract me. Anyways, I want to talk about him because I'm afraid he'll fade away if I don't. But I also never want to talk about him because that makes this entire hell experience real and it makes me feel my annoying feelings. If I shove it down, I can be numb. Does that make sense?"

He's totally going to complain to Mahler about me and get me fired after this. But maybe I can start some kind of Uber therapy business because I'm really enjoying this.

"I understand that more than I understand just about any-thing," he says.

And even though I'm about ten seconds away from falling asleep, my eyes snap open. Even though his car is dark and my vision is slightly blurry, I can still see the ghosts in his expres-sion . . . hear them in his voice.

"You do?"

He nods and takes a deep breath—slow in and even slower out. And just like the first time I saw him walk out onto the Mus-tangs field, awareness filters into every part of my body. I want to adjust my seat. Sit up and give him the same attentiveness he's given me, but I also don't want to distract him from the words he's obviously struggling to find. So instead, I sit as still as pos-sible, not even breathing.

"Yeah, I do. My—"

"You have now arrived at your final destination." His car—car!—interrupts him.

The British voice seems to startle whatever he was about to say right out of his head. His entire face transforms as he leans for-ward and looks out of his front window at my building. "Nice place."

Given I've seen his home and I'm still trying to catch my bear-ings after whatever that just was, I can't tell if he's being serious or not.

"You know, after all this time we've spent together, I still can't tell if you're being sarcastic or not."

"I'm not being sarcastic." He cranks the steering wheel and comes to a stop. "This looks really nice."

"Then thank you." I find the button to move the seat into a sitting position. "I bought it after I sold my dad's house."

I've decorated my condo . . . tried to make it feel like home, but it still doesn't and I'm not sure it ever will. After my dad died, I contemplated keeping his house. He loved that house. I loved that house. But as soon as he took his last breath, it stopped feeling like my home. Instead it just felt like a place I used to live. And when all of his medical bills started piling in, I knew I didn't have a choice. But now I don't have family. I have a house, but not a home. I just feel like I'm going to wander through the rest of my life. Like I have no place where I really belong.

I guess that will have to be a story for my next drunk taxi ride.

"I'm sure he'd be glad he was able to help you, even though he's not here."

"That's a nice way to look at it." I offer him a tight smile and try to get the focus off of me. Because after the loose lips section of drunk Elliot comes overly emotional Elliot and I cannot go down that road tonight. "What were you going to say before your navigation interrupted you?"

"Oh, it was nothing," he says, but the way his grip tightens around the steering wheel says otherwise.

"Are you sure?" I might be drunk, but that doesn't quiet the fixer in me. "Because I also don't care enough about what you will say to remember it tomorrow."

"Well, when you say it like that," he says, but the cobwebs of whatever was bothering him are gone and his smile manages to be bright in this dark car.

"Whatever, you know what I meant." I try to unbuckle the seat belt but I'm so uncoordinated that Quinton has to turn on the overhead lights to help me out. "Seriously, what is wrong with your car? I swear this is jammed."

This would never happen in a Toyota.

"Here." He wraps my hand in his and leans over to unbuckle my seat belt with the other.

When he touched me and I felt sparks earlier, I tried to convince myself that it was just the nerves because of the event. But the event is over. And with his face inches away and his hand on mine, I swear, the air thickens and crackles from the charged energy between us. Neither of us says anything, but my breathing deepens and my pulse quickens with every second that ticks by.

Until I can't take it anymore.

I close the distance between us and touch my lips to his.

And for a split second, he kisses me back.

Until he doesn't.

He drops my hand and pulls away. "Elliot . . ."

I've fallen in public before. I've replied all with a very personal email. I've embarrassed myself more than the average person. But nothing, NOTHING, compares to the utter mortification of this moment. Fire starts in the pit of my stomach and spreads right to my face. I take in the horrified look on Quinton's face and remember how he clearly stated, from our first meeting, that he was not interested in me. At all.

"Oh shit." I grab my purse off the floor of his car, my cheeks ablaze with humiliation. "I'm so, so sorry. I have no idea what came over me."

"Elliot." Pity is written all over his stupid, beautiful face. "I—"

"No, no. I get it. I'm sorry. I . . . Bye." I open the door, climbing out of his car faster than my drunk mind can keep up with, and run.

And I don't stop until the door to my condo is closed and locked behind me. But even that's not enough. I run to my bed and hide under my covers, hoping the tequila will at least let me forget that any of this ever happened.

When I said I had drunk mouth, this was *not* what I meant.

Eighteen

I DON'T KNOW WHAT WAKES ME UP FIRST.

Ripping my dry tongue off the roof of my mouth, the constant pounding in my head, or the insistent sound of text messages flooding my phone.

I do know, however, what keeps me up—the constant reminder of the horror on Quinton's face that plays on a loop every time I close my eyes. And the realization that not only did I kiss a guy who is not attracted to me, but I kissed a guy I work with. Like a fucking creep! If I was a man and drunk kissed a female employee I would be fired and publicly shamed . . . and rightfully so!

Ugh.

I've had moments where I wasn't my biggest fan, but I think this might be my baseline for self-loathing.

I'm terrified to check my phone and see missed calls from work or worse . . . Quinton. I'd much rather hide under my comforter for the next one hundred years, but I also need to know if I've been fired and/or have a sexual harassment case being lodged against me.

But even though I don't want to, I tap in my passcode. I'm not even going to attempt facial recognition with smeared makeup and a puffy hangover face. There are no missed calls. I'm taking that as a good sign that Quinton hasn't filed a formal complaint . . . yet.

There are, however, four new text messages. All from Brynn, Liv, Marie, and even Vonnie. If I wasn't mortified and in the midst of hating myself, I'd be flipping out that communication with Vonnie, aka My New Best Friend™, has progressed to text, but I do hate myself, so I only get a tiny bit excited.

The messages almost mirror each other.

> **Brynn:** Don't think the balloons distracted me enough to not see you leave with Q! You bring the details, I'll provide the whiskey.

I almost respond that while I appreciate the offer, she'd have a better chance of catching me with a hangover remedy and greasy burger.

> **Marie:** Heard through the grapevine that you hitched a ride with Quinton. Thought you hated him? What is that about? Meet at HERS. Need deets ASAP!

> **Liv:** Brynn told me that she saw your ass getting mighty comfy in Quinton's car. I knew there was something more going on there! I'll be at HERS at three. Be there or expect me to lead the gossip brigade to your front door.

That, I know, is not a threat but a promise. It makes me wonder what my life would've been like if my dad had just homeschooled me like he threatened that time I got a D in sixth grade. Or at least if I hadn't introduced Liv and Marie to each other.

> **Vonnie:** Biiiitch! I knew if you put up with Donny's ass that you liked Q! I want to hear everything! Be at HERS . . . or else.

I want to laugh at the "or else" part of Vonnie's message, but I saw her in full mom mode at the game. And while I have made some questionable life choices in the last twelve hours, underestimating Vonnie will not be one of them.

I add them all to a group text; my head hurts too much to stare at the bright screen any longer than necessary.

> **Elliot:** What happened to snitches get stitches? I'll be there at three, but not because I'm listening to any of you. I have to go pick up my car, which is close to HERS, and I need bar food.

I don't even get the chance to put my phone down and think of the ramifications that could come from these four women melding their powers together before my phone chimes with a new text message.

> **Vonnie:** Oh shit. The last time we had denial this strong, it was Brynn swearing there was nothing between her and Maxwell. I'm not missing a second of this! And I think I'm bringing Poppy. I wanna hear more about the balloons TK was bitching about on Instagram.

Yup.
This was a mistake.

My phone chimes again and I almost don't check it. I mean, a girl can only take so much. But this girl is also nosy AF and I do really want to meet Poppy.

But when I look at my phone, it's not the long string of names anymore. It's just one. The one that I don't want to see ever again. Just seeing his name causes my face to burn and my stomach to churn. And because I'm an adult, I do the mature thing. I clear the message without looking at it and pretend that it never happened.

Avoidance. That's my superpower.

SINCE I ALREADY planned to work from home today, the hours between me ignoring Quinton until I have to go get my car fly by. I send out press emails about last night, wrap up any lingering invoices, and check with Quinton's website woman to make sure everything is set to handle the amount of visitors he might get as he continues to announce more charities.

Everything is going so well that I forget about what a clusterfuck I've turned my life into. When I'm in the zone, nothing else matters. Football players have helmets to protect them, I have an abundance of emails. Same thing.

Then my alarm goes off and I'm snapped back to reality that means my afternoon is about to take a turn for the wild.

Lucky for me, my Uber driver seems to read my mood when I climb into the back of his car and doesn't say anything to me for the entire fortyish-minute drive downtown. I think about going to the Rue to see if Jen is there but then I remember the thing with her and Donny and decide not to press my—already bad—luck. Seeing Quinton would be bad. Seeing Donny would be worse.

When I get into my car, I contemplate ditching everyone at HERS and instead buying myself a dozen donuts and renting myself a hotel room until all of this blows over. But that seems extreme . . . even for me. So instead, I ignore the little voice in the back of my head telling me that a bacon and maple donut will solve all of my problems and crank my steering wheel in the direction of the interrogation I'm sure is waiting for me.

When I pull up to HERS just after noon, it's suspiciously empty. I parallel park right in front of the entrance and see the closed sign hanging on the door. I don't let myself get too excited. I might not know Brynn and Vonnie well, but I do know they wouldn't not tell me if they were canceling plans. So even though I want to accept this blessing and go get my donut, I know without a doubt this is terrible news for me.

I lean into the backseat to get my phone out of my purse. I signed Oprah's pledge not to text while I drive and I take that shit serious. I might disappoint myself on a daily basis, but my promise to Oprah is not something I take lightly. One of her tips was to keep your phone out of reach, and now, ten years later, it's just become a habit.

I find my phone at the bottom of my purse and see two missed calls and three text messages from Quinton. I know I deleted the one earlier, but I do work with him and I know I'm going to have to respond at some point. Might as well get it over with before I walk into a bar full of good booze and better people. But in a stroke of luck I've come to never expect, there's a loud bang on my window before I open my messages.

"Hey!" Brynn's innocent smile doesn't fool me for a second. "The Lady Mustangs had their meeting here today and I have to get everything reorganized again before I can open back up to the public."

I drop my phone into my bag, thanking all the stars in the sky for the excuse to avoid Quinton for a little bit longer, and pull my keys out of the ignition.

"Their meeting?" I walk around my car until I join her on the sidewalk. "Aren't you a Lady Mustang too?"

"Maybe technically, but not really." She pulls open the door for me. "I mainly do the bar stuff during meetings. I'm not an active member or anything."

"Is she trying to act like she's not a Lady Mustang?" Vonnie sets her martini on the table and even though I was a firm no when it came to drinking this morning, now I'm only slightly dedicated to that declaration.

I nod my head. "Yeah, she's basically saying she's just the host."

"And I am!" Brynn laughs and I think she was going for carefree, but sounds slightly hysterical instead.

"Tanya!" Vonnie yells across the room to one of the other servers. "How many drinks did Brynn make today?"

"Is that a trick question?" Tanya grabs a couple of empty glasses behind the bar. "Zero. You know she was talking about balloons for the holiday party the entire time."

"That doesn't prove anything," Brynn snaps before aiming her glare my way. "This is all your fault."

How did I get pulled into this? "My fault?"

"Yes." She puts her hands on her hips and says it in a way that's so matter-of-fact that maybe it *is* my fault. What do I know anyways? I'm still the dummy creep who kissed my kinda-boss. "If you hadn't made last night so amazing with those damn balloons everywhere, I wouldn't have gotten the bug to throw an event and I wouldn't have participated today. But you did, then I did, so it's your fault."

I don't know what I hate more—her flawed logic or that her flawed logic actually makes so much sense to me?

"So what about last month's meeting? Or all of the meetings last year? Your participation in those meetings is Elle's fault too?"

Phew! I was just about to take responsibility for it too!

"Shut up." Brynn collapses into the chair next to Vonnie. "You know I hate it when you're right and I'm called out."

Vonnie picks up her martini and stares Brynn down over the rim. "I'm always right, you should be used to it by now."

This is the adult version of "The Song That Never Ends." Brynn leans forward, ready to refute, when the front door opens. Liv's long legs walk in first, but Marie's voice leads the way.

As the owner of a cupcake bakery, she's just on a constant sugar high, I'm convinced. When she's not bouncing around, she's a total grump who needs to be fed. She's a toddler trapped in a grown woman's body. Which is probably how she's mastered making her money catering to the mom demographic of Denver. She's wearing her signature TOMS with cuffed jeans and oversized blouse. It's a stark contrast compared to the woman next to her.

Where Marie thrives on comfort, Liv thinks it's a four-letter word. I think the last time I saw her in flats was when we were in high school. And the pointy-toed stilettos she's wearing today are no exception. Her makeup is applied to contoured perfection and her long blonde hair falls down her back in flawless, glossy waves. And even with all of that, I have no idea if she came here from work, the gym, or a photo shoot. Liv is always on ten. It's why she makes such a killing in retail and with her blog.

"Hey hooker!" Marie drops her purse on the floor by an empty chair and wraps her arms around me. "You look terrible."

Gotta love friends who tell you how it is.

"Awww. Friends. Hugs. Wonderful," Brynn cuts in. "Is it time for details now?"

"Yeah, time to spill." Vonnie crosses her legs and leans back into her chair. "Poppy had a doctor's appointment, so we'll fill her pregnant ass in later."

I'm glad everyone else is so ready to take a deep dive into my personal life, but I so am not.

"Liv and I think it was a Cam Hall thing," Marie says. "Are we right?"

This is why you should end all friendships after high school and start fresh. No need to be in your thirties, already at a personal low, only to have your friends remind you that you've *always* been a disaster.

"Who the fuck is Cam Hall?" Vonnie asks.

"Oh. It's so good." Liv's eyes gloss over like they always do when the chance to gossip presents itself. She turns her chair to face Vonnie. "Cam went to high school with us and was ob-*sessed* with Elle. We all called it, but Elle didn't believe us. And when Cam finally told her he was into her, she freaked and ran away and literally avoided him until graduation."

"Okay, first of all? You know that's not what happened. Cam was just trying to weasel his way into our group because he liked Ruby. Second, I did not avoid him! He avoided me once I called him on his shit. You know I was the DUFF, I can't believe you're still telling that story."

"Oh my god! You were never the fucking DUFF!" Liv shouts as Marie groans.

Jeeeez. Glad I came in when this place was shut down after all.

"What the fuck is a DUFF?" Vonnie butts in, not here for high school tales and fucking same, Vonnie! "And why are we talking about Cam when we could be discussing Q's fine self and Elle's cute ass climbing in his car last night?"

"You know, a DUFF." I wave her off.

"Saying the word again does not clear this up," Vonnie says.

Of course super-stunning Vonnie has no idea what it is.

"It's the designated ugly fat friend," I decode, but I'm more focused on the tray of french fries and grilled cheese sandwiches that Tanya is dropping off on our table.

I knew Brynn was going to come through with the hangover food!

I reach across the table to grab some, but all I get is the taste of unexpected defeat. Brynn snatches the tray out of my reach.

"What the hell?" I ask, but when I look up, everyone at the table is wearing matching glares. "Umm . . . did I miss something?"

"Are you out of your ever-loving fucking mind?" Brynn puts the tray of fried goodness at the far end of the table. "Did you just call yourself ugly?"

"She did," Vonnie says to Brynn while staying laser focused on me. "That's exactly what she said."

I hate being the center of attention, it gives me hives. I flip through my PR playbook until I find something that I think will work here. "You guys, relax. I said *was* and it was a joke!"

I mean, do I still have some body image issues? Of course I do! Who doesn't? But it definitely doesn't need the attention it's getting right now.

Nobody says anything, they all just stare at me, trying to break me with their eyes. But I don't give in.

"I hope so," Brynn says at last, sliding a plate with a grilled cheese in front of me. "Because otherwise I have no problem locking you in here and telling you how wonderful you are until you believe it."

"We've done it before, so don't test us." Vonnie drains the last bit of her martini and I'm pretty sure I was the reason behind the sudden consumption.

"I fucking love you guys," Marie says to the table. "Anytime you want cupcakes, come see me. They're on the house."

"Okay." Liv claps her hands to get our attention. "Now that

that's under control, can we get back to the topic at hand?" She turns to look at me and I swear she can see into my soul. "What the fuck happened with you and Quinton last night?"

Now, as bad as the self-help, self-love intervention might've been, I know with one hundred percent certainty that it would've been more enjoyable than this.

"Are you already blushing?" Marie asks. "Holy shit. This is either really good or fucking terrible. Which one is it?"

I sit on the question for a minute. Not to build excitement or curiosity or anything. But because I have no freaking idea why I came here to subject myself to this nonsense in the first place.

"Terrible," I finally answer when I realize there's no way to make it back to my car without getting tackled first. "More than terrible. Mortifying might be better. And I think I might be a predator now."

"Well, crap!" a new voice says from behind me. "I skip out on one Wednesday meeting and this is what I miss?"

"Take a seat, Patterson." Vonnie gestures to the beautiful woman behind me cradling her adorable baby bump. "This shit's about to get good."

Nineteen

"*YOU* KISSED *HIM*?" LIV SAYS FOR WHAT FEELS LIKE THE TENTH TIME.

"Yes." My resolve not to drink has dropped to about negative three and I'm seriously eyeing the Johnnie Walker right about now.

"And he rejected you?" Vonnie asks . . . again.

I'm starting to feel like I'm stuck in some kind of time loop where only the last fifteen minutes repeat. And unlike all of the movies I watch where this happens, it's missing the zany appeal.

"And then you ran away and now you're ignoring his texts?" Marie not so helpfully points out.

"And calls," Liv, the freaking jerk, not so helpfully fills in. "Don't forget that she's ignoring his calls too."

You know, when I got swindled into meeting everyone here, I thought they would have a little restraint . . . maybe even be reluctant to open up in front of new people. Marie and Liv are my friends. They don't really know Brynn and Vonnie. Hell, *I* don't really know Brynn and Vonnie. How was I supposed to know that meddling in my life would bond them as though they've all known one another for lifetimes?

"Yes, okay?" I hit the table with a little more force than I intended, but none of them are helping and I'm reaching the end of my rope. "You've known me for half of my life. When have I ever not run from my problems?"

Therapy has helped me identify my issues and coping mechanisms. It has not, however, helped me change them.

"Something just isn't right here." Brynn leans back in her chair and folds her arms in front of her chest.

"I'm with you." Poppy—who is beautiful and lovely and meeting me at a personal low point—takes a sip of whatever nonalcoholic concoction Brynn made for her. "This doesn't make sense."

"How does it not make sense?" My nerves are raw and it's taking effort that I don't have not to snap at these well-meaning, but not all that helpful, women. "Quinton has now rejected me twice. Once when I wasn't even trying and again when I threw myself at him. I'm pretty sure the only thing that doesn't make sense is how surprised we all seem to be here."

"No. You're wrong. After the game on Sunday, his face fell when you weren't with Donny. Then, yesterday, I did not imagine the way he watched you from across the room or the way he trailed behind you just so, keeping his eyes plastered on you, but not in a creepy way." Brynn tosses her napkin on her now empty plate and pushes out of her chair. "And the way he was with your neighbor? That all said he wants you. He had huge donors begging to spend time with him and he ignored them all to talk to Mrs. Rafter."

Liv and Marie—my beautiful, loyal, concerned friends—suck in air through their teeth. The hiss of breath cuts through the air and slices my heart.

"Mrs. Rafter was there?" Marie asks.

"Who's Mrs. Rafter?" Vonnie's eyes bounce back and forth between me and Marie.

Liv ignores Vonnie's question. "You called her? Why wouldn't you tell us?" Liv's always solid and confident voice trembles.

"I didn't call her." I focus on the loose thread on the hem on my sweater. "I ran into her at Stanley's when I was meeting Quinton about the event. Hence why she was there, he got a front-row seat to our reunion."

"Oh fucking hell," Marie says on an exhale.

"I'm sure you handled that well." Liv picks up the drink she's been nursing and takes a giant gulp.

"Yup." My laugh shows just how well I did not handle it and that whiskey looks even better. "I flipped out. It was not my finest moment."

"Hold on!" Vonnie hits the table, not one to be ignored or left out. "Who is Mrs. Rafter and why do all of you look like you're about to fucking cry?"

Neither Marie nor Liv open their mouths to answer. Whatever I say is what they will go with. They're not going to push this. And it's on the tip of my tongue to say nobody and start to talk about Quinton again because I know that will distract them. But then I remember the way Vonnie cried in silence at the game when I first met her, and the way she worked so hard to hide it from everyone. I don't expect her to open up to me, I barely know her. But I know how concerned Brynn is and maybe, if I can talk about this, it will help her open up about whatever's been bothering her when the time is right. Lead by example, and all that other stuff I hated when my dad would tell me.

"Mrs. Rafter was my neighbor."

"Oooookay." She nods. "I got that part. So you moved? I don't understand why seeing an old neighbor is such a big deal."

"She was more like a grandma. She lived next door my entire life. She even spent Christmas mornings with us. But when my dad died last February, I sold the house and never went back. I also didn't answer or return her calls. I thought avoiding every-thing that reminded me of my dad would make coping easier."

Considering I never even told my therapist about Mrs. Rafter or the way I vanished after my dad's funeral, this is a really big deal for me. And from the way Vonnie's eyes go wide and then soft, she knows it too.

"Oh, fucking hell." Poppy grabs a napkin off the table and dabs her eyes. "I'm sorry. I'm not usually a crier, but when I'm preg-nant, my tear ducts don't go offline."

"I didn't know your dad died," Brynn says. She's sitting in her seat again.

"Yeah, cancer. We knew it was coming." I grab my water, re-ally, really wishing I'd given in and ordered booze. "Three days after the championship. The game was the last thing we did together before he fell asleep and didn't wake up again."

"Shit, girl." Vonnie closes her eyes. "I'm so sorry."

"'Tis life." I shrug, trying to keep my mask on and stay non-chalant about everything. *People die every day. It's the only guar-antee there is in life.*

Also, I do not need to cry in HERS.

"Wait." Brynn leans forward. "You're telling me that Quinton heard your reunion with your sweet, old lady neighbor?"

"That's what I'm telling you."

"During this reunion, did he hear any details about your dad?" she asks.

"Well, yeah." My eyebrows scrunch together. I have no idea where she's going with this. "I don't know exactly when he got there, but I'm pretty sure he heard it all."

"And I'm going to assume you cried?" she presses.

I shrug. I don't like to cry, but I feel like tears in that circum-stance were called for. "Well, yeah. Wouldn't you?"

"Yeah, yeah, sure." She waves me off, which I think is kind of rude, but when I look around the table and everyone is sitting up straighter and nodding along with Detective Sterling over here, I realize I'm the only one not following her. "So you're telling us that you had a full meltdown in front of Q about your dad with the neighbor who was like your grandma. And, instead of running or pretending he didn't hear any of it—which he could've done because you didn't realize he was there—he invited her to his exclusive event, blew off donors to make her feel comfortable, and placed her at the VIP table. All because why? He doesn't like you?" She jumps out of her chair looking like a freaking superhero with one arm raised to the sky before slamming it on the table and pointing an accusing finger at me. "Ha! I knew I was right! He's so into you!"

"Okay then, super sleuth." I place both elbows on the table. "If that's the case, then why has he rejected me not once"—I hold up my index finger—"but twice?" I ask, adding my middle finger.

"Looks like we have a mystery on our hands." She rubs her palms together. "And do you know what that means?"

I don't.

I have absolutely no freaking clue where the hell she is going with this. But apparently Vonnie and Poppy do.

"Oh fuck. I knew I was going to live to regret that," Vonnie groans.

Poppy on the other hand, well, she's clapping and her belly is bouncing in beat with her hair. "Ace is at his friend's house doing homework and TK took Posie to her swim class, so the whiteboard is free."

"The whiteboard?" Liv asks the question for me and Marie.

"Yes, my beautiful friends," Brynn says. "The whiteboard solves all."

Poppy grabs her purse off the chair and tosses it on her shoulder before leveling us all with a stare that I'm sure makes her children wither. "Snap snap! What are you waiting for? We have to get to my house and stake our claim before the rest of my motley crew tries to take it over."

I stand up and start following her, doing whatever it takes to avoid being yelled at and making a pregnant lady angry.

And I do it while silencing the buzzing in my purse by sending a call straight to voicemail . . . again.

Twenty

ONCE, WHEN I WAS IN COLLEGE, LIV AND I TOOK A TRIP TO NEW York City. It was amazing. We ate, we drank overpriced cocktails, we wore our skankiest dresses, and one day, while we were taking a stroll through Central Park, a squirrel chased me until I threw it the almonds I was snacking on.

That was a weird day.

But it still doesn't compare to today.

I turn my key in the lock and push open my front door, still trying to figure out what in the actual hell just happened.

When Brynn said whiteboard, I figured it was a euphemism for something. Spoiler alert! It wasn't. It was a literal whiteboard. A giant one that damn near took up an entire wall in Poppy's house, but was still just a dry-erase board nonetheless. I guess when Brynn had problems with Maxwell, the Lady Mustangs staged an intervention and used the whiteboard to help her see the light. And for some reason, she thought the same could be done for me and Quinton.

There was just one major problem.

Quinton and I are not Maxwell and Brynn. The main differ-ence being their relationship grew out of friendship and mutual respect. Quinton and I just started being able to stand in the same room as the other person and I'm pretty sure I assaulted him.

No whiteboard could help with that.

But we did break out into a very intense tic-tac-toe contest. Poppy's son, Ace, won. Which is total crap if you ask me because he's young and probably knows the algorithm. Thankfully for me, though, I didn't drink today so I had enough self-awareness not to say that thought out loud.

Oh.

And I also ignored two more texts from Quinton without reading.

Say it with me everybody: plausible deniability. But now that I'm home and don't have the Lady Mustangs, Liv, and Marie hovering over my shoulder, I'm going to have to be a grown-up and read them.

Sucks.

I hang my purse on the hook by the door and drop my keys in the bowl my dad painted the one time I was able to convince him to go to a pottery painting place with me. It's objectively terrible—an artist he was not—but it is easily one of my favorite pieces in my entire condo.

I toe off my shoes and leave them scattered across the rug pro-tecting the hardwood floors from the door to my kitchen. I'm usually pretty good about putting everything in its place, but I'm lacking the motivation to walk the extra fifteen feet to put them in my closet right now. A feeling I'm sure most people would share after the day—and night—I've had.

The plastic gas station bag holding the plethora of sugar coma–inducing treats bounces off my thigh with every step I take. I might have a Ben & Jerry's-sized bruise tomorrow and I'm honestly okay with that. It will be the most on-brand injury in the history of injuries.

In the kitchen, I empty the bag on the white countertops I had installed right after I moved in. The pint of peanut butter cup ice cream rolls off the counter and hits the ground with a plop. The lid pops off and white droplets of melted ice cream splatter across the hardwood floor that I'm still not sure how to properly take care of. I pick up the ice cream, not bothering to put it in the freezer, and wipe up the splatter art with a paper towel. I'll find a wood cleaner later, right now I'm in a race against room temperature to eat my ice cream.

I leave the rest of the candy sprawled out on the counter. There are a lot of perks to living alone, but the main one is that nobody will steal your snacks.

I grab a spoon out of my drawer and push it closed with my butt as I make my way straight toward my couch. If anything can ease the pain of the last twenty-four hours, it's reality TV and ice cream . . . and I plan on indulging in both.

But before my butt can meet the comfort it's yearning for and I can stuff my feelings down with the calorie-dense, only momentarily effective ice cream, there's a knock at the door.

"Fuck." I hiss, not wanting to talk about Quinton or Mrs. Rafter or anything actually, with Liv or Marie or whoever else followed me home. These women are relentless and the only reason I even open the door for them is because of the built-up guilt they aren't letting me repress.

"I'm out of wine and I'm not sharing my ice cream, so don't even ask." I swing open the door and then slam it shut when Quinton's stupid handsome face greets me on the other side.

What the fuck?! Can't this day just be over already?

"Ummm, Elle?" Quinton knocks on the door again. "If I

promise not to ask for some of your ice cream, will you open the door again?"

I wonder how much it would hurt if I jumped out of my bedroom window? I'm only on the second floor. I doubt I'd die or anything. A pair of snapped ankles maybe?

But, as appealing as broken bones sound at the moment, I do the thing Brynn talked about in quadrant four on the whiteboard. I act like an adult and open the door.

"Hi. I'm so sorry. I thought you were someone else. I mean, obviously I didn't think it was you. Why would I think it was you? And if I did think it was you I wouldn't have offered you ice cream, I just wouldn't have opened the door." My eyes feel like they are going to pop out of my head and I slap my hand across my mouth. "That's not what I meant! I would've opened the door, I just wouldn't have offered ice cream."

Stone-cold sober and still suffering from drunk mouth. What did I think was going to happen yesterday? I brought this on myself.

"Are you okay?" He sounds concerned, but even though his beard hides some of his amusement, it's for sure still there. I'm pretty sure he's about to laugh at me.

And maybe that'll be the icebreaker before he tells me I'm:

A. Fired

B. Having charges brought against me

C. Facing a public shaming for my abhorrent behavior

D. All of the above

It will be like a trifecta of shame.

I ignore his question because I'm very obviously not fucking okay. I'm a literal disaster and I will not humor him. I refuse.

"Umm, so . . ." I look over his shoulder for a stern man in a suit lingering behind him with a restraining order and let out a sigh of relief when I don't see one. Good sign. "Do you want to come in or something?"

"Yeah, that'd probably be good."

"Welcome, then." I scoot over and motion into my modest home.

He walks inside. Even in a Mustangs sweatshirt and matching sweatpants, his long, confident strides seem out of place in my little condo. Even though I really like his Afro fade, the orange beanie he's wearing looks good on him. All of this makes me even more furious for kissing him.

Before last night, I could mask my appreciation for his physical attributes with a roll of my eyes or a quick question. He never would've suspected a thing. But now? Now every time I catch his gaze, he's probably going to panic that I'm going to launch another attack.

I just started to accept my lust and I can't even partake in it anymore!

Life is so unfair.

I lock the door behind him, making sure my eyes absolutely do not linger on the way his ass fills out the loose sweatpants, and hurry in front of him.

"Sorry it's a mess." I bend down to grab my shoes and then toss them into the spare room that I turned into my office. "I wasn't expecting anyone."

My house is not a mess.

This is a lie I picked up from my dad. No matter how clean our house was, he always apologized for the mess when we had guests. He cleaned every single day. "If you stay on top of it, it will never get out of hand," he said. Advice, I should add, that also applies to the disaster that has become my entire freaking life.

"This is a mess?" He looks around the room, his eyes scanning my perfectly placed throw pillows and lined up remotes. "Seriously?"

"I haven't . . ." I look around for something to critique. "Dusted. I haven't dusted."

"Yeah, the dust in here is crazy. You should get on that." His sarcasm is well noted and not appreciated.

"Jerk." I roll my eyes and shake my head, but my heart's not really in it.

Awkward silence drifts between us. I know why he's here. He knows why he's here, but neither of us seem able to address the giant drunk elephant in the room.

But since I'm the cause of it, I decide to pull up my big-girl undies and face it.

"Listen—" I say at the exact moment that Quinton says, "About last night."

"No." I ball my hands into fists, my dull nails still managing to bite into the sweaty skin of my palms. "Let me, this is all my fault. I don't know what came over me last night." *Lie number one.* "I was drunk and not thinking clearly." *Half lie.* "I just haven't talked about my dad in a long time . . . Well, I've never really talked about him." *That's actually the truth! Besides in therapy, I never mention him.* "And I think between the emotions and the tequila I just blacked out a little bit. I honestly do not think of you like that at all." *Massive fucking lie.* "If anything, you drive me a little nuts. I have no idea what happened, but trust me, it will never happen again."

As soon as he leaves, I need to find the rosary Mrs. Rafter gave me and do some kind of praying because after all of that lying? I'm going to hell for sure.

"Okay, yeah." His shoulders slump down, the relief he must be feeling that he no longer needs to worry for his safety leaves his body. The small step he takes back, though, lets me know he's still not positive I'll be able to keep my hands to myself. "I just wanted to make sure things would be good between us. You weren't answering your phone and I didn't want you to quit over a mis-understanding."

"You called? I didn't even notice any missed calls."

I am *so* going to hell.

And by the look on Quinton's face, he knows I am too. An actress I am not.

"So we're alright? I felt like we were just getting to a really good place, I don't want to ruin that."

"No, I mean yeah." I crack my knuckles, a habit I always revert back to when I'm nervous. "We're good. It will never happen again. And I'd like it if we got along, because if you thought the work leading up to the launch was intense, you're in for a rude awakening."

Even though I stayed clear of the office today, I've been checking my emails all day. And the amount of interest in Quinton's foundation is wild. The inquiries about what he was talking about, what pension parity even is, were borderline overwhelming.

"I'm ready, I've been ready." He pulls the beanie off his head and toys with it between his hands.

I swear he's testing me. Letting me get a good look at him with and without the beanie. I could conduct a thesis and still not know which way he looks hotter.

"Good." After seeing his speech last night, I have no doubt he's telling the truth. If anything, I'll need to remind him to focus on the field. "So why don't we meet tomorrow after practice and plan on setting up meetings with Pro Players for Equal Treatment? Their cause is one a lot of people still need to be educated on. I was thinking I could set up a joint interview with you and their representative to really get the message out."

"Sounds good." He shoves his hat into his pocket as he heads for the door. I trail behind him, careful not to get too close, reminding myself of personal boundaries the entire ten-foot walk.

"Alright then." He lifts two fingers to his dark, full, always stern-looking brows, and salutes. "See you tomorrow . . . friend."

Friend? Awww, the friend zone. It's so cozy in here.

"Okay, yeah. Tomorrow—" I forget what words are and how they work. "We'll get to work then."

He walks out of the door and I watch him until he disappears into the stairwell. I close the door, only locking it by muscle memory, before walking back to my half-melted ice cream.

Friend? Did Quinton Howard Junior just call me his friend?

What in the entire fuck just happened?

I guess whatever it is, it's still better than being unemployed . . . or at least not for another two to three months.

Twenty-one

THE PING OF MY EMAIL IS ALMOST WHITE NOISE AT THIS POINT.

I knew coming back to the office after the launch party would be wild, but I still managed to underestimate just how wild it would be.

I was prepared for press inquiries. I had interviews set up. Press conferences for the next two weeks were scheduled. I was ready with Quinton's mission statement and the press kit we prepared before the launch. What I wasn't prepared for were the calls and emails from other teams' PR managers, telling me that their owners are starting to panic and I need to figure out a way to shut Quinton's protesting down and fast.

I wasn't prepared to hear from the players union about staying in my lane and telling Quinton if he was so worried about this, he should've done more than taking a knee and throwing them underneath the bus. That they had to worry about current players and now cleaning up his mess before they can actually protect the players he's claiming to be so worried about.

Even though I listened to Quinton as we set up the foundation, he always seemed to skate around the details of the individual charities he wanted to focus on. And he did a full-on dance routine when I tried to get him to tell me what, exactly, pension parity is and why it means so much to him.

On the surface, I get it. Equal pensions. Cool. Easy. But there's been a piece of this puzzle that's been missing since day one.

And figuring it out is why I've been ignoring my emails and why I continue to do so until my office phone begins to ring on my desk.

"This is Elliot," I say, half distracted reading about one of my dad's favorite players who is now struggling with ALS.

"Elliot, yes." The voice on the other end is familiar. "I have been sending you emails for the last twenty minutes. Mr. Mahler would like to see you in his office now," Gemma—I now recognize—says into the phone before disconnecting without a goodbye.

"Oh shit." I open my email and see seven new emails from the man upstairs.

"You alright?" Quinton's deep voice makes me jump in my seat.

"Fuck!" My vocabulary continues to spiral out of control when I check the clock and realize it's three minutes before I'm scheduled to meet with Quinton and of course he's not late, like a considerate person. "Shit." I shake my head, trying to clear out all of the profanity that is occupying my brain right now. "I mean, I'm so sorry. Mr. Mahler needs to meet with me."

His thick eyebrows arch to his hairline. "About what?"

"Another project I'm working on for him." I spin back to my computer, hoping to close all of the tabs I have open fast enough that Quinton won't see what I've been obsessing over. I'm sure the last thing he needs to be reminded of is a former player with ALS. "Don't worry, this one isn't about you."

He tries to neutralize his expression, but every time he gets angry, he gets this look like he just sucked on a sour candy. I'm not sure if he even knows he does it, but his chin tucks in and his lips purse out like he can taste whatever's bothering him so much. "Good for you. Makin' boss moves, I see."

I pretend not to notice how irritated he is. Working with him is great, but it's also consuming all of my time. Having another project to distract me from my very attractive friend with soft lips that I can't touch again will be good for all of us.

"I'm trying." I grab my iPad out of my drawer. "Why don't you head out and I can meet you at your place after this, if it isn't too late? If that's okay with you, of course."

Because "friend" or not, he's still pretty much my boss and my job still depends on our ability to work together and get things done.

"That's fine," he says. "Just give me a call when you're finished."

"Will do!" I call over my shoulder as I start to run down the hall. "And start thinking of a statement we can send to the players union! They're pissed!"

I don't turn around to see his reaction, but even without looking, I know there's a glare on his face. So even though I hate running, I run to Mr. Mahler's office with a smile on my face.

"Hey Gemma! Sorry about the emails," I yell as I blow past Mr. Mahler's secretary and barrel into his office. "Mr. Mahler, I heard you need me."

I'm out of breath when I say this and I can feel the edges of my hair beginning to curl from the sweat. I really need to work out more often.

"Yes." Mr. Mahler leans forward on the table, steepling his hands in front of his face. "I wanted to make sure you were still committed to the fundraiser I need organized. I know the other night was a bit . . . ." He pauses as he tries to find the word he's looking for. "Hectic."

Hectic? Out of everything that night was, hectic wouldn't have even registered with me . . . and I fucking kissed Quinton!

"Um, yes." I humor him. "A lot happened"—*understatement of the century*—"but I do remember agreeing to this and I'm looking forward to helping you create a wonderful and successful event."

"I knew I could count on you." He leans back into his leather chair and slaps a wrinkled, unnaturally tanned hand against his bare desk. "Take a seat, let's chat for a moment."

Satisfaction that I'm making myself known—and needed—within this organization causes a wave of pleasure that makes my skin flush.

I sit in the chair across from him—the same place I was sitting when he told me my job was on the line—ready to prove just how valuable I am. I swipe open the iPad screen and go straight to my notes app.

"Now, what exactly is this event for? Once I know that, we can come up with a theme and let ideas begin to form from there."

I love the details and even the technical aspects of an event, but the beginning stage, where I can let my imagination run wild, is my favorite part.

"Actually, my dear," he says, and I hope I hide the way I cringe from a person in power calling me by a term of endearment. Gross. "I can't tell you anything about this event until you sign an NDA. We want to make sure everything about this stays under lock and key until it happens."

I'm sure a nondisclosure agreement would throw most people, but I'm not most people. And as someone who has been on the other side of these situations, I understand the need to keep the details of a high-profile event under wraps.

To be honest, I always thought the people who signed them—no questions asked—were a little nutty. But now that I'm on the other side, I get it. It's kind of thrilling to be in the know on something so secretive and important. And after the way Quinton just stepped up to the plate, I can't wait to see what Mr. Mahler does next.

"Not a problem, Mr. Mahler. I understand your discretion and I have no problem signing an NDA." I sit up as straight as possible and hope my posture helps me come across as assertive. "But while we wait, basic details—like if it will be a formal sit-down dinner or more a cocktail hour with passed hors d'oeuvres, and what the anticipated guest count will be—will at least give me some kind of starting point. The date would be the most helpful. I can't even begin looking for a venue if I don't know when I'll need it."

"Oh, well, I guess I don't see the harm in that. The event won't take place until the first week of January. We want it to be a Friday so we won't have to worry about it interfering with the playoffs. It will be small, I'd say somewhere between thirty to forty guests. We want to keep it intimate." He folds his hands on the top of his desk. "I know you people love a big loud party, but sometimes it's better to keep it small."

My fingers stumble across the screen. *You people?* What the fuck? I'm hoping he means millennials. He has to mean that. Right? I tap the information into my notes, keeping my thoughts to myself, sure I'm turning his words into something they're not.

"Got it," I say when I'm finished. "When the nondisclosure is ready for me to sign, please let me know and I'll take care of that so we can get started planning immediately."

"Oh yes, very good." Mr. Mahler stands behind his oak desk, the corners of his mouth tilting up in a way that's anything but comforting. He's always reminded me a bit of a Disney villain, but even more so now as he reaches his hand across the table to shake my hand. "I'm looking forward to working with you."

I want to remind him that we already work together. Literally. He's my boss. But I don't.

"So am I." I stand from my seat and return his firm handshake. "Thank you for this opportunity."

"Oh, the pleasure is all mine." The smile on his face tenses a little bit as his fingers tighten around my hand. "I assure you."

I offer him my kindest smile before spinning on my heel and leaving his plush office.

"Bye, Gemma." I wave to the receptionist, who seems to have forgiven me from earlier. "Have a good evening."

"You too," she says, her normally warm smile back on her face.

I push open the heavy glass door and head into the window-lined hallway leading away from his office. When I'm at work, I tend to rush through everything. I don't tend to be seen as someone who can't keep up with the pace, so I move so quickly that I forget to slow down and breathe. But now that the halls are quiet and the parking lot is almost empty, I take this moment to stop and take in the view sprawling out in front of me. With everything that has happened in this last year, sometimes it's easy for me to ignore things like this. It's easy for me to forget that as bad as life has been, I still got my dream job. I did that. Even with the shit storm that has swirled around me.

There are things in life that we can't control. No matter how many positive affirmations we say or books we read or podcasts we listen to. Nothing I could've done would've stopped my dad from dying. It's a fact of life. Death comes for us all. And even though I feel like I've been stuck under the weight of the rubble that collapsed on me, I still managed to keep going and fought for the things I could have power over. Yeah, it hasn't gone exactly as planned, but I'm still doing it. And I need to appreciate that.

I need to appreciate myself.

With fall settling in, the sun is starting to set a little earlier each night. The sun fades behind the mountains, and the pink and orange clouds wisp across the sky above the perfectly maintained fields. In this moment of calm, a sense of peace I haven't felt in ages settles over me and I know that one day, I'll be okay again.

Gentle footsteps pull my attention from the view in front of me.

"Hey," Quinton says when I catch sight of him. "Everything alright?"

"Yeah, just taking in the view." I keep my gaze on the changing sky as the clouds dance across the horizon.

"It is pretty amazing." He closes the distance between us and stands beside me, taking in the view with me. "We had good ones in Dallas, but the mountains take them to another level."

"I forgot you're from Dallas. My mom's family lived there, I visited when I was a kid. It seemed nice from what I can remember."

I—admittedly—don't remember much besides missing my dad and not feeling like I fit in. I remember going for Thanksgiving break one year and just feeling lost the entire time. After my mom died, my dad had a really hard time being around her family. I still don't know if it's because it made him miss her more or if he felt guilty that he couldn't protect her. But when they invited us for Thanksgiving that year, he mysteriously had to go on a work trip and sent me by myself. I hated it. None of the food I normally ate at Thanksgiving was there, they didn't listen to any of the music I listened to, I got in trouble for using the hand towels in the bathroom. I was with family, but I felt like a stranger.

I didn't go back and they never came to Colorado to see me. Such is life.

"Yeah, it's nice. I'm not sure it prepared me for these Colorado winters everyone keeps warning me about, though. Atlanta's winters were pretty mild too."

"Pshhh. The winters are nothing." I wave him off. "It's the

spring that really bites you in the ass. Just when you think you escaped without a snowstorm? Bam! Blizzard. It's super fun. And, it's scientifically proven that they only come when I'm out of milk and bread."

Out of the corner of my eyes, I see his smile grow as his deep chuckle washes over me. I don't know what it is, but it's so soothing. He could start a Pandora station just of his laughter, and masseuses would play it while people got massages, it's that good.

"So if I keep you stocked, we'll be safe?"

"Yup, you can't argue with science." I stop and amend my statement. "Well, you shouldn't argue with science."

"Truth," he says.

We continue to stare out of the window until the blue starts to deepen and the pinks fade. Which reminds me that even though I'm only thirty-one, I already hate to drive in the dark. And also, that I told Quinton not to wait up.

"Why are you here anyway?" Once I hear the words out loud, I realize how rude they sound and cringe. He's going to think I'm incapable of being anything other than a bitch. "Nope, let me rewind. I thought you were going to head out. What made you stay?"

There. That was better . . . marginally.

"I went to talk to Jason about some extra stretches, my shoulder's been bothering me a little." He must see the panic that crosses my face. He might drive me nuts, but he can't be hurt, the Mustangs need him. "I'm fine, really. I just want to get ahead of it."

That seems like something a reasonable person who doesn't procrastinate would do. Not that I can relate to that in any way, shape, or form. What can I say? I make plans and life laughs—or punches me—in my face. And I've learned the punches hurt more when you're expecting a different outcome.

Expectations, kids. Don't have any.

"Okay, that's good." I take one last look out of the window before turning and starting to walk down the long hallway. "My fantasy team would not be happy if you weren't out there."

"I'm on your fantasy team?" he asks, a cocky, shit-eating grin pulling across his face.

"Don't let it go to your head. You were the only quarterback left. Definitely not my first choice." I lift my hand to pat his arm before remembering that I kissed him the other night, and all touching, no matter how innocent, should probably be off limits.

"Woooow." His laugh returns and my steps falter. "Okay, I see how it is."

"Whatever." I roll my eyes, hoping he doesn't notice how much he affects me. I never thought I'd say this, but it was so much easier being around him when I hated him. "Well, since you're still here, do you want to try and get some work done?"

"I'm actually starving." He pulls his phone out of his pocket and glances at the time. "It's not too late. Wanna go grab a bite somewhere first?"

We're just friends. He does not like you like that. This is not a date. It's a professional courtesy because despite what you initially thought of him, he's actually a decent guy. So calm the fuck down, Elliot.

Logically, I know what this is, but my stupid hormones don't seem to get the memo. My palms start to sweat and the place where my stomach used to be is replaced with butterflies.

"Um, yeah, sure." I keep my eyes trained in front of me. I'm convinced if I look at him, he'll be able to see that I'm still thinking about kissing him and run for the hills. "Dinner would be good."

"Cool." His voice is calm and steady, just like always. Which, of course it is. Just another reminder that I'm not his type and he doesn't see me in that light at all. "Since you picked the place last time and I didn't even get food, I'm picking this go-round. Wanna follow me there?"

I hate choosing restaurants, so this works for me. "Sounds good. Let me just go shut down everything and grab my purse."

"Great." He gives me that manly chin nod that all dudes seem to learn during puberty when they're too cool for words. "I'll pull my car around the front and wait there."

"Perfect, I'll be there in a sec."

He walks away and I only watch him for a second before I remember what I'm supposed to do. I head to my desk in a bit of a haze, only shutting down my computer from pure muscle memory as I try to get my mind right to have dinner with Quinton.

Hopefully I'll manage to not make a total fool out of myself . . . again.

Twenty-two

I FOLLOW QUINTON TO A RESTAURANT NOT FAR FROM HIS HOUSE.

I do this thinking he's much better at leading than I was when we went to Stanley's. He even passes up the parking spot right in front of the door and goes for the one that's a little further but has an open one right beside it. It's frustrating that when I really need to be focusing on reasons why I don't want to kiss him again, he seems to be going out of his way to be chivalrous.

"What is this place?" I ask as I push open my door.

Quinton is standing behind my car with his hands in his pocket and a smirk on his face. "You're a terrible driver."

Oh. Okay. Yeah. This is the ammunition I need.

"First of all, rude. Second of all, how dare you?" I climb out of my car and lock the doors before tossing my keys in my purse. "I'm a fantastic fucking driver. You, on the other hand, drive like a grandpa."

Whatever. Sure I just said he was nice to follow. I lied. Or am lying. Same difference.

He falls into step beside me as we cross the parking lot. "I had to be a grandpa because you rode so close to my bumper that if I went faster and had to stop, you would've killed us both."

"Whoa now, big fella. Playing it a little fast and loose with the exaggerations, don't you think?"

"Big fella?" His shoulders bounce with laughter as he pulls open the door. "We'll just have to agree to disagree."

"As long as we're agreeing that we disagree with what you said, that's fine with me." I approach the hostess, who is on her phone, before Quinton can retort. "Hi! Two please."

I don't mean to startle her, but by the way she fumbles her phone before it finally falls to the floor, that's what I do.

"Crap. I mean, sorry!" She grabs her phone and shoves it beneath the hostess stand before grabbing two menus. "Follow me."

I wasn't really paying attention when we were pulling in, so following her to the seat is the first time I really take in my surroundings. The restaurant isn't anything to write home about. There's a glassed-off area above the bar seating where you can see the chef rolling sushi. Japanese-inspired lanterns hang overhead, lighting the room. The tables are a light wood and there are lots of red and black decorations hung around the room. It's cute, someplace I could totally picture stopping on the way home from work when I don't feel like cooking (which is pretty much every day).

"Here you go." The hostess stops at a booth near the rear of the restaurant.

"Thank you." Quinton turns his attention to the hostess and directs his full, wonderful smile her way. She freezes midmotion, the menus hovering over the middle of the table as color fills her face. It isn't until he pulls them from her hands that her brain seems to kick back into gear and she damn near runs away from us.

Poor girl. Not that I can blame her. Out of everyone, I fully understand how being on the receiving end of Quinton's attention can scramble your brain.

I want to make a joke about what he does to people, but since I have been people in this situation, I keep my lips zipped . . . and to myself. Off to a great start!

"I probably should've asked if you liked sushi before, but—uh . . . do you like sushi? Or we can go grab Mexican . . . if you like Mexican food."

And fucking fuck me. How is he even more endearing like this? He just always has this air of confidence following him around like cologne. Even on the field while people are booing or in the conference room when reporters are grilling him, he never seems off balance. So seeing him stumble over his words, it makes me feel like I might be getting a glance at the real Quinton, not the practiced facade he puts on so well.

"First of all, I love sushi, this is perfect. Second, what kind of person doesn't like Mexican food?" The thought of people not liking the culinary gift of the gods honestly offends me. "You're in Colorado now, Howard. This is the home of Qdoba and Chipotle, where we have strived to get as much burrito in our mouths in the shortest amount of time. It's an institution!"

I don't mean for my voice to rise, but if there is one thing I'm undeniably passionate about, it's tacos.

"Damn, killer! I'm on your side, no need to attack." He drops the menu on the tiled tabletop and holds his hands in front of him, surrendering to my salsa-infused indignation.

I bite the inside of my cheek to stop the smile that's trying to overtake my face, but it's useless. I'm defenseless when it comes to playful Quinton. Lucky for me, though, before I can giggle or do something equally as mortifying, the waiter approaches the table.

"Mr. Howard, you're back!" the middle-aged man with a fantastic handlebar mustache says. "Do you want your usual?"

"Bobby, my man." Quinton shakes his hand. "I do, but I'm not sure what my friend wants."

There's that word again. "Friend." Blah.

Bobby turns his attention to me. His eyes are wide, but his smile is wider. "Oh yes, you brought a friend today! Can I get you something to drink?"

It's on the tip of my tongue to order something with sake. But I'm still scarred from the other night and will not be indulging in alcohol of any kind around Quinton.

"Can I have a Diet Coke?" I scan the menu, making sure they have my go-to order. "And I'll have a rainbow roll, please."

Bobby nods without writing down the order and takes our menus. Now, this would normally make me pretty nervous, but something about his mustache reassures me. I don't think you can be anything but dependable with a handlebar mustache that thick. He walks away, calling out his hellos to an older couple sitting in the opposite corner of the restaurant.

"And you thought you were special." I point to the couple who are now on the receiving end of Bobby's attention. "You're not his only favorite."

"I know I'm not." He rests his elbows on the table. "I don't think he has any clue who I am, it's why I always come. Well, that and their sushi is the shit."

"Sushi and anonymity, that's your kink?" As soon as I say the word, I want to fall under the table and roll myself out of the restaurant. I'm pretty sure if I touch my face, it will burn my hand. I could just die. There's no way he's not going to report me for harassment. Not a fucking chance. "Oh my god. No."

I hide my face behind my hands—not even caring a little bit about how smeared my makeup is getting—and keep them there until Quinton's unmistakable laughter fills the restaurant.

"I've never heard it that way before, but yeah, that's my kink," he says once I've peeled my hands off my face.

I fan my cheeks for a second before massaging my fingertips

into my temples. I don't know what's worse. Saying shit like this sober or making a drunken fool out of myself. I'm thinking they're equal.

I should've ordered the damn sake.

Bobby returns to the table with a tray carrying our drinks and edamame. I aim a grateful smile at him not only for the food, but the interruption as well.

"Moving on . . ." I take a deep gulp of my Diet Coke and my body rejoices. "So how have things been for you since the launch?"

Work is the only topic I think I might be safe discussing with him. It is, after all, the only reason we are speaking in the first place.

"Pretty good." He avoids eye contact when he talks. "A lot of questions."

I keep my response measured because even though he's trying to play it cool, I can tell something is bothering him. I've learned a lot about him over the last month or so, and one of the big things is that he shuts down when he gets uncomfortable.

"Oh yeah? What kind of questions?" I grab an edamame and shoot a few beans into my mouth.

"Mainly, they're trying to understand my issues with the League. Lots of personal questions. But I still have to clear up why I'm kneeling, remind them of systemic racism and police brutality." He shrugs before grabbing the soy sauce and spinning it around on the table. "It doesn't help that Glenn Chandler is still using me as one of his talking points. I don't understand why he's so intent on twisting what I'm doing."

"I don't know either. What I do know is that you can't make everyone happy. We expected this. There are still people who don't like Oprah. Oprah, Quinton! If the world can't agree on Oprah being the best, then there is no hope for any of us."

This is the pep talk I tell myself on almost a daily basis, but it doesn't seem to give him the same reassurance it gives me.

He sits up straight and meets my gaze again. "Can I ask you something?"

"Of course, it's literally my job." I drop the empty bean pod in the empty bowl next to the edamame. Shoving food in my mouth is one thing, talking with it in my mouth is another. I'm not a monster.

"I'd be blind not to see that a lot of people are pissed with my kneeling and that's fine. Like you said, I can't make everyone happy. But you made it pretty clear in the beginning that you weren't my biggest supporter and I'm not sure I ever really understood why. Does it still make you mad?"

His mouth is saying one thing—that he's curious and wants my opinion—but his eyes are saying something else. They are begging me to agree with him, pleading for me to tell him that I understand.

But I can't.

"Honestly?"

"Yeah." He fidgets with the sleeve of his sweatshirt. "I won't get mad, promise."

I hope not.

"It never made me mad." He opens his mouth to cut me off, probably thinking I'm blowing smoke up his ass right now. I hold a hand up and keep going. "It made me uncomfortable. I was just starting this new job . . . my dream job. I get why you're doing it. I understand your cause and what you want to accomplish and I support that. I even respect it. But for me, personally and selfishly, it put me in a really tough position. Siding with my boss and keeping my job, or siding with you and the important cause you're supporting. My job was kind of my bubble protecting me from the real world and you popped it."

"But that's the point. People are hiding in their bubbles and ignoring problems, letting things get worse. They go watch football games and pretend that the men they cheer for aren't killing themselves to entertain them. They think the League cares about players, when in reality they don't do shit." He no longer looks relaxed in the booth. Instead, every vein on his neck is bulging. His shoulders and arms are both stiff; no doubt he is trying to keep his words measured when he wants to yell. Serious conversations in public for the win! "And the racism! Every day when I turn on the news or look at Twitter, there's a new hashtag. Another Black life lost, and for what? For trying to live? And then I go work for rich white men who bank off our backs. Buying us, trading us, throwing us away when we're broken. Just to go back into a world that's moving backward instead of forward. I'm supposed to be quiet and thankful that they threw some money my way? Take it and shut up?"

Whoa.

I feel like I'm doing cartwheels in a minefield, but not just because of Quinton. My own mind is running wild and I don't like it.

"I don't know. What you're doing is messing with my head, okay? I think racism is the worst. But I've never known where I fit in this fight. I never felt like I belonged or was even welcome." If I could get away with pouring the soy sauce on his head, I would. I just wanted to eat and he has me talking about this. He's a jerk. A very hot jerk. "You're making me think about things I've avoided thinking about my entire life. I try to ignore race, and what you're doing is forcing me to examine things in a way I never have. I'm fucked up enough with everything else in my life without digging into the crazy parts of my brain."

So, remember how Quinton kept his voice down and only let his anger show through the tense lines of his muscle-covered body? Well, I do not have that skill. And by the end of my rant, not only is the old couple Bobby said hi to staring, but Quinton looks like he's about to laugh.

"So you're saying it really has nothing to do with me taking a knee and everything to do with you?"

And even though the soy sauce dumping might be unacceptable, I make the executive decision that throwing an edamame bean at him is fine. So I do. And it makes me feel better . . . until he catches it and pops it in his mouth like I did him a favor. "I hate you."

"Maybe, but that might have more to do with you than me too." He looks like he wants to say something else when his phone rings. He pulls it out of his pocket, looking at the screen for a split second before his shoulders tense up and he swipes his finger across the screen, putting it to his ear. "Angela." His deep voice caresses each syllable of her name. "Is everything okay?"

Ugh. Angela. I've bumped into her a few times since our first run-in outside of Quinton's house and every time she manages to seem even more beautiful and put together than before. Her long, naturally straight, perfectly highlighted blonde hair taunts me. Her cute little upturned nose is almost identical to the one I dreamed of when I begged my dad for a nose job. She's tall, skinny, and has curves that fit perfectly in her probably size-zero skirts.

And the thought of her makes the embarrassment from the other night rise up once more. I mean really, what was I thinking?

"Okay," he says and I tune back into his conversation. "I'm at dinner with a friend, but I'll check in as soon as I get home. Alright . . . bye."

I ignore the way him calling me a friend stings even more knowing Miss Perfect was on the other end of the phone. "Everything alright?"

"That? Oh yeah." He fidgets with the wrapped silverware and chopsticks on the table. "It's all good."

"Glad to hear that." I tread carefully with this subject; it's not one I love talking about considering our recent history. "How long have you two been together?"

"What?" His fingers freeze on the torn edges of the napkin he's fussed with. "No, we aren't together."

I want to roll my eyes and argue, but it's not my place . . . at all. Also, Bobby approaches our table with a tray full of food.

"Rainbow roll for the lady." He sets the long plate covered with the colorful roll in front of me.

"Yum." I fight to keep my eyes from rolling to the back of my head. "Thank you."

He puts Quinton's plate down in front of him. "Spider roll and salmon roll, neither with avocado for you."

"My man," Quinton says as he rubs his hands together like a super villain ready to take over the world.

And if I just heard him correctly, a villain he is. "No avocado?" I eye his plate with keen interest. "Why not?"

"I hate it," he says like he hasn't just lost all of his credibility for being a good judge of anything in life.

"I'm sorry, what?" I ask, giving him the chance to change his answer to the right one.

"Hate it," he repeats.

"Oh my god." My chopsticks fall out of my hand and I turn to see if Bobby is nearby.

It's one thing to force me to examine my own internal biases and to downplay his girlfriend situation, but it's another thing completely to disrespect avocados. Everything else we can discuss later, but this? I will not stand for it.

"Just so you know, as soon as we leave here, we're going to a

Mexican restaurant and I'm forcing you to eat guacamole." I pull out my phone to google the closest restaurant, even though my stomach is growling and I'm starving. "I can't work with a person who doesn't like avocados or guacamole. Unacceptable."

Priorities.

Twenty-three

"I BROUGHT FOOD!" I YELL AS SOON AS I WALK INTO QUINTON'S house.

I kick off my shoes and push them against the wall—the jolt of the freezing-cold cement floors never fails to shock me—before I head into his kitchen with the plastic bag filled with more tacos than he could possibly eat.

Or at least, I hope. He's like a bottomless pit.

But since he told me he didn't like avocados and I force-fed him guacamole, I just keep bringing them—and ignoring the fact that my pants are legitimately starting to get too tight from constantly eating them with him.

However, can I just say that I find it incredibly unfair that he's an actual endless pit and still looks as though he has no body fat. Yeah, sure, he works out like seven days a week. Whatever. The point still stands. It's bullshit.

"Did you get guacamole?" He shouts this ridiculous question from somewhere in this massive, cold, echoey house of his and misses the theatrical rolling of my eyes.

"Come on, Howard. I thought we talked about this."

When we stopped by the Mexican restaurant after sushi, I ordered chips and guac. When the waiter brought it to the table, it was like dealing with a fucking toddler. But when he finally tried it, his eyes lit up and he devoured the entire bowl. Apparently his mom used to always make face masks out of avocado when he was growing up and his aversion came from that.

And that's how I successfully converted him to the Church of Avocado. It is my proudest accomplishment to date.

I pull the tacos out of the bag and line them up on his pristine white countertops that are only pristine because he never cooks. And considering my life goal is to never have to worry about taking the meat out of the freezer and only cook when I want to—which is basically never—he's living my fucking dream.

I'm only a little bitter.

I look at everything lined up on the counter and there is one very noticeable thing missing.

"Crap!" I meant to stop at 7-Eleven on the way over here, but started to listen to my favorite podcast and totally forgot.

"What's wrong?" Quinton comes around the corner and even though we've been hanging around each other a lot recently, it's still always a jolt to my system to see his hotness up close and personal.

Plus, even though his beard was never short, he's stopped trimming it down and it just does things to me. *Things*. He's younger than me by more than a couple of years, but the beard just makes him look like a grown-ass man. A zaddy, if you will. And I am here for it.

"Nothing really." I walk to the cabinet that houses his dishes. "I just forgot to grab my Diet Coke on the way. I guess I can have water. My skin would probably appreciate that."

"Water is the better choice." He pulls two glasses down for us. "But I'm pretty sure I saw a Coke in my fridge earlier."

"No." I shake my head. I took the only one he had in there a few days ago. "I drank the one you had."

"Check again." He lifts his chin in the direction of his fridge. "Angela was over here yesterday, she might've left one."

Angela.

Blah.

So I know that Quinton and I are never going to happen. I get it. But it's one thing to know that and it's another to know that the reason why is because his "type" is the complete opposite of me. And while Quinton says they aren't together, I get the feeling that's just a technicality. Even though I'm an adult who lives in the time of Rihanna and body positivity and self-love, she still reminds me of all the times I was ignored while my skinny, blue-eyed, blonde friends were the envy of all. When all I wanted was to be one of those mixed girls who looked like both parents. The loose wavy hair or pixie nose or green eyes or something. Anything so that I could see myself in the people around me.

I swear, when Quinton asked why I didn't fully support him at first, he inadvertently opened a fucking floodgate in my mind. I've been remembering all of these things I thought I'd forgotten. I'm feeling things I'd learned to suppress. I hate feelings.

I pause in front of the fridge, squeezing my eyes shut to try to get myself under control and push everything to the back of my mind, where it belongs.

I open the door and sure enough, he's right. How Angela is consistently forgetting these blows my mind. I can't keep them stocked in my place. I almost feel bad for taking it.

But not that bad.

"You're right." I pull it out, not even waiting to get to the counter to crack it open. "Thanks."

"Hey," he says when I pull out the stool next to him. "You alright? You look . . . weird."

Another one for my ego!

"Wow, you sweet-talk all the girls like that?" I take a sip out of the can, looking at him over the aluminum rim.

He gets off his stool, shaking his head. "You know what I mean." He walks across the kitchen and pulls off a couple of paper towels before coming back. "You look like you were thinking about something and whatever it was, wasn't good."

"Oh no." I take a bite of my taco. There is no better stalling method than a mouthful of food. "I was just thinking about everything on my to-do list."

Even though that's a lie, I do have a shit ton of work to do.

"You still working on that thing for Mahler? What is it anyway?" he asks. His jaw clenches beneath his beard the way it always does when Mahler or any of the League's higher-ups are mentioned.

"Yup, still working on it." I take one of the napkins he brought over. "And I honestly don't know yet, but even if I did, couldn't tell you. I had to sign a nondisclosure agreement last week. So everything stays under wraps until the event itself."

"You know how I feel about him, so I won't say much. But I will say watch out, you can't trust him."

I don't tell him I think he's right, but I also don't tell him he's wrong. At this point, it's not really about trust, it's about building my résumé and not burning bridges. But Quinton wouldn't know this because I never told him that my job is out here just dangling by a thread. It doesn't matter that Quinton might actually be a friend (that word still haunts my dreams) of mine . . . or at least someone I'm friendly with, I'm not sure he would stop taking a knee for me. And more so, I wouldn't ask him to. It'd feel more manipulative telling him now that we're getting along than it would've when I hated him.

"It'll be fine." Considering my past experiences with Mr. Mahler and my luck in general, this might be a bit of an exaggeration. But no need to tell Quinton this—therefore increasing the size of his head—right now. "The entire thing is only for thirty to forty people. How much damage could it do?"

"Pretty sure that's the question the girl asks at the beginning of every horror movie." He takes a giant bite of his taco and gives me a chance to let his words sink in.

"You know what? I really don't like you." I throw my wadded-up napkin at his head and for once, I actually hit my target. But instead of the immense joy I thought would follow, it's more like a dull jolt of triumph for accuracy followed by disappointment from the lack of reaction from Quinton and the way it falls so gently to the floor.

"Do you feel better now?" He follows my gaze to the stupid, useless ball of paper on the floor.

"Not even a little bit." I hope he can hear the warning in my voice. "As an avid Bravo watcher, I've seen my fair share of items tossed in people's faces and I'm not afraid to step my game up."

"Is that where that one chick flipped the table and was yelling about prostitutes?"

Well fuck me.

Seriously.

I want him to do it.

He watches *Real Housewives*? He plays professional football, donates his salary to worthy causes, and watches Bravo. I've literally never been so attracted to a man in my entire freaking-ass life.

"You watch Bravo?" I ask, but I know it's too good to be true. That's probably one of the many things he does with Angela when she's over here forgetting about her Diet Cokes.

"I've watched." He shrugs before picking up another taco like he didn't just discover my love language. "My mom likes it, so I'll watch it with her."

The visual I get of him watching *Real Housewives* with his mom and not Angela does things to my insides that I'm not proud of. It's so sweet to picture him sitting with his mom, not caring what they watch, just wanting to spend time with her.

"I bet you can't wait to go back home to watch it with her. I'm sure watching the Dallas franchise is even more fun when you're there."

"Probably." He doesn't meet my eyes and shoves another bite into his mouth. I wonder if he dated one of the housewives? I'm pretty sure one of them was a cheerleader. His shoulders tense up and his jaw does that clenching thing before he tries to hide it with the phoniest smile that I have ever seen. Glad he can throw a football, because acting is def not an option for him. "Can't wait to go home to see."

He sounds like he's stepping on a nail and is doing everything he can not to show me just how much he never wants to go home. Between his dad not coming to the launch or being on the board and his reaction to me mentioning Dallas, something has to be going on. And as a person who understands the desire to keep all family matters under wraps, I drop it.

"Anyways, speaking of things I like to watch"—I really am the segue queen—"Vonnie invited me to go to the next Mustangs game with her. I wanted to run it by you since it's your box too. I didn't want it to be weird."

"Not weird at all. I can just give you one of my tickets if you want, that way you can ride on your own." All of the tension he was sporting is gone just as fast as it arrived. So much so that I wonder if I imagined it all. "I think that's the game right before Halloween. I'm not a kid expert, but I feel like Halloween makes kids nuts and you might want your own exit plan."

"Oh, uh—no. You don't need to do that." I try my best to sound convincing, but fail miserably. Probably because the giant lump that just materialized out of nowhere makes it hard for me to speak.

Because ugh. Halloween.

He places the taco in his hand back on his plate before pushing it to the side. "Hey." His voice is almost as soft as his eyes as he leans in closer to me. "Are you okay?"

I wave my hand in front of him. "Yeah, of course I am." I try to laugh it off as no big deal, but instead, my laugh mingles with the sob stuck in the back of my throat.

Oh my god.

I'm going to cry in front of him.

Again.

"Fuck." I slap my hands over my eyes when tears flood my vision and I realize there is no possible way to force them back down. "I'm so sorry." The words are smothered in my hands as my breathing hitches with each mortifying sob that takes over my body.

And before I know what's happening, heat envelopes me as long arms wrap around my shoulders and Quinton pulls me into his chest.

Any other time, I'm sure I would take note of his cologne and how his arms fit so perfectly around me. But instead, all I can think about is how crazy I must look and that there's a ninety percent likelihood of me ruining his shirt with either my mascara or snot.

Please, God, let it just be the mascara.

His hands start to rub circles along my back and he whispers words I can't comprehend in my ear.

The only thing I know, is that for the first time in a long time, I don't feel alone and it's that feeling . . . that realization . . . that slows my tears. Quinton's arms loosen as my body starts to relax, but he doesn't pull them away. His hands rest on my shoulders, and the heat and strength from his reassuring touch seeps into my body.

"I'm so sorry." I start to extract myself from his arms, but I don't make it far before his grip tightens.

"Don't you dare fucking apologize for that." He bends down so he's looking me straight in my eyes. "Are you okay?"

I start to say I'm fine. This is not what he signed up for . . . this isn't what *I* signed up for. But then I wonder when else I'll be able to share my feelings. When will I have this support and attention from someone offering to be a shoulder to lean on? My friends have been amazing throughout all of this, but I'm sure they can only take so much of my crying until they get sick of me. It might be nice to vent to a person I probably won't ever talk to again once I'm finished with this job.

But the real reason is that I'm so fucking tired of saying I'm fine when I'm not. I'm over being strong. I'm exhausted from the effort it takes to bury everything and walk around like nothing is bothering me. The smile I've been wearing is so heavy. I don't want to do it anymore.

"I've been pretending the holidays weren't going to come this year. I know it's only Halloween and it doesn't even count as a real holiday for most people. But once I got too old to trick-or-treat, I would pass out candy with my dad and as soon as we'd turn off the porch light, we'd watch a movie that gave me nightmares until the following Halloween. Even in college. I'd do the parties one night, but I always came home and did this with him." I look down at his stupid, bare cement floor that really needs a rug and wipe away the stray tears I don't try to stop from falling. "He's not here, the house is gone, and I can't even watch the movies because unless it airs on Disney—and not even always then—I get too freaked. And yes, I know how ridiculous this sounds."

"None of that sounds ridiculous." His fingers bite into my skin for a split second before his hands fall to his sides. "You miss your dad. The time of year when everyone is preaching about family is coming up. It'd sound ridiculous if you weren't feeling like this."

"Really?" I try to wipe away the remnants of melted mascara that's probably staining my cheeks and take a deep breath before meeting his gaze again.

And when I do?

Holy shit.

I might be drunk off feelings or the constant welling of tears has distorted my vision, but the way he's looking at me knocks what little air I do have right out of my system. I can't even pinpoint what I see. But it's not the look of pity or disinterest. He doesn't look irritated or annoyed that I broke down in his kitchen and he was forced to comfort me. It's none of those things. Understanding maybe? I'll never know.

"So . . ." He wiggles his eyebrows and looks cuter than anyone wiggling their eyebrows has a right to look. "Do you want that ticket and parking pass or nah?"

"Ugh." I groan and take a step away from him. My brain is struggling to function from all of the nearness and physical contact of a human male. "I mean, if you insist. It would be rude to turn you down."

"Thank you, I'm not sure my delicate ego could've taken the rejection." He grins and his white teeth just sparkle against his beautiful dark skin.

I nearly fall into a trance looking at him, so for the sake of self-preservation, I turn on a heel and book it out of there. Only slowing down to yell over my shoulder once I'm sure his smile magic can't take hold of me. "Hurry up, Howard. If you're done being so unprofessional, it's time to work."

I don't even make it around the corner before a wadded-up

paper towel—just like the one I hit him with earlier—whizzes by my head, just missing its mark.

Note to self—don't get into a throwing war with a professional fucking quarterback.

And not falling for him would be good too.

Twenty-four

EVEN THOUGH QUINTON GAVE ME A PARKING PASS ALONG WITH tickets—yes, plural, like I have friends who want to watch football with me—to the game, Vonnie insisted that we ride together. I gave in easily because there's free booze and having a designated driver works in my favor more than anyone else's.

What I didn't realize is the insanity that comes from riding in a car with three boys who have been strapped down in their seats for forty minutes after they have no doubt been sneaking Halloween candy for the last week.

And let me tell you, if I wasn't already planning on drinking, I sure as hell would be now.

"Mmmh. You see?" Vonnie says from inside the suite door as she watches me head straight for the bar. Her boys, who sprinted away from us as soon as we parked, are already sitting in their seats, plates piled high with goodies sitting on their laps. "You see why I made sure to make the woman who owns a bar my best friend?"

"I honestly don't know how you do it." I "accidentally" pour too much Jameson into my glass before topping it with a minuscule amount of ginger ale. "The fact that you can ignore and break up their fights and still manage to drive while not getting into a million accidents is a straight-up miracle."

After seeing the way Vonnie had to manage a million things at once, I'm not sure having kids is in the cards for me.

When Quinton said I wasn't a good driver, he wasn't exactly wrong. I mean, I'm not a *bad* driver, but I definitely cannot multitask when I drive. Putting on lipstick in traffic? Nope. Eating? Hell no. Even singing to the radio has its risks, it's why I got satellite radio. Talk radio saves lives, people.

"Thank you!" She throws her hands in the air. "Everybody acts like I have it so easy and this shit is hard. I love my boys, but fuck, can a girl get some support around here?"

Vonnie laughs as she navigates her way around the high-top table where she drops her clear purse before making her way to the bar. But even though her laugh is convincing and her smile is beautiful, I don't believe her. Normally, I would take this at face value and let it slide. Let's be honest, as evidenced by my own life, feelings aren't particularly my strong point. But this isn't the first time she's made a joke like this. I have a feeling that if Vonnie doesn't say something soon, she's going to explode.

I might not be much help when it comes to sorting things out, but I am the perfect person to commiserate with.

"Hey." I hand her a glass as she reaches for the vodka. "Is everything alright?"

"Yeah girl." She takes the glass from my hand without looking at me. "Of course everything is fine! Just a little mom venting, nothing a little cocktail and a lot of football can't handle."

As a person who has mastered the art of hiding my hurt behind a little self-deprecating humor, I know what she's doing maybe even more than she does.

"If you're sure." I keep my voice quiet—measured—but I don't

move to give her space. "Because I'm not sure if you've been paying attention these last few weeks, but I'm a total disaster and if
there is one person you can talk to who will not judge you, it's me."

I don't mention that I'm pretty sure Brynn would move heaven
and earth for her. I get how hard it is to talk to the people closest
to you. To feel like you're laying your burdens on them.

"You're sweet for offering, but I really am fine." She turns to
face me, taking a sip of a drink that has about a shot too much of
vodka for it to do anything but burn her esophagus. Her full lips
are painted the most gorgeous shade of red, her eyes are flawlessly
lined, and her highlighter makes her look like a glittering angel.
She is perfection.

But the highlighter also shows off the hollowness in her cheeks
that wasn't there a few weeks ago and the eyeliner points out the
sadness in her eyes. Her lipstick shows a smile that was painted
on for show.

Even her crystal-covered sweater falls off her shoulder in a way
that is not for fashion but because of weight I don't think she was
intending to lose. But all I can do is offer to be there, I don't want
to push her if she's not ready.

"Okay, if you're sure." I grab my glass off the table and turn
to go join her boys out in their seats.

"It's just that . . ." she starts and stops just as fast.

I change direction. Instead of opening the glass door to join
the masses as we wait to see our favorite team take the field, I
move to the long leather couch inside the box.

I fall onto the surprisingly plush couch not saying a word. I take
a small sip of my drink and keep my eyes locked with Vonnie's.

She closes her eyes and takes a deep breath as she lifts her glass
to her lips. Her feet look like they're coated in cement with how slow
and hesitant her steps are. But her eyes contradict her movements.

They might be red and glossed over from the tears she's been trying so hard to fight back, but the determined glint in them outshines everything else.

"My life has gone up in flames," she says as she takes a seat beside me on the couch. "I don't know how it happened or when it even began to change, but now things are so bad and I'm so overwhelmed with it all, that I don't even know if I can fix it."

My heart breaks for her as I see the carefully constructed facade she built crumble right in front of me.

I place my drink on the table next to the couch and grab her hand. "What's going on? What's so bad?"

"My mar-marriage." She chokes on the word and I know this is the first time she's given a voice to what she's been feeling. "I don't think we're going to make it. I don't even know who Justin is anymore and I'm pretty sure he hates me."

I'd like to say that loyalty is one of my best qualities. And even though I've only known Vonnie for a short period of time, we're on a nickname basis and she's my new bestie. But even if she wasn't, I still couldn't ignore the fact that she's a total badass who cares hard and deep for everyone around her, is funny, smart, and an amazing mom to three wild—but polite and wonderful—boys. How anyone could hate her, let alone her own freaking husband, makes my blood boil. But my anger won't help her.

"I'm sure that's not true." I squeeze her hand a little tighter. "I'm not sure if you know this or not, but you are pretty freaking phenomenal. I don't think anyone who knows you could hate you."

"Then maybe I hate myself?" She pulls her hand out of mine and runs it through her long, bone-straight hair. "I let myself become this woman I said I'd never become. Justin and I got married in college. It was a small wedding, we had fake flowers because they were all we could afford. He was still playing football and working on his undergrad. I was in law school. His major was childhood education. He wanted to be a teacher if he didn't make it to the League. I knew I would carry the financial burden and I was fine with that . . . he was fine with that."

I lean back on the couch, listening as she surrenders to everything she's been battling.

"Obviously he wanted to play in the League, but we're both smart. Justin was good, but he wasn't a standout in college and we both knew how quickly an injury could change everything. So when he was invited to the combine, we were pleasantly surprised. When he was drafted, we were ecstatic. He'd be able to live out his dream of being a football player and I'd live out mine as a lawyer. We figured he'd play for three, maybe five years, you know? The average career. What I didn't realize was the career I worked so hard for would become irrelevant."

The laugh that comes out of her mouth is the saddest sound I've ever heard. It's as if she put all of her hurt and regret into that one sound. I want to pull her into my arms and hug her, but she stands up before I get the chance. She paces in front of me, her high-heeled boots clicking against the wood-looking tile floors.

"I always wanted kids. Always. I know a lot of women feel pressured into having them, but not me. I couldn't wait. So when I got pregnant with Jagger, and Justin got his first big contract, it made sense that I would stay home. Then Jax and Jett came and I couldn't rationalize putting them all in daycare when they could be home with me. The thing is, as much as I'd always wanted to be a mom, I hate being a stay-at-home mom. But I can't say that. What kind of ungrateful, terrible mom can have as much money as we do and still complain about the fucking privilege to be home with my kids and watch them grow? How could I? And when I mentioned wanting to maybe get back into work to Justin, he basically reiterated what I was already afraid people would think. That I should be happy not having to work and he didn't want his boys gone when they could be with family."

"That doesn't make you a bad mom, Vonnie." I'd been trying to stay quiet, but when I see the pain and self-loathing in her grimace, I can't keep my mouth shut any longer. "You aren't just a mom, having kids doesn't mean you have to give up every single piece of yourself. Wanting to have the career you worked so hard for isn't something you should feel guilty about."

I don't know if I want to have kids. It's never been a goal of mine. I thought maybe I was broken and didn't have any maternal instincts because my mom died when I was so young. But as I got older, I realized part of it was because the way society acts like child-rearing is the only purpose of women pissed me right off. And, growing up being raised by a single dad, I need a partner willing—and wanting—to do just as much work as the mom, which is hard to find.

"Thank you!" She spins on her heels to face me. Her tearstained cheeks are filled with color, but somehow, her eyeliner and mascara are still perfectly in place. "Just because I took his last name when we got married doesn't mean I'm not still the same person I was before we met. Being married and a mom doesn't take that away. But after so long at home, my résumé didn't look as impressive and my independence had turned to dependence. I did the blogger thing for a while, but the Internet is scary and I wasn't comfortable with it anymore. So I knew I had to wait. Once the kids were all in school, it would be my time, right? Motherhood is a series of seasons, and for this season, I could suck it up and be the best stay-at-home mom possible."

I glance out the window at the Lamar boys, who are completely oblivious to the meltdown their poor mom is having. I may not be an expert on kids by any means, but I'm pretty sure they all look old as fuck. "But aren't your kids all in school?"

She waves her hands wide and looks at me with hard, angry eyes. "Exactly," she says—scratch that—she yells. "Herein lies the problem. The kids are in school and Justin is going into his hundredth year playing this stupid fucking sport and I'm still waiting. When I told Justin I was going to look into going back to work when Jax started kindergarten, I was still somehow convinced to stay home. Why would I want to miss all the field trips? Who would go to the teacher conferences? Wouldn't I feel terrible sending them to daycare after they already spent their day at school? Why would I want to miss any of this? I think it's why I jumped at the opportunity to be the president for the Lady Mustangs. It was the first opportunity I had to talk with adults and make things happen. And even though Justin will never admit it, he loved it because it was still focused around him. Because once I started getting outside opportunities based on it, he suddenly had a problem again.

"I don't know when the man I married became so keen on keeping me dependent on him. You know he called me selfish when I was working on the morning show?" she asks. I open my mouth to say something—something about what a dick Justin is being—but snap it shut when I realize she wasn't looking for an actual response. "I think it's a security thing for him, like I won't leave if I don't have a job. But what he doesn't realize is I probably am going to leave and he keeps pushing me to it."

She stops talking and her mouth hangs open, like her admission shocked her.

"Oh fuck." She falls back onto the couch and stares at me with wide eyes. But instead of seeing sadness and anger in her eyes, I see fear. "Can I leave him?"

"I'm not going to answer that for you." I twist my body so I can look her in her eyes. "I am going to say that life is too short to be unhappy. One day everything is fine, then the next day you're diagnosed with cancer. And then you're gone. If that happens. If, god forbid, you're taken from this earth tomorrow, would you be happy with the life you lived? Would your boys at least have the comfort of saying, *At least she lived her life the way she wanted to*? No matter what your happiness looks like, you can not only do it, you deserve it. It's your duty to show yourself and your boys how to live life to the fullest. And that happy life might be leaving Justin or it could be fighting for your marriage. But whatever it is, you're going to do it. Because you're still Lavonne fucking Lamar and you're alive and a badass."

"I'm a badass and I'm alive," she repeats after me, and a fire seems to have lit from within her. "Damn girl." She reaches for the drink she put down sometime during her rant. "You should be a therapist."

"Well"—I mimic her and take a sip of my drink too—"with as many as I've gone to, I was bound to pick up something."

Her eyes crinkle at the corners and for the first time today, a real smile crosses her face, but it falls away just as fast as it came. "I don't get it."

My eyebrows pull together. "Don't get what?"

She seemed to just have the breakthrough. Is she already trying to talk herself out of it?

"You seem to love dedicating your time and energy to other people. Me, Quinton, from what Liv and Marie said, them. You just talked me through shit I've been avoiding for months in a span of—what? Thirty minutes?" She puts a hand on my arm and I'm not sure if it's to offer support or keep me on the couch when she knows I want to run. "You said I deserve to be happy. That it's my duty to be happy. But where's that same energy when it comes to you helping yourself?"

Wait. Hold up.

How did she manage to flip this on me?

"I'm happy." I gesture to the suite that we're in. How can I not be happy and grateful for this? "My dad died. Of course that fucking sucks and I get sad. But death is part of life. I couldn't do anything about that. So you know what I did? I changed what I could. I got out of a toxic work environment and found my dream job. I love my job and I have great friends. I'm happy."

"You love your job? Really? The same job where some old man is threatening to fire you if you don't get a grown-ass man to stop fighting for causes he believes in?" She purses her lips and the red painted on them no longer looks like the perfect shade she found at a MAC counter. It looks like the blood of the people who tried to tell her half-truths.

Damn you, Vonnie Lamar, and your soul penetrating side-eye!

"Okay, well obviously that's not great. And some parts of my job suck." Knowing that Mr. Mahler doesn't really support Quinton is hard, but this is still a company and if it's hurting his bottom line, that's understandable. Money is still king. "But I'm working for the Mustangs! My dad can't be here for this, but he would've loved this and that makes me happy. Even if Quinton drove me crazy sometimes, planning his launch party was the most fun I've had in a long time. And now I get to do another event for Mr. Mahler. I love all of that."

"Okay, so what I'm hearing is that you're trying to connect with your dad through work while not dealing with the emotional ramifications of losing him and that you like event planning." She lets go of my arm and leans back against the couch. "I fail to see where I'm wrong."

"You know, I'm not sure I like you anymore." I almost roll my eyes at her, but like a small child, I wither under her warning glare.

"Mhmm." She lifts her drink to her lips, looking at me with bloodshot eyes over the rim of her glass. "Just like you don't like Quinton? It's hard to like the person shoving a mirror in your face."

I want to respond with something good. A snappy comeback that will make Vonnie question if she was right or missed the mark completely.

But instead, her lawyerly instincts have left me on the witness stand broken and battered.

See. This is why I should've kept my mouth shut. Help one person and they try and help you back.

Rude.

Twenty-five

AFTER VONNIE WENT INTO THE BATHROOM AND FIXED HER FACE—
her words, not mine—she came back out and we pledged not to
discuss any more heavy shit for the rest of the day. Preferably, the
rest of our lives.

What I didn't know was that soon, Brynn was going to bless
my soul with the most wondrous, enchanting woman I've ever
had the pleasure of meeting.

Ever.

In life.

"Greer, do you want a cocktail?" I offer, even though Brynn is
here and obviously makes way better drinks than I do. But it's the
thought, you know?

"Oh, thank you for offering, but I only drink if it's organic,"
she says. I can't tell if she's being serious or not, because I've literally never heard such a thing, but by the exaggerated roll of Vonnie's eyes, I realize that she is indeed serious.

I'm not sure why this surprises me.

Greer Francis—wife to Darren, the second-string safety—is

basically a living, breathing, motivational Instagram account. When she walked into the suite, she deemed that our energy was off and rolled us with whatever essential oil blend she carries in her purse before reciting her quote of the day. Her long, ash-brown hair falls down her back with loose curls. It's the kind of hair that convinces me she's worn a flower crown more than once in her life. Wearing ripped-at-the-knee jeans with a checkered button-up beneath a chunky sweater and distressed loafers that she for sure bought that way, I can guarantee she's ordered at least five pumpkin spice lattes this fall.

And that's not me being a hater. Because I'm a fan of ALL of it.

Being the most basic person ever is on my vision board . . . if I had a vision board. But that's just one more thing I'm sure Greer has that I'm here for.

"Really? Are there a lot of organic alcohol brands out there?" I ask because now I am truly curious.

The trip when I was chased by a squirrel through Central Park, I also went to the Church of Scientology. It was during the height of Tom Cruise and his crusade for his one true religion . . . it also had air-conditioning on a hot and humid day. When I sat down to stay for the movie they offered about the church, the eyes of the woman who worked there—maybe worked? Maybe volunteered? Who knows?—lit up like she finally caught a fresh one. And now, Greer has that same gleam in her eyes.

"There are!" She bounces in her probably vegan leather loafers. "I eliminated all GMO foods from my diet years ago. I did a ton of research and realized that even though my food was clean, my drinks weren't. People think all of the bad stuff is burned off when alcohol is distilled, but that's not the case. I just try to be very mindful of everything I put in my body and how it affects not only my health, but the environment as well."

"That's great." I nod, trying to remember the last time I was purposefully mindful of anything. "I had a Diet Coke and donut for breakfast."

This could be why Greer has skin that glows like the sun while mine is a confused mash-up of random breakouts and wrinkles.

"Diet Coke was the hardest thing for me to give up, but you can do it. If you want, I can send you the list of affirmations I told myself while I was quitting." She pulls out her phone and starts scrolling before I answer, but honestly, I'm not sure I could say no to this offer no matter what. Now that I know such a list exists, I need to know what anti–diet soda affirmations consist of.

Brynn shakes her head vigorously behind Greer, mouthing, "Don't encourage her."

This only makes me more interested in what she's selling.

"Thanks, I can't wait to see it," I tell her with complete sincerity. Brynn's consequent glare is merely the icing on the sugarless, organic cake.

Jack's—he's the announcer—voice has slightly less impact behind the glass wall of the suite as his voice drawls out through the stadium. They're introducing defense this week, so while the Lamar boys are chomping at the bit to see their dad, and Brynn is drooling to get a close-up of Maxwell, I stay inside to load up my plate with chips and guac and top off my drink.

Marie would be pissed if she saw me now, taking my time on snacks and ignoring the entrance I rushed her through the concessions to watch.

I do make sure to hurry out in time for the national anthem. Purely for work reasons.

Obviously.

Since his launch, Quinton has donated to a total of eight charities. He has given millions of dollars to these charities, but beyond that, he has introduced them to the public in a way that wouldn't have happened without him. He has opened up possibilities that they could've only dreamt of before. It's been amazing to witness. The foundation is doing what he and I wanted it to, but he's still taking a knee on the field and covering up the logo on his jersey.

I have set up hundreds of interviews and press conferences—that is only a slight exaggeration; I'm on a first-name basis with all the local news stations—for him to discuss his stance. He has spoken out many times about why he's doing what he's doing and he's putting a (not so) small fortune behind his actions, but that hasn't stopped people from trying to change the narrative.

Or, more accurately, it hasn't stopped people from going out of their way to deliberately misconstrue his mission. And the biggest culprit of this is still Glenn Chandler.

His popularity has been skyrocketing and his base has increased to a problematic level. During his last rally, he spent a record twenty minutes spewing his lies about Quinton, convincing his followers that Quinton is protesting the military and disrespecting our troops . . . despite Quinton stating multiple times why he's protesting—fairness and equality for all. *"If he cared about any of these causes, he'd quit throwing a football and sign up to serve his country. But the only person he's concerned about serving is himself. We aren't fooled!"* The crowd went crazy over that and the more conservative news stations have been playing it on what feels like a loop.

It's absurd. From what I've seen online, a lot of people are ready to grab their torches and burn things down. I'm really concerned about how that will translate to real life.

I slide open the glass door with my hip since my hands are occupied by an overabundance of snacks and a filled-to-the-rim glass. Nobody seems to notice my entrance, so I take a seat in the

back row. It will be easier for me to pay attention without someone pointing out how cute Quinton is (Brynn and Vonnie) or
telling me about all the chemicals in my tortilla chips (Greer).

"Please stand and remove your hats as Carol Langford per-
forms our national anthem," Jack says as a woman in a bright-red
dress settles into her position behind a microphone in front of the
Mustangs sideline.

A group of four military members in their uniforms stand behind her; the two in the middle are holding flags while the other
two hold what look like guns. Children and adults burst out running from the center of the field in different directions, all holding
onto a giant flag they're now spreading across the field. But even
with all of this, my attention is focused on one person and one
person only, Quinton Howard Junior.

I can't see the front of his jersey to see if he's used the tape or
not, but I know it's there. Then the music starts, and for a moment, he stays standing. My lungs stop working and even though
it doesn't make sense, dread that he might stay standing courses
through my body. I close my eyes, not able to watch. But when the
wave of boos fill the stadium, my eyes snap open and I see him on
one knee. Relief blooms from the tips of my toes to the crown of
my head even as Vonnie and Brynn both turn around, concern for
my livelihood evident on their beautiful faces. They offer me what
I'm sure are their best attempts at reassuring smiles, but what in
actuality look more like grimaces.

"It's fine." I get out of my seat and I walk down the few steps
to their row. "I'm really not worried, I promise."

Nobody says anything. I'm guessing that's their way of not
lying to me. I appreciate it all the same.

Carol finishes belting out the final note of the anthem and
Quinton stands up, clapping with the rest of the team as they rush
the sideline.

All of the tense, angry energy floating around the stadium seems to dissipate with a crescendo of cheers that builds as the special teams players—the players who come out during kicks and punts—take their positions on the field.

Cleveland's kicker runs forward, swinging his entire body as he makes contact with the football and sends it deep into our end zone. Davis, the Mustangs kick returner who clenched the position after his fourth return for a touchdown during preseason, positions himself beneath the ball and catches it with ease. But instead of dropping to his knee, he explodes into a full sprint.

Before I can check myself, I'm out of my seat with the rest of the stadium, screaming until my throat is sore, cheering as he breaks one tackle, spins past another one, and finds the hole his teammates have created with amazing blocking. He runs as fast as he can until a Cleveland player ends up bringing him down on our twenty-five yard line.

Everyone is on their feet, even Vonnie, who told me at the last game she saves her energy by sitting while everyone else stands. But this is why I love football so much. In the last hour, Vonnie was crying, I was put firmly in my place, and the crowd booed their quarterback, but thirty seconds in and everyone has forgotten it all. It's like their cleats have magical powers. Each step they take, every brutal hit they make, we're pulled out of reality and nothing else matters. For three glorious hours, all of our problems fade away.

Special teams clears the field as the Mustangs offense jogs out. Quinton is the portrait of confidence and grace. His body looks like it was made for this. Tall and lean, he fills out his uniform in a way that not a single other player on the field does. And even though I know I can't go there ever again, I can't help but notice how well he wears the uniform, blacked-out logo and all.

He just shouldn't look that way. Cropped spandex pants have no right looking that delicious on anybody.

He takes his position behind the center, squatting down before checking to his left, then his right. He stomps his legs and his head bounces around as he no doubt yells out instructions to the rest of the offense. This is his field. This is his team. And there's no mistaking that he has it under control.

The play clock is ticking down when he finally claps both hands together and the ball shoots between the center's legs and right into Quinton's strong grip. One lineman misses his block and a Cleveland defender slips through the line protecting Quinton. My breath catches in my throat and my stomach clenches as I brace for him to get hit. But at the last second, he fakes to the right before dodging to the left and sprinting out of the defender's grip. He runs toward the sideline, keeping his gaze down the field before spotting an open receiver in the end zone and snapping his arm back, firing the ball over the helmets heading straight for him.

It's not the longest pass, so we aren't kept in suspense as the ball whizzes to Beck, who doesn't even have to jump to catch it. Quinton, who never doubted that it would be caught, is already running toward Beck, jumping up and meeting him midair as they slam their shoulders into one another. If anyone in the crowd has a problem with Quinton's protest, they've put it to the side for now as they jump and scream, shaking the stadium floors.

The offense clears off the field as the special teams runs back on and Butler, the kicker, lines up behind the ball before kicking it directly between the goal posts.

The crowd cheers a little more—the poor kicker has all of the pressure but none of the glory—before finally settling into their seats. Their expectations for the game are set.

"Oh! Guacamole!" Greer pulls my attention off the game as she leans over and nabs one of my chips. She loads it with dip and shoves it in her mouth before I can say that I don't think any of it is organic.

"Just don't," Brynn says before I can warn Greer. "Trust me."

"I told you guys," Greer says after she's finished chewing on a most def not GMO-free chip. "Didn't I tell you?"

"Tell us what?" Vonnie is using the same tone she used with her kids when they were asking her what felt like twenty questions in the car.

"I gave Darren a list of positive affirmations to pass out to the guys last night so they could start reading them before bed and up until the game." She looks super fucking proud of herself as she grabs one more chip. "They're totally going to win today."

Vonnie just looks at her for a second before shaking her head and turning her attention to the game.

"This is why you are one of my favorite Lady Mustangs," Brynn says with no sarcasm in her voice. "You upped my vodka game at HERS and you do wild shit like that. We need more Greers in the world."

"Cosigned." I lift up my plate, giving her the option to dip, which she takes me up on.

And even though I've kind of resigned myself to the idea that I will not be working with the Mustangs come the end of the season, I really need to figure out a way to make sure these women are forced to stay friends with me.

I might be a bigger fan of the Lady Mustangs than I am of the actual Mustangs.

Twenty-six

I DON'T KNOW IF IT WAS THE POSITIVE AFFIRMATIONS LIKE GREER assured us or the Mustangs were just that much better than Cleveland, but it was a blowout. So much so that Jax fell asleep during the third quarter and I hitched a ride home with Vonnie in the middle of the fourth.

But despite the fact that we left early and I didn't drink nearly as much as I wanted to, thanks to Greer's judgy side-eye—even though she ate almost all of Jett's gummy bears and half of my chips—I still had a terrible case of the Mondays all week long. And now, of course, this is the bye week, so there is no game and I have two back-to-back meetings on a Saturday. I'm supposed to meet with Paul after them, but I fake being sick and cancel instead.

It has nothing to do with today still being Halloween, no matter how many times I tried to get it to not come this year.

Who am I kidding?

It has everything to do with it being Halloween. I've been teetering on the cusp of tears all week long. I had no idea the depths of grief until I experienced it myself. I wish I didn't know how the smallest things could set me off. Or how logic has failed me all day and I keep hoping my phone will ring and my dad will be on the other end. I wish I didn't resent all of my carefree coworkers and hate them when they wandered through the office with a painted face or ridiculous hat. I can't even talk about how much I wanted to punch Paul when he offered me a piece of candy from his pumpkin-shaped bowl yesterday. What he thought was nice felt like he was mocking my hurt.

I really need to call my therapist again because I am not properly equipped to handle this. Not even close.

I get home midday and kids are running all over the complex, probably counting down the minutes until they can trick or treat. I keep my sunglasses on as I make my way up the stairs, trying to decide whether or not I want to be a curmudgeon and keep my outside light off and eat the candy instead of handing it out.

I want the candy.

I unlock my door and I drop my keys into the bowl. I walk straight to my room, where I promptly kick off my shoes, unbutton my pants, and take off my bra before heading into my bathroom. I turn on the hot water, staring at the stream until I see the steam starting to billow up from the porcelain sink.

Even though I wear makeup every day, I don't love wearing it. Washing my face after work is one of my favorite parts of the day. I run the wet washcloth over my face, savoring the way the hot water stings before lathering my face wash between my palms.

After rinsing my face, I look into the mirror at my blotchy red skin that matches the red in my eyes. I just look so tired. The dark circles underneath my eyes that I've had since my dad's diagnosis have gotten darker and the worry lines on my forehead seem to have only gotten deeper. It's like all of the heavy shit in my life has made a permanent residence on my face.

It almost makes me want to put my makeup back on.

I guess if I do decide to pass out candy tonight, my makeup-free face could pass for a scary mask?

I'm putting away my face lotion when I hear a knock on my door.

I know they're starting trick-or-treating hours earlier these days, but this just seems excessive. Maybe they have special toddler hours.

"One second!" I call out as I run to my kitchen and grab the bag of candy I'm planning on finishing tonight. "Happy Ha—" I cut myself off when instead of a young trick-or-treater standing at my door, it's a not-so-young quarterback.

I really have to start using my fucking peephole!

"Quinton, um—hey." I cross my arms over my braless chest, trying to scrub the image of my makeup-less face from my memory. "What are you doing here?"

"Let's go, Reed." He claps his large hands together before barreling into my condo. "Get your shoes, we have shit to do."

"No we don't." I feel those frown lines I was just inspecting getting even deeper as my eyebrows scrunch together. "I didn't see anything on the calendar."

I might've been off my game today, but I'm positive we didn't have a meeting. Since the launch party, we had managed to go down to meetings twice a week and then quick get-togethers before an interview to go over talking points. But other than the meeting where we saw the Rue, we don't do Saturday meetings.

I watch him as he walks into my living room and falls onto my couch. "That's because it wasn't on the calendar." He spreads his arms across the top of my couch and his wingspan almost covers the entire length of it. "You said you have Halloween traditions and I have none, so I figured you could show me yours."

Holy.

Freaking.

Hell.

I might cry.

I forgot I even told him I was dreading Halloween. He not only remembered, but he's making sure I'm not going to be alone?

Oh yeah.

I'm for sure going to cry.

"You didn't need to do this." I forget about my appearance, lost in his kindness.

"I know I don't have to. I want to. Really. I've never really done the Halloween thing because my mom said it was the devil's holiday, so I'm excited to see what all the hype is about." He pushes off of my couch and comes to stand in front of me. "So are you going to get ready or am I going to have to figure it out on my own?"

"Oh man." A smile I didn't think would be possible today tugs on the corner of my mouth. "I hope you know what you're in for."

"With you, I'm not sure I ever know." He grabs me by the shoulders and turns me so I'm facing the hallway to my bedroom. "Hurry, we're losing sunlight."

THE FIRST THING I see when I walk into his house are two giant pumpkins decorating his normally empty kitchen island.

"You got pumpkins?"

"Yeah," he says as he walks in behind me. "Isn't that what you're supposed to do for Halloween? I got pumpkins, those carving books, and this drill the woman at Target said was a must-have."

Okay.

I know that I've covered the gamut when it comes to my feelings toward Quinton. I've hated him and wanted to kiss him—and was, admittedly, pretty bummed when he rejected me on that. But after this, if all I ever get to do is call Quinton a friend, I will take that and feel damn lucky to do so. Because this might be the nicest thing a person has ever done for me.

"You have no idea how much this means to me." I don't try to hide how my voice wavers. I'm a freaking emotional live wire right now, and I don't have it in me to pretend I'm not. "I was having a really hard day and this just made it so much better."

"Then it's all worth it." He squeezes my shoulder, letting his fingers linger before he lifts his chin and nods toward the kitchen. "Now, show me how to carve a pumpkin so I can beat you on my first-ever try."

"Oh, you wish. I might be grateful, but that doesn't mean I won't still kick your ass in pumpkin carving."

Just because he's the only professional athlete here doesn't mean he's the only competitive one. Once, Mrs. Rafter took me with her to her church group to decorate Christmas cookies. I turned it into a competition that I'm pretty sure nobody else participated in. My cookies kicked their asses. My sprinkle work was just—*chef's kiss*—so good. If I didn't take it easy on a bunch of old Catholic ladies, there's not a chance I'm easing up on this able-bodied male specimen.

And I don't.

"This is bullshit." He pouts as he looks at his pumpkin that is basically just a giant hole in the front because he wouldn't listen to me when I was telling him where to cut. "This is your fault, you sabotaged me. Look at yours next to mine."

I try not to laugh, I really do. But when I look at my beautiful pumpkin with a perfect witch carved into the front next to his . . . circle . . . I can't help it.

"If you would've listened to me, it would've been fine," I say once I've finished laughing. "Now grab it, we have to put it on your porch and turn on your light so trick-or-treaters know they're welcome here. Wait." I stop and turn to look at him. I forgot my candy at my place and Quinton better not be the jerk who gives out apples or protein bars. "Do you have candy?"

"Psssh. Do I have candy?" He walks past me with his sad pumpkin in his arms and a cocky smile on his face.

I follow him outside, putting my pumpkin on the other side of the steps so they frame his door and snap a quick picture before going back inside after him.

"Is this candy good enough for you?" He's standing next to his pantry door and when I make it next to him, I get my first look at what might be the entire candy section of Costco.

"Holy shit," I whisper, taking it all in. "You're like the fucking king of Halloween! Your house is so going to be the winner. A Mustangs player and an assortment of every full-size candy they could ask for!"

Dad and I were always generous with our handfuls, but there's just something extra special about getting a giant candy bar in your trick-or-treat bag.

"Did you just call me a king?" Mischief lights his dark brown eyes and I regret my words almost immediately.

"The king of Halloween. Not the king of like . . . life or anything." It's not my best comeback, but his thoughtfulness mixed with an overabundance of sugar has knocked me off my game.

"Say whatever you want, but a king is a king and I'll wear my crown with pride."

Oh god.

The pleased smugness in his eyes confuses me. I don't know if it makes him look hotter or makes me want to slap him.

Both.

Definitely both.

"I'm not doing this with you tonight." I grab the box of Milky Ways to be helpful, but also to snatch one when he isn't looking. "Do you have a big bowl we can dump these in?"

"No," he says behind me. "But I do have this."

I turn to see what he's talking about and he's pulling a fucking cauldron out of a giant dark red Target bag.

"You did not." I feel like my jaw is about to hit the floor. Every time I think he can't go any further with this Halloween surprise, he pulls something else out and shocks me again. "Why would you buy that? Don't you have a mixing bowl or something?"

"I don't cook much and I've never baked in my life, so I'm not sure." He walks toward me with the cauldron that covers his entire midsection. "Plus, the king of Halloween had to be prepared."

I brought this on myself. I had to open my big mouth.

"It's pretty dope, though," he says as he drops it in his entry-way. "I think I'm gonna bring it to the locker room. Fill it with protein bars or something."

"That's weird, but also nice." I tear open the box of Milky Ways and dump them into the cauldron. "I'm sure everyone will appreciate that."

He shrugs off my compliment. Something he does often. Even with his foundation, he always deflects praise and directs it to-ward the charities he's giving to. As a human, it's endearing. As a publicist, it's infuriating.

His doorbell goes off before I can point it out, though.

Quinton's eyes widen and an almost childlike smile lights his face. "They're here!" he whisper-shouts to me before swinging open the door and presenting the cauldron that still needs to be filled. "Happy Halloween!" he says, greeting the trick-or-treater.

The sun is still out and it's pretty early for trick-or-treaters, which is probably why the mom clasping the hand of her toddler outside Quinton's door is here. If I ever have kids, I'll want to hit the houses before the mad rush of sugar-hungry children starts busting down doors too.

"What do you say?" she asks her toddler, who is painfully cute dressed up as a dinosaur. The headpiece is falling over his face and he yanks his hand out of his mom's grasp to lift it out of his eyes.

"Twick-o-tweat!" he yells, raising his pumpkin candy basket in the air.

"Here you go, little man." Quinton reaches into the cauldron and when he pulls out the giant candy bar, the little boy's eyes get so round, I'm worried they might pop out of his little head.

Quinton drops it into his basket and it barely makes it in before the dinosaur is sprinting down to the sidewalk, where the man I'm assuming is his dad and not a random creep is recording it all with his phone.

"My gotta a BIG one!" he yells, ignoring his mom chasing after him shouting, "Don't forget to say thank you!" When it's clear there's no way her son is going to do anything except try to eat the candy bar on the sidewalk, the mom turns and waves. "Thank you!"

Quinton waves back before he closes the door and turns to me. "Fuck," he says, his smile even bigger than it was when he opened the door. "I get it now. This is great!"

I wish I was the kind of person who could refrain from saying "I told you so," but I am not.

"Told you so." I head back to his pantry to grab more candy while he looks out of the window next to the door, waiting for the next trick-or-treater.

I know he did this all for me—the thought still makes my stomach flip—but seeing how into it he is almost makes this feel like an equal partnership.

And even though Halloween will never be the same, Quinton has made it so the ache in my chest and the urge to cry are long gone. Just like the little dinosaur's candy bar.

Twenty-seven

"I CAN'T BELIEVE HOW MANY TRICK-OR-TREATERS YOU HAD." I PEEL open a Reese's cup and lean back on his stupid comfy couch.

I don't know why, but because his neighborhood is so fancy, I thought he wouldn't get many coming through. But I forgot that people drive to the fancy neighborhoods in hopes to find a house like Quinton's and get good candy. He almost ran out!

This could also be because once the kids realized who Quinton was, they came back like three or four times, until they worked up the nerve to ask for his autograph. And because Quinton was as into Halloween as they were, he gave them candy every single time.

I'm pretty sure that even the kids were calling him the king of Halloween by the end of the night too.

"I know." He grabs the remote before settling next to me on the couch. "I thought I was going overboard with the candy, but I'm glad I did."

He still has candy left over, but it was getting close. Thankfully, lights-off time came before he was cleaned out . . . and I still had my choice of candy.

"What movie do you want to watch?" I ask as he starts scrolling on his fancy smart TV.

He tosses me the remote. "Doesn't matter to me, you can pick."

Now, I can plan an entire event without help. What colors? No problem. Plan a menu? I got it handled. But when it comes to choosing what to watch? That's a different story.

There are just too many options and I always fall back to the same handful of shows.

"Ummm . . ." I hand him back the remote. "It's probably for the best if you pick. We'll be here all night if it's up to me."

"That'd be fine with me," he says before he starts clicking his way through movie options.

And lucky for me, he does this with his eyes trained on the TV because my jaw is just dangling helplessly while I openly stare at him.

That'd be fine with me? What the fuck does that even mean?!

I'm sure he just means that he'd be happy not to have to drive me back home or something meaningless like that. But another part of me, the part of me staring at his perfect profile with his parted, full lips and the way his Adam's apple bobs in his throat as he chews his candy, is hoping it means he wants me to spend the night because he wants to be with me.

"What about *Get Out*?" He startles me out of my thoughts and I snap my head around, hoping I wasn't caught staring at him.

"Um, yeah," I clear my throat and stare at the screen without really seeing. "That sounds good."

Now, if I was in my right state of mind, one where I wasn't just caught being a total freaking creep—again!—I would've remembered that I haven't seen *Get Out* because I'm a total scaredy-cat and I'm going to have to figure out a way to live my life, alone, in my condo again once this night is over.

Instead, I was too busy staring at his throat to have any cohesive thoughts float through my brain. Self-preservation is something I really need to get.

"Um, Elle?" Quinton asks not long after the movie starts. "Are you alright?"

I don't know just how long the movie has been playing, but I know we're getting to the part where shit's about to break loose. And being the person that I am, I'm not only covering my eyes . . . but plugging my ears as well.

"Yup! Totally fine." I give him a quick thumbs-up before putting my hand back over my face.

"You know we can watch something else." He wraps his long fingers around mine and pulls my hand from my face. And even though I'm sure someone is about to jump out from somewhere on the screen, all of my fear seems to fade away as all of my attention goes to the way he lets his hand linger on mine. "I just thought you said you watched scary movies."

We've touched before, but this feels different. Intimate even. After the night we had, I think it's almost impossible for me not to imagine him in a different light. One where he wasn't just a good friend trying to cheer me up, but an attentive boyfriend who has made it his job to be there for me.

Obviously, I know that's not the case and no matter how much I want it to be true, I won't make the mistake of crossing the line between us again.

"'Watch' might not have been the best word." I pull my hand out of his, even though it's the last thing I want to do. "More like I hide under the covers and scream every time the music gets scary or there's a creepy noise."

He shakes his head and even in the darkness of his living room, I can see him fighting back a smile. And I really do appreciate the effort.

"Then how about we start a new tradition where we pick

something you can actually enjoy." He exits out of *Get Out* and searches until *Hocus Pocus* comes on the screen. "I've never watched it, but everyone is always talking about it on Facebook, so I figure it's a safe choice."

"I love this movie!" I almost clap, but have just enough restraint not to. I don't, however, have the restraint not to yell, "Sisssstaaasss! 'Tis Time!"

His head jerks back and he looks at me like I've grown another head. "What the fuck was that?"

"That was my Sanderson sisters impression." I shimmy my shoulders. "It was a perfect fucking impression and you're going to be mad impressed when you see. But hold on!" Now that I'm not in danger of peeing my pants because I'm scared and can actually enjoy the movie, I need refreshments. I stand up, enjoying looking down at him for once. "I'm getting snacks. What do you want?"

I start to climb over his long, outstretched legs, but because I'm still a little drunk off fear and my legs fell asleep a little bit thanks to how tense I was, I trip over his feet like a total klutz.

"Shit!" My screech is higher and louder than I would ever like to hear again as I reach out for the couch. I've already embarrassed myself in front of Quinton enough to last a lifetime, I refuse to fall onto the ground.

Refuse.

But before I even get the chance to right myself, Quinton's hands latch onto my hips and pull me down onto his lap.

"Are you alright?" His gaze drifts down my body trying to see if I'm hurt. His hand reaches for my ankle that got caught up in between his legs.

"Ye—" I start, but the word gets stuck in my throat when his strong hands pull my legs onto the couch and start kneading into my ankle.

My mind goes blank and my eyes are glued to his fingers as they latch onto the hem of my leggings and slowly push them above my calf. He keeps his hands on my legs as he drags them back down to start his massage again.

Every muscle in my body—muscles I forgot I even had—are clenched. The silence in the room is only punctuated by the sound of my heavy breathing, which I can't seem to get under control. Goose bumps trail his every touch and my body is betraying me. No matter how hard I've tried to convince myself that I don't have feelings for him, one touch is all it took for me to forget it all.

The circles his fingers make across my skin are hypnotic. I couldn't look away even if I wanted to. Seeing his dark skin against mine is going to be what I dream about from now on. We look like the Reese's I just ate, chocolate and peanut butter . . . my favorite combination.

"You're so fucking beautiful," his hoarse voice whispers into my ear.

I'm pretty sure I have fallen into a sugar coma and this is all my imagination. I keep my eyes on his hands, afraid that if I look away, I'll shatter this wonderful fantasy I fell into.

But when his hand leaves my ankles and drifts to my chin, turning my face to meet his, I know this is real life. Because not in my deepest fantasy could I dream up the way he's looking at me right now. There's a fire behind his eyes that I've never seen before. He pulls his bottom lip between his teeth as his hand falls down my back, and we just stare at each other for what feels like an eternity.

Our breathing getting heavier with every second that passes by until he finally breaks the silence. "I'm going to kiss you." He leans in and his breath dancing across my lips causes shivers to run down my spine. "So if you don't want that, say it now."

I move my gaze from his full lips, wanting them to touch mine more than I've wanted just about anything in the entire world, and look him straight in his eyes. "I want it."

The words are still on my lips when his mouth touches mine.

I might've been drunk that last time we did this, but I was not wrong when I remembered how lush his mouth was.

The kiss starts out gentle. As though we are both waiting for the other person to say what a terrible idea this is and put a stop to it. Thank god, neither of us does.

His full, soft lips drop feather-light kisses onto my mouth. They are so sweet, I feel a pang in my chest. I twist in his lap, bringing my legs around so that I'm straddling him. I don't know if this will ever happen again, so while I have it, I'm taking it. All of it.

I link my hands behind his head, holding onto this ride for dear life and he seems to take that as a hint that I want more.

And how right he is.

His giant hands take up almost my entire back and pull me into him, pushing my chest into his and his mouth onto mine. Long gone are the gentle kisses. His tongue darts out, licking the crease of my lips and then takes advantage when my mouth instinctively falls open.

His firm tongue takes over. Dancing with mine as we explore this thing I've been wanting for so long. I let him take over as my hips grind against his. I'm at the mercy of his mouth. When he takes my lip between his teeth, letting it go ever so slowly as he tugs my ponytail, I think I might explode.

"Holy shit." I'm panting as though I've just finished sprinting. "I was not expecting that."

It was actually the last thing I ever expected to happen tonight. Which is why I'm sitting on his lap in leggings, a sweatshirt, and not a drop of makeup.

"It's all I've thought about since you kissed me in my car." There's a huskiness in his voice that would tell me just how affected he was by our kiss . . . if the bulge in his pants hadn't already clued me in. "Probably longer if I'm honest."

"What? You're such a liar." I lean back. I want to stay in this lust-filled bubble we're in, but I also know that's total bullshit and I can't not call him on his shit . . . no matter how good of a kisser he is. "The first time we met, you told me I wasn't your type. And you're the one who stopped the kiss last time!"

"I'm not a liar. At least, I'm not lying now." His fingertips sneak beneath the hem of my sweatshirt and start to draw lines across my back. "I was definitely lying when I told you you weren't my type. I was having a shit day and I was dreading meeting with the suit Mahler was sticking me with. The last thing I needed was him to walk in while I was flirting with a beautiful woman when I was supposed to be focused on damage control. And I only stopped the kiss because you seemed pretty drunk and I didn't want you to regret anything the next day."

The little bit of breath I have left leaves with a whoosh as I try to reevaluate our entire relationship.

"But you hated me." There is no way he wanted to kiss me this entire time. He didn't want to be in the same room as me, let alone stick his tongue in my mouth.

"You hated me. You made it clear from the beginning you thought I was an entitled asshole," he corrects me. "I'd be lying if I said I liked you all the time at the beginning, but things have changed over this last month. I consider you to be one of my friends."

"Friends?" I laugh as I rock my hips against the bulge that hasn't gone down at all. "You treat all your friends like this?"

"No," he says, but he's not laughing. "I don't."

"Good." I lean in and touch my lips to his, unable to bite back my smile that Quinton Howard Junior *likes me* likes me. "I don't either."

"I'm glad we're on the same page." He pulls his hands out of my sweatshirt before grabbing onto my butt and standing up, keeping me attached to him. "Now let's go get snacks so I can see what this movie is about and sneak some more kisses."

And just like that, this is no longer the first Halloween without my dad, but the first Halloween I have with Quinton.

And there's kissing.

Lots and lots of kissing.

He may have filled the ache in my heart, but he also created a new one between my legs. But I'm okay with that.

Twenty-eight

I WAS *THIS* CLOSE TO BLOWING OFF BEING AN ADULT AND SPENDing the night at Quinton's house last night when I remembered I had to meet with Mr. Mahler to look at venues and hopefully get the details needed so I can plan this event.

However, being an adult doesn't mean I didn't stay late and that Quinton didn't wake up with a few hickeys on his neck this morning. I would normally never do that, but he's Quinton and even though I'm not totally sure what's going on between us, I'd be crazy not to try and find one way to tell the world that he was mine.

I pull my car into the historic Denver neighborhood where I'm meeting Mr. Mahler and feel out of place almost immediately. Where Quinton's neighborhood is ridiculous and filled with mansions, I still don't have a complex driving my Camry there. But here? It's old money. It's filled to the brim with people looking for reasons to look down their noses at me. Which is the exact reason I know Mr. Mahler is going to love it.

I don't need my navigation to direct me to Fitz's Mansion.

Nestled deep in the heart of Denver, Fitz's Mansion was built in the early 1900s, something that is apparent as soon as I pull up. Thankfully, I don't think anyone will ever part ways with this architectural beauty to let someone else get their greedy modern hands on it. Without stepping foot on the property, you're aware of how special it is just from looking out of your car window. The beautiful stone covering the exterior isn't something you see anymore and neither is the ornate molding lining the tall windows and giant door. It isn't huge by any means, but that only makes it better. Only the most exclusive clients can have events here. And although I have other venues lined up, my fingers are crossed that Mr. Mahler will want Fitz's Mansion the second his old eyes land on it.

I'm walking up the stone-paved walkway when a Rolls-Royce turns onto the street. And even though I'm sure just about everyone in this neighborhood can afford one, Mr. Mahler is the only person who would be seen riding in one. The car comes to a stop and the driver steps out and opens the back door. Mr. Mahler climbs out, followed by the man I met at Quinton's event. I panic for a moment as I struggle to remember his name, but thankfully it comes to me just before I run out of time.

"Mr. Mahler, Mr. Carlin," I greet them.

An arrogant smile appears on Mr. Carlin's face, framing his yellowing teeth. He looks more like a super villain than I'd care to admit, but at least I know I got his name right.

"Elliot, how are you, darling?" Mr. Mahler leans in and kisses my cheek.

Gross.

This man really needs a lesson in personal space and talking to employees.

"I'm well, thank you." I suppress my shudder and start walking in step with him. His leathery skin somehow manages to seem even harsher beneath the bright Colorado sun. "Have you been to Fitz's Mansion before?"

"Once," he says as we step onto the patio that wraps around the building. "It was wonderful."

"Yes, the Ramsey event, wasn't it?" Mr. Carlin, clearly not one to be left out, adds. "That was a great event."

I take their mutual fawning as a good sign.

I open the door, holding it open for both men as we walk into the classic opulence of old money.

The entryway alone is enough to take my breath away. The owners take pride in the preservation of this estate; they boast that all features are still the originals. From the dark cherry staircase to the wide crown molding to the tiles on the floor, it's like stepping back in time—just with electricity and air-conditioning.

A door to the left opens and an older woman that I assume is Elizabeth Holding, the woman I've been speaking with for the past week, steps out to greet us. In a gray skirt suit with pearls resting at the base of her neck, Elizabeth is just how I imagined her. Her black hair is pulled up in a twist and her face is made-up in perfectly neutral tones. Even her closed-toed heels promise competence.

"Elliot? So nice to meet you." She reaches out her hand to shake mine. I want to point out the appropriate greeting to Mr. Mahler, but don't. He is in charge of my career, after all.

"It's nice to meet you as well. Thank you so much for taking the time to show us around." I shake her hand in return before stepping to the side to introduce the rest of my party. "This is Mr. Mahler and Mr. Carlin, they are the ones hosting the event. I want them to be able to see the space before making the final decision."

"Hello, gentlemen," Elizabeth aims a polite smile in their direction but makes no move to get closer. She must've seen the kiss out of the window and is keeping her distance. *Smart woman.* "I hope Fitz's Mansion is exactly what you're looking for for your event. Of course, if there is anything we can do to help, we would love to do just that. Fitz's Mansion has hosted some of our country's biggest names and most extraordinary leaders. We strive to make all events as perfect as possible."

Mr. Mahler and Mr. Carlin both nod, but keep their mouths shut. Something that brings me way too much joy.

"Could you give us a tour?" I really do want a tour, but Elizabeth's presence has also seemed to calm both of the men with me, and keeping her close is in my best interest.

When we talked on the phone, we discussed that Mr. Mahler and I would be able to walk around on our own and then go back to her with any questions once we finished looking around. I'm worried that she'll say no, but when her eyes soften and a sympathetic smile crosses her face, relief courses through me.

"I'd be happy to," she says. "Let me just grab a notebook so I can write some things down as we go."

She walks back into her office and when I turn around, Mr. Mahler and Mr. Carlin are huddled together, speaking in hushed tones.

Quinton's warning about not trusting Mr. Mahler pops into my mind unbidden.

The more I'm around Mr. Mahler, the less I like him. Neither one of these men gives me good vibes. I mean, I don't even want to walk around the venue alone with them, for goodness sake.

I don't know if it's because I can still taste Quinton's lips on mine or if I'm starting to recognize things I've been ignoring for the last couple of months, but I'm beginning to regret agreeing to plan this event for Mr. Mahler.

"SO," ELIZABETH COOS once we've made our way back to the entryway or, as Elizabeth calls it, the foyer. "What did you think? Will Fitz's Mansion be the site of your fundraising event?"

I hold my breath and cross my fingers behind my back. With every gold accent Elizabeth pointed out and historical anecdote she told, the doubts I had about working with Mr. Mahler faded. What could possibly be wrong with me getting to plan an event in this beautiful venue? Visions of centerpieces overflowing with every white flower I can get my hands on and white twinkly lights fill my mind. I can envision every piece of this event, all I need is Mr. Mahler's approval.

He leans over and whispers something in Mr. Carlin's ear and not surprisingly, Mr. Carlin nods yes to whatever he's hearing. During the tour, it became more apparent that even though Mr. Mahler introduced Mr. Carlin as a business partner at Quinton's launch, he doesn't hold any weight when it comes to this event. He basically just agreed with everything that Mr. Mahler said. Not saying I blame Mr. Mahler for bringing him. If I had a hype man, I too would bring them with me everywhere.

Mr. Mahler claps his hands together before revealing his freakishly white teeth. "Let's do it," he says. "This will be the perfect location for the fundraiser."

"I'm so glad! I knew you would just love this place." I can't hide my excitement. "If you want to wait here, I'll go confirm the date with Elizabeth and get her settled with the nondisclosure and then I'll meet you back in the dining room to tell you my vision."

"Perfect. We'll see you in a moment, dear." He turns to walk away but I'm so excited that he gave me the go-ahead to book the Fitz that I don't even care about him calling me "dear."

After I settle everything with Elizabeth, I take a little detour as I make my way back to Mr. Mahler. I walk down the empty hallways, listening as my stilettos echo against the mosaic marble floors. In school, history was always my favorite subject. There's just something about hearing stories about the way people used to live and how every decision had such massive repercussions on the world around them. Now, walking down this hallway, I can't help but imagine the world as it was when the Fitz family moved into this house and walked down this very hall every day.

I push open the heavy wooden door to the dining room, ready to get down to business. Like the ghosts of the Fitz women are helping me be the boss they weren't allowed to be, my spine straightens as I approach Mr. Mahler.

"So?" I gesture to the room around us. "What do you think of this being the location for the dinner?"

"Dining room" doesn't seem to really describe the room we're standing in. If we use long tables, we can easily fit forty people in here. The massive crystal chandelier falling from the center of the room catches the sun's rays from the window and covers the room in tiny rainbows.

"I think it's perfect. Just the kind of high-class event I knew we could pull together."

Just like at Quinton's event, his inclusion of himself where he did nothing irritates the shit out of me. Also like at Quinton's event, I bite my tongue and smile.

"I agree." It's so hard to say and I can feel my eye starting to twitch as the words leave my mouth. "Now, you still haven't given me many details, but from what I do know, I was thinking we could have the plated dinner in here and then move to the parlor after for entertainment and we can pass out different desserts. How does that sound?"

"That sounds marvelous." A phone ringing stops him from saying more. He looks at his phone and whatever he sees causes him to smile in a way that makes the sick feeling I had before the tour return with a vengeance. "One moment, I need to take this."

He puts the phone to his ear and walks out of the room with Mr. Carlin on his heels.

I'm sitting alone in the room, trying to focus on the beauty surrounding me and not letting my mind drift off to the place where worst-case scenarios live. I mean, it's a fundraiser . . . at the Fitz! How bad could it be?

The door opens and Mr. Mahler strides into the room. The look on his face makes my stomach twist and my palms sweat as my nerves go into overdrive. He's watching me closely, measuring my every move. The sadistic smile pulling on his lips makes me wish Elizabeth never left my side.

"I know you've been wondering when you'd get all of the details for this fundraiser and I've been a little . . . well, stingy with the details." This is an understatement. He hasn't told me anything other than the details I forced out of him. "Truth be told, I had to watch how you've handled the Howard boy before I could decide if I could trust you. But I saw the way he hesitated at the game this weekend and I appreciate how you've taken the narrative off my organization and onto him."

Something about the way he calls Quinton a boy rubs me the wrong way, and for once I can see why Donny didn't trust me. Also, if he saw the way I handled Quinton last night, I'm not sure Mahler would trust me at all.

"I'm glad you can see how hard I'm working to maintain both the organization and its players' integrity." I don't mention that I haven't ever discussed telling Quinton not to kneel and don't plan to.

Voices drift into the room from the hallway behind Mr. Mahler. The door opens and Mr. Carlin walks in, his unmistakable chuckle filling the room like my least favorite song. He's looking behind him at a man who looks so familiar. Someone I've been watching a lot of YouTube videos of lately.

Glenn Chandler.

The trash politician who has been dragging Quinton and just about every ethnic group through the mud.

And I'm planning a fundraiser for him.

"You must be the proud American working to get me elected." He extends his hand to shake mine.

Mr. Mahler is still watching me and I'm beginning to think this wasn't a job opportunity but a test of my loyalty. Everything in me wants to turn and run, but this is my job. It's what I've worked years to master. My personal feelings don't count. I just can't believe Mr. Mahler would support the man who has taken every chance he's gotten to disparage his starting quarterback.

I shake his hand and disgust makes it hard for me not to recoil at his touch. How am I going to do this? And what is Quinton going to think when he finds out?

Fuck.

I'm going to be sick.

Twenty-nine

AFTER MY MEETING WITH MR. MAHLER, ALL I WANTED TO DO WAS hide from the world. And also go back in time and say no to doing this event for him.

But as luck would have it, I couldn't do either.

Surprise, surprise.

Quinton and I already had plans to meet with Patricia and Bill Masterson from Pro Players for Equal Treatment to discuss what they're doing to fight for pension parity for retired players, and since the kissing happened, I can't even avoid him.

If it weren't for this stupid Glenn Chandler cloud hanging over my head, I would be really excited. Even though I've seen how passionate Quinton is about equality in the League for current and retired players, I'm still not exactly sure what all it entails. I've been looking forward to this meeting for a while. Working with Quinton has opened my eyes to issues I didn't know existed, and I've loved learning about them.

Because of the uptick in negative attention thanks to Chandler—who by the way, is just as greasy in person as he seems on TV—we moved the meeting from a restaurant to Quinton's house. He was worried we'd be interrupted and Patricia and Bill wouldn't feel comfortable enough to talk openly about the issues they're facing.

My hands are filled with groceries and I just manage to grab the doorknob without having to put down a bag. Yes, sure I parked in his driveway and could've just taken two easy trips, but I'd rather lose all feeling in my hands from bags on my wrists and arms than take multiple trips.

"You know, you really need to start locking your door!" I yell as I walk in.

"But then you wouldn't be able to just come and go when you want." His voice bounces off his empty walls, but he's nowhere to be found.

I start unloading all of the bags that I brought. I wasn't exactly sure what to bring, but I make killer charcuterie boards and they always look fancy as fuck. I figured it was a safe bet that there'd be at least one thing for everyone and the Mastersons would see that we put effort into the meeting.

"Damn, that's a lot of stuff."

Quinton comes up behind me and rests his hands on my hips before dropping a quick kiss on my cheek. His touch feels so right, but now, underneath it is this thread of guilt because of the fundraiser. All I want is to fully enjoy something . . . some*one* without feeling like impending doom isn't unavoidable. Is that too much to ask?

Ugh. My hate for Mahler and Chandler skyrockets by the minute.

"It looks like it, but it's just for a charcuterie board. I wanted to have a lot of options since I don't know what Patricia and Bill like." I point to the bag with sparkling waters still on the counter. "Can you put those in the fridge? Warm sparkling water is gross."

"I hate to break it to you, but sparkling water tastes like feet no matter the temperature," he whispers in my ear before backing away and forcing me to lose the comfort of having his heat against my back. "And I have no idea what the fuck charcuterie is."

I turn around with a log of salami in my hand, prepared to use it as a weapon against him for slandering sparkling water and being as old as he is and not knowing what a charcuterie board is. I mean, it's the age of Instagram! Doesn't everyone post pictures of their boards? There's no excuse.

However, all of my wrath fades to black with my first look at him.

Now listen, I've seen this man shoeless and in gray sweatpants more times than I can count. I'm pretty sure it's his outfit of choice, one that I fully stand behind and support. But right now, he's not in his standard home uniform. He's dressed in actual adult man clothes and holy fuck if it doesn't make my thighs clench together.

I feel like an athlete's build helps determine their position. Linemen are bigger, tight ends are taller, but still bulky in muscle. But quarterbacks. My, my, my. Quarterbacks. Quinton is tall and lean, but not bulky at all. I'm sure he's been told he's built like a basketball player many times in his life. And it's a build that wears dress pants and a tucked-in, button-up shirt so well that it actually robs me of my ability to speak. His dark gray pants were clearly altered to fit him just right. Snug around his thighs and slim cut all the way down to his ankles. I really want to make him turn around because I know his butt looks amazing.

But the pinnacle of this casual yet authoritative look, the part that just makes me want to scream "Yassss zaddy!" is the way he's taken the time to roll his sleeves up to his elbows. If you ask me, the most underrated part of the male body is the forearm. I don't know what it is, but seeing Quinton's forearms out, covered in just the right amount of hair and a fantastic watch, is the fantasy I never knew I had.

"Damn." I stare with my mouth hanging so wide open, I could catch flies, pointing a salami at him. "You look so hot."

The best thing about him kissing me last night is that I can finally say things like that aloud and stare at him until my heart is content.

"Thank you." He quirks the corner of his mouth before letting his gaze trail down my body, pausing at the salami. "What's going on with the meat stick?"

"Meat stick? Really?" It's good to know that no matter how hot he looks, he'll say things like that to bring me back to the reality that he's human. A very hot, but still dorky, human. "It's salami. I need a knife to slice it. You can open the rest of the packages so we can start building the board."

He pulls a knife out of the drawer and puts it on the counter next to the cutting board I brought because I wasn't sure he has one. "Would it be inappropriate to tell you how hot I think you are when you're bossing me around?"

I roll up on my tiptoes and drop a chaste kiss on his lips. Because I can do that now too! Kissing is the best. "Considering I just referred to you as a zaddy in my head, I'm going to say no."

"Zaddy?" he repeats after me before biting his lip and doing a terrible job at hiding his laughter.

"Anyways." I glare at him. "Would there happen to be a spare Diet Coke in your fridge? You know I can't work without one."

"Maybe," he says. "Let me check."

He turns to walk away and as he does, Angela's long legs and blonde hair flash in my mind. I know he's said in the past that nothing is going on between them. But maybe he meant nothing like the nothing I'm reading into between us.

"Um, hey?" The confidence I felt only moments ago is gone

and nerves have taken its place. I'm not saying I want to marry him or anything, but I would like to know if I've become an unintentional side chick. "I know you said nothing is going on between you and Angela, but the amount of sodas she forgets here says otherwise. Are you sure there's nothing going on between you?"

"Angela? What? I work with Angela, she's . . . well, I can't really say what she is. But nothing has ever happened between me and her. I know me and you got off to a bad start, but I wouldn't ever do what I did last night if I was seeing someone else." He closes the fridge and walks back over to me to grab my hand. "Let me show you something."

We hold hands as I follow him down the hallway and into his laundry room before he opens the door to his garage. I'd be lying if I said I wasn't getting more confused with every door he opens.

"Angela wasn't leaving the soda. I honestly don't even know if she drinks them." He pulls me over until he stops in front of another, not nearly as nice fridge. "You always had a Diet Coke with you, so I started buying them when I'd go to the store. I keep them in here and then move one into the kitchen before you come over."

I open my mouth to say something, but for the second time since I arrived, he has rendered me speechless. While I thought he was a jerk who hated me, he was going out of his way to do something nice for me. And he did it without taking any credit. The rules of the universe say that makes the act even kinder.

"It's not a big deal." He pulls a Diet Coke out of the fridge and hands it to me. "Like you said, it was pretty evident you worked better with one. I figured it'd be best to just have them on hand, you were mean that day you forgot it. It was self-preservation, re—"

I don't let him finish.

I wrap my arms around his neck and pull his face to mine. I don't even try to make it a gentle kiss. I slam my mouth onto his and meet his tongue as we continue our explorations from last night.

"You know . . ." I'm out of breath when we finally separate. "If you aren't careful, I might start telling people what a thoughtful person you are."

"You're the only one who didn't know." He winks before holding open the door for me. "The rest of the world loves me . . . well, most of them, at least."

I know he's thinking of Glenn Chandler and all of his followers, who are so intent on making their hate for him known. The guilt of the secret I'm hiding from him feels like I swallowed a brick. I have no idea how I'm going to keep this from him.

WE'VE JUST SET the charcuterie board on his coffee table when there's a knock at the door.

Quinton glances at his watch and I try not to stare at his exposed forearm . . . again. "Five on the dot, they're punctual."

He walks to the door and I run to the kitchen, pulling out four glasses, quickly filling them up with sparkling water.

"Patricia, Bill, this is Elliot Reed," Quinton introduces me to the stunning redhead and dapper man next to him. "She's the one who helped me organize my foundation so I could act on the commotion I caused."

"Mr. and Mrs. Masterson, it's so nice to meet you." I round the island and extend my hand to shake theirs, but I'm immediately wrapped up in Patricia Masterson's arms.

"Please, call me Patty," she says.

"And call me Bill," her husband says. "I might be old, but nothing makes me feel it like being called by my dad's name."

"Patty and Bill then." I nod, before gesturing to the glasses. "We have snacks, but would you like sparkling water before we sit?"

"That'd be wonderful, thank you," Patty says.

Everyone grabs a glass, even Quinton, who said he doesn't like it, before walking over to the living room. Peer pressure for the win!

Patty and Bill both sit on the couch, and Quinton and I sit in the chairs we set up across from the couch.

"Thank you for coming to talk with us." Quinton places his glass on one of the coasters I put down beforehand. "I really appreciate you coming all this way so we can work together to hopefully bring more awareness to this problem."

"It really is our pleasure," Patty says. "It's rare that we have current players come to us. Of course, your father played, so I'm sure you're much more aware of these issues than the average player."

Out of the corner of my eye, I see Quinton tense the way he does whenever his father is mentioned. I don't think Patty or Bill notice, but I wade in just in case.

"If you don't mind me asking, could you explain a little bit more about what pension parity is? I've heard Quinton say it a thousand times, but I'm still a little confused." At this table, I'm very much the odd one out. Sure I watch football, but I've never lived it the way the other three people around me have. If I can understand it, maybe I can help explain the importance of it to other people like me.

"Yes, of course." Patty looks to Bill and he motions his hand for her to take the lead. "In 1993, the players union and the League reworked the agreement between players so that once players retired, they'd be granted more benefits. These are benefits like severance packages, 401(k) retirement plans, access to health-care plans. Things that are needed. On top of all of that, the League started to take notice of all of the dangers in the game, changing the rules and trying to make it a safer game for players to participate in." As Patty speaks, the air of the carefree woman drifts away. She's all business and her passion for what she's speaking about reverberates through her every word. "Now, don't get me wrong, all of that is wonderful and so needed. The problem with this is they've completely forgotten about the players who retired before 1993."

"Okay." I try to take in the enormity of what she is saying. "So the men who retired before then aren't getting help from the League?"

This is hard for me to wrap my head around for so many reasons, but the main one is how often the League throws around the term "legends" and "honors" at past players. I just assumed that meant they were taking care of these men as well.

"Well, not exactly." She picks up her glass and takes a small sip and I feel like she's just giving me a few extra seconds to prepare. "You have to remember the pre-'93 players were also playing before they had full free agency, so the men also weren't making nearly as much as Quinton and his teammates are today. So while the men who qualified for a pension—about four thousand still living today—get one, it's not enough."

"You see on the news these stories about CTE being discovered. You might see a little blurb here or there about a former player passing away, but what you aren't seeing is the actual suffering that's going on." Bill leans forward. The smile he walked in with is gone, his jaw is set, and his mouth is a straight line. Talking about this clearly brings him no joy. "You don't hear about the dementia or the Alzheimer's or the ALS. You're not seeing the surgeries or the proud men who have been brought down to their knees and can't afford to even pay their bills. We fought for the guys to get what they're getting today and they deserve that. We just want to be able to take care of ourselves as well, to not be forgotten."

I look over at Quinton and I swear I can see the rigidness through every line in his body. His hands are balled in fists so tight, it'd be a miracle if he doesn't draw blood.

"The pension pre-'93 players are receiving is about one-third of what today's players are receiving. To put it this way, a basket-ball player who played for ten years and retired after 1965 receives around two hundred and fifteen thousand dollars a year at age sixty-two. A football player who played for ten years and retired before 1993 will receive a little over forty-three thousand dollars, pretax, at age fifty-five." Patty scoots to the edge of her chair; her kind eyes look tired. I know she has to be tired of feeling ignored. "Like Bill said, these are men who are suffering. They played the game when it was at its most vicious. The little money they are getting is going right back out of the door for medical bills and medicine, and some of them can't even afford to get the proper care. All we want is a pension for these men that's equal to those players are receiving today. Nothing else."

"More and more of us are dying every year," Bill says. "We want pension parity before we all disappear."

"Okay." I set my glass on the table, finally understanding why Quinton feels so strongly about this. "What can we do to help?"

Bill lifts his beardless chin Quinton's way. "Well, Quinton's doing a lot of it. People don't know this is a problem and because of that, the League doesn't feel any pressure to make changes."

Quinton is still as stoic as ever. With a stiff upper lip, he looks unbreakable, but something seems off. I know how unprofessional it is and I'll kick myself in the ass for it later, but I reach across the distance between us, and wrap one of his fists in my hand. I can't stand to see him fighting whatever demons he's fighting with-out knowing I have his back.

Patty's eyes follow my movement and a warm smile lights her face as she directs her attention to both of us. "With a new agreement getting ready to be worked out, all we want is a seat at the table during this negotiation."

"But in order to get that," Bill says, "we need Quinton to get more current players on board. I'm not sure they understand the power they wield."

I think back to all of those angry emails I've received from the players union and teams around the League and I finally understand why. Right now this is a Mustangs problem, but once people realize the way these retired players are being treated, this is going to be an issue all teams are going to start facing.

"I got you," Quinton says. "We owe this to you and I will do everything I can to get my peers on your side."

Underneath my hand, I finally feel some of the tension fall out of Quinton's body. It's like as soon as he has a call to action, purpose and determination take hold and nothing can stop him.

"Wonderful!" Patty claps her hands together. "Now can I dig into this board? I've never seen such a beautiful spread before."

As if I didn't like her enough already. Boards for the win!

Thirty

I FEEL LIKE I'M LIVING A DOUBLE LIFE.

And I'm really fucking terrible at it.

At the end of every day, I take a scalding-hot shower to try to wash the grime off me. I just don't know what to do.

Even though I want to, legally I can't tell Quinton what I'm doing for Mahler. And I might despise the man I'm planning this event for, but I can't help but try my hardest as I put in the work. This is still my job. And working in PR, I know there are times where I have to spin something I don't want to. And yes, this might hurt someone I really enjoy kissing, but I can't flush my career down the toilet over it.

But after two weeks of living like this, I'm on the verge of a nervous breakdown. I don't handle stress well at all. It manifests very physically and I almost drove myself to the emergency room last night when I was convinced I was having a heart attack. I have to tell someone.

"Vonnie!" I look into the camera on her doorbell. "Let me in!"

"Damn, girl." Vonnie pulls open her front door, looking glam as always, even at noon on a Thursday. "Is everything alright? Your texts were a little manic and you aren't looking much better in person."

She steps to the side as I bulldoze my way in. I'm so stressed that I can't even focus enough to drink in the grandiose decorating I know she has put into this house.

"You're a lawyer, right?" I ask instead of answering her question.

"Technically, I guess." She narrows her eyes before pointing a blood-red nail at me. "Why? Are you in trouble? Do you need legal advice?"

"I am in so much trouble that I don't even know what to do with myself." I tell her the god's honest truth.

"Oh shit. Come on, girl." She walks past me and I follow her as she makes her way to the kitchen. "Sit." She points at the stools lined up on her kitchen island and walks to the wine fridge a few feet away. "Champagne okay with you?"

"I'll take any and all things alcohol. I officially have no standards." *In life and in drink preference.*

She pops the cork with experienced precision and pours us each a glass before sitting on the stool next to me.

"Cheers." She taps her glass against mine. "I know we usually do this at HERS, but this will have to do in a pinch."

"I mean . . ." I take a look around at her beautiful kitchen, the pendant lights hanging above us, the two-toned cabinets with gold hardware, and the gorgeous tile backsplash beneath them is all immaculate. "This is hardly sloppy seconds."

"Thank you." She takes a small sip of her bubbly. "They've just been filming so much for *Love the Player* at HERS and I have too much shit going on in my life to even think about putting a damn mic on. Now that Aviana's husband got traded, those producers are working double-time to create drama and I know better than to fall into that trap."

I shudder at the thought of cameras catching anything that I'm about to admit to.

"That's a good call, what I'm about to tell you isn't something I'd want going around either."

"I'm intrigued, go on."

The stabbing chest pain that has been bothering me for the last week starts up again.

"I need you to agree to be my lawyer." I ignore the shocked look on Vonnie's face as I pull out my checkbook that Liv still mocks me for having. "How much should I give you?"

"Fuck. If you're enacting client-lawyer confidentiality on me, this is good enough to go pro bono." She leans over and snaps shut my checkbook. "I agree to take you on as a client, now spill."

"Okay." I take a deep breath, not even knowing where I should start this clusterfuck of a story. "Do you want the good or bad stuff first?"

"I would normally say bad, but by the way your lips look a little swollen and bruised, I'm going to assume the good has to do with Q. So I pick good."

I haven't told anyone about Quinton and me yet. We didn't make the decision not to say anything, but seeing as I'm a female in a male-dominated industry, it seems smarter for me to keep it on the down-low . . . even though I want to shout it from the rooftops.

"Quinton ca—" I don't even get the first sentence out before Vonnie's jumping off her seat and her scream is puncturing my eardrums.

"I knew it! I knew the good shit had to do with Q! What happened? How was it? How does that beard feel up close and personal? It has taken him from fine to finer and I'm loving it." I'm not sure she's taken a breath, let alone given me the chance to answer her rapid-fire questions.

"I was trying to get there when you went full rap verse on me. Like I was saying . . ." I take a deep gulp of my champagne, needing the liquid courage to get through all of this. "Quinton came over on Halloween. I'd mentioned to him before that I was dreading this holiday season and this was going to be my first Halloween not passing out candy with my dad and watching movies." The butterflies return to my stomach just thinking about how thoughtful he was that day. "So he took me to his house and he bought pumpkins for us to carve, candy to pass out to the kids, just everything. Then at the end of the night, we kissed."

"I knew it! I knew those lips looked fuller than usual!"

"Yeah, there's been a lot of kissing." I graze my fingers across my lips without realizing what I'm doing. "And it's been great. We cleared up a bunch of misunderstandings we both had and things are going really well."

Too well, one could say.

One being me.

We meet up at one of our places almost every night and eat dinner together. Then we either do some work for his foundation or talk when we say we're going to watch a movie. I'm starting to feel like we're in a real relationship and he's one of my best friends.

And then I remember I'm lying to him.

"Now for the bad news," I say.

"Oh lord. Hold on." Vonnie holds up her index finger as she drains the rest of her glass before filling it right back up again. "Poppy and Brynn were a pain in the ass, but I have a feeling you're about to blow them straight out of the water."

"You know how I agreed to plan the event for Mr. Mahler?"

"Yeah . . ." She drags out the word. "He's a creep, but you need him on your side if you're going to keep this job, and maybe even more if you don't make it past this season."

"Thank you!" I slap a hand on her granite countertops. "That's why I took this job with him. He had me sign an NDA, which is standard for these big events, so I didn't think much of it."

"Fuck the foreshadowing already, spill!"

"Okay, okay. Geez!" I really wish I would have asked for something stronger. "The day after we kissed for the first time, I met Mr. Mahler at the venue for the event and he finally shared all the details with me. The main one being it's a fundraiser for Glenn Chandler."

There.

I said it.

Mr. Mahler didn't appear out of thin air to sue me, and the world didn't explode.

"That disgusting son of a bitch who has been dragging Q every chance he gets? That fucking Glenn Chandler?" Vonnie shouts and the pendants I was just admiring rattle overhead.

So the world didn't explode, but I'm pretty sure Vonnie did.

"One and the same," I say. "I don't know what to do. Legally, I can't tell Quinton, but each time I'm with him and I don't tell him, I feel like I'm lying. And on top of that, I think this guy is a total prick! He's terrible and the last thing I want to do is plan an event that could help him. But I'm already skating on thin ice with Mahler, I can't not do it."

"Fucking hell." Vonnie sits back on her stool and just looks at me for a moment, not saying anything.

"Don't just stare at me! Tell me what to do!"

"I don't think I can tell you what to do on this one." She leans forward and rests her sweater-covered elbows on the granite. "I'm pretty sure this is a textbook definition of a lose-lose situation. The only question is which one are you okay losing? Q or your job?"

Is she crazy?

"Are you crazy? You think I should choose a guy I've literally only kissed over a job that I've worked my ass off for?"

I can't even wrap my mind around it. My dad would be so disappointed in me if I did that. He raised me to be strong and independent, not to give up everything for a guy who there's probably not even a future with.

"No, what I said was you need to choose what's important to you, because I don't see any way you can come out of this with your relationship *and* your job. What I didn't say is that you should choose Q over your job." Vonnie purses her lips the way she does before she yells at her kids, and I know I'm in for it. "Listen, we only met a couple of months ago, I'm not going to pretend like I know everything about you. But, from what I do know, this isn't about a job. If it was, I have a feeling you would've already started looking for a new one. First Mahler threatens your job and now he has very knowingly put you in a terrible position with Q."

"You were the first person I told about me and Quinton, Mahler has no idea what's going on." And I'd like to keep it that way, thank you very much. Just the thought of having to go to human resources and tell them makes me cringe.

"It doesn't matter that you two are doing whatever you're doing behind closed doors. Mahler gave you the job to get close to Q, which you have done. And even if he doesn't know the full extent of your relationship, just seeing the way Q has started to approach his protest in relation to his foundation is all the proof Mahler needs to know you've succeeded in gaining his trust. Mahler is doing this to fuck with him."

"Hey! I—" I try to defend myself, but Vonnie cuts me off before I can begin to state my case.

"I know you're good at your job. Damn good, according to the pictures I've seen and everything Brynn told me about the event I wasn't invited to." She cuts me with a fierce side-eye and I zip my lips closed. "What I'm saying is that Mahler could've found another person to put together this event, one who would not be put in a terrible position. Him making you do this—yes, making you—says a lot about him," she says when I open my mouth. "He is the owner of the organization you work for. He may have asked, but you know damn well you couldn't have said no."

"I guess you're right." I hang my head, hating just how right she is. But, if I ever decide to have kids, I'm so coming to her for lecture lessons.

"Of course I am." She raises an eyebrow like she can't believe I had the audacity to ever doubt her. "Now, the question is, what are you going to pick? It's not just your relationship with Q, it's your relationships period. Are you going to put a job that is slowly sucking away your soul over the relationships in your life? It's up to you, but you need to make this decision soon. The longer it goes on, the more damage it will cause."

It sounds like such an easy decision when she puts it like that, but she's missing one giant piece to this puzzle. My dad. This job feels like my last tangible link to my dad. Every time I walk through the doors of the Mustangs building, I feel like he's right next to me, taking it all in with me. And if I quit, I lose that. And I'm not sure I'm ready to throw it away.

Fuck.

Being an adult sucks.

Thirty-one

AFTER TALKING WITH VONNIE, I DECIDED THAT SHE WAS RIGHT . . . but also wrong.

Yes, I do need to make a decision, but what's the rush? It's nearing the end of November, but the event isn't until January. That gives me at least another month to weigh things out and choose what's actually right for me and not just base it on emotions.

And since Quinton asked me out on a date—like a real one, not at his house—I'll be even more well-informed before I pick.

"No," Liv says. "I refuse to let you wear leggings on your first date with Quinton fucking Howard."

Okay. So it'd be a safe assumption to say that I haven't been out with a guy in a long, long . . . long time. It wasn't a conscious decision I made or anything, but life got in the way. Plus, dating sucks these days. I was on the apps for a month before I deleted them all. I'd rather be a spinster than have to deal with that many dick pics. But that doesn't mean I need Liv to babysit me while I'm getting dressed.

This is what I get for opening my big mouth. I should've kept this a secret.

"He said to dress comfortable, and nothing is more comfortable than leggings." I know I'm not a style guru like Liv, but I think I look cute. It's November in Colorado. Boots, sweaters, and leggings are my go-to.

"Fine," she grumbles before going into my closet. "But at least wear these boots and not your UGGs. There's comfort and then there's pajamas. Leggings with UGGs is pajamas."

"I will agree to the boots, but not to your point. UGGs are the best and you're just a snob." I take the knee-high boots from her hands and set them next to my bed.

"How are you going to wear your hair? I think you should leave your curls, they're gorgeous and you never wear it like that."

I don't know how old I was when my dad realized he had no idea how to manage my tight curls and started taking me to get relaxers. If you don't know what relaxers are, bless you, child, and thank the heavens that your scalp never suffered. Relaxers are perms that chemically straighten your hair. Your stylist puts on gloves (probably the first sign that you don't want that junk on your head) and slathers the white cream directly to your roots. You then sit with it on your head as it starts to burn your scalp. Once the burn gets too intense—like it might start melting your brain at any second—you tell your stylist and they wash it out of your hair. The end result is perfectly straight, perfectly damaged hair.

I remember when I was in elementary school and another mixed girl came to my class. She had these beautiful ringlet curls and I wanted them so bad. And I'll never forget what happened when I asked my dad and the hairstylist if I could have curls like that. "Girl no," she said. "You don't got those good curls. Your hair's too nappy for that and your daddy can't handle all of that."

SNAPPED   259

They both laughed as she slipped on the gloves and started parting my hair.

I stopped getting relaxers in high school when I realized how much damage they were doing to my hair, but I never stopped straightening it. I love the way natural hair is being accepted and I think curly hair is beautiful, but I hate it on me and I always will.

I appreciate the compliment from Liv, though.

"Thanks, but I'm going to straighten it. You know I don't even know how to begin to style my curly hair."

"Fine." She sticks out her bottom lip, the same way she does every time I don't abide by her exact styling requests. "One day I'm going to convince you to go curly and you're going to regret not listening to me sooner."

She's been saying that since college. Still hasn't happened, but I do admire her tenacity.

"If that happens, feel free to throw it in my face."

"Like I need permission," she scoffs. "Okay, I have a photo shoot to get to. I need you to promise me you will not wear your UGGs."

"I promise." I roll my eyes. "I'll even send you a picture before I leave."

"Yes, I want one." She opens my bedroom door and walks through my condo. "Now, I know most people say don't go too far on the first date, but I'm going to say the opposite. You need to let loose and live a little. If the opportunity arises, go for it. You only live once and it's time for you to have some fun with yours."

"I'm pretty sure that's terrible advice." I unlock the front door and hold it open for her. "But I will keep it under consideration."

"That's all I ask," she says before spinning around. "Well, that and a bold lip. I left you three choices from MAC in your bathroom. I will find you on your date and apply it myself if I see any hint of clear lip gloss in the picture you send me."

"Leather boots and bold lip, promise." I push her out of my door; she's totally going to be late. "Now go, I think you're forgetting how bad traffic is . . . even on a Saturday."

"Fucking transplants," she groans as she stomps away.

I close the door on her, laughing at what an old lady she sounds like before checking the clock. T-minus two hours before my first real date with Quinton.

A KNOCK COMES on my door at four o'clock exactly. I would be impressed if I wasn't a nervous wreck. I even used the essential oils Greer gave me, but now I smell like a lavender plant and I hope I don't give Quinton a headache.

"Here I come!" I take one last look in the mirror, resisting the urge to wipe off the dark red lipstick and put on my clear gloss instead, before turning off the light and grabbing my purse. "Hey!" I pull open the door and get my first look at Quinton and man, it's like he gets better looking every single day.

I think I do a pretty good job not staring at how handsome he looks in his plaid button-up and puffy vest, a combination I didn't even know worked for me until this very moment. His beard is still on his face, but I can tell he's been to the barber recently because it's lined up so well that I swear it just creates a bull's-eye around his full lips. It's all very lumberjack in a way that makes my insides quiver.

"You look gorgeous." He leans in and drops a quick kiss on my red painted lips, his facial hair tickling against my face and making my mind drift to places it shouldn't . . . like what that beard would feel like against the inside of my thighs.

"Thank you," I say, hoping he'll think the blush in my cheeks is from the cold wind blowing around us. "You look very handsome as well. Very outdoorsy."

"I figured it was fitting for what I have planned today." He pulls a hand out of his pocket and wraps it around mine. It's such an innocent, sweet gesture that it makes my heart feel like it's going to explode.

"Outdoors?" I look at the deceptively cloudless sky and the bright Colorado sun. Sure it looks beautiful, but it's freezing outside. And I might not do heat, but I definitely do not do the cold. Plus, I brought my cute jacket, not my warm one. I'm not prepared for outdoors. "Isn't it a little cold for that?"

"Ouch, Elliot!" He brings his free hand to his chest and holds it over his heart. "You already don't trust me?"

"You're such a dork." I lean into him, shoving him with my shoulder. "Fine, I'll give."

"Good, because I think you're going to love it."

I look up at his wide smile and shining dark brown eyes and can't help but agree. "I'm sure I will."

He unlocks the doors to his fancy-ass BMW as soon as we approach. The dark blue paint glitters beneath the sun and I'm pretty sure he just got it washed, a mistake only a person new to Colorado would make. A native understands that you just give up hope of having a clean car until at least May. Especially when the forecast is calling for snow soon.

"So," he says as he pulls out of my complex. "I've been thinking about you a lot with the holidays coming up. I know Halloween had you nervous. How are you feeling about Thanksgiving?"

Usually this is the kind of topic I try to avoid, but after how amazing he was on Halloween, I'm glad he brought it up. It's like he somehow understands what I'm going through. I don't feel like a buzzkill when I talk to him about it like I do when Liv and Marie check in.

"Not great, but not terrible." I tell him the truth. "Brynn invited me over to her dad's house for dinner. I guess he goes big for the holidays. And Maxwell's mom is helping him cook. She said it would be a 'dinner for all tastes,' whatever that means. Plus, she told me I could bring Mrs. Rafter and whoever else I wanted to bring, which I'm pretty sure means you." I laugh thinking about how she didn't even try to play it cool. "So, if you want to come, I think it might be fun. Unless you already have plans or something."

"That sounds like fun." He reaches across the console and squeezes my thigh. "There was one thing I have planned earlier in the day, but I was going to ask you if you'd want to come with me. We could do that in the morning and then go pick up Mrs. Rafter and ride to Brynn's dad's together?" His fingers tense on my leg and even though he's staring at the road in front of him, I can still tell he looks anxious for some reason.

"I'd love that." I put my hand on top of his, enjoying that we're in a place where we welcome the other person's touch. I hope mine can comfort him as much as his seems to comfort me. "Thank you for thinking of me."

"I'm pretty much always thinking about you these days," he says. "Even when I'm trying not to."

I couldn't hide my smile even if I wanted to; his words make me happier than I can remember being in a long time. That undercurrent of guilt I've been feeling ever since my meeting with Mahler gets a little bit stronger before I shove it back down. I'm not doing anything wrong. What would be wrong is me making a permanent decision based on temporary emotions. If anyone would understand that, it's Quinton.

The cold must be keeping people inside today, because the drive downtown goes by in a flash. There wasn't even any traffic between Broadway and Sixth, which never happens anymore.

When we arrive in the heart of downtown, Quinton opens his phone and clicks on a few things before deciding to park in a partially empty parking lot on Twentieth.

"Where are we going?" I ask as Quinton guides us through the people on the sidewalks. I figure since we are downtown, the chances of us staying outside are slim to none, thank goodness, but now I'm even more curious about how his outdoorsy look was a clue.

"We're almost there." We round the corner and he points to a door. "What do you think?"

It takes a second for the words on the door to register. "Axe throwing?" I shout, startling the poor woman walking her dog as she passes us. "What if I kill you?"

I know I can be dramatic quite often, but seriously. What if I kill him? This seems like a terrible idea.

"You won't kill me." He opens the door and walks me inside. "I'm pretty sure they've taken the necessary steps to avoid that. It's going to be fun."

"I'm not convinced," I say as we walk up the stairs. "But I'll give it a go."

As soon as we reach the top of the stairs, I change my mind. The huge open space is a mix between industrial, artsy, and rustic. The brick walls and exposed air ducts on the ceilings somehow meld perfectly with the long wood tables going down the center of the room and framed art throughout the space. Six cages compiled of wood and metal wire house the bull's-eyes where people are throwing axes. The outside of each cage has a different mural painted on the wood base, and there is a huge bar boasting local beers at the end of the room.

Other than HERS, it's one of the coolest places I've ever been to.

"Hey, can I help you two?" A man approaches us and his eyes

widen just a fraction when he recognizes Quinton, but to his immense credit, he doesn't say anything.

"Yeah," Quinton says. "I have a reservation under Quinton for two hours."

Now it's my eyes going wide. Throwing axes for two hours? But also, spending time with Quinton for two hours? Yeah, I'm alright with that.

The man, also sporting a plaid flannel shirt and a beard, opens up an iPad and swipes around for a moment. "Quinton for two," he says. "Right this way."

He walks across the room to an empty cage in the back, but closer to the bar. "Alright, before we get going, we just need you to sign some waivers and then we have some rules and tips to go over. As I'm sure you can guess, we want to make sure everyone has a fun time and you can't do that if you get injured."

"Yes." I pull the iPad he's extended from his hands. "Please tell us how. Do you remember when Gavin Pope fell ice-skating? I cannot be responsible for something like that. Got it, Howard?"

"Got it," he says, but his laughter does not make me feel like he's taking me seriously.

"I'm serious." I look away from Quinton and aim my attention at our new bearded friend. "Tell him I'm serious. This cannot end with him losing a finger."

"We haven't lost any fingers yet, and I'll make sure it stays that way," he says, but also looking like he's going to laugh.

We're throwing freaking axes, for goodness' sakes! I can't be the only person who sees this going very, very badly!

I narrow my eyes at both of them before focusing on the man who works here. "I didn't get your name yet."

"Sorry about that," he says. "I'm Brett."

"Alright then, Brett." I move my finger between the two of them. "It is literally my job to spin stories in my favor. If this goes wrong, you and this guy"—I point to Quinton—"are going to be the only names mentioned. I was never even here."

"I promise that nothing will happen." Brett holds up three fingers in the air. "Scout's honor."

"Oh great." I roll my eyes as I start filling out the waiver form. "Like I haven't heard that before."

Thirty-two

"THAT WAS BULLSHIT AND YOU KNOW IT." I GLARE AT QUINTON from the passenger seat as he drives under the streetlight-lined highway.

"How so?" He laughs like he's been laughing since we got our total scores from axe throwing. "You're the one who made the bet, not me."

"Then you should've let me win and then lied about letting me win." I don't even know what I'm saying at this point. Losing brings out the worst in me.

"I don't think I'm wired to do that." He drops a hand from the steering wheel and rubs my leg. "Even for someone who looks as distracting in leggings as you did."

"I appreciate your attempt to distract me by implying that my butt looks good in leggings. I'll let it go . . . for now." Between the compliment and the way his hand is steadily moving north up my leg, he has discovered the only way to lick my wounds. "Just know that the next time we have a competition I get to pick the event and there will be no throwing involved."

"Fine by me," he says. "Just remember that I also lettered in track and swimming."

"Swimming?" I feel like I know a lot about him, but this is a total shock. "I would've assumed you played basketball."

"Nope, I was good at basketball, but I loved swimming." He squeezes my leg before putting his hands back on the wheel. "My mom signed me up for swim team when I was a kid. She said she wanted me to be a good swimmer because she didn't learn until she was an adult, but I'm pretty sure she just wanted to wake me up early and wear me out during the summers. I was actually really good at it. Got offered a scholarship and everything before deciding to go with football."

"Seriously?"

The world is so unfair. I had to write what felt like a billion essays to apply for scholarships and he just had them handed to him. And not only did he get all the football talent, but he got it in swimming too? Plus he's hot? What kinda bullshit is that?

"Yeah." He shrugs as he takes the exit to his place. "I wanted to find a place with a pool here, but it's almost impossible in Colorado."

"Yes, the harsh winters," I say. "That's the reason I'm not a great swimmer."

"Shit." He looks out the window as if only just realizing where we are. "I didn't even ask you. Do you want to come over or did you want me to take you home?"

"I'd love to come over if that's okay with you." I was secretly hoping we'd keep the date going, but I wasn't sure because his next game is away. "Don't you have to travel tomorrow?"

"Yeah, but we don't have to get to the facility until noon, so I'll be fine."

"If you're sure then." I pick at my nails, suddenly nervous even though I've been over to his house many times before.

"I'm sure." He links his hand in mine and his touch makes all of the nerves disappear.

We pull into his garage and he grabs me a Diet Coke before walking into his house. The fact that he's been buying them this entire time still blows my mind.

"Wanna order some food?" he asks as he kicks his shoes off in the laundry room that doubles as a mudroom.

"Sure." I'm never going to turn down food. Ever. "I'm not really in the mood for anything specific, so you can pick."

"There's a good Chinese place that I order from. Is that okay?"

"Yup." I follow him into his house. "I pretty much love all food, so that sounds good."

"A woman who eats, you must be after my heart," he says as he walks into his kitchen and pulls out a menu from one of his many drawers. And even though he hasn't decorated . . . like at all . . . it's nice to know he's still human enough to have a junk drawer filled with takeout menus.

"Oh yeah, you know me. Taking down men one order of fried rice at a time."

I have to admit, it's nice that we started out as friends—or not friends at all—and I was able to skip that whole awkward "should I order a salad or not" phase of a relationship.

"You want to pick something or do you want me to surprise you?" He waves the menu in front of my face.

"Surprise me," I say. "You've done a pretty good job of it so far."

"And there are so many surprises I've been hiding." He winks at me and I'm pretty sure my legs go numb. "Why don't you go ahead and pick something to watch?"

"Yeah, sure. I'll do that." I trip over my words, my brain is still stuck on what I think was sexual innuendo. I mean, I've been out of the game a long time, but that was an obvious hint at sex. Right?

I fucking hope so.

I think back to what Liv said before she left, and even though I waved her off, I have had a very, very long dry spell. Who better to break it than Quinton? We both like each other. He's hot as fuck. And we're grown. We can do what we want.

But on the other hand, he is Quinton Howard and he's hot as fuck. I'm . . . well I'm me. Maybe I should work my way up to Quinton. Work on my flexibility or something before we go at it.

"Food will be here in forty." Quinton sits down on the couch next to me, interrupting my sex thoughts. *I hope he can't read my mind!* "Did you find something to watch?"

"Um, yeah." I turn on Netflix and find my trusty *Scandal.* Shonda never does me wrong . . . except when she kills all my favorites. "Have you watched it before?"

He looks at the screen and his eyebrows scrunch together. "Not really. I've watched an episode or two."

"Oh good!" I pick season one, episode one. "Then we can start from the beginning."

I might not love scary movies, but even though there is way more murder than should ever be condoned on *Scandal*, I can't say no to a forbidden romance.

"Olivia is a fuckin' boss," Quinton says a little over halfway through the show.

"Right? She might be fictional, but she's totally my idol." It's hard for me not to tell him all the twists and turns that are coming, but I manage. "Shonda is a genius."

"Shonda?" Quinton stands up and pauses the TV when the doorbell rings. "Are you guys friends?"

"How dare you? Of course she's my friend." I follow him to the door. "She just isn't aware of it yet."

He opens the door and hands the deliveryman a tip that makes his eyes go wide before a smile splits his face. Just add that to the growing list in my head of reasons why I should pick this relationship over Mahler.

"I know you have your Diet Coke, but do you want anything else?" he asks as he unpacks too many boxes for just the two of us to eat. "I think I have wine in the top of my pantry."

I would normally be okay with just the Diet, but my shoulders are already starting to ache from that damn axe throwing, and a glass of wine sounds like a good idea.

"Wine actually sounds great, I'll go check your pantry."

I walk into his pantry and see the bottle shoved behind a cereal box on the top shelf.

"Where's your bottle opener?" I ask him as I walk back into the kitchen just in time to see him piling food onto two plates. "You know I'm never going to be able to eat all of that, right?"

He looks up at me with mischief in his eyes. "Wanna bet?"

"No!" An unexpected giggle falls from the back of my throat. "I'm not doing any more bets with you today. Now wine opener, stat."

ONE EMPTY BOTTLE of wine and what feels like twenty dumplings later, we're back on the couch watching Olivia as she fixes everything with her gladiators.

"I think Huck's my favorite," Quinton says.

"Yeah, he's pretty great." I roll my neck to try and loosen it. The ache in my shoulders from axe throwing has extended to my neck and back.

This is why I stay away from physical activities.

"You alright?" Quinton puts his hand on my neck and lightly massages it.

I don't know if it's the wine, the food, or that his hands just work that well, but my body goes slack underneath his touch.

"Thank you." I close my eyes and enjoy the way his strong fingers seem to find my pressure points without even trying. "I think two hours of axe throwing upset the muscles in my body that I've never used before."

"Come here then." He stands me up for a second before sitting me down between his legs. "Try to relax."

I've never loved being touched. I'd rather spend my money on just about anything other than a stranger rubbing my body for an hour. I got a massage one time with Liv and was so tense during it that my back wasn't right for a week afterwards. I actually broke up with a guy in college because he wanted to cuddle all the time and I couldn't take it.

But for some reason, I don't feel like that with Quinton. I already knew his hands were magic from when he helped my ankle, but this feels decadent.

My arms seem to go dead weight as they rest across the tops of my thighs. His hands make easy work of getting rid of the many knots I have in my back.

"Damn, girl," he says as he pushes his palms down my spine. "How stressed have you been lately?"

"You have no idea." I try to sound normal, but I accidentally moan out the last word when Quinton pushes his fingers into the spot just beneath my shoulder blade. "Why are you so good at this? Did your mom make you take massage lessons as a kid too?"

"Very funny." His voice sounds off. He clears his throat and repositions himself behind me before he answers. "No, I guess my big hands are good for something besides throwing a football."

"Thank you for that." I unroll my back and stretch my arms into the air. But as I do it, I scoot back against him and feel the reason his voice sounded the way it did. But instead of scooting forward and giving him space, something comes over me and I rock back against him instead.

"Fuck, Elle." His thick voice sounds strangled in his throat. His fingers clasp on to my hips, digging into the softness I've been so self-conscious about for so long. "You have no idea what you're doing to me, do you?"

Sitting on his couch, my makeup worn off, barefoot, and in leggings, I've never felt sexier.

"I hope I do." I stand up and turn around before straddling my legs over his lap. "Because you do the same thing to me."

He doesn't say anything.

His gaze drops to my mouth and he stares at my lips for a minute. "Then what are you waiting for?"

His hands reach into my hair, pulling out the ponytail I threw it into while we were axe throwing, and digging his fingers into my scalp, pulling my face to his before pushing his mouth onto mine.

We've done a lot of kissing since our first kiss on this very couch, but something feels different about this one. This feels like more. Every time his tongue circles mine, it feels like a promise of what's to come.

His hips thrust up beneath mine. The bulge in his pants aligns the zipper of his jeans perfectly against the seam on my leggings. He twists my hair around his hand and pulls my head back. My mouth falls open and my breathing speeds up as he moves his hips, hitting that spot with every thrust.

Like the rest of my body, my eyelids feel heavy and opening them is a struggle. But Quinton's breath is heavy against my throat as our moans begin to mix together. I know that if I don't see him beneath me as I fall apart, I'll regret it for the rest of my life.

I open my eyes and when I do, I'm met with the most beautiful sight in the entire world. Only inches away, Quinton is staring at me like I'm the only person in the entire world. His cocoa eyes are black as he watches me fall apart on top of him. And that's all I need to let go.

The friction between our bodies is too much to hold back anymore, and it's like all the heat from our bodies finds its way between my legs and explodes. A scream falls out of my mouth before Quinton's mouth is back on mine, drinking every sound that I make as my body shakes around him.

"So fucking beautiful," he rasps out once my breathing has evened out.

I think I should thank him or something, but instead, there's only one word that comes to my mind. "Bed," I say. "Let's go to your bed."

I don't have to repeat myself.

Quinton is off the couch, holding me against him as I lock my legs around his waist and he runs down the hallway, kicking open his bedroom door.

He slows down once we're in his room. His steps are measured and careful as he crosses the space and lowers me onto his bed.

"You're sure about this?" he asks. "We don't have to do anything you aren't comfortable with."

It's sweet of him and I appreciate him asking, but I've never been so sure of anything in my entire life.

I roll onto my elbows, taking in his giant height as he looms over me.

Oh yeah. I want this.

Bad.

"Take off your pants." I reach for the top button of his jeans, eager to see this fine specimen of a man naked. Needing to see it. Maybe needing it more than I need my next breath.

He steps out of my reach, taking over for my hands as he pulls down his zipper and slides the denim down his long, toned legs. I don't know what I expected, but the reality is still so much better than anything I could've imagined. He kicks them to the side and stands in front of me, not moving, like he understands how badly

I needed this moment. Like he understands my need to carve every moment of this into my brain.

He starts unbuttoning his shirt. One button at a time, revealing his smooth dark skin, inch by maddening inch, until the shirt is on the floor next to his jeans and he's standing in front of me in nothing but his black boxer briefs. His body looks like something out of Greek mythology. His muscles aren't exaggerated, but they are all there. The ridges of his abs, the thick curve of his thighs, and the broad expanse of his shoulders that lead his strong arms, it's all flawless.

He's flawless.

He takes a step toward the bed before bending down and reaching for the hem of my shirt. "Your turn," he whispers before dragging his teeth against my earlobe.

Goose bumps cover my body at the same time my nerves kick in. *Me? Get naked? In front of that? Seriously?!*

He must sense my hesitation because instead of waiting for me to do it, he stands back up . . . pulling me with him.

"Don't make me beg," he says into the dark room. "I'll do it, but don't make me."

He would beg to see me naked? Not that I'm complaining or anything, but something seems wrong with this scenario.

"I kind of want to see you beg now." I mean for it to come out as a joke, but I still haven't quite caught my breath from watching him take off his clothes and from the orgasm on the couch, so it comes out more as a whisper. A request.

And instead of him laughing, he drops to his knees. I try to tell him to get up, but I've forgotten how to speak. My brain has gone awry and all of the muscles that just stopped quivering tighten again. He doesn't even need to touch me. The sight of him, almost naked and on his knees, is enough.

But then he speaks.

"If you had any idea the amount of times I've walked into this room and pictured you right in this very spot, you'd think I was crazy." He curls his fingers into the waistband of my leggings. The scrape of his fingernails against my skin makes me shiver. "I've never met anyone like you. You are funny and infuriating and brilliant. You've brought me to my knees, literally. Please, let me see you."

My mouth has gone dry and I don't trust myself to say anything, so instead, I bite the inside of my lip to try and hide my nerves as I nod my head.

"Thank you," he says as he starts pulling down my leggings. He hasn't gone far before he lets out a hiss of air. "You aren't wearing underwear."

"They're legg—" I start to explain, but the explanation dies on my lips as soon as his mouth lands on me. "Oh my god."

My eyes slam shut and my mouth falls open as his tongue finds the target on his first try. I dig my hands into his coarse hair. I don't know if I'm doing it to pull him closer, push him away, or just to hold on.

"No!" I groan when he pulls his mouth away, but I'm only missing it for a second before he lifts me up and places me on the center of his bed. He climbs in after me, grabbing my ankles with his rough, calloused hands before putting them on his shoulders and covering my mound with his mouth. His talented, amazing mouth.

He sucks and licks and even nibbles until my back is arched so far off the bed I think I might be levitating. He digs his fingernails into my thighs so deep that there are going to be marks there tomorrow. And that's what does it. The thought of being marked by Quinton causes a wave of pleasure to wash over me that's so deep I might drown.

"Fuuuuck!" I moan as I shatter under his mouth.

But Quinton doesn't stop. His tongue swirls around on my core and only when my breathing has evened does he start to drop kisses down my thighs before sitting up on his knees.

"Holy shit. That was . . . That was . . ." Fuck. I don't even have a word for what that was. "What was that?"

"That was us just getting started." A mischievous smile that makes my insides tighten again crosses his face. "Now what do you say to us getting rid of the rest of these clothes?"

"Yes." I nod my head, all reservations and insecurities I had disappeared with the rest of my mind during that orgasm. "Let's do that. Now."

I pull my sweater over my head in record time, not wanting to miss a second of him pulling off his briefs.

And what a solid fucking decision it was.

Because when he pulls them off and reveals *all* of himself, I damn near faint. I knew he wasn't going to be small when I felt it beneath me on the couch, but this. Wow.

He reaches into the nightstand next to his bed, pulling out a condom, ripping it open, and then rolling it onto his perfect fucking penis.

"How are you real?" I breathe, not moving my eyes from his manhood as it stands at full attention in front of me, sheathed and ready to go.

"I was going to ask you the same thing." He climbs back onto the bed, positioning himself on top of me. "You have no idea how bad I wanted to get my hands on these. You're always wearing those silky tank tops and the curve of these"—he drops his head, running his tongue along the curve of my breasts before sucking my nipple into his mouth and releasing it with a pop—"they taunt me."

"Please." I wrap my ankles around his back, trying to pull him into me. "I need you inside me, now."

Droplets of sweat fall from his forehead as he rubs his manhood against my entrance and I can feel his muscles trembling beneath my fingers. "I'm not sure I can go slow."

I pull his face to mine, pressing my lips to his before biting his full, luscious bottom lip and tugging it between my teeth.

"Then don't." I lift my hips off the bed and kiss the soft skin on his neck. "I don't want gentle, Quinton. I want to feel every inch of you and I still want to feel it tomorrow when you're on that plane."

That does it.

He slams into me. His size and power catches me off guard. "Oh yes!" I moan as he pulls out and pushes back inside.

Every thrust feels different . . . amazing. Like he's waking up a part of me that's been asleep for so long. If I knew sex could be like this, I probably wouldn't have been able to have a dry spell for as long as I did.

He leans back on his knees, grabbing my legs from around him and slipping his hands down my calves until they reach my ankles. He wraps his long fingers around each ankle, forcing my legs apart as he thrusts inside of me, watching his every stroke as he enters me. With my legs spread wide, he gives me the perfect view of his abs as they contract with every movement he makes, but even that has nothing on the look on his face.

My fingers grab onto the sheets next to me as another orgasm begins to build. "Harder," I moan out even though I'm not sure my body can handle any harder.

Until he goes harder.

"Give it to me, Elle." His voice is hoarse with restraint and I know he's waiting for me.

He keeps driving into me at a maddening pace, never slowing, never easing up. Until I can't hold it back anymore.

Every muscle in my body goes taut, even my toes. My back arches as my head pushes back into his pillows and my knuckles go white clenching his sheets. My mouth falls open as I let out a strangled moan as every single nerve in my body explodes. The world goes black right before Quinton moans out and slams into me a final time before dropping my ankles and falling on top of me.

Even though my body feels as though my blood has turned into cement, I lift my legs and arms and wrap them around Quinton, holding him tight as our breathing returns to normal and we float back down to earth.

"Damn," he whispers, dropping a kiss onto my shoulder. "That was . . . That was . . ."

"Yeah, it was," I finish for him, because there are no words to describe what just happened between us.

I should've known he would be magic in bed.

As if my decision wasn't impossible enough already, I had to go and have the best sex of my entire life with him. I'm not one to think sex means love. Not at all. But maybe in this case, it does? Nobody has ever known what my body needs the way he did. And not just my body, but he's always one step ahead of me emotionally too.

How did I let this happen and what the hell am I going to do now?

Thirty-three

IF SOMEONE WOULD'VE TOLD ME THAT AFTER MY DAD PASSED away, I wouldn't be completely dreading my first Thanksgiving without him, I would've laughed in their face and asked them to share whatever they'd been smoking. Yet here I am.

Of course, there is still a gray cloud hanging over my day. A looming sadness that I don't even try to shake. A reminder that the most important person in my life will never share this day with me again. But instead of crumbling like I thought I would, I'm standing in front of my building, soaking in the sun on this surprisingly warm November day, watching as Quinton's sparkling blue BMW that he still insists on taking to the carwash glides into the empty parking spot in front of me.

"Happy Thanksgiving." I climb in and he meets me in the middle for a quick kiss.

"Happy Thanksgiving to you," he returns and glances at the clock. "I hope you weren't waiting long, I would've come sooner."

"I know you would've." I buckle my seat belt and settle in as he reverses out of the spot. "My place just felt too quiet and it's beautiful out. I figured I'd enjoy it before the weather switches up on us again."

He forces out a laugh. "This Colorado weather is giving me whiplash. It is a nice day outside, though."

Weather small talk? I thought we were beyond this. But as I look at the rigid lines in his shoulder and his white-knuckle grip on the steering wheel, it's obvious something is off. I wrack my brain, trying to think of anything that could've happened to make today so awkward, but I can't think of anything. He dropped me off at my place on Sunday morning before driving to the facility to meet the team and didn't get back into town until early Tuesday morning. We had dinner on Tuesday, but missed each other yesterday.

"Everything okay?" Maybe he's regretting giving his entire day over to me? We did just start seeing each other. This does feel like something a more serious couple would do. I wonder if he's afraid he's giving me the wrong idea?

"Yeah, great." He looks away from the road in front of him and offers me what I think is supposed to be a reassuring smile, but does the opposite. His mouth is so strained, it hurts me.

"I know we kinda just fell into this whole thing." I rest my hands on my legs as an attempt to stop my knee from bouncing. "If you're worried that I'm reading into this and going to become some crazy stalker, know that I won't."

Alright, so the no-stalking thing is a lie. We live in the time of the Internet and social media. I will for sure cyberstalk him. Torturing myself with thoughts of what could be and endless scrolling between the hours of twelve to three a.m. is my favorite pastime. But I won't like "show up at his house" stalk him or anything.

"No." He manages to pry one of his hands off the steering wheel and grab mine. "That's not it at all. If you couldn't tell, I'm really fucking into you. I want to see where this goes. I want you to read into this, I know I am."

My knee stops bouncing as my heart explodes into tiny little hearts in my chest. I'm not sure anyone has used the word "fucking" in such a sweet way, but it might be my love language. Well, that and Diet Coke, both of which Quinton has mastered.

"I'd like that too." Mr. Mahler crosses my mind, but I quickly shut it down. If I'm going to make a decision, I can't not be present when I'm with Quinton or at work. There's no way I can make up my mind if I'm checked out when I'm around them.

"Good." His fingers wind around mine and his jaw flexes beneath his thick beard. "Where we're going, I've never taken anyone. Ever. And I need you to know bringing you here isn't something I take lightly."

"Oookay," I drag out the word as I look at the nondescript neighborhood he's driving us through. The houses are nice, but cookie-cutter, typical for the suburbs. "Where are we going?"

He didn't tell me and I never asked. His surprises haven't let me down yet, so I didn't feel the need to ask until now.

"I've been pretty vague about my family life, but I'm a lot closer to them than you think." He flicks on his blinker, making the right-hand turn like it's second nature. Like these are streets he frequents. "I just like to keep my family private. It's not something I've ever wanted to advertise. And a few years ago, something happened and I grew even more private at my family's request."

"So I'm meeting your family?" The pieces of my heart slowly meld back together as it pounds against my chest and my palms begin to sweat. The way he is presenting this doesn't bode well for me. I feel like meeting the family should not contain this much dread.

"Yeah." He pulls to a stop in front of a ranch house with a white sedan parked in the driveway. The small tree in the grass is bare, its leaves long gone. It's every average house. "I . . . It's just . . . I need you to promise me that you will not share any of this with anyone."

Oh fuck.

He has a kid, doesn't he? He's taking me to meet his secret love child.

"I promise." I will a smile onto my face, hoping it looks more convincing than it feels.

It must work, because he takes a deep breath and I watch as the muscles in his body finally relax. "Alright then." He leans over and when he kisses me this time, it's more than the peck we had when I first got in the car. This one is deep and slow. It's him saying something that he couldn't quite put into words. I'm just still not sure what it is. When he pulls away, relief shines bright in his eyes. "Let's go."

I meet him on the sidewalk and he grabs my hand as we walk side by side to the front door. Quinton lifts his hand to knock on the blue-painted door, but it swings open before he can. And at the sight of the person on the other side, my stomach falls to my feet and my vision blurs.

"Hey!" Angela says. "Happy Thanksgiving!"

Unlike the first time we met, and the times since, her hair isn't down in perfect waves and her slim hips aren't wrapped in a pencil skirt. Instead, her long blonde hair is up in a bun that I think is supposed to look messy but instead looks high fashion, and her legs are encased in jeans that make them look even longer than they already are. Like a person would dress at home.

"Elliot, right?" she asks before leaning in and giving me a quick hug that I'm too shocked to reciprocate. "Nice to see you again."

"Um, yeah, you too," I say to the woman I'm beginning to

suspect is the mother of his child. I look at Quinton with wide eyes that hopefully say "What in the entire fuck is going on here?" when she steps to the side and gestures us inside.

Quinton doesn't say anything, but his fingers tighten around my hand as I try to pull it away. I freaking asked him if anything was going on between them and he said no!

"Q!" A beautiful Black woman who could pass for Angela Bassett's twin comes running into the room and wraps him in her arms. "You're early. I don't even have the appetizers ready yet."

"You know I'm always early, Mom," he says. "You and Dad drilled it into me."

"I know that's right." Her warm laughter fills the room so much that it unthaws my feet that have been frozen to the carpet beneath them. She turns her head and when she sees me, her mouth falls open for a second and then Quinton's smile appears on her wrinkle-free face. "You must be Elliot!" She forgets about Quinton and wraps me up in a hug much like the one she gave him. She pulls away, leaving her hands on my shoulders as she looks me over. It's hard not to shrink under her intense gaze. I swear she is looking into my soul right now. "I'm so glad he brought you. I've heard so much about you. It's nice to put a face to the woman who has made such a change in my son."

"Hi." I struggle to find my voice after the shock of seeing Angela and then meeting his mom wears off. "It's so nice to meet you, Mrs. Howard."

She glares at Quinton, and I'm so glad I'm not him, before looking back to me with that gorgeous smile of hers. "Please, call me Monica."

"And you can call me Elle." I feel my smile widen since I'm pretty sure I'm not meeting his secret love child. I'm still not sure why Angela is here, but as long as she didn't birth his offspring, I think I can handle anything.

"Alright, Mom." Quinton puts his arm around my waist and his fingers squeeze into my hips. I flush with the reminder of our night together. "Give her some space."

"Please." She brushes him off in a way only a mother can before pulling me out of his grip. "You knew this was going to happen. You've never brought anyone to meet me before. It's about time I had someone on my team when it comes to you and your father."

At the mention of his dad, his eyes soften and he looks at Angela. "How's he doing today?"

The smile falls from Angela's normally sunny face. "Not great."

Monica clears her throat and changes the subject. "Anyway, where are my manners? Can I get you something to drink? Q told me to grab Diet Coke, so we have some of that if you want."

I glance at Quinton and I swear, under that thick beard and beautiful skin, he's blushing.

Oh yeah, Diet Coke is definitely my love language.

"I'd love one, thank you." I look back at Monica and when I do, her eyes are glossed over and it looks like she might be on the verge of crying.

"Coming right up." She clasps her hands together and looks at Angela. "Come on, Angela, help me get this food together."

Angela follows her through the living room and as soon as they are out of our sight, I cut right to the chase. "Your mom is wonderful, but what in the world is going on here? Why is Angela here? Why are you asking her about your dad?"

"Angela runs a program that provides in-home care to dementia patients." He doesn't hesitate before answering. "She has gone above and beyond to make my family feel safe with their care for my dad, and she's become a close friend to my mom, hence her spending Thanksgiving here."

All of my breath leaves my body in one fell swoop.

"Dementia?" I ask as all of the pieces that I've been trying to place since the day he first covered his logo fall into place.

"After we got the diagnosis, he made us promise not to tell anyone, and I haven't, until you. It started off with little things. Falling down a lot, forgetting why he went to the store, not remembering phone numbers." He's looking at me, but he's not. It's almost like he's being pulled back in time. "Then he started getting mean. My parents didn't have me until after he retired. My dad wanted to be all in, not traveling or moving us around with trades. They wanted to be settled. He was at every single one of my football games, every school program. He was the best. But as he got older, his temper started getting shorter. My mom and I brushed it off in the beginning, but then news stories started coming out about other players committing suicide and getting diagnosed with all sorts of things."

I step in closer, grabbing onto his hands, trying to give him any kind of comfort that I can. My dad died. Yeah. And it fucking sucked. But my dad was the same person until the day he died. I can't even begin to imagine the horrors that come with watching the person you love disappear right in front of your eyes. And to suffer through all of this in silence? Hiding your pain from the entire world? It breaks my heart.

"My mom started reaching out to some of her friends from when my dad played and they were exchanging stories that resembled each other. One of them told her about the League sending her husband to see doctors. Neuromapping or whatever they call it." He rolls his eyes and I watch as his anger rises. "You know, the League pays these doctors and we're supposed to believe them? When they can't even get around to reimbursing you for seeing them? And we were the lucky ones. My dad kept jobs. He had made enough of a name for himself to earn money talking about sports, working short hours that he could manage. But once he couldn't work anymore, once things started going south, the money went fast and that measly pension the League gives him does nothing. And once he dies? My mom gets half of it. So I'm stuck working for this soulless corporation to provide for the family they should be paying. These men built this fucking league and now what? Now my dad can't even go to the bathroom by himself. He can't take walks without a nurse and my mom is stuck loving a man who disappeared a long time ago."

Guilt slams into me with the force of a tsunami. All of the times I judged him, resented him for not including his dad in his efforts. The times where I thought he was selfish and an asshole and I threw my dad in his face and he said nothing. Nothing about how the sport that I loved so much with my dad is the sport that stole his away. And the company that I work for is the same one who abandoned them when they needed support the most.

"I'm so sorry you have to go through this." I grab his face in my hands, hoping that he feels not only the sincerity of my words, but how grateful I am that he opened up to me. "I wish I could do something to make this better."

"You already have." He puts his hands on top of mine and places a kiss on my forehead. "You've been there for me in a way nobody else has and you've helped me find my voice in all of this."

"I didn't do anything, it's all been you." My stomach twists into knots and not for the first time, I feel dirty. Working for Mahler has me feeling gross.

But I can't lay that on Quinton. Not now. Not when I see the weight he already has on his shoulders. And I can't just up and quit with no plan either. I'll figure it out. I still have a month. I can make this work.

Somehow.

Thirty-four

"IS THAT HANDSOME QUARTERBACK YOU KEEP INSISTING ISN'T your fella going to be here tonight?" Mrs. Rafter asks from the passenger seat of my car.

After the wonderful early dinner with Quinton's mom and Angela—his dad was asleep the entire time, something Quinton reassured me was growing more and more normal for him—he dropped me off at home so he could get a quick workout in before eating again at Brynn's dad's. If I ever questioned if I had the dedication to be a professional athlete before, I now know the answer is a resounding no. Hell no.

Instead of working out, I just changed into my stretchy pants because priorities.

He offered to bring a change of clothes with him to the facility and pick me up right after, but I wanted to spend some time alone with Mrs. Rafter. Spending this morning with his family, seeing the strained smiles as their loved one was in the other room, slowly fading away, reminded me how important it is for me to cherish the people I love while I can. Plus, we still agreed on him coming back to my place after, so I'll still end the night with the only kind of workout I want to participate in.

"Yes." I put my old Camry in park behind the long line of luxury cars lining the street. "And I'm not insisting he isn't any-more. He definitely is."

"Oh good," she says. There's comfort in her voice that warms me from the inside. "Next time maybe you'll listen to an old lady instead of thinking you know better."

"I'll never doubt you again."

"That's all I ask." She opens her door and points to the ce-ramic pie dish that she has brought to every Thanksgiving we've spent together. "Do me a favor and grab the pie for me."

"Only if it's your bourbon pecan pie." It's the best pie on the planet . . . or at least the Denver metro area. She even has a couple of ribbons to prove it.

"Like I would spend this day with you and not make my girl her favorite pie." She clucks her tongue and wags a short, painted nail at me. "It's like you don't even know me."

"Of course I know you." I hurry around the car with the pie in my hands as we trek up the walkway to the front door. "And I know this will forever be the best pie in the world."

The beautiful weather from earlier is long gone. The forecast is calling for snow tonight and the chill in the air that's nipping at my ears believes it.

"Miss Elle!" a little voice yells just before the Lamar boys come piling out of the house.

"Another pie?" Jax says with wonder in his voice.

"This Thanksgiving is going to be so much better than when we went to Granny's house." Jett slams a hand over his mouth and looks around him, no doubt making sure his mom didn't hear that.

"I'll help you with that, Miss Elle," Jagger, such a little gentle-man, says.

"Thank you." I hand over the pie, leaning in to whisper in his ear. "But be careful, because this isn't just a pie, it's the *best* pie, and since you helped, I'll make sure to sneak you a piece."

"You're the best!" I'm pretty sure the only reason he is saying that is because the last time I saw him, I snuck him a few handfuls of gummy bears after Greer ate all of his. He leans in and gives me a shoulder hug, keeping both hands secure on the pie dish as he walks carefully into the beautiful house filled with loud voices and laughter.

"Hey!" Brynn calls out as soon as we walk into the house and runs to greet us. "You must be Mrs. Rafter! I'm so glad you could make it, thank you for coming."

"It smells like the pleasure is all mine," Mrs. Rafter says, and she is not wrong.

I wasn't sure if I'd be able to eat much after Quinton's mom practically force-fed me, but just smelling everything is making my stomach rumble.

"My dad and mother-in-law went wild." She puts her arm through the crook of Mrs. Rafter's. "Lets go get you something to drink and a few snacks to hold you over. They keep saying dinner's almost ready, but who knows anymore."

Brynn walks her into the kitchen, but just before they disappear, Brynn turns and points a very aggressive finger toward the stairs. And because I'm going to need her to make me the caramel apple cocktail she keeps telling me about, I follow directions.

When I reach the top of the stairs, there's a single door open with light and hushed voices spilling into the hallway. All heads turn to me when I walk in, but I focus on one face.

"Fuck." I rush over to Vonnie, who, for the first time since meeting her, doesn't have a drop of makeup on her face. "What happened?"

"I told him I couldn't do it anymore." She doesn't even try to wipe away the tears as they fall down her face. "I can't pretend to be happy with things the way they are anymore. I don't want to remodel the house again or do any of the other busywork I've been doing. I told him I'm tired of feeling like everything I care about is second to what he deems is most important."

I pile onto the twin-size bed with Greer and Poppy. "Good for you. What'd he say to that?"

She might not be happy with the way her marriage is going, but she still loves the man she married. Even though she's crying on what I can only assume is Brynn's childhood bed on Thanksgiving, a part of me is still hoping there's a chance this won't end in total heartbreak.

"He told me I was being ridiculous and that if I didn't like it, I could leave. Then he grabbed his car keys and drove to his mom's house without even saying bye to the boys."

"Are you fucking kidding me? What an asshole!" I know it's not what I'm supposed to say, but my filter has up and left me. My heart is broken for her and my anger is off the charts. How could he not realize that he had the best of the best?

"I can't believe he did that." Poppy leans back on her elbows, her sweet baby bump sticking out for all to see. "That doesn't sound like him."

"I don't even know if it *is* him anymore." Vonnie swipes at the tears on her face, leaving angry red marks in her wake. "He's so different now. I don't know if this is just the man he's grown into or if it's some brain thing. But what? Do I stick around and wait? If it is CTE, he's sick, right? So I should stay, like I promised in my marriage vows. But there's nothing to do to treat it, and you've seen what the women who have lived through CTE have said. Do I take that abuse and let my kids see it? Or do I protect myself and my boys? I don't think there's any way I can win in this situation."

"Alright." Brynn walks in and slams the door behind her.

"The Lamar boys are in the basement with Ace playing that dance game on the Xbox, which is hilarious by the way; TK has Posie; and Mrs. Rafter is being entertained by Maxwell. Should we FaceTime Charli and Aviana? I feel like we should. I hate this whole trading, different teams thing. None of my friends should be allowed to move. Can I make that a rule?"

"Oh my god!" Vonnie shouts, effectively cutting off Brynn's rambling. We all turn to look at her and when we do, she's not only no longer crying, but she is staring at me in a way that, frankly, terrifies me. "Q gave you that D!"

I feel the blush rise from my neck as my mouth sputters like a dying fish, but nothing comes out. How could she know?

"What?" I finally manage to spit out, but it's not the denial I was going for.

"She has a gift." Brynn pats me on the shoulder. "Don't fight it. She did it to me too."

I turn to Brynn, horrified by the idea of all this.

"I-I mean . . ." I start, not knowing where the hell I'm going with this, when the cutest boy with long golden curls barges into the room.

"Grandpa Sterling says it's time to eat!" He turns to Poppy. "Dad said he'll make your plate when you come down."

Ace sprints back out of the room without waiting for Poppy's answer.

"Ooooh, TK. Makin' plates and everything now." Vonnie stands up, pulling Poppy up after her. "You better be glad you found him before I left Justin because I'm telling you, all these years later and that man is still fine."

"Vonnie!" Greer sounds scandalized. "You can't say that about her husband."

"You want me to say it about yours?" Vonnie snaps back as she files out of the room. Brynn and I trail her, doing a terrible job disguising our laughter as coughs. "Hey Q," Vonnie says, and I'm not sure if she's serious or getting back at me for laughing until I turn the corner and see Q's long body leaning against the hallway wall.

"There you are." His eyes go soft when he sees me. He pushes off the wall and walks over to me. "You look beautiful . . . again." He drops his chin and touches his mouth to mine.

"You guys can go in my room, but no sexing on my childhood bed." Brynn motions two fingers from her eyes toward us. "Got it?"

"No sex in your room or the champagne room, got it."

We go into her room and close the door as she heads downstairs, warning people not to step on her PUMAs.

"I missed you." Quinton covers my mouth with his, but even though Brynn's bed is bumping into the back of my legs, he makes sure we stay on our feet.

"I missed you too," I admit, feeling silly saying it. I've never been the sappy type, but I guess that's changing like everything else in my life.

"I'm not sure I let you know just how much this morning meant to me," he whispers, the bristles of his beard tickling the shell of my ear. "You know how you said you were dreading the holidays?"

"Yeah." God. The amount of whining and complaining I did. I can't believe he doesn't just find me completely insufferable.

"That's how it's been for me. For years." He keeps his arms wrapped tight around me, like looking me in my eyes during this would be too much. A feeling I understand all too well. "I had to go put on a happy face and pretend I was fine, that everything was fine. Then I'd leave and bury it all because I couldn't put it on my mom. But today, for the first time, I wasn't alone. I don't have to carry that weight anymore. And that's because of you."

"I didn't do anything," I say. "You make it so easy for everyone in your life to depend on you. It's about time you start leaning on someone else. Nobody deserves that more."

"Donny had to convince me to come to Denver. I was dreading it." His gruff voice washes over me and he nuzzles his face into my hair. "Thank fuck I did, because I can't even imagine my life without you anymore."

Those words almost break me and the need to tell him about Glenn Chandler is overwhelming. But a lump forms at the base of my throat and when I go to confess, I feel like acid is dripping down the back of my throat. The fear of losing him and my job chokes me.

I'll figure out a way to tell him, to make him understand why I had to do it.

I have to.

"Lovebirds!" Brynn pushes open the door to her room with her foot, covering her eyes with both hands. "Mrs. Rafter is wondering where you are and Mrs. Lewis won't let anyone eat until we've all said grace. So hurry your hot asses."

"Let's go eat. We can continue this conversation later . . . with a king bed behind you instead." He waggles his eyebrows. He looks so young and carefree it's hard to remember the man I met at HERS a few months ago.

He intertwines his fingers with mine as we walk down the stairs and into the packed room. Because Brynn is Brynn, she couldn't just buy a few plastic foldout chairs from Walmart and call it a day. No, instead she went all out, ordering tables extending the entire expanse of her dad's living room. The table is beautifully set with a burnt-orange tablecloth and gold dinnerware that matches the gold seats we're assigned to. Food fills the table. Everything from the Thanksgivings I had with my dad, from mashed potatoes and green bean casserole to macaroni and cheese and collard greens. It's like the best of both worlds. I almost get teary-eyed taking it all in. I wish I had this growing up. Seeing people of all shades in one room, celebrating together, feeling as though I could exist in both worlds.

After Mrs. Lewis says grace, we all not so gracefully dig into the food in front of us. Ace and the Lamar trio pack their plates, and Mr. Sterling—Brynn's dad and America's favorite grandpa—encourages them to eat downstairs in front of the Xbox, despite the objections of both mothers. Mrs. Rafter is on the other end of the table, chatting it up with an older Black woman I haven't met yet.

"Did I sound convincing enough?" Vonnie whispers in my ear after the basement door shuts behind Jett. "Not having to fuss over them while I eat is a Thanksgiving miracle."

"You honestly deserve an award, I thought you were pissed."

"Misguided anger for the win." She takes a bite of the sweet potatoes with the candied pecan crust and moans. "Oh yes, try those next. And also one of these." She points to the nearly empty cocktail behind her plate. "I'm normally a vodka girl, but whatever Brynn put in this is a winner."

"I will, but maybe you should slow down a little bit? You don't usually drink this much."

Obviously, I know Vonnie drinks. We've done it together multiple times. But I've never seen her come close to being drunk. Even at the games with unlimited free booze, kids running around, and the Mustangs making a fourth quarter comeback, she's never had more than two drinks. Seeing her not only emotionally not herself, but under the influence on top of it, has me on edge AF. And call me selfish, but she's the only person who knows about what's going on with Glenn Chandler. Part of the reason she's the one I confided in is because she never gets like this.

"I know I don't." She picks up her drink like she's accepting the challenge I most definitely didn't give. "But I'm also not usually alone on Thanksgiving and in the midst of marital ruin. Plus"—she points to TK and Poppy—"those two offered to host a sleepover tonight, so the boys will be with them while I crash in Brynn's bed."

"Ace is so excited, he has deemed this the 'best Thanksgiving ever.' And we love having the Lamar boys over." Poppy has a bright smile on her face, but I can hear the worry in her voice. I'm not the only one who thinks this is way out of character for Vonnie.

Brynn clears her throat and waves her fork between Quinton and I. "So, I don't mean to make a scene," she says, no doubt about to cause a scene. "But does the hand-holding you two were doing as you walked down the stairs mean you've decided to admit you're into each other? And by that, I mean do I get to gloat because I was right and totally called this relationship from the beginning?"

I know that Brynn is just trying to get the focus off Vonnie, but as a person who thrives behind the scenes, having everyone staring at me in the middle of Thanksgiving dinner is something ripped from my nightmares. Luckily for me, though, the guy I'm falling head over heels for does his best work in front of a crowd and takes over for us.

"It does." He settles back into his seat and rests one arm across the back of my chair. He looks so comfortable sitting at a table with his coworkers and friends, talking about us. Confirming that there is an us. "But I don't know about you getting to gloat, though."

I don't know whether to be embarrassed that all eyes have turned to me—even Poppy's, which have only been on Vonnie or the plate that TK made her before we even said grace—or just give in to the giddy goodness that's filling me up more than the food in front of me ever could.

"That's fair," Brynn says. "You don't really know me too well, but I gloat. Like . . . a lot. And I did an entire whiteboard presentation trying to get her to acknowledge that you were into her, so I'm gonna go ahead and gloat."

Maxwell just stares at Brynn with a soft smile on his face as she talks, like every word that comes out of her mouth is the most interesting thing in the entire world. His love for her is written all over his face. It's disgustingly cute.

Quinton's hand freezes, his fork full of mac and cheese suspended midbite. "A whiteboard presentation?"

"Oh! You're Elliot?" TK asks. "I was wondering why your name was all over my board. Have you figured out the job thing yet? Or is Mahler still going to let you go?"

Because I have always been a huge Mustangs fan, TK was one of my favorite players. Not only was he a fantastic player, but he was so much fun to watch. He was one of those guys who actually looked like they loved what they did when they were on the field. Also, he's so hot it hurts my eyes to look at him and his Thor-adjacent face. In order not to make a total fool out of myself, I avoided meeting him when the chances arose.

Something I'm deeply regretting at the moment.

"Ummm . . . you know, not really, but—you know." I trip over my words. It's like I can feel Quinton's gaze burning a hole through my skin.

"No." Quinton sets his fork on his plate. "I don't know. Mahler is going to let you go?"

"It's not a big deal. Just when he assigned me to working with you, he said if you didn't stop protesting by playoffs, he'd have to let me go." I force a smile on my face and try to ignore everyone around us who are now also trying to look anywhere but at us and our awkward exchange. TK is cringing so hard that I'm almost positive Poppy is pinching him underneath the table. "He hasn't really mentioned it since, so I'm not even sure if he was serious or not."

The thick veins in Quinton's neck strain and I know he's trying not to make a scene. His distaste for Mahler is something I try to avoid whenever possible. Well, I try to avoid all conflict, to be honest. Hence my terrible decision-making skills.

He lets out a deep breath and moves his arm from the back of my chair to the top of my leg. "Alright," he says. "We can talk about it later if you want."

I nod in agreement.

Next to me, Vonnie finishes off her drink. "See, that's how a relationship works." She sounds a little unhinged and I have a terrible feeling that she is going to explode before the night is over. She's been holding it in for too long, it's bound to come out. "You guys talk to each other and value the other person's opinion. That's how things are supposed to be."

I hate the broken look in her eyes and the way her voice cracks at the end of her sentence. I'm about to tell Brynn to find childcare so we can whisk Vonnie away to some private island with no cell service when Quinton reaches behind me and grabs Vonnie's shoulder.

"You know if you need anything, I got you, right?"

She looks over, her throat working, but no words come out as her almost unrecognizable eyes—lacking both her long lashes and confident gaze—gloss over.

"Well, I'm glad you guys figured things out," Brynn cuts in, sounding much less gloaty than she did moments ago. I know I'm not a member of the Lady Mustangs and I've only been around them for a short time, but the one thing that has been clear from the beginning is how much they care about one another. When one of them is hurting, they're all hurting. And right now, the women surrounding Vonnie are breaking for her. And even though I hate being the center of attention, I will gladly take that for her. "I've seen a lot of bumpy roads, but you two may have beat everyone else out."

It's impossible not to laugh at that. "Bumpy" seems like such an understatement when I think back on just how much the man next to me drove me crazy. "You could say that," I say through my laughter.

"You don't even know." Quinton slips his hand on my thigh beneath the table. "But I think that now we've gotten everything out in the open between us, things are going to be good from here on out."

Well, almost everything.

I feel his eyes on me, but I can't meet them. Guilt over the secret I know I can't carry anymore makes it impossible.

"Oh thank god," Vonnie says and my vision blurs. She's moved on from her cocktail and is pouring herself a glass of wine from one of the many bottles sitting on the table, so she misses the way my eyes go wide, begging her to look my way. And I know it's only my fault. "I still can't believe Mahler had you planning a Glenn Chandler fundraiser."

Quinton jerks his hand from the top of my legs like the mere touch of me burned him. And maybe it did? The sting of what he must think is betrayal hurts. My stomach falls to my feet, and dread fills me to the point that I think everything I've eaten might make its way back up. I try to think of something to say, a way to explain to him what really happened. Anything to make him understand. But when I look at him and see the disgust written all over his face—disgust about *me*—my mind goes blank.

"How could he think you'd have no problem planning that trash fire? What an asshole." Vonnie takes a sip of her wine that she very clearly doesn't need, oblivious to the tension and anger radiating off Quinton.

"Quinton." My normally strong and assertive voice wavers over every syllable of his name. And even though I'm an expert at fighting back tears, the burning in my eyes is getting worse. "Just let—"

The legs of his chair scrape across the hardwood floors beneath them as Quinton shoots out of his seat, slamming his napkin on the table. "Thank you for inviting me, Brynn." He looks down the table, finding Brynn's dad and mother-in-law. "Mr. Sterling, Mrs. Lewis, this was wonderful."

Every line in his body is taut, stretching the soft fabric encasing the arms that I want to touch, the body that I want to hold on to. I reach out to grab him with shaking hands, but he cuts back away from me and steps out of my reach. My hand falls to my side. The weight of his rejection makes my arms feel like they weigh a hundred pounds. But it's the look in his eyes that hurts the most. Only moments ago, they looked at me with so much trust and affection, but now they're full of so much hurt and anger that his gaze is like a fucking knife to the heart.

"Fuck," Vonnie whispers as Quinton strides away from the table like he can't put distance between us fast enough. "I'm so sorry."

This isn't her fault. I knew how much she was going through and I still laid my burdens on her. This is exactly why I've learned to keep things to myself, figure my problems out on my own. I want to reassure her that I'm not mad at her, but I can't. I don't have time.

Because Quinton is storming out of the door and I have to go after him.

Thirty-five

UNLIKE QUINTON, I DON'T EXCUSE MYSELF FROM THE TABLE.

I run through the living room, catching the door just before it slams in my face. "Let me explain!" I yell after his retreating form.

He doesn't slow his steps; in fact, he might start moving faster.

I run after him, not even caring if the neighborhood is staring out of their windows, trying to catch a glimpse at a holiday disaster playing out somewhere besides their tables for once.

The lights to his car blink and he opens his door without missing a beat, without even looking back at me as I barrel full speed toward him.

"Stop, please! It's not what you think." I grab onto his arm, stopping him from getting into his car.

He jerks his arm out of my hand, spinning around and staring down at me. Nothing but disgust is written across his face. And I get that he's mad. He deserves to be. But that doesn't make it hurt any less.

"It's not?" His lip curls as he spits the words in my face. "I introduced you to my fucking dad, Elliot! I told you things I've never told anyone and you've been hiding this? How is it not what I think? Have you been fucking playing me this entire time?" His voice cracks, the anger fading and his hurt taking over for just long enough to effectively break my heart and make me feel like the scum of the earth.

"No, I haven't! I'm so, so sorry." The cold harsh winds bite against my cheeks and it feels like needles are poking my eyes. I can't fight back the tears anymore. They fall down my face like razor blades against my cheeks. "But it's not what you think, you just have to please let me explain. Listen to me for five minutes."

He looks at me for a minute before closing his car door and crossing his arms.

Relief overwhelms my system and it's like my lungs finally fill with air again. If he'll just listen, he'll understand. He has to.

"Thank you." I take a step toward him, but he holds out his arm, stopping me from coming any closer.

"No," he says. "Just talk so I can leave."

That glimpse of relief, hope that we'd work everything out, crumbles to dust, floating down the street with the stubborn leaves that are still falling.

"I didn't know it was Glenn Chandler's event. When Mr. Mahler asked me to plan it, he didn't tell me who it was for." Desperation filters my words, making what was supposed to sound like my defense a plea. "I didn't even find out who it was for until the day after Halloween."

"The day after Halloween?" Quinton looks as if I punched him as he repeats my words back to me. "You've known since Halloween? You've been coming to my house, forging into this relationship, all while going behind my back to plan an event for the guy who has done nothing but slam me in the press? You're supposed to try and help me! And you've been fighting for the guy who's done more damage to me than anyone else!"

Even when Quinton has been angry before, he's kept it contained. He'd shut down and get quiet. Having him standing in front of me, yelling in my face isn't just unexpected, it's scary. I know he'd never lay a hand on me. But the fact that he doesn't even care to restrain his anger? It tells me he doesn't think I'm worth the effort that the restraint would take. And that's fucking terrifying.

"I signed a nondisclosure, you know I couldn't tell you." Between the tears openly falling down my face and the snow starting to fall, my face is wet and freezing as I beg him to understand.

"I told you not to trust Mahler! From the very beginning, you didn't like what I had to say, but I told you. And you just refused to believe me!" he bellows, his words bouncing off the car-lined street. "And now you're working with Glenn fucking Chandler on top of everything? Two old, racist bastards that are determined to bring me down. And I'm supposed to trust you?"

"It's my job!" I snap back. I want to apologize for lying, but he, out of everyone in this world, should understand working for a person you don't like. He knows! It's fine for him, but I'm expected to give up everything and hold some moral high ground that I literally can't afford? He just wants to be mad at me. "What did you want me to do? Throw away my entire fucking career because you carved a fucking pumpkin with me?"

I hate myself the moment the words leave my mouth.

"Wow." Quinton rubs his hands through his hair and a humorless laugh falls out his mouth. "That's how you want to spin this? That's what the PR genius inside your head is doing now? Alright."

"Quinton, no, you know that's not what I meant, I just—"
He cuts me off.

"No, I get it." The smile on his face is colder than the snow falling on us and causes every muscle in my body to tense. The

Quinton I've gotten to know isn't in front of me anymore. And I'm the one who pushed him away. "You know, when you told me how my taking a knee made you uncomfortable because it made you reevaluate the way you saw the world, I dropped it. It was already clear to me you had some childhood issues I had no business touching, but I hoped it meant you'd start looking at yourself and how you view things."

At this point, I know he's not going to forgive me, and explaining myself is probably useless, but he has me confused with someone else if he thinks I'll just let him hit below the belt. "Seriously? I get you're mad, you have every right to be. But that's not okay. I don't have childhood issues."

"You don't?" He steps in closer, not needing space anymore now that it works for him. "Is that why you practically shove your fingers in your ears and close your eyes anytime anyone points out racism to you? I told you what Mahler was. I told you how racist and disgusting he was, and you refused to believe me. And still, here you are, lying to me, planning a fucking fundraiser for a guy who does nothing but spew racist shit every single day?"

"Just because I don't like to label everyone as a racist doesn't mean I have issues." The trembling in my hands has morphed from trembling to full-out shaking, but I don't know if it's because I'm so angry or cold. "How is me not wanting to throw that terrible label on everyone a bad thing?"

"It's not a bad thing," he says. As if the angry man in front of me was conjured by my imagination, every line in Quinton's body falls. Even his eyes that looked at me with so much hate only moments ago go soft. He reaches out for my hands and rubs them between his, causing feeling to come back into my fingertips before pulling me into a tight hug and tucking my head into his chest. "I think you've spent your entire life wanting so badly to fit in with the part of you people can't see, that you've conditioned yourself to excuse the hurtful things they say. You want them to accept you so bad, you've become blind to certain things. Even if I was the only Black person in my class, I still got to go home and fit in there. And I can't hold it against you for finding a way to protect yourself in a world I know nothing about."

He drops his face, his nose nuzzling into my hair, the kiss on my head speaking volumes. The tears that slowed pick up again, but before I can tighten my arms around him, he pulls away. Dropping his arms, he takes a step away from me and opens his car door.

"I can understand it, but it's not something that I can bring into my life," he says. Even after my dad died, nobody looked at me with the amount of pity that Quinton is looking at me with now. "I know this job is important to you and I'll make sure you can keep it. I hope you can find whatever validation you've been searching for, Elliot, but I know that I can't give it to you."

He folds his large body into his seat and starts his car, pulling away without even glancing my way. Not that it matters. I'm rooted to the spot he last touched me, wanting to rewind time and tell him everything before it came to this. Questions without any answers run through my mind. I can't move. I can't speak. I can't do anything. All I do is stare after him, watching as his taillights get further and further away, until I can't see him anymore . . . until he's gone.

"Come on, sweetie." Mrs. Rafter puts the strap of my purse over my shoulder and pulls my eyes away from the empty street in front of me. "Let's get you home."

I follow Mrs. Rafter out of the middle of the street and down the sidewalk until we reach my car.

Every step jostles me back to reality.

The reality where I had Quinton and lost him just as fast. The one where he took the liberty to try and tell me how and what I feel.

By the time we've reached my car, I'm so fucking pissed I can barely keep it in.

I mean, how fucking dare he? He has no idea how or what I think. And for him to tell me that I excuse racism is full-on bullshit. He has his opinions about people and just because I don't automatically agree with him means I'm not only wrong, but that I have some deep-seated issues I need fixed? Screw that.

I can understand that he was angry because I kept the fund-raiser from him. I really can, but the things he said were not only untrue, but unfair. But he was right about one thing—I can't be enough for anyone. I can't fit in anywhere. No matter what I do, I seem to be inherently letting half of myself down.

At least now I know trying is pointless.

Thirty-six

IF THERE'S ONE THING I'M BETTER AT THAN MOST PEOPLE, IT'S hiding.

Whether it's hiding my emotions from my coworkers or dodging Liv, Marie, and a gaggle of Lady Mustangs, I've been successful for the last two weeks.

I just wish I could avoid Quinton too.

Even though Paul is still clueless to the depths our relationship reached, there's no way he couldn't notice the difference in the way Quinton and I have been communicating since our Thanksgiving drama. Instead of weekly meetings, we've switched to emails. And by emails, I mean I send Quinton one with important information on Wednesdays and he never responds. I send him detailed itineraries of press conferences I set up for him during the week with statements and talking points that he never uses. I didn't realize how much he trusted me before to use the materials I sent him. Now it's like he thinks I'm trying to sabotage him.

But even though things are different between us, I still know I don't have to worry about him dropping the ball when it comes to his foundation. It may have been my idea in the beginning, but it is fully his now. I know how personally invested he is, I don't have any doubt that no matter how we turned out, we created something really special that will still be doing good years from now.

I wish the same could be said about my relationship with Mahler. Having to plan this event for Glenn Chandler is slowly ruining me.

It's like when Quinton threw all of that garbage in my face, he triggered a part of my brain to become hyperaware of all the things happening around me. Everywhere I look, I swear I see Glenn Chandler. I look on social media? Somebody is sharing the latest offensive thing he said. I turn on the news? It's a clip of one of his hate-filled rallies. I knew he wasn't good before, but I didn't realize he was this terrible. He must've gotten more confidence in the last couple of weeks and is getting more reckless. I want to believe Mr. Mahler has no idea what's happening, so I asked for a meeting today to talk about Chandler's recent antics.

"Elliot! Come sit," Mr. Mahler calls me into his office when he sees me approaching. "How've you been, dear? How's the big fundraiser coming?"

My heels tap against the plush rug as I enter the room, but the rush of nerves I used to feel coming in here is nowhere to be found. Maybe it's because the wooden walls and folded newspapers on his enormous desk have become so familiar that the room has lost its ability to overwhelm and intimidate me. More likely, however, I'm just too tired to care. I'm tired of him calling me "dear." I'm tired of acting like it doesn't bother me. I'm tired of letting him take credit for all of my ideas. I'm just tired.

"The vendors have all been fantastic. I talked with the florist, and the arrangements we have planned will be beautiful." I sit in the seat across from him, the same one I have been using for months now, and take out my iPad with all of my notes and plans on it.

"Very good." He taps his cigar in the ashtray on his desk. "But I know you asked for this meeting for a reason. Is there a problem?"

The only downside of being alone for two weeks is that I've been inside my own head for the majority of it. I've been over-analyzing everything that I say, do, or think. Conversations from the last few months, like Vonnie saying she thought I hated my job, repeat in my head like a bad song. And the only way I can think of to get them out is to confront what's been bothering me and prove to myself that I was right to give my loyalty to the organization that my dad and I both loved.

"There is, actually." I pull open the document I have filled with Glenn Chandler quotes and links to the videos or articles where he's being quoted and slide the iPad across the table. "I'm aware that this isn't an event under the Mustangs organization; however, as you're the owner, it will be touted as one no matter what. I understand that you're friendly with Mr. Chandler, but I'm not sure you're aware of some of the deeply problematic things he has said recently."

Mr. Mahler slips on his glasses as he takes the iPad from my hand. He starts reading the list, clicking on a few links as he does.

"I'm sure you understand that I'm just trying to protect your organization from the potential fallout that could come from you hosting a fundraiser while he's spouting some things that are, quite frankly, racist."

Take that, Quinton! I see racism and I call it out when I do!

Mr. Mahler takes off his glasses, tossing them on the table as he hands me back the iPad. "Racist? Come on. People are just too politically correct these days." The smug smile does a terrible job at masking the irritation in his voice. "That's what I love about

Glenn. He says what people are too afraid to say, he shakes things up."

"I'm sorry"—*not fucking sorry*—"but alluding that minorities are criminals and attacking immigrants is not just being politically incorrect. I can tell you, as a person of color, it is offensive."

"Oh lord." He huffs, leaning back in his chair. "Don't tell me you're pulling the race card."

"Excuse me?" I must've heard him wrong. There's no way he said what I thought he said. Right?

"You know what I mean, I thought you were different. Don't go getting all offended and pulling the race card on me now."

Wrong.

Heat blooms from deep within, my blood starting to boil with the rage that has been lingering beneath the surface for the last couple of weeks, as the final thread holding me together snaps.

First, I get Quinton accusing me of excusing racism. Then, when I do point out something that is glaringly racist, I get accused of using the race card. Whatever the fuck that is.

But more than the anger and shock of having him say those words to me, there's pain. Excruciating pain that comes with the realization that no matter what I do, no matter who I am, no matter how old I am, there are people who will never see deeper than the color of my skin.

Hurt causes my voice to shake. "If anything, I give more passes than most people and you should listen to me because that is not a term I throw around lightly."

"Sure it is," he scoffs. "Only when things aren't going your way, right?"

I have made an effort to not put labels on anybody for any reason. When something happens, I never factor race into it. And maybe that's naive of me. I never missed the way store clerks would follow me in stores, but never my friends. I witnessed the way officers handled pulling over my dad versus the Black men I dated. But I never attributed it to race . . . even when I knew deep down it was the reason.

Standing in this room, still reeling with the heartache of Quinton walking away, staring at a man who will never respect me, I feel like my entire life has been summed up in two moments. I just can't win. When I was a kid, my dad would say things about how we should all be color-blind. I can't help but resent those words now. It's how I've tried to live my life and it's impossible for me. I can't ignore color, I *am* color. Trying to do so has caused so much damage. What I should've been doing is acknowledging and accepting all of the pieces that make me who I am instead of trying to force myself into a box I'll never fit into.

Maybe Quinton was more right than I wanted to admit. Because when I think about it, I was so afraid that if I pointed out racism, I was inadvertently calling my family racist. I thought that I could protect myself from racism if I shielded myself in whiteness. But it doesn't matter how much I straighten my hair, how many stories I tell about my white dad, or if I never address racism ever in my life, some people won't see anything beyond my Blackness.

"You know what?" I stand up, ready to walk away from Mahler and Glenn Chandler. Vonnie was right, I hate this job. "I quit."

"You what?" He chokes on the cigar smoke he just inhaled. "You can't quit!"

"I can and I did." I grab my purse, not wanting to waste another second in the same room as this man who makes my skin crawl, and walk out of the room feeling ten feet tall.

I pull out my phone, first sending a text to Jen from the Rue to see if she's still looking for an in-house event planner, and then one to Marie and Liv, hoping they'll forgive me for ghosting them and show up when I need them . . . again.

THE GENTLE SNOWFLAKES falling make the cemetery look ethereal. It's so much different than the last time I was here, watching his coffin as it was lowered into the ground.

The empty space on the headstone that once only had my mom's name and dates is filled. My dad's name is etched into the granite stone and it just all seems so inconsequential. Their dates of birth and death, when it's really all of the living they did between those dates that matters the most. I close my eyes, thinking about my life. About the living that I'm doing, wondering if in the end, any of it will matter. Will anyone care if I spend the rest of my life pushing away everyone around me because I've been at odds with myself?

Even though it's freezing and there's no chance the flowers I brought will survive, I still empty the water bottle into the vase built into the headstone before I put the grocery store bouquet inside. I sit down in front of the large granite stone, and the cold from the grass seeps through the black trousers I wore to work today.

I trace my fingers over the carving of his name. "I think I'm mad at you."

I've come here many times before, but this is the first time I've ever spoken out loud. I never talked to my mom. It's just another thing on a long list of things I'm ashamed of. I was so young when she died and because of that, I never knew her. And how do you miss a person you never knew? And even though my dad always told me stories about her, she felt more like an idea than an actual person. "I'm mad that you guys figured out how to make life work for you, but you both left before I figured it out for myself. And now I'm a grown-ass woman who has tried to live life in this bubble that's done nothing except prevent anyone from getting close to me."

The sound of footsteps crunching against the frozen ground pulls my attention away from the stone in front of me. I glance over my shoulder and I'm so glad I'm already sitting, because the sight of Marie and Liv walking toward me makes my muscles go weak.

I push up off the hard ground and scrub away the tears with the back of my hands.

I wrap my arms around them, hoping they can feel how grateful I am for them. "Thank you guys for coming."

"Of course." Marie hands me a thermos mug. "Thank you for calling us."

I roll my eyes and take a sip of the hot chocolate she brought me. "Yes, because I'm sure a trip to the cemetery is the way you want to spend your Friday."

"Yes." Liv grabs my hand and bores into my eyes. "Supporting our friend who we've been worried about is exactly how we want to spend our Friday."

I'm not sure I've stopped crying since I drove through the gates of the cemetery, but the tears fall a little harder now.

Liv spreads out the blanket she always has in her trunk because we live in Colorado and she has a fear of being stuck in her car during a blizzard. Flanked by my closest friends, they take my hands as we sit on the blanket, staring at the headstone. They don't pressure me to say anything and I soak in the comfort they give me until I'm ready to talk.

I take a deep breath, exhaling slowly before breaking the silence. "Quinton broke up with me."

"We were able to piece together that much of the story," Marie says. "Vonnie feels terrible because she told him about some event you're planning and that's why he got angry."

Great. On top all of the hurt and confusion bouncing around my head, now I feel guilty too. I've been so wrapped up in my own feelings, I haven't even thought that Vonnie would blame herself. As if she's not already going through enough, I let her stew all this time, not telling her it had nothing to do with her.

"It wasn't Vonnie's fault that the event I was planning for Mahler was for Glenn Chandler." I cringe a little bit at the gasp that comes from both sides of me. "I know, I should've quit the moment I knew it was him and I should've stopped making excuses for Mahler then. I just wanted so badly to not believe the worst. But I quit today."

"You what?" Liv almost shouts. "I thought you loved that job!"

"I think I just loved the idea of the job. I loved thinking about what a kick out of it my dad would've gotten. But Mahler accused me of pulling the race card when I told him that I was offended by the racist shit Chandler has been quoted saying." I look at them and know that the red in their cheeks isn't just from the cold. "And one of the reasons Quinton said we couldn't work things out was because he thinks I excuse racism. I just feel like I can't win." I stare ahead of me, but when neither of them says anything, I look between the two of them exchanging worried glances. "Do you think I excuse it?"

"It's not that we think that you excuse it," Liv says like I'm some skittish cat she's approaching. "It's just that you don't seem to notice things."

"Like what? How long have you thought this and not said anything?"

"What were we supposed to say?" Marie asks. "We don't have any right to tell you how you're supposed to feel, so we stopped saying things. Even in high school, when people would call you an Oreo or how Ruby was always telling you she was Blacker than you for whatever stupid reason she came up with, even though she's white? You never seemed fazed, you always laughed it off."

"Just like when you were saying you were the DUFF," Liv says. "You always thought that and you would say little things about your nose being too wide or hating your hair and your hips. Why do you think I'm always trying to get you to wear your hair curly? I don't know what it must be like to be the only person in a room who looks different than everyone else, but I have seen the way it affected you. Maybe even more than you because I was on the outside looking in."

"We all go through a phase where we're insecure about our looks." I try to defend myself, even though she's right on.

"Of course we do, and we all build our defenses accordingly." Liv squeezes my hand. "And you did that by laughing off things that hurt you. You don't excuse racism, but you have learned to deflect and make excuses for people when they do things that are offensive."

"You know how much we loved your dad, right?" Marie says, and my lungs forget how to function as I brace for whatever she's about to say. "But remember when you were thinking about going to a historically Black university and your dad talked you out of it because he was disappointed you would go to a school that excluded people? And so you ended up miserable with us at the whitest college ever, where you had to build up your defenses even more every time someone asked you what sport you played or what you thought of affirmative action."

I haven't thought about that in such a long time that I almost forgot it happened. But now that Marie mentions it, I feel like it happened yesterday. I was so tired of sticking out all the time. Of the teachers looking to me for the "Black perspective" in history class and being overlooked by all the boys who loved my skinny, blue-eyed friends. I thought maybe, if I went somewhere I didn't stand out as soon as I walked through the door, maybe things would be different. The horrified look on my dad's face when I asked him broke me. I remember not feeling sad as much as I felt shame and guilt. *I thought I'd raised you to be different than that, I thought you'd want to go someplace that welcomed everyone,* he'd said. And that was the last we talked about it. I don't think he meant harm by what he said, but that doesn't mean it wasn't harmful. And I think I understand how he felt. Maybe he was afraid that I was ashamed of him, that I wanted to distance myself from him. But what he didn't understand, what I've never acknowledged, is that he made me feel the same way. It taught me to measure my thoughts, my feelings, and to place them beneath the feelings of everyone around me.

And that has gotten me here.

"I thought we had fun together in college." My deflections get weaker as their words continue to penetrate and break down my defenses.

"Sure, we had a blast together and you only remember that because you ignored the other shit you dealt with. And that wasn't wrong . . . but I also think maybe Quinton was more right than you want to admit."

Well, at least we can agree on that.

"Well crap, you guys." I fall back against the fleece blanket. "What am I going to do now?"

"Probably call your therapist because you have some shit to work through." Liv yanks me off the ground.

"But until then." Marie picks up my thermos and stands up. "How about we meet back at your house? I'll bring cupcakes and Liv will bring wine."

"That sounds like a plan I can get behind." I stand up and help Liv fold the blanket.

We walk back to our cars, navigating the headstones as we go.

Liv and Marie bicker over what movie we should watch, a crying one or a laughing one, and when I look over my shoulder at my parents' grave, the flowers already wilting in the vase, I feel a sense of peace starting to settle over me. It's a foreign feeling, but I'm ready to fight for it.

Thirty-seven

A KNOCK ON MY DOOR FORCES ME OFF THE COUCH.

"Pizza's here!" I yell to Marie and Liv, who are spread out across my living room, practically comatose from the amount of wine and junk we've consumed over the course of our sleepover.

I would also like to note that sleepovers are way better as an adult. You can eat what you want, watch what you want, and drink all you want. Way better than when I was a kid and my dad made us go to bed early . . . even though we're adults now and still wanted to go to bed early.

I swing the door open, holding out money for the tip, and freeze when the money is snatched out of my hand, but not by the delivery person.

"Thank you." Brynn shoves the money in her jeans pocket before pushing past me. "Even though I think we are owed much more than five dollars for how long you've ignored us."

For fuck's sake, Elliot! Use the goddamn peephole!

Poppy, Vonnie, and Greer all file in after Brynn as I stand dumbfounded by my open door.

"What are you guys doing here?"

"Well . . ." Brynn grabs a cupcake off of my coffee table and licks the frosting off like a toddler. "Since you weren't responding to our text messages, we decided we had to force our way into your house. It's a good thing you answered because I bought a lock-picking kit and was prepared to get in no matter what."

"I did not agree with that plan, so thank you for opening the door," Poppy says as she falls onto my spot on the couch. But considering she's like, a million months pregnant, I don't say anything.

Vonnie, who usually has at least something to say, looks like she's trying to blend in with the wall behind her. She's staring down at my runner and even though I think it's a great rug, it's not *that* interesting. Then I remember Liv and Marie telling me that she thinks I'm mad at her.

Ignoring everyone else in the room, even though I know their nosy asses aren't ignoring us, I walk over to Vonnie and put my hands on her shoulders. "Hey," I say when she won't meet my eyes. "I am not mad at you, not at all."

"I just feel so terrible." She closes her eyes and pushes her lips together. "I promised you I wouldn't tell and then I did it in front of a room full of people. You must have been so pissed at me."

"Please! If anything, you should be pissed at me." I hope she doesn't take me up on that, but I say it anyways because it's true, and a sad Vonnie is the most heartbreaking sight in the entire world. She's too full of life to ever be muted. "I should've never put that on your shoulders, it wasn't your secret to keep and I should've told him when you told me to."

"I thought you hated me," she says.

"Are you kidding me?" My incredulous laughter cannot be prevented no matter how hard I try. If anything, I was just waiting until they realized I was a visitor in their world and there was no reason for them to want to hang out with me when Quinton was out of the picture. "You are literally one of the best people I know. I thought you guys would've washed your hands of me already."

"Why the hell would we do that?" Brynn asks.

Poppy looks at me with big, sympathetic doe eyes, her curly hair bouncing as she shakes her head no.

"You know . . . I mean, we've only known each other for a short amount of time." I look to Marie and Liv to back me up, but the traitors say nothing. "I just assumed that because we only hung out because of Quinton, you wouldn't want to anymore."

"Oh yeah, that makes so much sense." Brynn's words drip with sarcasm. "You didn't even like Q when you guys met! Also, we're all grown women capable of creating and maintaining friendships that have nothing to do with our husbands or boyfriends."

"Preach." Vonnie snaps her fingers two times, the quiet woman who walked into my condo fading away.

"I get what you're saying." Poppy tries to take my side, ignoring Brynn's and Vonnie's glares while Greer just picks through the cupcakes, oblivious to it all. "When TK and I broke up, I felt the same way. But these women are like glitter, they never go away."

"I'm going to take that as a compliment," Brynn says.

"Same," Vonnie agrees. "Plus, Justin and I might not make it much longer, so then what? I'm not going to have any friends anymore? I think not."

Even though Vonnie is talking about her marriage ending, the sadness in her voice from minutes ago is gone and I'm so grateful to have her back. Even if it means her giving me a hard time.

Like Queen Lizzo says, truth hurts.

"Alright." Greer peels the wrapper off of the cupcake she finally decided on. "Are we going to tell her our intel from Maxwell now? Also, I brought sage to burn when we're finished. You know, good vibes only."

While someone offering to sage my house would usually be the thing that catches my attention, it isn't in this case.

"What intel?" I ask the Lady Mustangs taking over my living room. Even Liv and Marie are sitting up straight.

"I might've had Maxwell invite Q over to our place for dinner." Brynn has the decency to look a little embarrassed. "Hey, don't look at me like that! You weren't answering my phone calls, so I had to do what I had to do."

"That's fair," I say to Brynn before aiming a glare at Liv and Marie when I hear them laughing.

"I asked him about things between you two and he was super vague." She walks to my kitchen and sits on my stool as she pulls a bottle of whiskey out of her purse. And I'm not sure there's a more effective way to distract me from whatever bombshell she's about to drop. "But he said that he was worried about you losing your job, that he didn't want to be responsible."

I already know this since he said something along those lines before he drove away from me.

"Is that all?" I ask. "I quit yesterday, so it doesn't matter. Not that I think anything he says to Mahler would've changed his mind about letting me go."

"You what?" Vonnie grabs my arm and spins me around.

"Um, yeah. I finally realized you guys were right. Mahler is an asshole and I think I like event planning a lot more, so I quit." I thought out of everyone, Vonnie would be the happiest to hear that I made the decision to quit, so I'm taken aback by her reaction. "Isn't that a good thing?"

"It would be if Quinton didn't tell the world's slowest storyteller over there"—she glares at Brynn, who is glaring right back—"that he's planning on not taking a knee or wearing the tape for these final games so Mahler won't fire you," Vonnie says.

"Why would he do that?" The room starts to spin a little and

I stumble backward. "I never once told him to stand. After all of this, he's just going to stand? That doesn't even make sense!"

Greer takes a bite of her cupcake, oblivious to the mood in the room. "I think it's romantic."

"It's not romantic! It's stupid! Why would he risk his integrity for this? And why does he think I need him to save me?" By the looks on everyone's faces, I'm pretty sure I'm yelling. But seriously! "Why are men like this?"

"Age-old question, girl." Vonnie is the only one brave enough to answer.

"So," Marie says. "What are we going to do?"

"Seriously, you can't let him do this, especially when it won't even help you." Liv tells me something I already know.

I march over to the front door and grab my keys out of the bowl. "I'm going to go over to his house and yell at him! That's what I'm going to do."

"One problem with that plan." Brynn is in my kitchen, opening all of my cabinets until she finally finds my wine glasses. "They're at the hotel and it's like Fort Knox in that bitch, no way you're getting to him."

Tears spring to my eyes as I think about his parents, about Patricia and Bill, and about all of the people who are feeling so inspired by him. My heart aches as I imagine how let down he will be in himself for giving in.

I can't let that happen.

"I have to stop him." I will never forgive myself if he does this.

But even more than that, I won't forgive myself if I don't fight for him.

At first, I was so wrapped up in my righteous anger that he would use the things I confided in him about against me. I was so mad that it was easy to ignore that he wasn't trying to hurt me, he was trying to help me. He knew what I was struggling with,

ALEXA MARTIN

even when I didn't. And just like I've been doing for my entire life, I ran from those feelings instead of confronting them.

I'm done running.

I know he won't answer my calls. He might read my texts, but he deserves so much more than that. And I need to prove not only to him, but to myself, that I can fight for something, no matter how hard it might be. I have to see him.

"Oh goodness." Marie straightens from her slumped-over position on my couch. "That's your determined face. What are you thinking?"

"I'm not exactly sure, but I know I'm going to need all of your help." I've always been the person to help, not the person who asks for it. But I know if I'm going to be able to do this the right way, I have to get over myself.

"So she does know how to ask for help!" Brynn walks back into my living room. "Miracles do happen!"

That seems a little dramatic.

"Oooh!" Greer puts down her cupcake and claps. "I have the perfect list of power affirmations for this!"

"Do we need TK to bring the whiteboard?" Poppy rubs her ever-expanding belly with one hand and reaches for her phone with the other. "This feels like a whiteboard mission."

I hate to admit how much I love the idea of the whiteboard, but it's the mention of TK that really gets my mind working.

"I think we can manage without the whiteboard, but I might need you to call TK." I cross the room and grab my computer. "Does he still talk to some of the other players?"

"Umm . . . yeah." Poppy's eyes shift around the room as she struggles to sit up straight.

"Are you going to fill us in on what's going on in that mind of yours or are we supposed to guess?" Brynn, forever the smart-ass, asks. "The suspense is killing me."

"I need to show Quinton how much I believe in him and what he's fighting for." I sit down on an empty spot on my couch, trying to work this idea out in my head. "But I think I need to show him that it's not just me who believes in him. He's been fighting for everybody but himself and refuses to let anyone else help him."

"Something else you both have in common," Marie chimes in and gets nods of agreement from everyone in the room except for me.

"Rude." I try to glare at them, but I don't have it in me. "Fair. But still rude."

"Glad you're finally seeing the light." Vonnie leaves her post at the wall and sits on the arm of my couch. "Now what's the plan and how can we help?"

"I need you to help me get in touch with all the Mustangs. It's time Quinton has backup in this fight."

Vonnie stands back up, striding across the room until she reaches her purse and pulls out her phone. "Calling Justin now."

Obviously I know Vonnie isn't on the best of terms with Justin, so the fact that she would do this without hesitation makes my heart burst.

"We don't have Mustangs contacts." Liv grabs Marie's hand. "But we're in for whatever crazy plan you're dreaming up right now."

"Always and forever," Marie says.

God.

I thought I was alone—that I never fit in—while all along I was surrounded by the best friends a person could ask for. Even if Quinton and I never speak again, I will always be so grateful to him for waking me up to how lucky I really am. Not only did he hold my hand through one of the hardest times in my life, he introduced me to the most amazing women.

But before I go thanking him, I'm going to save him first.

"Okay." I put my communications hat back on as my fingers hit the keys on my computer. "I'm going to draft a script of sorts for you all. If you're on the phone, it's just a general list of talking points to help get the players on board. I'll also write an email that we can send out. I think an email will be the fastest, but obviously a phone call is more personal."

"Yeah, obviously." Greer is nodding along, but it's clear by the deer-in-headlights look she's sporting that she has no idea what's happening. And considering I'm making all of this up as I go, that's understandable. "So what exactly are we calling to ask for?"

"Help. That's how change is going to happen."

"I just got goose bumps." Vonnie shows me her arms, which are, in fact, covered in goose bumps. "That's amazing."

"It is," Brynn chimes in, and for once her tone is all business. I'm not sure I've ever heard her talk like this. "But we can do more. Why stop at the Mustangs? We all have friends on other teams. The guys all have friends playing on other teams. Hurry up and write the email. I'm going to call Maxwell, he'll get email addresses from all the guys, and then have them spread the message around the league."

"Wow." I breathe the word out, in awe of how these women not only support me, but make me better. Even if Quinton doesn't ever talk to me again, at least I'll be able to give him this. So I start typing and I don't stop until it's perfect, hoping the entire time I do, that this will work. And Quinton can finally see how much he means to everyone.

How much he means to me.

Thirty-eight

IF I GOT MORE THAN AN HOUR OF SLEEP LAST NIGHT, IT WAS ONLY by a few minutes.

Vonnie took Poppy home right before midnight. Brynn and Greer stayed until the wee hours of the morning. Liv and Marie, proving once again just how much they love me, camped out with me as we worked through the night.

The whole night, all I could think of was Quinton and how betrayed he must've felt not only that I was working with Glenn Chandler, but that I was always so quick to dismiss his feelings about Mahler. I don't know if he'll ever be able to forgive me for that—for how small I must've made him feel—but I hope that today will at least prove that I heard him and that I think his voice matters.

"Miss Elle." Jax tugs my sleeve and pulls my attention from the crowds starting to surround us as we make our way to the family and players' parking lot. I'm never sure if I feel like an old lady, a kindergarten teacher, or both when he calls me that, but he's cute enough that I don't think about it for too long. "Are you okay? You look kinda sleepy."

Nobody, and I mean NOBODY, in the entire world will tell you that you look like shit quicker than a child. I wish I could appreciate their honesty, but I'd much rather hang out with adults who know how to lie.

"She does, doesn't she?" Liv says from the front seat, the laughter in her eyes evident even through the rearview mirror. "That's what happens when you don't let your friends help you and then you're forced to stay up all night fixing things that could've been taken care of with a simple phone call."

I'd like to amend my previous statement. I'd much rather have friends who not only know how to lie, but do so often.

"Yup." Vonnie cosigns for Liv. "Listen to Miss Liv, this is good advice."

The car really isn't moving that fast. I'm sure I wouldn't get too hurt if I just jumped out.

"Hardy har har." I roll my eyes, not setting the best example for the impressionable eyes next to me. "You guys are so funny."

"Sarcasm is also a terrible defense mechanism," Marie, who I wasn't even annoyed with, pipes up from the row behind me.

But before I can say something snarky to her, Vonnie turns down the radio and starts to go over the plan for today again. "Alright boys, when we get to the stadium, you'll take Miss Liv and Miss Marie to the box. If I find out from either of them that you gave them a hard time, you won't have electronics for a month, and that includes Christmas, got me?"

"Yes, Mom," all three boys say in perfect synchronization. Even they know Santa's got no pull on Vonnie. Smart kids.

"Are you sure they'll let us in the tunnel?" I ask Vonnie. The confidence I had last night has withered away and melted into a rock in the pit of my stomach.

"I already told you yes. They love me here." She slows down, waving at the police officers guarding the players' lot. "Plus, I give them really good Christmas presents every year, they won't want to put those in jeopardy."

"Okay. Good. Yes." I've forgotten how to form sentences and I'm not even in the stadium yet. I hope this doesn't turn into a disaster. I really need this to work.

I spent so much time trying to hate Quinton that even when he managed to slide past my defenses, I still couldn't admit just how much he meant to me. It took him walking away and me really thinking about just how much he has been there for me to realize that the butterflies I felt every time he walked in the room, and the pressure in my chest every time he left, was love. I was just so convinced he would leave like everyone else seemed to, that I pushed him away. *A self-fulfilling prophecy*, as Greer not so helpfully informed me.

"Ready?" Vonnie asks as she pulls her gigantic SUV into the narrow parking spot surrounded by luxury cars.

But as nervous as I am, this feels different from everything else I've done. Because for once, I know I have an entire support system standing behind me. And if I fall, I know they'll pick me up again.

I close my eyes and take a deep breath. "I'm as ready as I'll ever be."

"Then let's go get your man back."

"WE HAVE THE stuff!" Brynn's voice echoes around us as she runs into the tunnel, waving a plastic bag above her head.

"Oh thank goodness." I take the bag from her, the weight of it surprisingly heavy . . . but that might just be the pressure of this grand plan I made.

I glance at my phone and check the time. I've never wanted a game delay more in my entire life. But of course, the one time I need Colorado's weather to go crazy, it's sunny and beautiful out-side. Cold . . . but still beautiful.

"Here." I reach into the bag, pulling out the rolls of tape and handing them to Vonnie, Brynn, and Greer. "You know what to do."

Greer grabs me by the shoulders and stares so deep into my eyes that I'm convinced she can actually see my soul. "Remember, 'You can't go back and change the beginning, but you can start where you are and change the ending.' This is you changing the ending and you can do this."

Whoa.

I never thought there was really any merit to motivational quotes and life coaches and whatever else everyone is always talk-ing about on Instagram, but Greer just hyped me all the way up. And it's exactly what I needed to hear before the click-clack of cleats echo against the cement floor as the team makes their way to the front of the tunnel.

"Rewrite the ending. Rewrite the ending," I chant and a very satisfied, bordering on smug smile pulls across Greer's beautiful face.

"You got this." Brynn wraps her fingers around my sweaty hand. "Maxwell texted me while we were in the car, everyone he talked to loves your plan. It's going to be amazing."

I'm sure we're a sight to be seen, the four of us huddled to-gether at the entrance of the tunnel when Patrick Dawson, one of the linemen, rounds the corner and sees us all.

"Elliot? I think you might have something for me." His soft smile is a stark contrast to the helmet he's holding and the pads encasing his body.

"I do." My voice wavers, but I'm not sure if it's from nerves or the overwhelming flood of emotions coursing through my system right now. "Thank you so much." I rip off a piece of tape and tears well in my eyes as he slaps it across the League's emblem at the top of his jersey.

"No, thank you," he returns. "I didn't realize how bad it was for the guys who paved the path for us. I'm proud to stand by Q's side."

After my plan started coming together last night, I reached out to Patricia from Pro Players for Equal Treatment. She sent over player testimonies of retired men all facing challenges like Quinton's dad. I included them in an email to every player whose address I could get my hands on. And then I proposed a call to action: take a stand alongside Quinton. By joining his fight, they will take him out of the equation and put the pressure on the people trying to twist his motives. There's power in numbers. It's up to them to make sure they're all taken care of, and that includes Quinton.

Even though Brynn and Vonnie have been trying to tell me everyone was on board, I still wasn't sure how this was going to go. But, with the first one down, my nerves fade and determination I've never felt before sets in. I bet this is how Wonder Woman feels.

The rest of the Mustangs players and coaches all make their way into the tunnel, stopping to get their piece of tape from one of us as they prepare to run out onto the field.

My cheeks hurt from smiling and I'm afraid I might run out of tape when strong fingers wrap around my wrist and navigate me through the crowded space until we're in a semisecluded corner.

"What are you doing here?"

I haven't seen Quinton since Thanksgiving. Whereas the time apart caused me to gain five pounds, break out like a thirteen-year-old, and get bags so dark beneath my eyes that I needed to order a special concealer, Quinton looks better than ever. His beard is longer than I've ever seen it and it's really unfair that he looks this good in a football uniform. Seeing him in it on TV or from up in the box really does it no justice. He's a work of art.

My stomach cramps as the nerves come rushing back. Even though I've missed him, maybe he's been better off without me. And even though I've been telling myself this isn't just about getting him back, but showing him how much he means to everyone around him, this is the first time it's really set in that this might not work. There's a good chance he won't forgive me.

I don't want to lose him.

I take a deep breath before the words fall out of my mouth. "Brynn told me you weren't going to take a knee. You have to take one."

His fingers tighten around the face mask of his helmet before he puts it on the ground. He moves his hands to his hips, and even though I know it's imperative for me to focus, I can't help the way I stare a little bit before moving my eyes back to his. And those dark eyes framed by his even darker lashes look anything but happy. "I told you I'd make sure you could keep your job and that's what I'm going to do."

"Okay, but—" I try to tell him that I quit, that this is pointless, but he talks over me.

"I hope you're doing well and I appreciate you coming here, but I know what I'm doing." He cracks his glove-covered knuckles and looks over my head as Jack starts announcing the players before him. "I was prepared for the fallout, but I'm not going to let that affect your job. You made it clear it's the only thing that matters to you. I won't be the reason you lose that too."

He can't keep the bitterness out of his words or his face when he talks about my job. And my heart aches that I made him feel like he wasn't as important as a stupid job. But even though I feel terrible, I can't help but be annoyed that he thinks I need to be rescued. So I latch on to that thread of irritation and hold on to it for dear life.

"Stop talking." I cover his mouth with my hand. "I quit.

Mahler's a jackass and you were right about everything. I'm not here just to tell you not to stand, I'm here to prove that you don't have to do this alone.

"You're always so concerned about taking care of everyone else that you never let anyone take care of you. And I understand if you never want to see me again. I get it. But I'm not going away until I prove to you just how important you are to me. To everyone." I hold up my nearly empty roll of tape. "All I had to do was show your teammates the things you've shown me. Every single one of them was proud to have your back. They're all going out there to kneel with you, to cover their emblems until the League is forced to make a change and all men"—I drop my voice so only he can hear me—"men like your father, get what's owed to them."

I take my hand off his mouth, but I still don't give him the opportunity to speak.

"I just need to tell you how much you mean to me. No matter what happens in the future, you've changed me. You made me face things I've spent forever hiding from, and I will always love you for that. I'm just so sorry that in that process I ignored your doubts and feelings just because I was scared to face my issues—"

"You love me?" His eyes go soft and I hope it's not from pity.

"I know it was fast and I get it if you don't—"

Before I can explain or even say yes, Quinton's mouth is on top of mine. The urgent, demanding kiss, forcing my mouth open as our tongues circle each other.

"I've been waiting to hear you say that," he whispers, his breath dancing across my lips. "Because even though you make me crazy, I love you too."

"Howard!" a security guard at the opening of the field yells. "You're next!"

Quinton grabs his helmet off the floor and intertwines his fingers in mine, running with me and only letting go of my hand

when his feet hit the turf. He jogs backward onto the field, bringing his hand to his mouth and blowing me a kiss before lifting his
helmet into the air and running into the middle of the circle of his
teammates, all with their black tape on their jerseys, as they cheer
for him along with the rest of the stadium.

I only wish I could see the look on Mahler's face right now.

"Sooo . . ." Brynn bumps her shoulder into mine. "How'd it go?"

Even though I'm sure the smile that has taken over my face gives
her the answer, it feels so good to say the words. "I love him."

"Girl, tell us something we don't already know!" Vonnie
stands besides us, the sun catching on the crystals of her shirt I
know she doesn't want to be wearing.

I look out at the field, watching Quinton as all of his teammates, with their logos blacked out, walk over to him and pat him
on the back before they line up on the sideline. "He loves me too."

"Fucking finally!" Greer—GREER!—shouts. "It took you
two long enough."

We all break out laughing and for the first time in a long time,
I feel free. There's no sadness lingering beneath my laugh, no
weight on my shoulders that I can't shake. I just feel happy. And,
as I look back to the field as the first notes of the anthem begin to
play and see everyone on the Mustangs' sideline, players and
coaches—and even some of Baltimore's players—drop to their
knees, a pride I didn't know was possible flows through my veins.

Knowing how pissed Mahler must be in his box is just the icing on the cake.

There's always been some booing when Quinton would take a
knee. But today, it seems like the crowd has been shocked into
silence. And even though it's not my job to figure out what they're
thinking anymore, part of me can't help but to step out of the
tunnel to look out into the sea of orange filling the stadium. And
when I do, I'm shocked at what I see.

It's a moment I'll never forget. Chills run down my spine and goose bumps cover my arms. So many people are slowly lowering themselves back into their seats, as if making the stand with the players. Some people are even taking off their jerseys and turning them inside out. As the final chords of the anthem blast from the speakers, cheers start to build from the stands. They start quietly, hesitantly even, but grow louder and louder until everyone is back on their feet shouting their support for the men on the field.

Who knows if this is something they've always wanted to do in support of Quinton. Maybe it's something they were inspired to do today after seeing all of the men they look up to also take a stand. But either way, it just goes to prove how much power comes with sticking together. Quinton has empowered all of these people to put action behind their thoughts. By doing something so small, but with more courage than most people could ever imagine, he's changing the League and the world.

But more than any of that, we've changed each other.

I always thought that I'd end up alone, but not anymore. Not only do I have this wild group of women, I also have Quinton by my side. And I've never been more excited to tackle life, because for the first time ever, I'm finally living it.

Epilogue

IF IT WASN'T SO INFURIATING, IT WOULD ALMOST BE COMICAL AT how quickly the media changed their tune once it wasn't just Quinton they had to go against. Apparently, it's a lot harder to twist the words of hundreds of people than it is just one person. In the two weeks since players from all across the League started kneeling with Quinton, it's like everything he was fighting for magically clicked.

Who would've thought?

Other than me, of course.

"Have you checked the news yet?" I flip all the switches and hit the buttons to make a coffee on Quinton's spaceship coffee machine.

He slides onto a stool at the counter. "You know I didn't."

Whereas the first thing I do when I wake up every morning is check my email and various social media sites, Quinton refuses to look at it before noon. I'm not saying he's an alien or anything, but he def has a healthier relationship with devices than I do.

"Well . . ." I slide my phone in front of him with my favorite article on the screen, "By Covering Up Their Logos, These Men Uncovered Mistreatment in the League." I try not to get too salty over the fact that they're acting like this has been a group effort all along and take the win.

In the article they discuss the mistreatment of the pre-'93 retired players, pointing out the way the League goes out of their way to honor them without putting in the work to actually care for them. They ask whether or not they are doing this on purpose and manipulating the public with halftime honors. But it doesn't stop there. They also delve into the racial stats of the League, questioning the fairness of the coaching standards by comparing the rate in which Black coaches are fired when white coaches with similar records are given more chances. It's everything Quinton has been discussing, but what everyone raked him over the coals for talking about.

"Wow." His eyebrows reach his hairline as he scrolls through the article. "They finally get it."

"Took them long enough." I grab the creamer out of the refrigerator so he can't see the way my eyes roll to the back of my head. Don't get me wrong, I'm glad my idea worked out and people are finally seeing his point, but I'm a bit of a Bitter Betty that it took them so long. And that they are glossing over Quinton starting the movement.

"Just because I can't see your face doesn't mean I don't know the face you're making right now." There's laughter in his voice and I do not appreciate it.

"I don't know why you're so amused by this." Forgetting the creamer, I turn and aim a glare at him with hands planted firmly on my hips. Something I'm sure would be more effective if I wasn't barefoot in his pajama pants that I rolled up approximately ten times. "It would've been so much easier if they just listened to you from the beginning."

"Maybe." He stands up and walks around the island. And even though we spent all of last night—and part of this morning—continuing to celebrate our official relationship status, seeing him without his shirt on and his eyes still hooded from sleep makes me want to jump back into bed with him. "But if they listened, I wouldn't have met you and this wouldn't feel nearly as sweet." He lowers his voice just as he drops a gentle kiss on my lips.

And I swear I swoon.

Maybe one day I'll get used to this, but I really hope not.

"YOU BOUGHT RUGS!" I yell as soon as I open Quinton's front door and cozy goodness is covering his cement floors.

Quinton closes the refrigerator and walks over to me with a Diet Coke in his hand. "You like it?"

"Do I like it?" I take the soda from his hand and roll on to my toes to drop a kiss on his mouth. "I freaking love it! Don't you?"

"I actually do, and look." He points to the living room floor that is also covered by a massive rug.

My eyes go wide and I shove my hand into his shoulder. "Is that the one I told you I loved when we were at the mall? You bought it?"

As a Mustangs fan, I was bummed when they got knocked out of the playoffs. As a girlfriend, I was thrilled. Because as much as I loved spending time with Quinton during the football season, having him to myself every day is so much better. If anything, now I'm the busy one.

Working at the Rue with Jen has been amazing. I can't believe I went so long thinking that hating so many parts of my job was normal. Now I get to go to work and love what I do. Even when we get a difficult client, I still come home with a smile on my face.

"Yeah." He sits on the couch and almost looks embarrassed.

"I snuck back in and ordered it while you were in line for ice cream."

"Sneaky, but I like it." I put my soda on a coaster and sit on the couch next to him. "It looks perfect in here."

He turns to me, his face suddenly serious as different scenarios race through my mind.

"You look perfect in here." He twists his body so that he's facing me and pulls me into his arms. "I used to hate coming home to this place. It was so empty, so cold. But the second you stepped through that door, things began to change. I know you've said your condo never felt right to you, so what do you say? Do you want to move in with me? We can turn this place into a home together."

I'm still in therapy. I have a lot of issues I still need to work my way through, but there is one thing that I know for sure—when I'm with Quinton, I feel safe. I fit and I belong. Whether it was the times we've spent laughing, crying, or even the time we were apart, he's always accepted me for me.

"Yes." I nod my head, watching as his face lights up just before our mouths touch, confirming what I already knew.

There's no place in the world I would rather be.

ACKNOWLEDGMENTS

The Playbook Series was originally only supposed to be three books. So, first and foremost, thank you to Berkley for giving me the opportunity to continue this series and tell this story.

Kristine Swartz, my badass editor, thank you for just being you. You make this entire process so wonderful and give me the courage to tell my stories, even if they might ruffle a few feathers. I'm so grateful that I get the opportunity to continue working with you. You are everything. Jessica Mangicaro, thank you for all of the amazing work you do and for making social media not seem scary and for basically holding my hand through all of it. And to the rest of the Berkley team, thank you, thank you, thank you. You are all so brilliant and talented, I still can't believe you took a chance on me.

My agent, Jessica Watterson. You are my biggest advocate and I will always be so thankful to be a part of Team Watterson. I could not ask for a better agent or a better friend.

Thank you to everyone at FAIR—Fairness for Athletes in Retirement—for the work you have done fighting for retired players and telling their stories. You have amplified their voices and finally let them be heard.

Lin and Lindsay. I could not have finished this book without your encouragement and hand-holding. Thank you for reading every chapter I sent you and telling me it wasn't a total dumpster fire. I love you both.

Andie J. Christopher. I wouldn't have had the courage to write this story without you. Thank you for being not only an amazing friend and someone I can always confide in, but also an inspiration.

Maxym. I'm not sure I've ever met someone and clicked with them so instantly. You are a superwoman and I'm so proud to call you a friend.

Abby, Taylor, and Natalie. I hope you know how much I love you. I talk a lot about strong female friendships in these books and that wouldn't be possible if I didn't have you all in my life, showing me just how important it is.

I'm writing these acknowledgments on day seven of social distancing for COVID-19. Hopefully by the time this book is out in the world, things will be back to normal and I will be home voluntarily. But right now, I think it's imperative that I thank all of you. This time is so wild and freaking scary, and the only thing that has brought me any comfort is seeing the way we've all come together on social media to comfort one another. Whether you've posted a funny meme or sent an encouraging message or voiced your fear so that someone else can feel like they aren't alone, thank you. The romance community is always the best, but I'm more aware of it than ever right now.

Now my kids, even though you have interrupted me approximately nine times while I'm writing this to ask for snacks, ask for water, or tell on your sibling, I couldn't love you more. You are sunshine and sparkle and everything good in this world. You are my everything. Even though being stuck inside is kind of a bummer, I'm so grateful for this time with you. I've loved slowing down and just enjoying you all without anything to interrupt us.

Derrick, thank you for being my partner through all of this. I love you.